Reel Echoes

Robert D Johnson

For Mom and Dad,
who built a world where love echoed louder than struggle,
and whose strength still reverberates through me.

For Matt, my oldest friend, literally.

For my Aunt Debbie,
whose laughter could brighten any room and whose spirit echoes
in the heart of everyone that has the privilege of knowing her.

And for all the people who inspired this tale,
your voices are the echoes I carry,
the memories that I refuse to let fade,
and the reason I believe some things are too precious to forget.

This story is for you…

Chapter 1 - This is My Home
(Summer 1961)

My name's Bobby Chandler. I had just turned nine in the Summer of '61. Back then my world wasn't made up of miles but of moments. I measured it by the rhythm of my bare feet thumpin' against the sun-soaked ground. From the ole farmhouse where the porch posts were held up by the roof instead of the other way around, my life unfurled in a winding patchwork of dirt paths and tree shadows. Each morning, just as the rooster's second crow called the sky into color, I would run out barefoot, the screen door slappin' behind me, even though dad had told me a hundred times to close it slowly. That red earth greeted me like an old friend. I used to say to myself, there was no better feelin' than the feelin' of that clay seepn' between my toes.

My journey really began at the edge of our property, where the Coldwater Creek curved lazy and glassy, cool even in the thick of summer. I knew its every bend, every root, and every tree that ya could jump from. The best part was the sandbar, a wide speck of soft white sand where time didn't tick but yawned and stretched. That's where we all grew from. From sunup to sundown, it was a slow parade of laughter and scraped knees, diggin' trenches and forts for battles we never quite finished, tradin' secrets that meant everythin' in the moment and nothin' a week later.

To get to town, we took a route that no map would ever show. It starts through Mr. Abernathy's pasture, where the grass grew tall enough to brush our knees as the cows would look up with the same sleepy disinterest every time…but not the bull, we steered clear of him. Then a quick hop over the splintered feed store fence, a quick run through the loadin' bay, and a final sprint down Gable's back alley, careful to keep to the left side, where the shadows fell just enough to avoid rousin' the barkin' hound that was tied up behind the trash barrels.

Just bout every mornin', our mom, most other people called her Ruth, would stand on the porch with a dish towel in hand, callin' after us, "You boys watch out for each other, ya hear?"

"Yes, ma'am!" We called back in chorus, not turnin', our sneakers scuffin' the path.

I'd grin, feelin' her words settle into me like a tether to our house, with its chipped gray sidin' and tomato plants curlin' in the backyard. "She always says that" I mutterd, kickin' a pebble.

"'Cause you're always gettin' lost," Matt teases, glancin' over his shoulder with a smirk.

"Ain't never been lost," I shoot back, though my cheeks warm. Not here, not in Mill Town, where the streets loop like verses in a church hymn, familiar yet full of surprises. Like a beetle I'd never seen playin' hide an seek under a rock, its shell glintin' like a lost pirate emerald, or a rusted nail pokin' from the boardwalk plank, six boards down from start of the riverwalk shorcut, darin' my bare foot to find it; a snatch of gossip floatin' from Mrs. Elma's bookstore window, where her typewriter ticks like a metronome.

Our route was a patchwork of shortcuts, a map only kids can read. We'd cut back through Mr. Abernathy's pasture, the grass ticklin' my calves, the air heavy with the musky scent of grazin' cows. Matt'd vault the splintered fence behind the feed store, landin' with a thud that sends sawdust into the sunlight. "C'mon, slowpoke!" he calls, halfway across the lot.

"I'm comin'!" I'd huff, scramblin' after him, my palms stingin' as I gripped the rough wood. A hound's bark erupts from the alley behind

2

Gable's Mercantile, all teeth and no courage, and my heart leaps as I dodge the invisible threat. "That dog's gonna eat us one day," I pant, laughin'.

"Nah, he's just loud," Matt says, grinnin'. "Like Eric when he's got jerky."

Eric Fulton lived a mile away, a half mile if ya knew the shortcut through ole Abernathey's property. Eric's dad worked deliverin' goods for Mr. Gable's. Eric's my best friend, but don't tell Lila though, cause she thinks it's her. Eric and I did just bout everythin' together.

The town unfolded around us, it was both a map and a mystery. From the other edge of town, we'd pass a lightnin'-struck pecan that stands like a sentinel, its gnarled branches cradlin' our treehouse, cobbled from scavenged planks and bent nails with a tire swing. We scramble up the rope ladder, our "meetin's" a sacred ritual of whispered plans and imagined invaders. The warped platform smells of sap and secrets, and I'd lean out, squintin' at the view: Main Street's clapboard storefronts, awnin's faded but proud; the grain tower's silhouette, stubborn against the sky; and beyond, the Blackwater River, a silver ribbon curlin' through the pines near Mainstreet.

"Bet I could hit the river with a rock from here," Matt says, pickin' at a blackberry splinter.

"You cain't hit the broad side of Gable's," I scoff, elbowin' him.

"Could too," he shoots back, but he doesn't throw. We'd sit a moment, the world was ours, until Matt nudges my shoulder. "Race you to the creek!"

We'd tumble down the ladder, sprintin' to Coldwater Creek, the air thick with the smell of wet bark and swamp mud.

"Looks like Eric's already there," Matt said pointin' to the fresh footprints in the mud. Yep, there he is with his BB gun slung over one shoulder, his laugh too loud for the quiet mornin'.

"Y'all er late!" he bellows, tossin' me a strip of jerky from his mom's pantry.

The salt bites my lips, sharp and warm. "Late for what?" I ask, chewin'.

"For glory!" Eric says, strikin' a pose like a radio announcer. "Matt Chandler, swamp king, leads his brave crew to hunt the almighty moccasin!"

Lila Hollis leaned against the half fallen cypress, her braid swingin' as she rolled her eyes. "Y'all are dumber than a screen door on a submarine," she'd say, but her grin gives her away. She's faster than most boys, smarter than all of us, and when I followed her slippin' off to climb the water tower for the fireworks last year, I knew she saw the world from angles I hadn't found yet.

"Gonna hunt snakes or just talk about it?" Lila asks, kickin' at the biggest pinecone I'd ever seen.

"Snakes don't stand a chance," Matt says, wieldin' a long stick like a spear, his old shoes squelchin' in the mud. Each step I took threatened to suck my shoe right off my foot. I follow, my heart hammerin', eyes wide for the ripple of a snake.

Eric narrated every step, "And here comes Matt, fearless in the swamp swingin what looks like a model 270 hickory long stick!" his voice bouncin' off the cypress knees until laughter drowns my fear.

"Shut up, Eric," Matt says, "You're scarin' the snakes." but Matt was grinnin' the entire time.

"Good, hope he does scare them," I mutter, grippin' my stick tighter.

"Matt, don't move!" Shouts Eric, as he spotted the biggest moccasin I've ever seen, and I'd seen lots of em. This monster was just three feet in front of em.

4

This was the granddaddy moccasin, at least six maybe seven feet long and as big around as my thigh. Matt just sees it, glances up at us, and smiles.

Eric see's Matt's face and loses at least three shades of color in his own "Don't do it!" Eric yells.

Matt smiles wider as he raises his stick up high slowly raisin' it even higher. I look down, my knees are deep in mud so I start lookin' for a quick exit. Bout the time I turn back to look at Matt, he swings that stick right on top of that snakes' head with a loud crack!

What none of us expected, was the stick to break in half. That moccasin wasn't very happy bout havin' some kids try to beat him for no good reason. He tore out after us. Matt was the first one to run. I just remember lookin' back and seein' that moccasin comin' stright for me, and I didn't even do nothin. I swear it was close enough for me to see it's huge yellow eyes as big as marbles, starin me down as it came at me with its white mouth open showin four inch long fangs drippin with venom. You ain't never seen four kids run so fast in knee deep mud before. I looked over just in time to see Eric laughin' at me, just as he runs face first into a juniper tree, nearly knockin himself out. After we collected ourselves about two hundred yards away, all drippin in mud and blood, we could finally laugh about it.

"You were so scared you nearly knocked yourself out!" Matt said laughing.

"Na uhh, I was laughin at Bobby's rooster tail of mud slingin' from his bare feet, that's how I knocked myself out." Eric shouted between breaths and laughter.

I think that was the last time we used sticks to go moccasin huntin'.

The creek was always a refuge from the heat durin' them dog days of summer. It glittered under the tree canopy, its water cool and clear, minnows flickerin' like sparks.

"Ahhh…" as my toes sunk into the sandbar reachin the water, the only sound was the hush of water, the buzz of dragonflies, and the weight of whatever secret was echoing inside.

The creek gave us everythin' we needed. We'd catch fish, swim, and laugh until our cheeks cramped up. It was our own little piece of heaven, not another soul for miles around. It was freedom.

When the sun raised up high and sweat turned sticky, we turned our attention to Mr. Collier's garden. Pillowcases slung over shoulders, we moved like ghosts across the field, barefoot, breath held, hearts thuddin'.

We'd argue over who's turn it was to get lunch "It's your turn!...I went last time."

"I know ya did, and ya left good tracks leadin' right back over here for Mr. Collier to find. I thought I told ya to walk on the grassy parts so ya wouldn't leave any tracks." Matt would say.

Eric snatched the bag from me, "fine, I'll go…I'm hungry."

Eric wasn't gone for more than three minutes when next thing we hear was a 'Boom!' Then here comes Eric with a full sack of watermelons screaming bloody murder runnin into every bush along the way, "Run!"

We all scatterd' into the swamp, those moccasins and gators were nothin' compared to that twelve gauge aimed right at us. 'Boom!' pellets rainin' around us.

I guess Mr. Collier didn't want to follow us no more cause he just cursed at us and turned around on the other side of the swamp. Just then Eric turned and dropped his shorts yellin' "Hey Mister Collier, Eat This!"

I swear I saw Mr. Collier smile as he raised his shotgun to his shoulder squeezing the trigger 'Boom!" Eric went to squeelin, rollin around on the ground holdin his behind, pants still around his knees.

"Now stay outta my garden!" Mr. Collier yelled back.

I ran over to Eric who was still rollin in the mud, not knowin what to do. Sensin it was safe, Matt and Lila came over too circlin Eric as he rolled in pain.

"Stop rollin around, Lemme see" Lila said.

Eric finally stopped squeelin' long enough for Lila to look close, "It's just rocksalt."

Eric looked at her, "Just rocksalt? Lemme shoot you with it and then hear ya say 'It's just rocksalt'" he said mimickin her.

Lila sneered back, "well, I didn't moon Mr. Collier after getting caught stealin his watermelons, now did I?"

We all sat and laughed down by the creek while eatin the crushed watermelon. Eric stood.

Some nights, when the air was thick and the moon was black in the sky, we would turn the dirt road into our theater of pranks. One of us would pull a rubber snake into the headlights of passin' cars with a fishin' line, tryin' not to laugh at the cars as they attempted in vain to kill it by backin' over it over and over, each time our laughin' grew harder and harder to contain. Another night, we stuffed a pair of jeans and shirt with straw.

"Whatcha wanna call him?" Eric said while starin at our masterpiece in his bedroom.

"Fred." Said Matt…"Dead Fred"

We all chuckled. That sounded good to us. We then laid Fred in the road with an old arrow stickin' out of his chest.

"Put sum ketchup on him…for good measure" insisted Lila.

We dumped an entire bottle of ketchup all over him. Just as we finished and were admirin' our work, headlights shined the top of the trees. We

7

dove into the ditch. We were only feet away when the entire road, includin' Fred layin there in the middle of the road was all lit up. The headlights went from dim to bright. Then the car came to a stop about thirty yards away. It just sat there for what seemed like forever. A minute or two later, Mr. Sheffield, a mean old man that lived down the road, opened the car door. He walked about ten yards away from Fred, then looked around at the woods, then quickly backed up to his car. He closed the door then put the car into gear. We were all just feet away from the road and could'a been easily seen by anyone that was really lookin. The car eased around Fred, then sped off. We waited until the car was around the corner before we all came out of hidin'.

"Did you see him?!? I bet he pooped all over himself." Eric laughed as we all joined in.

"It's a good thin' he didn't look too hard, cause we didn't have time to hide...we were right there!" I said pointin to a shallow ditch just off the road.

"Let's not let that happen again." Matt said.

That sounded like a good plan to us. We all broke limbs and bushes to make really good hidin spots then got into our hidin' positions. At least two other cars came by over the course of the next thirty minutes. They all slowed down, but nobody else stopped.

"Somethin's wrong, must not look real enough." Eric said.

We all came out to take a better look at Fred. I mean, sure you could see straw stickin out of his neck and his hands were old work gloves, but it still looked pretty convincin' to us. As luck would have it, the tops of the trees lit up again.

"Car!" Lila shouted.

"We had about two seconds to jump out of the road. This time we were separated, two of us on each side. This car came from the other direction and came to a stop. We were all frozen less than three feet

8

from the road. It was Mr. Sheffield again. This time he had his pistol in his hand. Then we heard it. Sirens. Eric was on my side of the road, Matt and Lila were on the other. It didn't take long before we saw the red flashin' lights shinin' on the tops of the trees. That's when things got serious. I looked at Eric, and he looked at me. I slowly pointed to the woods behind us. I could see Matt and Lila on the other side of the road doin the same. If Mr. Sheffield had cut his engine, he surely would have heard us. We had snuck through the woods plenty a times playin war with BB guns, but this time it was for real. We moved quiet as a church mouse through the woods. We weren't more than twenty yards away when the police got there. We were so close we could hear 'em talkin'.

"I know you're there, come on out! You've caused enough trouble tonight!" Officer Jefferson yelled as he scanned the bushes with his flashlight.

We had no intentions of bein' caught tonight. We continued our slow creep into the woods further and further. We could hear at least two other squad cars pull up. We were almost home free until Eric put his hand right in the middle of big ole fireant hill. He started huffin' and slappin' them off his arm, cain't blame him, I woulda done the same. Then we heard the sheriff movin' through the woods in our direction, fast. We had the advantage, we knew these woods like the backs of our hands, we bolted. Bein' quiet was completely out the window now…we sounded like a blind deer runnin' through a hubcap factory. We ran for a mile through blackberries and Jesus vines until we were sure they had given up the chase. We had splinters and thorns and were drippin' blood from every inch of our arms and legs. We spent the next two hours tryin' to evade the police that had staked out the roads just waitin' for us to cross to get back home. We just waited for a break and made a run for it.

"Did they see us?" I whispered to Eric on the other side of the hedge row.

"Nah, they were eatin donuts," Eric said tryin not to laugh too loud as we walked the rest of the way to the campsite.

Not more than five minutes after we got back to the campfire, so did Matt and Lila. We had gone over the road, they had gone under it, through the drain pipe. I shivered just thinkin' about all the creepie crawlies that were in there.

The rush, the thrill of nearly gettin' caught, became part of our language. We told the stories over and over, each time with new details, louder gasps, longer jumps, more darin' escapes. Truth blurred into legend.

Me and Matt weren't just brothers, we were part of a team. A unit. It wasn't always this way. We used to fight like cats and dogs, but we eventually got to likin bein' round each other. We built rafts out of oil drums and fence wire, floated them down the creek until they capsized and laughed about it anyway. We caught croakers in mason jars, laid out tin foil traps for raccoons, and argued for a week over what to name the scruffy mutt that followed us home one day. I called him Barney. Matt called him Fred. Barney eventually answered to both.

In Mill Town, childhood wasn't somethin' you were given. It was somethin' you *earned*. It was earned in blood, sweat, and skinned knees. It was baptized in whispered dares and death defyin stunts, and in the silence that followed the shared secret. It was the kind of life that settled deep in your bones, long after the laughter faded and the paths grew over, it still pulsed just under the surface. Like a heartbeat. Like home.

Back home there was always some chore to do. Because of that, Matt and I spent a lot of time out and about tryin' to get out of the house before we got roped into doing em.

I did always like plantin' the garden though. Mom always said the garden was where you learned patience, and the Lord's version of math, put one seed in, add some love, ya get a basket of squash out. She wore a wide-brimmed straw hat and an apron stained with tomato guts when she crouched down in the dirt beside me.

"Now dig a little well with your hand," she'd say, showin' me. "Not too deep. Seeds don't like bein' buried alive."

I poked my fingers into the warm soil and dropped in a seed.

"Now pat it, gentle, like you're sayin' goodnight to a baby."

She leaned back, brushin' hair off her forehead with her wrist. The sun painted her arms in gold and freckles, "Not every seed ya plant will grow, but they'll surely never grow if ya don't plant em'."

Then came a lesson about the crows.

"You hear that?" she asked, cockin' her head as a crow let out a ruckus from the power line.

"Yeah. He's squawkin' like he's seen a snake."

"He's lyin'. Crows lie. They holler like that just to spook you off your own dirt. Don't trust 'em."

I looked up at that black bird, shiftin' on the wire like he knew we was talkin' about him.

"What about owls?" I asked.

"Owls are saints," she said. "Night saints. But crows? Crows are smart, and born con men."

In the summer afternoons, thunder would rumble across the fields like a train too tired to stop. Then the power blinked off, and the house sighed into stillness.

We didn't light candles, we pulled out papa's old big lantern, the green Coleman with the hissin' mantle that smelled like campouts and history. Mom plated up cold meatloaf sandwiches, and Daddy poured sweet tea into Mason jars, the ice clinkin' like wind chimes.

Sometimes Matt would turn the battery radio on, the station fadin' in and out like it was chasin' the storm. "Nothin' on but preachers and fiddles," he muttered.

"Sounds about right," I said, grinnin'.

We ate those sandwiches slow, passin' the pickle jar round, the lantern glow flickerin' on the ceilin'. I remember thinkin' right then and there: *these are the nights I'll remember.* No buzz of fridge, no TV talkin' nonsense, just us. Together.

It was one of those dog days of summer, just too hot outside for anythin' other than the cicadas. I found myself diggin' through mom's junk drawer lookin' for a rubber band for a slingshot, I came across an old roll of film, dusty and soft around the edges.

"Mom, what's on this?" I asked.

She looked over from the sink and shrugged. "Could be Christmas. Could be my old Buick. Could be your dad in short shorts, God help us."

I was thinkin', this could be a treasure, "Can we get it developed?"

"Maybe." She replied.

But I didn't. Not right away. Part of me liked not knowin' what was on that roll. I'd unspool it just a little and hold it up to the light, tryin' to catch shadows like they were ghosts. I imagined all the memories trapped inside, curled up like messages in a bottle. That little roll lived in my sock drawer for years, a treasure too sacred to open. Sometimes I felt I was better just believin', than knowin'.

At night, when the town went quiet and the world shrank to the sound of my bedroom fan, I'd lie in bed watchin' my movies replay in my head from that day smilin', laughin' and sometimes wishin' I could share em'. They always took me to somewhere, sometimes to another time, and mostly just made me thankful for where I am.

I smiled I wondered what it'd be like to live in a place where people didn't wave from porches, where the grocery store stayed open past dark, and the sidewalks never rolled up.

"Maybe there's a town out there where the kids don't walk through cow pastures to get to school," I whispered to the dark.

Maybe. But maybe a town like that wouldn't smell like tomato vines and swamp water after a rain too. But, maybe a town like that wouldn't feel like home.

Too bad summer can't last forever…

Chapter 2 - Life was Simple
(Spring 1962)

That year, life wasn't measured in calendars or clocks. It ticked to the rhythm of screen doors, the crunch of gravel under bare feet, and the creak of the old school bell hangin' crooked above the front porch of Mill Town Elementary.

Most school mornin's started with me runnin' full speed down the dirt road, satchel flappin' like a busted window shutter and hair still wet from the pump out back. The red clay kicked up behind me like smoke off a fire. One mornin', I got halfway there when I realized I'd left my shoes sittin' right by the front door.

Miss Hollis took one look and said, "Bobby Chandler, you best turn yourself right back 'round. This ain't a barn."

So I jogged home. Mom waved to me from the kitchen window. "What are you doin' here, ain't you supposed to be at school?"

Lookin down at my bare feet, "I forgot my shoes again."

She smiled, "Bobby, I swear you'd forget your head if it wasn't attached. Here I just made some more cornbread, eat one before you go."

I sat at the table, just her and I talkin about the garden. I heard the school bell ring in the distance, "Oh no, I'm late!" as I bolted out the door.

I got back to class all huffin' and puffin' then looked down, still barefoot, grinnin' like I'd lost my report card.

Miss Hollis just sighed and muttered, "Lord, give me patience."

I think she meant it.

Recess was when the real learnin' happened. While the other boys were roughhousin' near the pump shed or flingin' rocks at the bell tower, I'd be under the big oak with Lila Hollis, Miss Hollis' niece and about the sharpest girl I ever met. We played marbles in the dust, knees dirty, eyes locked on the cat's eye we both swore was lucky.

"You sure you wanna lose again today?" she'd ask, smirkin'.

"Maybe I'm lettin' you win," I'd shoot back.

"You ain't that generous." She said slyly.

Some of the boys would walk by and snicker.

"Bobby's playin' with a girl," they'd whisper like it was a crime.

Lila would just shrug, not even lookin' up.

"Jealous boys throw the worst shade," she'd say.

And truth be told, I didn't care one lick. She beat me fair most days. And I liked watchin' the way her braid slid over her shoulder when she leaned down to shoot.

Lila liked drawin' horses. Not cartoony ones, real ones, with flowin' manes and strong legs, like they'd gallop right off the page if you didn't hold the paper down. She'd fill the margins of her spellin' tests with sketches, sometimes wearin' saddles, sometimes wild and free.

Me, I wasn't much of an artist. I mostly drew stick men climbin' trees or fallin' out of 'em. Sometimes I'd draw us, Matt, Eric, Lila, and me, all standin' on the sandbar like we'd discovered the New World. Miss Hollis didn't fuss about the doodles. She said imagination was the closest thing we had to wings.

Come afternoon, after the sun got tired and slid down behind the pine tops, Miss Hollis would crack open Charlotte's Web and read to us. Her voice drifted through the open windows, carried on the breeze like

15

it had some place to be. The whole room would go still, just the turnin' of pages, the sound of cicadas, and that sweet smell of school bakin' in the heat.

"You have been my friend," she read one day, slow and soft, "That in itself is a tremendous thing."

I remember glancin' at Lila. She didn't look back, but she was smilin'.

Lunch was always simple. Cornbread wrapped in wax paper. A jar of sweet tea sweatin' through a paper bag. Maybe a bruised peach or a chunk of apple if we were lucky. We'd sit out on the steps, backs to the wall, shoes kicked off, and pass the salt shaker Mom tucked in the satchel just in case.

"This cornbread's better than last time," Matt said once, mouth full.

"That's 'cause it's mine," I grinned.

Eric looked suspicious.

"You sure it ain't possum loaf?"

"Only one way to find out."

We laughed until we couldn't breathe, the kind of laughter that didn't need to ask permission, never had to explain itself, and had no regret.

Life didn't feel small. It felt *just right*. Big enough to hold wonder, small enough to know which mud holes were deep, and which weren't. We didn't know what we didn't know, and that was just fine. The days stretched out like the road to Coldwater Creek, dusty, sunlit, full of secrets and wonder…and most times horseflies too, just to make sure you keep movin' along.

And me? I was just a barefoot boy with a marble in my pocket and a camera in my mind, tryin' to soak it all in.

Come Friday nights, we'd haul blankets and canvas sheets and make tents outta clotheslines and fishin' poles down to the creek. No fancy gear, just rope, sticks, and hope. We'd camp right there on the banks, legs bitten up by skeeters and hearts full of whatever magic lived between a good catfish story and a dead flashlight. I'm sure we stayed up way too late, but nobody had a watch, and we liked it that way.

We'd usually slink back home in the mornin' when the sun rose above the juniper trees and started gettin' hot out. We all smelled like we slept in the fire instead of around it. Dad was usually there sittin on the front porch sippin mornin' coffee, wearin a big ol smile watchin us drag ourselves back through the front gate. We could smell the bacon and waffles from there. After a good breakfast and a quick cat nap under the oak, we were all ready to do it again.

Those evenin's at Coldwater Creek weren't just part of the day, they were the whole point of it. Soon as my chores were done and dad gave me that slow nod, the one that meant *alright, you earned it*. I'd hop on my bike and pedal like the devil was after me, but mostly just the horseflies. My tackle box bounced behind me, tied on with two belts and a shoestrin'. The road to the creek was more ruts than road, you had to watch the sandy spots too, but I could ride it blindfolded. That dusty trail knew me, and the Coldwater waited like an old friend, cool and still, like it had been holdin' its breath all day just for me. Even in the thick of summer, that water stayed cold as well pipe steel. It curled around my ankles like a secret, full of shadows and shine. Catfish hid beneath the undercut banks, motionless and clever, while minnows scattered near the surface like silver sparks catchin' the last light. Sometimes I'd wade out, toss a line in slow, and let the silence settle. No radio. No chatter. Just the song of the bullfrogs croakin' low and slow in the swamps behind me, the cicadas hummin' up in the trees, and the wind rustlin' through the cypress like some old woman whisperin' stories from the porch.

We made a ritual of those evenin's, me, Matt, Eric, sometimes Lila if she wasn't off drawin' horses or readin' under the oak. We'd catch fireflies in Mason jars, screwin' the lids on loose so they could breathe, watchin' 'em blink like tiny lanterns in the dusk. We'd get the fire goin

17

good and hot. If we didn't catch anythin', that was ok. We would just dig up some food. Behind the ole cypress stump we always kept buried about ten cans of beans and spam. Eric's idea. He said he was gettin' tired of haulin em back and forth.

For fun we'd usually throw one or two in the fire without openin 'em. Then see who would stay sittin by the fire the longest while that can of beans got good n' hot. If the fire was real hot, it wouldn't take more than a minute or two before the explosion. It'd send red hot beans and glowin' coals all over the sandbar. One time it even burned our tent down. That was the last time we ever took a tent. Mostly we just laid out under the stars anyway, they seemed to go on forever and ever. If the skeeters were bad, we'd just burry ourselves in the sand with a shirt over our face.

By day, we waged mock battles, duckin' behind logs with BB guns and shields made of plywood scraps we'd find in the woods from the last flood. We'd line up like soldiers and charge across the sandbar, hootin' and hollerin', smudged with mud like war paint.

"I got you!" Eric'd shout.
"Did not!" Matt'd yell back.
"OWWW, ya got me!" Lila would shout.
"You're dead, I shot you fair!" Eric would insist.
"You missed my *shoulder...see no mark*, I'm still in play!" Matt said pullin up his sleeve.

I don't think we ever finished a single battle without arguin' about the rules, mostly over how many pumps were allowed on Matt's air pump bb gun since the rest of us had single shot Red Riders.

We'd sit with our bare feet dug into the sand, toes wigglin' in the cool grit. The sun always seemed to bleed a little slower behind the treeline, like even it didn't wanna leave. That place made you feel like the world might actually hold still long enough to understand it.

18

We didn't need a welcome sign, you felt it the minute you stepped outta the truck. Folks waved from porches like it was their job, even if they didn't know your name. And if they *did*, they'd ask how your mom's tomato plants were doin' and whether your brother got over that stomach bug.

The barber, Mr. Lowell, knew every boy's cowlick, every man's credit tab, and which kid had cried last time he brought out the clippers.

"Sit still, Bobby," he'd say. "Ain't tryin' to shave a squirrel."
"You're the one with the blade," I'd mutter, wincin'.

He always smelled like talc and tobacco, and his little radio buzzed out gospel songs like it was tunin' in from heaven's own back porch.

Milk got left in glass bottles on our front step, sweat beadin' down the side like it missed bein' cold already. Mr. Timmons delivered it every Thursday before dawn, his old truck coughin' like it needed coffee. Mom said you could set your clock by him, if you had one that worked.

Miss Gables ran the general store, her fingers flyin' over that big brass register like she was playin' a hymn.

"You're growin' like a weed, Bobby," she'd say, slidin' me a licorice whip.
"Just tryin' to keep up with the beans," I'd grin.

That register dinged like a church bell, and her handwritten receipts curled like old letters in a drawer.

At Chandler Hardware, dad didn't say much, but he said just enough. Every customer got the same quiet greetin':

"What're we fixin' today?"

He didn't upsell. He didn't fuss. He'd just pull a part off the shelf, brush it off with a rag, and explain how to use it in twelve words or less.

19

You didn't need money in here, not all the time anyway. Some folks traded eggs for wire, greens for hinges, stories for change. The only currency that really mattered was trust.

Time moved different here. Sunrise told you when to start, rain told you when to pause, and the seasons told you everythin' else. Schedules didn't come from clocks or calendars, they came from dirt under your nails and the way folks bones felt when the wind shifted. The Saturday mornings we weren't out on the creek, meant biscuits at the diner with mom and dad. The air always smelled like sausage grease and burnt toast, and you couldn't sit down without elbowin' a neighbor. Farmers sat at the counter jawin' over black coffee, boots crusted in red clay, hats tipped back.
We kids took extra syrup when mom wasn't lookin'.

"You don't need all that," she'd scold.
"Syrup's the best part," I'd grin, dunkin' my biscuit like it was a donut.

Sundays were sacred, but not quiet. We'd all pile into Grandma's house in the mornin', the screen door bangin' as aunts and uncles arrived with casseroles and ties half-knotted. We'd ride to church together in a caravan of worn tires and shiny shoes, windows cracked for the breeze, the organ already hummin' in our heads. After service, the adults stood with Papa in a circle, talkin' about the sermon and politics like they were the same thing, while us kids made for the donut table like it was a race. Mill Town Bakery donuts were the best. Then it was barefoot chaos in the backyard, tree climbin', tag, and Lila tryin' to teach Eric how not to fall out of the swing.

Sunday afternoons settled soft like a hymn on a breeze. Porch naps, dogs snorin' under rockers, church windows still open wide enough to let out a few leftover hallelujahs. Pies cooled on sills, the sweet scent of apple and peach mixin' with fresh-cut grass and laundry soap.

We had no stoplights in our town. Just one caution bulb that blinked yellow like it was thinkin' about doin' more but decided not to bother. The town didn't have secrets, not really. But it had layers, soft ones, hidden in the creak of swings at dusk, in the way Mrs. Givens always left the porch light on even though she knew her son wasn't comin' home.

A boy could ride from one edge to the other in ten minutes flat, less if he didn't mind jumpin' curbs. But still, it felt like you'd traveled somewhere.

The town breathed. It forgave. It remembered.
And I still believe, if you listened real close, you could hear it speak.

Chapter 3 - The Summer Before
(Summer 1962)

That summer, the air hung so still you could hear your own thoughts rattle. Early June heat came and never left, settlin' into the bones of the town like an old wet quilt too stubborn to be shaken off. The dusty roads baked red and cracked, cicadas tuned up in the pines like they were practicin' for a concert with no end. We ran barefoot down clay lanes, feet slappin' earth, skin browned by sun, mouths sticky from store-bought orange slices and spit watermelon seeds.

Life moved slow, on purpose.

I spent my mornings helpin' out at dad's store, Chandler Hardware, sweepin' sawdust into neat little piles only for the breeze to scatter it all again. Dad had me refillin' bins, nails, bolts, screws, all by size, and carryin' the day's change over to mom in a little tobacco tin she kept in the drawer by the stove.

"Don't dawdle," dad would say, not lookin' up from his ledgers. "Wouldn't dream of it," I'd mutter, already jinglin' the tin like it was a treasure chest.

He never smiled at my jokes, but he always had sweet tea waitin' when I finished.

Memorial Day was a town event, whether you wanted it to be or not. Families dragged picnic baskets down to the Riverwalk, blankets spread under old oaks that had seen more stories than any newspaper. There'd be fried chicken, deviled eggs, sweet pickles, and lemonade so tart it curled your tongue. The Veterans always came in their crisp uniforms, hats tilted low, eyes distant but soft. A local boy plucked a banjo under the gazebo, while old Mrs. Gentry danced slow with her husband like the music had waited just for them.

Matt helped me hang little flags along the railin' of the store, whisperin',

"You think we'll have to go fightin one day?"
"You mean more than moccasins?" I shot back, elbowin' him.

He grinned, but there was somethin' else in his eyes that day, somethin' I wouldn't understand till much later.

When we got back home, mom was elbow-deep in the garden, her straw hat floppin' against her shoulders as she weeded the tomatoes, okra, snap beans and marigolds to keep the pests away.

"These'll keep the bugs out and the neighbors jealous," she said, pattin' the soil with the back of her trowel.

Matt had an old shortwave radio cracked open on the porch. He fiddled with the dials like he was tryin' to find messages from another planet.

"I heard Havana last night," he muttered, twistin' the knob.
"I heard you talkin' to yourself," I said.
Matt shot back, "Well, maybe I was sayin' somethin' worth hearin'."

I laughed out loud, too loud 'cause he hit me in my shoulder good for it.

Eric and I spent most afternoons down at Coldwater Creek, fishin' for whatever was dumb enough to bite and buildin' forts from driftwood like we were explorers on some half-forgotten frontier.

"If we find gold," Eric said, squintin' through binoculars made of toilet paper rolls,
"We ain't tellin' nobody."
"We'd tell Lila," I said.
"Yeah… but only if she promises not to *sell* it."

Evenin's belonged to the town. Church suppers with banana puddin' and chicken pot pie, soapbox races down Ridge Hill, and Friday night movies where the film'd pop and flicker and we'd all cheer anyway. Sometimes the movie didn't matter. It was the buttered popcorn, the sticky floors, the whispered bets about whether the reel would snap before the hero kissed the girl.

Main Street carried its own rhythm.
Uncle Don's repair shop hummed with electric fans and old radios.
Miss Elma rolled out crates of 5¢ comics, their covers cracked and smellin' like attic rain.
Chandler's Hardware front window always had a stack of seed packets on sale, mostly because the plantin' season had already passed.

Miss Elma handed me a copy of *Our Town* one afternoon. It was held together more by tape than paper.

"You like to watch things," she said. "That's good. But make sure you write it down, Bobby, or it'll vanish."

"Thank ya, mam." I replied.

I took it back to the hardware store and gently put it behind the counter, like it was the gospel. It was safe and sound sittin' next to dad's canon 8mm zoom camera he had won last month in the church raffle.

Just then, I saw Lila walkin' barefoot up the road to the diner, her sketchbook tucked under one arm, laughin' to herself like she knew a joke the rest of the world hadn't earned yet.

I looked at the camera, thinkin bout what Miss Elma said, then looked at dad. He was watchin' me and without me even sayin anythin' he said "Go ahead, just be careful."

I grabbed that 8mm camera and fidgeted with the dials. Dad showed me how to use it then I filmed her from across the street, her braid swingin', her toes dusted red, still laughin' as cicadas risin' behind her like sound turned visible.

24

Dad said "That should make for a good memory."

It was a golden summer, slow and syrupy and full of nothin' in the best way. It seemed like it was goin' to keep goin' forever. But lookin' back, I can remember it like it was yesterday.

The shadows started stretchin' longer just before the sun dipped. Because on a Tuesday in late June, I was just sittin' on the curb outside the theater, with that old book Miss Elma gave me in my lap flippin through the pages when a clean fancy black car with Atlanta plates and no mud marks on the tires pulled up to the inn. A woman in a clean white shirt with a briefcase and narrow eyes gracefully got out. I watched her step out, check her watch, and glance around like she'd just landed in a zoo.

Somethin' about the way the door shut told me, Summer wasn't gonna last forever.

Chapter 4 - Allied General
(Fall 1962)

Far from red clay and porch swings of Mill Town, in a high-rise of brushed steel and glass, the fate of our town was being plotted by people who'd never walked its streets. Inside Allied General's Atlanta boardroom, the air was chilled, the windows spotless, and the table large enough to seat two dozen comfortably, though only eight chairs were filled. A map stretched across the table, state lines and county roads lit beneath plastic lamination. Red pushpins dotted familiar places: Bay Springs, Monroe Ridge, Willow Fork. A new pin hovered in a VP's hand, hovered, then pressed into the paper over "Mill Town."

"Low competition," said a man in a dark blue tie, not looking up from his papers. "Infrastructure's dated. Closest franchise cluster is Pensacola, and that's diluted."

"Proximity to the highway makes it viable," another chimed in. "If we move fast, we get ahead of the bypass, land's still cheap."

The CEO, a sharp-browed man with cufflinks shaped like tiny dollar signs, didn't speak at first. He studied the map, tapping a pen against his palm.

"Let's make it clean," he finally said. "Carr, you're up. Handle permitting. Ease the friction. I want a full greenlight by year's end."

His voice didn't rise, but the room nodded like a sermon had been preached.

"What's the bonus this time?" Evelyn Carr asked, her voice smooth and careful.

"A Quarter this time. If it's seamless."

That sealed it. She leaned back in her chair and glanced at the map again. Her eyes lingered on the thin line labeled Mainstreet, like it was already a memory. Later that week, Evelyn sat alone in her office, flipping through aerial photos and zoning diagrams, sticky notes covering ordinances and demographic summaries. Civic meeting records. Property values. Business licenses. She flipped past one image and then backtracked. Mainstreet. Thatched awnings. Ghost signs. Little shops clinging to old paint.

"Charming," she muttered. "And brittle" she replied closing her binder.

Her visit to Mill Town was supposed to be quiet. She rented a room at the old inn near the square under the name *E. Carson*. Wore soft clothes and walking shoes. Took long morning strolls. Scribbled notes in the margins of a folded-up newspaper.

She passed Miss Elma's, counted parking spaces near Gable's, the width of alleyways. She even sat at the park for an hour counting the foot traffic past the storefronts.

That night, she reserved a private table by the fireplace at the inn's tiny restaurant. Mayor Heartwell arrived just after sunset, jacket folded over one arm, eyes wary but curious.

"You folks always do business over steak?" he asked, settling in.

"Only when we want to be taken seriously," Evelyn smiled.

They sipped red wine and danced around zoning and tax incentives like old friends catching up on weather. Slowly, she unfurled phrases like *"sales tax revenue," "job creation," "progressive,"* and *"regional growth."*

"The community might not be ready," the mayor said, dabbing his mouth with a linen napkin. "Folks here are… slow to change."

Evelyn placed her hand gently atop his.

"Progress needs a champion," she said. "And I think it could be you."

27

The music drifted on, soft and forgettable. The plates were cleared. The bill was never brought.

When the restaurant closed at 8, the mayor's car was still there.

The door to Evelyn's suite clicked shut, it sounded quieter than it should've. And yet, it echoed.

The deal had begun.

Change didn't usually happen too quick round here, but you could always tell when somethin' was about to change, not by what was said, but by what wasn't.

I was fishin' down by the creek on the other side of school when I saw 'em first. It started with a rusted pickup I didn't recognize, parked by the edge of the old orchard where the pecan trees leaned like old men restin' on canes. A couple fellas in clean khakis stepped out, clipboards in hand. I waved, but they didn't wave back. Didn't nod. Just looked around like the place was already theirs. Then one of 'em took out a can of spray paint and marked a tree, right across the trunk, a red 'X' line like a wound.

By the time I rode up on my bike to get a closer look, they were already walkin' back toward their truck, boots dusty, eyes straight ahead.

"Who were they?" I asked dad that night.

Dad was sittin' on the porch, legs stretched out, whittlin' something from an ole broom handle.

"Surveyors," he muttered.
"For what?" I quickly replied.
"Don't know. But folks usually don't paint trees unless they plan on movin' 'em. Or cuttin' 'em down."

Then came the letter at Gable's Mercantile. I think Mrs. Gables read it three times before she even showed it to Mr. Gable. I was standin' by the candy jars when she waved me over and tapped the corner of the paper.

"From a firm down in Mobile," she whispered, like the letter might hear her. "Ask if we'd ever consider a long-term lease."

"Lease for what?" I asked.

She just shook her head and said,

"That's the part they don't tell you up front."

Mr. Gable grumbled when he saw it. Didn't say much, just folded the letter slow and slipped it under the counter like it was somethin' indecent.

Over at Benny's Diner, the whispers started. Whispers and coffee go hand in hand here, but these had a different sound. Uncertain. Nervous. Too polite to be honest.

"Maybe they're extendin' the highway," one fella said, pickin' at his grits.
"Could be a new produce co-op," another added.
"Might mean more jobs," someone offered, though not convincingly.

Nobody said the word. Not yet.

But you could feel it hangin' in the air like heat before a storm. Folks stirrin' their coffee slower, starin' out the window like they were waitin' for somethin' they cain't name. They had all heard about them moving in on other small towns in Alabama.

That Sunday afternoon, Dad and I were at the store, doin' inventory since the rain had kept customers home. He was by the window, starin' across the square with a look I hadn't seen since the night the tornado skipped past the grain tower.

"What's wrong?" I asked, settin' a box of bolts on the counter.

He didn't answer right away, just motioned with his chin toward City Hall.

A Cadillac sat there, idle, paint too shiny for a Sunday. That same woman in a pressed blouse and high heels stepped out, carryin' a briefcase like it held something she didn't want anyone to read.

"City Hall don't open on Sundays," Dad said flat.
"Maybe she's lost?"
"Nobody gets lost with a briefcase," he said, and walked back to the stockroom.

A few days later, I took dads camera out past the pasture and stood on the rise just above the orchard, where the grass had turned gold under the heat.

I didn't really know why. It just seemed like the light was just good.

The trees stood there, still and familiar, every one of 'em part of some memory. The pecan tree where Matt and I hung a tire swing. The big oak that dropped branches in storms like it was throwin' tantrums. I panned the camera slow, the lens glidin' over trunks marked in red, the leaves shimmerin' in that lazy way summer leaves do.

There was no noise but the buzz of cicadas and the whirr of my camera.

But my chest felt tight.

I didn't know what was happenin'. Not really. But deep down, I knew I was filmmin' the end of somethin', even if I didn't know it yet.

Chapter 5 - The Arrival of Allied General
(Spring 1963)

There ain't no trumpet blast when the end of a town begins, just little signs, soft at first, like whispers before a shout. It started with little bitty flags. Red and orange, staked in the orchard like tiny warnings. They fluttered in the wind, bold as blood against the green. One was jabbed right where the pecan tree used to drop nuts into mom's apron. Another, right at the bend where us kids used to play war with pinecones and shouts. Nobody told us what they meant. Nobody had to. Flags don't go up for nothin'. If we really wanted to know what was going on, we knew where to go.

Back at Benny's Diner, the air felt different too. Quieter. Like folks were talkin' in code.

"State's probably widenin' the road," said one man, starin' deep into his coffee.
"Could be a packing plant. You know, vegetables or somethin' local," another offered.

The waitress topped off my tea without askin', her eyes flicking toward the window where you could just make out the tips of the orchard trees.

No one said the word.
Not *store*.
Not *superstore*.

But I swear it hovered in the air, waitin' for someone brave enough, or foolish enough, to name it.

That afternoon, Miss Elma waved me behind the counter at Gable's. She was holdin' a stiff white envelope like it was full of spiders.

"Came this mornin'," she said, handin' it to Mr. Gable.
"Typed letter. Atlanta firm. Wants to know if we'd ever consider... a sale."

He opened it slow, lips pressed thin, eyes movin' across the page like each word was a slap.

"Allied Holdings, LLC," he read aloud.
"Never heard of 'em," I said.
"Doesn't matter," he said. "Folks like this don't introduce themselves twice."

He folded the letter and slid it under the old brass register.
The kind you gotta punch with your whole hand to ring up a sale.

"Let's see them try and lease tradition," he muttered. "Ain't got a key for that."

Out past the orchard, the trees started lookin' different.
Orange 'X's painted across the bark, like they'd been sentenced.
Some trunks had deep cuts in 'em notched and marked, as if someone had already decided which day they'd fall.

I brought my camera. No plan, just feelin' like someone needed to remember.

I filmed the trees swayin' in the wind, that orange paint flarin' against their bark. It wasn't loud. Just quiet enough to feel sacred. The wind moved like breath through the branches, and I swear, those trees were sayin' goodbye.

Then came the bulldozers. Not with warning. Not with flyers or town meetings or even a posted notice. It was almost like they had sprouted from the ground itself. They were just there, one morning at dawn, growlin' across the southern edge of town. Big yellow machines belchin' diesel and shakin' the ground like thunder.

By noon, fourteen trees were down.
The air smelled like oil and sawdust and every memory those trees ever held, ripped up and flung aside.

I saw Eric standin' near the fenceline, arms crossed, shirt hangin' loose off his shoulder.

"Guess they ain't just plantin' cucumbers," he muttered.

Dad went to City Hall that same day. I know 'cause I watched him from the hardware store window, his shoulders squared like he was holdin' somethin' heavy and didn't want to drop it.

He came back an hour later, his brow dark and jaw tight.

"They say it's *preliminary development planning,*" he said.
"Nothing finalized," I repeated.
"Yeah," he replied, hangin' his cap on the hook.
"Funny how nothin's finalized but the trees are already gone."

He didn't say much more that day.
Didn't have to.

The church basement smelled like folding chairs, starch, and leftover casserole. That's where they held the meeting, not at City Hall, not at the courthouse, but below St. Luke's, where the fellowship hall still had old Vacation Bible School banners curled up in the corners.

By the time I arrived, it was standing room only. Folks packed shoulder to shoulder, fanning themselves with hymnals, whisperin' about what was comin' and hopin' someone would say it out loud.

I had my camera on my lap, already rollin' before the mayor stepped up.

Mayor Heartwell looked like a man who'd rather be anywhere else, tie too tight, collar too stiff, fingers clamped around the mic like it might wiggle away.

"Thank you all for coming tonight," he began, voice thin and formal. "We're pleased to welcome representatives from Allied General. Here to answer questions and... provide clarity."

He stepped aside, like someone lettin' a snake out of a box.

Three men in dark suits stood behind him like shadows that carried briefcases. Then there she was, Evelyn Carr. The same woman I had seen at the Inn.

She didn't smile. Just nodded once and stepped forward, sharp in a gray suit with buttons that caught the light. Her voice was like clean paper, smooth, practiced, not a word outta place.

"Allied General is committed to regional investment," she said. "We believe in opportunity, accessibility, and community partnerships."

She said it like she meant it. But it didn't feel like she meant *us*.

Mr. Abernathy was first to stand. Big man, hands calloused from decades of swingin' feed bags and balin' wire.

"What about jobs?" he asked. "For our folks, not outsiders."

Evelyn nodded politely, hands folded.

"We expect to create dozens of permanent positions across departments. Hiring will begin with local applicants."

Some clapped. Most didn't.

Miss Elma stood next, glasses slid to the end of her nose, arms crossed like she'd already heard what was comin'.

"What happens to stores like mine?" she asked. "We've kept this town fed and clothed for near a century."

Evelyn didn't blink. "Healthy competition fosters innovation," she said. "It strengthens resilience."

Someone near me whispered under their breath, "That means 'we win, you close.'"

Then Dad stood up, Thomas Chandler, the quiet one folks listen to when he speaks 'cause he don't do it often.

"I'd like to know," he said slowly, "how a bulldozer cleared four acres before a single permit was signed."

That one landed. The room stiffened. Evelyn's team shifted in their loafers. But she kept her face even.

"All preliminary work is conducted within legal thresholds," she said. "We're committed to transparency and full compliance."

Dad nodded once and sat. But I saw it in his eyes. He wasn't satisfied. Not even close, he had just opened the door to the lion's cage.

From the back row, I filmed it all. My lens caught sweat beadin' on brows, hands twitchin' in laps, and jaws clenched hard enough to creak. Some faces looked mad. Some confused. Some already looked beat. And then there was Mrs. Elanor, she was a young mother with two youngins'. She stood up with a baby on her hip and asked, voice soft but steady: "Will the new store have baby supplies?"

Evelyn turned to her like it was a press conference. "We believe in bringing affordable products that otherwise may be difficult or sometimes impossible for you to attain with current means."

The mother sat down, eyes full of a future she hadn't planned for.

The mayor nodded along like he believed it all. But his eyes... they kept drifting toward the floor.

And I thought, right then, that our world was like that last row of trees marked in orange, still standing, but not for long.

Supper was quiet that night.

Not the kind of quiet where people are tired or thinkin'. This was that sharp, silverware-on-ceramic kind of silence, where every clink of a fork sounds too loud and every chew feels like an interruption. We sat there under the yellow glow of the kitchen light, mashed potatoes settlin' on the plate like wet plaster.

Mom asked "Bobby, did you finish you're homework?" but she didn't look up when she said it.

"Almost," I muttered.

Matt passed the butter without askin'. Dad didn't say much. Just cut his roast slow, each slice cleaner than the last, like he was tryin' to make sense of somethin' he couldn't fix. And nobody mentioned the meeting. Later that night, I heard them in the kitchen. Mom was drying a plate like it had insulted her.

"It's already decided," Dad said softly.

She didn't answer right away. Just kept wiping the plate till it squeaked.

"They don't build things that fast unless the papers were signed before they asked."
"They never asked," she said, finally.

And that was the end of it. I went out to the porch, sat down on the swing that creaked just enough to remind you it was still holdin' you up. The air smelled like dirt and sawdust and somethin' else, loss, maybe, though I didn't have that word for it yet…kinda hard to explain.

I opened my notebook and wrote: "They call it growth, but it doesn't feel like growin'. It feels like clearin'."

Next day, Lila and I walked down Main Street, the afternoon sun slantin' long between the awnings. Her sketchbook was under her arm, but she wasn't drawin'. Just walkin'. We passed Miss Elma sweepin' her storefront, and Mr. Gable watchin' the sky like he was checkin' for a forecast no radio would ever report.

"They smiled too much last night," Lila said, her voice low. "When adults smile like that, while they're talkin' about something, it usually means they're lyin'."

"How do you know?" I asked.

"My daddy used to smile like that when he was leavin."

She didn't look at me when she said it. Didn't need to.

Matt didn't come to the meeting, but he had opinions all the same.

"Maybe it'll be good," he said later, flippin' through a car magazine on the couch.
"Some folks could use lower prices."

But his voice didn't match his words. Not quite. It was the kind of voice you use when you're tryin' to convince yourself.

"You think Dad believes that?" I asked.

Matt quickly replied, "I think Dad's gonna fight either way."

The next mornin, when I biked into town, I passed the repair shop.

Uncle Don was in the window, pinning up a handwritten sign. Big block letters, thick black marker:

LOCALLY OWNED. NOT FOR SALE.

He didn't say a word when I stopped and watched.
Just nodded once, then went back inside.

I took my camera to the orchard again, though it didn't feel like the orchard anymore.
All the trees were gone except a few here and there.

The ones that stood looked smaller, lonelier, like they were next in line. I aimed the lens up as a crane's claw swung one of them through the air, its roots dangling like broken fingers.

One last pecan tree remained, the one with the swing rope we used to climb like monkeys. The crane wrapped it's metal fingers around it's trunk. With a loud crack it was over. The tire was danglin' from the crane, swayin' back and forth in the breeze like it was tryin' to escape.

I filmed it all.

Zoomed in on the torn roots, the red slash across the bark, the way the branches looked like arms outstretched.

And I whispered to the tape: "This is the first funeral I've ever filmed."

Chapter 6 - Stars, Stripes and Savings (July 1963)

Sometimes you can just feel a storm comin' on a sunny day, even if the sky is perfectly clear. Something in the air just tells ya that it's comin'. That's what those posters felt like. They showed up without fanfare, slick, glossy things with red, white, and blue letters that practically screamed off the page. The first one was taped lopsided to the post office door. I remember the corners curled in the humidity, edges smudged with dust and fingerprints, like they'd already been handled too much.

Big bold letters at the top:

"FREEDOM FESTIVAL – JULY 4th at Allied General!"
"Music! Fireworks! Family Fun!"

A kid near me read it out loud like it was a Christmas miracle.

"They're gonna have fried elephant ears," he told his little sister.
"Ewww" she balked.
"I dunno, some kid said they were really good" he shrugged. "But it sounds kinda gross."

Soon enough, those posters were everywhere. Pinned to telephone poles, stuck to storefront windows, even tucked between hymnals at First Baptist like they were tryin' to baptize the whole town in patriotism.

"Come celebrate Mill Town's bright future," one read.
"Live music! Free food! Games for the whole family!"
"Proudly sponsored by Allied General."

They printed 'em thick too, the kind that crackled when you bent 'em, slick as magazine pages. The ink bled a little in the heat, and the tape melted on windshields where folks had found 'em left like parking tickets.

The scent of hot paper and citrus glue followed you around like a dog starvin' for attention.

The talk started soon after.

At Gable's, folks murmured near the cash register, eyes darting to the flyer taped up outside.

At Benny's Diner, the waitresses passed out eggs and gossip in equal portions.

"They say there's gonna be fireworks that put the fairgrounds to shame."
"Heard they're handin' out free radios."
"One fella told me you can get hired just by shakin' hands."

The air buzzed, not from truth but from possibility, like the town was bein' offered a present it wasn't allowed to unwrap yet, but everyone was guessing what was inside.

Jason couldn't contain himself. He lived two farms over from us, and I found him that afternoon leaning against his rusted pickup, studying a flyer like it was a treasure map.

"This is it, Bobby," he said, not looking up. "This is my chance."

"For what?" I asked, though I already knew. Jason had been talking about getting out of farming ever since I could remember.

"For everything." He smoothed the paper against his truck's hood. "They're hiring stockers, cashiers, even department managers. With benefits, Bobby. Health insurance, paid vacation." His eyes shone. "I put my application in yesterday."

"But what about your dad's farm?"

Jason's jaw tightened. "What about it? Another bad season and we'll lose it anyway. Least this way I'll have steady money. Maybe even enough for a new truck by Christmas."

I raised my camera. "Can I film you? With the flyer?"

He straightened his shoulders, held the paper up like a diploma. Through the lens, I saw what he wanted to see, a future written in red, white, and blue promises. But I also caught the tremor in his hands, the way his eyes darted toward his family's fields stretching brown and thirsty behind him.

"You know what the best part is?" Jason said as I lowered the camera. "They're calling it a celebration of the American Dream. And that's what it is, right? The chance to make something better of yourself?"

The words tasted bitter as the dust in the air. I thought of my father's hardware store, of Main Street's shops that had weathered decades of lean times and fat. What kind of opportunity celebrated itself by replacing what already was?

But I just nodded, watching Jason fold the flyer carefully and tuck it into his shirt pocket, right over his heart.

I spent the rest of the day walkin' town with my camera. People leaned in close when I asked about the festival, like they didn't want the microphone to catch the part they didn't say.

At the hardware store, Mr. Gable wiped his hands on his apron, looked straight into the lens, and said: "It'll be good for business… unless it isn't."

Miss Elma stood in her doorway with the bell behind her janglin' softly in the breeze. "I've seen festivals before. But not like this. This one feels bought."

A group of boys hollered in the background, kickin' a can across the street. One of 'em paused just long enough to say: "I hope they got hot dogs."

The heat sat heavy on our shoulders, the kind that made your shirt cling and your thoughts stick. And all around, the town felt...like it was holdin' its breath for the wrong reason. That night, I played back what people were sayin in my head. Heard the way folks talked about the "celebration" like it was somethin' they were supposed to be excited for, but didn't quite seem to trust.

I wrote in my notebook: A firework lights up the sky just before it disappears then all you're left with, is trash. Maybe that's what this is.

The first thing you noticed was the flags.

Big ones. real big, hangin' off every light pole like sails catchin' wind that wasn't there. Red, white, and blue everywhere you looked, from the laminated banners that lined the fences to the little paper hats they handed out to kids. The Riverwalk had been transformed into somethin' between a carnival and a campaign rally. There were folding chairs in uneven rows, balloons bobbin' on strings, and loudspeakers propped on milk crates blarin' country tunes and radio jingles.

They called it the Freedom Festival.
But it didn't feel like freedom to me.
It felt like a sale with fireworks.

Someone'd built a makeshift stage from shipping pallets, strung with red, white, and blue bunting that flapped in the breeze like it was tryin' too hard. Up top, a local DJ in a cowboy hat introduced acts every fifteen minutes, shouting like folks cain't hear him from five feet away.

"Next up, Mill Town's own Lonesome Pine Ramblers!"

A few folks clapped. A few didn't. Some sat with arms folded and brows drawn, eyes scanning the horizon like they were waitin' for somethin' more honest to arrive.

The smell of barbecue hung thick in the air, heavy with wood smoke and sweet sauce, and I'll admit, it pulled me in for a minute.
Hot dogs hissed on flat tops, and "Freedom Burgers" were wrapped in crisp Allied General paper, stamped with a flag and a slogan: *"Proud to Serve America."* Each one came with a cup of cola and a plastic flag toothpick stabbed in the bun like we were conquering lunch.

Kids darted between the legs of grown-ups, sticky hands clutchin' helium balloons, each one tied off with a tag that read *Welcome to the Future.* Greeters in crisp Allied collared shirts handed 'em out like they were givin' away hope in rubber form.

Everywhere you turned, there was somethin', a prize wheel, a dunk tank, sack races, a raffle booth shoutin' about a brand-new transistor radio or an electric toaster. The sound of tinny music and canned applause carried over the concrete parking lot, floatin' with the smell of cotton candy and diesel fumes.

Folks were laughin', takin' pictures, holdin' hands, but underneath it all, you could feel it. Like someone had handed us a party with a string tied to it. And they were all lined up waitin' their turn to pull.

I walked the edge of it all with dads camera hangin' around my neck, film clickin' every so often. I caught a few scenes.

A little girl, couldn't have been more than five, stood near the hot dog cart, her pigtails tied with ribbon that matched the balloons bobbin' above her. She clutched a paper plate like it held treasure, a Freedom Dog buried under relish and enough mustard to paint a porch. She took one bite too eager and, **splat**, a fat ribbon of mustard slid off the edge, landing right on the front of her white cotton dress, leaving a gold streak like a crooked lightning bolt. For a second, everyone near her froze, waitin' to see if she'd cry. But she didn't.

She looked down at the mess, let out a laugh that bubbled up like a soda fizz, and said real loud: "I guess my dress wanted a bite too!"

Then she took another chomp like nothin' had happened, mustard and all, her tiny shoulders shakin' with joy. Her mom tried to dab at the stain with a napkin, mutterin' about vinegar and bleach, but that little girl just kept grinnin' like the whole day was still perfect.

Near the edge of the crowd, Mrs. Elanor knelt beside a stroller, adjusting a sunhat on her squirmy toddler while tryin' to balance a snow cone in her other hand. The boy clutched a red helium balloon, the string tied loose around his chubby wrist, just tight enough to feel safe, but not tight enough to hold.

There was a gust, just a lazy, sweet-scented wind that rolled off the barbecue pits, and then the knot slipped.

The boy didn't notice at first. But I did. The balloon lifted slow, rose over the stroller like it was shy about leaving. Then, as if it had made up its mind, it caught a bit of breeze and darted up, swayin' left and right, a dot of red in the blue July sky.

It floated higher, past the tops of the parked trucks and vendor tents, past the strings of pennant flags flappin' in rhythm. Then over the rooftops of Main Street, where the paint still peeled on the barbershop and the post office's awning flapped on one corner.

The mother looked up, squinted, and then gave a small, sad smile.

The little boy reached up too late and let out a soft "Oh…"

But he didn't cry. Just watched it go, both hands now empty, the way kids do when somethin' slips away and they ain't old enough yet to chase it.

"That's ok, they're free, we'll get you another one." She said. He instantly stopped crying.

In my notebook later, I wrote: "They gave us balloons and fireworks. But nobody asked why we needed 'em."

By the time the sun peeked up over the pines, families were already staking out spots along the grassy stretch of the Riverwalk, chairs creakin' open, quilts laid out like claims on memory. The smell of damp earth mingled with charcoal, and the Blackwater shimmered beside them, still and wide like it was holdin' its breath.

Kids ran barefoot through the grass, gigglin' and tossin' pebbles toward the water while their parents unfolded aluminum chairs and swatted at gnats. Coolers clicked open, full of coleslaw and store-bought cookies. Flags fluttered from picnic baskets. Radios played scratchy country tunes in between bursts of static.

It looked like every Fourth of July I'd ever known. Only now, the banners all said Allied General.

Matt was at the edge of the field, helpin' park cars along the dirt access road that snaked around the back side of the Riverwalk. A man in a bright Allied polo handed him a cap and a thank-you voucher for a "future meal discount."

"Thanks for steppin' up," the man said, clappin' Matt on the back.

"No problem," Matt muttered, already sweatin' through his shirt.

The cap was stiff with fresh embroidery, the kind that leaves a red line across your forehead. The voucher fluttered in the breeze, unpromised.

Miss Elma stood near the gazebo, arms crossed, her wide straw hat throwin' a shadow over eyes that didn't blink much. She watched the whole thing like a schoolteacher waitin' for someone to fess up. She didn't take a flyer. Didn't sit for the music. Just stared like she was tryin' to see past the bunting and balloons to whatever was comin' next.

Mayor Heartwell wandered through the crowd in a seersucker suit, shakin' hands and noddin' like a bobblehead. But his eyes kept trailin' Evelyn Carr, who moved through the tents like she was already back in Atlanta.

He caught up with her by the refreshments table, tried to ask about zoning or ribbon cuttings, his voice just loud enough to make it seem casual.

She gave a soft laugh and glanced at her watch.

"Let's enjoy the festival, Mayor," she said with a smile that didn't reach her eyes. "There'll be plenty of time for business after."

Then she turned to greet someone else, leaving him there with his paper cup and a face that said he'd been dismissed. I wandered through the crowd with my camera, catchin' the quiet moments between the music and the speeches.

Folks were everywhere, smilin', snackin', listenin' to fiddles, but underneath it all, I swear you could feel the hush of worry. Like the town knew this celebration had a cost…They just hadn't figured out who'd be payin' for it.

By mid-mornin', families were already settin' up along the edges of the Riverwalk, foldin' lawn chairs open with loud snaps, shufflin' picnic blankets onto hot pavement like it was a summer parade on Main Street. Kids ran wild, eyes wide with sugar and helium, their feet slapping across the grass.

Folks brought coolers, bug spray, and the kind of hope you don't say out loud, hope that maybe this thing really was for them. Some wore their Sunday best like they were attendin' a fair. Others came in overalls and swim shorts, leanin' into the promise of free food and maybe, just maybe, a better tomorrow.

Matt was out in the heat, workin' the gravel turn-in as a volunteer, flaggin' cars into makeshift rows while the sun baked his neck red. Some manager in a blue Allied polo gave him a paper voucher and a branded baseball cap with the company's name stitched in bright red thread.

"Appreciate your help," the man said like he meant it.

"Sure," Matt replied, tugging the cap lower to block the glare.

Matt showed it to me. The voucher said "Future Meal Discount – One Per Customer", but no one said where or when the meal would be, or if it'd ever come at all. Miss Elma stood near the fence line, arms folded tight over her chest, a wide-brimmed hat shading her eyes. She didn't clap. Didn't sit. Just stared across the parking lot like it had betrayed her. When I walked by with my camera, she didn't speak just gave me a nod, slow and solemn, like we both knew somethin' wasn't sittin' right.

Dad didn't come at all. He stayed back at the house, said the fan belt needed replacin' on the mower, but I knew better. His silence was louder than fireworks.

From the center of it all, Mayor Heartwell moved like a man tryin' to look important, shakin' hands and adjustin' his tie even though the heat was meltin' it flat. I caught him on camera a few times, hoverin' near Evelyn Carr like a moth to porch light.

But she wasn't havin' it.

She moved through the crowd in that sharp gray dress like she was already thinkin' about her next project. When the mayor tried to corner her near the water table, she smiled quick, made an excuse about *scheduling*, and slipped off toward the back tents. He stood there with two lemonades in his hands, lookin' like someone who'd just realized he'd been thanked and forgotten in the same breath.

Everywhere I looked, people were wipin' sweat, smilin' too hard, and lookin' around like they were searchin' for the catch. Like this party was free, but the bill was comin' later.

The lot was full, but it wasn't with joy.

The music stopped mid-song, just cut off in the middle of a chorus and the voice from the speakers came on, smooth as syrup but colder.

"Ladies and gentlemen, we invite you to turn your attention to the main stage for a special announcement from our regional manager."

The crowd, still chewin' barbecue and wipin' mustard off kids' cheeks, turned toward the stage with paper fans and sunburned squints.

The DJ stepped back. And then Evelyn Carr walked up.

She moved like she'd rehearsed every step, like each heel tap on the plywood stage was planned. Hair tucked neat behind her ear, suit tailored sharp enough to slice sunlight. She didn't even flinch at the squeal of the mic.

"Happy Fourth of July, Mill Town," she said, her voice carryin' crisp and clear across the Riverwalk, wrapped in confidence like a ribbon on a package.
"What a beautiful day to celebrate partnership and progress."

Some folks clapped. Others just shifted in their chairs.

She went on, thankin' us for "embracing change," for "believing in opportunity," and for being "a community that values future growth."

"Allied General is proud to be part of your story," she said, hands folded like a preacher's. "Together, we're building something strong. Something sustainable. A brighter tomorrow for Mill Town families."

That word again. *Tomorrow.* Like today or yesterday didn't count anymore. The applause came, soft and uneven, like folks weren't sure if it was time to clap or time to worry. I turned my camera toward the crowd. Some smiled politely. Others didn't smile at all.

Then the real show began. Behind Evelyn, a large white tarp tugged loose from a scaffold just beside the stage. It unfurled with a snap of rope and wind, revealing a billboard big enough to cover half the feed store.

HELP BUILD THE FUTURE

Big block letters.
Underneath, a colorful chart of job openings, over 50 of them, printed in bright fonts like candy wrappers:

- Stockroom Attendant
- Seasonal Cashier
- Loss Prevention Assistant
- Overnight Receiving Crew
- Breakroom Associate

And next to it, a row of white tents popped up like mushrooms after rain.

One was marked HUMAN RESOURCES, with folks already standin' in line. Some held resumes. Others just held hope.

Another tent had folding tables with plastic signs that read:

FREE RESUME HELP
ON-THE-SPOT INTERVIEWS TODAY!

Clipboards, staplers, lemonade in paper cups, like a job fair and a bake sale had a baby.

I filmed it all. Every bit.

From Evelyn's shiny smile, to the hired clappers in Allied polos, to the man near the back who crossed his arms and said under his breath:

"So this was the real reason."

Back at the riverbank, the sun kept slippin' lower, and the smell of scorched burgers floated behind me as I walked away from the crowd. The music came back on a minute later, cheerier than before, but it couldn't cover the sound of the future bein' sold in tidy bullet points.

Not long after Evelyn stepped off stage, the crowds shifted, not toward the music or the games, but toward the billboard. Toward the future, printed in ink and stapled under a banner. It was like watchin' a slow tide roll in.

Mom stood near the job board, a paper plate in one hand, the other resting light on her purse strap. She didn't say anything. Didn't move much either. Just watched. A few feet away, Mrs Elenor's daughter, a young mother knelt on the grass, babies in laps and pens in hand, filling out applications against diaper bags and clipboards borrowed from the HR tent. One of 'em had a stain on her blouse and a look that said she didn't care anymore. The other one kept checkin' her watch between questions.

Mom's eyes never left them. Not once. She just stood there like she was holdin' her breath.

Matt stood at the side of the board, arms crossed, the brim of his Allied cap bent low to block the light. He looked at each listing like it was a test he hadn't studied for.

"You think I should?" he asked me softly, eyes still locked on the board.

I didn't answer. Not 'cause I didn't care. But 'cause I wasn't sure what he was really askin'.

He looked torn between shame and hope, like takin' one of those jobs meant givin' up… but not takin' one might mean fallin' behind.

Lila showed up a minute later, barefoot in the grass, a sketchbook under her arm. She stopped next to me, stared at the line of folks by the application tent, and shook her head. "They're calling it opportunity," she said. "But it feels like surrender."

I didn't argue. I didn't have to.

She opened her sketchbook and started drawing, not the billboard, not the smiling HR rep, but the people waiting in line. Bent shoulders. Folded arms. A child asleep on her mom's chest.

I had the camera in my hand, already rollin'.

I zoomed in on the line, slow and steady. Faces half-lit by sunset, half-shadowed by something none of us could name yet. Then I cut.

I didn't need to say a word. The film would speak for me.

By the time the sky turned lavender and the last sunbeam melted behind the trees, the whole Riverwalk had gone still.

Families settled on blankets and truck beds, bug spray in the air, mason jars full of tea resting in the grass. Kids climbed onto shoulders, babies yawned in their grandmoms' arms. Somewhere down by the picnic benches, a transistor radio buzzed with static before fading into silence.

I found a spot near the tall cypress with Lila, my camera already rollin'.

Then the speakers kicked in, patriotic music loud enough to shake the leaves.
John Philip Sousa led the charge, brass and drums gallopin' through the air. Then came "God Bless America," piped in like a hymn on parade.

Right after that, without a single pause, came a cheery jingle in a bright, tinny voice: "Allied General, building your future, one neighbor at a time!"

Some folks clapped. Some didn't seem to notice. But I felt the shift, like a spoonful of syrup followin' vinegar.

And then the sky bloomed.

The first firework rose fast and clean, BOOM!, a red starburst that popped like it'd been waitin' all day to make its entrance. Then blue. Then gold. Then a spinning white wheel that shimmered like a thousand dandelions caught in moonlight.

Children squealed. Moms smiled. Dads clapped with barbecue grease still on their fingers. For a moment, the whole town tilted their faces upward, eyes wide and mouths slack. And it was beautiful, I won't lie. Even I forgot, for just a heartbeat.

But then I turned my camera away from the sky. I filmed the crowd instead, the way the colors danced across their faces, turnin' joy into wonder, wonder into silence. How the bangs echoed against the other riverbank just out of frame, the hum of the current steady and old, as if it had seen this kind of magic before and knew better.

Later, when I edited the footage, I wouldn't use the Sousa march or the jingle.

Instead, I'd lay the film over the low hiss of the river, and the crackle of Mom's old radio, the one with the frayed dial and wood frame.

Because fireworks fade quickly, but rivers always remember.

We left before the grand finale. We didn't feel like stayin' to watch the sky get loud one more time. The three of us me, Lila, and Matt, slipped away through the side alley, our footsteps soft in the grass, then crunchin' steady along the road.

Behind us, the Riverwalk still pulsed with color and cheers. But up ahead, Main Street was quiet as a church pew after Sunday service.

The storefronts we passed looked like they were holdin' their breath. Gable's Mercantile, shuttered for the night. Miss Elma's Bookstore, windows dark and dust-fogged. Even the light above Uncle Don's repair shop was out for once. No neon signs. No foot traffic. Just us and the hum of the crickets…and the explosions in the background. Lila didn't say much. Matt kept his hands in his pockets, kickin' a pebble as he walked.

I held my camera at my side, not rollin'. Just carryin' it like it was part of me now. Like it could see in the dark even when I cain't. As we turned the corner near the square, I stopped.

There, barely stirrin' in the warm night breeze, was a single American flag hangin' over the front door of Chandler Hardware. The light from the streetlamp flickered just enough to catch it, a sliver of red and white against the blackened glass.

It didn't wave. It just hung there. Quiet. Still. Present.

I lifted my camera slowly and framed the shot, my finger hoverin' over the shutter. Then I whispered it, mostly to myself, but loud enough for them to hear.

"They lit up the sky. But they didn't light anything down here."

Nobody answered. We didn't need to.

Chapter 7 - The Grand Opening
(November 1963)

The air in town was hot that Veterans Day like summer just wasn't
ready to take a vacation. Flags sprouted overnight like wildflowers,
their reds and blues vivid against every porch post, every shop window
along Main Street, even danglin' from the rusted grain tower, its
silhouette loomin' solemn, as if it's whisperin' gratitude to the sky.

By sunrise, the town hummed different, alive with purpose, starched
uniforms snap as veterans tug them on, the low scrape of boots bein'
polished in kitchens echoes, fathers and grandfathers sittin' silent at oak
tables, their faces lined, eyes distant. Gold stars hung solemnly in some
of the windows. Mothers move quiet, pourin' coffee, its bitter aroma
thick, steam swirlin' beside velvet boxes cradlin' medals, their brass
glintin' under bare bulbs. Outside, behind the First Baptist Church, the
school band's tunin' up, clarinets squeakin' off-key, trumpets blarin'
"America the Beautiful" in three clashin' tempos, the notes tanglin'
with the laughter of kids clutchin' paper flags, wavin' them like wands.

I stand on the corner of Main and Elm, same as every year, my 8mm
camera heavy in my hands, its leather strap creaking, the lens cold
against my palm, ready to catch the parade's heart, soldiers' steps, kids'
grins, the town's pride. But today, somethin's off, a stillness in the air
like the sky's holdin' its breath, watchin' us. The crowd's here, but
thinner, familiar faces missing, old Mr. Gable's not by his store, Miss
Lorraine's scarf nowhere in sight. I adjust the focus, the viewfinder
framin' parents tuggin' collars straight, pattin' shoulders, their voices
low, urgent.

"Stand tall when they pass, Jimmy," Mrs. Carter says, her gloved hand
brushin' her son's jacket, his paper flag drooping.

"Yes, ma'am," he mumbles, scuffin' his sneakers, the gravel crunchin' soft.

A whisper cuts through, soft, hesitant, from two women nearby, their coats buttoned tight, paper coffee cups steaming.

"They're not endin' at the war memorial this year…?" Mrs. Elma says, her voice trailing, eyes flickin' to her friend, who frowns.

Her friend, leanin' closer. "Heard they're marchin' down to Allied for the grand openin'," she murmurs, barely audible, like it's a secret she's not sure she should share.

I freeze, my finger pausin' on the camera's trigger, the whir of film stopping, the world sharpening, coffee's tang, leaves' rustle, the band's trumpet hittin' a sour note. I lower the camera, its weight pullin' at my neck, and look down Main Street, where the parade always ends, the Veterans Memorial's granite stones gleaming, names chiseled in careful hands, poppies and daisies usually laid at its base by noon, their petals bright against the gray.

"Allied?" I mutter, half to myself, the word bitter, my breath clouding.

Tommy Carter, my old friend, sidles up, his tie loose, hands in his pockets, catchin' my look. "You hear that, Bobby?" he says, voice low, noddin' toward the women. "They're skippin' the memorial for that damn factory." His jaw tightens, the air between us heavy, the snap of a flag overhead loud.

"Ain't right," I say, shakin' my head, the camera dangling, my fingers itchin' to roll again but stuck, Mom's voice, *Tell the truth, Bobby*, echoin' in my mind.

"Since when does a company trump our soldiers?" Tommy kicks a pebble, its skitter sharp.

I quickly retorted, "Since Allied General started wavin' checks, I reckon."

Down the block, Allied's banners flap in the breeze, their red-and-blue logos bold, gaudy, strung across storefronts like they've always belonged, their plastic sheen clashin' with the faded paint of Gable's Mercantile, the barbershop's spinnin' pole.

"Look at that," Lila says, appearin' beside me, her sketchpad tucked underarm, her denim jacket zipped, her dark hair catchin' the light. "They're turnin' our day into their ribbon-cuttin'." Her voice was sharp, but her eyes are wet, her pencil smudged from sketchin' the crowd.

"Mom's going to be pissed," I say.

Lila nods, "wonder if she's up there now." We share a look, the band strikin' up "Yankee Doodle," the notes brassy, uneven, the crowd cheering, kids wavin' flags harder, their tin bells jingling.

"Who decided this?" I ask, louder, turnin' to Tommy, my camera swinging.

He shrugs, "Mayor, probably. Allied's got deep pockets."

Lila scoffs, "Deep enough to bury what matters." Her words sting, the air stiller now, the sky graying, a hawk circlin' slow overhead, its cry faint. I lift the camera, frame the banners, their flutter mockin' the memorial's quiet stones, the lens catchin' a kid droppin' his flag, its paper crumplin' in the dirt.

"They can't just erase it," I say, voice low, rollin' film again, the whir steady. The parade starts, boots marching, uniforms crisp, but the whispers linger, the memorial's absence a shadow, Allied's banners louder than the band.

Nobody said a word about changin' the route. No flyers. No bulletin notice at First Baptist. Not even a whisper at the feed store. But somehow, everyone in charge knew. The band stepped off from the church like always, drums thumpin', flags wavin', uniforms shinin' in the November sun. Kids tossed peppermint candies from hay bales. A cardboard tank made out of appliance boxes rolled past, squeakin' on its wagon wheels. I filmed from the edge of Main, same as always, waitin' for them to turn up north toward the square. Toward the old Veterans Memorial, where every parade had ended since before I was born.

But they didn't turn.

The band kept marchin' straight down the middle of town, past Uncle Don's repair shop, past Elma's bookstore, past the empty barber's chair behind the fogged window. Then they turned. But not toward the memorial. They turned West. Toward the big freshly paved Allied General parkin' lot, where red, white, and blue balloons bobbed in the wind and a banner above the storefront read:

"Proud Sponsor of Mill Town's Future."

It was like watchin' the whole town follow the wrong song.
Like we'd all been rerouted and no one thought to ask why.

The color guard led the way, their boots clackin' like clockwork on new pavement. Behind them, the school floats rolled slow, crepe paper rustlin' like dry leaves, kids wavin' to an audience they couldn't see. They marched right past the memorial at the square, never even slowin' down.

I turned my camera fast.

There, near the edge of the Square, where the tall grass thinned out around the stone war marker and flagpole, knelt Mr. Jennings. He wore his uniform proudly, he didn't speak. Didn't shift.

Three service medals were pinned neat and straight to the left side of his shirt, though the fabric sagged a little from age. The wind tugged at the tiny American flag beside him, but he didn't look up at it. His eyes were closed, and his hands were folded together, not clutched, not pressed, just restin' like a man who'd learned that silence could be louder than talkin'.

I zoomed in close as a single tear trickled down his face catchin' the sunlight. I didn't want to disturb him. I didn't dare say a word.

Behind him, in the background the music from the fadin' band marchin' away played somethin' patriotic, but he didn't move. Just breathed. And for a second, he looked like part of the earth, weathered, rooted, and maybe a little forgotten.

It was just a few seconds of film. But it said more than any speech I heard that day.

I left Mr. Jennings to his remembrance and walked back to the parade route, camera still rollin. A veteran in a wool coat with two ribbons pinned above his heart stopped marchin'. He turned his head and stared down the side street toward the memorial, confused, like maybe he'd misremembered the way. Another behind him did the same. But the line kept movin'. And they had no choice but to follow. I kept filmin', my hands steady even when my stomach wasn't. In the viewfinder, Mainstreet blurred into the background.

And in my head, maybe in the film too, I heard the line rise up like breath behind my tongue, I quietly spoke, *"Rememberin' what ya lost is sometimes more important than thinkin' bout what ya gain."*

When I got to the AG parkin' lot, it looked like Veterans Day, a county fair and a circus all collided in one place, and somehow lost the theme in the wreckage. The AG parkin' lot was a full-blown red-white-and-blue carnival, where we used to play in our treehouse and eat pecans laughin' and caryin' on. Now it was smoothed out, painted in fresh stripes, and gleamin' like a stage set. Balloon arches two stories high stretched across the entrance, bobbin' like jellyfish in the hot wind, tethered down by sandbags with Allied's logo stenciled on 'em. You couldn't see the sky without seein' stars and stripes.

Pop-up booths flanked the lot, foldin' tables covered in branded vinyl and coolers stocked with meltin' ice and soggy condiments.

"Free hot dogs! Fresh lemonade! Coke-a-cola!"

All of it passed out by cheerful Allied employees, every one of 'em wearin' crisp polos and plastic name tags with first names only and a little flag printed beneath. They smiled too hard. Like someone had told them to smile with their whole face, even if it hurt. The music blasted loud from mounted speakers, Sousa marches, mashed up with company slogans in between like a station that couldn't decide if it was sellin' freedom or light bulbs.

"Allied General, servin' your community with pride!"
Bum-ba-da-dum!

"Come on in, folks, beat the heat!" A greeter in khakis and white teeth waved people in like a preacher callin' folks to the altar.
"Air conditioned and fully stocked!"

His voice bounced off the concrete, sweet and hollow at the same time. Like a spell you didn't know you were under.

I stood near the edge, camera in hand, not sure whether to film it or run from it.

It may have looked like the future. But it didn't feel like home.

The doors kept openin' schhhhk, psshhhht like the place was breathin'. And with every sigh, more people poured in. Eyes wide, mouths open just a little, like they were walkin' into the kingdom of heaven with pocketbooks full of coupons. I stood by the entrance for a minute, camera propped against my shoulder, watchin' the flow, moms with strollers, daddies with calloused hands, teenagers in Sunday jeans holdin' leaky paper snow cones. Most looked dazed. All looked curious.

Just inside, under the bright hum of fluorescent lights, I heard "Bobby! Bobby, over here!"

It was Jason, grinnin' from ear to ear in a brand-new Allied vest, blue and yellow with a laminated name tag pinned crooked to his chest. He was wavin' both arms like a man on a ship tryin' to signal home.

"Ain't this somethin'?" he hollered, arms spread wide as if he owned the place. "They put me in Sportin' Goods, I got keys to the ammo cabinet and everythin'!"

I waved back, forced a smile, but my gut twisted like fishin' line in a motor. I stepped through the threshold, and it hit me all at once. Cool air. Bright lights.

Shoppin' carts sparkled in rows, their chrome sides catchin' the sun like mirrors in a funhouse. Inside, some folks pushed 'em already filled with toilet paper, extension cords, canned ham like they were marchin' toward prosperity, one aisle at a time. Others wandered in with dazed looks, drawn in by the smell of popcorn, the freezin' cold blast of air comin' out of the automatic doors, or just the feelin' that this was where the future had landed. It was unnatural and inviting, like steppin' into a world where everythin' was clean and color-coded. Behind the glass: neat aisles, fluorescent lights, refrigerated shelves hummin' like lullabies.

A smell like plastic and cinnamon and cardboard all at once. And rows. Endless rows. Toasters stacked three high. Typewriters boxed in tidy towers. Rockin' chairs shrink-wrapped like prize cattle. Rifles mounted in locked displays like museum pieces waitin' to be adopted.

Children crowded the toy aisle, mouths hangin' open at dollhouses with real electric lights, slot cars zoomin' on demo tracks, puzzle boxes with glittery cartoons they didn't even know they wanted yet.

"They got canned peaches in five brands!" someone yelled over the intercom music.

"I swear," a woman whispered by the linens, "these four sheets and towels cost less than what I paid for one at Gable's."

Her husband nodded, holdin' the tag between two fingers like it was proof the world had changed for good. I filmed as I walked slowly, tryin' to take it in and still keep my distance.

"Five brands of canned peaches," someone hollered from down the aisle like it was a miracle.

And maybe to some folks, it was.

Their carts were full. But it seemed their expressions were kinda hollow.

It wasn't joy. It was novelty. It wasn't survival, it was somethin' else. It was somethin' that felt a whole lot like defeat dressed up as a discount. I passed Jason again. He was helpin' a lady find batteries, his vest crooked, his grin tight now. I didn't stop him. Later, when I watched the footage back, I wrote one sentence under the reel: "it wasn't sold, it was just replaced"

Main Street always felt a little lonely after a parade, like a stage after the play's over. But this time… it felt hollow somehow. Flags still fluttered, tied to porch rails and lamp posts, but there was no breeze to give them purpose. Just the slow wave of cloth and the sound of wind that wasn't there. The sidewalks? They were completely empty. No kids chasin' leftover candy. No old-timers comparin' uniforms or smokin' by the corner barber pole. Just silence, the kind that don't ask for attention but gets it anyway. I wandered down the block with my camera hangin' at my side, too tired to film, too full to cry. The heat pressed down like a heavy truth. And up near the square, the Veterans Memorial stood alone.

The few wreaths that had been laid quietly that mornin' now wilted in the sun, their ribbons saggin', flowers gone limp and brown-edged. One had blown sideways and was lyin' half crooked. Not a soul in sight.

Just the statue, kneelin' in bronze.
Still holdin' his helmet.
Still waitin' for someone to say thank you.

I took out my camera one more time. I did a closeup of the wreath wilted and hangin sideways. Then I focused out and over to the Allied General banner flyin' in the background in perfect condition with the whole town it seemed at a carnival in it's parkin' lot in the distance.

Just then, I felt a hand on my shoulder and heard "keep it rolling."

It startled me and I looked back, it was Mr Jennings smilin' at me.

"Didn't mean to scare you, Bobby," he said, his voice low and warm, like a radio turned down soft. "Just saw you workin' that camera like you was born to it. You're catchin' somethin' special here, ain't you?"

I swallowed, my cheeks flushin'. "Just tryin' to get the wreath and the carnival," I mumbled, glancin' back at the viewfinder. "The way it all looks together."

Mr. Jennings nodded, his eyes followin' mine to the scene. "That's more than a picture, son. That's progress speakin to you. The wreath's old and crooked, but it's still hangin' on. And that banner? It's new, proud as you please, with everybody laughin' and carryin' on behind it. You're seein' the whole story, past, present and future, all in one scene."

I blinked, not sure what to say. Mr. Jennings always had a way of makin' things sound bigger than they were, like he could see the world in a grain of sand, the way mom read poems sometimes. "You think so?" I asked, my voice small.

"I know so," he said, givin' my shoulder a gentle squeeze before lettin' go. "You keep that camera hummin'. Years from now, you'll look back and remember what it felt like to be a kid, with your whole life stretchin' out b'fore you like a promise. Ain't too many folks can capture that."

I turned back to the camera, my hands a little steadier now. The wreath was still there, lopsided but stubborn, and the banner still flew high, the carnival hummin' with life. I pressed the record button, and for a few seconds, it felt like I'd trapped time itself. The sounds of the carnival, kids laughin', the clink of bottles at the ring toss, the distant pop of another firecracker, seemed to sharpen, like the world was posin' just for me.

I spotted Miss Elma before she spotted me. She was sittin' on the bench in front of her bookstore, the same one she'd owned since before I could read. Shop was closed. Sign turned around. But she was there, arms folded, hat tilted just enough to block the sun from her eyes. She wasn't readin'. She was watchin', watchin' the Allied lot from three blocks away.

I eased down beside her, not sayin' much. The wood creaked under me. My shirt stuck to my back. Her hands were folded over a notebook, but she hadn't opened it. She didn't turn to look at me. Just nodded once and said: "They didn't follow the band, Bobby. They followed the honey."

She didn't need to explain.

I looked down toward the glint of chrome and helium in the distance, where the parkin' lot buzzed like a beehive with lights flashin and folks wheelin their carts like they were pushin' promises home.

I looked back at the memorial, silent, sunbaked, and forgotten by most everyone but the stone it stood on and Mr. Jennings.

And then I looked at Elma. She didn't blink. Didn't cry. Just watched.

Chapter 8 - The Day Everythin' Stopped
(November 1963)

It was November 22, 1963. I was eleven. That Friday started ordinary enough, we had already made plans for campin' that night. The air turned crisp, smellin' of fallen leaves and chimney smoke, the kind of cold that nips your fingers but don't quite settle in. I was at school, sittin' in Miss Carver's history class, doodlin' a treehouse in the margin of my notebook while she droned on about the Civil War. Lila was flickin' paper wads at Eric when Miss Carver wasn't lookin'. The clock above the chalkboard ticked lazy, like it was in no hurry to get to lunch.

Then the intercom crackled, a sound we were used to for fire drills or lunch menus. But this time, Principal Hargrove's voice came through, shaky, like he was tryin' to swallow with somethin' stuck in his throat. "Teachers, students," he said, and there was a long pause, so long I looked up from my doodle. "I have… terrible news. President Kennedy has been shot in Dallas. He's… he's been taken to a hospital. We don't know much more. Please, let's all pray for him."

The room went still, like the air itself forgot to move. Miss Carver's chalk froze mid-word, leavin' "Gettysbu" half-written on the board. A girl in the front row, Sarah Beth, gasped, her hand flyin' to her mouth. Lila's paper wad dropped to the floor, forgotten. I felt my stomach twist, like I'd swallowed a rock, and I looked at Eric, hopin' he'd have some smart-aleck remark to make it less real. But his face was blank, his eyes wide, like he was seein' somethin' I couldn't.

"Is he gonna be okay?" Eric whispered, his voice small, like he was six again.

Miss Carver turned, her face pale as the chalk dust on her hands. "We don't know, Eric," she said, her voice waverin'. "We just... we pray."

The bell rang for lunch, but nobody moved. It was like we were all waitin' for someone to tell us it was a mistake, a bad dream we could shake off. Finally, Miss Carver cleared her throat. "Go on, kids," she said, though she didn't sound sure. "Go to the cafeteria. I'll... I'll let you know if there's news."

We shuffled out, quiet as ghosts, the usual chatter and shovin' gone. In the cafeteria, the smell of mashed potatoes and gravy was there, but nobody was eatin'. Kids just sat, starin' at their trays or whisperin' in tight knots. Lila, who'd outrun me in a race just last week, sat alone at a table, her braid undone, her eyes red like she'd been cryin'. I wanted to say somethin' to her, but my tongue felt glued to the roof of my mouth.

"Think it's true?" Matt asked, slidin' onto the bench beside me, his voice low.

"Gotta be," I said, though I didn't want it to be. "Mr. Hargrove wouldn't lie."

Matt nodded, pickin' at a crack in the table. "Why'd someone do that? Shoot the President?"

I didn't have an answer. All I could think of was the news clips I had seen, Kennedy smilin' with that easy grin, talkin' about goin' to the moon, makin' us feel like anythin' was possible. Now he was lyin' in a hospital, maybe dyin', and my world felt smaller than it ever had.

By the time the final bell rang, word had spread like wildfire. Principal Hargrove came back on the intercom, his voice heavier now, like it was carryin' a load too big for one man. "All, I'm sorry to tell you... President Kennedy has passed away. School's dismissed early. Go straight home to your families."

A wail broke out from somewhere in the hall, sharp and raw, like an animal caught in a trap. Kids started cryin', some quiet, some loud, and even the tough ones, the ones who'd dare you to jump off the water tower, looked lost, their shoulders hunched like they were tryin' to shrink away. Matt grabbed my arm, his grip tight. "Let's go," he said, and we bolted, not even stoppin' for our books.

Outside, town limits was different, like someone had drained the color from it. The streets were quiet, no screen doors slappin', no kids racin' bicycles. Folks stood in clumps, talkin' low, their faces drawn. Mrs. Elma stood outside her bookstore, her typewriter silent for once, huggin' a shawl around her shoulders. "Oh, boys," she said as we passed, her voice thick. "Ain't it awful?"

"Yes, ma'am," I mumbled, not knowin' what else to say. Matt just nodded, his jaw tight.

At the hardware store, dad was behind the counter, the radio on low, a newsman's voice cracklin' through the static, repeatin' the same terrible words: *President John F. Kennedy, assassinated in Dallas.* A couple of old farmers stood by the nail bins, hats in their hands, like they were at a funeral. Dad looked up as we came in, his eyes red-rimmed, and for the first time, he didn't ask me to sweep the floor or check the stock.

"Come here, boys," he said, his voice rough. He pulled us into a hug, his arms strong but shakin', and I could smell the sawdust and oil on his apron, the familiar scent that usually meant everythin' was right in the world. But not today. "It's a dark day," he said, lettin' us go. "You stay close to home, you hear?"

"Yes, sir," we said together, and I felt a lump in my throat, like I might cry if I opened my mouth again.

When we got home, mom was in the kitchen, her apron twisted in her hands, the radio on the counter blarin' the same news. She turned as we came in, her face crumplin' like she'd been holdin' it together till she saw us. "Oh, my boys," she said, pullin' us into her arms. She smelled of flour and lavender, and I buried my face in her shoulder, wishin' I could stay there forever. "I can't believe it," she whispered. "He was so young, so full of hope."

We sat around the table, nobody eatin' the cornbread she'd baked that mornin'. The radio kept talkin', about Dallas, about a man named Oswald, about Mrs. Kennedy in her pink suit, stained with blood. Mom kept wipin' her eyes with the corner of her apron, and dad, when he got home, just sat with his head in his hands, starin' at the floor like it held answers.

"Why'd it happen, dad?" I asked, my voice barely above a whisper.

He looked up, his eyes tired. "Some folks can't stand to see a man like that, Bobby. A man who wants to change things, make 'em better. It scares 'em, so they lash out. But it don't make it right."

That night, Mill Town was quieter than I'd ever heard it. Even the crickets were silent, no screen doors, no laughter from the sandbar. Matt and I sat on the porch, the cold seepin' through our jackets, starin' at the stars like they might tell us what to do next. "You think things'll ever be the same?" I asked, my breath puffin' out in the chilly air.

Matt was quiet a long time, then shook his head. "Nope," he said. "Somethins' broke. Ain't just the President. It's... everythin'."

His answer was unexpected, but I nodded, feelin' the truth of it settle heavy in my chest. I thought of my camera, sittin' on my dresser, and wished I could take a picture of the town before today, when it was still whole, when we were still kids who thought nothin' could touch us. But the world had shifted, and I wasn't sure how to map it anymore.

The next day, the town moved slow, like it was wadin' through molasses. Folks gathered at the church, even though it wasn't Sunday, and pastor Williams led a prayer for Kennedy, for the country, for us all. Mrs. Elma put a black ribbon on her bookstore door, and Mr. Collier closed his diner, a sign in the window readin', *Closed in Honor of JFK.* Even the kids stayed quiet, no moccasin hunts or ditch-divin' stunts, just hushed voices and eyes that didn't meet.

I walked to the sandbar alone, the creek glintin' under a gray sky. I sat on the cold sand, my knees pulled up, and thought about Kennedy, about his grin, about the moon he'd promised we'd reach. I wondered if we'd still get there, or if that dream had died with him. The water lapped at the bank, steady as ever, and I wished I could be like it, movin' forward, no matter what.

Life would go on, I knew that. We'd laugh again, run through the pastures again, tell stories that grew bigger with each tellin'. But somethin' had changed, a crack in the heart of our little world. And as I sat there, the wind carryin' the faint scent of pine and loss, I felt older than ten, like I'd seen the edge of somethin' I couldn't unsee. The map of Mill Town was still mine, but it was different now, and I'd have to learn to navigate it all over again.

Chapter 9 - Consumer Confessions
(November 1963)

It was nearly Christmas and the streets weren't empty, not exactly. Folks still shuffled along, their boots scrapin' the cracked pavement, their breath puffin' out like little clouds. But the talk was different, hushed and quick, like they were tradin' secrets they didn't want to own. I lingered by the lamppost near Gable's Mercantile, pretendin' to adjust my camera, but really listenin' to the whispers that floated like leaves in the wind.

"You can get wrappin' paper three rolls for a nickel at Allied," Mrs. Tate said to her sister, her voice low, like she was confessin' to stealin'.

She clutched a worn purse, her knuckles white, and I could see the shame in her eyes, like she'd rather be anywhere but sayin' those words.

"Plastic ornaments, whole set, two bucks," Mr. McGreggor added, leanin' against his restaurant's wall, his apron stained with grease. He shook his head, like the price was a punch he couldn't dodge. "Ain't seen a deal like that at Gable's in years."

"They even got turkeys cheaper than the co-op used to," Mrs. Hollis, Lila's mom chimed in, her shoppin' list crumpled in her hand.

Her voice was flat, like she was readin' a sentence she didn't believe. "Dollar less than last year, can you imagine?"

I glanced across the street and caught Lila's eye. She was standin' by Benny's Diner, her braid tucked under a knit cap, her hands stuffed in her jacket pockets. She'd heard it all, same as me, and her face was tight, like she'd bitten into somethin' sour. Just then,

Mrs. Tate leaned closer to her sister, her voice droppin' even lower. "I hate goin' there, but what choice do we have?" she said, and Lila's eyes flicked to mine, sharp with understandin'. Allied General was a giant, swallowin' Main Street whole, and we were all feedin' it, one cheap roll of wrappin' paper and excuse at a time.

I wandered into the Diner, the bell jinglin' as I pushed through the door. The air was thick with the smell of coffee and fried onions, but the usual hum of stories and laughter was gone, replaced by a different kind of talk, cold like the numbers on a ledger. Folks hunched over the counter, their voices low, comparin' prices like they were sizin' up enemies. "Allied's got canned cranberries for half what Gable's chargin'," Mr. Abernathy said, stirrin' his coffee with a spoon that clinked too loud.

"And their Christmas lights don't tangle like the ones at Chandler's," another man added, glancin' at me quick, then away, like he'd just remembered I was Thomas's boy.

I slid into a booth, orderin' a Coke I didn't really want, the bottle cold against my palm. Lila slipped in across from me, her cheeks pink from the chill outside.

"It's all they talk about," she said, noddin' at the counter. "Prices, deals, Allied. Nobody's talkin' about Christmas, or… I dunno, each other."

"Yeah," I said, spinnin' the bottle between my hands, watchin' the bubbles fizz slow. "Feels like we're all shoppin' just to see how much we can save, not to celebrate."

She leaned back, her eyes narrowin'. "You think it's always gonna be like this? Everybody just… givin' up on Main Street?"

I didn't answer right away, thinkin' of dad out there every mornin', stringin' up them same old Christmas lights at Chandler Hardware, even though half the bulbs were dead.

"Hope not," I said finally. "But it's hard to fight a giant when it's sellin' turkeys for a dollar less."

Lila snorted, but it wasn't a real laugh. "My mom's been goin' to Allied every week," she said, her voice quieter now. "Says it's just till we get back on our feet. But I see her face when she comes home. She don't like it any more than Mrs. Tate does."

I nodded, thinkin' of mom at home, sittin' at the kitchen table with a stack of Allied's circulars spread out like a bad hand of cards. She'd sigh, her pencil circlin' items, wrappin' paper, canned yams, a set of plastic ornaments, not 'cause she wanted to, but 'cause we couldn't afford not to since the hardware store is dryin' up.

"Turkeys for a dollar less than last year," she'd muttered last night, her voice flat, no pride in it like when she used to barter with Mr. Gable for flour or pick out ribbons at the co-op. "And they got stockin' stuffers cheap, too."

I'd watched her, my chest tight, knowin' she was doin' what she had to, but hatin' how it made her look smaller, like she was shrinkin' into someone I didn't know.

"You goin' to Allied, mom?" I'd asked, settin' my camera on the counter, its weight a comfort against the ache.

She'd looked up, her eyes tired but still hers, still mom's. "Have to, Bobby," she said, her voice soft but heavy. "We can't afford not to. But I swear, it feels like betrayin' somethin', your dad, Mr. Gable, all of 'em."

"Dad ain't givin' up," I'd said, thinkin' of them flickerin' lights, stubborn as he was. "He's still puttin' up them lights, even if nobody sees 'em."

Dad smiled, faint but real, reachin' over to squeeze my hand. "Your dad's always been stubborn. Maybe that's what keeps us goin'."

71

Now, in the diner, I looked at Lila, her face half-lit by the weak sunlight slantin' through the window. "my mom's doin' the same as your mom," I said. "Checkin' circulars, circlin' stuff. But she hates it. Says it feels like betrayin' everyone."

Lila nodded, her fingers tracin' a crack in the tabletop. "Maybe that's the worst part," she said. "Feelin' like you're lettin' down the folks you love, just to get by, because ya have to. Like they created a problem only they can solve."

We sat there a minute, the clink of spoons and the low hum of price talk fillin' the silence. I thought about takin' a picture of the diner, capturin' the way folks sat, heads bent, talkin' about nickels and dimes instead of dreams or memories. But I didn't. Some things didn't need a picture to stick with you.

"Wanna walk Main Street?" I asked, pushin' my Coke aside. "I'm tryin' to get a few more shots before the light's gone."

"Sure," Lila said, her grin creepin' back, though it didn't reach her eyes, "but don't you dare take my picture…"

"I know, you ain't fixed your hair today" I finished for her.

We laughed, the sound feelin' strange, like it'd been locked away too long.

"Deal," I said, and we headed out, the bell jinglin' behind us. Outside, the whispers kept goin', folks tradin' their consumer confessions like they were prayin' for forgiveness.

"Three rolls for a nickel," someone said again, and I saw Mrs. Hollis nod, her list still in hand, her face a mirror of mom's.

I raised my camera, framin' the street: the lamppost with its lopsided wreath, the faint glow of Dad's lights flickerin' in the distance. Lila walked beside me, quiet but steady, and for a moment, I felt like we were holdin' onto somethin' not the old Mill Town, maybe, but

72

somethin' new, built from whispers and stubborn lights and the hope that we'd find our way through.

Main Street was dressed up for Christmas, but it was a hollow kind of cheer. Lila suggested we go by the ole Christmas tree lot at the edge of town. It was an annual tradition, that was where the Mill Town Christmas Tree lot stood, fenced in by weathered boards and a family's pride that like the rest of the town, was startin' to fray.

The lot was run by the Hendersons, three generations deep, a patch of ground that'd been sellin' trees since before my dad was born. Rows of pine and fir leaned in the cold, bundled tight in twine, their branches saggin' under the weight of frost. They stood like soldiers waitin' for a battle that never came, their needles dryin' at the edges, some already scatterin' on the ground like forgotten confetti. The air was thick with the scent of pine, sharp and strong, but it wasn't the joyful smell of Christmas I remembered from when I was a kid. It was mournful, like the trees knew they were bein' left behind.

A hand-painted sign hung above the gate, its letters faded but still bold: *Mill Town Christmas Trees – Fresh-Cut Tradition Since 1931.* I could picture it in its heyday, the lot buzzin' with families, hot cocoa in thermoses, kids like me and Matt runnin' between the rows, laughin' as we hunted for "the one", the perfect tree, not too tall, not too sparse, just right for the livin' room. Mom'd trail behind, her scarf flutterin', while dad'd haggle with old Mr. Henderson, both of 'em grinnin' like it was part of the fun. The lot'd be alive with voices, the clink of coins, the rustle of trees bein' dragged to car roofs. But now, as I stood at the gate, the lot was eerily still, like a photograph left too long in the sun.

Only a handful of cars stopped by these days, their tires crunchin' slow on the gravel. Even fewer trees were taken. I saw a pickup pull in earlier, a man and his boy climbin' out, but they left empty-handed, the boy kickin' at the dirt like he was mad at it. Mr. Henderson, young Mr. Henderson now, since his dad passed last spring, stood by the shed, his hands in his pockets, watchin' 'em go.

73

"I shouldn't tell you this, but Allied's sellin' trees for half our price," I overheard him tell dad at the store last week, his voice flat, like he was too tired to be angry. "Plastic ones, too. Folks don't want the mess of needles no more."

I walked the rows alone, my sneakers sinkin' into the soft earth, the cold bitin' my fingertips as I held my camera. The trees loomed around me, their branches brushin' my jacket, and I could hear the faint creak of twine as the wind tugged at 'em. Fallen price tags littered the ground, handwritten in Mr. Henderson's careful scrawl, *$5 for a 6-footer, $7 for an 8*, some smudged by frost, others crumpled like they'd been stepped on. I knelt down, snappin' a shot of one tag half-buried in needles, the ink bleedin' into the paper. Then I stood, pannin' the camera across the rows, catchin' the way the trees leaned, silent and waitin', their shadows stretchin' long in the weak afternoon light.

I stopped by a small pine, no taller than me, its branches uneven but full. It reminded me of the tree we'd picked when I was eight, the one Matt swore was too scrawny but mom loved 'cause it "had character." I raised the camera, framin' it against the darkenin' gray sky, the fence in the background, and clicked the shutter. The pine scent filled my lungs, sharp and heavy, but it didn't lift my spirits like it used to. It felt like sayin' goodbye to somethin' I couldn't name.

"Hey, Bobby," a voice called, soft but familiar. I turned to see Mr. Henderson by the shed, his flannel coat buttoned crooked, a thermos of coffee in his hand. "Takin' pictures of my trees?"

"Yes, sir," I said, lowerin' the camera, my cheeks warm despite the cold. "They're... still pretty, even if folks..."

He nodded, his eyes crinklin' with a sad kind of smile. "They are that. Been cuttin' these trees since I was your age, haulin' 'em down from the hills with my pa. Thought my boy'd do the same one day." He glanced at the empty lot, his smile fadin'. "But times are chang'n, aren't they?"

74

"Yes, sir," I said, my voice quiet. I wanted to say somethin' more, somethin' to make it better, but the words wouldn't come. Instead, I raised the camera again, snappin' a shot of him standin' there, the shed behind him, the sign above the gate just in frame. He didn't seem to mind, just took a sip of his coffee and looked out at the trees, like he was tryin' to memorize 'em.

I walked on, the rows stretchin' out like a maze I didn't want to leave. The pine scent clung to me, mournful but stubborn, like the town itself. I thought of the families that used to fill this lot, their laughter echoin' through the cold, and wondered if we'd ever get that back. Allied General was sellin' trees now, cheap and plastic, no needles to sweep up, no tradition to carry. Maybe that's what folks wanted, somethin' easy, somethin' that didn't ask 'em to remember, somethin' that didn't bother them, ya know…convenient.

As I reached the gate, I turned for one last shot, capturin' the whole lot: the rows of trees, the faded sign, the empty gravel where cars used to park. I felt a pang in my chest, like I was sealin' away a whisper of history that might not make it to next Christmas, the end of a family tradition. The wind picked up, scatterin' a few more needles across the ground, and I headed home, the scent of pine followin' me like a ghost that didn't want to let go.

I went to AG, not 'cause I wanted to, but 'cause mom needed me to pick up some wrappin' paper, three rolls for a nickel, she'd said, her voice heavy with the kind of practicality that hurt to hear. The store was a world away from Main Street, all gleamin' tile and fluorescent lights that buzzed like a swarm of bees. The aisles were stacked high with pre-lit artificial trees, their plastic branches shiny and perfect, not a needle out of place. They were the same cost as Hendersons' fresh-cut pines, and folks milled around 'em, their carts piled with tinsel and canned cranberries. The air smelled of plastic and floor wax, nothin' like the pine scent of the local lot.

I wandered down the Christmas aisle, my camera in my hand, feelin' like a stranger in my own town. A kid, maybe six, tugged at his mom's coat, his eyes wide as he pointed at a tree that spun slow on a stand, playin' "Silent Night" in a tinny chime.

"Can we get this one, Ma? It spins and plays music!" he begged, his voice loud enough to turn heads.

His ma shushed him, checkin' the price tag, but I could see her soften, like the convenience was winnin' her over. I raised my camera, catchin' a shot of the boy, his face lit up by the tree's fake glow, the aisle stretchin' behind him like a tunnel of glitter and bargains. The camera was hummin', and I felt a twist in my gut, knowin' this was what we were choosin' now, somethin' easy, somethin' that didn't ask us to really care.

The Christmas spirit in town was fadin' fast, just like the rest of the community, like a fire left untended. The school Christmas play, a tradition since I was in short pants, got canceled "due to fundin'," the principal said, his voice cracklin' over the intercom. Instead, they set up a community film night in the school gym, showin' an Allied General promotional cartoon about a singin' snowman playin' with all the toys that AG had for sale. Kids sat on foldin' chairs, munchin' popcorn, while parents whispered about their latest Allied bargain purchase. I didn't go, couldn't stomach it, but Matt said it was like watchin' a commercial that'd swallowed Christmas whole.

Instead, I took my chance at the church basement, where Preacher Daniels let me screen a short reel I'd put together from my camera's film. It was footage I'd been savin', clips of past parades with marchin' bands and paper floats, tree lightings on Main Street with kids singin' carols, holiday markets where mom'd haggle for pecans and Mrs. Elma'd sell books tied with twine. The basement was dim, the projector whirrin' as the images flickered on a bedsheet hung on the wall. A small crowd gathered, mom and dad, Lila, a few old-timers, and Mrs. Elma, her shawl pulled tight around her shoulders.

The reel played, and I watched their faces, lit by the soft glow. There was the 1961 Christmas parade, me and Matt wavin' from the back of dad's truck, grins wide as the Blackwater River. Then the tree lightin' from '60, dad flippin' the switch while folks cheered, the bulbs blazin' against the night. The market scenes showed mom laughin' with Mrs. Hollis, their baskets full, and kids runnin' through the stalls, chasin' each other with candy canes like they were guns. The room was mostly just quiet. I guess people rememberin' what it was like, and how it is.

When the reel ended, the silence lingered, heavy as the frost outside. I stood by the projector, my hands sweaty, waitin' for someone to say somethin'. Then Mrs. Elma's voice broke through, a whisper that carried like a bell. "We used to shine, didn't we?" she said, her eyes glassy, starin' at the blank sheet where the images had been.

"Yes, ma'am," I said, my throat tight. "We did."

Nobody else spoke, but I saw mom reach for dad's hand, and Lila gave me a small nod, like she knew what I was tryin' to do, hold onto how we'd been, even if it was just in pictures. The crowd shuffled out slow, their footsteps echoin' in the basement, and I packed up the projector, feelin' like maybe I'd given 'em somethin', even if it wasn't enough to fix what was broken.

The next day, I found Matt outside Benny's, helpin' string Christmas lights on the awning. The bulbs were new, brighter than dad's, but Matt's face was grim, his hands movin' like he was just goin' through the motions. "Feels like stringin' tinsel on hope," he muttered, loopin' a strand over a nail.

I stopped, my camera hangin' heavy. "You think it's that bad?" I asked, though looking at the vacant sidewalks, I knew the answer.

He looked at me, his eyes older than fourteen oughta be. "Unless somethin' changes. I've been putting up lights for the past three years, you remember. Now, everyone says they couldn't afford to take on help this season unless sales pick up. I'm doin' this just to help out Benny."

I didn't have an answer, so I raised my camera, snappin' a shot of him against the diner's awning, the lights glowin' but not warm a contrast to the rest of the dark Mainstreet. The shutter clicked, and I thought of Mrs. Elma's words, *We used to shine*. Maybe we still could, in some small way, but it was gonna take more than lights or pictures to bring it back. I lowered the camera, the cold pressin' in, and followed Matt inside, hopin' the warmth of the diner might thaw us out.

Chapter 10 - Hollow Holidays
(December 1963)

Mill Town felt like a house with the lights on but nobody home. Winter was creepin' in, and the air had a bite now, carryin' the scent of fallen leaves and chimney smoke. The gutters along Main Street were choked with red and gold leaves.

At the hardware store, dad was out front on a ladder, stringin' up the same Christmas lights we'd used for years, tangled strands of red and green bulbs, some flickerin', some dead, but he wouldn't hear of replacin' 'em.

"They still shine," he'd say, his breath puffin' out in the cold as he wrestled with the cords.

I watched him from the sidewalk, my hands stuffed in my jacket pockets, wonderin' if anybody'd even notice the lights this year. The store's windows were bare, no garlands or paper snowflakes like the other shops, but dad didn't care about that. "Lights are enough," he muttered, hammerin' a nail to secure the strand. I didn't argue, but it felt like he was tryin' to hold onto somethin' that was already slippin' away.

Main Street was still dressed up for tradition's sake, like a tired actor goin' through the motions. Shop windows sported garlands of pine, handmade wreaths with red ribbons, and faded paper snowflakes that'd hung there since I was a kid. But the cheer felt thin, like a coat too worn to keep out the cold. The church bells rang on Thanksgivin' mornin', their deep toll callin' folks to service, but the pews were half-empty. Fewer casseroles were carried to potlucks, and more cars crowded the Allied General parkin' lot, folks stockin' up on canned goods and Christmas hams instead of prayin' or sharin' stories. It was like the town was movin' toward winter, but not together, not the way it used to.

Downtown had a strange kind of liveliness, like a pulse that didn't know it was fadin'. Folks still strolled Main Street out of habit, their boots scrapin' the cracked sidewalks. Older couples walked arm in arm, their scarves flutterin' in the wind, noddin' to each other but not talkin' much. Mothers pushed strollers, their faces tired, while kids in mittens dragged their hands across the cold shop windows, leavin' smudges on the glass. I walked among 'em, my camera in hand. I'd already takin' six or seven rolls of video this fall, tryin' to catch the way the town looked now, like ghosts reenactin' a life they'd already lost.

Mrs. Elma's Book Nook had her "12 Books of Christmas" display in the window, a tradition she'd kept up since before I was born. Twelve books, each wrapped in brown paper with a red ribbon, stacked like presents under a tiny fake tree dusted with tinsel. But her front door stayed locked, the "Closed" sign hangin' crooked, and the typewriter that used to tick like a heartbeat every morning, was silent. I pressed my face to the glass, squintin' past the display to the dark inside, where shelves loomed like shadows. "You still readin', Mrs. Elma?" I whispered, my breath foggin' the window. Nobody answered, but I snapped a picture anyway, the whirrin' of the shutter loud in the quiet street.

Gable's Mercantile was tryin' harder, a tinny speaker outside playin' "Jingle Bells" on a loop, the notes warblin' like they were tired of themselves. The store was open, but nobody went in. I stood under the awning, watchin' a couple of kids chase each other past, their laughter sharp but quick, like it didn't have the strength to last.

"Ain't nobody buyin' nothin'," I heard Mr. Gable mutter to his clerk inside, his voice carryin' through the open door.

"They're all at Allied." The clerk replied solemnly.

80

I happened to catch Mr. Gables expression which said it all.

I kept walkin', my sneakers crunchin' on stray leaves, the camera bumpin' against my leg. Main Street felt like a stage set, all dressed up but empty, the actors gone home. I stopped at the corner by the theater, where the wind carried the faint scent of diesel and decay, and looked back at the street. It was a picture I'd taken a hundred times, storefronts, lampposts, the church steeple pokin' above the pines, but now it felt hollow, like I was seein' it through a cracked lens. I raised the camera, framin' the scene: an old man in a wool coat shufflin' past Gable's, a kid kickin' a can down the sidewalk, the Christmas lights flickerin' above dad's store. I pressed the shutter, hopin' to catch the strange emptiness inside the motion, the way the place was still movin' but not livin'.

"Hey, Bobby!" a voice called, and I turned to see Lila joggin' toward me, her braid bouncin' under a knit cap. She was taller now, her eyes sharper, but she still had that grin that could make you forget the cold. "You still makin' movies of this sad old street?" she asked, stoppin' beside me, her breath puffin' out like smoke.

"Tryin' to," I said, lowerin' the camera. "It's… different now, ain't it?"

She nodded, her grin fadin'. "Yeah. Feels like everybody's just goin' through the motions. Like we're supposed to be happy 'cause it's Christmas, but…" She trailed off, kickin' at a pile of leaves. "You think it's 'cause of Kennedy?"

I shrugged, the weight of that day still heavy in my chest. "Maybe. Or maybe it's just… everythin'. Allied's takin' over, shops are closin'. Even Mrs. Elma's gone quiet."

Lila looked toward the bookstore, her eyes narrowin'. "She's still in there, you know. I saw her yesterday, sittin' in the back with a book. Didn't even look up when I knocked."

"Think she'll open again?" I asked, my voice quieter than I meant.

"Dunno," Lila said. "But I hope so. This town needs her stories."

We stood there a minute, the wind whippin' at our jackets, the faint jangle of "Jingle Bells" driftin' from Gable's. "Wanna walk with me?" I asked, holdin' up the camera. "I'm tryin' to get the whole street before the light's gone."

"Sure," she said, her grin creepin' back. "But you better not get me this time. I ain't fixed my hair today."

I laughed, the sound feelin' strange in my throat, like it'd been locked away too long.

"Deal," I said, and we started down Main Street, side by side.

I caught a few more shots, a wreath hangin' lopsided on a lamppost, a kid's mitten left on a bench, the church steeple framed against a sky turnin' gray with snow clouds. Lila didn't say much, but her bein' there made the emptiness feel a little less heavy, like maybe we could still find somethin' worth holdin' onto.

Back home that night, the farmhouse was warm, the smell of mom's cornbread fillin' the kitchen. But even there, the holiday felt hollow. The radio played carols, but mom kept turnin' it down, like the cheer was too much. dad sat at the table, starin' at a ledger, his pencil still, and Matt was upstairs, not even botherin' to tease me like usual. I sat by the window, lookin' out at the dark, thinkin' about the images I had hopefully captured.

"What you seein' out there, Bobby?" mom asked, settin' a plate of cornbread in front of me.

"Nothin'," I said, then shook my head. "I mean… everythin'. It's all still there, the lights, the wreaths. But it feels like it's slippin' away."

She sat across from me, her hands folded, her eyes soft. "Things change, honey," she said. "They always do. But you're catchin' it with that camera of yours, holdin' onto what matters. That's somethin'."

I nodded, pickin' at the cornbread, the warmth of it steadyin' me. "You think we'll ever feel like us again? Like it used to be?"

Mom reached over, squeezin' my hand. "Maybe not the same," she said. "But we'll find a new way to be us. Takes time, is all."

I looked out the window again, at the faint glow of our Christmas lights, flickerin' like they were tryin' to say somethin'. It was quieter now, its heart beat slower, but it was still there, stubborn as ever. And as I sat there, the taste of cornbread on my tongue, I thought maybe mom was right. Maybe we'd find our way, one picture, one step, one hollow holiday at a time.

Chapter 11 - Heart of Christmas
(December 1963)

It was Christmas mornin'. I woke up, early with the smell of dad's waffles driftin' through the house. The air was chilly, the kind that makes you pull the quilt tighter, but I could hear the clatter of dishes and dad's low chuckle from the kitchen, so I knew it was time to get movin'. Christmas in Mill Town used to feel like magic, like the whole world was holdin' its breath for somethin' good. But this year, after Kennedy's death and Allied General's shadow creepin' over, it felt different, like the heart of it had gone missin'.

I shuffled downstairs, my socks slippin' on the worn wood, and found the family gathered in the livin' room. The tree, a majestic pine from Henderson's lot, a bit lopsided but ours, stood in the corner, strung with popcorn and a few glass ornaments mom'd saved from her own childhood. The lights blinked weak, but they were tryin', just like us. Mom was in her apron, her hair still pinned up, passin' out presents from a modest pile under the tree. Dad sat in his chair, a mug of coffee steamin' in his hand, while Matt sprawled on the rug, already tearin' into a package.

"Merry Christmas, Bobby," mom said, handin' me a box wrapped in brown paper, the kind Allied sold three rolls for a nickel. Her smile was warm, but there was a tiredness in her eyes, like she was pushin' through the holiday for our sakes.

"Thanks, mom," I said, takin' the box. I peeled it open, findin' a new pair of gloves, wool with a red stripe, practical and sturdy. "They're nice," I said, and I meant it, but somethin' felt off. The gloves were fine, but they didn't feel like mom had picked 'em special, like she used to when she'd knit socks with my initials or slip a handwritten note in with a gift. It was like she'd grabbed 'em 'cause they were on sale, not 'cause they were me.

Matt was next, rippin' open a package to reveal a pocketknife, shiny and new, the kind Allied had stacked in their aisles. "Cool," he said, flippin' the blade out, but his grin faded quick, like the knife was just a thing, not a story. Mom handed dad a new thermos, and he nodded, sayin', "This'll do fine," but his voice didn't have the spark it used to when he'd unwrap a scarf mom'd spent weeks knittin'. My gift to Matt was a pack of baseball cards, and he got me a notebook for school, both bought at Allied, both useful, but neither felt like us.

I knew it had been a tough time lately and I tried to smile, to feel the Christmas spirit I remembered from when I was a kid, runnin' to the tree with Matt, laughin' over gifts that meant somethin' 'cause they came from thought, from heart. But this year, it was different. I was grateful for everythin' they did, but the presents gave a quick jolt of satisfaction, like a sip of Coke on a hot day, but it fizzled fast, leavin' me empty afterward. It wasn't the gifts themselves, it was the why behind 'em. They felt like things we needed, not things we wanted to give, like Allied's bargains had replaced the love we used to wrap 'em in. Honestly, I would have been happier receiving a rock kept from when we all went to the lake in Texas. I sat there, my gloves in my lap, feelin' a knot in my chest, wonderin' if this was what Christmas was now, just temporary, just enough to get by.

"Bobby," dad said, his voice pullin' me out of my thoughts. He was standin' by the tree, holdin' a small box wrapped in plain paper, tied with a piece of twine. Mom was beside him, her hands clasped, and they exchanged a look, a quiet smile passin' between 'em that I hadn't seen all mornin'. "Got one more for you," dad said, handin' me the box.

I took it, the weight light but solid, and my fingers fumbled with the twine, my heart pickin' up like it knew somethin' was different. I tore the paper, revealin' a worn leather case, scuffed at the edges but familiar as my own hands. I opened it, and there it was, dad's camera, the one I'd been usin', the one he'd let me borrow for years, its lens still clear as a creek and familiar as that worn trail to town. My breath caught, and I looked up at dad, his eyes crinklin' with a warmth I hadn't seen in weeks.

He kind of looked embarrassed not knowin what I would say, "I know it's not much, thing's have been tough.."

I stopped him there and hugged him as tight as I could.

He continued, "...but it's official now," he said, his voice steady but full of somethin' deeper, like pride, like love. "That camera's yours, Bobby. You're doin' somethin' with it, seein' the world, holdin' onto what matters. It's time you had it for good."

I ran my fingers over the camera, feelin' the scratches, the weight of years in its frame. This wasn't just a thing, it was a true gift, his trust in me. It was mom's nod from across the room, her smile sayin' she'd known this was comin'. It was the thought I'd been missin' all mornin', the heart that'd been drowned out by Allied's deals and Main Street's fade. I looked at dad, then mom, and felt my throat tighten, not with sadness but with hope, like a spark catchin' in dry kindlin'.

"Thanks, dad," I said, my voice rough. "This... this means everythin'."

He clapped a hand on my shoulder, his grip firm. "You keep makin' those movies, son. Remind us who we are."

Matt looked over, his pocketknife forgotten, and grinned, a real one this time. "Now you're stuck with that thing," he teased, but there was no bite in it.

Mom laughed, soft and warm, and for a moment, the room felt like Christmas again, like the home I remembered, full of heart and meanin'. I held the camera, my camera now, and thought to myself, *This is what I was talkin' about.* Not the gloves or the thermos or the baseball cards, but this, a gift that carried us in it, that said we were still here, still fightin' to be us. Maybe there was hope yet, maybe there was some heart left, still flickerin' like dad's lights, still waitin' for us to fan it into flame.

I set the camera on the table, careful, like it was made of glass, then went to the backside of the tree where I had one last gift that I wasn't sure I was gonna give.

"This one is for the whole family…" I said holdin' out a round disk shaped package with brown paper wrapped around it barely staying on.

"You mean we gotta share?" Matt said with a smile.

Mom reached out "What is it?" She opened it carefully. It was a reel of film.

"It's just something to remember us all here together, bits and pieces from birthdays and just messin round." I said timidly.

"I'm takin that notebook back." Matt said grabbin at my new notebook.

I snatched them away and smiled, then I reached for a waffle, the sweetness fillin' my mouth as the mornin' sun slanted through the window. The pile of wrappin' paper was still there, the gifts still practical, but that one small box had changed everythin'. I looked at my family, mom stirrin' her coffee, dad leanin' back in his chair, Matt flippin' through his cards, and felt like we could face whatever came next, together. Now this, I thought, this is what Christmas is.

Maybe there was still some heart left in this world. Maybe it just needed help rememberin its way back.

Chapter 12 - Temperatures Risin'
(February 1964)

It was February 1964, and Mill Town was teeterin' on the edge of somethin' nobody could name. The air was brittle, carryin' the sting of frost and the faint smoke of fireplaces, but it wasn't just the cold makin' folks uneasy. A notice went up early that week, tacked to the post office door, the church bulletin board, and the front of the hardware store, its words stark in black ink: *Emergency Town Meeting – Wednesday, 6 PM – Community Hall – All Welcome*. I saw it at dad's store, the paper flutterin' in the wind, and felt a knot in my gut.

Rumors spread faster than a brushfire. At Benny's Diner, folks leaned over coffee cups, whisperin' about unpaid business taxes, broken promises from the town council, missin' school funds that were supposed to pay for new books and the Christmas play. I overheard Mr. Radcliffe outside the post office, his voice low and sharp. "It's about time someone demanded answers," he muttered, adjustin' his hat like he was gearin' up for a fight. Nobody knew what the meetin' was really about, but it felt big, like a storm brewin' just out of sight. I tucked my camera under my jacket, unsure if I was headin' to film a reckonin' or a surrender, but knowin' I had to be there, lens ready.

Wednesday evenin', the church basement was packed, the air thick with the smell of damp coats and stale coffee. Foldin' chairs were set up in uneven rows, creakin' under the weight of a crowd that filled the room fast, shopkeepers, farmers, teachers, folks who hadn't been to a town meetin' in years. The mood was tense, like a rope pulled too tight. Store owners like Mr. Gable and Mr. Collier sat in clusters, whisperin' about their dwindlin' sales, their eyes dartin' to the front. Teachers fidgeted, clutchin' notepads, worryin' about the school budget. Old veterans, their arms folded tight across flannel shirts, stared straight ahead, their faces hard as the oak pews upstairs. Dad was near the back, his jaw set, mom beside him, her hands folded but restless. Matt slouched next to me, mutterin' about how this better not take long.

At the front, a wobbly table held Mayor Heartwell, sweatin' under his tie, the School Board Chair, Mrs. Tate, twistin' a handkerchief, and two town council members who sat silent, their faces blank as slate. An empty chair sat beside 'em, a name placard propped on it: *Evelyn Carr – Regional Liaison, Allied General.* The sight of it sent a murmur through the crowd, like a match flarin' in dry grass. Allied's shadow loomed over town, its cheap goods drainin' Main Street dry, and that empty chair felt like a taunt, like they knew they didn't even need to show up to win.

The church basement was a powder keg that evening. I sat in the back row, my 8mm camera hummin' soft, tryin' to capture the storm brewin' in the crowd. The foldin' chairs groaned under restless bodies, shopkeepers, teachers, farmers, all packed in tight, their whispers sharp as the cold seepin' through the walls. At the front, Mayor Heartwell stood, sweatin' under the bare bulbs, flanked by Mrs. Jenkins, the school board chair, and two stone-faced council members. That empty chair with *Evelyn Carr – Regional Liaison, Allied General* on its placard sat like a dare, fuelin' the tension.

The mayor cleared his throat, clutchin' a crumpled paper, his voice waverin' as he read a pre-written statement. "We're facin' some… growin' pains," he said, the words limp, like he didn't believe 'em himself. "Allied General's promised pendin' cooperation, and we're workin' to address the tax issues, the school funds…" He trailed off, wipin' his brow, as murmurs rippled through the crowd, low and angry, like a hive stirred up. I zoomed in with my camera, catchin' the mayor's nervous tic, the way his hands shook, then panned to the crowd, noddin' heads, furrowed brows, eyes narrow with distrust.

Mrs. Jenkins took the mic next, her voice strained, like it was pushin' through a wall of grief. "We were promised new textbooks, updated heatin' systems, a music program by spring," she said, her knuckles white on the podium. "It's nearly May, and we got nothin' but excuses."

Gasps broke out, sharp and jagged, followed by a swell of murmurs, parents clutchin' their coats, teachers shakin' their heads. I kept filmin', the lens sweepin' over frustrated faces, a mother whisperin' to her neighbor, a veteran's arms crossed tighter. The camera caught it all, the raw edge of a town betrayed.

"Is the school short on money?" Mr. Collier called out, his voice cuttin' through the mayor's preamble. "We paid our taxes, but the kids got no books, no play this year. Where's it goin'?"

Mrs. Tate flinched, her handkerchief twistin' tighter. "We're… investigatin'," she said, her voice thin. "There's been some… discrepancies."

"Discrepancies?" Mrs. Hollis stood, her arms crossed, her eyes blazin'. "My girl's usin' a history book from 1949, and you're tellin' me discrepancies? What about the taxes we're bleedin' to pay while Allied gets breaks?"

The room erupted, voices overlappin', shopkeepers shoutin' about no holiday sales, farmers grumblin' about crop prices, parents demandin' answers for their kids. Dad stayed quiet, but his hand tightened on mom's, and I could see the strain in his jaw, like he was holdin' back a flood. Matt leaned over, whisperin', "This is a mess, Bobby. They don't know nothin'."

The murmurs turned to shouts when the business owners had their say, a swell of voices that couldn't be held back no more. Uncle Don stood first, his broad shoulders squared, his voice steady but heavy. "I've fixed this town's appliances since before some of y'all could drive," he said, lookin' out at the crowd. "Washers, radios, you name it. For the

90

past four months, I've had ten customers comin in, they just want estimates. Allied's sellin' new appliances nearly the same price than I can fix the old ones for." His words landed like a hammer, and I zoomed in, catchin' the pain in his eyes, the way his hands flexed like he was still holdin' a wrench. The crowd nodded, some clappin', their faces mirrorin' his loss.

Miss Elma was next, standin' frail but fierce, shakin' a handwritten ledger like it was evidence in a trial. "Last month? Three customers," she said, her voice crackin' but strong. "Three. And two of 'em were my cousins, buyin' out of pity."

A few gasps, a few bitter laughs, and I filmed her, the ledger tremblin' in her hands, the weight of her empty bookstore hangin' in the air. She'd been Main Street's storyteller for as long as I knew.

A man in the back stood, his voice rough, cuttin' through the noise. "Have you been down Main Street lately? I drove by last Friday at four p.m., and there was a possum layin' on a bench."

The room went quiet for a beat, then erupted in grim chuckles and nods, the image too real to deny. I swung the camera to him, catchin' his weathered face, the way he pointed like he could still see that possum, a symbol of how far we'd fallen.

Mr. Radcliffe rose, his voice boomin', his finger jabbin' at the empty Allied chair. "I warned you about bringin' 'em in," he said, his eyes blazin'. "Now they're here, and you won't be able to get rid of 'em. They're killin' us, and you let 'em through the gate. Ya know the Robinson-Patman Act was supposed to protect small businesses like ours against companies like AG, but them Washington folks choose to have their pockets lined by a few big companies instead of lots of little ones, so they ignore it like it don't exist. We may not have enough money to lobby our congressman, but we sure as heck can vote you out." The crowd roared, some leapin' to their feet, their applause sharp but not unanimous, some sat still, heads bowed.

Mr. Gable from the mercantile shouted over the din, his face red. "We were told Allied would bring traffic! Traffic away from Mainstreet is all they brought!" His words sparked another wave of applause, louder now, but still fractured, some folks clappin', others just starin', their hands still. I kept filmin', pannin' across the crowd, catchin' the split, those ready to fight, those already givin' up. The camera lingered on Dad, noddin' slow, and mom beside him, her eyes fierce but wet, like she was holdin' onto hope and grief at the same time.

Mr. Radcliffe stood, his voice boomin'. "We're losin' Main Street 'cause Allied's got the politicians, including you in its pocket! Why ain't their liaison here, answerin' for this?" He pointed at the empty chair, and the crowd roared, some clappin', others yellin' agreement.

The mayor tried to respond, stammerin' about "schedulin' conflicts," but it only made the room hotter.

Mr. Radcliffe wasn't done yet, "You know corporations got a fiduciary responsibility to their shareholders to do what's best for them, not what's best for us, right? If they got a choice tween doin' what's best for us, or them, well, ya see the answer to that question right in front of ya."

The room was alive with anger, but it felt fragile, like a fire that could burn out or burn everythin' down. I lowered the camera, my arms achin', knowin' I'd caught somethin' real, the town's heart, beatin' hard but bruised, demandin' to be heard. Mayor Heartwell tried to speak again, but the voices drowned him out, and I wondered if this was the start of a stand or the last cry of a town too broken to rise.

Jason, who lived just down the road, stood, his Allied vest wrinkled but proud, his voice steady despite the glares. "I finally got a job that don't depend on weather or someone dyin' to open a slot," he said, hands in his pockets. "Stockin' shelves at Allied means I can plan now, buy a truck from you're lot" He said lookin' at Mr Deeds. "and maybe even save a little. That's more'n I ever got haulin' hay." A few nodded, mostly younger folks, but the shopkeepers stared, their jaws tight. I zoomed in, catchin' Jason's defiant chin, the way his eyes flicked to the crowd, darin' 'em to argue.

Mrs. Elanor stood next, another baby on her hip, her coat patched at the elbows. "I can finally afford diapers again," she said, her voice soft but firm, the baby fussin' against her shoulder. "And shoes for my kids. We ain't all shop owners. Some of us just needed some help." Her words hung there, honest and heavy, and I filmed her, the camera lingerin' on her tired eyes, the baby's tiny hand clutchin' her collar. The room was quieter now, some noddin', others lookin' away, like her truth was too hard to face.

Vinny Deeds from the Ford dealership rose, his tie loose, his voice boomin'. "We've been sellin' near twenty percent more cars since Allied opened," he said, gesturin' wide. "Folks got more money to spend now, and they need bigger trunks to haul it all. That's money in my pocket, and back to the community, and I ain't ashamed to say it." A few clapped, but the sound was thin, drowned by grumbles from the back. I panned the crowd, catchin' the split, hopeful faces against hardened ones, a town pullin' apart.

Matt sat beside me, slouchin' in his chair, his Allied work shirt peekin' from under his jacket. He was uncomfortable, his fingers tappin' his knee, and when he met my eyes, his look was heavy, like he wanted to speak but couldn't. He stayed silent, and I didn't push, just kept filmin', the camera's hum a steady anchor.

Lila leaned over, her breath warm against my ear. "This is how towns split, right down the middle," she whispered, her voice low but sharp. I nodded, feelin' the truth of it, the way Jason's job, cheap diapers, Vinny's cars were pittin' neighbor against neighbor. I filmed the crowd again, zoomin' in on Matt's tense jaw, Lila's narrowed eyes, the empty Allied chair, knowin' this was the story, the town tearin' itself in two.

Mayor Heartwell reclaimed the floor, smoothin' his tie with tremblin' fingers, his face slick with sweat. "We hear you," he said, his voice strainin' for calm. "That's why I'm announcin' the creation of a Town

Economic Advisory Committee to study this transition and recommend actions." He paused, like he expected applause, but the room stayed taut. "We'll have public input sessions, rotatin' leadership, an open-door policy. And I assure you, Allied General ain't abandoned the partnership, despite Ms. Carr's absence tonight." He gestured at the empty chair, like it was proof of somethin', but his words felt hollow, like a promise written in the sand at the beach.

Some clapped, a scatterin' of hands, mostly from folks like Vinny or Jason. Others shook their heads, their faces sour, and a few, Mr. Radcliffe among 'em, stood and walked out, their boots echoin' on the concrete. I filmed the exodus, the camera catchin' their slumped shoulders, the way the door swung shut behind 'em, a quiet rebuke to the mayor's plan.

As the crowd spilled out into the cold, I stayed, interviewin' folks with my camera rollin', their voices raw against the night. "It's too late for a committee," Mr. Collier said, his apron balled in his fist. "We needed action six months ago." Mrs. Hollis shook her head, her scarf tight around her neck. "They'll bury us in studies while Main Street dies quietly." A farmer I didn't know spat on the ground, mutterin', "Allied's laughin' at us, and Heartwell's holdin' the door open for them." I filmed it all, their words cuttin' deep, each one a nail in the town's coffin.

Before leavin', I turned the camera to the front, zoomin' in on that empty chair, *Evelyn Carr*'s name tag stark under the flickerin' light. It sat alone, a silent player in the chaos, speakin' louder than any voice in the room. I packed up, the cold bitin' as I stepped outside, the footage heavy in my hands.

Later, in my room, I rewatched the film, the projector whirrin' as faces and voices flickered on the wall. I scribbled a voiceover in my notebook, my pencil scratchin' in the dark: "Sometimes the loudest sound in a room is the person who ain't there to speak." The words felt true, like they carried the weight of Jason's job, a mother's relief, dad's pain, and that empty chair, all tangled in Mill Town's fight to survive. I leaned back, the reel still spinnin',

The next week, the air in the hardware store was thick with sawdust and tension, the faint buzz of Main Street seepin' through the open door as I swept the floor, bristles scratchin' the worn boards. It was a week after the town hall, where folks had aired their gripes 'bout Allied General siphonin' customers from family businesses, and Matt was pacin' near the counter, his work apron loose, his face tight with nerves. He caught my eye, his voice low, urgent, as he leaned close. "Bobby, it's been rough here," he said, glancin' at the empty aisles, the shelves of nails and tools gatherin' dust since Allied General opened. "Hardly any customers, and college is comin' fast. I gotta save money, but the only place hirin' in town's AG."

He rubbed his neck, his eyes dartin' to the back door where Dad was stackin' crates. "I applied last week, had an interview yesterday durin' my lunch break," he said, his voice droppin' softer. "They hired me on the spot, startin' next week. But now I gotta tell Dad I won't be here at the store much, that I'm workin' for AG." His jaw clenched, his feet shufflin', the weight of betrayin' Dad's shop clear in his slumped shoulders. I nodded, keepin' my broom movin', my stomach knotty, knowin' Dad's pride in the store ran deep as that Blackwater River out back.

"Let me know when you tell him, I wanna' to film it." I said with a smile.

"Thanks for the help," as he hit me in the shoulder.

The next day, I was sweepin' again, the store quiet save for the creak of floorboards, when Matt called Dad out back, his voice steady but strained. This is it! I eased closer to the open door, the broom still in my hands, overhearin' their talk over the hum of cicadas outside.

"Dad, I got a job at Allied General," Matt said, his words rushin' out. "I gotta cut my hours here. It's the only way I can save for college." The air went heavy.

I peeked through the crack, seein' Dad's face fall, his hands pausin' on a crate, disappointment creasin' his brow. But he exhaled, slow, his voice calm, weathered. "I understand, son," he said, lookin' Matt in the eye. "Life's got droughts and floods, Matt. A man's gotta prepare for both, do his best without losin' sight of the here and now. I'm proud you're tryin'."

Matt nodded, his shoulders easin', and I gripped the broom tighter, feelin' Dad's wisdom settle. As Matt walked away, dad's expression changed to worry, like these changes, aren't just temporary, that somethin' had changed for good.., and now he knew it.

Chapter 13 – Lost Time (1964)

The summer of 1964 hung heavy over Mill Town, the air thick with the scent of river mud and wilting magnolias, Main Street's pulse fading like a heartbeat slowing. With my camera in my hands, its leather strap biting my neck as I filmed downtown, the lens catchin' the decline in stark frames, Gable's Mercantile with its paint peelin' like old skin, the barbershop's pole spinnin' slower, its red and white dulled, the hardware store's dust gatherin' on the sills. But the Blackwater murmurs just the same, its ripples glintin' under a bruised sky, but the town feels hollow. I pan to the Crazy Horse saloon, its neon flickerin', fewer cars parked out front, then to the grain tower, its rust bleedin' through faded paint, a flag drooping limp.

"Ain't the same," I mutter, rewindin' the reel, the whir soft, the weight of change pressin'.

The Civil Rights Act passes in July, and the town stirs, a mix of hope and tension cracklin' like static.

At the diner, Mr. Gable slams a newspaper down, "Equal rights, signed and done," he says, voice gruff, coffee steaming.

Miss Lorraine, her scarf knotted tight, nods, "About time, but some folks won't take kindly."

Mr Abernathy chimed it, "Law's one thing, hearts another," he mutters, eyes sharp. Whispers ripple, some cheer quietly, others scowl.

"Government meddlin'," a farmer grumbles, his boots scuffing.

That Sunday at Reverend Williams' church, a small clapboard sanctuary by the river, fills beyond its pews, the air warm with sweat and hymnals' musty tang. Mom, her quilted purse clutched, leads us, Dad, Matt, me, through the crowd, her eyes fierce, "We stand together to show our support. Sometimes change is the right thing to do." she says, voice steady. Dad nods, his button up shirt patch crisp, Old Spice sharp. Other neighbors pack in, Miss Elma, Gable, Lila's family, even Eric's dad, his suit starched, showing support, their hands clasped, voices rising in "Amazing Grace," the organ's chords trembling, the creek's murmur a soft echo.

Reverend Williams, his robes swaying, preaches, "Justice is God's work, and ours too," his words a spark, the congregation's "Amen" a vow, Mom's hand squeezing mine, the wood pew creaking, the town's heart beating, uneven but alive.

Matt's starting high school, his grin wide as he laces new cleats, ready for football with Tommy Carter and the boys, their laughter loud at practice, the field's grass clipped, smelling fresh.

"Gonna smear em', Bobby," he says, posin' with the ball under one arm with his other straight out in front of em', his hair curling wild, eyes bright. I nod, happy for him.

My first day of school feels emptier, the school's halls echoing, the linoleum's wax sharp in my nose, Matt's absence a hole. My locker clangs, books heavy, and I shuffle to class, the chalkboard's dust chalky, the teacher's voice distant. Lila finds me at lunch, her sketchpad tucked underarm, her braid swinging,

"Chin up, Bobby, you're not rid of us yet." She grins, passing me a cookie, its oatmeal sweetness warm.

Eric, as loud as ever saunters over, "School's kinda quiet this year, huh, Hollywood?" His tease lifts me, and we laugh, the courtyard's oak leaves rustlin' above in the breeze.

"Want to go to the creek after school?" Eric says lookin' at us.

"Can't, Ma lost her job and took a night shift at AG stockin' shelves, so I gotta help out at home." Lila said with her head tilted down lookin at the table.

"Well…guess we're comin over to help then." Eric said pokin' me in the ribs with his elbow.

She's quieter, her sketches fewer, but every week or two she still meets us by the creek, her pencil tracing the river's curve, "Gotta keep drawin', right? Keeps me sane." I nod, filming her, the camera catching the water's gurgle and sparkles as it reflects on her face as she's drawin'. Just then Eric sticks his head right in between with a funny face shaking his cheeks with his tongue out waggin like a dog.

Just before Thanksgiving, Dad organized a meeting at our house one evening. The living room cramped, the air heavy with coffee and cigarette smoke. Mom's pecan pie cooling on the table, its nutty sweetness a faint comfort.

Mr. Gable, his tie loose, paces, "Last Christmas was a bust, sales down over seventy percent."

Miss Lorraine, her scarf slipping, sighs, "Bank's been breathin' down my neck, sayin' I'll close by spring."

Dad leans forward, his calluses catching the lamplight, "We need a big push, how bout a Christmas Festival, lights, music, the works, like we used to?" Mom nods, "Bring the whole town back together, show em we're still here."

There's a new energy in the room. They're eyes light up like kids on Christmas mornin'. They plan, a parade, carols, a tree in the square, the scent of pine and tinsel imagined, their voices hopeful but strained.

"I'm in, but if sales are like last year, I'm afraid I'll have no other choice," Mr. Gable warns, "we're done."

Mom's eyes were fierce, urging a fight, "remember the flood of '54, we all thought we were done? You were only two. We never thought the town would be the same. Remember that hurricane in '49? We always come back!"

There was a flurry of activity in the two weeks followin'. Matt and I both helped paint store fronts, dad donated materials to help fix doors and windows that had been neglected. The day before the festival the floats were all ready, Cray paper surrounding them with cardboard deer and sleighs made of wood. Mainstreet had a complete makeover ready for the whole town to come and see. I got my camera out just in time to catch Dad standin' in the middle of mainstreet with Mr. Gables admiring their work, smiling for the first time in months.

"Hope is a wonderful thing, but best shared with those around ya" I spoke quietly into the camera.

The morning of the festival, the day dawn. I see dad standin' on the front porch. I step out onto the porch, it's a warm humid morning with a stiff breeze blowin from the south with a grey overcast sky. Dad has a worried look on his face.

Dad's looking at the sky, "storm's coming."

He was right, by noon, the clouds turn black and swollen. The wind suddenly shifts out of the North unleashing freezing rain that pelts Main Street, the sidewalks slick, the air biting with ice and wet cedar. The red-and-white awnings sag, bunting tears, flags droop, the square's spruce tilting, its ornaments, glass balls, tinsel, shattering on the cobblestones, their shards glinting like broken promises. Vendors huddle under leaking tents who's edges are covered in icecycles, their hot cider steaming, unsold, the scent souring, the band's instruments silent, cases soaked. Kids, bundled in scarves, slip on ice, their paper snowflakes wilting, parents pulling them back.

"It's no use, let's go!" Miss Lorraine, her coat drenched, shakes her head, "Ain't nobody commin' for a festival in this, Bobby."

Mr. Gable, his hat sodden, mutters, "Bank'll have my keys by New Year."

I film it all, my lens fogging, the rain's patter loud on my hood, the camera catching the storm's howl, the crowd's murmurs fading, the festival a bust, the town's hope drowning.

Dad's hand on my shoulder, "Keep rollin', Bobby. Anyone can smile in the sun, but it's the hard times that make up who we are."

At home, the fire crackles, its smoky warmth faint against the damp chill seeping through the windows, the living room's lamplight casting shadows on Mom's quilt, folded on her chair. Matt, sprawled on the couch, his cleats muddy, says,

"Football's the only thing this town's got going for it, Bobby. Coach says I'm startin' next game, bring your camera!" His grin's half-hearted.

I could tell he was tryin' to lift us up. I guess that's what we do though, when times are tough.

Dad sips coffee, the mug's steam curling, "We'll try again, son. Town's tougher than one bad day." Mom, her apron dusted with flour, nods, "We're small, not weak, like the creek, we keep movin' forward."

I think of Lila, her mom's late shifts. She calls later, her voice tired, "Saw the mess, Bobby. Mama says we'll make it, but it hurts."

"I sure hope so. Let me know if ya need anythin'." then I quietly hang up the phone, knowin' this winter was going to be bleaker than usual.

Chapter 14 – Makin Movies
(January 1965)

Main Street was still bleedin' out. They hung in there for two holiday seasons. Just barely though. Now the businesses were shutterin' one by one like candles snuffed in a storm. I carried my 8mm camera everywhere, filmin' the end as it came, not 'cause I wanted to, but 'cause it felt like someone had to bear witness. Dad, Matt, and I helped out where we could, movin' boxes, haulin' shelves, but every trip felt like goin' to a funeral, the air thick with loss and the kind of quiet that hurts more than words.

First to go was Mrs. Elma's Book Nook, its "12 Books of Christmas" display long since packed away. She'd locked the door for good in January, her typewriter silent, the shelves emptied of stories. We helped her move out on a gray mornin', carryin' crates of books to her nephew's truck.

"These were my life," she said, her voice crackin' as she patted a box, her shawl slippin' off one shoulder.

I filmed her standin' in the doorway, the "Closed" sign swayin' behind her, the footage shaky 'cause my hands weren't steady. The bookstore had been a heartbeat, a place where kids like me learned to dream through pages. Without it, Main Street felt like it'd lost its dreams.

Gable's Mercantile went next, its tinny Christmas speaker finally unplugged. Mr. Gable's shelves, once stuffed with flour sacks and ribbon bolts, stood bare, the floor scuffed from years of footsteps. We hauled crates to a storage shed, Matt gruntin' under the weight, dad wipin' sweat from his brow. "Forty years," Mr. Gable muttered, lockin' the door for the last time. "Now it's just a building." I caught that moment on film, the click of the lock echoin' in the empty store, the camera lingerin' on his slumped shoulders. Gable's had been where folks traded gossip with their groceries, where mom'd barter for thread. Its closin' left a hole, like losin' the town's kitchen.

McGregor's Restaurant held on longer, but by June, it was done. The counter where shopkeepers once swapped plans over coffee was cleared, the jukebox silent. We helped Mr. McGregor pack up, stackin' stools, rollin' up faded menus, the smell of grease still clingin' to the air.

"Thought I'd retire on my terms," Benny said, his voice gruff, tossin' a spatula into a box.

I filmed the empty booths, the neon sign out front gone dark, tryin' to capture the diner's soul before it was gone. Mr. McGregor's had been our gatherin' place on Friday evenings, where stories were served with pie, where the town felt like family. Now, it was just another shell, leavin' us to eat our meals alone.

The Henderson's Christmas tree lot didn't close, not exactly, but Mr. Henderson stopped cuttin' trees, the fenced lot left to weeds and rust. We helped him clear the last of the mulch, the trailer creakin' under the load.

"No point," he said, kickin' at the dirt. "Allied's got the market now."

I filmed the empty lot, the faded sign, *Fresh-Cut Tradition Since 1931'* tilted in the wind, the ground littered with brittle needles. That lot had been Christmas itself, kids runnin' through rows, families laughin'. Its absence made winter feel colder, like we'd lost the spark that lit the season.

Each move was a funeral, and we were the pallbearers. Dad worked quiet, his jaw tight, like he was carryin' more than boxes. Matt threw himself into the labor, but his usual jokes were gone, his eyes distant. I filmed when I could, the camera's whir a small comfort, catchin' moments like Mrs. Elma's tremblin' hands, Mr. Gable's final lock, Mr McGregor's empty checkout counter. The footage was raw, silent except for the shuffle of feet or the creak of a door, but it held the weight of what we were losin'.

These businesses weren't just shops, they were roots, growin' deep into our lives. The bookstore gave us stories, the mercantile gave us community, the restaurant across the street gave us warmth, the tree lot gave us joy. Their closin' didn't just empty downtown; it kinda emptied us, leavin' gaps where laughter and connection used to be, leavin just memories. Allied General's red sign glowed brighter with every shuttered door, its aisles fillin' the void with cheap goods, but no soul.

As we hauled the last of Mr. McGregor's chairs to his truck, dad put a hand on my shoulder, his grip firm but shakin'. "It's hard, Bobby," he said, his voice low. "But we keep goin'. For them, for us."

I nodded, my camera hangin' heavy, knowin' my films were more than pictures now, they were proof we'd been somethin' once, somethin' worth fightin' for. Matt looked back at the diner's dark windows, then away, like it hurt too much to linger. We walked home, the street quiet, the ghosts of Main Street followin' close, their absence louder than any farewell.

By the spring of 1965, town was slippin' further into the shadows, and I was there with my camera, now mine for good, tryin' to catch what was left before it was all gone. I'd started filmin', its whir a steady companion as I walked Main Street. The town wasn't dead, not yet, but it was quiet, like it was holdin' its breath, waitin' for a miracle that just hadn't shown up yet.

I'd take long, slow pannin' shots, the lens sweepin' over once bustlin' clean as a whistle, but now empty sidewalks where weeds pushed through the cracks. Bare windows stared back like closed eyes, some still had boxes piled up inside. "Open" signs swayed in doorways, creakin' in the breeze, but no one came. Gable's Mercantile had one, its red paint faded to pink, hangin' crooked above a locked door. I'd linger

104

on it, the camera hummin', lettin' the silence speak louder than any voice could. The footage was stark, no music, no chatter, just the wind and the occasional caw of a crow, like the town was narratin' its own fall.

The decay showed up in small things, too, and I caught those in close-ups. A fallen banner from last year's Fourth of July lay crumpled in an alley, its stars and stripes torn, the words *Mill Town Proud* barely readable. A rusted bike rack stood alone by the empty diner, its bars bent, no bikes to hold. One evenin', I filmed a streetlight that used to glow at dusk, its bulb dark now, the pole leanin' like it was tired of standin'. The camera didn't lie, it showed the town as it was, not as I wished it could be.

Back home, I'd sit at the kitchen table, a notebook open, scribblin' ideas for voiceovers to go with the footage. I wasn't sure if I'd ever record 'em, but writin' helped me make sense of what I was seein'. "This is Main Street," I wrote one night, my pencil scratchin' in the quiet, "where folks used to wave, where stores closed for lunch. Now it's a ghost town, but the ghosts don't know they're gone." Another page had fragments, like, "The banner fell, and nobody picked it up," or "The light's out, and the dark feels heavier for it." I'd read 'em back, tryin' different tones in my head, somber, angry, maybe even hopeful, though hope was hard to come by.

Sometimes I'd show Matt a clip, the projector whirrin' in our bedroom, the images flickerin' on the wall. "It's grim, Bobby," he'd say, leanin' back on his bed, but he'd watch, his eyes fixed on the empty sidewalks. "You gonna show this to anybody?"

"Dunno," I'd say, windin' the film back. "Maybe someday. Just feels like I gotta keep filmin', you know? Like it's not done yet. Maybe I just keep waitin for a happy endin'."

He'd nod, not pushin' it, and I'd go back to my notebook, writin' lines like, "Town's still here, but it's whisperin' now, not shoutin'." The camera was my way of listenin', of holdin' onto the pieces, rusted racks, fallen banners, lights that didn't flicker no more. It wasn't about savin' Main Street, not anymore. It was about rememberin' it, givin' it a voice, even if it was just mine, scratchin' in a notebook under the dim glow of a lamp.

Matt came barging into my room late one night while I was reviewing a film. Matt and Eric had hatched the plan to haul Dad's old canoe down for a campin' trip "In stead of watchin' other people's memories, we're gonna make our own! We're going campin' in style this time, like those fancy people from outta town!"

Through the week we piled gear in the garage. Fishin' poles with tangled lines, sleeping bags musty from storage, a tin of worms dug from the garden, their earthy wriggle ticklin' our palms, and a dented cooler stuffed with soda and bacon, its ice sloshing. Lila even brought some old lawn chairs. This was the most gear we had ever assembled for a campin' trip. The canoe, a beat-up beast, weighed a ton, its hull scratched from years of river scrapes, but dreams of frying fat bass over a fire kept us grinnin' as we lugged it through the woods, sweat soaking our T-shirts, the scent of cedar and anticipation sharp. Lila, her braid swingin', carried the bait bucket, teasing, "Y'all better catch somethin' worth eatin', or I'm stickin' to beans!" Eric, his limp barely slowing him, laughed, "Better keep pushin, artist, or we'll leave you for the gators!" We reached the creek, dropped our gear on the sandy bank, the water's cool kiss on our toes a relief, and launched the canoe, its bow slicing the surface, paddles splashin', our whoops echoing off the cypress knees as we fished 'til sundown, rods whipping, the air hummin' with dragonflies. Lila, triumphant, hooked a scrawny bass, its scales glinting silver, "Only one who's eatin' tonight!" she crowed, while Matt groaned, "That ain't even a snack!" The sun dipped, paintin' the sky tangerine, but the wind shifted, the puffy white clouds started turnin' dark. Storm clouds rolled in, thunder rumblin' like a warnin' drum, the air electric, heavy with coming rain.

"We best get back to the sandbar before that storm hits." Matt said while starin' at the sky.

We all nodded and turned the canoe around. As tired as we were, with each lightning strike we paddled harder the mile upstream back to a sandbar. The canoe's hull scraping gravel, our arms burning, the creek's murmur drowned by thunder's growl. The first fat raindrops pelting our shoulders as we scrambled to shore. We barely sparked a fire under the large juniper tree, its smoky crackle frail under the storm's roar, the coals barely strong enough to heat up the cast iron pan Eric had brought, bass sizzling in the frying pan. Its fishy tang was mixing with wet wood ash, before the clouds unleashed a deluge, rain hissing, dousing the flames, the air cold and raw. The frying pan nearly instantly turned into a bowl, making fish soup. We flipped the canoe, its metal clanging, and huddled beneath, the four of us, Matt, Eric, Lila, me crammed tight. The rain was blowin in sideways, our knees knocking, fighting over who'd stay driest, the creek's swell lapping close.

"My leg's gettin' soaked, Eric!" Lila snapped, shoving his shoulder, her braid dripping.

Eric, grinning, "Better'n your sketchpad, ain't it?"

Matt, his hair plastered, grumbled, "This was your dumb idea, soldier!"

I laughed, "Y'all quit whinin', or I'm swimmin' home! And no fartin'!"

None of us admitted defeat, pride stubborn. It was a long sleepless night but as the sky purpled, lightnin' flashin', we unanimously called it. Our gear, sleepin' bags soppin' wet, poles tangled, a soggy mess tossed into the canoe. We waded, chin-deep, pushing the canoe through the swollen swamp, then pushed and dragged it down the muddy road like a sled, the mud's slick suck pullin' at our sneakers. When we got to Red Hill, the only real hill near home, we all stared up at its summit. The rain poured, turnin' the clay to a slippery slimy beast. The canoe was more like a thousand-pound anchor. We pushed, grunting, feet slippin', clay smearin' our faces, my hands raw.

We were half way up when I glanced at Lila, clay drippin' from her chin, and burst out laughin', "You look like a mud monster!"

Matt turned, chuckling, when a blindin' orange bolt of lightning cracked ten yards away, thunder explodin', knockin' us to our knees, hearts poundin'. "Let's get outta here!" Matt yelled, "Heave!" as he leaned into the rope pullin' the canoe from the front.

Adrenaline surged, and we shoved, muscles screamin', the canoe inchin' up, clay suckin', until we crested, panting, soaked, triumphant. We pushed our rain soaked gear home, rain relentless.

Afte what seemed like eternity, we saw our gate. Dad was on the front porch, coffee steaming, his grin wide, "Y'all look a little wet. Hose off and come on in."

We didn't need an invitation. We hosed off all the mud, just as mom brought some warm towels out to the garage. I still remember the smell of those towels and the warmth I felt.

Shiverin' we all drug ourselves inside where we were welcomed with a big pile of waffles. Nature's lesson still fresh in our mind and etched in our mud-caked smiles, one sopping step at a time. As we ate, we recanted our story in boisterous unison like we had just returned from an epic adventure.

By the end of summer of 1965, I was spendin' every spare moment with my 8mm camera. I'd film us all down at the creek swingin from trees like tarzan, hootin' n hollarin'. I got a real good clip when Eric was swingin from the tree and didn't let go the rope in time smackin' on the cypress root, as soon as we knew he was ok, I nearly dropped the camera in the creek from laughing so hard.

But mostly I was filmin' the slow fade, tryin' to hold onto what was left. But it wasn't just the empty sidewalks or boarded windows I was capturin', it was the people, their stories, the way their words made the town's decline feel real, like a wound you don't notice till it starts to bleed. Talkin' one-on-one with folks deepened what I saw, turnin' my lens from a tool into a mirror. It didn't take long before people started hearin' bout what I was doin'. I guess folks had somethin' still to say.

One afternoon, I sat with Uncle Don on his porch, the paint peelin' like old skin. He'd been the town's handyman forever, fixin' just bout any kind of appliance. Now, his tools sat rusty in a shed, and his hands were idle, folded in his lap. "Used to be I'd work sunup to sundown," he said, his voice rough, starin' at the horizon where Allied's sign glowed. "Folks'd call me for every squeak and crack. They weren't just callin' a repair man, sometimes I'd sit for an hour over coffee after the job was done, just catchin' up. Bobby. Now... I ain't repairin' nothin'. People just throw it out and git another these days." His eyes were cloudy, like he was seein' a town that didn't exist no more. I didn't film him, some moments are too raw, but I scribbled his words in my notebook, feelin' the weight of a man whose purpose had been stolen.

Miss Elma invited me into her house one evenin', the first time I'd seen her since her bookstore closed. Her livin' room smelled of dust and lavender, and she pulled out old ledgers, their pages yellowed, crammed with her neat handwriting. "Every customer's name," she said, tracin' a finger over the ink. "Mrs. Tate bought *Little Women* for her girl. Mr. Collier got a dictionary for his boy." Her voice broke, and tears spilled down her cheeks. "I knew 'em all, Bobby. Now they're just names." She wept, and I filmed her gently, the camera hummin' soft, catchin' the way her hands shook as she closed the ledger. Her shop had been more than books, it was a landmark, it was the town's unwritten history, and losin' it left us all a little lost.

Lila joined me one day at golden hour, when the light turned Main Street soft and warm, like it was tryin' to apologize. We walked slow, her boots scuffin' the pavement, my camera whirrin' away.

"I remember when I had to step off the curb to make room," she said, her voice quiet, her braid swayin' as she looked at the empty street.

"Folks'd be laughin', carryin' bags, callin' to each other. Now it's just… nothin'.""

Her words hung there, and I filmed the street as she spoke, the lens catchin' the deserted storefronts bathed in amber light, her silhouette at the edge of the frame. Lila's memory was a thread, tyin' me to a town I'd almost forgotten, I felt like I was archivin', tryin not to forget, so we remembered what's possible.

I stopped bein' just a witness and became somethin' else, a keeper of what was. Every evenin', I'd shoot footage of the storefronts in fadin' light, their signs creakin', their windows dark, Gable's, Benny's, the barbershop with its pole still but unlit. I filmed mom at her kitchen window, her face soft as she stared at the garden, and dad at the hardware counter, countin' nails like they were all he had left. Even Matt, wipin' his hands on a rag after night shifts at Allied, got caught on film, his jaw tight, his eyes avoidin' the lens. Back in my room, I'd edit short segments on dad's old reel-to-reel setup, splicin' tape by lamplight, tryin' to weave the clips into somethin' that told the truth without breakin' me.

Somethin' shifted that summer, not just in town but in how folks saw me. I wasn't just Bobby with a camera anymore, I was a documentarian, carryin' the town's story. One mornin', while Mr. Abernathy closed up his feed store, he waved me over, hammer in hand. "Make sure you get this, son," he said, his voice gruff but steady, as he drove a nail into the plywood. "Let 'em see what happened here so they don't forget," his voice crackin' a little. I filmed him, the camera steady, catchin' the sweat on his brow, the finality of each nail. His store had fed livestock and families for decades, and now it was just wood and nails, sealed shut.

A young girl, maybe seven, ran up to me one day outside the old diner, her pigtails bouncin'. She held out a crayon drawin' of Main Street, stick-figure people, bright storefronts, a sun smilin' overhead. "For your movie," she said, her voice small but sure. I took the drawin', my throat tight, and nodded. "I'll keep it safe," I promised, tuckin' it into my notebook. That night, I filmed the drawin' by lamplight, its colors vivid against the reality I was capturin'. Her gift made the work feel bigger, like it wasn't just for me anymore.

I started losin' sleep, my dreams turnin' to black-and-white stills, reels spinnin' with no sound, empty sidewalks, Miss Elma's ledgers, Lila's silhouette against a dyin' street. I'd wake up sweatin', the camera still in my lap, the weight of it all pressin' down. One night, mom found me asleep at my desk, the projector whirrin', footage of Miss Elma loopin' silent on the wall, her hands on the ledger, her tears catchin' the light. Mom didn't say nothin', just draped a quilt over my shoulders and turned off the projector, her hand lingerin' on my head like she knew what I was carryin'.

I kept filmin', kept writin', kept editin', 'cause I felt like stoppin' would mean lettin' go. The conversations, the drawin', the way folks looked at me now, they made me feel like I was holdin' somethin' sacred, somethin' that could outlast the boarded windows and the rust. My lens was awake, and so was I, archivin' a town that was fightin' to be remembered, even as it faded into the dusk.

Chapter 15 - A Smaller Celebration (May 1965)

It was Memorial Day mornin', 1965, and the town woke to a quieter kind of reverence, like a song played with half the notes missin'. I was out early with my 8mm camera, walkin' Main Street to capture what was left of our traditions. The air was warm, carryin' the scent of cut grass and distant barbecues, but the street felt hollow, its pulse weaker than I remembered.

Dad had hung flags along Main Street, their red, white, and blue flappin' gentle in the breeze, but the line was sparse. Where every lamppost used to sport one, now gaps stood out, like missin' teeth. Fewer homes joined in, too, porches that once flew Old Glory proud were the same as they were the month before, their owners either gone or just forgot. Several houses, like the Fultons' and old Mrs. Tate's, stayed undecorated for the first time since I could remember, their windows dark, their yards tired, like the overall feelin' in town. I filmed the flags, pannin' slow across the street, the camera's hum mixin' with the rustle of fabric, catchin' the way the colors looked brave but lonesome.

The town band gathered in front of the church, their instruments glintin' in the mornin' sun, but the group was smaller now. Mr. Hollis, who'd played trumpet since I was a kid, was gone, workin' stock at Allied. The drummer, young Tommy, had moved to Raleigh with his folks after their store closed up. The remainin' band members tuned up, their notes waverin' but determined, practicin' "Sweet America" for the service. I filmed 'em from across the street, zoomin' in on the clarinet player's furrowed brow, the way the bandleader's baton shook just a little. The music was still there, but it felt thinner, like a memory tryin' to hold its shape.

Church bells rang out, deep and steady, callin' folks to the memorial service at the statue in the town square, a bronze soldier, rifle in hand, standin' watch since 1919. A small crowd assembled, maybe thirty souls, far less than the hundreds who'd once packed the square a few years ago. Veterans in faded caps stood upfront, their medals pinned proud, but their faces were heavy, like they felt the weight of wars past. Families clustered in twos and threes, kids fidgetin', their parents whisperin' about who wasn't there. The energy was subdued, not the proud swell of years gone by, but a quiet nod to duty, like showin' up was all they had left.

I filmed it all, keepin' to the edges, the camera's lens sweepin' over the crowd, catchin' the veterans' stiff salutes, Mrs. Smith wipin' her eyes, the band's haltin' rendition of "Taps." In my notebook, I jotted names of folks missin', Mr. Collier, whose diner had closed; Lila's ma, workin' a double at Allied; even Eric, who'd always worn his dad's old army hat to the service but was nowhere now. Their absence stung, like an old threadbare blanket that used to be soft and warm.

As the preacher started his prayer, I spotted Mr. Jennings near the statue, his uniform crisp with medals displayed proudly. He'd been at every Memorial Day since I could remember, always with a story about his brother lost in Korea. He caught my eye, his weathered face softenin', and gave a quick smile, like he was glad I was there, filmin' what mattered. I nodded back, adjustin' the camera, and zoomed in for a moment, catchin' the way his smile held both pride and sorrow, a flicker of the spark still alive in him.

The service ended with a final note from the band, the crowd dispersin' slow, their footsteps muffled on the grass. I lowered the camera, my notebook heavy with names and absences, knowin' this Memorial Day was smaller, quieter, but still ours. Mr. Jennings' smile stuck with me, a reminder that some folks hadn't given up, even if the flags were fewer and the crowd was thin.

Under a heavy sun, Mainstreet tried to muster some of its old spark, but it felt like a candle flickerin' in a storm. I wandered with my camera, filmin'. The festivities, if you could call 'em that, were a pale shadow of what they'd been.

At Chandler Hardware, Dad had done somethin' new, a Memorial Day discount sign hung in the window, offerin' ten percent off nails and tools. The store usually closed for the holiday, dad and mom joinin' the service at the statue, but this year, he stayed open, his face tight as he adjusted the sign. "Gotta try to sell somethin'," he'd said that mornin', his voice low, like he was betrayin' somethin' by workin today. I filmed the sign, the camera lingerin' on its uneven letters, dad's shadow movin' behind the glass. It wasn't just a sale, it was a plea, and it hurt to see. I knew he would never miss Memorial Day if he didn't have to.

Later, at the church basement potluck, mom carried in a pecan pie, her pride and joy, but the spread was thin, only half the usual dishes lined the tables, and most had Allied stickers on their plastic containers, like even the potluck had lost some of its soul. I filmed the table, the camera lingerin' on the store-bought cakes next to mom's homemade pie, a quiet battle between what was… and what we'd settled for.

Lila, standin' nearby, caught my eye and said, "It's like a town puttin' on its old clothes, hopin' they still fit."

Her voice was soft, and I nodded, knowin' she'd named the ache I couldn't.

I found Mr. Abernathy outside, leanin' against the church wall, and asked if I could interview him. He sighed, his eyes squintin' at the horizon. "Used to be I couldn't keep up with sales by noon on Memorial Day," he said, his voice gravelly. "Now I count change for the same two customers all mornin'." I filmed him, the camera steady, catchin' the lines in his face, the way he gestured at the empty street.

"Allied's got a big sale this weekend," he added, spittin' the words. "Patriot Discounts, they call it, grills, flags, soda. Folks are there, not here." His words were a mirror, showin' how Allied was stealin' even our holidays.

Back at the church, I saw Matt slip in for lunch, still in his Allied uniform, on break from a shift. He looked out of place, his shoulders hunched like he knew it. Mrs. Clara, greeted him warm, settin' a piece of pie in front of him. "Good to see you, hon," she said, then quieter, "You're missed over here." Matt gave a tight smile, his eyes flickin' to the empty booths, and I filmed from a distance, catchin' the way he gripped the mug, like he was holdin' onto somethin' he couldn't keep. He didn't stay long, headin' back to Allied before his pie was gone.

The day lingered in Mill Town like a half-forgotten promise, the downtown square a faded stage for a ritual losin' its fire. I moved through the crowd with my camera, capturin' what was left of the day's heart. The square, once packed shoulder-to-shoulder, now held fewer lawn chairs, scattered in small clumps, with wide stretches of empty grass between groups. Families sat apart, their conversations low, their picnic baskets sparse. I panned the camera slow across the scene, the lens takin' in the gaps, the quiet, the way the square felt more like a memory than a moment.

Near the fountain, a handful of kids chased each other, splashin' in the shallow water, but their laughter was thin, distracted, like they were playin' out of habit. A boy tossed a pebble, watchin' it sink without a smile, and I filmed him, the camera lingerin' on his small, bored frown, the fountain's trickle louder than the kids' voices. The energy wasn't what it used to be, when me, Matt, Eric and Lila would run wild here, dodgin' knees and borrowin' cookies from picnic spreads.

The high school choir took the makeshift stage, their voices risin' for "America the Beautiful," but the performance faltered. Several singers looked nervous, missin' notes or glancin' at each other, unprepared. The school's arts fundin' had been slashed, leavin' 'em with no music teacher, no rehearsals worth mentionin'. I filmed their effort, the camera catchin' a girl's shaky hands, a boy's eyes dartin' to the crowd, the melody brave but frayed.

Mayor Heartwell stepped up next, his tie loose, his speech short and forgettable. He spoke of "economic promise" and "new opportunities," barely mentionin' the soldiers the day was meant to honor. His words drifted over the crowd, landin' flat, like coins in a dry well. I filmed him, zoomin' in on his forced smile, the way his hands fidgeted with his notes, then panned to the crowd, veterans starin' stone-faced, mothers shiftin' in their chairs, unimpressed. The mayor's promises felt like a dodge, a way to skirt the sacrifice we were there to remember.

The undercurrents ran deeper than the speeches. Dad stood in the doorway of Chandler Hardware, his arms crossed, watchin' the foot traffic trickle past like water through a sieve. His discount sign swayed in the breeze, but few stopped, their eyes on the ground or the horizon where Allied's sale was pullin' 'em away. I filmed him from across the square, the camera holdin' his still figure, the store's shadow stretchin' long behind him, a man tied to a town, an era, that was movin on, leavin' him behind.

As the service wrapped, I caught mom slowly lookin' around, wipin' a tear, her hand quick to hide it. I didn't ask why, didn't need to. Her face said it all: grief for the fallen, for the way things used to be. I filmed her from a distance, the camera gentle, catchin' the glint of sunlight on her cheek, the way she squared her shoulders after, like she was bracin' for what came next.

Lila sat on a bench near the shuttered bookstore, sketchin' in a small pad, her pencil movin' fast. I leaned over, seein' not the people but the emptiness, bare sidewalks, dark windows, the spaces where crowds used to be. "Drawin' what's gone?" I asked, keepin' my voice low.

She nodded, not lookin' up. "It's louder than the rest." I didn't film her, just let her words settle, knowin' she was seein' the same town I was, one that was fadin' faster than we could hold.

Uncle Don found me near the fountain, his toolbelt swapped for a clean shirt, his face lined deeper than last year. "It ain't a celebration if nobody remembers what it's for," he muttered, his eyes on the thinnin' crowd. "This day used to mean somethin', honor, loss, us. Now it's just... goin' through the motions and sales." I filmed him, the camera catchin' his clenched jaw, the way he shook his head, his words a truth that nobody wanted to admit.

The next weekend', I sat in my room, editin' the footage from that day, thinkin' of the images that told the day's story. Smilin' veterans saluted beside empty shop windows; kids played near a quiet fountain; dad stood alone in his doorway. I titled the reel *Memorial Day, Assembly No Longer Required*, the words bitter but true. In my notebook, I scratched a closin' narration: "Once, we gathered to remember. Now we gather 'cause we forgot how not to. But each year, the crowd thins, and the echo grows."

I leaned back, the projector's hum fillin' the dark, watchin' the footage loop, mom's tear, Lila's sketch, Uncle Don's mutter, the choir's shaky song. My lens had caught a community tryin' to honor its past while its present slipped away, a celebration smaller and sadder, but still stubborn, like a flag flyin' on a broken pole. The reel ended, and I sat in the silence, hopin' my film could keep the echo from fadin' completely. I started to feel the weight of it all.

Chapter 16 - There's Still Some Life Left
(July 1965)

It was a sticky mornin' in July 1965, the kind where the air hugs you too tight and the cicadas hum like they're plannin' a takeover. I was sittin' on the porch, my 8mm camera idle in my lap, its lens pointed at nothin'. The town's decline had been weighin' on me, each reel I shot, empty storefronts, rusted bike racks, Miss Elma's tears, pilin' up like stones in my chest. I was lost in it, the ache of a town fadin' faster than I could film, when I heard the rumble of an engine and the crunch of gravel.

Eric's dad's old Ford truck rolled up, its fenders speckled with rust, Eric peerin' over the steerin' wheel, grinnin' like he'd just won a bet.

Lila was in the passenger seat, her braid bouncin' as she leaned out the window, wavin' like a parade queen. "Get your sorry self up, Bobby Chandler!" she hollered, her voice bright as the sun glarin' off the hood. "We're kidnappin' you for the day!"

I squinted, shieldin' my eyes. "Kidnappin'? What's this about?"

Eric leaned on the horn, a quick bleat that startled a crow from the oak. "You been mopin' around with that camera, filmin' every sad corner of this town," he said. "We're here to get your head out of the gloom. You can't fix everythin' all by yourself, but you can show folks there's still some life left!"

Lila hopped out, her sneakers kickin' up dust, and grabbed my arm. "Come on, Bobby. We're gonna have *fun*. Remember what that is?

Laughin'? Not thinkin' about nothin?" Her eyes sparkled, darin' me to argue, and I couldn't help but crack a smile, the first real one in weeks.

"Alright, alright," I said, settin' the camera on the porch rail.

"Where's Matt?" Eric asked.

"He's workin today" I replied.

"Figures, well, we're gonna have fun for em'" Eric shouted.

I was afraid to ask, "What's the plan?"

Eric revved the engine, a low growl that sounded like trouble. "Muddin'," he said, his grin widenin'. "Borrowed Pop's truck while he's off workin' in Pensacola. He's gone all day, so we got the wheels. Let's tear up the woods!"

"Borrowed?" I raised an eyebrow, climbin' into the cab, Lila squeezin' in between us. "You mean stole."

"Well, he was the one that left the keys on the counter, like he was just beggin' me to do it." Eric corrected, throwin' the truck into gear. "Beggin us to have a blast. Now hold on!"

We roared out of the driveway, the truck rattlin' like it might shake apart, headin' for the woods beyond the Coldwater. Eric cranked the radio, some twangy country tune blarin' through static, and Lila sang along, off-key but loud, her elbow jabbin' me every time she hit a high note. "You're gonna thank us, Bobby!" she shouted over the music. "This is what livin' looks like!"

The woods were a maze of pines and red clay, the trails slick from last night's rain. Eric gunned the truck into the first mudhole, tires spinnin', mud flyin' like chocolate syrup, splatterin' the windshield. We whooped and hollered, the cab shakin' as we fishtailed through the slop. "That's how you do it!" Eric yelled, slappin' the steerin' wheel, his face lit up like a kid on Christmas. Lila leaned out the window, scoopin' a handful of mud and flingin' it at me, laughin' when it hit my cheek.

"You're dead, Hollis!" I shouted, wipin' the muck off, but I was laughin' too, the kind of laugh that hurts your sides and makes you forget everythin' else. We hit mudhole after mudhole, the truck slidin' and groanin', our voices echoin' through the trees. For a while, it was just us, the mud, and the thrill, no Main Street, no Allied, no weight of a town slippin' away.

We ended up at the sandbar by the river, the truck parked crooked under a juniper, its fenders caked in clay. We sprawled on the sand, passin' a warm bottle of Coke, the water lappin' soft against the bank. The sun was high, paintin' the creek gold, and we talked about high school, just a month away. "Gonna be weird, huh?" Lila said, diggin' her toes into the sand. "New teachers, new rules. Think we'll still be us?"

"Course we will," Eric said, tossin' a pebble into the water. "We'll run that place. Bobby'll probably film the whole school fallin' apart, though."

I chuckled, leanin' back on my elbows. "Maybe. But today, I ain't filmin' nothin'. This is enough."

We stayed till the light started to soften, talkin' about dumb stuff, pranks we'd pull, teachers we'd avoid, whether Lila could sneak into the boys' locker room to steal Matt's clothes while he was takin a shower. It was easy, like the world was just the three of us, the river, and a truck that smelled like swamp. But time don't wait, and Eric checked his watch, his face droppin'. "Dad'll be home in twenty minutes," he said, scramblin' up. "We gotta haul."

We piled into the truck, the engine coughin' to life, and tore back through the woods, mud still flyin'. Everythin' was fine till we hit the last mudhole, a deep, soupy pit we'd dodged earlier. Eric gunned it, but the tires spun useless, the truck sinkin' till the axles were buried. Mud oozed up to our knees as we climbed out, starin' at the mess.

"Oh, we're dead," Eric groaned, kickin' the tire, which just sprayed more mud on his jeans. "Pop's gonna skin me alive if he sees this!"

Lila laughed, wadin' into the muck, her shorts already ruined. "You're such a genius, Fulton. 'Borrowed,' my butt. Now what?"

I looked at the truck, then at Eric's panicked face, and couldn't help it, I busted out laughin', the kind that makes your eyes water. "We're knee-deep in it, and you're worried about your pop? We ain't gettin' this out in twenty minutes!"

"Quit cacklin' and help!" Eric snapped, but he was grinnin' now, shovelin' mud with his hands like that'd do anythin'. Lila grabbed a stick, pokin' at the tires, mutterin' about how boys always mess things up. We pushed, pulled, and cursed, the truck budgin' an inch before sinkin' deeper, our clothes soaked, our faces streaked with clay.

"Alright, new plan," Lila said, wipin' her brow, leavin' a muddy smear. "We hide the truck, tell your pop it was stolen, and move to Mexico."

"Great idea, Hollis," Eric shot back, flingin' a clump of mud at her. "You're payin' for the tacos."

We were still laughin', half-panicked, when we heard another engine, a farmer's tractor rumblin' down the trail. Old Mr. Jenkins leaned out, squintin' at us. "Y'all stuck?" he called, his voice dry as the sandbar.

"Yessir," I said, tryin' to sound less guilty. "Little trouble here."

He shook his head, hookin' a chain to the truck, and yanked us out in five minutes flat, the Ford drippin' like a drowned dog. "You bess' get this cleaned up 'fore your pop sees it," he said to Eric, a knowin' glint in his eye, then drove off.

We raced to Eric's, hosin' down the truck just as his dad's car pulled in. The truck was still drippin' with a halo of red clay surroundin' it.

Pop didn't notice a thing, and we collapsed in the yard, muddy, exhausted, and alive in a way I hadn't felt in months. "See?" Lila said, pokin' my ribs. "Told you we'd show you some fun."

"Yeah," I said, grinnin', the ache in my chest lighter. "Maybe there's still some life left to film." I didn't grab my camera, but I knew I'd remember this, mud, laughter, and two friends who pulled me out of the dark, even if we almost got stuck doin' it

Chapter 17 - High School
(September 1966)

It was September 1966, and I stepped into Mill Town High School, feelin' like I had somehow grown years over a single summer. I hated to admit it, but it felt good to be back in the same school as Matt. The hallways echoed with fewer footsteps than I'd expected, the air carryin' a faint musty smell, like old books and forgotten promises. Lockers lined the walls, their hinges rustin', some stuck shut, others hangin' open, empty. I moved through the crowd, smaller than it should've been, my backpack heavy, my camera left at home, untouched for weeks.

The bell tower still worked, its chime ringin' out sharp across the schoolyard, I looked up, but nobody else did anymore. It was just noise, not a call to attention, like the town itself had stopped listenin'. In classrooms, teachers greeted us with forced smiles, their chalkboards worn, their lessons pulled from textbooks at least a decade old, history books that ended before Kennedy was elected, science books with faded diagrams of atoms nobody cared to update. I sat in the back, noticin' how the teachers' voices carried a strain, like they were tryin' to teach hope but weren't sure it was there.

The cafeteria was worse than I imagined it. The linoleum was scuffed and dull. Kids clustered in small groups, their trays holdin' thin sandwiches or watery soup, the kind of food that said the budget was stretched past breakin'. I ate with Lila, Eric, and a couple others, but the chatter was quiet, less laughin' than I remembered from middle school. Matt even came by, if not just to punch me on the shoulder. Outside, the football field's grass was patchy and brittle, the goalposts leanin' slightly, but a sign for tryouts was tacked to the bulletin board,

123

written in bold marker, like someone still believed the team could rally. I passed it without stoppin', my mind overwhelmed with the new energy.

When that last bell rang, the schoolyard was a mass of kids walkin' different directions. It was different here, many kinda just gathered in small circles talkin. I looked at em kinda confused. I saw Eric and Lila huddled together and walked over, formin' a triangle instead of a circle. We talked bout our classes and teachers. Then started walkin' home. Main Street was quieter than ever, a ghost of what it'd been. But, the hardware store, the Majestic Theater and Henson's Drug Store were still open, their signs flickerin' like the last stars before dawn. Every other storefront was shuttered or papered over, their windows cloudy, their "Closed" signs permanent. The theater's marquee cycled the same three films for weeks, *Ride the Wild Surf*, *The Sons of Katie Elder*, *That Darn Cat!*, the letters crooked, some missin', like even the movies were tired of tryin'. I'd go with Lila sometimes, sharin' a popcorn we couldn't really afford, but it wasn't the same as when the theater was packed, kids shoutin' at the screen…maybe we were gettin' older, or was it the town that was gettin' older?

Henson's Drug Store had become a rare hub, its soda fountain drawin' teenagers not to buy but to linger. We'd sit on the stools, nursin' a single Coke between three of us, the jukebox playin' faint tunes nobody danced to. The counter had a permeant coatin' of "somethin' sticky", the stools wobbly, but it was a place to be, a holdout against the emptiness creepin' over town. The last island of community in a sea of efficiency. Mr. Henson would watch us, his apron stained, his smile forced, knowin' we weren't spendin' enough to keep him afloat, but just happy we were there.

I was busy with friends and Lila, caught up in the newness of high school, the way she'd nudge my shoulder when we walked or laugh at my bad jokes. My camera was gatherin' dust, its film unloaded, its lens gatherin' dust. I hadn't filmed in weeks, not the rusted lockers, not the empty cafeteria, not the shuttered stores or the theater's tired marquee.

Part of me wanted to, knew I should, but the weight of capturin' the decline felt heavier than I could carry. I was livin' in the moment, holdin' onto the small joys of Lila's smile or a shared soda, lettin' the town's fade blur into the background.

Standin' outside the hardward store one evenin', Lila kicked a pebble across the sidewalk, her eyes on the dark windows of what used to be Gable's Mercantile. "Feels like we're playin' pretend," she said, her voice low. "Like we're still a town, but we're just actin'." I nodded, feelin' it, I quickly thought about my camera, but buried it just as quickly. For the first time, I wasn't sure I wanted to see the town dying through a lens, maybe 'cause I was afraid of what it'd show me, or maybe 'cause I was too busy tryin' to hold onto what little was left.

I was tryin' to find my place in this quieter town, and Matt seemed to think he knew where it was. One muggy afternoon, he cornered me on the porch, his football pads slung over one shoulder, his hair still damp from practice. "Bobby, you gotta join the team," he said, tossin' a football at me, the leather smackin' my chest before I caught it. "Better to hit somethin' than sit around doin' nothin'. Besides, if you are playin ball, you won't have to work at the hardware store every afternoon."

I fumbled the ball, scowlin'. "Football? Me? I ain't built like you, Matt. I'd get flattened."

He grinned, that cocky big-brother grin that made me wanna punch him and hug him at the same time. "Flattened? Nah, you're scrappy. Besides, you're carryin' all that gloom in your head, take it out on some runnin' back. Come on, what else you doin'? Writin' sad poems about this town?"

"Shut up," I said, tossin' the ball back, but I was smilin' a little, 'cause he wasn't wrong. "Fine, I'll try out. But if I break somethin', you're explainin' it to mom."

"Deal!" he hollered, slappin' my shoulder hard enough to make me stumble. "You're gonna love it, little man. Sweat, mud, and glory!"

Tryouts were brutal, the football field's patchy grass slippin' under my sneakers, the air thick with the smell of dirt and teenage sweat. I was smaller than most, but Coach Carl, a bear of a man with a whistle that could wake the dead, didn't care. "Chandler!" he barked, pointin' at me. "You run like you're scared of hittin'! Hit the sled like you mean it!" I did, my shoulders burnin', my breath comin' in gasps, and found somethin' unexpected, a release, raw and simple, in the crunch of contact, the sting of mud in my face. Each tackle, each sprint, shook loose the knot in my chest, the one tied to empty storefronts and dad's tired eyes.

I made the team, barely, and practice became a ritual. The game was blunt, no room for overthinkin', just you, the guy with the ball tryin' his best to avoid being tacked. I'd dive into a play, mud smearin' my jersey, and for those moments, the town's fade didn't exist. Matt was there, a junior now, playin' linebacker too, his helmet glintin' under the field lights. He'd nod at me across the field, never sayin' much, but I could feel him watchin', makin' sure I didn't quit. Playin ball, I learned one good thing, how to turn my brain off. I found the more I thought about somethin', the worse I played. I learned to stop thinkin' bout anythin'.

After practice, we'd pile into Matt's old Ford Falcon, a beat-up blue beast with a radio that only got three stations. The windows were down, the night air rushin' in, cool against our sweaty skin, and Matt would crank the music loud, Chuck Berry or the Beach Boys blastin' through crackly speakers. "Ain't that better than filmin' sad stuff?" he'd yell over the guitar riffs, weavin' the Falcon down backroads, the engine rattlin' like it was singin' along.

"Better'n gettin' hit by you, that's for sure!" I'd shoot back, dodgin' his playful swipe. "You tryin' to kill me out there?"

"Nah, just toughenin' you up!" he'd say, laughin', his eyes bright in the dashboard glow. "You're holdin' your own, kid. Didn't think you had it in ya."

126

"Gee, thanks," I'd mutter, but I was grinnin', the music and the wind makin' everythin' feel lighter. We'd belt out "Surfin' U.S.A." like we were California kids, not stuck in a dyin' town, the Falcon's tires hummin' on the asphalt. For those rides, it was just us, brothers, the road, and a beat that drowned out the world.

On game days, Coach Carl would single me out, his voice boomin' across the field. "Chandler! That's the grit I wanna see! Keep hittin' like that, you'll start someday!" I'd nod, my face hot under the helmet, feelin' a spark of pride I hadn't known in months. Matt never said much, just patted my helmet after a good play, his hand heavy but sure. "Good game," he'd mumble, then walk off, like words were too much. But that pat, that quick glance, said more than he ever would.

For a brief while, football gave me somethin' to hold onto, a place where I wasn't just the kid with the camera, archivin' loss. I was part of the team, part of the sweat and the mud, the roar of a tackle, the rhythm of a play. Ridin' home with Matt, music blarin', the Falcon's engine rattlin' like our own heartbeat, I felt like I belonged again, like this place still had a pulse, even if it was faint.

One night, as we pulled into the driveway, Matt cut the radio, the silence sudden. "You're doin' alright out there, Bobby," he said, his voice low, like he didn't want the dark to hear. "Keep at it."

I nodded, my throat tight. "Thanks, Matt. Means a lot."

He just grunted, climbin' out, but I sat there a moment, the Falcon's engine tickin' as it cooled, feelin' like maybe, just maybe, I'd found a way to hit back at the world, one play at a time.

By October, my weekends had taken a sharp turn from the quiet creek walks and voiceovers I used to lose myself in. Mill Town High School had pulled me into its orbit, and with football and new friends, I was spendin' Saturday nights chasin' a different kind of light. My camera sat untouched on my desk, its film unloaded, while I traded the hum of the projector for the roar of bonfires and truck trails deep in the woods.

It started with a nudge from Tommy, a wiry sophomore on the football team, who caught me after practice one Friday, his helmet danglin' from his hand. "Hey, Bobby, you comin' to the bonfire tomorrow with Matt?" he asked, his grin all mischief. "Out by the river, past the old mill. Gonna be trucks, tunes, and a whole lotta fun. You in?"

I shrugged, wipin' sweat from my brow. "Dunno, man. Ain't that just a bunch of kids actin' dumb in the dark?"

He laughed, sluggin' my shoulder. "Exactly! Actin' dumb's the point! Bring that football grit, leave that depressin' camera at home. We're livin', not filmin'."

"Alright, twist my arm," I said, smilin' despite myself. "But if I end up stuck in a ditch, I'm blamin' you."

"Deal!" he hollered, joggin' off. "Bring Lila, too! She needs to loosen up!"

That Saturday, I piled into Tommy's pickup with a half-dozen other kids, the bed crammed with coolers and blankets, the radio blastin' Elvis Presley's "Hound Dog" so loud it rattled my teeth. We tore down backroads, tires spinnin' deep in the clay, mud flyin' like we were racin' the devil. "This is livin'!" Tommy shouted, leanin' out the window, a beer in one hand, steerin' with the other. "Screw this town, let's tear it up!"

"Heck yeah!" yelled Sarah, a cheerleader wedged next to me, her hair wild in the wind. She passed me a beer, cold and fizzy, but I caught a whiff of somethin' stronger in her cup. "Drink up, Chandler! You're too quiet back there!"

I took a swig, the bitterness cuttin' through the dust in my throat, and laughed, feelin' the truck lurch as we hit a mudhole. "Y'all are gonna kill us!" I shouted, but I was grinnin', the music and the speed pullin' me out of my head. Lila was there, sittin' across from me, her arms crossed, her smile tight. She'd come 'cause I'd begged, but I could tell

128

she wasn't feelin' it, her eyes flickin' to the beer cans rollin' in the truck bed.

The bonfire was a beast, flames lickin' high in a clearin' by the river, sparks dancin' against the pines. Kids piled out of trucks, hollerin', some swiggin' beer, others sneakin' sips of somethin' harder from flasks passed in the dark. The air smelled of smoke, pine, and spilled beer, the radio now blarin' the Rolling Stones' "Satisfaction," the bass thumpin' like a heartbeat. We went muddin' again, trucks churnin' through the trails, tires slingin' clay, lights flashin' through the trees, kids whoopin' as we slid and spun. "Faster, Tommy!" Sarah screamed, bangin' the cab, her laugh wild. "Let's get stuck and stay here forever!"

"Forever's a long time in this dump!" Tommy shot back, yankin' the wheel, the truck fishtailin' through a puddle that soaked us all. I laughed, loud and raw, my shirt clingin' to my skin, the mud cool against the heat of the night.

Lila stayed by the fire, pokin' a stick in the embers, her face half-lit. I dropped next to her, still buzzin' from the ride. "You okay?" I asked, nudgin' her shoulder. "This ain't so bad, right?"

She sighed, tossin' the stick into the flames. "It's loud, Bobby. And... I dunno, it feels like we're pretendin' everythin's fine. Beer and mud don't fix anythin'." Her voice was soft, but it cut through the noise, and I felt a pang, like she'd seen somethin' I was tryin' to ignore.

"Come on, Lila," I said, tryin' to keep it light. "Just one night. Let's have fun, forget your troubles for just a lil' bit."

She gave me a look, half-sad, half-knowin'. "You're forgettin' more than that," she said, then stood, brushin' off her jeans. "I'm headin' home. See you tomorrow." She walked off, hitchin' a ride with a sober kid headin' back, leavin' me by the fire, her words stickin' like burrs.

I stayed, though, longer each time we went to those bonfires. The laughter came easier, louder, the muddin' wilder, the music drownin' out the quiet I'd carried. I'd shout with Tommy, wrestle in the clay with Sarah, let the night pull me under till I was free, untethered, forgettin' the shuttered stores, dad's discount signs. My camera just sittin' on my desk collectin' dust. One night, deep in the woods, some kid I didn't know leaned against a truck, his voice slurrin' through the dark. "Ain't nothin' left in town but sparks and dust," he said, liftin' his beer can like a toast.

I laughed, caught in the haze, my head fuzzy from too many beers and the smoke. "Sparks and dust, man!" I echoed, clinkin' my can against his, but as the words faded, I forgot why they'd felt funny, why they'd stung. The fire crackled, the trucks roared, and I kept goin', chasin' the rush, lettin' the night erase what I'd meant to remember.

Back home, my camera stayed silent, its lens dusty, no film loaded. I wasn't filmin' the bonfires, the mud, the way we laughed like nothin' was wrong. I wasn't filmin' Lila's quiet exit or the kid's words about sparks and dust. I was livin', or at least it felt like it at the time, and for those nights, it felt like enough. But somewhere, in the back of my mind, I knew somethin' was slippin', the town, my lens, maybe even myself, and I wasn't sure how to find it again.

Chapter 18 - War Comes Home
(April 1968)

Spring 1968 swept into Mill Town with a burst of life, the azaleas bloomin' early, their pink and white petals dustin' the ground like confetti. The air was thick with the earthy mix of pollen and cut grass, and spring football hummed in the background, kids shoutin' from the field while radios crackled with baseball play-by-plays. But somethin' felt off, like a song playin' just out of tune. The world was shiftin', and even the ordinary moments, kids laughin' by lockers, teachers scribblin' on chalkboards, but there was somethin' I just couldn't shake.

I wandered the school, my shoes echoin' in the corridors, seein' things I'd passed a hundred times but now noticed different. A freshman droppin' her books, her giggle nervous but bright; Ryan and Donny arm-wrestlin' in the courtyard, their grins fierce but fleeting; Miss Elma's old bookshop poster in the library, its edges curled like it was tired of holdin' on. Each moment felt heavier, like I was filmin' a scene I didn't understand yet. I imagined settin' up my camera on the football field, where practice was startin' soon, the ground still muddy from last night's rain, cleats diggin' in like anchors to a world that was slippin' beneath us. I could see it in my head, slow pans of players runnin' drills, their breaths puffin' in the cool air, the mud splatterin' their jerseys, holdin' onto somethin' solid while everythin' else moved too fast.

At lunch, I sat with my tray, half-listenin' to Tommy jabber about the baseball team's new pitcher, when I caught a different kind of talk at the seniors' table nearby. Their voices were low, their eyes serious, not the usual loud braggin' about cars or girls. I leaned closer, pickin' up scraps of their words, *Vietnam, draft, ain't comin' back*. One of 'em,

Jimmy Tate, a linebacker with a buzz cut, leaned over his tray, his voice rough but quiet. "Noah Jennings came home in a box Tuesday," he said, his words landin' like a punch. "Ain't just news no more."

The table went still, no jokes, no shovin', just stares, their forks frozen mid-bite. Noah had graduated last year, a track star who'd enlisted right after graduation, all grins and promises to write. Now he was a name in the paper, a flag-draped coffin, and the war wasn't just grainy footage on the evenin' news, it was here, in our town, sittin' at our lunch table. I gripped my milk carton, my stomach twistin', tryin' to picture Noah's face but comin' up blank, the silence louder than the cafeteria's usual roar.

In history class later, Miss Hollis stood by the Vietnam map pinned to the wall, its red ink markin' "conflict zones" like wounds on the paper. She paused longer than usual, her pointer hoverin' over names like Hanoi and Saigon, her voice quieter than when she taught about the Civil War. "This is happenin' now," she said, her eyes scannin' the room, lingerin' on us like she was countin' who might not be here next year. "It's not just history, it's happenin' right now." Nobody spoke, not even Tommy, who'd usually crack a joke. The map's red lines burned into me, and I thought of Noah, of Jimmy's low voice, of the football field where we'd run drills like nothin' could touch us.

After school, I walked home, the spring air warm but heavy. I felt like filmin' it all, the muddy field, the quiet lunch table, Miss Hollis's map, but I didn't know how to capture what wasn't there. The fear was creepin' into town like a fog. Dad behind the counter at the hardware store with the radio on, mom's gumbo waitin' at home, but the war's whispers were gettin' louder, and I knew, even at fifteen, that the world shiftin' under me wasn't gonna stop. I kept thinkin' maybe, just maybe, I could capture this feelin'.

The Vietnam War was no longer a distant hum on the evening news but a shadow cast over our streets. As the town grappled with loss, its heart heavy with the death of Noah Jennings, a track star turned soldier who'd come home in a box. The funeral and the days that followed cut deep, makin' the war real in ways we couldn't ignore, from church pews to the football locker room.

The morning of Noah's funeral, church bells rang sharp in the crisp air, their toll slicing through the gray skies. The whole football team gathered at First Baptist, shoulder to shoulder in our Sunday best, ties knotted tight, our faces pale against the pews. The war wasn't just a map in Miss Hollis's classroom anymore, it was here, in the packed church, in the way our breaths caught as we stared at the casket, draped in an American flag, its folds stark against the polished wood. I had dusted off my camera and I stood at the back, my camera hummin' soft, my hands tremblin' as I filmed, tryin' to hold steady while the weight of the moment pressed down.

The preacher's voice wavered as he spoke of sacrifice, his words about Noah's bravery, "a son of Mill Town, who gave all", breakin' on the edges. In the front row, Noah's mother sobbed uncontrollably, her cries raw, a sound that made my chest ache. I zoomed in, catchin' her hands clutchin' a tissue, her shoulders shakin', then panned to the team, boys I knew, their faces solemn, eyes fixed on the floor like they could avoid the truth. The honor guard outside stepped forward, their rifles firin' three shots, each crack joltin' the room, followed by a bugle's taps, its notes slow and mournful, lingerin' like a goodbye nobody wanted to say. I kept filmin', my lens on Matt, standin' tall but rigid, his cap pressed to his chest, his jaw clenched so tight I thought he'd crack, holdin' back a scream. A scream I could feel in my own throat.

I didn't stop the camera, capturin' it all, the flag, the sobs, the faces of boys turned men too soon, knowin' this was our reality now, a time where spring blooms and the realization that church bells could carry both grief, and joy.

The next week, after practice, the football locker room hummed with a tension thicker than the sweat and mud clingin' to our gear. I sat near the wall, my pads off, listenin' as the seniors clustered by the benches, their voices low but heavy.

Jimmy Tate pulled a letter from his bag, its edges worn, and read aloud, his voice rough. "My cousin's in Da Nang," he said, squintin' at the scrawl. Says, "It ain't like the movies, man. It's worse. Mud, bugs, and you're waitin' for somethin' to hit you every second, cant sleep."

Another senior, Stuart, leaned against a locker, his towel draped over his shoulder. "My brother's out there, too," he said, his voice quieter, eyes on the floor. "Says he sleeps with his boots on, 'cause you never know when you gotta run. Jungle swallows everythin', tents, plans, people, lives."

The room stilled, the usual post-practice chatter gone, replaced by a weight we couldn't shake. Tommy, a junior, spoke up, his voice shakin' just a touch. "Y'all think it'll be goin' on next year? The war, I mean. When we're seniors, when…" He trailed off, the question hangin' like smoke.

No one answered, the silence deafening, louder than the showers hissin' in the corner or the clank of lockers. I gripped my helmet, thinkin' of Noah's casket, the flag, Matt's clenched jaw, and felt the war creep closer, its shadow stretchin' over the field, the locker room, our futures. I wanted to film this, too, their voices, their fear, but my camera was still in my bag, and some moments were too raw for a lens. All I could do was listen, holdin' onto their words, knowin' the war was no longer just whispers, it was here, waitin' for us, and we weren't ready.

The seniors were facin' a fork in the road, their post-graduation paths split between hope and dread, and I was startin' to see how fast the world could change. After practice one humid afternoon, the locker room was a mix of sweat, liniment, and tension, the air thick with more than just the pungent musky smell and usual banter. I sat on the bench by my locker, unlacin' my cleats, listenin' as the seniors sprawled nearby, their voices bouncin' between bravado and doubt. The talk turned to what came after graduation, each word carryin' the war's shadow. Stuart Tate, his towel slung over his shoulder, grinned wide. "My dad's got me set at the saw mill," he said, punchin' Carl's arm. "Good money, steady work. I'll be runnin' that place by thirty, y'all watch!"

Carl laughed, shakin' his head as he stuffed his gear in a bag. "Saw mill? Man, I'm headin' to Auburn, partial scholarship for track. Gonna study business, maybe open a shop someday. Beats cutin' lumber all day, Stuart."

The others nodded, some clappin' Carl's back, but then Eddie, a quiet lineman with a buzz cut, spoke up, his voice low, cuttin' through the noise. "I enlisted, ship out day after graduation'," he said, his eyes on his locker, his hands still. "Figure might as well choose how you go, 'stead of waitin' for the letter to come in the mail and not have a choice. At least I'll have some say."

The room went quiet, the laughter dyin' fast, like air sucked outta the space. Jimmy's grin faded, Carl's bag hit the floor with a thud, and I felt my stomach twist, thinkin' of Noah's flag-draped casket, the bugle's taps. Nobody said nothin', just stared, at Eddie, at the floor, at nothin'. Matt, sittin' across from me, listened but stayed silent, his jaw tight, his hands grippin' his helmet like it could hold him in time, knowin' he would have to make the same choice next year.

Later, as we walked home, the sun sinkin' behind the pines, Matt finally spoke, his voice low, unsteady. "I'm thinkin' about college, Bobby," he said, kickin' a pebble down the road. "Maybe engineerin', somewhere like Florida State. But... nothin' feels real anymore. Not after Noah, not with the war breathin' down our necks. Like, what's the point of plannin' when it could all get yanked away?"

I nodded, wishin' I could film the weight in his voice, the way his shoulders slumped. When we were kids, all we wanted to do was to work the hardware store with dad. "Yeah," I said, my throat tight.

"Feels like we're all waitin' for somethin' to happen, good or bad. But college sounds right, Matt. You'd kill it."

He gave a half-smile, but it didn't reach his eyes. "Maybe. Just gotta get there first."

A few days later, in the locker room, the seniors were back at it, jokin' about girls and cars, tryin' to keep the mood light. I leaned against the wall, smilin' at their dumb bets over who'd get a date first, when I noticed Eddie again, sittin' alone on a bench, starin' at his cleats like they held answers. His face was blank, distant, like he was already halfway across the world, marchin' through jungles instead of muddy football fields. The sight hit me hard, a reminder of how fast things were splittin', some to mills, some to schools, some to war.

That night, I opened my notebook, the pencil scratchin' slow as I wrote: "Graduation used to mean beginnings. Now it just feels like a countdown." The words felt true, sharp, like the crack of rifles at Noah's funeral, like Eddie's quiet choice, like Matt's doubt. There seemed to be a fork in the road where some boys stood, some laughin', some starin', all wonderin' what was waitin' on the other side.

Chapter 19 - A Shattering Shift
(Summer of 1968)

It was a warm July evenin' in 1968, the kind where the air hangs thick with the scent of honeysuckle and the hum of crickets feels like a lullaby. I was sittin' at the kitchen table with mom, dad, and Matt, the clink of forks against plates mixin' with soft laughter. Mom had just teased me about a tackle I had made last year on a runnin' back that didn't have the ball. Her eyes crinklin' the way they did when she was tryin' not to laugh too hard. "Bobby, you gonna tackle the kid with the ball or just the rest of the team next game?" she'd said, and I was grinnin', ready to fire back, when it happened.

She reached for a towel hangin' by the sink, still chucklin' faint, and then her knees buckled. It was like watchin' a string cut, her body folded, the plate in her hand clatterin' to the floor, shards skitterin' across the linoleum. She slumped, a sound too soft for the weight it carried, and for a moment, none of us moved. The kitchen went still for what seemed like an eternity, like time itself stopped, then the sound of crickets outside louder than my heartbeat hammerin' in my ears.

"Ruth!" dad's voice snapped the silence, rough and sharp. He was out of his chair before I could blink, kneelin' beside her, his hands gentle but sure, like he'd done this before, though I couldn't imagine when. His face was set, eyes unreadable, a mask of calm over somethin' I didn't want to name. "Bobby, grab her shoes, and the keys" he said, his voice low, no room for questions. He lifted her like she weighed nothin', her head restin' against his chest, and headed for the door.

I scrambled, grabbin' her worn loafers from the mat, my hands shakin' so bad I nearly dropped 'em. Matt was frozen at the table, his fork still in his hand, starin' at the broken plate like it held answers. "Move,

Matt!" I barked, and he blinked, followin' me out to dad's truck, the gravel crunchin' under our feet. Dad settled mom in the passenger seat, her breath shallow but there, and climbed in without a word. No one called an ambulance, that wasn't how things were done. The truck roared to life, Matt and I jumped in the back, tires spittin' gravel in the fadin' light, and we were gone.

The hospital room was cold, its flickerin' fluorescent lights buzzin' like a trapped fly. We'd sat in plastic chairs, mom's hand in dad's, while the doctor, a young guy with a clipboard and no warmth, laid it out plain. "It's spread but we'll try," he'd said, his voice clinical, like he was readin' a weather report. "We can operate, then most likely chemotherapy." The words felt like a theft, stealin' Thanksgivings, Christmases, all the days we'd taken for granted.

Cancer, the words landed like dust on a coffin, light, but final, settlin' into every corner of the room. I felt my pulse in my ears, a dull roar that drowned out the crickets. Matt kept starin' at the floor, his hands balled into fists, like he could punch the truth away. Dad nodded once, slow, his jaw tight, like he was translatin' the doctor's clipboard into somethin' solid, somethin' he could carry. But there was no version of this that held together, not this time.

Mom's response was what broke me. She'd listened, her face calm, her hands folded like she was at church. Then she'd looked at the doctor and asked, "What about Thanksgiving? Can I still make my gumbo?" Not a question about chemo, not survival, just gumbo, her recipe with oysters, chicken and okra, the one we'd eaten every year since I was old enough to hold a spoon, and probably even before that. The doctor hesitated, mumblin' somethin' about diet and strength, but Mom just smiled, a small, stubborn curve of her lips, like courage was just another dish she'd memorized years ago.

"Gumbo?" I said now, my voice crackin', the room spinnin' around me. "Mom, you're talkin' about gumbo?"

She reached for my hand, her fingers cool but firm. "Bobby, honey, I'm gonna make whatever I got, count. Gumbo's part of that. You'll see." Her eyes were bright, not with tears but with somethin' fiercer, like she was darin' the cancer to take her joy.

"Ruth, you don't gotta," Dad started, his voice rough, but she cut him off with a look, one of those looks that could stop a train.

"Thomas, I'm makin' gumbo," she said, final as a slammed door. "And you're gonna eat it, and so are these boys. We ain't quittin' on livin' just 'cause the doc's got a clipboard."

Matt let out a sound, half-laugh, half-sob, still starin' at the floor. "Mom, you're somethin' else," he muttered, his voice thick, and I saw his shoulders shake, just once, before he locked it down.

I couldn't speak, my throat too tight, my mind stuck on "cancer". I thought of my camera, sittin' unused, and wished I'd filmed more of us together, her laugh, her hands kneadin' dough, the way she'd hum hymns while hangin' laundry. Now, it felt like time was slippin' through my fingers, and I hadn't caught enough of her to keep.

Dad stood, his chair scrapin' the floor, and put a hand on mom's shoulder, then mine, then Matt's, like he was anchorin' us all. "We're gonna get through this," he said, his voice steady but raw, like he was willin' it to be true. "Together. Ain't no other way."

Mom nodded, leanin' into him, her smile still there, small but unshaken. "Together," she echoed, and for a moment, the room felt solid again, like we could hold onto each other even if the world was crumblin'.

But as I lay in bed that night, the dark pressin' in, I kept hearin' the clatter of that plate, seein' mom's body slump, the doctor's calm, cold words. My pulse pounded, a rhythm of fear and loss, and I knew nothin' would ever be the same. The town had been fadin' for years, but this, this was a shatterin' shift, one that'd break us or bind us, and I wasn't sure which. All I knew was mom's gumbo was comin', and I'd eat every bite I could, holdin' onto her courage like it was the last light in the house.

The farmhouse we'd called home all my life had turned into a stranger. The air in the house had changed, like someone had twisted the volume knob down till all that was left was a hum. No more squabblin' over who left muddy boots by the door, no more laughter spillin' from the kitchen where mom used to sing while bakin'. Just footsteps on creaky boards, whispered prayers slippin' under bedroom doors, and the occasional clink of silverware at meals nobody really felt like eatin'.

Dad became mom's caretaker, his days reshaped around her needs with a quiet that scared me. He started wakin' before dawn, tendin' to her garden, pullin' weeds, waterin' her tomatoes, like he was proving if he could keep' 'em alive, he could do the same for her. He fed the hens, their clucks the only chatter in the yard, and took to ironin' his own shirts, the hiss of the iron fillin' the mornin' silence. When he folded mom's blankets, he did it slow, reverent, like each crease was a prayer. His hands, seemed gentler now, movin' careful, like he was afraid of breakin' somethin' sacred. "You sleep alright, Ruth?" he'd ask, his voice soft as he tucked the quilt around her, and she'd nod, her smile a flicker in the dim room.

Matt drifted inward, like he was tryin' to hide from the truth. He stopped goin' to the Saturday bonfires, leavin' his buddies' calls unanswered, their voices cracklin' on the phone we all ignored. Instead, he stayed late at Allied General, stackin' shelves till midnight, his Allied vest wrinkled and his eyes hollow. Some nights, I'd see him sittin' in his Ford Falcon out front, engine off, starin' at the porch light like it was a puzzle he couldn't solve. "You comin' in?" I asked once, leanin' out the door, my voice sharper than I meant.

He didn't look at me, just gripped the steerin' wheel. "In a minute," he muttered, his voice flat, like he was talkin' to the dark. I shut the door, leavin' him to his ghosts, knowin' he was as scared as I was but too stubborn to say it.

Me, I escaped into noise, anythin' to drown out the silence chokin' the house. I started goin' to more parties, mud trails, tearin' through the woods, bonfires roarin' by the river, the chaos of kids shoutin' and music blarin'. The cheerin', the firelight, the sting of cheap beer, it didn't heal nothin', but it muffled the quiet, made me forget the way mom's hands shook now, the way dad's eyes didn't meet mine. "Chug it, Bobby!" Tommy'd yell, tossin' me a can, his grin wild in the fire's glow. "Let's keep this alive!"

"Hell yeah!" I'd holler back, tippin' the can, the bitter fizz burnin' my throat like medicine. I'd laugh too loud, dance too wild, let the night swallow me whole. But Lila noticed, her eyes narrowin' when she and Eric saw me at the drug store, my shirt half-untucked, my words slurrin'. "You're runnin', Bobby," she said one day in the hallway, her voice cuttin' through the haze. "This ain't you."

"Mind your own, Lila," I snapped, harsher than I meant. Eric looked at me and just shook his head, then they walked off, Lila's braid swingin', leavin' a gap between us that grew wider each week. We stopped talkin' much after that, and I told myself it didn't matter, but it did, like losin' another piece of home.

Mom, though, she kept smilin', a light that refused to go out, even as it flickered. She still set the table, her hands tremblin' as she placed each plate, still hummed hymns like "Amazing Grace," her voice thin but steady. She folded napkins with care, though her appetite was gone, her plate often untouched. Before dinner, she'd insist on grace, her words soft but firm: "Lord, thank you for this food, this family, this day." Even when the pastor came, his Bible tucked under his arm, she'd joke with him, her laugh faint but real. "Don't you go prayin' me out of my gumbo recipe, now," she'd say, and he'd chuckle, but his eyes were wet.

She was the only light left in the room, and we all clung to it, knowin' it couldn't last. "You boys keep eatin'," she'd say at supper, pushin' the cornbread toward us, her smile darin' us to argue. "I ain't raisin' skinny men." Matt'd force a grin, shovelin' a bite, and I'd try to match her smile, but it felt like lyin'.

My camera hung on the wall, its lens capped, untouched in what felt like years. I couldn't bring myself to film this, not mom's tremblin' hands, not dad's gentle rituals, not the way Matt walked slower now, like he was carryin' a weight nobody could see. It wasn't that I didn't care, it was that I cared too much, too raw, to trap this pain in a reel, the thought that I may have to relive this moment again, was too much. The thought of pointin' the lens at mom, capturin' her fade, felt like stealin' what little she had left. So it stayed there, silent, while I ran to bonfires and beer, tryin' to fill a hole that had developed inside.

One night, after a party, I stumbled home, the beer still buzzin' in my head, and found mom awake, sittin' in the livin' room, a quilt over her lap. "Bobby," she said, her voice soft but clear, "you smell like a brewery. Sit down."

I froze, my cheeks burnin', then sank into the couch, avoidin' her eyes. "Sorry, mom," I mumbled, my words slurrin' just enough to make me wince.

She reached for my hand, her fingers cool but strong. "You're hurtin', I know," she said, her eyes searchin' mine. "But don't lose yourself in that noise. You got a gift, Bobby, seein' the world, holdin' onto it. Don't let it go, not for me, not for this."

I swallowed, my throat tight, her words cuttin' through the haze. "I can'd film dis, mom," I said, my voice breakin'. "Not you. Not... diss."

She squeezed my hand, her smile faint but fierce. "You don't have to film me, honey. Film what's still here, the good, the hard, the true. That's what you do." She leaned back, her breath shallow, and I sat there, the quiet creepin' back, but softer now, like it was holdin' us instead of chokin' us.

I didn't touch the camera that night, or the next, but her words stuck, a seed planted deep, but not too deep. The house stayed silent, Dad's gentle hands, Matt's idlin' car, my escape into noise, all of it a dance around mom's light, flickerin' but stubborn. I didn't know how to hold onto it, or how to face what was comin', but for the first time in weeks, I felt like maybe I could try, if only to make her proud before I may not have a chance to.

It was a humid September night, the kind where the air feels like ya could drink it, and the stars hid behind a layer of Florida haze. Lila had been keepin' her distance since I'd started snappin' at folks, but that night, she showed up at the farmhouse, her braid loose, her eyes searchin' mine like she was tryin' to find the Bobby she used to know.

We stood on the porch, the crickets hummin' loud, and she leaned against the rail, her voice soft but steady. "Bobby, how you holdin' up?" she asked, like it was a simple question, like I could answer without crackin' open. I bristled, the weight of everythin', mom's tremblin' hands, dad's quiet new rituals, Matt's idlin' car pressin' down till I couldn't breathe.

"What do you want me to say, Lila?" I snapped, my voice sharper than a switch. "I'm fine, alright? Stop actin' like you get it!" I immediately regretted it, but it was too late.

Her eyes flashed, hurt and anger mixin' like storm clouds. "You think you're the only one losin' somethin'?" she shot back, her voice risin'. "My mom's workin' doubles at Allied just to keep our lights on and food on the table, my brother's gone to Charlotte, and you're out here drownin' in beer and self-pity! You ain't the only one hurtin', Bobby Chandler!"

I froze, her words cuttin' deep, but my pride was louder.

"Then leave me be!" I shouted, steppin' back, my hands balled into fists.

She stared at me, her jaw tight, then turned and walked away, her sneakers scuffin' the gravel, the sound fadin' into the dark. I didn't follow. I couldn't, my pride wouldn't let me. Instead, I grabbed my coat from the hook, the screen door slammin' behind me, and headed out, my heart poundin' like a drum I couldn't silence.

I didn't drive to the bonfire just down the road, I ended up at the riverwalk, the old path along the Blackwater where me and Lila used to skip stones as kids. It was cracked now, overgrown with weeds in places, the lamplight flickerin' like it was too tired to stay lit. Shadows danced on empty benches and broken fences, the wood splintered, the paint peeled away. The river glowed faint under an orange sky, movin' slow, like time in a house full of pain. I walked alone, my boots crunchin' on gravel, the quiet pressin' in, louder than the bonfires I'd been chasin'.

I found the bench we'd claimed as ours back when we were ten, its iron frame rusted but still standin'. We'd sit there, tellin' stories about pirates and spaceships, laughin' till our sides hurt, the world nothin' but possibility. I sank onto it now, restin' my elbows on my knees, starin' into the dark. The river murmured, a soft whisper against the bank, and I imagined my camera rollin', but this time, I was in the frame. Just a boy on a bench, surrounded by memories louder than the world around him. In my head, I sketched the shot: a boy, small in the frame, hunched under a sky burnin' orange. The river below, reflectin' light like a promise it couldn't keep. The town behind him, its shuttered stores and faded signs a ghost in the distance. Silence all around, except the screamin' in his head, a roar of grief, anger, and guilt, for mom, for Lila, for the town he'd stopped filmin', but mostly mad at himself, like he didn't recognize himself anymore. The image was stark, raw, the kind of shot that'd make you feel the weight of a life turnin' on its axis.

I sat there, the bench cold against my back, Lila's words echoin', *You ain't the only one hurtin'*. She was right, and I'd pushed her away for it, too scared to face the truth. Mom's smile, dad's gentle hands, Matt's silence, they were all part of this, and I'd been runnin', leavin' myself to gather dust 'cause I couldn't bear to see it clear. But sittin' by the river, the quiet wasn't suffocatin', it was callin'. I felt somethin' shift, like a door unlockin'.

I whispered to myself, my voice barely a breath, "Time to stop runnin'." The words hung in the air, small but heavy, like a vow I wasn't sure I could keep. I didn't have my camera, didn't need it yet, just the thought was enough, the seed was growing. The river kept movin', the lamplight flickered, and I sat a little longer, the screamin' in my head softenin', not gone but bearable, like maybe I could face it again, even if it was breakin'.

Chapter 20 - Newcomers
(Fall 1968)

Mill Town seemed to be stretchin' thin, like a piece of cloth pulled till the threads started to snap. I was carryin' the weight of mom's cancer diagnosis and a camera I'd only just started to pick up again after what seemed like years of leavin' it to gather dust. The town I'd grown up in, the one I'd filmed through its slow decline, was changin' faster now, not dyin' but morphin' into somethin' I barely recognized. Newcomers were movin' in, old families were movin' out, and the land itself seemed to be shiftin' under our feet. It started with the rumble of construction crews, their yellow bulldozers and dump trucks roarin' in from the highway. I'd see 'em on my way to school, their engines rattlin' the quiet mornin', but they weren't here to fix Main Street's shuttered stores or patch up the cracked sidewalks. They were pavin' new roads, wide and black, cuttin' through what used to be pastureland where cows grazed and kids like me and Matt once chased fireflies. I'd stop sometimes, my camera recording, watchin' 'em tear up the earth, the red clay churnin' like an open wound. "What's this for?" I asked a worker one day, his hard hat tilted back, sweat beadin' on his brow.

"Progress," he said, spittin' tobacco into the dirt. "Folks want houses, not cows. You'll see."

Progress. The word tasted bitter, like the dust cloudin' the air. Those pastures were bein' bulldozed into cul-de-sacs and subdivisions with names like *Oak Meadows* and *Creekside Pines*, signs staked into the ground with fancy script, promisin' somethin' green and alive. But the meadows had just been bulldozed, no more creeks tricklin' through, just ditches and flat, scraped land, the soil packed hard under new concrete. More lies in the name of progress. I filmed it one afternoon, the camera's hum steady as I panned across a field where a backhoe was clawin' up roots, the horizon jagged with half-built houses. The footage was stark, no sound but the machine's growl and a crow's lonely caw.

The ancient oaks that'd shaded those fields were gone, too, the ones where barefoot boys like me used to climb, where cattle dozed in the heat. They'd been cut down, their trunks hauled off, leavin' behind stumps like huge gravestones in the flattened silence. I'd walk by 'em on my way home, my sneakers scuffin' the new asphalt, and feel a pang, like losin' a friend. One evenin', I filmed a stump, its rings wide and weathered, countin' decades of storms and summers. I thought to myself how much that tree must have seen, wonderin' if it like it when kids used to play on its branches, or rather be left alone. Sometimes I wished they could talk, but right now, I was glad it couldn't. "Used to be nice," I muttered to myself, the camera rollin', knowin' no one would hear it but me.

Nobody walked anymore, not like they used to. The town had sprawled too far, the new subdivisions stretchin' out where farms once stood on the outskirts of town, too much distance for a stroll to the store or a neighbor's porch. Kids rode buses from farther out, their faces pressed to the windows, starin' at houses that all looked the same, brick boxes with tiny lawns, nothin' like the weathered farmhouses they'd replaced. Teenagers drove to school, to Henson's Drug Store, to each other, their pickups and hand-me-down sedans cloggin' the new roads. We even got two redlights.

I'd see some kids from school at the soda fountain, laughin' over Cokes, but it wasn't the same as when downtown buzzed with folks on foot, wavin' to each other like family.

"Town's gettin' big, huh?" Matt said one mornin', leanin' against his Ford Falcon as I climbed in for a ride to school. His Allied vest was wrinkled and starting to show it's age, his eyes tired from late shifts, but he was tryin' to sound light.

"Big, crowded with cars, but empty," I said, slumpin' in the seat, my camera in my lap. "All these houses, but where's the town? Ain't no center no more."

He grunted, turnin' the key, the engine coughin' to life. "Folks gotta live somewhere, Bobby. Ain't our fields no more."

I didn't answer, just stared out the window as we passed the Abernathy's pasture we used to run through on the way to town, now *Creekside Pines*, its sign already fadin' in the sun, no creek in sight. I thought of dad, still tendin' mom's garden, his hands gentle with her tomatoes, and mom, smilin' through her pain, hummin' hymns in a house gone quiet. The hardware store closed half the time now, hardly anyone went by there anyway. The new roads, the cul-de-sacs, the stumps, they were takin' the town's shape and twistin' it, leavin' us to navigate a place that didn't feel like ours. The town felt like it was losin' the threads that'd held it together, the small, familiar things that made it feel like home. The changes weren't loud, no big announcements, no parades, just a quiet unravelin', like a quilt comin' apart stitch by stitch.

The footpaths we'd worn into the grass as kids, windin' from house to house, were gone, overgrown, fenced, or paved over by the new roads cuttin' through old pastures. Front-porch conversations, where folks used to swap stories over sweet tea, had faded, replaced by the hum of pickup trucks and station wagons rollin' to the new subdivisions. Bicycles, once racin' down Main Street with kids hollerin', were rare now, their bells silenced. Links in the sidewalk gossip, the kind that carried news faster than a newspaper, had gone missin', leavin' just the growl of engines and the glare of headlights. I'd walk past houses at dusk, seein' folks pull into their driveways, doors closin' quick, no wave, no nod. "Ain't nobody got time to talk no more," dad said one evenin', his voice low, and I felt it, the loss of a town that used to breathe together.

Mrs. Clara's Family Restaurant, the last family-owned restaurant in town, closed on a Thursday in October, quiet as a sigh. I was passin' by when I saw the note taped to the door, handwritten in Mrs. Clara's neat script: *Thank you for the memories. We were proud to feed this town.* The words hit like a punch, and I stood there, my breath catchin', rememberin' the eating there with mom and dad and Matt before a football game, the clink of forks, the way Mrs. Clara'd call me "sugar" when she slid a plate of fried steaks my way. It had been a heartbeat, a place where shopkeepers planned, kids laughed, and even mom, before she got sick, would linger over pie with her friends. Now, its windows were dark, the neon sign unplugged, the tables empty.

I lifted my camera, the hum steady as I filmed the note, pannin' slow across the door, the faded paint, the "Closed" sign swayin' in the breeze. My hands shook, not from cold but from the weight of capturin' another piece of the puzzle, gone. I zoomed in on the note's last line, *We were proud*, and felt my throat tighten, knowin' this was more than a diner closin'. It was the death of the familiar, the end of a place where we'd been us.

Six months later, a corporate sandwich chain moved in, same address but a new smell, sterile, like bleach and plastic, nothin' like the hometown cookin' of Mrs. Clara's. The old sign was scraped off the window, the family name peeled away like skin, and a new one went up, bright and glossy, promisin' "Fresh Subs Daily!" I was there, camera in hand, filmin' the worker scrapin' away the last of Mrs. Clara's, the letters flakin' into dust. The footage was raw, the sound of the scraper sharp against the quiet street, but when they started hangin' the new sign, I turned the camera off. I couldn't watch it, couldn't record the moment we traded our social bedrock for a chain that didn't know our names.

"Progress, huh?" Matt said when I told him, leanin' against his car, his Allied vest still on from a late shift. His voice was bitter, like he was spittin' the word out.

"Ain't progress," I said, clutchin' the camera, my voice low. "It's erasure."

He nodded, kickin' a pebble across the lot, and we didn't say more, but I knew he felt it too, the way the footpaths, the porches, the diner were slippin' away, replaced by things that didn't seem to belong. I walked home, the camera heavy, the footage of Mrs Clara's note burnin' in my mind. I didn't know if I'd ever show it, but I knew I'd keep it, a piece of the familiar I could hold onto, even as it forgot itself.

High School was a maze of rusted lockers and half-empty hallways, but I'd found a corner of it that felt like mine. I was still reelin' from mom's cancer and the way the town was slippin' into somethin' unfamiliar, with new roads and impersonal chain stores replacin' the dirt foot paths and family diners I'd known. My camera, quiet for too long, was back in my hands, and when I saw a flyer for a new Film Club tacked to the bulletin board in the hallway, somethin' sparked. I signed up, hopin' to find a place where I could make the world make sense again, even if just through a lens. Maybe I'd be able to develop my film there too.

The Film Club met in a cramped room at the back of the school, its walls lined with shelves of old reels and a clunky projector that hummed like a tired engine. The group was small, a handful of misfits and quiet kids, like Sarah with her thick glasses, always doodlin' in her notebook, and Jake, who mumbled but knew every knob on the soundboard. We learned to splice reels, the scissors snippin' clean through film, and check microphones, tappin' 'em till the static cleared. It wasn't glamorous, but it was ours, and I felt a pull toward it, like comin' home after a long walk.

The dark editin' room became my refuge, a closet-sized space with a single bulb and a splicin' table that smelled of dust and celluloid. I'd sit there for hours, the door shut, the world outside gone. Things could be rewound, paused, trimmed, moments shaped into somethin' I could control in a world I couldn't, like mom's tremblin' hands or the bulldozers tearin' up pastures. Best of all, the school did cover the cost of developin' film, a relief for a kid scrapin' by on odd jobs and dad's dwindlin' hardware sales. I'd splice together practice shots, trees swayin' in the wind, kids laughin' in the cafeteria, my fingers steady, the rhythm of it soothin' the ache in my chest.

Mr. Tolley, our teacher, was a wiry man with a grayin' beard and a voice that carried quiet conviction. He'd been a photographer in Raleigh before teachin', and he saw somethin' in my work, the way I framed shots to catch the emotion of a moment. One afternoon, as I was threadin' a reel through the projector, he leaned against the table, his arms crossed. "Bobby, you got a knack for this," he said, his eyes sharp behind his glasses. "There's a statewide film competition comin' up, short films, five minutes max. Stick with it. Show 'em what you see."

I paused, the reel clickin' in my hands, my stomach twistin'. "I dunno, Mr. Tolley," I said, keepin' my voice low. "Not sure I got anythin' worth showin'."

He raised an eyebrow, not buyin' it. "You're filmin' all the time, kid. That footage you showed me last week, the empty lot where the diner used to be? That's got weight. Make somethin' real. Ain't nobody else seein' this town like you do."

I nodded, but my mind was racin'. I'd been thinkin' about a film on the town, somethin' to capture its fade, the shuttered stores, the new cul-de-sacs, the way folks didn't talk no more. I had reels of it: Mrs. Clara's Diner's closin' note, the stumps of old oaks, mom's garden still growin' despite her sickness. But hesitancy gnawed at me. Would people want to see what I saw? The loss, the quiet, the truth of a town stretchin' thin? Or would they turn away, like I'd turned away from Lila when she'd tried to pull me back?

That night, I sat in the editin' room, the projector whirrin', watchin' a test reel flicker on the wall, Main Street's empty sidewalks, a kid ridin' a bike past a boarded window. The images were stark, honest, but they felt heavy, like stones I wasn't sure I could carry. "Maybe it's too much," I muttered, splicin' a frame, the snip of the scissors loud in the dark. But Mr. Tolley's words stuck, and so did mom's, from that night she'd told me to keep filmin' the true. I didn't know if I was ready to make the film, to show something so personal to a world that might not care, but sittin' in that dark room, the hum of the projector like a heartbeat, I felt closer to tryin' than I had in months.

Chapter 21 - Family and Friends
(November 1968)

Thanksgiving 1968 rolled into town like a quiet guest, settin' down at the Chandler table with a weight we all felt but didn't name. I was filmin again, capturin' the town's changes, but today was more personal. It was about capturing our family. The kitchen smelled of mom's chicken oyster gumbo, a long family tradition, a rich, briny warmth that'd always meant home, but the mood was different this year, softer, like a song played too slow. Mom's cancer hung over us, her smile still bright but her hands shakin' as she stirred the pot. Aunt Debbie, mom's sister from Mobile, had come for a visit, her laugh loud and her hugs tighter than usual, fillin' the house with a spark we hadn't had in months.

"Ruth, you look like a picture!" Aunt Debbie hollered, bustin' through the door with a pecan pie in one hand and a suitcase in the other, her hair messy from the drive. "Now, don't you go fussin' over that gumbo, I brought enough food to feed an army!"

Mom turned from the stove, her apron tied loose, her face lightin' up like it used to. "Debbie, you hush and get over here," she said, her voice thin but warm, pullin' her sister into a hug. "Ain't no army eatin' my gumbo but this family, and you know it."

I grinned, settin' the table, the clink of plates mixin' with their chatter. Mom ate less now, her appetite fadin' with her strength after each round of chemo, but she'd insisted on cookin', standin' at the stove for hours, her hands steadyin' on the spoon like it was a lifeline. "Nobody's touchin' my roux," she'd told dad that mornin', shooing him out of the kitchen. "Cancer ain't takin' my gumbo, Thomas."

152

We sat down, the table crowded with gumbo, cornbread, green beans, and Debbie's pie, the steam risin' like a prayer. Matt was there, quieter than usual, his Allied vest swapped for a clean shirt, his eyes flickin' to mom every few seconds. Dad carved the turkey, his knife steady, his face set but softer when he looked at mom. Aunt Debbie kept the talk goin', her voice a bright thread in the room's heavy weave.

"Bobby, tell me about school!" Debbie said, ladlin' gumbo onto the rice in my bowl, her eyes bright despite the shadows under 'em. "You still runnin' with that football team? And what's this I hear about a film club?"

I took a spoonful, the oysters warm and salty, and nodded. "Yes mam, football's keepin' me busy. Coach says I got grit, whatever that means. Film club's better, though, bunch of us messin' with reels, splicin' 'em, makin' short movies. Mr. Tolley's got us usin' real microphones, and I don't gotta pay for film no more."

"Sounds like you're a regular Hollywood man!" Aunt Debbie said, wavin' her fork. "You gonna put us all in a movie, Bobby? Make me a star?"

I laughed, the sound feelin' good, like a crack in the quiet. "Maybe, Aunt Debbie, but you'd steal the show, and I ain't ready for that kinda trouble."

Mom chuckled, a soft sound that warmed the room, but she pushed her bowl away, barely touched. Dad watched her, his fork still, and I saw Matt's jaw tighten, like he was holdin' back a storm.

Dad cleared his throat, his voice low but steady. "You filmin' the new neighborhoods, Bobby? All them cul-de-sacs poppin' up?"

I paused, the gumbo sittin' heavy in my mouth. "Naw, they all look the same, brick houses, no trees, no nothin'. If you've seen one, ya seen em all, ain't worth wastin the film."

Mom looked at me, her smile gentle, her eyes seein' deeper than I wanted. "So did the old houses, includin' this one, if you weren't from here," she said, her voice quiet but firm, like she was remindin' me of somethin' I'd forgotten. "Every place has a past, present, and future."

Her words hung there, and the table went still, the clink of spoons fadin'. Nobody mentioned downtown or the lack of income from the store, but we didn't have to. Its absence was in the air, a ghost sittin' at the table with us, like mom's gumbo, holdin' us to a town that was slippin' away.

Aunt Debbie broke the silence, her voice softer now. "Y'all remember Thanksgivin' when we were kids, Ruth? Mom'd make us shell peas and pecans till our fingers hurt, and we'd sneak bites of cornbread when she wasn't lookin'."

Mom laughed, a real laugh, her hand restin' on dad's. "And you'd eat half the pan, Debbie, then blame me when Mom caught us!"

We chuckled, the memory a small light, but it didn't chase the shadows far. Dad set his napkin down, his eyes on me. "Bobby, I need a favor," he said, his voice steady but heavy. "I'm takin' your mom to the doctor tomorrow, checkup, nothin' big. Can you mind the store while we're gone?"

I nodded, my throat tight. "Yeah, dad. I got it."

"Good boy," he said, his hand squeezin' mom's, and she smiled at me, her eyes sayin' more than words could.

We finished the meal, the gumbo coolin' in our bowls, Aunt Debbie's stories keepin' us tethered to the past. I'd mind the store, keep filmin', hold onto the stories, 'cause even if the town was changin', Mom was right, every place had a heart, and I wasn't ready to let ours go, not while we still had her light at the table.

The day after Thanksgiving dawned cold and gray, the air sharp with the promise of winter. I was up early, pullin' on my jacket to head to the store, takin' over for dad while he drove mom to her doctor's appointment. I had my camera with me this time. I followed dad's routine, one I'd seen a million times, unlock the front door, flip the "Open" sign, sweep the floor, check the register. The motions were automatic, like a prayer, but the store felt different now, quieter, its shelves half-stocked, the hum of Main Street long gone.

It was still early, the sun barely peekin' over the horizon, castin' long shadows across the counter. I walked behind it, my boots echoin' on the worn wood, and stopped at the picture of Grandad, hung crooked above the register. His stern face stared out from the black-and-white frame, the man who'd built this place when the town was barely even a town. I straightened it, my fingers lingerin' on the glass, feelin' the weight of his legacy and dad's struggle to keep it alive. The store was empty, no jingle of the bell, no clatter of tools, just the tick of the clock and the faint creak of the building settlin'.

The bell chimed, startlin' me, and I turned to see Lila step in, her braid tucked under a knit cap, her cheeks pink from the cold. She hesitated in the doorway, her eyes searchin' mine, and I felt a pang, rememberin' our fight on the porch that night, the way I'd snapped at her for carin'. "Hey," she said, her voice soft, like she wasn't sure she was welcome.

"Hey," I said, steppin' out from behind the counter, my hands fidgety. "Lila, I… I'm sorry. For what I said that night, for bein' selfish, actin' like I'm the only one hurtin'. I was wrong, and I hate how I pushed you away."

She looked at me, her eyes softenin', a small smile tuggin' at her lips. "You were a jerk, Bobby Chandler," she said, but there was no bite in it. "But I get it. This," she gestured vaguely, meanin' mom, the town, everythin', "it's a lot. Apology accepted."

I exhaled, relief washin' over me like a warm wave. "Thanks, Lila. For real." I leaned against the counter, my voice earnest. "How you holdin' up? Your mom, your brother, how's it goin'?"

Her smile faded, but she didn't look away. "It's hard," she admitted, pullin' off her cap, her fingers twistin' it. "Mom's workin' herself to death at Allied, and Tommy's in Charlotte, chasin' a job that might not pan out. Feels like we're all just… hangin' on. But I'm okay, Bobby. Keepin' busy with school, drawin' when I can. You?"

I nodded, grateful for her honesty, wantin' to rebuild what we'd had. "Same, I guess. Mom's fightin', dad's holdin' it together, but it's heavy. Been filmin' again, though, and… there's this thing at school. Film Club's got a statewide competition, short films. Mr. Tolley's pushin' me to submit somethin'."

Her eyes lit up, bright as the sun breakin' through clouds. "Bobby, that's huge!" she said, steppin' closer, her voice bubblin' with excitement. "You're gonna do it, right? Show 'em the town, all of it, the good, the bad, the true? Oh, you gotta, Bobby! Show em what you see!"

I laughed, her enthusiasm catchin' like a spark. "I'm thinkin' about it," I said, rubbin' the back of my neck. "Got tons of reels of the town, McGregor's closin', the new roads, the riverwalk. Just… not sure folks'll wanna see what I see."

"They will," she said, fierce, leanin' on the counter. "Your films, they're like… like holdin' a mirror up. People need that, even if it stings. You're gonna win that contest, Bobby Chandler, I know it!"

"Easy, Hollis," I teased, but I was grinnin', her belief warmin' me like mom's gumbo. "Ain't won nothin' yet. Gotta make the film first."

"Then get to it!" she said, pokin' my chest, her smile wide. "I'll be your cheerleader, but you better not slack off."

We talked all afternoon, the hours slippin' by as we leaned on the counter, tradin' stories about school, football, her sketches, my footage. She told me about a drawin' she'd done of the old oaks before they were cut, and I told her about splicin' reels in the dark editin' room, how it felt like controllin' time. The store stayed quiet, the bell never ringin', but with Lila there, it didn't feel so empty.

As the sun dipped low, paintin' the windows gold, Lila glanced around, her brow furrowin'. "Bobby," she said, her voice droppin', "It's been great talkin' but ain't a single customer come in all day, have they?"

I followed her gaze, takin' in the dusty shelves, the untouched tools, the silence where Main Street's bustle used to be. "Nope," I said, my voice steady but heavy. "Not a one."

I locked up as the light faded, Lila waitin' by the door, and I grabbed my camera.

"Come with me," I said, a sudden need stirrin' in me.

We walked to the riverwalk, the path cracked and overgrown, the lamplight flickerin' on empty benches. Downtown loomed behind us, its shuttered stores and faded signs a ghost of what was. I set up the camera, the hum steady, and filmed, the river's slow glow, the broken fences, the dark windows of what used to be McGregor's Diner, now a sandwich chain.

Lila stood beside me, quiet, watchin' the lens work. "What's this gonna be?" she asked, her voice soft in the dusk.

"Dunno yet," I said, zoomin' in on a bench where we'd told stories as kids. "Maybe the start of that contest film. Maybe just… to remember this day."

She nodded, her hand brushin' mine. I kept filmin', the riverwalk and downtown stretchin' out, neglected but still ours. The store's empty day, Lila's forgiveness, the spark of the contest, they were pushin' me to see again, to capture somethin' before I couldn't again. The camera rolled, and for the first time in months, I felt like I was holdin' onto somethin' real, somethin' worth fightin' for, even if it was just a reel of a community that remembered how to be.

Chapter 22 - The Last Turn of the Wrench
(January 1969)

Christmas had come and gone. Matt and I were preparing for school to start back up. It was the kind of day where the sun shines but don't warm you, and the family gathered after church, holdin' onto what was left of our traditions. The kitchen table was heavy with mom's roast chicken, biscuits fluffy as clouds, and collards simmerin' with ham hock, their steam curlin' like a prayer. The house smelled of comfort, but the air was tight, mom's cancer and the town's fade pressin' in like uninvited guests.

Mom brought out sweet tea, the pitcher clinkin' with ice, and a peach cobbler, its crust golden and bubblin'. "Y'all better save room," she said, her voice softer now, her smile still a light in the room despite her tremblin' hands.

I set up chairs on the porch for after, the wood creakin' under my hands, knowin' we'd need the open air to breathe through whatever this day held.

Lila was there, helpin' in the kitchen as she had done more and more lately, her braid swingin' as she stirred the collards, her eyes catchin' mine with a quiet understandin'. She'd been around more since our talk at the hardware store, sensin' the tension in our house before words even named it, but I knew the stress she had at home too.

"Smells like heaven in here, Mrs. Chandler," she said, settin' a bowl on the table, but her glance at mom was careful, like she was measurin' how much strength was left.

Uncle Don arrived late, his truck rattlin' into the drive, his hat in hand as he stepped through the door. His face was drawn, lines deeper than I remembered, and when he hugged mom, he held on a little longer, his arms tight like he was afraid to let go. "Sorry I'm late, Ruth," he said, his voice gruff but warm. "Roads ain't what they used to be."

"You're here now, Don," dad said, giving Uncle Don a hug. "That's what counts. Sit, eat."

We gathered 'round, dad at the head, Matt slouchin' but present, his Allied shifts leavin' him quieter these days. The food was a comfort, the chicken tender, the biscuits meltin' in our mouths, but the talk was light, careful, like we were all dancin' around somethin' heavy. Lila passed the collards, her smile easy, but I saw her watchin' Uncle Don, sensin' the storm in his silence. Uncle Don asked both Matt and I about our school and he asked how mom was doin'.

As the meal wound down, the plates half-cleared, Uncle Don looked at me, and asked if I would get my camera so he could see it. I thought it was a strange request, but said "Yes sir."

He waited until I got back, then asked if I could film him. I must have had a strange look on my face, because he gave me a look that implied I needed to do it. "Yes sir."

Uncle Don set his fork down, the clink loud in the hush. He cleared his throat, his hands foldin' tight, and looked around the table, his eyes heavy. "I need to talk to y'all," he said, his voice low, like he was pullin' the words from deep. "The bank's done givin' me time. It's sell or face foreclosure. My shop… it's over."

The room went still, the air sucked out like a vacuum, just the sound of my camera whirrin'. Mom's hand froze on her glass, Matt's jaw twitched, and Lila's eyes flicked to me, wide with the weight of it.

Don kept goin', his voice steady but raw. "Been holdin' out, hopin' things'd turn around, new customers, somethin'. But they haven't. Allied's taken the trade, and I can't keep up. It's just time to let it go."

I widened the shot and looked to dad, waitin' for him to say somethin', to fight like he always did for the store, for us. But he stayed silent, chewin' slow, his jaw tight, his eyes fixed on his plate like it held answers. Mom reached for Don's hand, her fingers thin but firm. "You did all you could, Don," she said, her voice soft but sure. "Ain't no shame in that."

Uncle Don nodded, but his shoulders sagged, like the fight had drained out of him. "Just wanted to tell y'all myself," he said, almost a whisper. "Before the papers get signed." I stopped the recordin'.

We cleared the table quiet, Lila helpin' mom with the dishes, her glances at me full of questions we didn't voice. Matt slipped out, mutterin' about checkin' the car, but I knew he was runnin' from the truth. I followed dad and Uncle Don to the porch, where they sat on the steps, coffee mugs in hand, the steam risin' into the cold air. The trees swayed in the wind, their bare branches scratchin' the sky, and for a while, neither man spoke, just stared out, lettin' the silence hold 'em.

Dad finally broke it, his voice rough but steady. "You held the line longer than most, Don," he said, his eyes on the horizon. "Most woulda folded years ago."

Don took a sip of coffee, his hands steady but his voice shakin' just a touch. "It ain't about pride anymore, Thomas. It's about what's left of my name. Sellin' feels like givin' up, but losin' it to the bank… that's worse."

Dad nodded, slow, his fingers tight around his mug. "We ain't far behind you," he said, so soft I almost missed it, his words carryin' the weight of Chandler Hardware's empty days, the customers who didn't come any more. "Store's hangin' by a thread. Don't know how long I can keep it before..."

Neither man looked at the other, their eyes fixed on the trees, the wind whirlin' through the yard like it was carryin' away the last of their fight. I stood in the doorway, my heart heavy, I didn't notice Lila beside me, her hand grabbin' mine, a quiet anchor. "They're losin' everythin'," I whispered, my voice barely there.

"Not everythin'," she whispered back, her eyes on mom inside, hummin' faint as she stacked plates. "They got each other. That's somethin'."

I nodded, but the ache didn't ease. Uncle Don's shop, dad's store, they were our rock, and now they were breakin'. The porch creaked under dad and Uncle Don, their coffee coolin', their silence a kind of understandin' deeper than words. I didn't film it, didn't need to. This was the last turn of the wrench, the moment we all knew the town we'd fought for was slippin' away, and all we could do was sit together, listenin' to the wind, holdin' onto the family that was still ours, for as long as it lasted.

The mornin' after that heavy Sunday lunch, Uncle Don faced a task harder than any repair he'd ever tackled. Uncle Don had asked if I would come and film it, so people could see, but insisted I be respectful, that not all people want the world to see them. To see them for who they really were in the worst of times. I filmed Uncle Don as he opened his shop early, the air sharp with frost, the neon sign flickerin' for the last time above the door that read *Don's Fix-It*. The shelves were near empty, tools sold off to cover debts, and the smell of oil and sawdust lingered like a ghost. He'd called his employees, folks who'd been with him through lean years, to meet him at dawn, before the bank's deadline loomed.

Uncle Don told the crew that I was filmin' for a school project. They all waved as they gathered in the shop's main room, the concrete floor scuffed from years of boots and dropped wrenches. There was Hank, gray-haired and steady, who'd fixed near everythin' since I was a kid; Jimmy, wiry and quick with a laugh, always hummin' a tune; Carl,

161

quiet but strong, his hands scarred from years of labor; and Ellen, the newest, a young mother with a newborn at home, her eyes tired but fierce. Uncle Don stood before 'em, his work apron swapped for a clean flannel, his hat crumpled in his hands, his face etched with lines deeper than the day before.

Uncle Don cleared his throat, the sound echoin' in the near-empty space, and tried to meet their eyes, but his gaze kept slippin', like the words were too heavy to carry. "Y'all," he started, his voice thick, chokin' back emotion, "y'all gave me more than I could ever pay back. Your sweat, your time, your trust, this shop was ours 'cause of you. But I can't keep fightin' a storm that won't pass. I mortgaged everythin' just to keep us going, but now we gotta close shop before the bank takes it."

The room went still, the kind of quiet that hurts. Hank stepped forward, his calloused hand restin' on Don's shoulder, his grip firm but gentle. "You did right by us, Don," he said, his voice gravelly but sure. "Ain't no one coulda fought harder."

Jimmy stared at the floor, his hands stuffed in his pockets, his usual hum gone, like the shop's silence had swallowed it. Carl stood rigid, his jaw tight, his eyes fixed on a crack in the concrete, like he could anchor himself to it. Ellen's face crumpled, tears spillin' as she clutched her coat, her breath hitchin' soft, thinkin' of her baby and the bills waitin' at home.

Don moved to each one, shakin' their hands, his grip lingerin' like he was memorizin' the feel of 'em. He hugged 'em after, quick but fierce, his voice low as he repeated their names. "Hank, you kept us runnin' smooth," he said, his hand on the older man's arm. "Jimmy, your laugh got us through the worst days. Carl, you were the backbone, always. Ellen, you brought heart to this place, and I'm so damn sorry it's endin' like this" tears streaming down his face.

He pulled out final checks, scribbled on yellow paper, his handwritin' shaky but clear, and passed 'em out, his fingers brushin' theirs like a

162

last connection. "If I had the means," he said, his voice breakin' now, "we'd run it another fifty years. Build things, fix things, keep this town turnin'. But it ain't right to string y'all along, not when the bank's got its claws in me."

Ellen sobbed, clutchin' her check, and Hank pulled her into a side hug, his own eyes wet. "We'll be alright, Don," he said, though his voice wavered, like he was tryin' to believe it. "You gave us more than a job. You gave us a place."

Uncle Don nodded, his throat workin', but he couldn't speak no more. He stood there as they filed out, the bell above the door jinglin' faint, each chime a goodbye. The shop was empty then, just Uncle Don and the echoes of a life's work, the tools gone, the future sold. Don swept the floor one last time, like he wanted to leave it clean for whatever came next.

Uncle Don stood alone in the husk of *Don's Fix-It*, the shop that had been his life's work. The air was cold, heavy with the scent of oil and sawdust, a faint echo of the years when the place hummed with noise and laughter. Now, the shelves stood bare, the tools sold to pay debts, the neon sign above the door dark forever. He walked through one last time, his boots scuffin' soft on the concrete, each step a farewell to a world he'd built.

His fingers brushed the workbenches, scarred from decades of repairs, their wood worn smooth by hands that trusted him to mend what was broken. He paused at a shelf, empty now, and ran his thumb along its edge, as if greetin' an old friend who couldn't answer back.

A memory stirred, "I remember Ruby Anne, eight months pregnant, waddlin' in to pick up a shovel I had repaired for her, her water breakin' right there by the counter. The whole town had roared, jokin' she needed the shovel to bury her husband for gettin' her in that state."

Don's lips curved, a faint smile breakin' through the ache, the ghost of her laugh lingerin' in the silence.

In the back, his eyes caught on his son's old toolbox Don mounted to the wall, left from summers when the boy, still young, learned to turn a wrench at his side. The initials carved in the lid stared back, a reminder of a bond stretched thin by time and distance, his son now in Raleigh, chasin' a life beyond this dyin' town. Don's hand hovered, then fell, the weight of absence too heavy to touch.

He moved to the door, his shadow long across the floor, and flicked off the lights. I captured the shop as it was plunged into darkness, a final breath held and released. He lingered, his hand on the knob, the metal cold against his palm, then turned the key, the lock's click sharp and final, severin' the past from what came next. Outside, he hung a sign in the window, its words simple, handwritten in black ink: *Closed. Thank you for the years.* It swayed in the breeze, a quiet epitaph for a place that had fixed more than machines.

I filmed Don as he climbed into his old truck, the door groanin' as it shut, and placed both hands on the wheel, knuckles pale, his breath shallow. He didn't start it, not for a long time, his eyes fixed on the shop, as if he could etch its shape into his bones. I moved across the street, I stood unseen, my camera hummin' soft, filmin' from a distance, respectful, silent. I didn't want to intrude, but I needed to hold this moment, for Don, for all of us, for the story I was still learnin' to tell.

When the engine finally coughed to life, the truck eased away, and I zoomed in, the lens catchin' the reflection of the *Closed* sign in the background, its letters stark against the mornin' gray. Inside the cab, Uncle Don drove, tears tracin' silent paths down his cheeks, his face turned just slightly toward the passenger seat, where a ghost must have been sitting.

Later, in the quiet of my room, I drafted a voiceover, my pencil slow across the page: "Sometimes, goodbye doesn't mean turnin' your back, it means lockin' the door, so the memories don't slip out." The reel spun, Don's truck fadin' into the gray, and I knew this was more than a shop closin'. It was another heart breakin' again, leavin' us to carry the echoes of Ruby Anne's laugh, a toolbox of memories, and a sign that thanked the years, even as they ended.

Chapter 23 - Legacy Fading
(May 1969)

I tried to capture the town's unravelin', but nothin' quite prepared us for what happened that day. Dad'd risen early, like always, to open the store, his boots heavy on the porch as he left the house where mom rested, her cancer stealin' more of her each day. The air was crisp, the sun just breakin' over the horizon, but when he reached the store, the world tilted.

Dad stopped short at the sight of the front door, slightly ajar, the brass bell that'd jingled for decades missin' from its hook. His breath caught, a low sound like a man bracin' for pain. He pushed the door open, slow, and stepped inside, his eyes takin' in the ruin. Glass shards glittered on the floor under the display window, shattered in the night, their edges catchin' the mornin' light like cruel stars. A crowbar lay discarded nearby, its iron dull but guilty, tossed by hands that didn't care what they broke.

The shelves were ransacked, once-neat rows of hammers, nails, and wrenches now gaps and chaos. Tools were gone, anything of value, stolen, likely to be pawned in some town past the bypass. The cash drawer hung open, emptied, though there'd been little in it, just a handful of bills from a day when no customers came. Dad stood in the wreckage, his hands at his sides, his face unreadable but heavy, like the weight of the store's slow death had finally crushed what was left.

The police arrived, two officers in stiff uniforms, their notepads out but their eyes already wanderin'. "Probably kids from out past the bypass," one said, kickin' a shard of glass with his boot. "Joyride gone too far. You're lucky it wasn't worse, Mr. Chandler."

Dad didn't answer, just nodded once, his jaw tight. The officers scribbled a report, promisin' to look into it, but their voices carried no hope, and they left as quick as they came, their cruiser's engine fadin' down Main Street. Dad stayed, alone in the mess, and picked up a broom. He swept the glass, the bristles hissin' soft against the floor, each stroke deliberate, like he could sweep away the loss itself. The shards clinked into a pile, a broken mirror of the store he'd fought to keep alive, and he worked in silence, his shadow long across the empty shelves.

I wasn't there when he found it, but he told me later, his voice low, the words comin' slow like they hurt. "It ain't the tools or the money, Bobby," he said, his eyes on the horizon. "It's the bell. That bell rang for your grandpa, for me, for every soul who walked through that door as a greeting. Now it's gone."

I didn't know what to say, just stood there, my camera heavy in my hands, wishin' I could film the bell back into place, could rewind the night and lock the door tighter. Chandler Hardware had been hangin' by a thread, but this, the burglary, the broken door, the missin' bell, was a cut too deep, a sign that even the bones of the town were bein' picked clean. Dad kept sweepin', the broom's rhythm a quiet dirge, and I knew, without him sayin', that the store's days were numbered, its heart stolen long before the crowbar broke the window.

The hardware store was a shadow, its pulse so faint it barely registered. The store once a town's focal point, dad's pride, Granddad's legacy was slippin' away faster than I could film it. Heavy as the May heat, there was no escapin' the truth that our family, like the town, was fadin'.

Sales had dwindled to nothin', weeks passin' without a single customer crossin' the threshold. The bell, stolen in the burglary, left the door silent, but it didn't matter, no one came to ring it. Dust settled on the shelves, coatin' the few remainin' tools like a shroud, the hammers and wrenches untouched, the register closed tight. Dad would open each mornin', flip the "Open" sign out of habit, but the store was a tomb, its quiet broken only by the creak of the floor under his boots. I'd pass by after school, seein' him standin' behind the counter, starin' at the empty street, and I'd keep walkin', too ashamed to face the void where Main Street's bustle used to be.

The bank called again one afternoon, their voice cracklin' through the phone like a judge passin' sentence. The next morning, we were all sitting down eating breakfast like we had done millions of times before, Dad spoke, "the last loan, meant to float the store through winter, is long overdue, and winter had come and gone." Dad told us we had thirty days to settle or the bank would foreclose. Dad looked straight ahead, his hands shakin' as he put his hands together to keep em still. "The debt had been pilin' higher than the hospital bills already chokin' us."

I never even asked to see if I could help. I had been too worried about myself, and what I felt. I felt selfish that I had let him carry such a load and not done more.

Matt broke the silence, "is there anything we can do?" his voice solemn.

"No, I think it's time. It will give us more time to help your mom, to focus on what's really important. We'll sell off the back pasture to that developer that keeps callin, it'll pay the bills and then some." He said with a forced smile.

Mom's health was worsenin', each day stealin' a little more of her light. Hospital visits came more often, the drive to the clinic a grim routine. Dad helpin' her into the truck, her steps slow, her smile fadin' but still there, stubborn as ever. The bills stacked up on the kitchen table, unopened envelopes mockin' us with numbers we couldn't pay. Mom's treatments, her pain meds, the specialists who offered no hope but charged plenty, they were drainin' what little we had left, leavin' dad to carry the store and her care on shoulders that looked more bowed each day.

One evenin', Matt came home from Allied, his vest crumpled, holdin' a letter that changed everythin'. He sat at the table, starin' at it, till mom noticed, her hands tremblin' as she reached for his. "What's that, honey?" she asked, her voice soft but sharp with hope.

"Engineering college," Matt said, his voice low, like he was afraid to believe it. "Full ride. They want me, mom. Startin' in the fall."

Mom's eyes lit up, a spark in the dimness, and she gripped his hand, her frail fingers fierce. "You're goin'," she said, no room for argument. "Promise me, no matter what, Matt. You're gonna build things, make a life. This town ain't your end."

Matt nodded, his jaw tight, tears glistenin' but not fallin'. "I promise, mom," he whispered, and I saw dad look away, his face a mix of pride and pain, knowin' Matt's chance was a light in the dark but a step away from us.

I was proud of him, but felt almost like the day he moved on to High School leavin' me behind. I knew it was the nature of things, but still felt a little sad.

I was soon lost in the blur of high school. Football and film club kept me busy. From the muddy field to splicin' reels in the dark editin' room, chasin' the statewide competition. I wasn't sure I'd ever finish the film about the town's fade. Football practice left me bruised and alive, the sweat and tackles a release from the weight at home. And girls, Sarah from film club with her shy smile, Jenny from the cheer squad with her laugh, they pulled me into moments where I could forget the store's empty shelves, mom's cough, dad's silence. I was distant from the hardware store, avoidin' its fadin' reality, tellin' myself I was too busy to help, too young to fix what was broken. But deep down, I knew I was runnin', leavin' dad to carry the load alone.

One night, I came home late, the house quiet except for mom's soft hummin' from her room. dad was at the table, the bank's letter open, his hands folded like he was prayin'. "Bobby," he said, not lookin' up, "store's done. Ain't no comin' back from this."

I stood there, my throat tight, the truth landin' like a stone. The store, mom's health, Matt's leavin', my own driftin', it was all too much, a strain I couldn't seem to shrug off. I wanted to say somethin', to promise I'd help, but the words wouldn't come. Instead, I nodded, turned to my room, and left dad in the dark, the mounting weight of our losses settlin' deeper, with no way to lift it.

Chandler Hardware, dad's heart and Granddad's legacy, was bleedin' out. Dinner that night was simple, mom's cornbread and a pot of beans, her hands too weak to do more, but we sat together, the four of us, in a kitchen that felt smaller each day. Mom's cough echoed soft, Matt's fork scraped his plate, and Dad's silence was louder than the chorus of frogs and crickets outside.

As we cleared the dishes, dad stood at the sink, his back to us, his shoulders squared like he was bracin' for a storm. He didn't turn, didn't raise his voice, just spoke, plain and final, like he was layin' down a stone. "It's time," he said. "Store's closin'. Ain't no more fight left."

The words landed soft but heavy, like dirt on a coffin. Mom nodded, her eyes fixed on the table, her hands folded tight, not liftin' her gaze, as if lookin' up would make it real. Her face was pale, the cancer stealin' her color, but her nod was steady, a quiet acceptance that cut deeper than tears.

Matt set his plate down, his jaw tight, and said, "I'll help you pack it up, dad. Whatever you need."

"Me too," I chimed in.

His voice was low, practical, but I heard the crack in it, the boy who'd grown up sweepin' those floors now facin' their end. I stood frozen, my hands grippin' the chair, words stuck in my throat. The store was dad's life, our family's anchor, and losin' it felt like losin' the ground beneath us. I thought of my camera, the reels I'd shot of Main Street's fade, and a need stirred, sharp and urgent.

"Dad," I said, my voice quiet, almost lost in the hum of the fridge, "can I film it? The closin'?"

Dad turned then, his eyes meetin' mine, tired but clear, like he'd seen this comin' and already made his peace. "Yeah, Bobby," he said, his voice rough but steady. "But don't point that thing at me. Film the store, the shelves, what's left. Not me."

I nodded, my throat tight, understandin' he didn't want his pain trapped in a frame, didn't want the lens to catch the breakin' of a man who'd fought so long. Mom reached for Dad's hand, her fingers thin but firm, and gave a small smile, the kind that held more courage than words could carry. Matt looked at me, his eyes sayin' what his mouth didn't, that this was ours to carry now, together, even if it hurt.

No one said more. The decision was made, no fanfare, no fuss, just a family facin' the end of an era in a kitchen lit by a single bulb. I thought of the store's empty shelves, the stolen bell, the bank's cold calls, and knew this was more than closin' a door, it was buryin' a piece of ourselves. My camera would capture it, not Dad's face but the store's bones, the last of Chandler Hardware, so the memories wouldn't slip away, even as we locked up for good.

Chandler Hardware was breathin' its last. My camera hummin' soft as I stood in the store's dim light, filmin' the end of an era. The burglary, the empty weeks, the bank's cold grip, they'd all led to this, Dad's decision to close what Granddad had built. The air was thick with dust and memory, and as Dad and Matt worked to shut it down, it felt like we were buryin' a piece of ourselves, right there on Main Street. Dad and Matt moved through the store, boxin' up inventory that hadn't budged in months, nails rusted in their bins, socket sets no one needed, oil lamps gatherin' cobwebs in a world lit by electric bulbs. "Who even buys these anymore?" Matt muttered, holdin' up a lamp, its glass cloudy, his voice half-jokin' but heavy.

171

Dad chuckled, low and sad, tapin' a box shut. "Folks used to swear by 'em, son. Said they kept the dark honest. Now they just sit, like us, waitin' for a miracle."

They worked steady, their hands sure but slow, like they were handlin' relics. Behind the counter, Dad paused at the coffee mugs, each chipped and labeled with regulars' names, *Hank, Mrs. Clara, Old Joe*, etched in faded marker from years of mornin' chats. He wrapped 'em in newspaper, gentle as if they were mom's fine china. "Gotta keep these," he said, his voice thick. "Ain't much, but they're proof folks came here, laughed here."

Matt nodded, settin' a mug aside. "Reckon we oughta bury 'em out back, give 'em a proper send-off. 'Here lies Joe's coffee, gone but not forgotten.'"

I snorted, the camera steady in my hands, catchin' dad's faint grin. "Careful, Matt," I said, zoomin' in on a mug. "You'll have us holdin' a funeral for the whole store. Preacher'd have to bless the screwdrivers."

"Wouldn't be the worst idea," dad said, his eyes crinklin' just a touch. "Might get more folks here than we've seen in a year."

The pegboard tools came down next, one by one, their hooks leavin' dust trails like ghosts on the wall. Hammers, pliers, chisels, each clinked into boxes, their metal dull but heavy with years of fixin' fences, buildin' barns, mendin' lives. The store creaked under dad's and Matt's boots, the floor groanin' like it knew this was goodbye. I filmed it all in wide shots, quiet angles, long silences, no music, just the raw sound of the end, tape rippin', boxes thud-din', the occasional cough from dad as the dust got to him. My lens stayed off him, like he'd asked, focusin' on the shelves, the counter, the life leavin' the place.

When everythin' was boxed or stacked, the store stripped to its bones, one thing remained on the wall: a black-and-white photograph of Grandpa Chandler, the man who'd opened the store in 1937. He stood in front of the original storefront, sleeves rolled, smile crooked, a hammer in hand like he was ready to build the world. The frame was worn, the glass smudged, but his eyes seemed to watch us, steady and proud, even now.

Dad stepped forward, his breath catchin', and reached for the frame, slow, his fingers tremblin' like they were touchin' somethin' holy. He lifted it from the nail, the wall bare behind it, a pale square where time hadn't touched. He brushed the dust from the glass, his thumb lingerin' on Grandpa's face, and held the photo to his chest, his shoulders shakin' just once before he stilled. There was a prominent silhouette where the picture hung, like the spirit of the picture refused to leave.

"Dad," Matt said, his voice soft, steppin' closer, "he'd be proud of you. Hell, he'd probably say you held on too long, stubborn as he was."

Dad let out a breath, half-laugh, half-sob. "He'd say I'm a damn fool, Matt. 'Thomas, you let my store go to kids with crowbars?'" He shook his head, clutchin' the frame tighter. "But he'd understand. He'd know I tried."

I lowered the camera, my throat tight, the lens too small for this kind of hurt. "We could hang it at home," I said, my voice barely above a whisper. "Right in the kitchen."

Dad nodded, his eyes wet but clear. "Yeah, Bobby. That's fittin'. He'd like that, keepin' watch over us."

We stood there, the three of us, in the hollowed-out store, the boxes stacked like tombstones, the photo in dad's hands a last link to the past. "Reckon we oughta have a wake," Matt said, tryin' to lighten the air, his voice crackin'. "Pour out some coffee for the mugs, sing a hymn for the hammers."

"Lord, Matt," I said, managin' a smile, "you'll have us dancin' with the brooms next."

"Let's not give the bank any ideas," dad said, his voice steady now, a flicker of his old fight. He tucked the photo under his arm, his steps slow as he headed for the door. "Come on, boys. Let's go home."

I filmed the last shot, a wide view of the empty store, the bare pegboard, the counter where mugs used to sit, the floor still creakin' under ghosts. The camera hummed, holdin' the silence, and I knew this wasn't just the end of Chandler Hardware. It was boxed up with chipped mugs and a crooked smile, carried home to mom, where we'd try to keep livin', even as the dust settled behind us.

It was the last day of May 1969, and Chandler Hardware was no more, its shelves had been emptied, its heart packed into boxes. The store was a husk now, stripped of tools, mugs, and the bell stolen by thieves, but the act of closin' it felt heavier than all that loss combined. It was like buryin' a friend, and we moved through it quiet, solemn, knowin' we would never be the same.

Dad turned and stood at the counter one last time, his hands restin' on the worn wood, then walked to the front, slow and deliberate, his boots echoin' in the empty space. He paused beneath the doorframe, a long moment where time seemed to hold its breath. His shoulders were bowed, his face etched with years of fight and failure, but he stood tall, like a man facin' a storm he couldn't outrun. I watched from the back, my camera hummin' soft, capturin' the weight of his stillness, the store's bare walls a backdrop to his goodbye. I could see that he was watching a lifetime of memories flash in his mind, the laughter, the sorrow, the joy…all flooding at once.

He reached for the light switch, his fingers steady but slow, and turned out the lights. The last bulbs flickered, a weak protest, then faded, plungin' the store into shadow. The air went still, the hum of the place silenced forever. Dad moved to the "OPEN" sign, its letters faded from years of use, and removed it for the final time, not to "CLOSED," but to empty glass, a blank face that said nothin' at all, 'cause there was nothin' left to say.

Outside, I stepped onto the sidewalk, the camera steady as Dad locked the door. The key turned with a soft click, final as a heartbeat stoppin', and he slipped it into his pocket, his hand lingerin' there like he could hold onto what it meant. He didn't look back, just squared his shoulders and walked to the truck, his steps even but heavy, leavin' the store behind like a soldier leavin' a battlefield. I filmed it all, the lens catchin' the dark storefront, the locked door, the silence of Main Street stretchin' out, its other shops long shuttered, their windows black. The last heartbeat of the town was gone, and the quiet was deafening.

Back at home, the kitchen was warm, mom's presence a faint light despite her frailty. Dad carried Granddad's photograph, the sepia image of the man who'd opened the store in 1937, his crooked smile and hammer, an ode to better days. Dad hung it on the wall above the kitchen table, careful, his hands steady, the frame settlin' into place like it belonged there. He stepped back, starin' at it, his eyes distant, holdin' memories I couldn't touch.

He sat down without speakin', the chair creakin' under him, and mom brought him tea, her steps slow, her hand tremblin' as she set the cup before him. She placed a hand on his shoulder, her touch light but sure, a silent vow that they'd carry this together. Dad's fingers brushed hers, a small gesture, but it held a world of love and loss.

I stood by the table, my camera still in hand, starin' at Grandpa's photo, his sleeves rolled, his smile defiant, like he was darin' the world to break him. I lifted the camera, then lowered it, turnin' it off with a soft click. Some moments were too raw for film, too sacred for a reel. I didn't need the lens to hold this, the image of Dad's silence, mom's hand, the photograph watchin' over us like a ghost who'd understand.

Later that night, in my room, I opened my notebook, the pencil scratchin' slow as I wrote: "hope, fadin'." The words felt small, not enough to carry the noise of the silence, Dad's pocketed key, or mom's touch in the quiet kitchen. But they were true, a marker for the day Chandler Hardware locked its door, leavin' us to face a town without its pulse, with only a photograph and each other to keep the hope from fadin' entirely.

Chapter 24 - The King Has Arrived
(May 1969)

The air at home was heavy still, but overnight, somethin' new shook the stillness, a loud, brash arrival that didn't care about our losses. A giant red-and-yellow banner unfurled across from Allied General, screamin' in bold letters: *COMING SOON – BBQ-GRILLED FLAVOR HAS A NEW HOME!*

I stopped dead on my way to school, my camera slung over my shoulder, starin' at the lot where that banner staked its claim. It'd been an empty field just weeks ago, a stretch of weeds where kids flew kites and old men tossed horseshoes. Now, it was paved and fenced, swarmin' with construction crews in hard hats, their equipment rattlin' like a war drum. I lifted my camera, the hum steady, filmin' the transformation as a drive-thru frame rose, all steel and sharp angles, like scaffoldin' for a new way of life. "What the hell's this?" I muttered, zoomin' in on a worker weldin' a beam, sparks flyin' like tiny stars.

"Hamburger King, WoooHooo!" hollered Tommy, ridin' past on his bike, a paper crown made from notebook paper wobblin' on his head. He grinned, wavin' like a king himself, joined by a pack of kids chantin', "Humdinger and fries! Humdinger and fries!" Their voices echoed, half-mockin', half-excited, as they pedaled down Main Street, their crowns catchin' the sun.

I shook my head, lowerin' the camera. "Y'all look like you're joinin' a circus," I called after 'em, but I was smilin', their energy a jolt in the town's gray haze. Still, the sight of that banner, that lot, felt like a stranger kickin' down our door, and I wasn't sure I liked it.

The advertisin' blitz hit like a tidal wave, loud and relentless. Mailboxes overflowed with glossy coupons, their colors screamin', *Buy One Get One Free! $1 Kids Meals! Grand Openin' Giveaway!*, like promises of a better life wrapped in wax paper. I pulled one from our mailbox, the paper slick under my fingers, and showed it to Matt at breakfast. "They're givin' away free food," I said, tossin' it on the table. "Think it's a trap?"

Matt snorted, pourin' coffee, his Allied vest already on for a shift. "Trap? Nah, just capitalism, Bobby. They'll hook us with cheap burgers, then we're all eatin' Humdingers for supper. Mom'll have a fit."

"Only if they start sellin' gumbo," I shot back, grinnin', but the thought of Ma, frail but fierce, facin' off with a fast-food chain made me laugh for the first time in days.

The invasion didn't stop there. One afternoon, a flatbed truck rolled down Main Street, blastin' "Sweet Caroline" so loud it rattled the empty storefronts. Kids ran after it, cheerin' as workers tossed free T-shirts and more paper crowns into the crowd. "Get your Hamburger King treasure!" a guy in a red polo shouted, flingin' a shirt that landed on Lila's head as we watched from the sidewalk.

She yanked it off, holdin' it like it was radioactive. "What is this nonsense, Bobby?" she said, her eyes narrowin' at the truck. "They're actin' like they're savin' the town with fries and T-shirts!"

"More like killin' it," I said, liftin' my camera to film the chaos, the lens catchin' kids divin' for crowns, their laughs sharp against the street's silence. "But you gotta admit, it's a hell of a show."

"Show's all it is," Lila muttered, stuffin' the T-shirt in her bag. "Main Street's a ghost, and they're throwin' a parade on its grave."

The local radio station piled on, runnin' ads every hour with trumpets and a voice like a carnival barker: "Bigger! Juicier! BBQ-grilled and

178

right here in Mill Town! Hamburger King's bringin' the flavor, grand openin' this June!" I'd hear it at Henson's Drug Store, the jukebox drowned out by the fanfare, and old Mr. Henson would shake his head, mutterin', "BBQ-grilled my foot. Ain't no soul in that food."

One evenin', I biked to the edge of town, where a new billboard loomed over the highway, its red-and-yellow logo glowin' like a second sun. *Hamburger King – Coming Soon!* it declared, with a picture of a Humdinger so shiny it looked fake. I set up my camera, framin' the shot careful, lettin' Main Street blur in the background, its dark storefronts, its faded signs, a ghost town behind the promise of fast food. The footage was stark, the billboard's glare a knife in the heart of the town I'd grown up in.

"Looks like the king's takin' over," I said to myself, the camera hummin', my voice low. "But he ain't gonna rule me."

I packed up, the coupons and crowns and radio jingles spinnin' in my head, a loud, colorful storm that didn't care about mom's gumbo, dad's store, or the place we were losin'. I biked home, the banner's words, *BBQ Grilled Flavor*, burnin' behind my eyes, knowin' I'd film it all, the invasion, the change, 'cause even if the king was here, I was still holdin' the lens, tellin' our story, one reel at a time.

May 1969 had brought a red-and-yellow storm to town, and by the time Hamburger King's grand openin' hit, the whole town was buzzin' like a hive. The new fast-food joint was a loud intruder, and its arrival was shakin' up every corner of our lives, from schoolyards to empty diners. At school, the cafeteria was half-empty one lunch period, kids ditchin' their trays to bike over to Hamburger King, their laughter echoin' down the halls. I sat with Lila, pokin' at my mashed potatoes, watchin' the chaos through the window. A table nearby was loud with freshmen tradin' Humdinger wrappers like baseball cards, their voices high with excitement. "Yo, I got two already!" bragged Tommy, wavin' a greasy wrapper. "Ate mine in, like, three bites. It's like we're a real town now!"

I snorted, stabbin' my fork into my plate. "A real town?" I muttered, low enough so only Lila heard. "What, 'cause we got burgers instead of history?"

Lila raised an eyebrow, her milk carton paused mid-sip. "They're kids, Bobby. They don't know what they're tradin' away."

Eric leaned in, "Ya know, they're only two years younger than us right?"

Across the room, Mrs. Carter, our history teacher, leaned against the wall, her arms crossed, her voice drippin' sarcasm as she spoke to another teacher. "Well, ain't we fancy now? Upgraded from heritage to hamburgers. Next thing, they'll pave the riverwalk for a second drive-thru."

"Tell me about it," the other teacher chuckled, but it was a tired sound, like she felt the loss too.

Lila nudged me, her eyes searchin' mine. "You're quieter than usual, Bobby. What's eatin' you?"

I leaned back, my voice low, bitter. "Even the kids are cheerin' their own inheritance gettin' pawned. Main Street's dyin', mom's sick, and they're actin' like a Humdinger's gonna save us all."

She nodded, her hand brushin' mine, a small comfort. "It's loud, but it's temporary. Folks'll miss Benny's Diner when the shine wears off."

Benny's was feelin' it already, its afternoon crowd gone, the jukebox playin' "Stand By Me" to empty booths. I'd passed by after school, seein' the waitresses leanin' on the counter, their aprons limp, the smell of coffee fadin' with no one to drink it. "Used to be packed this time of day," I heard one say, her voice flat. "Now it's just us and the flies."

At home, Matt drove mom past the Hamburger King one day, her eyes lingerin' on the bright sign, and sighed, a sound that carried years of fight. Later, I found her at the kitchen table, circlin' menu items in an

Allied flyer, her pencil slow, cost-conscious even now. "Gotta stretch what we got," she said, catchin' me watchin', her smile faint but stubborn. "Ain't no Humdinger worth breakin' the bank."

Dad, restockin' what was left of our home's tools, overheard the radio's Hamburger King ad blarin' about *BBQ-grilled flavor*. He scoffed, settin' a hammer down hard. "BBQ-grilled? They don't even know what real BBQ tastes like," he said, his voice gruff but edged with somethin' sad. "Buncha city folks sellin' us our own hunger." He turned back to his work, quiet, the weight of the closed store still heavy on him.

Grand openin' day was a circus. A man in a plastic Hamburger King crown costume waved on the corner, his cape flappin' as cars snaked through the drive-thru, horns honkin' like it was a parade. Parents pulled kids outta school early, linin' up for free kids' meals and photo ops with the mascot, their laughter loud against the hum of engines. I stood across the street, my camera hummin', framin' the King against Allied General's massive sign, its shadow loomin' over the lot like a giant claimin' its prize.

I caught Matt in the lens, walkin' into Hamburger King, his Allied vest swapped for a red-and-yellow uniform, his face unreadable as he headed for a shift. "You workin' *there* now too?" I called, lowerin' the camera, my voice half-teasin', half-stunned.

He shrugged, not meetin' my eyes. "Allied cut hours. Gotta save money for college, Bobby. Ain't personal."

I nodded, but it stung, seein' him in that uniform, like he was surrenderin' to the same wave drownin' our town. I turned the camera back to the crowd, catchin' an elderly couple at the corner, stoppin' to stare at the noise and motion. The man shook his head, his wife's hand tight on his arm, and they turned around, walkin' back toward the quiet end of Main Street, their steps slow, like they were leavin' a world they didn't know.

My lens lingered on a kid draggin' a Hamburger King balloon past Chandler Hardware's empty bench, the red string bouncin' against the cracked wood where Dad used to sit. The image was sharp, cruel, the bright balloon, the dark store, a town cheerin' its own fade. I kept filmin', my heart heavy, knowin' this was our town now: kids with paper crowns, a jukebox playin' to ghosts, and a family holdin' tight to what little we had left, while the King waved us into a future that didn't feel like ours anymore.

Chapter 25 - Matts Going to College
(June 1969)

In our kitchen, a spark of hope flickered, bright and fierce, as Matt held a thick envelope from Florida State University, his ticket out of this place. We were gathered 'round the table, the smell of mom's oyster gumbo lingerin' despite her bein' too weak to cook much these days. Matt ripped open the packet, his hands steady but his eyes wide, like he was holdin' a treasure map. "It's official!" he hollered, wavin' the letter, his grin splittin' his face. "Enrollment confirmed, y'all! I'm headin' to Tallahassee for engineerin'!"

I leaned forward, my chair creakin', catchin' his excitement like a fever. "No kiddin', Matt? You're gonna be buildin' bridges and skyscrapers? Hot damn, that's big-time!"

He laughed, flippin' through the packet, his voice bubblin' as he read aloud. "Listen to this, mom, 'Florida State's engineerin' program offers hands-on trainin' in structural design, mechanics, and innovative tech.' They got labs, Bobby, real labs with machines I ain't never seen! Says here I'll be workin' on projects that could change cities!"

Mom's smile lit the room, her frail hand pressin' his, her eyes shinin' despite the shadows under 'em. "Oh, Matt, that's somethin' else!" she said, her voice soft but warm, like a hug. "You're gonna make us proud, buildin' things that last. Ain't that right, Thomas?"

Dad nodded, his face quiet but his eyes softer than usual, pride breakin' through his usual reserve. "It's the right choice, son," he said, his voice low and sure. "You go down there and show 'em what a Chandler's made of."

Matt's grin didn't fade, his fingers tappin' the letter like it was a drum. "They've got a good school, mom, and it's close enough I can come back on weekends. Ain't leavin' y'all high and dry, promise! I'll be home haulin' groceries and eatin' your cornbread before you know it!"

"Better bring some of that fancy learnin' back with you," I teased, leanin' back, my arms crossed but my heart racin' for him. "Don't go gettin' all city-fied, forgettin' how to fix a tractor."

"Forget a tractor?" Matt shot back, pointin' at me, his eyes sparklin'. "Boy, I'll be designin' tractors that'll plow circles around anything you've seen! You just keep filmin' your sad little movies, Bobby, while I'm out changin' the world!"

"Sad movies?" I laughed, tossin' a napkin at him. "I'll film you fallin' off one of them skyscrapers, big shot!"

Mom chuckled, her hand still on Matt's, her smile a lifeline in the dim kitchen. "Y'all hush now," she said, but her voice was bright, like she was soakin' in this moment. "Matt, you go to that college and learn everythin' you can. We'll be right here, cheerin' you on."

Dad leaned forward, his voice steady but warm. "You got a full ride, son. That's rare. Build somethin', for you, for us, for this town, even if it's just a memory."

Matt nodded, his grin softenin' into somethin' serious, like he felt the real meaning of their words. "I'm gonna do it."

I watched 'em, the packet on the table, mom's smile, dad's quiet pride, and felt a lift in my chest, like a breeze after a long, hot day. Matt was leavin', chasin' a future bigger than this town's broken streets. I was proud of him, even though I would never admit it to him.

That summer seemed to fly by and August was a furnace, the heat pressin' down on us as we prepared to send Matt off to Florida State University. Matt's acceptance to college was a light we all clung to, a chance for one of us to break free. The farmhouse buzzed with purpose

184

as we packed him up, each of us movin' careful, like we were handlin' somethin' fragile.

In Matt's room, boxes piled high, stuffed with clothes, books, and dreams. I dragged an old suitcase from the attic, its leather worn but sturdy, dust cloudin' the air as I thumped it down. "This thing's older than dad," I said, wipin' my hands, grinnin' at Matt as he sorted cables for his radio. "You sure it'll make it to Tallahassee?"

Matt laughed, tossin' a coil of wire into a box. "It'll outlast your sorry camera, Bobby. Help me label these, will ya? Don't want my tools gettin' mixed up with your film junk."

"Film junk?" I shot back, grabbin' a marker to scrawl *Matt's Gear* on a box. "These cables'll be collectin' dust while I'm winnin' awards, big shot. You just focus on not flunkin' engineerin'."

"Flunk? Me?" He smirked, tapin' a box shut. "I'll be designin' bridges before you figure out how to focus that lens proper."

We kept at it, jokin' to keep the ache at bay, my hands steady as I labeled his tools, screwdrivers, a wrench, the stuff he'd used at dad's store before it closed. Each item felt like a piece of home he was takin', and I wondered if Tallahassee would know what to make of a Chandler's grit.

In the kitchen, mom was at the ironin' board, her hands tremblin' as she pressed Matt's shirts, the steam risin' like a soft prayer. She'd insisted on doin' it herself, though her strength was fadin' fast, her face pale but set. "Mom, let me take over," I said, steppin' close, worry tight in my chest. "You don't gotta do this."

She waved me off, her smile stubborn as ever. "Bobby, these shirts are goin' with my boy to college," she said, her voice soft but firm, the iron hissin' under her hand. "They'll be crisp as my cornbread, cancer or not. Ain't no machine gonna outshine a mother's touch."

I nodded, swallowin' hard, and let her work, knowin' this was her way of sendin' Matt off right, of holdin' onto him a little longer.

Outside, dad was circlin' Matt's old Ford Falcon, the car'd that'd carry him to College. He checked the tires, tappin' 'em with a wrench, then popped the hood to eye the oil, his hands movin' slow, deliberate. He did it twice, like he could keep Matt safe by makin' sure every bolt was tight. "You watchin' this, Matt?" he called, wipin' his brow, his voice gruff but warm. "Don't go drivin' this thing dry, or you'll be walkin' to Tallahassee."

Matt leaned against the porch rail, grinnin'. "I got it, dad! Oil, tires, all good. You gone over all it at least twice now. You gonna check the wipers next, make sure I don't get wet in a drizzle? Besides, if I'm walkin so are you, you're followin' me still aren't ya?"

"Don't tempt me, boy," dad said, a rare chuckle breakin' through, but his eyes lingered on the car, like he was memorizin' it, knowin' it was takin' his son to a world he couldn't follow. Dad walked to the shed shaking his head, probably to get some more tools.

Lila stopped by that afternoon, her braid loose, a small package in her hands. She found Matt on the porch, sortin' socks, and held it out, her smile shy but bright. "Here," she said, pushin' it toward him. "A goin'-away gift. Don't open it till you're in Tallahassee, but... it's a notepad for all them fancy engineerin' ideas, and a lucky penny, 'cause you're gonna need some luck with Bobby as your brother."

Matt laughed, takin' the gift, his eyes soft. "Thanks, Lila. This penny's gonna get me through exams, I bet. You make sure you keep Bobby in line while I'm gone."

"Hey!" I called from the doorway, pretendin' to scowl. "I don't need babysittin', and you don't need luck, you're gonna own that college, Matt!"

Lila grinned, nudgin' me. "He better, or I'm keepin' that notepad for my sketches. Go big, Matt. Make us all proud."

"I will," Matt said, his voice quieter now, the gift tucked under his arm like a promise. We stood there, the suitcase packed, the shirts ironed, the car ready, and for a moment, the weight of mom's illness and the town's fade eased, replaced by the hum of somethin' new, Matt's departure, a road to a future we could all believe in, even if we had to stay behind to cheer him on.

The day we took Matt to Florida State University felt heavier than the heat. Matt's full ride to college was a lifeline, a chance for him to build somethin'. We helped mom into Dad's truck to follow Matt for the two-hour drive to Tallahassee, the whole family mom, dad, me, and Matt, windin' through roads flanked by pine stands and empty storefronts, the world blurin' past like a reel I couldn't pause. We talked about how much Matt was gonna enjoy class like he always did. Matt always aced all his classes.

"Good thing he learned to work hard," mom would say.

Dad would reassure her, "He'll do just fine…"

I watched the small towns blur by out the window, snaking through a few downtowns that looked eerily familiar. They all had boarded up storefronts and there was always a big box store just beyond the city limits with huge half empty parkin lots with shiny signs by the road. I asked dad if we could stop at a few on the way back if mom was feelin' up to it.

One thing for sure, the Chandler family was on the move, drivin' to Tallahassee to drop Matt off at Florida State University. I was ridin' in the middle of dad's truck, while Matt led the way in his old Ford Falcon, packed with boxes and dreams. Mom sat beside me, her hands folded tight, her breathin' shallow from the cancer that clung to her like a shadow. Dad gripped the wheel, keepin' Matt's taillights in sight as we wound through pine stands and past empty storefronts, the road stretchin' long and quiet. But the silence didn't last, mom's worry spilled out, and dad tried to hold it back, their voices mixin' with the hum of the engine.

"Thomas, he's so young," mom said, her voice thin but sharp, her eyes fixed on Matt's car ahead. "Barely nineteen, drivin' off to a city we ain't never seen. What if he gets lost? Or lonely? Tallahassee's a big place, and he's never been on his own."

Dad glanced at her, his jaw soft but his hands steady on the wheel. "Ruth, Matt's tougher than a pine knot. He's got a good head on him, same one that got him that full ride. He ain't gonna get lost, not with that map you folded up for him. And lonely? Boy'll be too busy to mope."

Mom shook her head, her fingers twistin' the hem of her dress, her voice tremblin' just a touch. "Busy don't mean happy, Thomas. He's leavin' everythin', us and the only home he's known. What if he don't fit in? All them city kids, with their fancy clothes and big talk. Matt's got his heart, but he's still our boy."

Dad chuckled low, tryin' to lighten the air, his eyes flickin' to the road. "Fit in? Ruth, Matt's gonna stand out, and that's better. He's got grit they don't teach in no city school. And experiences? Lord, he's gonna have a time down there. Classes with machines we ain't never heard of, buildin' things that'll last longer than what we got on Main Street. He'll be in labs, tinkerin', makin' friends who think like him."

Mom's lips pressed tight, her gaze still on Matt's car, its bumper glintin' in the sun. "Friends are fine, but it's the rest I worry about. All them new things pullin' him away. He's never had to fend for himself, laundry, meals, nobody to nudge him awake for church."

"Aw, Ruth," Dad said, his voice warm, teasin' now, "you think Matt's gonna starve? Boy's been eatin' at Allied's lunch counter since he started there. And laundry? He'll figure it out when his socks start walkin' on their own. Besides, FSU's crawlin' with girls, smart ones,

188

pretty ones, all studyin' to be teachers or nurses. Matt's gonna have his pick, smilin' at 'em with that Chandler charm. He'll be too busy courtin' to miss church."

Mom's eyes widened, her hand flyin' to her chest, her voice risin' sharp. "Girls? Thomas Chandler, that ain't helpin'! My boy don't need no Tallahassee girls battin' their eyes, distractin' him from his studies! He's there to build bridges, not chase skirts! Oh, Lord, now I'm picturin' him flunkin' out 'cause some city girl's got him all moony!"

Dad laughed, a deep, rare sound, shakin' his head. "Ruth, I'm just sayin' he'll be fine. Girls or no, Matt's got your stubborn streak. He promised you he'd make it, and he will. Ain't no co-ed gonna derail that boy, not when he's got your voice in his head, tellin' him to keep his nose clean."

Mom sighed, her shoulders easin' just a fraction, but her eyes stayed on Matt's car, like she could will him safe. "I just want him to be okay, Thomas," she said, softer now, her voice thick. "He's carryin' so much, our hopes, this family's name. I don't want him to feel alone."

Dad reached over, his hand coverin' hers, his voice low and steady. "He ain't alone, Ruth. He's got us, even three hours away. We raised him right, strong, kind, ready for what's comin'. He'll stumble, sure, but he'll stand up taller for it. And he'll be back, eatin' your cornbread before you know it."

Mom nodded, her hand squeezin' his, a small smile breakin' through. "He better," she said, her voice firmer now. "I ain't raisin' no city boy who forgets his mom's cookin'."

I couldn't help but listen, I tried to stare straight ahead, but the pretended like I wasn't there anyway. Mom's worry, dad's reassurin', their voices wove a net to catch Matt, even as he drove ahead, out of our reach. The road stretched on, pines blurrin' past, and I knew mom's fears wouldn't fade, but dad's faith in Matt, in all of us, was a light we could follow, no matter how far the road took him.

The campus was a sprawl of red-brick buildings and kids haulin' boxes, their voices loud with new beginnings. We helped Matt settle into his dorm, a small room with two beds and a window lookin' out on a courtyard. His roommate, a lanky kid from Miami named Carlos, was already there, unpackin' a radio and lookin' as out of place as we felt. "Hey, uh, you Matt?" he asked, pushin' up his glasses, his voice soft but friendly.

"Yup, that's me," Matt said, droppin' a box on his bed, flashin' a grin. "You're stuck with me, Carlos. Hope you like country music, 'cause I'm bringin' Mill Town with me."

Carlos chuckled, shruggin'. "Man, I'm all about Santana, but I'll deal. Welcome to FSU."

Carlos looked around at the family. Matt introduced all of us. Carlos said it was great to meet all of us. Then he sensed the moment and excused himself lettin' Matt settle in.

Mom moved through the room, her steps slow, her breath shallow but her eyes takin' it all in. She touched the desk, smoothin' her hand over its edge, then folded a towel from Matt's bag, placin' it neat on the bed. "This is a good place, Matt," she said, her voice barely above a whisper, like she was memorizin' the space for him. "You'll do big things here."

Matt nodded, his throat workin', and I saw him blink fast, holdin' back what he didn't wanna show. We unpacked his suitcase, the one we'd pulled from the attic, stuffin' drawers with shirts mom had ironed, her tremblin' hands leavin' love in every crease. Dad set up a lamp, checkin' the bulb twice, his hands steady but his silence loud, like he was buildin' a wall to keep his heart from breakin'.

At the curb, the goodbye came too fast. Mom hugged Matt tight, her thin arms fierce despite her frailty, her face buried in his shoulder. She whispered somethin', her words too soft for me or Dad to hear, but Matt's eyes glistened, and he nodded, holdin' her like he could carry her strength with him. "I love you, mom," he said, his voice crackin', loud enough for us to hear, and she smiled, a flicker of her old fire.

Dad stepped up, clappin' Matt's shoulder firm, his hand lingerin' as he looked him in the eye, one long look that said more than words ever could. "You're ready, son," he said, his voice rough but sure. "Don't look back. Just go."

Matt nodded, his jaw tight, and turned to me last, his grin half-forced but real. I leaned against the truck, tryin' to play it cool, my hands in my pockets. "Don't let 'em fix you too much, city boy," I said, smirkin', but my voice wobbled, betrayin' me. "Tallahassee don't know what it's gettin'."

He laughed, his eyes red but bright, and pulled me into a quick hug, his voice low. "Keep filmin', Bobby. Show 'em Mill Town's still kickin'. I'll be back to hide your camera again before ya know it."

"Fat chance," I shot back, but I held on a second longer, feelin' the gap he was leavin' already widenin'. We stepped back, and Matt stood there, his suitcase at his feet, the dorm loomin' behind him, a new world we couldn't follow him into.

We left him there, waving by the curb, the dorm towerin' behind him. The drive home was next, but this moment, the hugs, the jokes, the tearful grins, felt like a wake for the Matt we knew, the one we were sendin' off to become someone new. Mom's whisper, dad's look, my dumb funeral analogy, they were our way of buryin' the boy and blessin' the man, hopin' he'd carry Mill Town's heart, even as he left it behind.

The drive home was silent for miles, the truck's rumble the only sound, the radio playin' faint country tunes we ignored. Mom sat between Dad and me, her hands folded, her breathin' shallow but steady. We passed a Hamburger King billboard, its red-and-yellow glare mockin' us with promises of *BBQ-grilled flavor*. Mom glanced at it, then away, her voice soft but certain. "He'll be fine," she said, like she was speakin' to herself as much as us. "Matt's gonna shine."

Dad nodded, his eyes fixed on the road, his hands tight on the wheel. "He will," he said, his voice low, a vow as much as a hope.

I leaned against the window, watchin' the treetops blur, their green a smear against the sky. My fingers traced storyboards in my notebook, idle sketches of Matt's dorm, the road, mom's hug, images I'd never film but couldn't shake. The truck carried us back to home, to a house quieter without Matt's laugh, but mom's words echoed, a small light in the dark. He'd be fine, and maybe, just maybe, we'd find a way to be too, holdin' onto the hope he'd taken with him, out there on a path we'd all helped him start down.

Mill Town seemed like it was a different place, its heart reshaped by loss and new arrivals like Hamburger King's neon glow. Home was where the real story unfolded. With the hardware store closed, Dad turned his hands to a new purpose, carin' for mom, whose cancer was stealin' her breath but not her spirit. The farmhouse became their world, a quiet stage for rituals that held us together.

Dad's days revolved around mom now, his old store routine traded for a tighter schedule. Tuesdays meant chemo, the hospital's sterile smell clingin' to their clothes as they returned. He'd fix her soup and saltines afterward, settin' the tray careful by her bed, the radio tuned to gospel in the afternoons, its hymns a soft backdrop to her rest. "You feelin' alright, Ruth?" he'd ask, his voice low, stirrin' her soup like it was a potion to keep her here.

"Better now, Thomas," she'd say, her smile faint but real, sippin' the broth despite its thinness. Some nights, he'd sit by her bedside, readin' from a worn Bible or an old Western, his voice steady even when his eyes weren't. He'd fix her tea, always with too much sugar, the spoon clinkin' loud in the quiet. She never corrected him, just sipped it slow, her hand restin' on his, a silent thank-you for his tryin'.

When dad was too tired, his shoulders slumped from sleepless nights, I'd drive them to the hospital, my hands tight on the wheel. I'd sneak my camera out, filmin' through the rearview mirror, capturin' the small rituals that defined their days, Mom's scarf tied neat, dad's hand on her knee, the way they'd share a look when a gospel song hit just right. "You filmin' us again, Bobby?" Mom asked once, catchin' me, her voice teasin' but warm.

"Just practicin', Ma," I said, smilin' back, but I kept the lens rollin', knowin' these moments were the truest thing I'd ever shoot.

"I'd assume it'd be best if you dropped us at the hospital than an ambulance to take us all, keep your eyes on the road, Bobby." She said with a smile.

School kicked off again in the fall, and football season roared back with it, but the field felt hollow without Matt's name echoin' through the stands. At least now, when the announcer called "Chandler", it was just me they meant, a bittersweet clarity. Matt was the one who'd gotten me into the game, his fire pushin' me to lace up my cleats, but with him off at Florida State, I was playin' for my teammates, my heart only half in it. I kept pushin' through the drills, the tackles, but my mind was elsewhere, on mom, cancer stealin' her strength, and on holdin' things together at home, where every day felt like a battle to keep our family steady.

One night, I joined the guys for a bonfire on River Road, across the river from downtown's dark storefronts, the fire cracklin' under a sky thick with stars. I brought my camera this time, not a six-pack, wantin' to see clear, to hold onto somethin' real. The crowd was lively, people sprawled on blankets, their voices loud with excitement about the town's changes. "Man, Hamburger King's just the start!" Tommy said, tossin' a stick into the flames, his paper crown from the grand openin' still tucked in his pocket. "Heard they're plannin' a mall out by the bypass. We're gonna be like Pensacola soon, y'all!"

"Pensacola?" Lila scoffed, sittin' cross-legged, her sketchbook in her lap. "Tommy, a mall ain't gonna bring back here. It's just more noise, coverin' up what's gone."

I nodded, settin' my camera on a log, filmin' the fire's glow on their faces. "She's right," I said, my voice low. "All this new stuff, drive-thrus, billboards, it's like puttin' a Band-Aid on a broken leg. Ain't fixin' what's hurt."

Some kids shrugged, too caught up in the shine of progress and the haze of beer. "C'mon, Bobby, lighten up," Jenny said, laughin', her cheerleader ponytail bouncin'. "We got Humdingers now! That's somethin'! Beats eatin' at Benny's with the same old jukebox."

"Speak for yourself," I muttered, but I let it go, the fire's heat keepin' us close. Talk turned heavier, the war in Vietnam creepin' into the chatter, rumors of the indoctrination letters hangin' like smoke. "Heard they're pullin' numbers faster now," Carl said, his voice quiet, starin' into the flames. "My cousin got called up last month. Don't know if he's comin' back."

Lila's pencil stopped, her eyes dark. "It's gettin' closer, ain't it? Feels like the world's spinnin' too fast, war, malls, all of it. What's left for us?"

I didn't answer, just zoomed in on the fire, the sparks dancin' like questions we couldn't solve. We stayed late, talkin' 'til the flames died, the future a shadow we couldn't outrun.

Back home, I stood on the porch alone, the light fadin' over the empty road, the hum of cicadas louder than usual, a chorus for a town half-gone. I set my camera on the railin', my finger hoverin' over the record button, but I didn't press it. Some things were too big for film, too raw for a reel. Inside, dad's faint laugh drifted out, answerin' somethin' Ma said, fragile but real, a sound that held more life than all the bonfires on River Road.

I pulled out my notebook, the pencil scratchin' slow as I wrote: "It's strange what passes for strength now. Not marchin'. Not shoutin'. Just... stayin'." The words felt true, like mom's tea, dad's readin', the way we kept goin' despite the losses. I closed the notebook, the crickets singin' on, and stepped inside, where the faint glow of home was enough to keep the dark at bay, at least for tonight.

Chapter 26 - The Concrete Snake
(December 1969)

Thanksgiving 1969 rolled into Mill Town with a cool breeze and a spark of hope we hadn't felt in months. Matt was comin' home from Florida State University, his first break since leavin' for Tallahassee, and mom, feelin' better than she had in a while, was determined to fill the house with her famous oyster chicken gumbo.

The kitchen was alive, the air thick with the briny, spicy scent of gumbo simmerin' on the stove. Mom stood at the counter, her apron tied tight, her hands steadier than they'd been in weeks as she stirred the pot, the roux bubblin' like a promise. "This gumbo's gonna bring Matt right back home," she said, her voice bright, a smile lightin' her face. "Ain't no college cafeteria toppin' my oysters, you hear?"

I grinned, settin' the table, the clink of plates mixin' with her hummin'. "Ma, you're gonna have him ditchin' Tallahassee for good with that gumbo. They don't know gumbo like this over there!"

"Better not!" she teased, wavin' a spoon at me. "I'm countin' on you to keep him fed when I'm restin', Bobby. Don't go burnin' my recipe!"

Dad chuckled from the doorway, his sleeves rolled up, carryin' firewood for later. "Ruth, you got enough spice in there to wake the whole county. Matt'll be smellin' it from the highway."

The front door swung open, and Matt burst in, his duffel slung over his shoulder, his grin wide as the river. "Y'all talkin' about me already?" he hollered, droppin' his bag and pullin' mom into a hug, careful but fierce. "Mom, you look like a million bucks! And that gumbo, Lord, I been dreamin' of it since I crossed into the county line!"

Mom laughed, her eyes shinin' as she held him tight. "Oh, my boy, you're too skinny! Them college folks ain't feedin' you right. Sit down, we're eatin' soon as this pot's ready!"

We gathered 'round the table, the gumbo steamin' in bowls, cornbread golden on the side, and sweet tea clinkin' with ice. Matt dug in, his spoon movin' fast, his voice bubblin' as he told us about school. "Y'all, FSU's wild!" he said, wipin' his mouth, his eyes sparklin'. "My engineerin' classes are tough, but the labs are on a whole nother level. We're buildin' models of bridges, testin' 'em till they snap! And my friends, there's Carlos, my roommate, y'all met him, he plays guitar like nobody's business, and Jenny, she's studyin' physics, smart as a whip. We stay up late arguin' about designs, eatin' pizza at two a.m.!"

"Pizza at two a.m.?" I said, leanin' back, grinnin'. "Matt, you're livin' like a rock star! Next you'll be tellin' us you're in a band, serenadin' all them Tallahassee girls."

He laughed, pointin' his spoon at me. "Don't tempt me, Bobby! I'm keepin' it to bridges for now, but the girls? Let's just say I ain't lonely. They like a country boy with a wrench and a smile."

Dad raised an eyebrow, a rare smirk tuggin' at his lips. "You focus on them bridges, son. Girls'll wait. But sounds like you're fittin' in just fine."

"More than fittin' in, dad!" Matt said, his voice loud with excitement. "I'm learnin' stuff that's gonna change things. Oh, and get this, they're buildin' a new interstate, comin' this way soon. I saw the plans in class, all these big roads linkin' towns like ours to the cities. Mill Town's gonna be on the map, y'all!"

"An interstate?" Ma said, her spoon pausin', her smile soft but curious. "Well, ain't that somethin'? Maybe it'll bring some life back to Main Street."

"Or more Hamburger Kings," I muttered, half-jokin', but I winked at Matt, keepin' it light. "You gonna design that road, big shot? Make sure it don't pave over mom's garden?"

"Not a chance!" Matt shot back, laughin'. "I'm plannin' a detour just for her tomatoes. But for real, Bobby, it's gonna be big, trucks, cars, folks passin' through. We ain't done yet!"

We ate and talked, the gumbo warm in our bellies, Matt's stories fillin' the room like music. Mom's laughter was a gift, her strength a miracle for the day, and dad's quiet nods held pride deeper than words. "This is what I needed," Matt said, leanin' back, his bowl empty. "Y'all, this gumbo, this table, it's home. I'm comin' back every chance I get."

"You better," mom said, her voice firm but warm, reachin' for his hand. "This table's waitin' for you, Matt. Always will be."

I looked around, the kitchen glowin' with the light of us together, and felt the ache of the past year ease, just a little. Matt's college life, his friends, the interstate comin', it was a new world, loud and bright, and for one night, with mom's gumbo and our laughter, it felt like the town could hold its own, a home worth comin' back to, no matter how far the road led.

It was a great Thanksgiving, especially havin' the whole family together. Mom has had her good days and bad, I'm just glad that she had a string of good one's while Matt was here.

The morning Matt had to get back to college I was standing on the porch filming, Dad was already out lookin at Matt's falcon with the hood raised checkin the oil. "Matt, you're a quart low, can you go get one from the shed?" he yelled out.

"Yes sir!" Matt started back to the shed when half way there he stopped cold in his tracks. He stooped over and pecked at the ground with his fingers. I zoomed in.

I yelled over "Whatcha find?"

Matt pulled up an ole BB case we must have dropped on our way out camping years ago. The memories must have come flooding back. Matt took a slow distant look around like he was comparing the pictures in his mind, to what he saw in front of him. Like his mind was coming to terms that time is pluggin along, sometimes it's too slow to notice, but then too fast when you do.

"He replied back, "nothin, just an ole BB case," but then I saw him stuff it in his pocket.

Matt promised to be back for Christmas if he could, we all understood. We all said our goodbyes and waved until he was out of sight. We all walked back inside. The house went quiet again.

It was early spring 1970, and the town was stirrin' under a new kind of change, one that didn't care about our shuttered stores or mom's fight with cancer. I was always filmin' the town's shift as the world pushed in. Chandler Hardware was a memory, and Hamburger King's neon glow was old news, but somethin' bigger was brewin', a new interstate, its shadow creepin' closer, promisin' progress but leavin' us wonderin' what it'd cost.

South of town, survey stakes sprouted like weeds in the farmland, their neon ribbons flappin' in the breeze, each one tagged with numbers like markers for a grave. I biked out one mornin', my camera hummin', filmin' the brush bein' cleared, slow-movin' excavators growlin' through fields that once held picnics and hay bales, their blades slicin' paths where we used to catch redfish down by the bay. The footage was stark, the green torn open, dust risin' like smoke from a wound. Old Man Tucker, a farmer whose land bordered the site, leaned on his fence, watchin' the machines with eyes like storm clouds.

"What you filmin', Bobby?" he asked, his voice rough, spittin' tobacco into the dirt.

"The change, Mr. Tucker," I said, zoomin' in on a stake, its ribbon a slash of pink against the brown. "They're callin' it progress."

He snorted, his hat low over his brow. "Progress? It's a snake through the heart of the state, boy. And it's hungry. Gonna eat these fields, our history, and spit out asphalt. You mark my words."

I nodded, my throat tight, lettin' the camera linger on the excavator's claw, Tucker's words echoin' as word spread through town: "It's the new interstate. Runnin' clean from Mobile to Jacksonville." The news was everywhere, in Benny's Diner, at the gas station, whispered like a secret no one could keep.

A week later, Mayor Heartwell called a public meetin' at the town hall, the room packed with farmers, shopkeepers, and kids like me, all cranin' to see what was comin'. Large maps hung at the front, bold red lines tracin' the interstate's path, cuttin' through fields and skirtin' town like a river rerouted. Heartwell stood tall, his tie loose, his voice boomin' with a salesman's grin. "Folks, this is our future!" he said, slappin' a map. "The interstate's gonna bring life back here, motorists, money, maybe even a motel or two!"

A Department of Transportation rep, a slick fella in a gray suit, stepped up, his pointer tappin' the map like a drum. "Jobs, folks!" he said, his voice loud, city-smooth. "Construction crews, gas stations, diners to feed 'em all. Ease of travel, modernization, y'all are gonna be a hub, not a dot on the map!"

One council member, Mrs. Ellis, clapped her hands, her eyes bright. "This could put us back on the map, Mayor!" she said, her voice high with hope. "Folks'll stop here, spend here. We'll be more than just a bypass!"

I stood at the back, my camera filming with my eyes sharp, noticin' what they didn't say. The map's red line curved around the town, not through it, leavin' Main Street, already dark with empty stores, out of the picture. No one mentioned it, their voices too caught up in promises of jobs and travelers. I shifted, my boots scuffin' the floor, feelin' the omission like a stone in my gut.

Heartwell kept goin', his hands wavin' like he was conductin' an orchestra. "Think of the motorists, folks! Hundreds, thousands, drivin' through, needin' gas, food, a place to stretch their legs. We're gonna be a destination, not a detour!"

"Destination for what?" muttered Old Man Tucker, sittin' near me, his arms crossed. "More Hamburger Kings? They ain't stoppin' for our ghosts."

I nodded, leanin' close. "They're talkin' like Main Street don't exist no more, Mr. Tucker. Like it's already gone."

He grunted, his eyes on the map. "It is, boy. They're just drawin' the coffin now."

Mr. Radcliffe raised a hand, his voice cuttin' through the chatter like a blade. "Mayor, if this new off-ramp's two miles south," he said, squintin' at the map, "why would anyone stop here? They'll zip right by, headin' to Pensacola or Tallahassee. We ain't got no fancy signs to pull 'em in."

The room went quiet, heads noddin' as his words sank in. A local business owner, Mrs. Perry, who ran the flower shop next to Benny's Diner, stood up, her hands wringin' her scarf. "He's right," she said, her voice shakin' but firm. "We're not a destination, never were. We were a pass-through, folks stopped for gas, coffee, a wrench. What happens when they don't gotta pass through anymore? My shop's already hurtin'. This interstate's gonna bury us."

The Department of Transportation rep, still in his slick gray suit, flashed a big smile, the kind that showed every tooth but don't reach the eyes. "Progress doesn't always feel like progress at first," he said, his voice smooth as oil, dodgin' their fears like a politician. "Give it time, folks. The jobs, the travelers, they'll come. You'll see."

The crowd murmured, some noddin', others frownin', but his answer felt like a shrug, leavin' Radcliffe and Perry to sit down, their questions hangin' unanswered. I caught Lila's eye across the room, her sketchbook tucked under her arm, her face set hard. Later, as we walked out into the cool night, she muttered, "Liar. Main Street, our shops, us, they're pavin' it all under progress."

Those that didn't have a stake in the town were actually happy that a new inter

I nodded, my camera bag heavy on my shoulder, feelin' the truth in her words. The interstate was comin', but Radcliffe's question, Perry's fear, and Lila's sharp insight lingered, like dust that wouldn't settle, warnin' us that this town's heart might not survive the map's bold red lines.

The meetin' ended with claps and chatter, folks excited about jobs and modernization, but I left quiet, my camera heavy in my bag. The interstate was comin', a snake through the state, and while Heartwell saw dollar signs, I saw fields torn up, Main Street forgotten, and a town changin' faster than my lens could catch. I biked home, Tucker's words in my head, knowin' I'd film it all, the stakes, the maps, the hunger, 'cause even if the interstate put us on the map, it was leavin' behind the community we'd fought to keep.

The town was bracin' for a change that felt more like a wound than a win. The air hummed with the rumble of machines and the weight of what was bein' lost. Bulldozers roared south of town, their engines a low growl as they tore the earth into segments, leavin' scars where wildflowers used to sway. Rebar rose from the red clay like bones, the skeleton of an overpass takin' shape in the haze. I filmed it one mornin', standin' at the edge of a field, the lens catchin' the churned dirt and the machines' relentless push. The local feed store, just down the road, closed two days early, its owner, Mr. Gibbs, loadin' his last sacks of grain into a truck. "I'm sellin' out," he told me, wipin' sweat from his brow, his voice flat. "Ain't waitin' for the dust to settle. This road's gonna choke what's left of us."

I nodded, my camera hummin', feelin' his words settle heavy. Later, I drove to an old scenic overlook on Pine Hill, a spot that once showed the town's sprawl, Main Street's lights, the river's curve. Now, the view ended at a concrete divider, gray and final, blockin' the horizon like a slammed door. I set up my camera, capturin' a slow pan of the new overpass risin' in the distance, its shadow splittin' the sky in half, a monument to a future that didn't include us.

The town's mood shifted with the construction, emotions runnin' like undercurrents beneath the noise. At dusk, dad walked the length of Main Street, his boots scuffin' the cracked sidewalk, stoppin' at the corner to stare toward the glow of work lights where the interstate was takin' shape. He didn't say nothin', just stood there, hands in his pockets, his face carved with a grief I couldn't film.

At dinner, mom prayed aloud, her voice soft but clear, her hands clasped tight. "Lord, give us guidance in a time of vanishin'," she said, her eyes closed, the words a plea for the town, for her, for us. "Help us hold fast to what matters." dad reached for her hand, his fingers steady, and I bowed my head, feelin' the weight of her prayer like a stone.

The next day at school I was talking with Lila about the interstate and what's been happening. She told me she overheard a woman at the post office, her voice tired but sharp: "I hate goin' to Allied General, but what choice do we have? Benny's is half-empty, and I can't afford to wait." The words stuck with Lila, her sketchbook full of drawings of Main Street's dark windows, like she was tryin' to save it on paper.

In Benny's Diner, conversations turned to comparisons, not connection, folks sizin' up Allied's prices against the few local shops left, their voices low, resigned. "Allied's got deals, but it ain't quite the same," one man said, stirrin' his coffee. Another laughed, bitter but tryin' to lighten it. "Maybe we can open a gas station at the ramp, call it 'Last Chance.' Get 'em to stop before they zoom past."

Mom, practical as ever, sat at the kitchen table one night, sighin' as she checked Allied's circulars, circlin' items with a pencil, canned goods, soap, things we needed, not wanted. "Used to shop with pride," she muttered, her voice low, "now it's just numbers." I watched, my heart tight, knowin' she was fightin' to keep us afloat, even as the town sank.

Mom sat at the kitchen table, her hands wrapped around a mug of tea, her voice tinged with a mix of nostalgia and frustration as she spoke. "When people needed help before, they used to barter, trade work, or whatever they had, eggs, a day's labor, a quilt stitched by hand. Neighbors leaned on each other, fixed each other's fences, shared what little they had. Now?" She shook her head, her eyes flickin' to the window, where the quiet streets lay under the glow of a new billboard. "Now they just stick their hand out to the government, waitin' for a check like it's owed 'em." Dad, standin' by the sink, his sleeves rolled up from washin' dishes, grunted in agreement, his jaw set hard. "Ain't no government gonna provide for my family while I'm still standin'," he said, his voice low but fierce, the words a vow he'd carved into his bones. "This is my family, my responsibility, not some fella in a suit decidin' what we're worth. Long as I got breath, I'll carry us, no handouts needed." His hands stilled in the soapy water, and mom's gaze softened, knowin' his pride was both their strength and their burden in a town where bartering was fadin' and government aid was becomin' the new neighbor nobody wanted to need.

I sketched a new film segment in my notebook, the title sharp: *How to Slowly Poison a Town... Just Coat It with Sugar.* The interstate, Allied, Hamburger King, it was all sweet promises over a bitter truth, and I wanted my lens to show it.

One evenin', Lila and I climbed the water tower at the edge of town, my camera slung over my shoulder, the metal rungs cold under my hands. From up high, I filmed a bird's-eye shot of the old highway, quiet and narrow, windin' through fields like a forgotten path. In the distance, the interstate snaked through the woods, wide and gleamin', its asphalt never curvin' close enough to touch town. My narration, scribbled later, came slow: "The road, it used to bring people here.

Now it carries them around us, like a stream findin' a faster route. And the banks are startin' to dry."

Even before the interstate was done, a billboard went up near the exit site, its words bold against the dusk: *Exit Now! Just 2 miles, Turn Left for Allied General, Turn Right for the King!* I filmed it, the sign's glare mockin' the town's quiet, a beacon for a world that didn't need us. The camera hummed, holdin' the truth, our town was bein' bypassed, its heart left to beat alone, while the interstate roared on, hungry and unyielding.

Chapter 27 - Homecoming
(Summer of 1970)

The Summer of 1970 was a golden haze in Mill Town, a fleeting season of long days and warm nights before the world pushed us into adulthood. I was eighteen, mom's cancer treatments kept her fightin', dad's care for her a quiet strength, and the interstate's rumble was a reminder of change that seemed to be comin' too fast. But for at least one afternoon, the last summer before graduation felt like a gift, a chance to hold onto the way things are with my friends, Eric and Lila, in a beat-up truck and a cloud of dust.

I was on the porch, fiddlin' with my camera lens, when I heard the rumble of a familiar engine, a deep growl that could only be Eric's dad's old green Ford. It rolled into the driveway, kickin' up gravel, Eric behind the wheel, his elbow hangin' out the window like he was born to drive. "Yo, Chandler!" he hollered, his grin wide, sunglasses perched on his nose. "Quit polishin' that camera and get your butt in here! We're goin' on a mission, man!"

Lila leaned over from the passenger seat, barefoot, her sketchbook open in her lap, her hair tied back with a faded red ribbon that fluttered in the breeze. She waved, her smile bright but mischievous. "C'mon, Bobby, don't leave me alone with this gearhead!" she called, holdin' up her pencil like a sword. "He's already tried singin' Johnny Cash, and my ears are bleedin'!"

I laughed, grabbin' my camera and a bag, my boots hittin' the steps as I ran out, the summer heat kissin' my skin. "Y'all ain't leavin' without me!" I shouted, 'move-over' I said slidin' into the truck's benchseat, the vinyl hot and sticky. "But if Eric's singin', I'm filmin' it for blackmail, Lila!"

"Deal!" she said, her laugh ringin' like a bell. Eric gunned the engine, the Ford lurchin' forward, and we bounced down the old dirt trail toward Coldwater Creek, no need to ask where we were headed. It was our spot, the one we'd claimed since we were kids, swimmin' holes, bonfires, secrets, all shared under the stars.

As we rattled along, the windows down, dust swirlin' behind us, we traded stories and dumb jokes, the kind that only make sense when you're young and free. "Remember when we stole that canoe from Old Man Tucker?" Eric said, glancin' at me in the rearview, his voice loud over the engine. "Thought we were pirates till it sank in the creek! Swore he'd tan our hides!"

"Yeah, and you cried like a baby when we had to swim back through the swamp!" Lila shot back, sketchin' a quick doodle of a soggy Eric, holdin' it up for me to see. "Look, Bobby, it's Captain Sob-a-Lot!"

I cracked up, leanin' forward, my camera bouncin' on my knee. "Man, I shoulda filmed that! Coulda called it *Pirates of the Mud Puddle*! Eric, you still owe me for not rattin' you out!"

"Owes me too!" Lila said, nudgin' him, her ribbon slippin' loose. "I had to bribe Tucker with my mom's cornbread to keep him quiet!"

Eric laughed, swervin' just enough to make us yelp, his grin wicked. "Y'all are brutal! But fine, today's my treat, soda and chips at the creek, and I ain't singin' no more, so quit your whinin'!"

We kept goin', the trail windin' through pines, the radio blastin' Creedence Clearwater, our voices overlappin' with stories of summers past, sneakin' into the drive-in, racin' bikes down Main Street, Lila's first sketch of the river that won her a ribbon at the fair. The creek came into view, its water sparklin' under the sun, as we all seemed to exhale at the same time.

We parked under the shade of a the big juniper, the creek windin' the same as ever, its water glistenin' like a promise, though the trees were taller now, their branches stretchin' farther, like they were reachin' for somethin' just outta grasp. Our shoes were already off as we trudged to the sandbar, the sand warm under our toes, dragonflies buzzin' like summer prayers. It was familiar, same current, same hum of cicadas, but distant, too, like we were relivin' a memory on purpose, knowin' it'd never feel quite the same. Not a single sound of the world beyond.

Lila stopped short, her bare feet sinkin' in the sand, her eyes lockin' on a cypress leanin' over the water. "Holy cow, y'all, look!" she said, pointin' at a carving etched deep in the bark, four initials, E, L, B, M, wrapped in a heart with a crooked arrow, cut with Eric's pocketknife when we were seven.

"We were such dorks!" she laughed, tracin' the lines, her ribbon slippin' loose. "Thought we'd be pirates forever, rulin' this creek!"

Eric snorted, droppin' his shoes and joggin' over, his sunglasses slidin' down his nose. "Pirates? Lila, you cried when we got stuck in the mud!" he said, dodgin' her playful swat. "But damn, that's our mark, ain't it? Lil' warn but still holdin' up, like us!"

I grinned, liftin' my camera to film the carving, the lens catchin' the heart's wobbly edge. "Y'all were gonna get married, right?" I teased, zoomin' in on Lila's mock glare. "Eric and Lila, king and queen of Coldwater Creek, livin' off fish and bad ideas!"

"Shut it, Bobby!" Lila said, chuckin' a pebble at me, her laugh bright. "You were the one writin' love poems to Jenny in your notebook, don't lie!"

"Poems? Man, I was writin' scripts for my Oscar speech!" I shot back, duckin' her next throw, the sandbar alive with our noise. But the carving sobered me, its initials a reminder of kids who didn't know about wars or shuttered stores. "Feels like a lifetime ago," I said, quieter, the camera lowerin'. "You think we'll come back here, after… everythin'?"

Eric didn't answer right away, his grin fadin' as he turned to a tree stump nearby, the one we'd used as a hideout for our "survival supplies" when we were kids. "Hold that thought, Bobby," he said, droppin' to his knees and diggin' in the dirt, his hands flingin' sand like a dog after a bone. "If this is still here, we're golden!"

Lila raised an eyebrow, leanin' against the cypress, her sketchbook tucked under her arm. "Eric, you're chasin' ghosts," she said, but her eyes sparkled, watchin' him. "That stash is long gone, probably eaten by squirrels!"

"No faith, woman!" Eric hollered, his voice muffled as he dug deeper, then let out a whoop that echoed across the creek. "Ha! Got it!" He held up a half-rusted can of beans, its label faded but intact, glintin' in the sun like buried treasure. We howled with laughter, collapsin' onto the sand, our voices bouncin' off the water.

"I told y'all I buried it deep!" Eric crowed, wavin' the can like a trophy, his grin wide as the creek. "This is history, right here! Survivor beans, class of '71!"

"You nearly buried it in the water table, you nut!" Lila said, snatchin' the can, inspectin' it like a scientist. "Look at this rust! We'd die eatin' this now. Some survival plan, Captain Genius!"

I filmed it all, the camera shakin' as I laughed, zoomin' in on Eric's proud strut and Lila's eye-roll. "This is goin' in the sequel," I said, wipin' my eyes. *Mill Town Treasure: The Great Bean Heist*! Y'all are gonna make me famous!"

"Famous for filmin' idiots," Lila teased, tossin' the can back to Eric, but her smile softened, her voice droppin'. "This place, though... it's still ours, right? Even with the interstate, the war, all of it waitin'?"

Eric sat on the stump, the can in his hands, his sunglasses pushed up, his voice serious for once. "Yeah, it's ours," he said, lookin' at the creek, the carving, us. "It's not changin, we sure are. Mill's hirin', but I hear the draft's gettin' closer. Ain't sure what's next."

I lowered the camera, my heart tight, the war's shadow creepin' in even here. "We got this summer," I said, forcin' a grin. "Let's make it count, beans, bad jokes, all of it. Deal?"

"Deal," Lila said, her hand out, and Eric slapped it, then mine, our laughter risin' again, pushin' back the heavy stuff. We stayed on the sandbar till the sun dipped, tradin' stories, skippin' rocks, the rusted can our trophy for one last summer, holdin' onto the creek, the heart, and each other, before the world grew up and took us with it.

"Too bad Matt's workin…as usual…he's gonna miss this." I said quietly.

On the sandbar, we stretched out, gazin' up at the tree canopy, and talked of tomorrows, our voices soft with the choices of what was comin'. We spread a worn blanket on the sand, the creek's murmur mixin' with the buzz of dragonflies, the tree branches above weavin' a green roof against the sky. We lay back, shoulder to shoulder eating snacks, like we had a hundred times as kids, our shoes piled nearby, the air warm and heavy with summer's end. The canopy swayed, light dappled through, and for a moment, it was just us, the creek, and the future hangin' like a question nobody wanted to ask first.

Eric broke the silence, his hands behind his head, his voice easy but thoughtful. "I'm stayin' right here," he said, starin' up at the leaves. "Gonna take Dad's truck, maybe start a delivery service or an odd-jobs business. A man with a truck can make somethin' happen, y'know? Haul lumber, fix fences, whatever folks need. Ain't glamorous, but it'll be mine."

I turned my head, the sand cool against my cheek, smilin' faint. "You, a businessman? Eric, you couldn't even sell that canoe we sank!" I teased, but my voice softened. "Sounds solid, though. You'll be runnin' this town while the rest of us are still figurin' it out."

He chuckled, nudgin' my arm. "Damn right, Bobby. You'll be filmin' my empire one day, callin' me 'sir'! But for real… I can't leave. This place is home, busted or not. What about you, Lila? You ditchin' us for some fancy city?"

Lila lay on her side, her sketchbook open but untouched, her ribbon loose in her hair. She sighed, her voice dreamy but firm. "Art school," she said, tracin' a finger through the sand. "Maybe Atlanta, maybe somewhere bigger. I wanna study paintin', learn how to make light move on a canvas. After that? Could teach, could just keep drawin'. Don't care, long as I'm makin' somethin' that feels true." She paused, her eyes on the canopy, reflective. "This town taught me to see beauty in the broken stuff. I'm takin' that with me."

I nodded, her words hittin' deep, thinkin' of my film, the way I'd tried to capture that same beauty in Main Street's cracks. "You're gonna kill it, Lila," I said, my voice low. "Your sketches already make this place look like a masterpiece. Ain't no art school ready for you."

She smiled, but her eyes turned to me, searchin'. "What about you, Bobby? You're always filmin' everybody else's story, what's yours? What's next?"

I went quiet, my hands foldin' over my chest, the sky above feelin' too big, too open. The question had been gnawin' at me, but I hadn't faced it till now. "I got no idea," I admitted, my voice barely above the creek's ripple. "Feels like I've been recordin' everybody else's story, mom's fight, dad's store, Miss Elma's books, and forgot to figure out my own. The films… it's all about the past, but what future does that leave for me? Just a kid with a camera and no map."

The air stilled, Eric's usual jokes absent, Lila's hand findin' mine, her squeeze warm and steady. "That *is* your story, Bobby," she said, her voice soft but sure, like she saw somethin' I didn't. "You're the one holdin' the lens, showin' us what matters. Every frame you shoot, that's you figurin' it out. You don't need a map, you're makin' one, frame by frame."

211

Eric nodded, his voice quieter than usual, reflective. "She's right, man. You're tellin' the truth nobody else sees. Those films of yours? It's not just the town's heart, it's yours, too. Ain't many folks can do that. Me, I got a truck. Lila's got her pencils. You? You got a whole damn world in your mind that somehow you manage to show us through that camera."

I swallowed, my throat tight, their words settlin' like stones in a river, heavy but right. "Y'all make it sound easy," I said, a half-laugh escapin'. "But… yeah, maybe you're right. Maybe I'm findin' my way, even if it's just filmin' the mess we're in."

"Mess is where the good stuff hides," Lila said, her smile warm, squeezin' my hand again before lettin' go. "Keep filmin', Bobby. We're all waitin' to see what you make next."

We lay there, the canopy swayin', the creek singin' soft, talkin' of tomorrows, Eric's truck, Lila's art, my uncertain lens. The war loomed, the interstate grew, but for now, we were just three kids on a blanket, holdin' onto the last summer, reflectin' on paths we couldn't see but were startin' to choose, our voices weavin' a promise to carry with us, no matter where the road led.

As the sun sank, the creek held us close, its waters glowin' with the last light of a season we'd never get back, and we said goodbye to the sandbar, knowin' we were leavin' more than just a place.

The sun dipped behind the pines, paintin' the sky in streaks of orange and pink, shadows stretchin' long across the sandbar like fingers reachin' for the water. We stood by the old cypress, its heart-carved initials, E, L, B, M, worn but clear, our arms slung around each other, older now but still tethered by the creek, the tree, the years of secrets and dumb jokes. The air was coolin', the dragonflies had gone quiet and the skeeters were movin' in. Eric's odd jobs, Lila's art school, my uncertain future, hung soft but real.

Eric broke the silence, his smirk flashin' as he picked up the half-rusted can of beans we'd dug up, holdin' it like a trophy one last time. "Well, ol' friend," he said, tossin' it in his hand, "you survived the squirrels, but it's time to retire." He put it back in the hole and covered it up, "My you rust in pieces…time to leave some things behind, y'all."

Lila laughed, her ribbon slippin' loose, her arm tight around my shoulder. "Eric, you're gonna pollute the whole creek with your bad ideas!" she teased, but her voice softened, her eyes on the ripples. "Still… feels right, lettin' go a little. We're not those kids buryin' snacks anymore, are we?"

"Nope," I said, my voice low, feelin' the ache of it, the way the sandbar seemed smaller now, the trees taller, like they'd outgrown us or we'd outgrown it. "But this place, it's us, always will be. War, college, work, whatever comes, this is ours." I pulled my camera from my bag, the weight familiar, steady. "Hold still, y'all," I said, steppin' back balancing the camera on the tree stump, framin' them against the creek, the sunlight catchin' Lila's hair, Eric's grin, the water glowin' gold behind 'em. I moved into frame, looked at them and said, "Just in case we forget what real looks like."

Eric struck a pose, flexin' like a bodybuilder, his sunglasses crooked. "Make me look like a movie star, Bobby!" he hollered, laughin' as Lila shoved him, her smile wide but her eyes wet. "You're gonna break his camera, you goof!" she said, then turned to me, her voice quieter. "Get it right, Bobby. This is… this is home."

We may be moving on, but that moment was frozen in time, Lila's ribbon, Eric's smirk, the creek's shimmer, the cypress standin' watch. "I think I got it," I said, my throat tight, runnin' back to the camera. "Ain't forgettin' this, not ever."

We stood there a moment longer, arms linked, the sun gone now, the sky fadin' to purple, the creek's murmur a soft goodbye. Eric's kick, Lila's laugh, my picture, they were our way of markin' the end, of holdin' onto the sandbar before we stepped into the world waitin' beyond the pines. Eric slapped his ear tryin' to swat a skeeter, "time to go, while we still have some blood left." We grabbed our shoes, the blanket, and headed to the truck, our shadows mergin' into one, tethered still, ready or not for whatever came next, but carryin' the creek's light with us, always.

This was our last summer, one final run before graduation, before Eric's job at the mill, Lila's art school dreams, my own uncertain path. We didn't talk about the war, the interstate, or mom's sickness, not today. Instead, we laughed, splashed, traded dumb jokes, the truck's engine coolin' in the shade, holdin' onto what we had for one more golden day, knowin' the world was growin' up without askin', but not quite ready to let us go.

Chapter 28 - My Senior Year
(Fall 1970)

School was back, and bein' seniors felt like standin' on a ledge, excitin', scary, and heavy with the sense that nothin' would be the same. The first day back, the school bell clanged loud and hollow, echoin' through the worn halls of Mill Town High, its sound sharper than I remembered. We were seniors now, walkin' paths we'd known since freshman year, but the corridors felt different, fewer kids, more silence, like the town's fade had crept into the walls. Lockers still slammed, sneakers squeaked, but the chatter was quieter, new faces looked younger, as if we all sensed the clock tickin' down. I adjusted my camera, slung across my chest, my eyes already huntin' for what the year might try to hide, a laugh in the courtyard, a teacher's tired smile, a story worth filmin'.

Lila was there before homeroom, leanin' against a locker, her sketchpad already open, her pencil dancin' across the page. She was drawin' the shadows cast through the library's cracked windows, their jagged lines spillin' like ink. "Mornin', Bobby," she said, not lookin' up, her ribbon tied loose in her hair. "These shadows got more to say than half our teachers. You filmin' this dump yet?"

I grinned, liftin' my camera, pretendin' to frame her. "Dump? Lila, I'm makin' you the star of *Senior Year Saga*!" I said, zoomin' in on her smirk. "But yeah, I'm lookin'. This place feels… empty, don't it? Like it's holdin' its breath."

She nodded, her pencil pausin'. "Yeah. Fewer faces, more ghosts. But we're here, so let's make it count." Her voice was firm, her eyes flickin' to me, a spark of the creek's summer promise in 'em.

Eric strutted in then, his fresh buzz cut gleamin' under the hall lights, his usual grin plastered wide, actin' like nothin' ever changed. "Ladies and gentlemen, your king has arrived!" he hollered, spinnin' his backpack like a showman, dodgin' a freshman who scurried past. "Senior year, baby! We own this joint, Bobby, you filmin' my grand entrance or what?"

I laughed, swingin' the camera his way, catchin' his mock salute. "Eric, you're a walkin' disaster reel!" I said, but my grin faded a touch, knowin' we all felt it, the war's shadow, the town's shrinkin', the way his strut hid a worry we didn't name. "You plannin' to rule the school or just the cafeteria line?"

"Cafeteria first, then the world!" he shot back, slingin' an arm around Lila, who shoved him off, laughin'. "Get off, you oaf!" she said, wavin' her sketchpad. "I'm drawin' art, not your ego!" But her smile was real, and Eric's laugh bounced off the lockers, a sound that warmed the hollow halls.

We headed to class, the three of us fallin' into step, Lila's pencil scratchin', Eric's jokes flyin', my camera ready for whatever this year would show, new faces, old wounds, or maybe just the way the light hit the cracked windows. Senior year was here.

Football called me back for one last season, a pull I couldn't quite shake, though its hold on me was fadin', leavin' me torn between the game I'd loved and the new path I was findin'.

Before school started, Coach pulled me aside in the gym, his clipboard tucked under his arm, his eyes squintin' like he could see right through me.

"Chandler, you're comin' back for your last season, right?" he asked, his voice gruff but warm. "Team needs you, son." I shifted, my feet scrapin' the floor, my heart caught between the field and everythin' else, mom, the film club, the war's shadow.

"I ain't sure, Coach," I said, rubbin' my neck. "Got a lot goin' on."

He nodded, clappin' my shoulder. "Pads are waitin' in the locker room anyway. You know where to find 'em."

I showed up, couldn't help it. The locker room hit me like a memory, the smell of sweat, athletic tape, and that sour dirty sock mildew clingin' to the air, a mix that never left, no matter how much you scrubbed. Part of me felt like I belonged there, pullin' on my jersey, lacin' up cleats, the routine as familiar as breathin'. My name, "Chandler," was stitched on the back, no longer Matt's shadow but mine alone, and it stirred somethin', pride, maybe, or just the ghost of who I'd been when football was everythin'.

Under those Friday night lights, with cleats diggin' into the sod and my name echoin' from the stands, "Chandler, get-em!", I remembered how it used to matter.

The crowd's roar, the snap of the ball, the thud of a tackle, it was now the town's heartbeat, a place where we were kings, untouchable, even as the war took boys like Peter Jennings. I ran hard, my breath puffin' in the cool air, but my mind drifted, to mom's tired smile, dad's quiet readin' at her bedside, the film club where my camera felt more like home. The game was still magic, but it didn't feel like it was mine anymore, not fully.

When the season ended, a close loss in the final game under a sky full of stars, I walked off the field, the cheers fadin', my chest tight with a strange ache. That same evening, I turned in my pads, stackin' 'em in the locker room like I had seen seniors do before me. It was now my turn, my hands lingerin' on the worn leather, scuffed from years of hits.

"You ready, Bobby?" Coach asked, leanin' in the doorway, his voice soft.

I nodded, swallowin' hard. "Yeah, Coach. It's time." Sadness hit me, sharp and real, football had been Matt's gift to me, a piece of us I'd carry with me, but as I walked out, I felt almost thankful, like I was settin' down somethin' that'd grown too heavy, makin' room for the stories I'd tell through my lens.

I left the locker room, the mildew smell fadin' behind me, the pads no longer mine. Senior year stretched ahead, and though the lights would shine again, I was ready to chase a different kind of glow, one frame at a time.

Nothin' hit harder than the three funerals that fall, boys barely older than us, seniors from recent years, comin' home from Vietnam in flag-wrapped boxes, leavin' our town to mourn under gray skies.

The first was Tommy Reed, class of '69, a wide receiver with a laugh that filled the locker room. Then Carl Hayes, '67, who'd sung in the choir, his voice deep enough to rattle the pews. Last was Stuart Tate's brother, Eddie, 68' just twenty, a lineman who'd enlisted to "choose his way." Each funeral packed First Baptist, the church bells tollin' sharp, their sound cuttin' through the crisp air like a cry. Lila, Eric, and I stood together, our Sunday shirts stiff, collars tight, feelin' like intruders in a grief too big for us. We watched classmates and cousins carry caskets, their faces pale, shoulders bent under a weight they didn't deserve, boys turned pallbearers too soon.

At Carl's service, Lila held my hand, her grip strong but tremblin', her ribbon tied neat but her eyes wet.

"This ain't fair, Bobby," she whispered, her voice breakin' as the honor guard folded the flag, their movements sharp, final. "He was s'posed to come back, sing at the fair, not... this."

I squeezed her hand, my throat too tight to answer, the crack of the rifle salute makin' us flinch.

Eric stood on my other side, silent, his usual grin gone, wipin' his eyes with his sleeve. He looked up at the sky, gray and heavy, like it might answer why Eddie, why Carl, why any of 'em. "Ain't right," he muttered after, his voice rough, barely audible over the bugle's taps. "Just… ain't right."

I brought my camera, couldn't help it, its weight a reflex. I filmed the church bells swayin', their clangs echoin' over the crowd; the folded flags, crisp against the caskets; the quiet sobs ripplin' through the pews, a sound that hurt worse than silence. But I didn't film the faces, Tommy's mom collapsin' into her sister's arms, Carl's little brother starin' blank at the altar, Jimmy's red eyes as he carried Eddie's casket. Some moments ain't meant for reels, too sacred, too heavy for a lens to hold. I lowered the camera, lettin' it hang, my hands shakin' as I stood with Lila and Eric, our shoulders touchin', a silent pact to carry this grief together.

After the funerals, we'd walk to the creek or Benny's, not sayin' much, just sittin' close, Lila's sketchbook still, Eric's jokes absent. The war was for us even more real now, not just locker room letters or Miss Hollis's maps, but names we knew, boys who'd run the same fields, laughed in the same halls. Senior year pressed on, but those funerals, Tommy, Carl, Eddie, stayed with us, a reminder of what waited beyond the town's border in a few months time, and a call to hold tighter to the time we had.

The film club became my refuge, a place where I could shape my story to how I saw it, and with Lila and Eric by my side, I found a new rhythm, filmin' the change, the loss, and the breath still left in our quiet streets. The film club room became my second home, its darkroom hummin' with chemicals and the projector's flicker lightin' up my evenings after school. The air smelled of developer and dust, the walls lined with old reels and posters of movies we'd never make. I'd stay late, splicin' footage or screenin' rough cuts, the click of the projector a heartbeat I could count on. Mr. Tolley, my sponsor, would lean in the doorway, watchin' me work, his glasses glintin'. "Bobby, you got a documentarian's eye," he'd say, his voice warm but firm, like he was namin' a fact. "You see what folks miss, the soul of things."

I'd shrug, my hands busy with a reel, a half-smile hidin' how much it meant. "Ain't about titles, Mr. Tolley," I said, windin' film careful, like it was mom's scarf. "I just wanna tell the story."

He'd nod, leavin' me to it, and I dove into a new reel, one I hadn't planned but felt like it was waitin' for me. This one was about change, the interstate's rebar risin' like bones, the empty storefronts where laughter used to spill; loss, the funerals of Tommy, Carl, Eddie, their flags folded tight; and the way the town still breathed under all that quiet, in mom's garden overgrown with weeds, dad's new porch, the kids still racin' bikes down the riverwalk. I filmed early mornings, the fog over Coldwater Creek; late afternoons, the sun hittin' the school's cracked bleachers; moments that felt like it had a pulse, faint but stubborn.

Lila was there most nights, her sketchbook open on the table, her pencil scratchin' out title cards or sketches for my reel, Main Street's silhouette, a cypress by the creek, a flag at dusk.

"You need somethin' to tie it together, Bobby," she said one evenin', holdin' up a drawing of a broken bell, her ribbon loose in her hair. "This one's for the end, somethin' quiet, like the town's whisperin' back."

I grinned, tapin' her sketch to the wall, its lines perfect. "Lila, you're makin' this look like art," I said, half-teasin'. "Folks'll think I'm fancy, not just some kid with a camera."

"You *are* fancy," she shot back, smirkin', her pencil pokin' my arm. "Fancy enough to make em' cry. Keep goin'."

Eric would sometimes show up, too, his usual strut softer in the darkroom, his hands clumsy but eager when I taught him the tripod.

"Alright, Bobby, I'm camera two, yeah?" he said, adjustin' the legs, his buzz cut catchin' the projector's glow. "Point me at somethin' cool, like Lila's drawings or… I dunno, the janitor's mop!"

Lila laughed, tossin' a crumpled paper at him. "Eric, you'll film your own foot and call it a masterpiece!" she said, but her eyes were warm, proud of him tryin'.

"Nah, I'm a pro!" Eric said, swingin' the tripod, nearly knockin' over a lamp. "Watch out, Hollywood, Eric's comin' for ya!" But he settled, holdin' the camera steady as I filmed a shot of the school's flagpole, the wind rattlin' the chain, his focus real, like he knew this mattered.

Together, we built the reel, my footage, Lila's sketches, Eric's shaky but earnest shots, a story of the town's fight to stay alive. The film club was more than a room; it was where I found my voice, where Lila's art and Eric's heart met mine, where we remembered things right, frame by frame, holdin' onto the town we loved, even as it changed under our feet.

Matt rolled in the day before Thanksgiving, his old Ford Falcon rumblin' into the driveway, his shoulders broader from college life, his eyes wearier from late nights and exams. But when mom hugged him, her arms tight despite her frailty, he smiled the same, wide, boyish, like the kid who'd tossed footballs in the yard. "mom, not so hard!" he teased, spinnin' her gentle, her laugh a spark that lit the house.

"Missed you, Matt" she said, pattin' his cheek, her scarf slippin' as she beamed.

We gathered 'round the table that night, the kitchen warm with the smell of mom's oyster chicken gumbo, cornbread, and Lila's pecan pie, her contribution since she'd joined us, her sketchbook left at home for once. Lila fit like family, her laugh fillin' the space like she'd never left, her ribbon bright against her sweater.

"Matt, you better not be eatin' dorm slop all year," she said, passin' him a bowl, her eyes teasin'. "I'm expectin' you to bring some fancy college recipes next time!"

"Fancy?" Matt laughed, spoonin' gumbo, his grin wide. "Lila, I'm livin' on rice and hope! But this?" He nodded at the table, mom's smile, dad's steady gaze. "This is what I been dreamin' of. Y'all are spoilin' me."

Dad chuckled, cuttin' cornbread, his voice low but warm. "Good. Keeps you comin' back, son." I watched 'em, my heart full, knowin' these moments, Matt's laugh, Lila's jab, mom's eyes shinin', were what made home, home, stronger than any loss.

Out back, dad had built a new porch, a surprise for mom, finished just before the holiday. He'd worked weekends, hammerin' boards, sandin' 'em smooth, tellin' me it was so mom could sit and watch her garden without leanin' on the old, wobbly post. "Your mom deserves a proper seat," he'd said, his hands rough but careful, the wood gleamin' like a promise. Every mornin', mom was out there, wrapped in her shawl, tea in hand, starin' at the squash vines climbin' the trellis, their green curls like secrets only she could hear.

"Look at 'em grow, Bobby," she'd say, her voice soft, a smile playin' on her lips. "Ain't no sickness gonna stop this garden."

Thanksgiving dinner stretched late, our voices mixin' with clinkin' glasses, stories of Matt's bridge designs, Lila's latest sketch, Eric's absence noted but forgiven, he was haulin' lumber for extra cash. We stepped onto the porch after, mom settlin' in her new chair, dad's arm around her, Matt sprawlin' on the steps, Lila leanin' on the rail, me sittin' cross-legged, the night cool and quiet.

"This is it," Matt said, lookin' at the stars, his voice low. "Family, friends, a porch. Ain't nothin' better."

Lila nodded, her eyes on mom's garden. "Here's to keepin' it, always."

I didn't film it, this was just for us. The porch, mom's shawl, Matt's weary smile, Lila's laugh, they were etched in me, a frame brighter than any reel, holdin' us together as senior year rolled on and the world waited beyond the vines.

Chapter 29 - A Door Opens
(January 1971)

January was colder than usual. The new gray stretch in Mill Town, the interstate's rumble a constant hum beyond the fields, and mom's cancer a quiet fight we faced each day. Most had forgotten completely about Main Street. Now it was just something you tried not to look at when you drove through town. Now that football season was over I was able to spend more time on film club. Mr. Tolley, my film club sponsor, pulled me aside after class one afternoon, settin' me on a path I hadn't seen comin'.

The classroom was empty, the chalkboard still dusty from algebra, when Mr. Tolley leaned against his desk, his glasses low on his nose, his voice low but electric.

"Bobby Chandler, hold up a sec!" he called, wavin' me over, his grin wide like he was holdin' a secret. "I've seen what you capture with that camera of yours, kid. You ain't just pointin' a lens, you're tellin' the truth, raw and real. Them shots of Main Street, the riverwalk, the way you caught old Tucker's face by them survey stakes? That's soul right there!"

I shifted, my camera bag heavy on my shoulder, a half-smile tuggin' at my lips. "Aw, Mr. Tolley, it's just footage," I said, rubbin' my neck. "Nothin' special. Just me messin' around, tryin' to keep things from fadin'."

"Messin' around?" He laughed, slappin' his desk, his eyes sparklin' like he'd struck gold. "Boy, you're spinnin' stories that'd make Hollywood jealous! That reel you showed last week, the one with the empty storefronts set to that gospel track? Had me near tears, Bobby! You got a gift, and I'm tellin' ya, you gotta share it! I know you've

224

entered before, but I want you to know, you really got a shot, if ya want it."

I shrugged, hesitant, the weight of his words settlin' uneasy. "Share it where? Ain't nobody outside this town gonna care about our busted benches or closed shops."

"That's where you're wrong!" he said, leanin' forward, his voice risin' with excitement. "The senior regional student documentary contest is comin' up, and you're enterin'. Your film's got heart, Bobby, it's the kinda truth that cuts through. I know you could win this thing, show the state what our town's made of! Hell, maybe even get some eyes on what's happenin' here! Not only here, but all over the country. We're selling our souls, and don't even realize it."

I froze, my heart racin', doubt and hope wrestlin' in my chest. "I dunno, Mr. Tolley," I said, my voice low. "Last time I entered, I didn't even place. And I'm still splicin' reels, tryin' to make it all fit. What if it ain't good enough?"

He stepped closer, his hand on my shoulder, his voice steady but fierce. "I didn't feel like your heart was really in it then, but now? Good enough? Bobby, you owe it to this place, to your dad's store, your mom's fight, every soul on Main Street, to tell their story. You're not just filmin' a town; you're savin' us from ourselves, frame by frame. Get that film in, kid. Show 'em we're still kickin'!"

I nodded, a grin breakin' through, his words lightin' a fire I hadn't felt in months. "Alright, Mr. Tolley, you got me!" I said, laughin', my hands up like I was surrenderin'. "I'll do it! I'll polish them reels till they shine, make 'em see this place like we do!"

"That's my boy!" he said, clappin' my back, his grin wide as the river. "You're gonna knock their socks off, Bobby Chandler! Now get to that editin' room and make some magic!"

I left the classroom, my steps lighter, Mr. Tolley's faith buzzin' in my head like a summer bee. The contest was a long shot, but his words, *you owe it to this place*, stuck with me, a call to turn my camera's truth into somethin' bigger. I'd splice those reels, pour our heart into every frame, and maybe, just maybe, show the world what we were losin', and what we were still fightin' to keep.

Mr. Tolley's push to enter the regional student documentary contest had lit a fire in me, and after days of thinkin', I knew what my film had to be, not just a record of Mill Town's fade, but a love letter to what it was, and a raw look at what it felt like to watch it change.

I sat in my room one night, the house quiet except for mom's soft hummin' from the kitchen and dad's chair creakin' as he read. My notebook was open, the pencil scratchin' as I poured out the idea that'd been brewin'. This film wouldn't linger on Hamburger King's neon or the interstate's rebar, it'd dig deeper, to the heart of what a community was before the world sped up. I wrote questions, each one a hook to pull out the town's soul: *What was Mill Town like in 1950? What's the one thing you miss the most? Do you think the town can ever come back?* The words stared back, simple but heavy, like keys to a door I hadn't opened yet.

I hauled out my old reels, dusty boxes of footage I'd shot over the years, Main Street's Fourth of July parade in '66, the riverwalk packed with families, Dad behind the counter at Chandler Hardware, grinnin' as he handed a kid a free nail. Talkin with the neighbors standing around drinkin coffee. Each reel was a piece of the home I loved, the one that lived in stories mom told about dance halls and dad's memories of farmers barterin' tools. I wanted my film to weave those memories with the ache of now, to show the town's bones and its bruises.

In the barn, I set up a makeshift studio, my camera on a tripod like a priest waitin' for confession. I dragged in a stool, a single lamp castin' a warm glow, and let the silence settle, heavy and invitin'. It was a booth for truth, a place where folks could sit and answer questions, their voices carryin' the weight of what we'd lost and what we still held. I tested the setup, sittin' on the stool myself, the lamp hot on my face, whisperin' my own answers to the dark: "Mill Town in '50? Alive, loud, and everybody knew your name. What I miss? The bell on Dad's store. Can it come back? Don't know… but I'm filmin' so it don't disappear completely."

The setup felt right, sacred almost, like I was buildin' a church for memories. I'd ask mom first, her stories of gumbo suppers and jukebox nights, then dad, his tales of the store's heyday. I'd find Mr. Tucker, Mrs. Perry, maybe even Lila, get their voices on film, their answers spliced with old reels to show the town that was, vibrant, close-knit, ours, and the one we were losin' to asphalt and chain stores. My notebook filled with shots I'd need: the empty bench outside the store, the interstate's shadow, mom's hands stirrin' a pot, all tied to those questions that burned in me.

I closed the barn door, the cold bitin' at my fingers, and looked out at the town's dark skyline, the water tower a faint silhouette. The contest was a chance, but this film was more, a way to save what mattered, to tell the truth Mr. Tolley saw in me. I'd make it not for judges, but for us, for the community that lived in our bones, and for the hope that, maybe, by showin' what we were, we could find a way to fight for what we could still be.

My barn studio was ready, a stool, a lamp, silence like a held breath, and I'd started invitin' folks to sit before my lens, answerin' questions to weave the town's past with its achin' present. First up was Miss Elma, the bookshop owner, whose voice carried decades of the town's soul.

Miss Elma settled onto the stool, her hands folded neat in her lap, her gray hair pinned up like always, her eyes sharp but soft under the lamp's glow. I adjusted the camera, the hum steady, and gave her a nod. "Alright, Miss Elma, whenever you're ready," I said, my voice low, tryin' to keep the moment easy. "Tell me, what was Mill Town like in 1950?"

She leaned back, a smile curlin' slow, her gaze driftin' like she was steppin' into a memory. "Oh, Bobby, in '50, this town was a hummin' hive," she said, her voice warm, rich with the past. "We had a bakery pumpin' out sourdough you could smell from the river, a tailor who'd mend your Sunday best in a day, a shoe man who shined boots till they gleamed, and four different grocers, each with their own secrets, Mrs. Clara's tomatoes, Mr. Hale's honey. Nobody ever went hungry, not with neighbors sharin' what they had."

I smiled behind the camera, picturin' it, the lens catchin' the light in her eyes. "Sounds like paradise," I said, leanin' in. "What'd you do back then, Miss Elma? Where'd you fit in?"

Her smile turned wistful, her fingers smoothin' her skirt. "The bookshop wasn't mine yet, that was Mrs. Longstreet's domain, all oak shelves and ink. I was just a girl, sixteen, alphabetizin' her poetry section after school, dustin' off Frost and Whitman while she brewed tea. I'd sneak a read when she wasn't lookin', dreamin' I'd run that shop one day." She chuckled, soft, like the memory was a treasure. "Took me twenty years, but I got there."

I nodded, my throat tight, thinkin' of her shop now, half-empty, its windows dark with boxes still piled up. I shifted to the harder question, my voice gentle but steady. "Miss Elma, what's the town feel like now? To you, I mean."

Her eyes dropped, her hands stillin', the air heavy with the shift. She took a breath, her voice quieter, like she was speakin' to the barn's shadows. "It feels… like an echo, Bobby. Still here, just quieter. The bakery's gone, the tailor's boarded up, and folks shop at Allied 'stead of sharin' tomatoes. You hear the old laughter sometimes, in the wind, but it's fadin', like a song you can't quite catch. Folks are always in a hurry. We don't stop and talk like we used to. Nobody just sits and waves from their front porch anymore. I miss it…"

The camera hummed, holdin' her words, her wistful smile, the way her eyes held both love and loss. I swallowed, keepin' the lens steady, knowin' her echo was the heart of my film, Mill Town in '50, alive and full, now a whisper fightin' to be heard. "Thank you, Miss Elma," I said, my voice thick. "That's... that's exactly what I needed."

She nodded, pattin' my arm as she stood, her smile returnin', faint but kind. "You keep filmin', Bobby. Don't let our echo die." I watched her go, the barn door creakin' shut, and rewound the reel, her voice already splicin' into the story I'd tell, a town that was, a town that's fadin', and the truth of what it meant to stay and remember.

With Miss Elma's words already on reel, I turned to Mr. Abernathy, the old feed store owner, and mom, whose heart held the town's truest stories, each voice addin' to a film that felt like savin' a piece of home.

Mr. Abernathy shuffled into the barn, his dentures clickin' as he settled on the stool, his overalls worn but clean, his eyes twinklin' with memories. I started the camera, its hum a soft welcome, and leaned in. "Mr. Abernathy, tell me about Mill Town in the '50s," I said, smilin' to ease him in. "What was it like at your feed store back then?"

He chuckled, a warm, rattly sound, leanin' back like he was steppin' into a sunlit day. "Oh, Bobby, that store was the heart of it all!" he said, his voice lively, hands wavin'. "We used to line up out front for sacks of seed like it was payday at the bank, farmers jostlin' for the best corn blend. Boys'd perch on the hay bales, talkin' tractors 'til sundown, John Deere this, Massey that, arguin' like it was scripture. You could hear the laughter from Main Street, smell the grain dust mixin' with coffee from Benny's."

I grinned, the camera catchin' his spark, picturin' the scene. "Sounds like a party every day," I said.

He quickly corrected me, "No, no, it was hard, but we had each other. Everyday was another challenge, but we faced it together. You remember when that twister came through? It may have been before

229

you were born, but it destroyed dozens of homes on the north side, killed seventeen people. The government wouldn't do nothin' because it didn't damage enough municipal buildings. Many didn't have insurance back then. We rebuilt every one of those houses together. Your dad pitched in most of the tools and supplies. The whole town closed for two weeks while we all mended homes. We got those poor people back into their homes as quickly as we could, they had been through enough."

"What's it feel like now, Mr. Abernathy? The town, I mean."

He leaned forward, his chuckle fadin', his eyes sharp but heavy. "Now? I see more plastic than people, Bobby. Bags from Allied, wrappers from that Hamburger King, ain't no hay bales left. And the names... I don't hear 'em no more. No Hales, no Tuckers, just strangers passin' through, headin' to that interstate." His voice dropped, the barn quiet except for the camera's hum, holdin' his truth like a weight.

I nodded, my throat tight, and thanked him as he shuffled out, his words echoin', plastic over people, names lost. The reel was growin', but I needed mom's voice, her stories of Mill Town's warmth, to anchor it. She'd hesitated, her cancer makin' her shy of the spotlight, but one evenin' she agreed, sittin' on the stool, her scarf tied neat, her hands folded like she was prayin'.

"Ma, tell me about the old days," I said, my voice soft, the lamp glowin' on her pale face. "What was Mill Town like when you were my age?"

She smiled, her eyes far off, her voice steady despite her frailty. "It was a family, Bobby," she said, her words warm, like her gumbo. "When someone got sick, folks'd leave casseroles on their porch, chicken and rice, green beans, all homemade, not a frozen box in sight. You'd find a dish waitin', no name, just love. We took care of each other, no questions asked."

I leaned in, the camera hummin', her words paintin' a town I ached to know. "What's different now, Ma?" I asked, gentle, knowin' the answer'd hurt.

Her smile faded, her eyes glistenin' as she spoke, her voice soft but raw. "People used to come to the church basement just to be with each other, singin', laughin', sharin' stories over coffee. Now they go where the coupons are, Allied, Hamburger King, places that don't know their names." A tear slipped down her cheek, quiet, and she looked away, her hands tremblin' in her lap.

I turned the camera off, the click loud in the silence, and sat with her, no words needed. We stayed there, mom's breathin' soft, the barn holdin' us like it held the town's memories. Her tears, Mr. Abernathy's lost names, the casseroles gone cold, they were the town's echo, fadin' but still here, and my film would carry them, a truth louder than any interstate's roar.

The interstate's rumble was gettin' louder in the distance, mom's cancer a quiet battle, but in the school's AV room, I found a kind of peace, editin' late into the night, shapin' a film that'd show what home really was, and what it was becomin'.

I stayed after hours, the AV room a dim cave lit by the flicker of my projector, the air smellin' of dust and old film. The janitor, Mr. Rawls, swept around me, his broom hissin' soft against the floor, givin' me a nod as he worked. "Burnin' the midnight oil, Bobby?" he called, his voice echoin' in the empty room, a grin tuggin' at his lips.

"Gotta get this right, Mr. Rawls!" I said, my eyes on the splicer, my hands steady as I cut a strip of film. "This film's gotta sing, you know? Make 'em feel it!"

He chuckled, leanin' on his broom. "You're doin' right by this town, kid. Keep at it, I'll lock up when you're done."

I nodded, divin' back into the reels, splicin' together childhood footage, me and Matt runnin' through the riverwalk in '65, Main Street's Fourth of July parade with flags wavin', and present-day stills of empty benches, boarded shops, the interstate's rebar clawin' at the sky. Black-and-white memories faded into colorless storefronts, the contrast sharp, like a heartbeat slowin' down. I worked slow, deliberate, each cut a choice to show the town's soul, its laughter, its losses, its stubborn pulse.

For sound, I overlaid old music, pullin' from tapes I'd scavenged: church hymns from mom's gospel station, their voices risin' like a prayer; radio jingles from the '50s, cheerful ads for soda shops long gone; porch fiddles from a reel of Dad's uncle playin' at a barn dance. The music wove through the images, a thread of warmth against the cold of now. I leaned into the mic, my voice steady but raw, recordin' my narration: "This is a story about a place that's still here, but not in the way we remember. Not in the way we need."

The words echoed in the AV room, mixin' with the projector's hum, and I played it back, watchin' Miss Elma's wistful smile, Mr. Abernathy's dentured chuckle, mom's tearful truth about casseroles and church basements. The film was takin' shape, a mosaic of the town's past and its pain, the hymns and fiddles carryin' it like a river. I spliced late into the night, Mr. Rawls' broom a soft rhythm, my hands shakin' with the weight of what I was makin', not just a contest entry, but a love letter to a town fightin' to be remembered, a truth that'd outlast the interstate's roar and the silence it left behind.

Chapter 30 - The Private Showin
(February 1971)

With the regional student documentary contest just weeks away and my 8mm film, *Mill Town Echoes*, finally ready. My nights spent splicin' reels in the AV room, pourin' the town's soul into every frame, mom's stories, Miss Elma's wistful smile, Mr. Abernathy's lost names. Before sendin' it to the judges, I wanted to test it, to see if it carried the weight I felt, so I invited the film club to a private screenin' and of course Lila, in the school's media room, a small space with just eight foldin' chairs and a borrowed projector, but big enough for truth.

The media room was dim, the air cool and heavy with the smell of old books and metal. I set up the projector, my hands shakin' as I threaded the reel, while the film club, Lila, Jenny, Tommy, and a few others, filed in, their chatter fadin' as they took their seats. Mr. Tolley stood by the door, his glasses glintin' in the low light, his grin wide but proud. He clapped his hands, his voice boomin' in the small space.

"Alright, y'all, settle in!" he said, gesturin' to me. "This is *Mill Town*, through Bobby Chandler's eyes. He's poured his heart into this, and you're about to see why. Bobby, take it away!"

I nodded, my throat tight, and mumbled, "Hope y'all like it," before flickin' off the lights.

The projector hummed to life, the reel spinnin', and the room fell silent, thick with feelin' as the images rolled. Slow pans of Coldwater Creek flickered first, its water glintin' under summer sun, then the broken bell at the school, its silence louder than any chime. The image of dad handing out candy from the hardware store with granddad's picture behind him, then faded to an empty store counter with the silhouette of grandad's picture, then mom's quiet gaze filled the screen, her hands

233

folded as she spoke of casseroles and church basements, her voice a soft ache as a tear fell. Miss Elma's dusty shelves followed, her words about 1950's grocers and poetry lingerin' like a hymn. Matt's reflection in Hamburger King's drive-thru window cut through, his face unreadable in his new uniform, a boy caught between worlds. Mr. Jennings solemn remembrance at the memorial while everyone carried on in the background.

No one spoke, no one shifted, the room holdin' its breath as the footage wove the town's past with its pain, Main Street's parades fadin' into boarded windows, gospel music mixin' with the interstate's distant roar. My narration, raw and steady, tied it together: "This is a story about a place that's still here, but not in the way we remember. Not in the way we need." I glanced at Lila, her eyes fixed on the screen, her sketchbook still, and felt my heart pound, hopin' they felt what I did.

The closin' shot faded in, a flag over Main Street at dusk, tattered but still hangin', its frayed edges catchin' the last light. The screen went dark, and my voice, recorded late in the AV room, closed it out: "This was Mill Town. And maybe it still is. If we remember."

The projector's film slapped the table, a rhythmic *thwap-thwap* echoin' for five seconds, each beat loud in the dark, until a final click brought it to a stop. No one moved, the eight foldin' chairs holdin' us like statues, the silence thick as fog. My hands gripped the camera in my lap, my heart poundin', waitin' for somethin', a word, a sound, anythin' to tell me they'd felt it.

Jenny sniffed, wipin' her eyes, and Tommy let out a low whistle, breakin' the spell. "Damn, Bobby," he said, his voice soft but awed. "That's... that's our town, man. You made the truth hurt, but it's beautiful."

Lila turned to me, her eyes wet but fierce. "You didn't just film it, Bobby," she said, her voice steady. "You saved it. That's Main Street, Ma, all of us, right there. You gotta win this thing."

Sarah, one of the younger club members, barely fifteen, leaned forward, her voice a whisper but clear as a bell. "Bobby," she said, her eyes wide, "you made it real. Like… I could feel Main Street, the people, everythin'. It's all right there."

Mr. Tolley clapped, his grin wide as he flicked the lights on. "Told y'all he had it!" he said, pointin' at me. "Bobby, that's a gut-punch and a love song all at once. You're ready for the contest, kid. The town's ridin' with you."

I smiled, my face hot, the weight of their words liftin' me up. "Thanks, y'all," I said, my voice thick. "I just… I needed to show what we're losin', what we still got. Hope it's enough."

"It's more than enough," Lila said, squeezin' my arm, and the others nodded, their faces lit with the same fire I'd felt editin' those reels.

The screenin' was small, just eight chairs, but it felt huge, like I'd given what had just been a feelin', a voice, a chance to be remembered. As we folded the chairs, I knew this film wasn't just for the contest, it was for all of us, and every echo still hangin' on, fightin' to be heard.

The media room had cleared out, the film club's tears and whispers still echoin' in my head as I packed up the projector, my camera bag slung over my shoulder.

Mr. Tolley caught me in the hallway, his footsteps quick, his face set with a fire I hadn't seen before. "Bobby Chandler, hold up!" he called, his voice bouncin' off the lockers, his glasses glintin' under the fluorescent lights. "We gotta talk about that film."

I stopped, shiftin' my bag, a half-smile hidin' my nerves. "What about it, Mr. Tolley?" I said, keepin' it light. "They liked it, didn't they? That's enough for me."

He stepped closer, his arms foldin', his eyes lockin' onto mine like he could see through my shrug. "Liked it? Bobby, they laughed, then they were wrecked, tears, silence, the whole room felt it. This ain't just a

235

school project, kid. It's a piece of truth, a town's heart, its hurt, all of it. And the world needs to see it, not just eight kids in a media room."

I looked down, kickin' at a scuff on the floor, my voice low. "I didn't make it for them, Mr. Tolley. I made it for us, for mom, dad, Main Street. For the town. Ain't sure it's meant for strangers, judgin' it like their visiting a zoo."

He didn't budge, his arms still crossed, his voice firm but warm, like a coach pushin' you to run one more lap. "That's exactly why it's gotta go out there, Bobby. You made it for the town, but it's bigger than that now. Your film's got power, those shots of Coldwater Creek, your mom's voice, that damn flag at dusk, it's a wake-up call. If you don't send this to the contest, you're hidin' the truth. And I ain't lettin' you do that anymore."

I shifted, my throat tight, his words hittin' like a shove. "What if they don't get it?" I said, my voice quieter. "What if they just see another dyin' small town and move on?"

"Then that's their loss, if that's all they get outta it," he said, leanin' in, his tone fierce. "But you don't get to decide that for 'em. You've got one week to submit it, Bobby. If you don't, I'm doin' it myself, entry form, reel, all of it. I'll mail it with my own damn stamps."

I stared at him, his ultimatum hangin' heavy, part of me wantin' to argue, part of me knowin' he was right. My film was Mill Town's voice, and maybe it did belong out there, where it could shout for all of us. I sighed, a grin tuggin' at my lips despite myself. "Alright, Mr. Tolley, you win," I said, shakin' my head. "You're a hard man to say no to."

"Damn right," he said, clappin' my shoulder, his grin wide. "Get that form signed, kid. You're about to show the world what heart is really made of."

The next day, I showed up to the AV room, the entry form in hand, my pencil hoverin' before I scrawled my name, reluctant but resolved. I handed it to Mr. Tolley, my heart racin' but steady. "Here's your truth, sir," I said, half-smilin'. "Hope it's ready for the big leagues."

"It's ready," he said, takin' the form, his eyes proud. "And so are you." As I walked out, the weight of the contest felt real, but so did the purpose, my film, our story, was headin' out to speak, and I was ready to let it, thanks to a teacher who wouldn't let me hide.

Chapter 31 - The Call
(March 1971)

Life had settled into a fragile pattern. Mom went for the doctor every Tuesday, Dad drivin' her with a thermos of sweet tea, his hands steady on the wheel like he could steer her through the pain. She'd come home pale but smilin', her shawl wrapped tight, and dad would read to her, old Westerns or her favorite Psalms, his voice a low comfort. Sometimes I would hear her throwin' up at night. She always apologized for wakin' us up.

Matt's letters from Tallahassee arrived like clockwork, scribbled tales of finals and dorm food that made mom laugh. "Bobby, listen to this," she'd read at dinner, holdin' up his latest. "Says the cafeteria tried 'mystery meat' again, thinks it's roadkill this time!" mom's giggle was a gift, dad's nod a quiet pride, keepin' us tethered while the town felt emptier every day.

The talk in the hallways and lunchroom had turned sharp, all about the draft, the word itself heavy as a slammed locker. Seniors whispered over trays, their eyes dartin' like they could dodge the news. Several football players, guys I'd run drills with, like Troy and Rod, started gettin' induction notices, their birthdays called by a government that didn't know their faces, just the day when they took their first breath. Nate showed me his letter one day, folded tight in his pocket, his voice low. "Got two months, Bobby," he said, his usual swagger gone. "Then it's me and a rifle, somewhere I can't even spell." he nodded, my gut twistin', knowin' each notice was a clock tickin' down.

Eric got his, too, the paper delivered to his house like a bad report card. He told me and Lila at Benny's, his grin forced, his fingers tappin' the counter. "I'm deferred, but day after graduation, I'm gone," he said, his voice flat, like he was tryin' to outrun the truth. "Army's callin', and I ain't got the cash to duck it like some rich kid."

Lila's face fell, her sketchbook still, her voice soft. "Eric, we ain't losin' you."

He nodded, but his eyes were on the floor, and I felt the air shift, the war no longer just a story. It was now a thief stealin' my friend.

I was nervous, too, I couldn't watch those drawin's on TV anymore, so took to checkin' the mailbox daily, my heart racin' at every envelope, dreadin' my own notice. At night, I'd lie awake, thinkin' of Tommy, Carl, Eddie, boys in boxes, their funerals still raw. "What if it's me, or Eric next?" I muttered to Lila one day by the creek, my camera idle. She squeezed my arm, her voice fierce. "Don't you dare think it, Bobby. You're stayin' right here, filmin' our story." But the fear stuck, a shadow I couldn't shake, makin' every day feel like a countdown.

I filmed less those months, my camera restin' on my desk more than in my hands. It wasn't defeat, *Mill Town Echoes* had taken all I had, spillin' mom's stories, Miss Elma's echoes, and Mr. Abernathy's lost names onto the reel. Now I was waitin', like a fisherman watchin' a still line, hopin' the contest might give a tug. I'd walk Main Street, eyein' the boarded shops, or sit by the river with Lila and Eric, their chatter fillin' the quiet, but my lens stayed mostly still, savin' its strength for what might come.

One quiet mornin', durin' second period English, I was slumped over *Wuthering Heights*, the teacher's voice a hum, when the intercom crackled, sharp and jarrin'. "Robert Chandler, please report to the principal's office," it blared, cuttin' through the room. The class stirred, heads turnin', a few kids whisperin'. Jason leaned over, his grin sly. "What'd you do, Chandler? Steal the principal's stapler?"

I snorted, stuffin' my book in my bag, my heart kickin' up despite my shrug. "If I did, I'd aim higher, his coffee mug, maybe," I said, keepin' it light, but my stomach twisted as I stood. The principal's office wasn't my scene, I wasn't a troublemaker, and the call felt wrong, like a reel skippin' its track. Was it mom? Had her treatment gone bad? My mind was reeling and I was startin to sweat. My shoes echoin' in the empty hall, confusion doggin' my steps. The air felt charged, like the moment before a storm, and as I headed to the office, I braced for whatever was waitin', knowin' it'd probably change somethin', one way or another.

My mind was still spinnin', was something wrong with mom? Had something happened to Matt? The draft, or somethin' worse? The receptionist said they were waiting for me. They? I knocked softly, my hand shakin', and pushed the door open, the creak loud in the quiet. Inside, Principal Harris sat at his desk, Mr. Tolley stood by the window, and three strangers, two men and a woman, sharply dressed in city clothes, sat in chairs, their eyes turnin' to me. They stood as I entered, the air shiftin', and the woman stepped forward, her hand outstretched, her smile warm but professional.

"Bobby, I'm Ava Klein," she said, her grip firm, her voice clear, like she was used to bein' heard. "This is Jordan and Reed. We're producers from Sun Studios in Los Angeles. And we saw your film."

I froze, my bag slippin' in my hand, the words hittin' me in the chest like a missed a catch. *Mill Town Echoes*, my reel of mom's stories, Main Street's fade, the creek's glow, had reached further than I'd dreamed, but the draft's shadow, Eric's notice, and the war's weight made the moment feel surreal, like I was standin' in two worlds at once. Mr. Tolley grinned, his eyes proud, but I just stood there, heart poundin', tryin' to find my voice in a room that suddenly felt too big for a High School Principal's office.

My shoes seemed to be rooted to the floor, facin' three strangers from Sun Studios, Ava Klein, Jordan, and Reed, their sharp city clothes out of place in the school's faded walls. Mr. Tolley leaned against the window, his grin barely hidin' pride, while Ava spoke, her voice clear and warm. "Bobby, we were on the judging panel for the documentary

240

competition," she said, her eyes lockin' on mine. "We watched dozens of entries, good ones, polished ones, but yours? *Mill Town Echoes* hit something we didn't expect."

Jordan, lean and bespectacled, nodded, leanin' forward. "It's not just a film," he said, his voice earnest. "It's a requiem for a place, a warning about what's being lost, and it moved every single one of us. Your shots, the creek, the empty shops, your mom's voice, it's raw, real. You made us feel your town's heart, and that is something special."

I blinked, my breath catchin', their words landin' like stones in a still pond. Ava smiled, her hands clasped. "We're offerin' you a full scholarship to our partner film school in Los Angeles," she said, her tone steady but warm, "plus a one-year understudy placement with our studio's nonfiction division. You'd learn, work, and hopefully grow with us." She paused, her eyes soft but fierce. "You've got talent, Bobby, no doubt. We don't just want to teach you, we want to help you tell more stories like this."

The room spun, my heart poundin' so loud I thought they'd hear it. A scholarship? Los Angeles? Me, a kid from Mill Town, with a camera and a town's worth of grief? I glanced at Mr. Tolley, his small, proud nod anchorin' me, his eyes sayin' what he'd told me months ago: *You owe it to this place.* My mouth opened, but nothin' came out, the weight of it, Eric's indocrination notice, mom's cancer all mixin' with a hope I hadn't dared to feel.

Reed, the quiet one, spoke gently, sensin' my stun. "We understand this is a lot, Bobby," he said, his voice calm. "Take your time, talk to your family. But we hope you'll seriously consider it. The world needs your voice, kid."

I managed a whisper, my throat tight. "Thank you." It was all I could get out, my hands shakin' as I gripped my bag.

Ava slid a folder across the principal's desk, its edges crisp, flight information, scholarship details, a contact number, all real, all for me.

As they stood to leave, she paused, her eyes meetin' mine again. "That final shot," she said, her voice soft, "of the old, tattered flag over boarded up Main Street, waving at dusk? That'll stay with me for the rest of my life."

They left, the door clickin' shut, and I stood there, the folder in my hands, Mr. Tolley's hand on my shoulder, his voice low. "You did this, Bobby. You told our story, our real story."

I nodded, still stunned, the offer a door swingin' wide to a world I'd never imagined, film school, a studio, a chance to keep tellin' stories. But something held me back, makin' the choice feel bigger than me, a leap I'd have to weigh with the ones I loved most.

The offer from Sun Studios, a full scholarship to film school in Los Angeles, a year workin' with their nonfiction division, sat like a live wire in my hands, a chance I'd never dreamed of, but one that meant leavin' home, mom, dad, Lila, and Eric, who was facin' his own departure to the war. At lunch, I faced my best friends, the weight of our futures hangin' between us, and confessed the news that'd change everythin'.

I slid into the booth across from Lila and Eric at lunch, the cafeteria's hum a dull roar around us. The letter from Sun Studios, folded neat in my back pocket, felt like it was burnin' a hole through my jeans, each word, *scholarship*, *Los Angeles*, *understudy*, echoin' in my head since the principal's office. Lila was doodlin' on a napkin, her ribbon loose, while Eric shoveled fries, his buzz cut fresh for graduation. I took a breath, my hands grippin' the table, and let it out. "I got in," I said, my voice low but clear. "Full ride. LA. Film school and a studio gig."

Lila blinked once, her pencil stoppin', her eyes lockin' on mine like she was seein' through me, past the words to the choice I hadn't made yet. "Los Angeles?" she said, her voice soft, testin' the words like they were fragile. "Bobby, that's… that's huge. Your film did this?"

I nodded, my throat tight, pullin' the letter out and settin' it on the table, its creases worn from readin'. "*Mill Town Echoes*," I said. "They saw it, said it moved 'em. Want me to tell more stories like it. Start after summer."

Eric's grin, usually quick and wide, faded slow, his fork settin' down soft on his tray, the clink loud in our corner. "So you're leavin'," he said, his voice flat, eyes droppin' to the letter. "And I'm goin' over there." His draft notice, set for two days after graduation, hung unspoken, the war's shadow darkenin' his face. "Vietnam and Hollywood, huh? Ain't that a hell of a split."

The silence between us was loud, thicker than the diner's chatter, heavier than the ketchup bottles and half-eaten burgers. Lila's sketchbook, always open, stayed closed, her hands still, her breath caught. Eric forced a smile then, crooked and brave, leanin' back like he could shrug off the weight. "Hell, someone's gotta make a movie about me, right?" he said, his voice tryin' for light but crackin' on the edges. "Eric the War Hero, directed by Bobby Chandler. Get me a good actor, man, someone with my charm!"

I laughed, a short, choked sound, grateful for his try but feelin' the ache. "Yeah, Eric, gonna need a whole studio to catch that ego," I said, forcin' a grin, but my eyes stung, thinkin' of him in a uniform, halfway across the world, while I'd be in a city I couldn't even picture.

"You better write, man. I'm holdin' you to it," as he hit my shoulder.

Lila's gaze hadn't left me, her eyes wet but steady, her voice a whisper that cut through the noise. "You always said the camera was your way out, Bobby," she said, her words slow, like she was piecin' together a puzzle. "Now it really is. You're gonna go, aren't you? Leave this place, show the world what you see."

I swallowed, my hands twistin' the letter's edge, her words hittin' deep. "I don't know yet," I said, honest, my voice shakin'. "mom's sick, dad needs me, and y'all… you're my home. But this, this chance, it's what I've been filmin' for, ain't it? To make our story matter."

She nodded, reachin' across the table, her hand coverin' mine, warm and firm. "It's your story, too, Bobby," she said, her voice fierce despite the tears. "You take it to LA, you hear? Make 'em see what you do, the creek, all of it. Don't you dare stay for us."

Eric leaned in, his smirk softer now, his eyes serious. "She's right, man. You go make them fancy films, but you better put me and Lila in the credits," he said, tappin' the table. "We're your crew, always. Even if I'm dodgin' bullets and she's paintin' masterpieces. Besides, if you hang around here, it will be you in the foxhole down the line too."

I looked at 'em, Lila's steady grip, Eric's brave front, the letter between us, and felt the pull of two worlds, home's roots and LA's open door. The diner's hum faded, leavin' just us, tethered by years of laughter, promises, and a summer's pact. "Y'all are in every frame," I said, my voice thick, meanin' it. "No matter where I go."

We sat there, the letter untouched, the future unwritten, knowin' Eric's war and my chance were takin' us apart but not breakin' us. Lila squeezed my hand, Eric raised his soda in a mock toast, and we held on, the moment, each other, for as long as we could before the world called us away.

Headin' home to face mom and dad, I wrestled with a choice that felt too big, my steps slow, the gravel under my feet echoin' my doubt. I didn't feel like celebratin', not yet, despite the offer bein' the kind of dream I'd barely dared to name. The lane to our house stretched long, the afternoon sun slantin' through the pines, and I kicked gravel with every step, each stone skitterin' like the thoughts I was rehearsin'. How do I tell them I might leave? How do I look mom and dad in the eye and say I'm headin' to LA when they're fightin' mom's cancer day by day? The letter, folded tight in my pocket, felt heavy as a brick, its words, *scholarship*, *studio*, *stories*, mixin' with guilt that gnawed at me.

Mom had been movin' slower lately, her strength ebbin' like a tide goin' out but never quite coming all the way back in after every treatment. She spent more time sittin' on dad's new porch, wrapped in her shawl, sippin' tea and watchin' her squash vines, than stirrin' gumbo or sweepin' the kitchen. Her smile was still there, bright as ever, but her hands trembled now, and dad's quiet care, refillin' her tea, readin' to her at night, showed how much she leaned on him. I pictured her on that porch, her eyes soft but searchin', and my chest tightened. What kind of son leaves right when she needs him most? I kicked another stone, harder, its clatter loud in the quiet lane, my mind spinnin'. This was my chance to make *Mill Town Echoes* mean somethin', to tell stories for her, for our town, but leavin' felt like betrayin' the woman who'd taught me to see the world worth filmin'.

I stopped halfway home, the fields stretchin' gold under the sky, the interstate's faint hum a reminder of everythin' changin'. I pulled out the letter, unfoldin' it, Ava Klein's words starin' back: *We want to help you tell more stories like this, before there's no one left to tell them.* Mom's voice echoed in my head, from a night she'd watched my film, her hand on mine, "You got a gift, Bobby. Don't you hide it." But hidin' was easier than leavin', and as I folded the letter back, the gravel crunched under my boots, each step a question I'd have to answer when I faced mom and dad, their love the only thing heavier than the choice in my hands.

I gripped the letter through supper prep, helpin' mom chop green beans while dad set the table, my thumb wearin' down the paper's corner, its words, *scholarship*, *Los Angeles*, burnin' in my mind. I didn't say a word, not yet, my voice caught somewhere between fear and hope. Mom moved slow, her shawl slippin' as she stirred the chicken and dumplin's, her best dish, the kitchen warm with its smell, mixin' with cornbread and beans. I watched her, her hands shakin' just a touch, and kept quiet, the letter hidden in my pocket like a secret I wasn't ready to share.

We sat to eat, the table creakin' under the weight of plates, mom's smile soft but tired, dad's eyes steady as he passed the cornbread. The radio hummed low behind us, some old country tune, its twang fillin' the pauses.

Dad asked 'bout school, his voice easy. "How's that film club treatin' you, Bobby?" he said, spoonin' dumplin's. "Tolley still pushin' you hard?"

"Yeah," I said, my voice tight, pokin' at my beans. "Got us editin' a new reel. Keeps me busy." I glanced at mom, her plate barely touched, her fork restin' more than movin', and my chest ached, the letter feelin' heavier.

"Matt wrote," mom said, her voice liftin' a bit, a spark in her eyes. "Says he'll be home for Christmas, bringin' some new bridge designs to show off. Boy's gonna build the world, Thomas."

Dad chuckled, noddin'. "He's makin' us proud, Ruth. Just like Bobby with that camera." His words hit soft, proud, and I swallowed, the letter's weight unbearable now, the cornbread half gone, crumbs scattered like my nerve.

I took a breath, my hand slippin' to my pocket, pullin' out the folded paper, its creases worn. "I got called to the principals office today," I said, my voice stickin' in my throat, the words scrapin' out slow.

Dad looked at me sternly, then his expression softened, "Everything ok?"

"I got a scholarship to Film school. California. Full ride." I set it on the table, the paper stark against the checkered cloth, my eyes dartin' between mom's wide gaze and dad's still face. "They saw my film, *Mill Town Echoes*. Want me to study with 'em, work at their studio. Starting after summer."

The radio's hum was all I heard for a moment, mom's fork frozen, dad's hand pausin' mid-bite. Mom's eyes, tired but sharp, locked on mine, her shawl slippin' as she leaned forward. I swear waiting for me to say I was kiddin.

"California?" she whispered, her voice a mix of wonder and somethin' else, fear, maybe, or pride, I couldn't tell. Dad set his fork down, slow, his jaw tight, but he didn't speak, waitin', like he always did, for the truth to settle.

I pushed the letter toward 'em, my hands shakin'. "It's a chance," I said, my voice steadier now, though my heart raced. "To tell more stories, like you taught me, mom. But... I don't know if I can leave y'all. Not now." The words hung, raw, the radio's twang a faint echo of the choice I'd laid bare, waitin' for either one to say something.

The kitchen was quiet, the radio's country twang fadin' under the weight of my confession, *film school, California, full ride.* The letter sat on the checkered tablecloth, its creases worn, chicken and dumplin's forgotten, mom's plate barely touched. Mom looked up slow, her eyes full but dry, shinin' with somethin' deeper than tears, pride, fear, love all tangled. "They see what I see in you, then," she said, her voice soft but steady, each word landin' like a stone in my chest. "That fire, Bobby. That way you make the world mean somethin' through that lens. I always knew it'd take you far."

I swallowed, my throat tight, her words hittin' hard. "Mom, I don't know if I can go," I said, my voice crackin', leanin' forward, my hands twistin' the napkin. "You're fightin' so hard, and I'm s'posed to just... leave? Head to some city while you're here, hurtin'?" The guilt spilled out, raw, my eyes stingin' as I looked at her, her shawl loose, her face pale but fierce.

Dad nodded once, proud and quiet, his fork still, his eyes steady on me. "You got a story to tell, Bobby," he said, his voice low, rough with feelin'. "Not just ours, but yours. Don't let it sit too long, son. Ain't no good in holdin' back what you were made to do." He paused, his jaw tight, like he was fightin' his own ache. "We'll be here, holdin' the fort. Always."

247

Nobody said the word *abandon*, but it hung there, a ghost in the air, twistin' my gut. I shook my head, my voice barely a whisper. "What kinda son walks away now? Mom, you're… you're everythin'. This film, it's 'cause of you, your stories, your heart. How do I leave that? The film can wait."

Mom reached across the table, her hand findin' mine, her grip warm despite the tremble, her smile soft, the kind that'd always pulled me through. "Go on, baby," she said, her voice breakin' just a touch, tears glistenin' but not fallin'. "You ain't leavin' me, you're takin' me with you. Every frame you shoot, that's us, this town, right there in your heart." She squeezed tighter, her eyes fierce now, a mother's love stronger than any sickness. "You make me a promise, you go, no matter what. Just make sure we're in the credits, you hear? Ruth and Thomas Chandler, biggest fans."

I laughed, a choked sound, wipin' my eyes with my sleeve, her smile pullin' me back from the edge. "You're gonna be the star, mom," I said, my voice thick, holdin' her hand like it was the only thing keepin' me steady. "And dad, you're gettin' a whole scene, readin' them Westerns."

Dad chuckled, his eyes wet but warm, leanin' back. "Better make it quick, son. I ain't got the face for long shots." But his nod said more, go, be you, we'll be okay.

The letter lay between us, no longer a weight but a bridge, their words givin' me resolve I hadn't found alone. Mom's hand, dad's nod, they were permission, a blessing to chase the stories I was born to tell, carryin' our spirit, their love, and their strength to a city I'd make my own.

Chapter 32 - Senior Bash
(May 1971)

May of 1971 was a blaze of endings in Mill Town, the final bell of my senior year ringin' out like a farewell to the life I'd known. I was eighteen, my 8mm camera a steady companion, the Sun Studios offer, a full scholarship to film school in Los Angeles, set to pull me from mom's cancer fight, dad's quiet strength, and the town's fadin' pulse. Eric's draft notice loomed, Lila's art school waited, and as I walked out of that old door for the last time, the weight of goodbyes mixed with a spark of what was comin', my heart torn but ready.

The last day of school was bright, sunlight spillin' across the cracked steps, warmin' the concrete where we'd stood a thousand times. The final bell clanged, sharp and free, and seniors spilled out, hollerin', tossin' papers into the air, math notes, essays, schedules flutterin' like confetti, catchin' the breeze. The school felt smaller already, its red-brick walls and squeaky halls shrinkin' behind us, like a reel fadin' to black. I stood on the steps, my camera bag slung over my shoulder, watchin' kids hug, laugh, some cryin', knowin' we were leavin' more than a building.

Mr. Radcliffe, the Economics teacher who'd pushed me to write what I saw, caught me by the door, his tie loose, his eyes crinkled. He shook my hand, his grip firm, his voice low but clear. "You told the truth, Bobby," he said, noddin' toward my camera. "*Mill Town Echoes*, that was real. Don't stop, you hear? The world needs that kinda honest, don't let anyone change the truth just because they don't like it or afraid of it."

I nodded, my throat tight, his words landin' deep. "Thank you, sir," I said, my voice steady but thick. "Tryin' to keep it, like you taught me."

He smiled, clappin' my arm, and stepped back, lettin' the crowd swirl around us. Then Mr. Tolley was there, my film club sponsor, his glasses glintin' in the sun, his hand restin' heavy on my shoulder. "You're gonna make us all proud, Bobby," he said, his voice warm, proud, like he was sendin' off a son. "Los Angeles ain't ready for you, but you're ready for it. Go show 'em what we're made of. Don't let them change who you are."

I laughed, a short, grateful sound, my eyes stingin' as I met his gaze. "Hope I don't mess it up, Mr. Tolley," I said, half-jokin', but his nod was sure, his hand squeezin' tighter before lettin' go.

"You won't," he said. "You got the eye, the heart. Just keep filmin'."

I turned, takin' one last look at the empty hallway through the open door, lockers dented, posters curled, the echo of our voices already fadin'. My camera bag felt heavier, packed with reels of memories, mom's voice, Lila's sketches, Eric's grin, all ready to follow me to LA. The steps were crowded, seniors scatterin' to cars, to plans, to futures, but I stood a moment longer, the sunlight warm, the papers still fallin'. I wasn't just leavin' a school; I was leavin' a piece of me, but carryin' its truth forward, frame by frame, with Radcliffe's charge and Tolley's faith to guide me into whatever lay beyond those cracked steps.

Word spread fast after graduation, like wildfire through the grapevine: one last party at Coldwater Creek, under the bridge where we'd jump off in the dead of summer into three foot of crystal clear, cool flowin' water. By dusk, the creek was alive, cars parked under the bridge and on the hill, their radios blastin' Creedence and Skynyrd, mixin' with the chirp of crickets and in the distance a lone whippoorwill. Coolers brimmed with root beer, a jug of moonshine smuggled in by Tommy's cousin, its recipe a secret shared in paper cups. A bonfire roared, its flames dancin' high, lightin' faces I'd known forever, kids from algebra, the football team, the film club, all here to mark the end, and the beginning.

Matt surprised me, rollin' in from Tallahassee in his Ford Falcon, his grin wide as he stepped out, holdin' his old baseball glove and a six-pack of root beer. "Couldn't miss the big send-off, little brother!" he said, tossin' me a bottle, his college swagger softenin' as he hugged me tight. "Heard you're Hollywood-bound, Bobby. You bring that glove, we'll play catch for old times' sake!" I laughed, my chest warm, clinkin' my root beer against his. "You're on, Matt, but I'm filmin' you strikin' out first!"

The creek buzzed with life, kids leaped from rope swings, splashin' into the cool water with whoops that echoed in the dark; couples danced barefoot in the sand, swayin' to the radio's slow tunes, their shadows long in the firelight. Jenny's brother brought a guitar, strummin' a rough "Sweet Home Alabama," and voices joined in, off-key but loud, the night holdin' us like a promise. I moved through it all, my camera hummin' quiet, catchin' moments between sips of root beer, friends laughin' by the coolers, their faces bright; Lila sketchin' faces in the firelight, her pencil flyin', her ribbon glowin' red against her hair; Eric starin' at the stars, his draft card in his pocket, his eyes far off but a smile tuggin' at his lips.

I paused by Lila, sittin' on a log, her sketchbook open to a drawin' of the bonfire, faces blurred but alive. "You're missin' the party, artist," I teased, filmin' her quick, her smile flashin' in the lens.

"Gotta catch this light, Bobby," she said, her voice soft, eyes meetin' mine. "It's us, right here, one last time. You're gettin' it too, ain't ya?"

I nodded, my throat tight, the camera lowerin'. "Every frame," I said, meanin' it, knowin' this reel was for us, for me, for the creek that'd always be home.

Eric found me later, a soda in hand, his grin softer now, the fire castin' shadows on his face. "Look at this, man," he said, noddin' at the crowd, the swings, the guitar. "We did good, didn't we? One hell of a goodbye." His voice cracked, the draft's weight heavy.

I gripped his shoulder, my voice low., "When you come back, Eric, and we'll do it again. Bigger fire, better moonshine."

He laughed, clappin' my back. "Deal, Hollywood. Film it for me."

The bonfire's glow softened, the crowd thinnin' as kids drifted to cars, their radios fadin' into the night. Lila caught my arm, her sketchbook tucked under her elbow, her ribbon loose in the moonlight. "Walk with me, Bobby," she said, her voice quiet but sure, noddin' toward the water's edge. We strolled along the creek, the sand cool under our bare feet, the water lappin' soft, dragonflies long gone. She stopped, her eyes glintin', and slipped a folded note into my pocket, her fingers quick, deliberate. "Don't read it till you're gone," she said, her voice low, a mix of firm and fragile. "It's… just somethin' to take with you. So you remember us."

I touched the note, my throat tight, wantin' to pull her close but noddin' instead.

"Lila, I ain't forgettin' you," I said, my voice thick. "You're in every reel I shoot, every damn frame."

She smiled, small but real, and bumped my shoulder, her laugh soft. "Better be, Bobby Chandler. Go make us proud." We stood there, the creek whisperin', her note a secret I'd carry to LA, a piece of her heart to keep me grounded.

Eric found me later, leanin' against a pine, the fire's embers castin' shadows on his face. He held out his favorite worn camouflage cap, its edges frayed, the one he'd worn fishin', racin', livin'.

"Here," he said, pushin' it into my hands, his grin crooked but his eyes serious. "If you ever make it big, don't forget us small-timers. This is for good luck, Hollywood." His voice cracked on the last word, the draft's weight heavy, his departure just hours away.

I took the cap, my fingers tracin' the stitches, my chest achin'. "Eric, you're the star of my first big film," I said, forcin' a laugh, but my eyes stung. "You come back, and I'll put this cap on a statue of you, right on Main Street."

He laughed, pullin' me into a quick hug, his voice low. "Deal, man. Keep that camera rollin' for me." I nodded, slippin' the cap into my bag, knowin' it'd ride with me to LA, a talisman for his safe return.

Matt was last, waitin' by his car, a root beer in hand. I climbed up beside him on the trunk, the creek glintin' behind us, the night cool and still. He looked at me, his college-weary eyes soft, older brother knowin'.

"You can leave Mill Town, but it never quite leaves you," he said, his voice steady, sippin' his drink. "Trust me, I know. Tallahassee's got nothin' on this place, Mom's gumbo, dad's porch, this creek. It's in your bones, Bobby."

I nodded, my hands grippin' the tailgate, the bonfire's last sparks fadin'. "I'm scared, Matt," I admitted, my voice low, the words spillin' out. "LA's huge, and mom... what if I'm not here when...she needs me?"

He clapped my shoulder, his grip firm. "You're takin' her with you, little brother. Every film you make, that's her, dad, all of us. Go be you." His smile was warm, sure, and I leaned into it, the creek's murmur a backdrop to his words, anchorin' me for the road ahead.

The bonfire's firelight flickered on the few faces left, its crackle softenin' as the night grew late, laughter turnin' quieter, like a song fadin' out. Kids drifted off, one by one, their shadows slippin' into the pines, Jenny huggin' Lila, Tommy's cousin haulin' the moonshine jug, car radios hummin' as they pulled away. The creek's sandbar, once alive with rope swings and guitar strums hours ago, settled into a hush, the coolers empty, the guitar gone silent. I stayed behind, my camera hummin' soft, filmin' the last embers, their orange glow dancin' on the sand, a final frame of the night that'd held us all.

I set the camera down, its weight a relief, and sat in the dark, the creek's murmur the only sound, its water glintin' under the moon. For a moment, I didn't feel excited about LA, or scared of leavin' mom, dad, or home. I was just… still, like the world had paused, lettin' me breathe in the place that'd shaped me. The air was cool, the junipers whisperin', and I leaned back, my hands in the sand, Lila's note in my pocket, Eric's camo cap in my bag, Matt's words, *Mill Town never leaves you*, echoin' soft.

I found a quiet spot by the creek. I just sat there for a bit. I looked to the heavens just in time to see a heron cross the moon above Creek, its wings a silent arc against the silver light, and a train sounded far off, its whistle low, mournful, like it was callin' us away. I whispered, "It's time," the words barely a breath, my heart steady but full, knowin' this was the end of one chapter and the start of another.

Matt and Eric appeared then, their steps squeekin' on the sand, their grins lit by the dyin' fire. They each were smilin' from ear to ear, "One last jump, Bobby?" Matt said, noddin' toward the old bridge over the creek, where we'd leaped off as kids, fearless and free. Eric slapped my back, his eyes bright despite the draft's shadow. "C'mon, Hollywood, let's go out with a splash!" he said, his voice loud, darin' the night to take him.

I laughed, standin', the stillness breakin' into somethin' alive. "Y'all ain't leavin' me behind," I said. The three of us racin' to the bridge, its surface littered with broken glass. We climbed the rail, the creek below dark and invitin', the moon watchin'.

"Together," Matt said, his voice firm, and we nodded, hands clasped, Matt's steady grip, Eric's calloused palm, my own shakin' but sure.

"One, two, three!" Eric hollered, and we jumped, sailin' through the night air, the water rushin' up cold and wild, swallowin' us in a splash that echoed like a vow.

We surfaced, laughin', sputterin', the creek holdin' us one last time, our voices bouncin' off the bridge. Matt slung an arm around me, Eric splashed us both, and we stood in the shallows, the embers gone. That jump, me, Matt, Eric, together, was our goodbye to innocence, to our youth, to home, carryin' its light to LA, to war, to college, to wherever we'd go, we'd always be tethered forever by a memory.

Chapter 33 - Leaving Home
(July 1971)

Before dawn, it was already 80 degrees out, the family gathered in the yard, the sky still dark, stars fadin' slow, dew glistenin' on the grass like tears the earth hadn't shed yet. Mom wrapped herself in her shawl, her frame small against the summer heat, her hands tremblin' but her smile steady as she handed me a thermos of coffee.

"For the road, baby," she said, her voice soft, her eyes holdin' mine like she was memorizin' me. I took it, my throat tight, wantin' to say a thousand things but I just nodded instead, huggin' her close, her shawl's wool scratchin' my cheek.

Dad loaded my luggage into the bed of the truck, careful as if it were glass, his hands movin' slow, deliberate, stackin' my suitcase and duffel with the same care he'd built mom's porch.

"Got everythin' you need, Bobby?" he asked, his voice low, his eyes catchin' mine in the dim porch light. "Camera's safe?"

I nodded, pattin' my carry-on, Eric's cap inside. "Safe, dad. Ready as I'll get." Matt, home from Tallahassee, double-checked my bag, riflin' through for my ticket, his grin forced but warm.

"Don't lose this, little brother," he said, slappin' my shoulder. "LA's waitin', and you ain't walkin' there."

We piled into the truck, dad drivin', mom beside him, Matt and me sittin against the bed in the back, the engine's rumble the only sound as we pulled outta the drive. The road to the airport stretched dark, pine trees blurrin' past the windows, their shadows long and lean. I could hear mom humming a hymn softly to herself out the window,

"Amazing Grace," her voice thin but clear, fillin' the cab with a comfort that hurt as much as it healed. dad's hands gripped the wheel, steady as always, his silence loud with pride and ache. Matt stared out his window, his jaw tight, like he was fightin' his own goodbye.

I watched the road, the yellow lines fadin' under the headlights, but my mind was elsewhere, the creek, its water glintin' under moonlight, where we'd jumped one last time; Main Street, its empty shops and tattered flag wavin' in my film; the family under the porch light at home, mom's garden growin' despite her sickness, dad's voice readin' to her, Matt's laugh over gumbo. Every mile took me further from 'em, from Lila's sketches, Eric's grin, the sandbar's embers. I touched Lila's note in my pocket, unopened, savin' it for the plane like she'd asked, and felt the weight of leavin', not just a place, but a piece of my soul.

The truck rolled on, mom's hum carryin' us, the pines givin' way to open fields, the airport somewhere ahead. I didn't speak, didn't need to. The quiet held us, a family bound by love and loss, sendin' me to chase stories for our town, for mom, for all of us, with the dawn creepin' closer and the road leadin' me to a gate I'd walk through alone, but never empty.

We pulled into the airport lot, the sky just blushin' pink, the terminal's lights harsh against the soft dawn. Mom was too weak to walk through, her body betrayin' her strength, so she stayed in the front seat, the window down, her shawl wrapped tight despite the summer warmth. Her soft smile masked the pain in her eyes, but I saw it, the way her hands trembled, the way she leaned against the door. Dad stood by the truck, unloadin' my bags, his silence a wall of support, while Matt checked my ticket, his voice low, keepin' busy to dodge the ache.

I knelt beside the car window, the gravel bitin' my knee, my face level with mom's, her breath shallow but her gaze fierce, like she was pourin' all her love into this moment. She reached out, her hand tremblin' as it touched my cheek, her fingers cool but steady, tracin' the line of my jaw like she was memorizin' me.

"You've always seen more than most, Bobby," she said, her voice hoarse but warm. "That's a gift. Don't be afraid to use it."

Tears welled, burnin' my eyes, but I blinked 'em back, my throat so tight I could barely breathe. "Mom," I started, my voice crackin', "what if I never, " The fear spilled out, raw, the thought of losin' her, of bein' in LA when she needed me, chokin' me.

She interrupted, her hand firm on my cheek, her eyes lockin' mine. "You made a promise," she said, her voice fierce now, cuttin' through my doubt. "You're tellin' our story, our town's, mine, your dad's. I couldn't ask for anythin' better than that." Her smile softened, but her grip didn't waver, her love stronger than the sickness stealin' her strength. "Follow your dreams, Bobby. Life's shorter than you think."

I nodded, tears spillin' now, no stoppin' 'em, my hand coverin' hers, holdin' tight like I could keep her forever. "I'm scared, mom," I whispered, the words barely audible, my head bowin' against the window's edge. "Scared I won't make you proud, scared I'll lose you."

She leaned forward, her shawl slippin', and kissed my forehead, her lips warm, a mother's seal. "You already made me proud," she said, her voice a rasp but sure, squeezin' my hand one last time. "Go show the world what you see. I'm right here, in every frame." She let go, her hand fallin' slow, her smile steady, a lighthouse in the dawn.

I stood, wipin' my face, my heart full and breakin', her words a fire I'd carry to LA. Dad clapped my shoulder, Matt hugged me quick, but mom's touch, her voice, were what I held as I grabbed my bags, the terminal waitin'. I looked back once, her silhouette in the truck, shawl and smile, and knew she was right, life was short, but her love, our story, would live in every reel I shot, pushin' me through the gate to chase the dreams she'd blessed.

Dad and Matt walked me through the airport's echoin' halls, the fluorescent lights harsh, the hum of voices and rollin' suitcases a

258

strange new rhythm. We said little, just quiet steps, our shoes tappin' the linoleum, small talk fillin' the space to keep the ache at bay.

"You got your ticket handy?" Matt asked, his voice casual, checkin' my bag again.

"Yeah, right here," I said, pattin' my pocket, my other hand grippin' my camera bag, its weight a tether to home.

Dad nodded at a sign. "Gate's up ahead, Bobby. Flight's on time." His voice was steady, but his eyes flicked to mine, holdin' more than he said.

At the gate, the crowd thinned, the plane's nose visible through the window, a beast waitin' to carry me west. Matt stopped, turnin' to me, his college-weary grin soft but real. He shook my hand, his grip firm, lingerin'. "Call me if you need anythin'," he said, his voice low, eyes steady. "Or if you don't. I'm your brother, Bobby, anytime." I nodded, my throat tight, squeezin' his hand back.

"Will do, Matt. Keep that Falcon runnin' for me." He laughed, a quick sound, clappin' my shoulder, his way of sayin' he'd be there, no matter the miles.

Dad stepped forward, his face weathered, his hands rough from years at the store, the porch, mom's care. His hug was strong and still, pullin' me close, his arms a wall I'd always leaned on. "You remember who you are out there," he said, his voice low, rough with feelin', his breath warm against my ear. "And where you came from. Don't forget we're so proud of you, son." He pulled back, his eyes mistin' over, a sheen I hadn't seen since I was a kid, his jaw tight to hold it in. No words left, just a nod, his hand lingerin' on my arm, sayin' what words couldn't.

I nodded back, my own eyes burnin', my voice gone. "I won't, dad," I managed, barely a whisper, my heart full of his pride, Mom's blessing. They stepped back, Matt's hand on Dad's shoulder, their silhouettes steady against the terminal's glare, as I turned to the gate.

As I walked toward the plane, my ticket in hand, I turned for one last look. Matt stood tall, his hand still on dad's shoulder, his grin brave but strained. Through the airport fence, I could see the truck in the parkin' lot, mom in the front seat, her shawl loose, her hand over her mouth, watchin' me through the windshield, her eyes fixed like she could see me across the distance. The sun had risen now, washin' the sky in soft gold, its light catchin' her face, dad's nod, Matt's wave, a final frame I didn't need my camera to keep.

I sat down on the plane for my first plane trip. The force pushin' me back in the seat as the plane's engines roarin'. We climbed higher and higher, the gold sky stretchin' endless outside the window. I could see how small our town really was from up here as it shrank below, the river, Main Street, the porch where mom sat, but it never left me, etched in my bones, in Lila's note, Eric's cap, the family I carried. Home was behind me, LA ahead, and as the plane soared, I whispered mom's words, *Life's shorter than you think.*

Halfway through the flight, I remembered the note, my fingers brushin' the folded paper in my pocket. I pulled it out, the note square smudged with pencil lead, Lila's tape seal intact, her voice, Don't read it till you're gone, clear as the creek. My hands, calloused from football and filmin', trembled as I broke the tape, unfoldin' the note slow, my breath catchin'. My eyes, red from holdin' back tears at the airport. I felt my jaw tightened, a mix of ache and resolve, my fingers tracin' the fold lines as the plane carried me further from home. I folded the note back just like it was and sealed it back up with the tape, unread. It was something meant just for me, hope and a dream that anythin' is possible.

Chapter 34 - The City of Angels
(July 1971)

My trip from home dropped me into Los Angeles, where a full scholarship to film school and a year with Sun Studios' nonfiction division lay ahead. I was just eighteen, images of home still echoed in my mind, holdin' Eric's camo cap, Lila's unread note, and mom's words, *Follow your dreams, life's shorter than you think*, echoed in my head. Steppin' off the plane at LAX, I was hit by a world so loud and alive it made the freight train by the old ice factory feel like a whisper, both thrillin' and overwhelmin' as I took my first steps into the City of Angels.

The terminal was a storm of motion. A chaos of noise. Folks rushin' past. Suitcases clatterin'. Voices bouncin' off the high ceilings in a mix of accents I couldn't place. It felt massive, like the whole world had crammed into one room, nothin' like Mill Town's stillness. The loudest thing there was a tractor or the church bell on Sunday. My worn shoes scuffed the shiny floor. My starched shirt seemed out of place. I clutched my camera bag, it reminded me what I was here for, mom's stories, dad's nod, the sandbar's firelight. It was keepin' me from driftin' in the tide of LAX. Part of me wanted to find a quiet corner to sit in, the other part was amazed by all the activity and stories each person could tell.

I weaved through the crowd, my heart thumpin', when I saw a driver in a crisp suit, holdin' a sign: "Bobby Chandler." That's my name! It was bold in black marker. It looked like it belonged to a stranger, the gesture so surreal it felt cinematic, straight outta the movies Mr. Tolley showed in film club. "That's me," I said, steppin' up, my voice half-swallowed by the din. The driver, a wiry guy with a quick smile, nodded. "Welcome to LA, Bobby. You got any bags?"

261

"I'm Bobby Chandler!" I said probably a little too loud while holding out my hand. "Yeah, I got two," I said, then paused, realizin' I had no idea where they were.

He just looked behind me, "Did you bring them with you?" he smiled.

"Uh… I think so," As I shrugged my shoulders.

He chuckled, not missin' a beat. "First time flyin', huh? Name's Ray, C'mon, let's hit baggage claim. I'll show you the ropes kid."

He led me back through the terminal, pointin' out the conveyor belts, explainin' how to spot my bags among the sea of luggage.

"Yours will come around eventually," he said, leanin' against a pillar. "Look for the ones that scream small town.'"

I laughed, easin' up, and we grabbed my beat-up suitcase and duffel, the driver slingin' one over his shoulder like it was nothin'.

We headed out, my bags in tow, toward the automatic doors, their glass slidin' open with a smooth whoosh that sent a shiver down my spine. I remembered the first time I'd seen 'em, at the AG store back home, starin' like they were magic, dad laughin' at my wide eyes. Now they were real, openin' to a city I'd only seen in grainy reels, and I shivered again. Outside, the air was cool but crisp, no trace of home's sticky summer.

"This is summer here?" I said, a half-smile tuggin' at me. "It's like outdoor air conditionin'."

Ray just smiled.

Ray loaded my bags into a sleek black car, the kind I've only seen in the movies. The city sprawlin' beyond, palm trees, freeways, a pulse that hummed louder than Main Street ever could. I gripped my camera bag. LAX was just the start, a gate to a world I'd learn to frame, to tell our story and mine, as the car pulled away, LA unfolded before me.

I slid into the back of the black sedan, Ray, a wiry guy, his name stitched on his shirt, glancin' at me in the rearview. "First time in LA, kid?" he asked, his voice rough but friendly, pullin' outta the airport lot.

I nodded, my camera bag on my lap, still clutchin' it like it might keep me from gettin' lost. "Yeah, just flew in from Mill Town. Small town, just outside of Pensacola, nothin' like this." I gestured out the window, where palm trees spiked the sky, their fronds swayin' against glass towers. "These trees, man, they're like somethin' off a postcard. And all this concrete? Feels like the whole city's movin'."

Ray chuckled, mergin' onto a freeway, cars zipin' past like fish in a river. "LA's a beast, Bobby," he said, catchin' my name from the sign he'd held. "Born and raised here myself. Came up in Ecino Park, driving cabs to pay for music school till life had other plans. You get used to the rush, but it never stops surprising you." His eyes crinkled, sensin' my awe, and I leaned forward, eager for more.

"What's it like, livin' here? Everybody's goin' somewhere, ain't they?" I said with hushed amazement.

"They think they are," Ray said, noddin'. "Everybody's chasing something, a gig, a dream, a break. You'll fit right in with that camera." He grinned, tappin' the wheel as we slowed near a mural-splashed wall, bright colors shoutin' stories of struggle and hope. I stared, my fingers itchin' for my lens, the city unfoldin' like a reel outside the window, food trucks slingin' tacos, their smoky smells driftin' in; glass towers glintin' like giants; skateboarders weavin' through crowds, their boards clatterin' on sidewalks. Life moved at full speed, a rhythm I'd never heard in home's quiet lanes.

I pressed my face to the glass, takin' it in, vendors hawkin fruit, old men playin' chess on crates, a street performer blowin' a saxophone, its wail cuttin' through the honks. Every corner sparked possibility, like each street was a story waitin' for my camera. "This place," I said, half to Ray, half to myself, "it's alive, ain't it? Like it's darin' you to keep up."

Ray laughed, turnin' onto a boulevard lined with more palms. "That's LA, kid. It'll chew you up or lift you up. You kid, got the look of someone who's going to fly."

The taxi rolled on, the city's pulse syncin' with my own, mom's words, *You've always seen more*, echoin' as I saw home's heart in every mural, every face. I gripped my camera bag, Lila's note and Eric's cap inside, ready to frame this new world, to make it sing like I'd made Main Street glow. LA was openin' wide, and I was already filmin' it in my head, one shot at a time.

The taxi slowed, turnin' off the boulevard, and rolled through wrought-iron gates, the words "Sun Studios" gleamin' in gold letters on a white arch, like a portal to another realm. I leaned forward, readin' the sign, my breath catchin' as it hit me, this was real, not some reel I'd watched in film club with Mr. Tolley. The lot stretched wide, soundstages loomin' like giants, palm trees framin' the sky, my head was stickin clean out the window, Ray, grinned. "Welcome to the big leagues, Bobby," he said, pullin' up to a sleek buildin' with glass doors.

I stepped out, my shoes hittin' the pavement, the air cool and dry, LA's pulse still buzzin' from the ride. Ava Klein, the producer who'd shaken my hand in Mill Town High's principal's office, waited by the entrance, poised and warm, her dark hair pulled back, a clipboard in hand. Her smile was bright, like she'd been expectin' me all along.

"Bobby Chandler," she said, her voice smooth, extendin' a hand. "Welcome to Sun Studios. Are you ready to make some stories?" Her eyes sparkled, knowin' the weight of what she'd offered, a scholarship, a chance, a new world, a life.

I shook her hand, my palm sweaty, my grin half-nervous, half-thrilled. "Yes, ma'am," I said, my voice steadier than I felt. "Still pinchin' myself, but I'm here, I think."

264

She laughed, soft, and waved over a lanky kid, about my age, with shaggy hair and a skateboard under his arm. "This is my son, Grant," Ava said, her tone fond but firm. "He'll give you the lay of the land, show you where you'll be stayin' and workin'. Grant, make sure Bobby doesn't get lost in the backlot, alright?"

Grant nodded, flashin' a grin that felt like Eric's, easy and a little sly. "C'mon, man, let's roll," he said, tuckin' his board under his arm, noddin' toward a path lined with trailers and soundstages. I slung my camera bag over my shoulder, glancin' back at Ava, who gave a small wave, her clipboard gleamin' in the sun. The gates of Sun Studios stood behind me, the gold sign a promise, and as I followed Grant, the lot buzzin' with crew calls and movin' lights, I felt every frame I'd shoot in this cinematic world unfoldin' before me.

Grant and I clicked the moment he led me from Ava's welcome, his skateboard tucked under his arm, his shaggy hair fallin' into his eyes. "So, Bobby, you're from some cowboy town or what?" he teased, dodgin' a movin' light rig as we headed toward the backlots. "Bet you rode a horse to school, right?"

I snorted, the first real laugh I'd let out in weeks, the sound surprisin' me, easin' the knot in my chest. "Naw, man, just a truck," I shot back, slingin' my camera bag higher. "Mill Town's got creeks, not corrals. You ever seen a real fishin' hole, city boy?"

He grinned, wide and genuine, like Eric when we'd race to Coldwater Creek, and I felt a tug of somethin' familiar, a friend-shaped hole startin' to fill.

"Fishing hole? I'd probably fall in," Grant said, laughin' as he waved me through a gate to the backlots. He showed me the studio's heart, sprawlin' sets where dust kicked up on a western town, its saloon doors swingin' like in dad's old novels; green screens glowin' under lights, ready to morph into any world; sound stages hummin' with crew shouts, mics danglin' like spiders. "This is where the magic happens,"

Grant said, pointin' to a sci-fi ship, its hull gleamin' fake but real enough to touch. "You're going to love this."

My curiosity sparked again, a fire I hadn't felt since filmin' *Mill Town Echoes*. My eyes lit up with every turn, takin' in the western sets, wooden storefronts, hitchin' posts, like Main Street reborn; the costume department, racks of glittering gowns and battered armor, stories waitin' to be worn; a prop room stuffed with ray guns and antique lamps, each a piece of a tale. "This is… unreal," I said, my voice low, runnin' my hand over a fake boulder, my camera bag bumpin' my hip. "Back home, I filmed a creek and a flag. Here? It's like the whole world's right here, in one lot."

Grant nodded, kickin' his skateboard up to catch it. "That's the game, man," he said, his eyes bright. "You take what's in your head and make it real. Mom says your film's got soul, I'm sure you'll make this place sing." His words hit deep, mom's voice, *You've always seen more*, echoin' as the studio surrounded me, the world I'd imagined through my lens now solid, alive, darin' me to frame it.

I followed Grant, my laugh comin' easier, my heart lighter despite the ache for home, mom, dad, Eric, Lila. This fast friendship, born in the shadow of soundstages, was a new reel startin' to roll, one where I'd learn to shoot the stories I'd carried, hometown heart, now mixin' with LA's glow.

Grant seemed as curious about me as I was of him. He kept sayin' he'd found somethin' rare, but I didn't know what that meant. He was pure LA, weaned on backlots, but his eyes had a hunger for somethin' else, not just Hollywood shine. After the day's orientation, he caught me by the campus fountain, his backpack bulgin' with film scraps and sketches, his voice lit up. "Bobby, you've got to room with me," he said, leanin' in, freckles dancin' across his nose. "I'm talking to Mom about the pool house. You're cool, man, like… real. Not some poser churning out car chase scripts. Say you're in!"

266

I laughed, my southern drawl feelin' thick, my hands stuffed in my pockets. "Grant, I'm just a small-town kid with a beat-up ole camera," I said, half-smilin'. "Your mom's gonna want more than that to let me crash." He grinned, slingin' his bag, already plottin'. "Nah, you've got that Southern charm thing. Mom's a pushover for honest. Let's go!"

We drove to his family's house that afternoon, a sleek spread of glass and manicured lawns, worlds away from home's saggin' porches. Ava Klein met us at the door, her silver-streaked bob gleamin', her slate-blue eyes sharp behind tinted sunglasses, a silk scarf loose at her neck. I shook her hand, standin' tall, my voice steady despite the nerves. "Mrs. Klein, thank you for seein' me," I said, meetin' her gaze. "It's an honor to be invited to your home." Grant jumped in, his plea a mix of charm and urgency. "Mom, Bobby's the guy, his film's got the profs buzzing. He's polite, won't trash the place, I swear! Pool house, please?"

Ava's lips curved, her eyes readin' me like a script, impressed by my quiet presence, the way I didn't push or preen. "You've definitely got a certain gravity, Bobby," she said, her voice low, a faint German lilt in her words. "Alright, the pool house is yours. Keep Grant out of trouble, yes?" I nodded, relief floodin' me. "Yes, ma'am, I'll try my best," I said, and Grant whooped, flailin' his arms 'round' like we'd pulled off a heist.

The pool house was a haven, clean white walls, big windows spillin' golden LA light, the pool's soft ripple outside, a bed and desk waitin' for my camera. It was more than a dorm's stale bunk, privacy to think, space to breathe, and Grant's restless energy, a friendship that felt like a lifeline. I moved in that evenin', my suitcase still zipped, set by the bed. I wasn't quite ready to unpack home's weight, but Grant's voice, "Bobby, you settled in or what? Got a projector to test!", cracked the ice.

"Comin'," I called, a smile tuggin' at me, my heart slowly unfreezin', the pool house a place to start, where LA's glow met Mill Town's

267

roots, and I could build somethin' new with a friend who seemed to understand me.

Settlin' into LA, I got swept up in the city's glow, a golden day with new friends stretchin' on, then it hit, sharp as a missed step, a creepin' realization that cut through the laughter: I never called home. I'd promised mom, kneelin' by the truck at the airport, her hand on my cheek, her voice firm, *Call when you get settled in, Bobby, let me know you're safe.* It was her way of holdin' on, of knowin' I was okay in a city she'd never see. My stomach twisted, guilt floodin' in, So much had happened since I left just hours ago, it had slipped my mind in the city's rush. I asked Grant if I could use the phone to call home.

He smiled "Use it all you want, we get free long distance! You're going to love it here."

The night had settled over Mill Town, dark and heavy, the town's heartbeat slow, its streets empty under a sky pricked with stars. The old Chandler house sat at the lane's end, its clapboard walls silvered by the full moons light, the porch dad built for mom creakin' soft in the breeze. Crickets and frogs sung a chorus, their song fillin' the quiet where Main Street's bustle used to be, the interstate's distant growl a faint scar on the silence. The garden's squash vines curled in the dark, mom's pride, but no light spilled from the windows, no warmth to greet the night.

Inside, the farmhouse was still, the air thick with absence. In mom and dad's room, the nightstand held a glass of water, a worn Bible, mom's shawl folded neat. The phone rang, sharp and jarrin', its trill cuttin' through the dark, a call from LA, from me, finally rememberin' my promise. It rang again, echoin' off the walls, the sound lonely, searchin'. The bed was still made, its quilt smooth, untouched, no one there to stir, to answer. Mom's absence, dad's too, hung like a held breath, the house a shell without their voices, their steps.

The phone rang on, unanswered, each note a plea that faded into the night. No one came, no hand reached for the receiver, the dial tone risin' slow, a mournful hum that filled the room, the house, the town. The crickets sang, the porch creaked, but the silence was louder, a weight that pressed against the walls, holdin' mom's laughter, dad's steady readin', my childhood in its shadows. The moment stretched, the dial tone lingerin', a sound that carried all I didn't yet know, all I'd left behind.

The scene faded to black, the dial tone hangin' in the air, a thread cut too soon, leavin' home still, the Chandler house empty, and me in LA, unaware, chasin' a golden day while home waited, silent, for a call that came too late.

Restless worry over the missed phone call to mom gnawed at me, chasin' sleep away as Los Angeles' unfamiliar clamor jolted me awake every few minutes. The guttural roar of motorcycles as they rumbled down the boulevard, their engines snarin' like chained beasts, while heavy trucks growled past, shakin' the pool house's thin walls. Above, helicopters thumped through the night sky, their blades slicin' the air, and airplanes droned high, a ceaseless hum that yanked me from shallow dreams. Each sound was a thief, stealin' rest, leavin' my heart racin' in the dark. Well before dawn, I gave up, risin' early, the sky still inky, no hint of the sunrise yet. I stepped outside the pool house, the air cool, carryin' a faint tang of chlorine and city dust. The pool shimmered under a full moon's silver gaze, its surface ripplin' like liquid glass, catchin' the light in soft, dancin' waves. The city had finally surrendered to silence, its pulse slowed, as if it, too, had collapsed into sleep. I stood barefoot on the dew-slick tiles, starin' up at the moon, its glow a quiet ache. I thought of Eric, likely still in basic trainin' somewhere, maybe sprawled in a bunk, body heavy from marchin' under a burnin' sun, his breath slow, dreamin' of the creek. Then my mind turned to mom and dad, the unanswered phone a knot in my gut, why hadn't they picked up? The house, the porch, mom's shawl, all felt far, too still. I'd try again when Grant stirred, his snores faint through the pool house wall. I laid back, in the hush, time stretched, the quiet wrappin' me like a memory of sittin' on the bench by the Riverwalk, the river's murmur my only company, leavin' me to wrestle with thoughts of home, heavy and clear under the moon's unblinkin' eye.

Grant loomed over me, his shadow dancin' across my face, pokin' my arm with a stick like he was testin' a campfire log. "Yo, Bobby, you still breathin' or what?" he teased, his sandy hair flappin' in the breeze, freckles poppin' across his grin. The Los Angeles sun blazed down, its heat pressin' on my skin as I must have dozed off in the pool chair, Eric's hat tipped over my eyes, the faint ripple of the pool a lullaby. He laughed, slingin' his beat-up backpack over his shoulder. "Man, you want a tent out here instead of that fancy bed?" I stirred, squintin' up at him, my neck stiff, and he yanked me to my feet, leadin' me into the cool shade of the house for breakfast. At the table, Ava's silver-streaked bob caught the mornin' light, her slate-blue eyes flickin' over us as she sipped coffee, while Grant shoveled pancakes, chatterin' about a broken projector.

The smell of syrup and bacon filled the air, just like home, just then a jolt hit me, mom, the unanswered call, her frail smile at the airport. "May I be excused? I gotta call home to make sure mom's ok." I asked, my voice quick, standin' before I thought it through.

Ava's lips curved, her gaze softenin' at my manners, my tie to family clear in my rush. "Of course, Bobby," she said, noddin'.

As I stepped out, her voice followed, low and firm, to Grant: "Stick by him, son. You two might learn a thing or two from each other." I pushed through the door, the weight of home pullin' me to the phone, mom's voice is all I needed to hear.

In the quiet of the pool house, the Los Angeles sun creepin' through the windows, I clutched the phone, my heart racin' as I dialed home, the unanswered call from yesterday twistin' my gut. After two rings, Dad's voice came through, steady but tired. "Chandler residence," he said, and I blurted out, "Dad, is everythin' okay? Why didn't nobody answer last night? Is mom alright?" My voice shook, picturin' mom's frail

270

frame, the empty house. Dad chuckled soft, calmin' me. "Easy, Bobby. Your mom's fine. She just couldn't bear goin' home to an empty house yet, not with you gone. She wanted to see the ocean, so we drove to Pensacola Beach for the night." Relief flooded me, my breath easin', and mom's voice came on, warm but hoarse. "Oh, Bobby, the waves, I had forgotten about how they roll in like a lullaby, I'd forgotten, soothin' and endless, and the moon was so bright the white the sand glowed. We walked the shore last night, me leanin' on your dad, just listenin'." She paused, her smile carryin' through the line. "How you holdin' up, baby? You settled in that big city?" I grinned, leanin' against the wall, the pool's shimmer outside. "Gettin' there, mom. Got a place with a friend, my camera's ready. It's... different." Her voice softened, proud and fierce. "I'm so proud of you, Bobby. Don't you worry 'bout us, we'll all be okay. You go show them what you see." I nodded, tears prickin', her words a balm,

Later that day was a blur of discovery, the film school campus alive with kids like me, dreamers with scripts, cameras, and stories to tell. Grant introduced me to a group from my class, their voices loud, their laughter easy, pullin' me into a day of explorin' LA. We wandered Venice Beach, the boardwalk buzzin' with skaters, musicians, and salt air, then hit a diner for burgers, talkin' films, Hitchcock, Cassavetes. I couldn't believe when one of them mentioned my own *Mill Town Echoes* sparkin' their questions. They said the teacher had shown it a few weeks ago as a lesson of how to show emotion through a lens without overdoin it. "A whole town in one reel?" a girl named Sarah asked, her eyes wide. "Bobby, that's raw."

I grinned, sharin' mom's stories, the creek's glow, feelin' home come back alive in my words. They said my face would light up every time I talked about home.

The day stretched on, golden, almost too perfect, palm trees swayin', the sun paintin' everythin' in a warm haze, LA's pulse was so different from Mill Town's slow beat. We laughed over arcade games, traded dreams on the pier, the ocean glitterin' like it held secrets.

271

Chapter 35 - Learning the Craft
(October 1971)

Grant was my guide, his wiry frame and restless grin leadin' me through film school's chaos like he'd been born with a clapperboard in hand. One crisp mornin', he hauled me to a campus workshop, his sandy hair flopping under a faded baseball cap, his Converse squeaking on the linoleum. "Time to get serious, Bobby," he said, unpackin' a Bolex 16mm camera, its chrome glintin' like a prize. "Your 8mm's got heart, but this baby's the real deal." He showed me how to mount it on a tripod, steady as dad's workbench, and adjust the lens for crisp focus, teachin' me to track a subject without jerkin' the shot. We rigged lights, big, hot Klieg lamps and softer Fresnels, castin' glows that could mimic mom's porch at dusk. In the editin' room, he walked me through a Steenbeck flatbed, its reels whirrin' as we spliced film strips with razor blades and tape. "Look here," he said, trimmin' a frame, his beaded bracelet clinkin'. "Cut tight, you keep the story movin'. You're painting a picture, but with precision." I soaked it up, my hands quick to copy his moves, my mind spinnin' with ways to frame water shimmerin', Lila's sketches, Eric's laugh. I was a fast learner, hungry for every tip, each reel a step toward makin' my stories breathe.

The Sun Studios lot was a livin' stage, and Grant, weaned on its backlots, snuck me into its heart. I stood behind soundstages, watchin' directors bark orders, their voices cuttin' through the clatter of C-stands and cables. One day, a wiry director with a cigar caught me peerin' from a prop crate, his eyes narrowin'. "You lost, kid, or you workin'?" he snapped. I stood straight, my voice steady. "Workin', sir. Wanna make films that mean somethin'." He smirked, puffin' smoke. "Then watch close and keep quiet." I did, studyin' how he angled shots, coaxed actors, turned a bare set into a world, skills I'd use to capture emotion. My notebook filled with jotted angles and lightin' tricks, each one tied to home.

A month later, Grant's biggest move came one afternoon when he leaned into the pool house, his plaid shorts rumpled, his eyes sparklin' like he'd found gold.

"Mom's pitchin' a project at Sun Studios today," he said, tossin' me a lanyard with a studio pass. "You're taggin' along, Bobby. Don't blow it."

I followed, my stomach knottin', to a polished boardroom where Ava Klein held court, her silver-streaked bob sharp under fluorescent lights, her slate-blue eyes scannin' a table of slick producers and jittery writers. I stood in the corner, quiet, watchin' her wield her father's legacy like a blade, her voice low, her faint German lilt edgin' her words.

"This script's got no guts," she said, slappin' a page, her ink-stained fingers firm. "You're just selling flash, not a story. Dig deeper or it's dead."

A producer argued, and she leaned forward, her scarf slippin', her gaze unyieldin'. "Sun Studios doesn't churn out noise, we make truth something to make us believe. I want a film that makes me feel something. Rewrite it." I scribbled notes, her fire echoin' mom's charge to tell our story, my own resolve hardenin' to carve a place in rooms like this, where stories lived or died.

Nights in the pool house, Grant and I worked late, testin' camera rigs, cuttin' practice reels on a rickety splicer, his quick wit keepin' me sharp. "You're getting real good, Bobby," he said one night, threadin' film, his freckles faint in the lamplight. "Your stuff's raw, but it's alive, same story, but now it's got studio snap."

I grinned, windin' a reel. The lot, the lessons, Ava's steel, they were tools to lift my home's truth, and with Grant's hand showin' me the ropes, I was learnin' to wield 'em, buildin' a craft that'd carry voices across the miles, one careful frame at a time. It was the first time I realized that immortality does exist.

One Friday evening, Grant burst into the pool house, his sandy hair wild, his Converse floppin' as he dangled his car keys. "Get up, Bobby, we're hittin' the road!" he said, his freckles poppin' with a grin. "Pacific Coast Highway's callin', and you ain't seen LA till you've felt it."

I grabbed my jacket, half-laughin', and we piled into his beat-up Chevy convertible, the engine sputterin' as we peeled out toward the coast. The sea breeze hit me hard, cool and salty, rushin' through the open top, tanglin' my hair as the highway curved along the ocean, its waves glintin' under a settin' sun. Neon signs flickered to life, diners, motels, gas stations, their pink and blue glow mixin' with distant music, a jukebox wail driftin' from some beachside joint. I leaned back, the sights and sounds washin' over me, so different from back home, yet stirrin' the same ache for somethin' real.

We parked at the Santa Monica Pier, its Ferris wheel spinnin' slow against the twilight, the boardwalk alive with laughter and the sizzle of fry stands. Grant handed me a fish taco, the tortilla warm, the fish crisp, and we walked the creakin' planks, dodgin' kids with cotton candy and couples swayin' to a street band's twang.

"So, Bobby," Grant said, leanin' on the rail, the ocean dark and endless below, "what's the big dream? Are you going to make a Hollywood epic?" His voice was light, but his eyes, sharp as ever, waited for truth.

I chewed slow, starin' at the waves, the taco's spice fadin' as my fears spilled out. "I wanna tell stories, Grant, mom's, dad's, my town's, every small town's," I said, my voice low, the pier's noise dullin' around me. "But sometimes I'm scared, Scared I'll get lost out here, forget where I came from. This place, it's all lights and noise. What if it swallows me, and I start makin' films that don't mean nothin' just to make a buck?" The words hung, raw, my hand grippin' the rail.

Grant tossed his taco wrapper in a can, his beaded bracelet clinkin' as he turned, his face serious, no trace of his usual quips. "Listen, Bobby," he said, his voice firm, cuttin' through the boardwalk's hum. "Hollywood's full of facades, fake fronts, empty scripts, folks chasin' fame over truth. But what the people really crave, deep down, is authenticity. Your stories? Your town, your mom, that creek, they're real. Stay true to that, and you'll cut through the noise." He clapped my shoulder, his grin returnin', softer now. "Keep telling stories that hit like yours do. Nobody will ever be able to take that away from you."

I nodded, the sea breeze cool on my face, his words settlin' like a reel findin' its frame. The pier's lights danced, the music played on, but I saw mom's porch, dad's nod, Eric's laugh, Lila's sketches, Matt tossin a ball, all clear as the ocean's roll. "Thanks, Grant," I said, my voice steadier, a smile tuggin'. "Guess I just gotta keep filmin'…my own way."

He laughed, nudgin' me toward the Ferris wheel. "Damn right, man. Now c'mon, let's ride this thing before you get all sappy!"

We ran, the night alive, my fears easin' under the neon glow, home was still beatin' strong, ready to shine in every story I'd tell, authentic and unyieldin', just as Grant said. Maybe Matt was right, we could leave Mill Town, but it never really left us.

The Sun Studios lot was my classroom, its sprawl of sets and cables a maze I learned by heart. I spent my days soakin' up everythin' I could, shadowin' crews with my notebook clutched tight. I watched directors block scenes, their hands shapin' air like sculptors, placin' actors just so, a tilt of a hat, a step to the left, to catch the story's pulse. One mornin', a cinematographer, grizzled and squintin' through a viewfinder, let me peer through his lens, showin' me how to balance light and shadow for a diner scene's mood. "See that glow?" he said, adjustin' a Fresnel lamp. "It's gotta feel like heartbreak, kid." I nodded, thinkin' of mom's porch at dusk, and later helped frame second-unit shots, holdin' a light meter steady, my hands learnin' to paint with sun

276

and steel. The work was hard, the hours long, but each moment, grippin' a dolly, checkin' a focus pull, felt like buildin' somethin' real, a bridge from that small town's stories to the screen.

The lingo came natural, slippin' into my talk like it'd always been there. "We need more coverage on this beat," I'd say, pointin' at a script, or "Check continuity, her scarf's flipped," noticin' a mismatch between takes. Grant caught me one day, mid-sentence, and laughed, his sandy hair floppin' as he slung an arm around me. "Listen to you, Bobby, tossing 'coverage' like a pro!" he teased, his freckles dancing. "You're becoming the real deal, man." I grinned, my chest warm, knowin' I was shapin' up, the kid with a shaky 8mm turnin' into someone who could hold his own on a set.

Grant treated me like a brother, his quick wit and studio tricks keepin' me sharp. He'd joke while threadin' a Steenbeck editor, callin' me "Mill Town Kubrick," then slow down to show me how to splice a reel clean, his beaded bracelet clinkin' as he worked. "Keep your cuts tight," he'd say, his voice earnest, "like your creek stories, every frame's gotta count." When I fumbled a rig, he'd nudge me, smilin'. "You'll get it, Bobby. You got the eye." His encouragement, his late-night talks over Cokes in the pool house, made LA feel like home, his belief in me a fire that matched mom's pride.

Ava was my guardian, her mentorship steady as dad's hands, her warmth a quiet strength. She'd call me to her office, her silver-streaked bob sharp under lamplight, her slate-blue eyes readin' me like a script. One day, she slid a contract across her desk, her ink-stained fingers tappin' it. "Read every line, Bobby," she said, her voice low, a faint German lilt edgin' her words. "You're here to create, not get chewed up by fine print in a contract." She guided me through clauses, taught me to spot traps, her advice clear: protect your story.

"You have something that's rare. Others may not recognize it, don't let them change your vision in editing because a suit thinks it would sell better that way." She said with conviction, like it was coming from somewhere deep, a personal experience maybe.

Another time, over coffee, she asked about my next project, listenin' as I sketched a film about a boy growin up in a small town.

"Hold that truth," she said, her scarf slippin', her gaze fierce. "Don't let this town polish it away." Her faith, her care, echoed mom's charge to tell our story, pushin' me to grow without losin' myself.

The lot's chaos, Grant's brotherhood, Ava's wisdom, they were shapin' me, turnin' my hunger into skill. I stood on set one evening, framin' a shot, the camera was humming. Suddenly, I saw myself filming like I was watchin' myself from a distance. I was becomin' a real filmmaker, my roots not just holdin' me but liftin' me, preparing me to tell stories that'd carry a small town's heart across the years.

Chapter 36 - A Visitor from Home
(July 1972)

I was in the studio's editing bay, splicing a reel, when Grant yelled across the floor, his voice cutting through the projector's hum. "Hey, Bobby, phone for you!"

I jogged over, grabbing the receiver, and Matt's voice came through, warm but tired, like he'd been carrying something heavy. "Bobby, it's me," he said. "I was thinking of flying out there next week for a few days. Need to clear my head, see what your big-shot LA life's like." His laugh was quick, but it didn't reach far, and I gripped the phone, my heart lifting despite the edge in his tone.

"Matt, that's great!" I said, lighting up, my grin wide enough for Grant to raise an eyebrow. "You'll love it, palm trees, studios, the whole deal. I'll pick you up at LAX. When's your flight?" We set the details, and I hung up, thrilled, picturing Matt's easy grin, his Falcon's rumble, our last creek jump.

"My brother's coming," I told Grant, already planning to show Matt the backlots, maybe sneak him into a sound stage. But a small knot stayed in my gut, Matt's voice echoing, *clear my head*, like there was more he wasn't saying.

One week later, I stood in LAX's terminal, the same chaotic swirl I'd faced a year ago, my shoes scuffing the floor, eyes locked on the escalator. Matt came down, his duffel slung over his shoulder, his hair longer now, college life marking his frame. For a split second, his face tightened, like a grimace, a flash of something raw, maybe pain or worry, before it melted into his familiar smile, wide and warm. "Little brother!" he called, pulling me into a hug, his arms strong but quick, like he was rushing past that first look.

I hugged him back, laughing, but sensed something wrong, a shadow in his eyes, the way his grip lingered a beat too long. "Good to see you, man," I said, stepping back, searching his face. "Flight okay?"

He nodded, slinging his bag higher, his smile holding but not deep. "Yeah, smooth. LA's wild already, look at this place!" His voice was bright, dodging deeper waters, and we headed to the car, chatting about his classes at Florida State, bridge designs he was drafting.

"How's mom and dad?" I asked, testing the ground, knowing mom's treatments were rough.

"Same as ever," he said, quick, his eyes flicking away. "Dad's readin' her Zane Grey, mom's bossin' the garden. Tell me 'bout these studios, Bobby, what's the big shot life like?"

He changed the subject fast, his laugh forced, and I let it slide, though the knot in my gut tightened. Matt's grimace, his quick dodge, told me something was off, home, school, maybe something deeper, but he wasn't ready to spill. I drove us into LA, pointing out murals and food trucks, keeping it light, hoping the city's glow and our brotherly bond would coax out whatever he was carrying, knowing whatever it was I would get out of him eventually. I was just glad he was here, under LA's sun.

In the car from LAX to the house, where I stayed near the studio, Matt fired off questions like he was racing to fill the silence.

"How big is that lot again, Bobby?" he asked, leaning forward, his eyes darting to the palm-lined streets. "What's it, acres? And you get to eat with actors and stuff, right? Like, real movie stars?" His voice was loud, eager, but I caught the edge, less curiosity, more deflection, like he was building a wall with words. I answered, keeping it light, my hands tight on the wheel.

"Lot's huge, maybe ten acres, soundstages everywhere. No actors in the cafeteria yet, but I saw a guy who looked like John Wayne's stunt double." Matt laughed, quick and sharp, but his eyes flicked away, dodging mine in the rearview.

I tried probing, soft. "You good, man? School treating you right?"

He shrugged, staring out the window at a mural flashing by. "Yeah, bridges and math, you know. Same old. Tell me 'bout your films, what's the next big hit?" His tone shut the door, and I let it go, the knot in my gut growing as we pulled up to Ava's.

Grant met us at the door, his shaggy hair falling over a wide grin. "Matt, welcome to the LA!" he said, clapping his shoulder. "Stay as long as you like. We got room, and Mom's cool with it." Matt nodded, his smile easing a bit, but I saw the strain, like he was holding something back even from Grant's warmth.

Later, we hopped a bus to the beach, seeking a break from the city's hum, Matt's idea to "see the ocean before I'm stuck in a library again."

He leaned back in the bus seat, his baseball cap pulled low, shielding his eyes. I watched him in the window's reflection, searching for clues behind his forced grin, the way his jaw tightened when he thought I wasn't looking. The city rolled by, taco stands sizzling with grease, neon-lit motels blinking pink and blue, the curling edge of LA's sprawl giving way to glimpses of the Pacific.

"Man, this place doesn't stop, does it?" Matt said, a touch of awe in his voice, his cap tipping back as he stared at a street performer juggling fire. "It's like Tallahassee got plugged into a socket."

I nodded, smiling, but kept watching, his awe feeling like another dodge. "Yeah, LA's a live wire," I said, leaning closer. "But you ain't gotta play it cool with me, Matt. What's going on? Something with home? School?"

He stiffened, his grin fading for a beat, then flicked his cap lower. "Just needed a break, little brother," he said, too quick. "Let's hit that beach, alright?" His voice closed the door again, but I saw the shadow in his eyes, a piece of Mill Town's weight, maybe mom's sickness, dad's worry, or something else, carrying over, even here.

The bus rumbled on, the ocean nearing, and I held my question, hoping the waves and our bond would loosen whatever Matt was burying.

The bus hissed to a stop near Santa Monica Pier, and the second we stepped off, the scent of salt air hit us, sharp and clean, riding a breeze that cut through LA's heat. I inhaled deeply, closing my eyes, a smile spreading wide as the Pacific sparkled ahead, its waves crashing soft against the sand. "Almost smells like Pensacola," I said, my voice light, the briny tang pulling me back to the snow white sands and emerald colored water, summer surfing trips with Matt when he wasn't working. The Pacific seemed bigger, wilder, but that salt was a thread to home, the life I'd left.

Matt laughed, a real laugh, the first since he'd landed, his baseball cap tipping back as he squinted at the horizon, his shoulders easing for the first time. "Almost like home, huh, well except, for the rocks?" he said, his grin breaking through the shadow I'd seen at the airport. "Let's see if these California waves are as tough as the Gulf, little brother. Bet I can still beat you!" His voice had a spark, the old Matt who'd tossed footballs and raced me to the creek, and he tugged off his shoes, already heading for the sand.

I followed, kicking off my own shoes, the warm sand shifting under my feet, the pier's bright wheel spinning slow in the distance. Matt's laugh, his loosened stride, felt like a crack in the wall he'd built, though I still sensed the weight he carried, mom's sickness, maybe, or something from school he wouldn't name. For now, I let it go, racing him to the water's edge, the salt air filling my lungs, the waves daring us to dive in. Matt splashed into the surf, hollering "Man that's cold, this definitely ain't the Gulf!", I grinned, hoping the ocean's pull would loosen the truth he was holding back, brother to brother under the wide California sky.

We ambled to a weathered shack near the pier, the kind with faded paint and a sun-bleached sign reading "Surf's Up Rentals." A lanky guy with a sunburned nose leaned on the counter, chewing a toothpick. "Yo, dudes, what's the vibe? Shortboards for tricks or longboards for cruising?" he drawled, sizing us up. I grinned, pointing to a sleek shortboard, its red stripes gleaming like a racecar. "Gimme that one, man," I said. "Wanna carve some waves, show this place how we do it back home!" Matt laughed, slapping my shoulder, and grabbed a longboard, wide and steady, just like we'd done back in Pensacola. "Slow and smooth, little brother," he teased, hoisting it under his arm. "You'll be suckin' my spray while I glide this hog!"

We paid and hit the sand, the sky beginning its golden descent, painting the Pacific in hues of fire and peach. We paddled out, the water cold and alive, slapping our boards like a familiar joke, its chill biting through but waking me up. "Holy hell, this is colder than the Gulf in February!" Matt hollered, shaking water from his hair, his baseball cap left on shore. "These Cali waves better be worth it, Bobby, or I'm haulin' you back to Florida for some real surf!" His grin was wide, the shadow from LAX fading in the ocean's pull, his voice carrying the old Matt, the one who'd raced me to the creek.

I laughed, paddling harder, the board slicing through the swell. "Keep talking, big shot!" I shouted, spotting a set coming in. "Bet I'll catch this one and leave you chokin' on foam!" The water surged, alive under us, and we pushed forward, the sun dipping low, its gold light dancing on the crests. Matt's longboard caught the wave first, his stance steady, hollering, "Watch the master, kid!" as he glided, while I fumbled my shortboard, wiping out in a salty tumble, laughing through the crash. The ocean was our old friend, pulling us back to Pensacola's shores, back home, but I still saw the flicker in Matt's eyes, a secret he wasn't spilling, even as we rode the waves, brothers bound by the tide, daring the truth to surface under Santa Monica's glowing sky.

We floated side-by-side on our boards in the lineup, the shortboard under me, Matt's longboard steady, the Pacific's swell rocking us gentle as we scanned for the next set. The sun hung low, its gold light spilling across the water, the pier's wheel lit up, spinning slow in the distance reflecting off the water. Matt grinned, his face salt-streaked. "Remember that rip current at the Pass that almost took you into Alabama?" he teased, splashing water at me, his voice light, like we were back on Pensacola's shores. "Thought we'd have to send a boat for you, screamin' like a seagull!"

I laughed, flicking water back, my board wobbling under me. "I remember *you* screaming like it did!" I fired back, dodging his splash. "Hollerin' for dad like the Gulf was gonna swallow us both! Took mom's gumbo to shut you up after." His laugh boomed, real and deep, the kind I hadn't heard since our last creek jump, and for a second, his eyes lost their shadow, sparkling like the kid who'd raced me to the creek.

A wave rose, clean and curling, and we locked eyes, nodding without words, paddling hard. "Go, Bobby!" Matt shouted, his longboard catching first, but I was right with him, my shortboard gliding down the face. We rode together, the water roaring under us, the wind whipping our faces, the sun painting the wave gold. For those brief moments, we weren't in LA, not carrying news of mom's sickness, my guilt for leaving, or whatever pressure Matt was hiding. We were just two brothers surfing under a golden sky,

The wave faded, dropping us into the foam, and we paddled back, grinning, the ocean's cold bite a reminder we were alive. Matt's shadow lingered, a secret still unshared, but that ride, that rewind to childhood, was a gift, a frame I'd carry like my camera's reels, keeping us close as I faced LA's sprawl and he faced whatever waited back home.

Matt grew quiet, his grin from our childhood banter gone, his eyes fixed on the horizon where the pier's lights flickered on. The laughter we'd shared, teasing 'bout rip currents and Gulf swims, faded into the rhythm of crashing surf, each wave a low roar that filled the space he left empty. I sensed it, the air turning heavy, and let the silence linger, my hands gripping the board, waiting for whatever was weighing him down. A wave rose, curling clean, but we didn't chase it, our boards bobbing still, the moment too thick to move.

Matt finally spoke, his voice low, rough, like it hurt to push out. "Eric's home." The words hung, simple but sharp, cutting through the surf's hum. I spun on my board, nearly tipping into the water, my heart leaping with joy, a grin splitting my face. "Eric's back?!" I said, my voice loud, ecstatic, the image of his crooked grin, his camo cap, flooding me. "Why didn't you say anything, man? That's amazing! When'd he get home? Is he, "

Matt's shoulders sank, his face tight, eyes dropping to the water, and my words died. "He's pretty banged up, lost his leg," he said, his voice barely above the waves, each syllable heavy, like stones sinkin' in the tide. The sound of the surf suddenly felt louder, a roar that drowned everythin' else, the boards bobbin' with the tide as the joy drained from my face, leavin' a cold ache. Eric, my best friend, the one who'd jumped off the creek bridge, who'd dared me to film the world, home, but broken, the war takin' a piece of him I'd never get back.

I swallowed hard, my throat burnin', starin' at the water, seein' Eric's laugh, his strut, now changed. Matt's voice came again, rougher, tryin' to hold steady. "He looks the same, but different," he said, his eyes wet, glintin' in the dusk. "Got that same dumb grin, still talkin' 'bout his truck. But... he's alive, Bobby. That's somethin', right?" He looked at me, searchin', like he needed me to say it was enough.

"Yeah," I managed, barely noddin', my voice thick, the word feelin' small against the ocean's vastness. "That's somethin'." The waves kept crashin', the boards kept bobbin', and I gripped my board tighter, Eric's cap in my bag back on shore, his absence now a wound I hadn't felt till now. Matt's silence, his grimace at LAX, made sense, carryin' this news, protectin' me till he couldn't. We just floated there watchin' the sun disappear into the ocean, brothers.

We floated on our boards, the Pacific's swell rockin' us, the sky now a deep amber as the sun sank beneath the horizon. We rode a few more waves, neither speakin' much, the crash of water fillin' the space where our laughter had been. My shortboard cut through a curl, but my heart wasn't in it, my mind on Eric, his grin, his truck, the leg he'd left in a war I couldn't picture. On one wave, I leaned too far, tumblin' into the cold churn, the water closin' over me. I didn't scramble to get back up, lettin' the tide hold me a moment, the sting of the cold salt water mixin' with the ache burnin in my chest, before I surfaced, gaspin', and hauled myself back on the board. Matt glanced over, his longboard steady, his eyes shadowed but not pushin' me to talk.

"Best get in 'fore the sharks come out" I shouted to Matt over the sound of the waves breaking.

We paddled in, the shore comin' closer, the pier's lights glowin' against the dusk. On the sand, we carried our boards back slowly, the mood heavy, the boards' weight matchin' the news we carried. My toes sank in the sand, Matt's steps beside me quiet, his baseball cap back on, pulled low. Eric's loss, his leg, his old self, felt like a reel I couldn't edit to make it right, a story I didn't know how to tell. The surf shack loomed ahead, the rental guy wavin' lazy, but we didn't speak, just handed over the boards, the ocean's roar fadin' behind us.

Matt broke the silence, his voice low, like an olive branch. "Let's get some of those fish tacos I've been hearin' about," he said, noddin' toward a food truck up the boardwalk, its neon sign blinkin', the smell of grilled meat driftin' over. His tone was soft, tryin' to pull us back from the edge, to find somethin' normal in the hurt.

I didn't respond right away, my hands stuffed in my pockets, Eric's face flashin', laughin' at the creek, now different, changed. I swallowed, the ache still there, but nodded, my voice rough. "Yeah. Let's eat."

It had been a great week, showin' Matt around LA. He got to meet all my new friends and see where I was studyin'. We even called mom and dad, both on the same call. It was almost like we were all back home sittin' round the table at breakfast eatin' waffles, talkin' like we had done thousands of times before. I realized I didn't appreciate it as much as I should've. Made me think, in twenty years from now, what would I say I should've done in *this* moment?

The freeway stretched quiet under an early mornin' haze, the LA skyline blurred in soft grays, nothin' like the banter-filled drives we'd shared back home, laughin' over radio tunes or creek memories. I gripped the wheel, my eyes on the road, but my mind was on Eric, his grin gone quiet, his leg lost to war, the news still churnin' like the Pacific's waves. Matt sat beside me, his duffel in the back, starin' out the window, his baseball cap low, his usual spark dimmed. The ocean, where we'd laughed and rode waves, was just another memory now, its salt air replaced by the city's hum, both of us lost in thought.

At the departure terminal, I pulled to the curb, the airport's buzz muted in the dawn. Matt grabbed his duffel from the back, slingin' it over his shoulder, and stood beside the car, his boots scuffin' the pavement. For a moment, neither of us said anythin', the silence thick, like the haze over the city, holdin' all we hadn't voiced, mom's sickness, Eric's pain, the distance growin' between us. I stepped out, leanin' against the car, my hands stuffed in my pockets, waitin' for words that didn't come easy.

Matt finally broke the silence, his voice low, rough, like it took effort to push out. "You should come back, Bobby," he said, his eyes meetin' mine, steady but heavy. "For a little while." He shifted his bag, his jaw tight, and kept goin'. "We missed you at Christmas. Eric's not talkin' much. Barely eatin'. He's… stuck, man. Needs somethin' familiar, somethin' to pull him back." He hesitated, his voice droppin' softer, almost a plea. "Maybe seein' you will pull him out of whatever this is."

His words hit like a wave, cold and sharp, stirrin' the guilt I'd carried since leavin' Mill Town. I nodded, my throat tight, seein' Eric's face, his camo cap, the creek jumps we'd shared, now shadowed by war's cost. "Yeah," I said, my voice thick, barely above the airport's hum. "I'll come. For Eric. For all y'all."

Matt's eyes softened, a flicker of relief, and he clapped my shoulder, his grip firm but brief. "Good. He needs to be reminded of what's still here."

Matt stood by the curb, his duffel slung over his shoulder, the early mornin' haze softenin' LAX's edges, his eyes holdin' mine after urgin' me to return for Eric's sake. He leaned in, his voice softer this time, almost a whisper, like he was sharin' a secret too heavy for the open air. "And Mom…" he said, his gaze steady but raw, "she's tryin' to stay strong, but you know she's... She misses you, Bobby. Talks 'bout your films, your letters, like they're keepin' her goin'." His words cut deep, mom's frail hug at the airport flashin' back, her shawl, her smile tryin to mask the cancer's toll.

I swallowed hard, my throat burnin', noddin' 'cause words wouldn't come, my hands clenched in my pockets. Mom's face, her eyes bright despite the pain, her voice tellin' me to chase my dreams, filled my mind, mixin' with guilt for leavin', for bein' here while she fought, while Eric struggled, while dad tried to hold it all together. I wanted to say I'd be there, that I'd drop everythin', but the weight of it, film school, Sun Studios, the stories I was learnin to build, choked me, leavin' just a nod, my eyes stingin' as I looked at Matt.

He stepped back, slingin' his duffel higher, and headed for the terminal doors, the glass glintin' in the risin' sun. Halfway there, he looked back, his voice clear, carryin' over the airport's hum. "Don't wait too long, Bobby," he said, his eyes fierce, a brother's plea. "Sometimes the story ain't the only thing that needs finishin'."

Matt vanished through the doors, and I stood by the car, the haze liftin' as the city woke. Matt's warning was heavy, a truth I couldn't dodge.

I'd go home, not just for them, but to face the story I'd left unfinished, before time ran out, before the frame faded to black. I climbed into the car, the road to Sun Studios waitin', but home's call was stronger now, a promise I'd keep, soon, for the ones who'd shaped every shot I'd ever take.

Chapter 37 - The Pitch
(July 1972)

It was late, the studio quiet, just me and Grant in the editin' bay, the hum of LA muted beyond the windows. We'd been messin' with a school project, but somethin' in me, maybe Matt's plea to come home, maybe Eric's shadow, pushed me to dig deeper. I pulled my 8mm reel from my bag, its canister worn from countless viewings, and looked at Grant, his shaggy hair fallin' over curious eyes. "I wanna show you somethin'," I said, my voice low, a mix of nerves and pride. "It's my film, the extended edition of *Mill Town Echoes*. Ain't quite done, but… it's bout as real as it gets."

I threaded the reel, the projector clickin' to life, and the screen glowed with Mill Town's faded streets, Main Street's empty shops, Coldwater Creek's shimmer, mom's voice tellin' stories of her garden, dad's hands fixin' a porch, the tattered flag wavin' at dusk. Grant leaned forward, his skateboard propped against the wall, and watched, silent and still, his usual quick grin gone. The film rolled, Eric laughin' by the creek, Lila sketchin' faces, Mr Jennings at the memorial, the town's quiet ache under the interstate's hum, and I saw his eyes glisten, his breath catch, the weight of it hittin' him like it had me every time I watched.

When the screen went dark, the projector's hum fadin', Grant sat back, his voice soft but fierce. "Dude… this is real," he said, turnin' to me, his eyes wide, raw. "This ain't just a film, Bobby. This is art. It's… it's like you pulled the heart outta that place and put it up there. People *need* to see this." His words hit deep, not praisin' my cuts or shots, but seein' the love, the loss, the truth I'd poured into every frame, mom's strength, Eric's spirit, Lila's light…soul.

I swallowed, my throat tight, feelin' seen, not for my technique but for my heart, the part of me that'd filmed to keep home alive. "Thanks, man," I said, my voice rough, a half-smile breakin' through. "Been carryin' this place with me, y'know? They're why I'm here."

Grant nodded, clappin' my shoulder, his grip sure. "Then you gotta finish it." The night stretched quiet, the reel back in its canister, but Grant's words lit a fire, pushin' me to polish *Mill Town Echoes*, to share its truth with LA, with the world, a promise that their story would shine, no matter how far I'd roamed.

We sat in the editin' bay, the projector still warm from *Mill Town Echoes*. Grant leaned back, his shaggy hair fallin' over eyes lit with excitement, his skateboard propped nearby. "Bobby, this film's a knockout," he said, his voice buzzin', "but we could make it sing even louder. Picture this: enhanced color grading to pop the creek's greens, the flag's reds. An original score, something soft, like a guitar, to carry your mom's voice. Smoother transitions, maybe a fade to echo the town's quiet." He leaned forward, hands movin' fast. "And a pro sound mix, clear up the wind noise, make every word hit.

I froze, my hand tight on the reel's canister, a flicker of doubt hittin' me. "I dunno, Grant," I said, my voice low, shakin' my head. "This is home, raw and real, mom's stories, dad's hands, Eric's grin. I don't wanna Hollywood-ize it, y'know? Make it some slick thing that ain't *us*." The thought of changin' *Mill Town Echoes* felt like betrayin' a memory, the sandbar, the heart I'd poured into every frame, filmed on a camera that knew Mill Town's dust.

Grant's grin softened, his eyes steady, readin' my worry. "Hey, man, I hear you," he said, leanin' closer, his voice earnest. "We're not changing your story, Bobby. It's yours. We're just lifting it up, giving it the polish it deserves so the world can't look away. Think of it like... cleaning the lens, not pointing it in a different direction." He tapped the table, his excitement quiet but sure. "Your heart's still the star. We're just making sure everybody sees it clear."

291

I exhaled, my grip easin' on the canister, his words settlin' like dust after a breeze. He was right, *Mill Town Echoes* was my truth, but a little shine could make mom's voice carry further, Eric's laugh ring louder, the flag's wave hit harder. "Alright," I said, a half-smile breakin' through, my voice steadier. "Let's do it. But no fancy stuff that drowns 'em out, yeah? It's gotta stay Mill Town."

Grant nodded, slapping my shoulder, his grin wide. "Deal, director. Let's make it glow." We dove in, sketchin' ideas, color tones to match the creek's dusk, a guitar score to weave through dad's silences, a sound mix to lift Lila's sketches. Our partnership took root, Grant's LA savvy blendin' with my Mill Town grit, a creative bridge between home and here.

In Sun Studios's editin' room, the air was thick with the smell of celluloid and coffee, the Steenbeck flatbed's whir a steady pulse as Grant and I hunched over reels, our eyes bleary but burnin'. My old 8mm footage, Main Street's tattered flag, Coldwater Creek's shimmer, mom's smile on the porch, spilled across the table. Grant's hands, quick and sure, trimmed frames with a razor, his beaded bracelet clinkin' as he taped splices.

"This fade's got to linger a little longer for effect," he said, threadin' a reel, his sandy hair floppin'. "Like your creek at dusk, soft, but it sticks."

I nodded, adjustin' a color wheel on the grader, shiftin' the film's hues to match Mill Town's golden haze, the greens of mom's garden, the gray of empty shops. We layered music, a lonesome guitar track from a studio vault, its twang echoin' Lila's sketches, Eric's laugh, cuttin' it to swell just right, each note tyin' the frames to home. Days bled into nights, our fingers stained with developer, our voices hoarse from arguin' cuts.

"Too long here," I'd say, markin' a shot of dad's porch. "Keep it tight, like you taught me."

Grant'd grin, his freckles faint in the lamplight, and counter, "Trust me, Bobby, this shot's of your mom, it's needs to breathe."

We'd compromise, shapin' ten minutes that held years: Mill Town's fade, its fight, its heart. When we finished, the reels were tight, the fades smooth, the colors true, the music a pulse that carried it all.

We screened the final cut in a dim projection room, just us, the projector's clatter fillin' the quiet. The screen lit up, Main Street's flag wavin' slow, the creek glintin', mom's voice narratin' a memory in the background, fading to her image, her strength clear despite her frailty. Eric's grin flashed, Lila's sketches moved in a montage, the town's pulse alive in grainy color. Ten minutes, short as a breath, but it hit harder than *Gone with the Wind*, its heart raw, real, every frame a piece of art, a piece of Mill Town's soul. I leaned back, my throat tight, seein' mom's pride, dad's nod, Lila's hope in every shot. Grant whistled low, his Converse tappin'. "Bobby, we did it," he said, his voice soft, awed. "This ain't just a film, it's pure emotion."

He turned, his eyes sharp, his grin bold. "Mom's gonna flip for this," he said, leanin' forward. "I'm bettin' Sun Studios greenlights it, no question. But here's the deal, I wanna produce it, make sure it's done right, keep the suits from messin' with it. And you, Bobby, you're the director. This is your vision, your town. We call the shots, you and me."

I blinked, the weight of it landin', my heart racin' with hope and nerves. "Producer and director?" I said, my voice low. "Grant, you sure we can pull that off?"

He clapped my shoulder, his laugh bright. "Sure as hell, man. This film's got truth, Mom'll see it, and we'll make it sing. You in?"

I nodded, a smile breakin', seein' Mill Town's story in his eyes, ready to lead it with him, our ten minutes just the start of somethin' bigger, built on heart and held by trust.

I looked at Grant as I stood outside Ava's office, my hands stuffed in my jeans, heart racin'.

"You ready?" he announced lookin' me in the eye. It was more a statement than a question. Grant burst into Ava's office at Sun Studios, his sandy hair floppin' as he wheeled in a clunky Bell & Howell projector, its metal frame rattlin' on the linoleum. I trailed behind, my arms full with a roll-up screen, my heart thumpin' like a bass drum. Ava looked up from her desk, her silver-streaked bob catchin' the light, her slate-blue eyes sparklin' with a quiet smile, her silk scarf loose at her neck. "Boys," she said, her voice low, a faint German lilt edgin' her words, "this better be worth the interruption." Grant grinned, his freckles poppin'. "Oh, it's worth it, Mom. Bobby's got somethin' special."

I stepped forward, my hands steady despite the nerves, and placed a folder on her desk, on its cover was that worn stick-figure drawin' of Main Street, a gift from a little girl in Mill Town years ago, her crayon lines capturin' the town's soul better than any LA artist. The folder held our storyboards, every shot sketched out: the creek's glint, mom's porch, the tattered flag wavin' slow. Ava didn't say a word, just leaned back in her chair, her ink-stained fingers thumbin' through the pages, her eyes scannin' my pencil lines, Grant's notes, the heart we'd poured in. I set up the screen, my shoes scuffin' soft, while Grant threaded the projector, his beaded bracelet clinkin' as he worked. We dimmed the lights, the room fallin' hushed, and I hit the switch, lettin' the film roll.

The projector's clatter filled the space, castin' grainy images on the screen, Main Street's fade, Coldwater Creek's ripple, mom's voice narratin' a memory, her strength clear in every word. I watched Ava, her face lit by the flicker, all business now, her warmth tucked behind a producer's focus. She scribbled notes on the storyboards, her pen movin' quick, markin' shots, timin', music swells, a guitar's lonesome twang we'd layered in. Eric's grin flashed, Lila's sketches danced, the town's pulse alive in ten short minutes. When the screen went dark, the projector's hum faded, leavin' a silence thick with weight.

294

Grant leaned forward, his Converse squeakin', his voice eager but steady. "Well, Mom, what do you think?" he asked, his eyes searchin' hers, hopin' for the greenlight we'd dreamed of.

Ava set down her pen, her scarf slippin' as she leaned back, her gaze shiftin' between us, sharp but warm, like she was weighin' more than the film. "What is it you want me to think?" she said, her voice calm, a challenge wrapped in a question, her lips curvin' just enough to hint at pride.

I swallowed, my hands grippin' the folder's edge, knowin' this was our moment to prove the film's truth, Mill Town's heart, our heart, was worth her trust.

Grant leaned on her desk, his freckles poppin' with excitement, his voice bright. "Mom, we gotta go back to Mill Town," he said, his Converse tappin'. "Bobby's film, it's not done. We need to shoot the rest, the real stuff, the creek, the streets, the people holdin' on. It's gonna be somethin' special, I know it!"

Ava set down her pen, her slate-blue eyes sharp but warm, her ink-stained fingers foldin' as she leaned back, listenin' careful, like she was splicin' a reel in her mind. She glanced at me, her gaze readin' my quiet hope, then nodded, a small smile breakin'. "I think it would be a great project," she said, her voice low, her faint German lilt carryin' weight. "You're right, you boys have something real here, a story that cuts through the noise. Let's do it right."

My breath caught, and Grant whooped, his grin wide enough to light the room. "You mean it, Mom?" he asked, leanin' forward, his beaded bracelet clinkin'. "We can go? Shoot it proper?"

Ava stood, her scarf slippin' as she rounded the desk, her presence steady, like mom's on her best days. "I'll sponsor it," she said, her tone firm but warm. "Travel, production costs, equipment, whatever you need. Sun Studios's behind you." She looked at me, her eyes fierce with belief. "This isn't just a favor, Bobby. It's an investment. This film, your vision, it's the kind of story my father built this studio for. You're going to make him proud we're a part of it."

I stepped forward, my throat tight, my voice shakin' but full of hope. "Mrs. Klein, I don't know how to thank you," I said, meetin' her gaze. "This film, it's my home. I wanna do it right, make 'em proud."

Ava's smile grew, her hand restin' on my shoulder, a mentor's touch. "You will, Bobby," she said, her voice soft but sure. "You've got the eye, the heart. Go back, finish it, show the world what we've forgotten."

Grant clapped my back, his laugh bubblin' up. "I finally get to see this town you've been talking about all this time, man!" he said, his eyes sparklin'. "You, me, the camera, we'll make it sing, Bobby. Your town's going to be a star!"

I grinned, my chest light, seein' Coldwater Creek, mom's porch, Lila's sketches in vivid color, ready to come alive. Ava watched us, her nod a promise, her support, a greenlight not just for the film, but her trust in us.

Later that day, in the Sun Studios conference room, the mid day sun slanted through the windows, castin' a warm glow on the rotary phone as Grant sprawled on the couch, his sandy hair floppin', his Converse propped on a crate. He dialed with a flourish, his freckles dancin' as he grinned at me, the phone cord twistin' in his fingers. "Time to make this official, Bobby," he said, his voice bright, like he was born for this. I sat on the floor, my back against the wall, my heart racin' as he called Mill Town's Mayor and Chamber of Commerce, the line cracklin' with distance, connectin' LA's shine to home's quiet streets.

"Afternoon, this is Grant Klein with Sun Studios out in LA," he said, his tone smooth as a radio DJ, leanin' back like he owned the room. "I'm calling about a major motion picture film we're planning to shoot in Mill Town, directed by one of your own, Bobby Chandler. We'll be on-site in four months to capture your town's story, and we'd love your support." His beaded bracelet clinked as he gestured, his words confident, carryin' the weight of Sun Studios's name. I watched in awe, my jaw slack, as he charmed 'em, paintin' our project with big-screen promise. The Mayor's voice buzzed through, eager, promisin' permits, locations, even a welcome from the town. Doors that'd seemed locked tight in Mill Town swung open with a few of Grant's bold words, his Hollywood polish workin' magic I'd never seen.

Grant hung up, the receiver clunkin' back, and spun to me, his grin wide enough to light the room. "That's how things are done in Hollywood, Bobby!" he said, laughin', his eyes sparklin' with mischief and pride. "We got the greenlight, the town's on board, and you're going to be a Director for your own film. Directing a film in your home town, man! They're rolling out the red carpet for their hometown kid!" He clapped my shoulder, his Converse squeakin' as he stood, already plotting our next move.

I leaned back, a smile breakin' through, my chest light with hope and wonder. "Grant, you just talked to the Mayor like he was your neighbor," I said, shakin' my head, still seein' Mill Town's dusty streets, the Chamber's stuffy office, now waitin' for us. "Four months, and we're filmin' home. I can't believe it's real."

He laughed, tossin' me a Coke from the fridge. "Believe it, Bobby. Your story's going to sing, and we're making it happen, Sun Studios style."

I caught the bottle, the cold glass steady in my hand, making good on a promise, set to roll in the place that made me, coming from another place that polished me.

I stood in the conference room alone after Grant left to go start organizing. The mornin' sun filterin' through the blinds, my palms sweaty on the rotary phone's receiver as I dialed home. The line rang twice, each trill tightenin' my chest, till dad's voice came through, gruff like he'd been wrenchin' on the truck even if it was runnin' fine.

297

"Chandler residence," he said, and I grinned, the sound of him steady as ever.

"Hey, Dad, it's me," I said, my voice bright, pausin' to let it land. "I'm comin' home... We're gonna shoot a film there, not just *about* Mill Town, but *from* it, right there."

He didn't speak, just breathed heavy, like he was holdin' the world's weight on his chest, his silence louder than words. In the background, the screen door creaked, I heard mom's voice floatin' through, soft but knowin'. "Who's that, Thomas?" she asked, like her heart already guessed. Dad's chuckle rumbled low. "It's your boy," he said, handin' off the phone. "Says he's bringin' that camera home."

Ma's voice lit up the line, bright as spring after a hard frost, warmin' me through the static. "Bobby Chandler, if you're foolin' me, I'll tan your hide, film star or not!" she said, her laugh shakin' with joy, her rocker creakin' as she settled in.

I laughed, my eyes stingin', leanin' against the wall. "I ain't foolin', mom," I said, my voice soft but sure. "I wanna tell our story right. I can't do that from out here. It's gotta be back home."

She got quiet, the rocker's creak slowin', a sound I'd memorized long before I ever held a camera. "Oh, Bobby," she said, her voice thick, like she was holdin' back tears. "You come home when you're ready, but don't you forget, you got more than footage waitin' here. You got folks who love you, prayin' for you every night." Her words wrapped me like her shawl, steady and warm, and I nodded, though she couldn't see, my heart full.

Dad took the phone back, clearin' his throat, his voice rough but soft. "I'll patch that porch roof before you get here," he said, a smile in his tone. "Just don't go trippin' over that camera cord, son, or I'll never hear the end of it."

I laughed, the sound bubblin' up, echoin' old times, us on the porch, jokin' over supper, the creek hummin' nearby. "Deal, dad," I said, grinnin'. "I'll keep the cord clear, but you keep that gumbo ready." He chuckled, deep and warm. "You know I will, Bobby."

We hung up, the line clickin' soft, but their voices stayed, fillin' the conference room with light. I leaned back, knowin' the story started in Mill Town, mom's strength, dad's hands, the town's fight, and it wasn't done yet. With Sun Studios's backing and Grant's fire, I was bringin' the camera home, not just to film but to hold my folks close, their love the heart of every frame, ready to shine under Mill Town's sky again. I could almost smell the river and pine pitch.

Chapter 38 - Prepare for Take-off
(August 1972)

In the pool house, the air buzzed with our excitement, the late mornin' sun spillin' through the windows, lightin' up my dog-eared notebook and Grant's stack of production notes. I was electrified, my heart racin' at the thought of goin' home. To show the world what I see. Years of filmin' on shaky 8mm, nights wrestlin' with guilt over leavin' mom and dad, moments of doubt in LA's glare, all felt validated, like every frame I'd shot was leadin' to this.

I leaned back, grinnin' at Grant, my voice bright. "Man, we're doin' it, Grant. Can't believe my town's gonna live on that screen, every crack, every hope. I can't believe it's happenin'."

Grant was just as lit up, his sandy hair floppin' as he paced, his freckles poppin' with a grin that could power the lot. "This is it, Bobby!" he said, his Converse squeakin', his beaded bracelet clinkin' as he waved a pencil. "My first full production lead, me, callin' shots, not just Mom's kid fetchin' coffee. I'm gonna prove I can make this sing, man, and your story's the one to do it with." His eyes gleamed, his hunger to step outta Ava's shadow matchin' my own to honor home, our dual excitement a spark that'd carry us back to Mill Town.

We moved to a Sun Studios studio office, a cramped room smellin' of mimeograph ink and old coffee, to map out the shoot. Grant hauled out whiteboards, production calendars, and call sheets, spreadin' 'em across a rickety table like a general plannin' a campaign. "Alright, Bobby, let's build this thing," he said, scribblin' dates, his voice all business but warm.

I jotted names in my notebook, Lila for sketches, Mr. Tolley for interviews, the creek, the diner, mom and dad's porch, places and folks who'd make the film breathe. "We need the heart in every shot," I said, tappin' my pen, seein' Mill Town's dust in my mind. "No polish, just truth."

Grant nodded, markin' locations. "Got it. We'll keep it raw, like your 8mm stuff."

We hit a snag, runnin' a shoot this size needed someone who could tame chaos like it was nothin'. Grant snapped his fingers, his grin flashin'. "Jesus," he said, like it was obvious. "Jesus Morales, the logistics wizard. Guy's a veteran, ran shoots from Borneo to Brazil, makes madness look like a Sunday drive." I raised an eyebrow, half-laughin'.

"You serious? We're gettin' a guy named Jesus?"

Grant winked, grabbin' the rotary phone. "His family is from Mexico, Watch and learn, Bobby."

He dialed, the line cracklin', and Jesus answered, his voice boomed through, a backyard barbecue sizzlin' in the background. "Klein, what's the job?" he said, laughin' over clinkin' bottles. "Another jungle epic?"

Grant leaned into the phone, his tone smooth. "Nah, Jesus, this one's in Florida in two weeks. Small-town story, big heart, directed by my pal Bobby Chandler. We need you to keep the trains running for us. You're the only one that can do it. You in?"

Jesus chuckled, the sound warm, easy. "Wait, it's not in Africa this time? Hell, sign me up! I'm there, Klein, just don't let your kid director lose my grip kit."

Grant hung up, tossin' me a look, his grin wide. "I told you, Bobby. Crew's coming together."

I laughed, leanin' back, the chalkboard's scribbles of possible locations. "We're really doin' this, Grant," I said, my voice soft, full of wonder. "Home's gonna see itself, clear as day."

He clapped my shoulder, his eyes bright. "Damn right, man. You direct, I produce, Jesus runs the show, we're gonna make Mill Town a legend." The office hummed, our crew takin' shape, my hometown's story no longer a dream but a plan, ready to roll in four months, carried by our shared fire and the promise of truth.

Within a month, the Sun Studios lot buzzed with purpose, a warehouse corner piled high with gear as our shoot took shape. Crates filled fast, Arri 16mm cameras with heavy lenses, tripods and gimbals for smooth pans, Klieg lights and Fresnels to catch the creek's glint, generators hummin' like the interstate back home. I walked among 'em, my boots echoin' on the concrete, my eyes wide at the sheer scale, a far cry from my bedroom floor where I'd spliced 8mm reels with tape and hope.

"This is really happenin'," I said, half to myself, runnin' a hand over a camera case, thinkin'.

Grant caught my look, his sandy hair floppin' as he hauled a light stand, his freckles poppin' with a grin. "Told you, Bobby, this isn't just a backyard film. We're bringing your story to the big screen!"

I paused by an open crate, my old 8mm, I slipped it from my bag, its weight familiar, and nestled it among the studio gear, my voice soft but sure. "For backup," I said, meetin' Grant's raised eyebrow.

He laughed, clappin' my shoulder, his beaded bracelet clinkin'. "Backup, huh? Bring it, it will be a homecoming for both of you."

I grinned, the camera's presence was somehow comforting, ready to roll beside the big rigs.

We labeled the crates, *Mill Town Project, Florida*, their wooden sides stamped with Sun Studios's logo, sealed tight with nails and tape. Forklifts hummed, movin' 'em to air freight for Florida, the lot's clatter echoin' like a train leavin' the station. I watched 'em go, my chest tight with awe and hope, seein' dad's nod, mom's voice, the creek's flow in every box. Grant stood beside me, wipin' sweat from his brow, his Converse scuffed from haulin' gear. He turned to Jesus Morales, our logistics wizard, a stocky veteran with a cigar stub and a clipboard, barkin' orders to the crew. Grant handed him the manifest, his smirk wide. "It's all yours now, Jesus," he said, his voice light but trusting. "Don't let our cameras end up in Timbuktu."

Jesus chuckled, his eyes crinklin' as he tucked the papers under his arm. "Relax, Klein, I promised that would never happen again." he said smiling, his voice gravelly, warm. "Nah, I've run shoots in worse spots than Florida. Your gear'll be waitin' in Mill Town, right on time."

Grant nodded, tossin' me a look, his grin sayin' we were really doin' this. I touched my old camera's case, one last time, its scratches whisperin', all packed and ready to fly home.

In a Sun Studios office, the air thick with coffee and mimeograph ink, Grant and I met with Jesus to pick the advance team, a lean crew to hit Mill Town first and set the scene. Grant leaned on a table, his sandy hair floppin', scribblin' names on a call sheet. "We need a tight group," he said, his freckles poppin' with focus. "Location scouts to nail Main Street and the creek, electricians to rig lights for that dusk glow you want, Bobby, and a fixer who can charm a small town."

Jesus nodded, his cigar stub chewin' as he flipped through a roster. "Got just the guy, Hank Riley, our fixer. Grew up in a speck like Mill Town, talks slow, knows how to drink coffee with the locals and *get 'em smilin'*." I grinned, relievin' the thought of someone who could speak my town's language, not just Hollywood's.

I leaned forward, my notebook open, my voice firm but warm. "This has gotta be authentic, y'all," I said, tappin' my pen. "Mill Town ain't just a backdrop, it's the story. I want the team to touch base with the Mayor, get his blessin' on shootin' downtown. Talk to the school principal, 'cause we're filmin' the kids, the hallways, the real pulse.

And swing by Mr. Abernathy's. He knows everybody, and they trust him. If he's in, the town's in."

Grant raised an eyebrow, his Converse squeakin' as he shifted. "Your neighbor, huh? That's your secret weapon?"

I laughed, noddin'. "You bet. This is how we get things done in Mill Town" with a wink.

Jesus jotted it down, his chuckle low. "Mayor, principal, Abernathy, got it, Bobby," he said, his eyes crinklin'. "Hank'll work his magic, shake hands, buy a few sodas at the diner. We'll have Mill Town ready for your cameras, no shortcuts." He clapped the roster shut, his voice steady. "Scouts'll map every alley, electricians'll wire it to glow like your 8mm stuff. This ain't my first rodeo, kid." I nodded, my chest light with trust, seein' Main Street's cracked pavement, the school's dented lockers, all waitin' to come alive, true to themselves.

Grant slung an arm around me, his beaded bracelet clinkin', his grin wide. "We're settin' the stage, Bobby," he said, his voice bright. "Your town's gonna shine, and we're doin' it right, no fake fronts, just Mill Town, raw and real."

I smiled, the advance team pavin' the way. The fixer, the scouts, the sparks, they'd carry my vision, touchin' base with the folks who made Mill Town home, ensurin' every frame we shot would pulse with its truth, no less than it deserved.

It seemed like just yesterday we got the greenlight from Ava, but here we were, three months later. The pool house was quiet, the late afternoon sun slantin' through the windows, castin' soft gold on the white walls, the desk where my camera rested, the crates waitin' for the trip. I stepped inside, my shoes scuffin' soft on the floor, takin' a final look around the space that'd been my haven since leavin' Mill Town. The bed was made, my suitcase half-packed, a few dog-eared scripts stacked by the lamp. It felt like pausin' a reel, this LA chapter closin' as I prepped to bring my film home. My eyes drifted to a shelf in the corner, where Eric's camouflage hat sat, its faded green and brown a relic from our last summer, his grin flashin' in my mind, him tossin' it to me at the creek, sayin', "Keep it for luck, Hollywood."

I crossed the room, my heart tight, and picked it up, the fabric worn soft, a faint smell of creek water and sweat lingerin'. Dust clung to its brim, a sign of months untouched, and I brushed it gentle with my thumb, like cleanin' a lens. There was a small hole in the side, from where I accidentally hooked him one day while we were out fishin' in the swamp. I smiled thinkin' bout how mad he was that I scared the fish away, not about his hat. Eric was home waitin' for me too, his laugh silenced by the draft's weight. I held the hat, seein' our last jump off the bridge, his voice darin' me to leap. With a slow breath, I set it on my head, the fit snug, reverent, like carryin' a piece of him back home to 'em. "This one's for you, man," I whispered, my voice low, the hat a promise to keep his spirit in the film, his grin, his courage, his sacrifice, his place in our town's story.

I stood there, the hat's weight steadyin' me, my fingers tracin' its stitches. The pool house seemed to urge me to go, the sun's glow soft, it was time. I grabbed my bag, my notebooks, and stepped out, ready to head home, the hat a quiet vow to tell our story right, with every piece of heart it deserved, for Eric, for all of us.

Outside the pool house, the mornin' air was warm, the sun climbin' slow, castin' long shadows across the Klein's manicured lawn. I stood with my suitcase in one hand, my bag slung over my shoulder, its strap snug against my jacket, Eric's camo cap fittin' just right. A sleek black limousine idled by the curb, its chrome glintin' like a promise, sent by Sun Studios to carry us to the airport.

Grant was already inside, his sandy hair pokin' out the open window, his freckles poppin' with a grin wide as a kid headin' to summer camp. "C'mon, Bobby!" he called, his Converse tappin', his beaded bracelet clinkin' as he waved me in. "Home's waiting, man, let's make it a blockbuster!"

I laughed, slidin' into the leather seat beside him, the limo's cool dark a world away from Mill Town's dusty pickup trucks. Grant leaned back, tossin' me a Coke from a cooler, his eyes sparklin'. "You ready to direct your hometown epic, Chandler?" he teased, his voice light but proud.

I nodded, poppin' the bottle's cap, my heart racin' with hope. "Ready as I'll ever be," I said, my voice steady, in my mind I was already home.

"You ready to produce you first major Hollywood hit? This ain't just a film, Grant, it's home, and I know we're gonna do it right."

The limo pulled away, the pool house and LA's sprawl fadin' behind us, the city's skyline glimmerin' in the distance, towers and neon signs catchin' the sun, a world I'd learned but never owned. I didn't look back, my eyes fixed forward through the windshield, the highway stretchin' toward the airport, toward Mill Town. The limo hummed, Grant hummin' a Skynyrd tune beside me, and I touched Eric's cap, feelin' Lila's words, Mom's pride, dad's nod ridin' with me. This was no goodbye to LA but a new beginnin', my camera ready to capture Mill Town's truth, every frame a step toward home, where the story I was born to tell waited under that big Florida open sky…I'm goin' home.

Chapter 39 - Homecoming
(November 1972)

The plane dipped low. I swear I could feel the Gulf Coast's warmth and humidity seepin' through even before we landed, the air thick with salt and pine, a feel I'd missed in LA's dry sprawl. I pressed my face to the window, my breath foggin' the glass, heart poundin' like a drum as the patchwork of green fields, red clay, and glintin' creeks came into view. Pensacola's runway stretched below, so close to home I could almost see mom's porch, the creek where we swam.

"There it is," I whispered, my voice shakin', nervous but lit up. "Home, Grant. I'm really back." I turned to him, my hands grippin' the armrest, my eyes wide. "What if I mess this up, man? What if the town don't want cameras in their face?"

Grant looked up from his notebook, his sandy hair floppin' under a Sun Studios cap, his freckles standin' out as he flashed a grin, though his pencil tapped fast, betrayin' his own nerves. "Mess this up and your town'll probably shun you, Mom will wonder why she ever took a chance on a kid like you, and Hollywood will probably shun you too." he said, his voice bright but quick, "I'm joking! You just listen to that voice inside and we'll be laughing at the Oscars!" He flipped a page, showin' a minute-by-minute agenda, call times, scout meets, diner lunch with the Mayor, scrawled in his messy hand. "Look, I got us covered. We land, we meet Jesus and the advance team, we hit the ground running. You focus on directing, I'll handle the chaos. We're gonna nail this, right?" His beaded bracelet clinked as he nudged me, his eyes sparklin' but searchin', like he needed me to believe it too.

I nodded, swallowin' hard, my fingers tracin' Eric's cap, its stitches, that small hole. "Yeah, we're nailin' it," I said, forcin' a grin, my voice edgin' toward sure. "Just... feels big, ya know? Mom and dad waitin', Lila, Eric, the whole town watchin'. Gotta make 'em proud."

Grant laughed, slappin' his notebook shut, his Converse tappin' the floor. "Proud? Bobby, you're going to have the whole world crying in the bathrooms. This film's got your heart, your town's heart. We're bringing it home, man, no sweat." His words, half-cocky, half-kind, eased my jitters, his agenda a map through the nerves.

The plane's wheels hit the runway, the jolt rattlin' my bones, and I took a deep breath, the Gulf's humid air already callin' me. "Alright, let's do this," I said, my voice steadier, excitement winnin' over fear. "Home's waitin', and I ain't lettin' it down."

Grant clapped my shoulder, his grin wide. "That's my director! Let's roll, Chandler, time to make a masterpiece!" As we taxied in, Pensacola's heat was already huggin' us, I could feel the pull of home.

We walked through the Pensacola airport's gate, even in November, the Gulf Coast's humid air thick with the scent of salt and jet fuel, my heart still racin' from the descent. A large crowd waited, their chatter hummin' low, a mix of local press in crumpled suits, town officials clutchin' clipboards, and townsfolk in their Sunday best, all eyein' us with eager grins. Front and center stood Mayor Hargrove, his tie loose, his handshake ready, and Mrs. Tillman, President of the Chamber of Commerce, her smile wide under a floral hat. Handmade signs bobbed above 'em, *Welcome Home Bobby!* in bold red paint, *Mill Town on the Map!* with glitter sparklin' in the fluorescent light. I froze, my camera strap diggin' into my shoulder, my voice catchin'. "Grant, look at this," I said, my eyes wide, nerves mixin' with a grin. "They're all here for us?"

Grant nudged me "Get used to it!", his sandy hair peekin' under his Sun Studios cap, his freckles poppin' as he laughed, though his voice had a nervous edge. "Told you, Bobby, you're their hometown hero!" he said, slingin' his notebook under his arm, his beaded bracelet clinkin'. "Smile, man, you're on! Let's do it!"

308

I nodded, swallowin' hard, steppin' forward as the Mayor grabbed my hand, pumpin' it like I'd won an election. "Bobby Chandler, Mill Town's own!" he boomed, his drawl warm. "We're tickled to have you back, son, filmin' our story!"

"Good to be home, sir," I said, loud enough for the press to hear.

Mrs. Tillman hugged me, her perfume strong, her voice bright. "You're puttin' us in the pictures, Bobby, we can't wait to see it shine!"

My eyes scanned the crowd, the press snappin' photos, their flashbulbs poppin', townsfolk wavin', but then I saw her, Lila, standin' just behind, her ribbon loose in her hair, holdin' a hand-painted sign that read *Bobby's Back!* in swirlin' blues and greens, like the creek we loved. Her smile broke through the noise, warm and familiar, the first true comfort in this sea of new attention, her eyes sparklin' like they held every memory of our summer nights. "Lila," I said, my voice soft, wavin' as I pushed through the crowd, my heart liftin'. "You're here!" She laughed, her sign bobbin', her voice clear over the crowd. "Course I'm here, Bobby Chandler! You think I'd miss you comin' home to make us famous?" Her grin steadied me, like sittin' on the creek bank, and I felt those roots wrap tight.

Grant clapped my back, his Converse squeakin' as he leaned in, his voice half-teasin', half-nervous. "See, Bobby? Your town's all in, Lila's leadin' the cheer squad!" he said, noddin' at her sign. I chuckled, my nerves easin', the crowd's warmth sinkin' in.

Grant, this is Lila, the one I been tellin' you about," I said, my voice warm, noddin' toward her as she stood there holding her hand-painted sign, still bobbin'.

Lila's cheeks flushed pink, her ribbon slippin' loose in her hair, her eyes flickerin' with a shy smile. Grant stuck out his hand, his freckles poppin' under his Sun Studios cap, but Lila ignored it, steppin' forward to wrap him in a big, heartfelt hug, her arms tight like she'd known him forever. "Thank you for lookin' after him," she whispered, her voice soft but fierce, her breath catchin' as she held on. Grant's grin faltered for a split second, his eyes widenin' as her words sank in, his expression shiftin' to somethin' deeper, like he finally understood what I was trying to save.

The Pensacola gate was still alive, the crowd's chatter minglin' with the flash of press cameras. Grant's grin kept me movin', but my eyes darted through the throng, searchin' for Eric, hopin' to see his cocky smirk, his arm slung 'round his ma, maybe even his dad. I wanted his laugh, him makin fun of my new clothes, I wanted him to carry us back to our creek days. Then, I spotted dad, standin' near the back, his work boots planted firm, his flannel shirt tucked neat, his face proud but tired, lines deeper 'round his eyes, like he had been using all his strength trying to hold things together for too long.

Eric wasn't there, nor was his mom, their absence a gap in the crowd, sharp as a missed frame. A quiet, sinkin' feelin' settled in my chest, heavy like the still humid air, whisperin' fears. I clutched my bag strap, my throat tight, tryin' to shake the thoughts. Grant was still smilin' as he was shaking hands.

The crowd's cheers minglin' with the snap of press shutters still. Grant stepped forward, his sandy hair neat under his Sun Studios cap, his freckles poppin' as he flashed a polished grin, shakin' hands with the Mayor and Mrs. Tillman from the Chamber. "Grant Klein, Sun Studios," he said, his voice smooth as a radio ad, his beaded bracelet clinkin' soft. "We're honored to be here, filmin' our town's story with Bobby Chandler, your own hometown talent. This project's gonna shine." The crowd clapped, the Mayor noddin', and Grant's Hollywood charm worked its magic, settin' the stage like he was born for it.

I stepped up beside him, my shoes scuffin', my heart full but steady, and broke the script we'd rehearsed. "Folks, if ya haven't met him yet, this is Grant," I said, my voice clear, cuttin' through the hum, my hand on his shoulder. "Not just the producer, he's my friend, the reason I'm doin' this right. Y'all make sure ya treat him right. We're here to capture what each of ya already knows, now, let's share it with the world"

The crowd clapped, smilin', and Grant's grin faltered, his eyes widenin' with surprise, then softenin' with pride. He nudged me, his voice low, teasin' but warm. "Aw, Bobby, you're gonna make me blush in front of the Mayor!"

Lila laughed from the crowd.

Then I saw dad, pushin' through the crowd, his flannel shirt tucked, his face weathered but proud. Without a word, he walked up and grabbed my suitcase, his weathered hand grippin' the handle, knuckles rough from years at the hardware store. The gesture hit me like a reel spinnin' back, him carryin' my bag as a kid, teachin' me to fish, waitin' at the airport when I left for LA. It was forgiveness, quiet and strong, for the time I'd been gone, for the worry I'd caused. I met his gaze, my throat tight, and managed, "Thanks, dad," my voice soft but sure. He nodded, a faint smile creasin' his face, his hand steady, sayin' more than words could.

Grant clapped my back, his Converse squeakin' as he leaned in. "Your dad's a man of few words, huh?" he said, his grin warm.

"But that grip's worth a speech." I nodded, watchin' dad head toward the exit, my bag in hand, Lila's smile still glowin', the crowd's welcome lingerin'.

The group moved through the Pensacola terminal, a jumble of flashin' press cameras and townsfolk offerin' awkward, warm hugs, their voices mixin' with the clatter of luggage carts. Lila walked nearby, her hand-painted sign tucked under her arm, her ribbon flutterin', while dad carried my suitcase, his steady steps leadin' the way. Grant was ahead, shakin' hands, his sandy hair bouncin' under his Sun Studios cap, his freckles poppin' as he charmed the crowd. My feet slowed as the exit doors slid open, the Gulf Coast's humid air rushin' in, thick with salt and promise, my heart thumpin' with the weight of bein' home.

Outside, a sleek limousine idled by the curb, its black chrome gleamin' under the airport lights, engine hummin' low like a Hollywood dream. Grant beelined for it, his Converse squeakin', his grin wide as he yanked open the door and slid inside, leanin' back like a big-shot producer. "C'mon, Bobby, let's roll in style!" he called, his beaded bracelet clinkin', his voice bright but carryin' a hint of LA gloss. I paused, my boots rooted to the pavement, my bag strap diggin' into my shoulder, in it was all the material things that really mattered in the world.

I looked at the limo, its shine temptin' but cold, then turned to dad, standin' by his dusty old pickup truck parked just behind, its faded green paint chipped, the bed littered with hardware store tarps. His weathered face watched me, his smile beginning to fade, proud but waitin', his hand still grippin' my suitcase. A question of truth hit me, Mill Town's story wasn't limos; it was creek mud, porch creaks, dad's calloused hands. I met Grant's eyes, my voice steady but teasin', a nervous edge betrayin' my hope. "You want a real ride, Grant," I said, noddin' to the truck, "or another façade?"

Grant blinked, surprised, his grin fadin' for a beat as he read the moment, his eyes flickin' to dad, the truck, then back to me. He saw it, the truth we'd sworn to tell, not Hollywood's polish but home's grit. Without hesitation, he climbed out, slammin' the limo door with a thud, his freckles poppin' as his grin returned, softer now, real. "Hell, Bobby, you're right," he said, his voice warm, a laugh bubblin' up as he jogged over, his Converse slappin' the pavement. "Let's ride!" Dad was grinnin' ear to ear, chuckled low, tossin' my bag in the bed, and Lila's smile glowed, her nod sayin' I'd passed the test.

I climbed into the truck's cab, the vinyl seat crackin' under me, Grant pilin' in beside, his notebook tucked away, his eyes bright with the thrill of home. Dad started the engine, its rumble familiar as a creek's flow, and we pulled away, the limo and crowd fadin' behind.

312

Dad steered the old pickup through Mill Town's outskirts, the engine's low rumble fillin' the silence after we'd left Grant at the hotel with the rest of the crew, his grin and wave fadin' in the rearview as he hauled his bag inside. The cab felt heavier now, no cameras flashin', no press chatter, just me and dad, the weight of months apart settlin' between us like dust on the dashboard. Outside, the humid night pressed close, pine trees blurrin' past, their shadows dancin' under a half-moon, the road to home stretchin' familiar yet new. I glanced at dad, his weathered hands grippin' the wheel, his flannel shirt rolled at the sleeves, his face tired but proud.

We didn't speak, the silence not empty but full, an unspoken understandin' carryin' what words couldn't. I'd left for LA, chasin' dreams that'd pulled me from here, from him and mom, and though dad's nod at the airport, his grip on my suitcase, had been forgiveness, this quiet drive was somethin' more, a mendin'. The strain of my absence, the worry I'd caused, the letters I hadn't written enough, all hung in the cab, but so did his pride, his steady hand takin' me home. I shifted, Eric's cap snug, and cleared my throat, my voice low, testin' the air. "Dad, I... I'm glad to be back," I said, soft, meanin' more than the words. He didn't look over, just nodded, a small hum in his throat, his hand easin' on the wheel, like he'd heard the apology, the love, in my tone.

The truck rolled past Main Street's darkened shops, the hardware store's sign still creakin' faint, and I saw us years back, me sweepin' the store's floor, dad teachin' me to measure lumber, our laughter over Cokes. That bond, stretched thin by time, was stitchin' itself back, thread by thread, in the cab's quiet, the shared rhythm of the road.

"Your mom's waitin'," he said finally, his voice rough but warm, breakin' the silence as we neared the house. "She's been talkin' 'bout this film of yours non-stop."

I smiled, my chest light, feelin' the mend. "I'm gonna make y'all proud, dad," I said, my voice sure. He glanced at me then, his eyes soft, a nod sealin' it.

The old pickup eased down the dirt road, its headlights sweepin' across the pine trees that'd stood sentinel since I was a kid, their needles glintin' silver in the dark, the weathered porch comin' into view, its posts saggin' but proud. The gravel crunched under the tires, a sound sharp and clear, same as when I'd race home from the creek, my sneakers kickin' up dust, mom callin' me for supper. Each pop and grind was a memory, dad teachin' me to drive this truck, me and Eric pilin' in the back, Lila sketchin' by the porch steps. I leaned forward, my breath catchin', Eric's cap snug, all the memories came flooding back.

Through the front window, mom's silhouette moved behind the thin curtains, her frame slight, a shawl draped loose over her shoulders. The headlights caught her just for a moment, her face older now, pale from the cancer's toll, but lit with a warmth that could outshine the sun. She peered out, her eyes searchin' the dark, landin' on the truck, on me. Her smile, faint but fierce, broke through the glass, a beacon that'd guided me since before I could remember, through fevers, the fights, my leavin' for LA. "There she is," I whispered, my voice thick, my hand grippin' the door handle, heart racin' with love and ache for all the time I'd missed.

Dad cut the engine, the truck settlin' with a groan, and the gravel's last crunch faded, leavin' the night's quiet and the hum of the season's last crickets. He glanced at me, his weathered face soft, noddin' toward the house. "Go on, son," he said, his voice low, warm. "Your mom's been waitin'."

I nodded, my throat tight, pushin' the door open, the air heavy with pine and home. Mom's silhouette shifted, the curtain fallin' back, and I stepped out, the porch waitin', her warmth pullin' me like a fishin' reel pullin' me forward, ready to hold her, just like the gravel drive that'd always led me back.

I took Eric's hat off and kicked my shoes off, out of habit as I rushed inside, the screen door slappin' shut, movin' down the hallway without a word, my feet felt home on the worn runner. The house wrapped me in memory, the cedar smell from the old mill, the stairs we used to slide down in boxes when nobody was watchin', my favorite seat on the fireplace hearth, the smell of the coffee lingerin' from dad's coffee pot, the faint floral whiff of mom's lilac soap that'd cradled me since I was small. Each step echoed summers with Eric, nights sketchin' with Lila, Matt's taunts, mom's voice callin' us all to dinner. The barks from all the dogs over the years that are now silent, now all laying under the old pecan tree out back. I pushed open the bedroom door, the dim light of a single lamp castin' soft shadows, and there was mom, propped on pillows, her frame frail under a quilt, her shawl loose. She shifted, tryin' to rise, her pale face strainin'. "Don't get up," I said softly, my voice catchin' as I lowered myself beside her, the mattress creakin' under my weight.

She reached for my hand, her fingers thin but warm, grippin' mine like she'd never let go. "I'm sorry I wasn't there today, Bobby," she whispered, her voice hoarse, her eyes searchin' mine, heavy with guilt for missin' the airport welcome. I squeezed her hand, leanin' close, Eric's cap still in my other hand, my heart full.

"You were, mom," I said, my voice steady, true. "I saw you every time I closed my eyes. You were right there."

Her lips trembled, a smile breakin' through, and I felt her love, like always, bridgin' the gaps of time.

Dad stood in the doorway, his arms crossed, not cold but holdin' in a tide of feelin', his flannel shirt rumpled, his weathered face soft in the lamplight. I looked up, my voice firm but warm, "I came back to finish what I started," I said, meetin' their eyes. "To tell the truth, our story, no polish, the good, the bad, the sad, the happy…real life. I'm not gonna sugar coat nothin'." mom's eyes filled with tears, her hand tightenin' on mine, her breath catchin'. "I'm so proud of you, Bobby," she said, her voice thick, shinin' with love. Dad shifted, his throat workin', a nod sayin' he felt it too, his silence loud with pride.

Dad, watching out for mom, piped in, "Bobby, you're old room is ready for you whenever you are."

I took dad's que, mom needed her rest. "Mom get some rest and we'll catch up in the mornin'."

I pushed open the door to my old bedroom, the hinge givin' a familiar squeak, the air carryin' a faint dust-and-cedar smell, like my room was just waiting for me to return. The room was a museum of who I once was, faded posters of *Easy Rider* and Hendrix concerts curled at the edges, pinned to the wood-paneled walls, their colors dulled but proud. My bookshelf sagged under dog-eared comics, a Hardy Boys stack, and a worn copy of *Huck Finn*, untouched since I'd left for LA. The bedspread was new, a crisp blue quilt Ma must've laid out, replacin' the old checkered one I'd worn thin, but the bedframe was the same, its iron creakin' as I brushed past, a sound that echoed sleepovers with Eric when we were kids, we would tie on capes and jump on the bed pretendin' we were flyin'. Smiling, I set Eric's hat on my desk.

I then sat on the edge of the bed, the mattress saggin' soft, my hands restin' on my knees. I felt older, LA's hustle and the film's responsibility was making me sink deeper than I remembered, or maybe it was just from all those churros I was eating from the studio cart. I replayed the movie in my mind, me as a kid dreaming of movies under these very posters, sneakin' a flashlight to read past midnight. The room still fit, its shadows familiar, its quiet a mirror to the boy who'd filmed Main Street on that shaky 8mm, hopin' to catch somethin' true. It still felt like mine, every inch a piece of my heart as much as the town's, both ready for the story I'd come back to tell.

My foot shifted, and the floorboard creaked, the same sharp groan from years of pacin', plannin', dreamin'. I froze, smilin' soft, the sound pullin' me back, runnin' in from the creek, mom hollerin' to Matt and I to watch out for each other, Eric's laugh bouncin' off these walls. "Still here," I whispered, my voice low, my fingers tracin' the quilt's stitches, Lila's unread note crinklin' in my pocket.

I heard the crunch of car tires on the driveway as Lila's old car rolled up to the house just as the moon hung high, honkin' twice, sharp and bright, like she'd done a hundred times when we were kids, callin' me to the creek. I stepped out into the cool night air, smilin', She leaned out the window, her ribbon loose, her grin teasin'.

"You didn't think I'd let you brood alone, did you, Bobby Chandler?" she said, her voice warm, her eyes sparklin' like the river in the moonlight.

I laughed, slidin' into the passenger seat, the vinyl creakin', the air smellin' of her lilac perfume and motor oil.

"Wouldn't dream of it, Lila," I said, my heart light but nervous. "Where we headed?"

She winked, pullin' onto the road. "Diner, like old times. You owe me a story, Hollywood."

At the diner, the jukebox hummin' Skynyrd, we sat in our old booth, the air thick with coffee and fry grease, small talk flowin' easy, her art classes, my LA hustle, the film's big plans. But my mind drifted to Eric, his absence at the airport a hollow ache. I leaned forward, my voice low, testin' the water.

"Lila, Matt came by in LA, told me 'bout Eric… his leg," I said, my fingers tracin' the mug's rim, nervous for what she'd say.

Her smile faded, her eyes droppin' to her cup, her hands still. "Eric hasn't been the same, Bobby," she said softly, her voice heavy, like she'd carried it too long.

I nodded, my throat tight, "Matt mentioned it, from the war," I said, hopin' that was all. Lila shook her head, her ribbon slippin', her voice quieter now.

"It's not just the leg, Bobby. He gets angry, quick, like a storm rollin' in. Says no one understands what it was like over there, in Vietnam." She paused, her fingers twistin' a napkin. "He won't talk to his folks, barely talks to me anymore. Keeps sayin' this town, this life, it's all fake, like we're livin' in a movie." A chill settlin' in my chest, Eric's grin from our creek days fadin' in my mind.

I leaned back, stunned, my voice shakin'. "He said that? Like we're in a movie?" I asked, my eyes searchin' hers, hopin' I'd heard wrong. Lila nodded slow, her gaze steady but sad. "He's not all there, Bobby. No pun intended," she said, a faint smile tryin' to break through. "But sometimes... I see a flicker, like the old Eric's still in there, under all that hurt he's keepin inside." Her voice softened, I felt helpless, guilty, for not bein' there for 'em.

I took a breath, my resolve stirrin', my voice quiet but sure. "Maybe if I could get him to talk, make me understand, maybe I could help him, Lila," I said, my eyes meetin' hers, nervous but hopin'. "Maybe it'll remind him who he is."

Lila looked up, her smile small but real, her voice warm. "Maybe, Bobby. Or maybe he just needs to see someone who never gave up on him." Her words landed soft, a spark of possibility, and I nodded, seein' Eric's laugh, his place in our film, a way to reach him.

We left the diner, headin' downtown, walkin' the riverwalk under soft yellow streetlights, the Blackwater ripplin' beside us, its murmur like a song we both knew. Laughter came easy, echoin' old days, fishin' with bent rods, skippin' stones till dark, sneakin' milkshakes from the diner's back door.

Lila nudged me, her eyes glintin' sideways. "You've changed, Bobby, but you haven't," she said, her voice teasin' but kind. "You're still you, just a little more grown up now."

I watched the water, its ripples catchin' the light, and smiled, my voice steady, knowin'. "I just finally figured out what that means, Lila, bein' me, tellin' our truth."

She drove me home, the car's engine rattlin' as she pulled up to the gate, the night quiet, crickets hummin'. She cut the key, silence settlin', and looked at me, her eyes soft, her voice warm. "It's great to have you back, Bobby," she said, pausin' like she meant more than words could hold.

I smiled, my heart full. "I'll see you in the mornin', Lila," I said, steppin' out, she nodded. I looked up at the clear night sky, "I'll trade these ones for the ones in LA anytime."

Chapter 40 - Settin' the Stage
(November 1972)

The dark of my childhood room held me close before dawn, the light just startin' to creep through the old curtains, their faded blue flowers glowin' soft as the sky turned from purple to pink. The crickets were still chirpin' outside, a familiar chorus mixin' with the faint creak of the house settlin', the air thick with the scent of damp wood and ironed sheets, crisp from mom's laundry. It was quiet in that sacred way, the world takin' one last deep breath before the day's bustle, dad's heavy footsteps on the wood floors, mom's skillet sizzlin'. I lay still, Lila's words from last night echoin', her worry for Eric, his silence since comin' home, the things left unsaid, sittin' heavy on my chest like river mud. I swung my legs over the bed, the floorboards cool under my feet, and pulled on a flannel.

Downstairs, the kitchen was a warm glow, the smell of grits and bacon curlin' through the air, mixin' with the bitter tang of dad's weak coffee. Mom stood at the stove, stirrin' a pot of grits with a wooden spoon, her shawl loose over her shoulders, her movements slower but steady, like she'd never missed a beat despite the cancer's toll. Dad sat at the table, readin' the paper slow, his glasses low on his nose, a half-finished mug beside him, the steam risin' in lazy swirls. I slid into my old chair, the wood creakin' familiar, and cleared my throat.

"Mornin', I sure missed this." I said just standin' in the doorway takin' it all in. Dad jumped up and threw a huge helpin' of eggs on my plate and two biscuits. Mom looked at me and smiled, "Did ya sleep alright?"

"Never better." I replied solemnly as I sat down at the table.

Mom poured a huge helpin' of grits on my plate 'til it nearly spilled over, "You best' eat up, ya gotta big day ahead of ya."

At the kitchen table, the steam from dad's eggs, mom's grits and bacon risin' soft, they all sat down. Dad looked around the table and smiled, his weathered hands foldin' as he bowed his head, the morning light catchin' the gray I hadn't noticed before in his hair. "Let's pray," he said, his voice low and steady, the room fallin' hushed but for the faint hum of cicadas outside. "Lord, we thank you for this food, for your provision, and for Bobby sittin' here with us, home safe from his journey. We're grateful for this family, together again, and we ask you to watch over us all today, Ruth, Bobby, me, and all our kin. Guide us, keep us, and let your love hold us tight. Amen." His words, simple but deep, wrapped the table like a warm quilt, and I lifted my head, mom's soft smile and dad's nod told me I was ready for the day ahead.

"Mom, Dad," I said, my voice soft, testin' the quiet, "y'all think Eric's okay? I mean, *really* okay?"

Dad didn't look up at first, his eyes fixed on his plate, he set his fork down. "Boy's carryin' more than his rucksack, that's for sure," he finally said, his voice low, rough, like he was weighin' every word. "A boy goes to war, a man comes back. The man that comes back never quite see's things the same, Bobby. It changes ya." His eyes meetin' mine, steady but shadowed, knowin' Eric's leg, his spirit, had paid a price I couldn't yet grasp.

Mom turned from the stove, her spoon pausin', her eyes soft but sure, carryin' the same strength that'd blessed my LA dreams. "You talk to him when he gets home from Gainesville Friday," she said, her voice warm, firm, cuttin' through my worry. "Till then, keep your hands busy and your head steady, baby. You got your film to make, and this town's waitin' for you to tell its story." her hand brushin' my shoulder, light but anchorin'.

I nodded, sippin' my coffee slow, its bitter heat groundin' me as mom's words settled, dad's truth lingerin'.

The kitchen held us, the tick of the clock, the clink of dad's mug, the sizzle of mom's skillet a quiet symphony. I set my mug down, the ceramic warm.

As I got up to walk out I looked back, "Dad, now that is still the weakest cup of coffee I think I've ever had. Are you sure you put grounds in there?" I said with a grin.

He looked at me and smiled, "that's how I like it."

As I drove to town, my mind had already begun shiftin', lenses and light angles, the way Main Street's cracked windows might catch the dawn, how the Blackwater River's mist could frame Eric's silence, mom's fight, the town's fade. The bell above Benny's Diner door jingled sharp as I stepped in, the familiar scent of burnt bacon and old grease hittin' me like a memory, pullin' me back to high school nights with Matt, Eric and Lila, laughin' over fries. The jukebox hummed a low Merle Haggard tune, its notes mixin' with the clatter of plates and the hiss of coffee pourin'. The air was warm, thick with fry oil and the faint tang of lemon cleaner, the checkered floor scuffed from years of boots. Grant waved me over from a corner booth, his shaggy hair fallin' over a notepad scribbled with shot lists, a pile of clipboards beside his plate of half-eaten eggs, the yolk poolin' like the dawn we were chasin'.

I slid into the booth, my clipboard thumpin' the table, my backpack plopped on the floor, the vinyl seat creakin' under my flannel. "Alright," I said, leanin' forward, my voice low but firm, eyes flickin' between Grant, Jesus and Ryan the main camera op. "We're doin' it at first light, two shots, wide and true. Not staged. Not sweetened. Just real. Main Street's gotta breathe, empty shops, cracked windows, the flag's frayed edge. Like the town's whisperin' its own story." My fingers tapped the table, seein' dad's hardware store, the dusty bookstore across the street.

Grant nodded, his pencil scratchin' notes, his eyes bright with the same fire we'd had polishin' *Echoes* in LA. "Wide shot from the feed store, catchin' the sunrise over the Blackwater," he said, sketchin' an angle on a map. "Then a tighter one, maybe trackin' past the diner, low angle, showin' the decay. We'll use the Mitchell 35mm, 50mm lens for depth, keep the f-stop low for that soft dawn glow." Ryan leaned in, his coffee mug steamin', and chimed in, "Exposure's tricky at first light, sun's gonna flare fast. We'll need to meter quick, maybe bracket the shots." Their words bounced like kids buildin' a dream outta spare parts and borrowed time, the diner's hum fadin' as we carved out Mill Town's soul.

Jesus set his mug down, his eyes narrowin' with focus. "Bobby, show me the exact spots you wanna shoot from," he said, his voice direct, pullin' out a crumpled map of downtown. "Walk me through it, where's the camera standin', what's in the frame?" I nodded, spreadin' the map, my finger tracin' Main Street's curve. "Here, by the feed store's porch, wide shot facin' east, river in the back. Then here," I tapped the diner's corner, "trackin' dolly shot, startin' at the barbershop, endin' on dad's hardware sign, swayin' in the breeze. Gotta feel like you're walkin' through a ghost town that's still alive." My voice steadied, the shots clear in my head,

The diner's lights flickered, the bell jinglin' as a trucker left, and we kept plannin', lenses and angles spillin' like creek water, Grant's sketches, Ryan's notes on light meters, my vision of Mill Town's raw truth. The coffee grew cold, the eggs forgotten, but the dream took shape, a plan to catch dawn's first light, to make Main Street sing through the Mitchell's lens, with a crew that believed in my story, ready to roll when the sun brakes tomorrow.

The air was cool and damp, smellin' of river mud and fallen leaves as we stepped outta Benny's Diner, the bell's jingle fadin' behind us. The sun was just beginning to rise over the cypress trees on the other side of the river, its light spillin' soft gold through bare limbs, castin' long shadows across Main Street's cracked pavement. I led the way, my shoes scuffin' the asphalt, clipboard tucked under my arm. Grant and Jesus both had notepads in hand, and Ryan, slingin' a light meter over his shoulder, followed close, their breaths puffin' white in the mornin' chill, ready to map the shots we'd planned over coffee.

I stopped at the Blackwater River's bend, where cypress tree knees filled the bank, their branches swayin' like curtains in the breeze, the water's surface glintin' faint under a risin' fog. "First camera goes right here," I said, pointin' to a spot under the tree, my voice low, reverent. "Get the light comin' through the mornin' fog, still, quiet, sacred. Wide shot, 35mm lens, catch the river's mist, the sunrise just breakin' over the trees." I crouched, framin' the shot with my hands, seein' the Mitchell 35mm's lens drinkin' in the haze. Ryan nodded, checkin' the light meter, mutterin' 'bout exposure, while Grant sketched the angle, his pencil scratchin' fast. Jesus stuck an orange flag in the ground markin' the location.

I stared at the flag for a moment, thinkin' back to when I first saw them in the pecan orchard all those years ago.

We moved on, crossin' to the corner by Gable's Mercantile, its boarded windows starin' blank, the air carryin' a whiff of dust and old twine from inside. "Second camera's dead center," I said, plantin' my feet in the street, pointin' straight down Main Street's length, where faded shops and the diner's sign stood like ghosts. "Lookin' right down the heart, 50mm lens, low angle. Gotta be outta frame from the river shot, but close enough to feel the same hush." I turned, checkin' the sightlines, makin' sure the shots would weave together, the Blackwater's quiet flowin' into the street's silence. Jesus paced the spot with chalk, eyein' the pavement for tripod marks, while Grant jotted notes, mutterin', "We'll need to flag the sun to avoid lens flare."

I walked the street slow, eyes squintin' against the low sun, my hand stretched like a viewfinder, framin' the shot in my head. The pavement was worn, grass pokin' through cracks, the faint creak of Chandler's Hardware sign, dad's shop, carryin' on the breeze. "Then once that shot's done, we run the dolly tracks right here as quick as we can," I said, tracin' the center line with my boot, from Gable's to the diner's edge. "Chrome rails, Mitchell on a dolly, one shot, unbroken. I wanna walk the length of it, town as it is, no sugar, just the truth." I saw it clear, the camera glidin' past empty stores, cracked glass, the flag's frayed wave, art in a single, steady roll.

Grant clapped my shoulder, his grin flashin'. "Man, you do know this town huh?" Ryan nodded, slappin' his light meter against his palm. "Let's mark it and lock it, boss." We paced the route again, the sun climbin', the Blackwater's murmur a steady pulse, my heart racin' with the shots we'd catch, Mill Town's raw, unbroken soul, ready to live on 35mm, directed by the kid who'd always seen it, now with a crew to make it real.

We stood on Main Street's cracked pavement, the Blackwater River's murmur fadin' as the sun climbed past the grain tower, its light glintin' off the boarded-up shops. Ryan, scribbled notes in his spiral-bound pad, his pencil scratchin' quick as he nodded, his light meter slung over his shoulder.

"We'll have the racks laid and dolly greased before the sun gets too high, as long as all the other shots are on time," Jesus said, his voice steady, already picturin' the chrome rails for the Mitchell 35mm, the dolly's rubber treads ready to glide down the street's center line. His eyes flicked to the route we'd scouted, from the river's cypress to Gable's corner, endin' at Chandler's Hardware, makin' sure every angle was locked.

"Good," I said, turnin' to face him and Grant, my voice firmer than usual, cuttin' through the mornin' chill, the air sharp with the scent of rust and dry leaves. "But don't let nobody touch a damn thing." My words hung, heavy, my feet planted firm, my clipboard tight under my arm.

Jesus looked up, his pencil pausin', brow furrowin'. "No props?" he asked, puzzled, thinkin' I'd want to stage the street, maybe add a chair or a sign to dress it up.

"No props," I said, my voice low, unyieldin'. "No cleanin'. No straightenin' shelves or sweepin' porches. No addin anything or takin away anything, I want the dust on Elma's books, the rust on Gable's tins, the mess inside Chandler's. Let it tell the truth, every crack, every cobweb, every damn thing that says this town's been raped."

I pointed to the empty window of Chandler's Hardware, dad's shop, its glass smudged, the faded sign creakin' soft in the breeze, carryin' the faint whiff of sawdust and loss. This was Mill Town, raw and broken, and I wouldn't let it be softened or fluffed up, not for the camera, not for anyone.

Grant smiled, his grin flashin' but his eyes serious. I think he was seein' the heart of what I meant.

"It's gonna hurt to see it like that, Bobby," he said, his voice soft, knowin' the pain of filmin' the town's fade without a filter. His hand lingered, steady, like he was holdin' me up.

"Yeah," I said, lookin' up at Chandler's window, the glass reflectin' a ghost of dad's pride, and mom's love. "But it's gonna hurt worse if we don't." My voice cracked, just a bit, but I stood taller. Jesus nodded, scribblin' again, his nod sayin' he got it, the Mitchell's lens would catch the truth, no polish, just the town's soul. We turned back to the street, the dolly's path waitin', ready to roll at dawn, to frame Mill Town's hurt, its heart, its unvarnished story, one raw, real shot at a time.

Chapter 41 - Shooting Begins
(November 1972)

I woke before the alarm, my eyes snappin' open in the dark of my old bedroom, heart racin' like a projector on double speed, excitement and nerves tanglin' tight. The faded *Easy Rider* poster stared down, the room still a museum of the kid I'd been, but today I was a director, filmin' my town with real gear, real people. I paced the creaky floor, rehearsin' directions in my head, "Track the creek slow, catch the dawn light, let mom's voiceover breathe", each word a prayer to get it right. The thought of Main Street, Lila's sketches, dad's store under studio lights thrilled me, but the responsibility, the eyes of Mill Town watchin', made my hands shake. What if I let 'em down? I muttered, "You got this, Bobby. You were born to do this." half-convincin' myself, my voice low in the quiet.

I started downstairs, the stairs groanin' familiar, but stopped, my heart tuggin'. I turned back, grabbin' Eric's camo cap from the shelf, its faded green a piece of him, now a piece of me. "Ain't doin' this without you," I whispered, puttin' it in my bag. Downstairs, the kitchen glowed soft, the smell of bacon and coffee fillin' the air, a surprise waitin'. Mom, pale but smilin' in her robe, stood by the stove, dad settin' a plate of waffles and biscuits at the table, his flannel shirt rumpled, his eyes proud.

"Didn't think we'd let you start this big day hungry, did you?" mom said, her voice warm, teasin'.

I grinned, my nerves easin', and sat, the plate a gift. "Y'all didn't have to," I said, my voice thick, "but I'm glad you did."

Dad leaned back, his hands folded, his voice low but sure. "You'll do us proud."

Mom touched my arm, her fingers frail but firm. "You've always seen the heart of things, Bobby. Trust that today."

I nodded, my throat tight, their words a shield against the jitters. "I will, mom, dad," I said, my voice steady,

"This film's for all of us." We shared a quiet smile, their encouragement a spark, and I grabbed my bike from the porch, ready to ride to the set.

The mornin' was cool, a cloudless sky stretchin' wide, stars still beamin' bright, sharp as pinpricks in the velvet dark, a soft breeze carryin' the scent of pine and dew, whisperin' of the sunrise to come. I pedaled down the drive, the gravel crunchin' under my tires, the air crisp against my face. Mill Town slept, its houses dark, but the promise of dawn lit my path, the set waitin', Main Street, the creek, Grant's grin, Lila's hope. My heart raced, nerves dancin' with excitement, but mom's warmth, dad's nod, Eric's shadow rode with me, ready for the first shot, a frame to hold Mill Town's truth under Florida's risin' light.

I pedaled into downtown, the cool mornin' air still carryin' stars, Main Street glowin' soft under streetlights as the set came alive. Gear was already set, tripods planted firm, jibs swingin' slow, reflectors propped against shopfronts, and light panels castin' a warm haze. Cables snaked across the riverwalk, twistin' like vines, while generators hummed low in the background, a pulse under the quiet. Grant, stood in the middle, as he barked orders, orchestratin' the chaos like a general before battle. "Move that jib left! Watch the cables, don't trip!" he growled, his clipboard wavin', his eyes sharp, makin' the sprawl look easy. I leaned my bike against a lamppost, my heart racin', It nearly took my breath away, the scale of it, real rigs, real crew, my town, both firin' me up and knotting my stomach.

Locals peered from their porches, sippin' coffee in flannel shirts and curlers, their faces curious but respectful, watchin' their street turn into a stage. Old Mr. Tolley waved from his stoop, his mug steamin', and I waved back, smilin' to hide my nerves, knowin' his eyes'd be on every frame. I spotted Grant near a monitor rig, his sandy hair mussed, his Sun Studios cap crooked, checkin' a call sheet. I jogged over, my shoes clompin', my voice light, expectin' his usual spark.

"Hey, Grant, how'd you sleep?" I said, grinnin', figurin' he'd say he slept like a baby, ready to conquer the shoot.

He looked up, his freckles faint in the dawn light, his beaded bracelet clinkin' as he rubbed his eyes, a half-smile tuggin'.

"Sleep? Man, I didn't catch a wink," he said, his voice rough but teasin'. "All that racket, crickets chirpin' like a choir, frogs croakin' louder than a jukebox. Small towns, Bobby, they're noisy as hell!"

I laughed, my nerves easin', his city-boy gripe, so Grant it steadied me. "You'll get used to it," I said, nudgin' him. "That's Mill Town's lullaby, keepin' you honest."

He chuckled, slappin' my shoulder, his eyes bright despite the bags. "Honest, huh? Let's make this film sing louder than those damn frogs, then. Hey, have you tried these donuts from the bakery down the road? They're the best I've ever had, and that's saying a lot since I grew up on a set!" Grant said holding up a half-eaten chocolate glazed donut.

The crew buzzed 'round us, haulin' lights, testin' panels, their chatter mixin' with the generators' hum. I drifted toward the center where the main camera was set up focused on Main Street's cracked pavement, the diner's unlit neon sign, the flag hangin' limp. But I hesitated, my hands stuffed in my pockets, unsure where to stand, director or just Bobby, the kid who'd filmed this street on a shaky 8mm. Jesus caught my eye, noddin' sharp, and Grant leaned in, his voice low, warm. "You're the boss, Bobby. Pick a spot, call the shot." I nodded, I opened my bag, took out Eric's cap and put it on then stepped forward, my nerves burnin' into focus, I could hear Eric's voice in my head "Film it for me." Now I was ready to frame Mill Town's truth as the town woke, its heart beatin' under the dawn's first light.

The air bit with a Florida winter's edge, sharp and clean, carryin' the damp scent of river mud and pine as we set up on the Blackwater's bank before first light. The crew moved quiet, their breaths puffin' white in the chill, boots crunchin' on frost-kissed grass, the camera rig's metal cold under my fingers. I stood by the main camera, my scarf loose, heart racin' as the sky hinted gray, the river a dark ribbon snakin' through bare trees, their skeletal branches clawin' at the fadin' stars. Grant, adjusted the lens, his gloved hands steady, while the sound guy caught the water's soft gurgle, a low hymn under the mornin's hush.

Grant caught my eye, his shaggy hair tucked under a cap, his LA confidence soft but sure as he stepped close, sensin' my hesitation. "This is your home, Bobby," he said quietly, his voice steady, cuttin' through the crew's hum. "Show it in its present state, focus on the loss of soul, the quiet it's got now. You've already directed this town with a camera and a dream. Now you've just got the team to match."

I remembered mom sayin', *You've always seen more*, and I nodded, this was our story, and I knew it best.

Grant grinned, grabbin' the director's chair from beside a light rig, its canvas creakin' as he pulled it over and patted the seat. "Time to take your place, Director," he said, his eyes bright, darin' me to step up. I hesitated a beat, then sat, the chair solid under me, my eyes scannin' the small but bustlin' set, cameras angled, crew waitin', Main Street stretchin' out like a reel ready to roll

"Bring the camera in closer and lower. Focus just above the surface of the water twenty degrees left of the sun, then wait for my call. Give it five seconds then gently pan up and focus in on downtown" My voice echoing off the other side of the bank.

"Ready on the set!" Everyone took their positions. I watched the sun began its climb, a shy amber glow crestin' above the treeline, spillin' gold across the Blackwater.

"Action!" I belted out.

The only sound I could hear was the humming of the camera. Within a few seconds, the sun illuminated the mist as it curled above the water, delicate as lace, dancin' like breath in the mornin' light, each wisp catchin' the dawn's warmth and glowin' soft, like ghosts risin' to greet the day. The camera continued to roll, its hum a heartbeat, capturin' the river's shimmer, flecks of gold on its surface, ripples kissin' the mossy bank, a heron's shadow flittin' silent in the haze. I held my breath, the shot feelin' sacred, like filmin', the river wakin' to whisper its story.

The shot panned slow, the lens tiltin' up to reveal downtown Mill Town, quiet and worn, its silhouette etched against the risin' sun. The winter trees stood bare, their naked limbs reflectin' the town's mortality, a stark mirror to the empty shops, rusted and saggin' roofs along Main Street. The cracked façades of the old stores, the hardware store sign hanging at an angle, the barber sign missing a letter like a missing front tooth, the diner, all illuminated by the dawn's gold, their cracked windows glintin' like fractured eyes, holdin' stories of better days. The paint peeled in curls, the brick faded to a dusty red, and the air carried a faint whiff of rust and old wood, the town's pulse faint but stubborn, breathin' under the frost.

A flicker of movement broke the stillness, near the curb, a lone rabbit, thirty yards out, its soft gray fur catchin' the light like a ghost in the dust. "Keep rollin'!" I hissed to Ryan through the headset, leanin' forward, my voice a tight whisper. "Zoom in on that rabbit, nice and easy, don't spook it." The Arri's lens purred, the operator nudgin' the Panavision 50mm, trackin' the rabbit as it hopped into the road, its nose quiverin', ears twitchin'. It nibbled grass sproutin' through a jagged crack in the asphalt, the street split like a wound, the green blades stark against the gray decay, dust motes dancin' in the lens flare.

Grant nodded silent, his shadow still, the camera glidin' smooth, capturin' the rabbit's delicate chew, its eyes glintin' like tiny black beads, unaware of the crew's hushed hustle, the clink of a light stand, the rustle of the soundman's windscreen.

331

"Now, zoom out slow," I murmured, my hands clenchin' the chair's arms, "widen to the whole street, show the emptiness."

Ryan eased the lens back, the frame stretchin' to take in Main Street's desolation, shuttered windows, faded signs. You could almost see the ghost of the diner's lone waitress wipin' a counter through a cracked window pane. Just then, a stiff breeze kicked up, sharp with the scent of dry earth, whippin' red and orange leaves across Main Street coming from the crape myrtle outside the bookstore, their rustle like a sigh. The rabbit froze, ears boltin' upright, then scampered, a gray blur divin' into a hole under a saggin' fence. "Cut!" I called, a grin breakin' through, my voice echoin' off the empty street, knowin' that shot, life clingin' to a broken place, would be the films first heartbeat.

The crew relaxed, the clapperboard snappin' shut, the soundman mutterin' about wind noise, but I felt it, all in that rabbit, that crack, that breeze.

Grant clapped my shoulder, his grin wide. "That's the shot, Bobby. Pure. No way we'd get that on a lot, not in a million years."

I nodded, the chair creakin' as I stood, ready to call the next shot, directin' my town's truth with a team that was beginning to see its soul, framin' its loss, its pulse, for a world that needed to remember what it lost.

"Great shot everybody!" I yelled out.

"Now all we need is another twenty shots like that!" Grant yelled as he walked away.

"Let's keep it going. Reposition!" I yelled, not wanting to lose the light.

The second camera was set up just out of frame on Main Street. I walked quickly over. Main Street was a ghost of itself, it looked even more run down than I remembered, empty storefronts and cracked sidewalks exaggerated by the early morning sunlight, the tattered flag still wavin' over the diner, its soul drained.

I took a breath, my voice findin' its edge, and yelled, "Ready on the set!"

The crew froze, heads turnin', and a beat later, everyone snapped to their places, grips steppin' back, the sound guy raisin' his boom, Ryan noddin'. I leaned forward, heart poundin', I looked behind me, over my shoulder "Lights off!", I heard the lights click off. I paused for a few more seconds…and called, "Action!" The set sprang to life, cameras rollin' catchin' the first rays of sunlight hittin' the empty storefronts, illuminating the dust in the empty windows, the flag's frayed edges highlighted by the light, the lone handprint on the inside of the old bookstore window, like a memory yearning to escape. The crew moved like a dance, capturin' what was left of the town, its soul drained but still there, in the cracks, the quiet, the stories I'd always filmed.

"Cut…Next shot, lets not lose the light, otherwise we'll have to do it all over again tomorrow!" I belted out.

Grant stood nearby, his nod quiet but proud, and I felt it all in this moment, this frame. It was all about the timing, with the sunlight just coming through the trees right at that exact moment as it crested above the rooftops flooding through the windows of the shops illuminating their neglected interiors with over exaggerated shadows on the dust textured floors.

Jesus went into action, and techs began layin' chrome rails down the sidewalk. Main Street lay quiet in that early morning, the air crisp with the scent of old brick, the cracked pavement glintin' where the sun hit chrome rails bein' bolted down by the crew.

"We're ready for the dolly!" Jesus yelled out to one of the techs by the crates. It was like military precision, no wasted movements, it was fluid like they had done this a thousand times.

I stood in the middle of the street, clipboard in hand. The rails, laid for a dolly shot, stretched from the feed store's saggin' porch to Chandler's Hardware, Dad's old shop, its sign faded but proud. I crouched beside a

grip, his hands wrenchin' a heavy Mitchell 35mm camera onto a
wheeled platform, its rubber treads scuffin' the asphalt. "Make sure the
dolly's level," I called, my voice firm but calm, checkin' the mount's
balance, the camera's lens glintin' like an eye ready to open for the first
time.

Two gaffers hustled nearby, rollin' out thick power cords from behind
the old barbershop, its striped pole chipped and still. The cables snaked
across the street like veins, feedin' juice to the Arriflex lights perched
on stands, their beams waitin' to carve the shot's mood, and to a Nagra
tape recorder hummin' soft, its reels ready for ambient sound, wind
through bare trees, a distant dog's bark. The air smelled of diesel and
metal, mixin' with the faint must of abandoned shops, their broken
windows catchin' the sun's glare. I pulled my grease-pencil-marked
viewfinder from my pocket, its scratched glass framin' the street, and
checked the angle, my breath puffin' in the cold. "We roll from the feed
store to Chandler's," I said, pointin' down the rails, my voice steady,
eyes on the crew. "Smooth. Eye level. Like a ghost walkin' memory's
shoes."

The grip nodded, adjustin' the Mitchell's focus, while a sound tech
tested the Nagra, its tape hissin' as it caught Main Street's quiet, a
creak from the diner's sign, the rustle of a stray leaf. Grant, stood by
the dolly, his cap low, givin' me a quick nod, his faith in my vision a
spark. I stepped back, clipboard under my arm, headset slippin' on, the
crew's rustle fadin' as I pictured the shot: the camera glidin' slow,
capturin' the feed store's warped boards, the barbershop's decay and
ghostly lone chair, warm but covered in dust. The dolly rolled silently
past Chandler's faded sign, all stitched into the frame. The sun shifted,
softenin' the light, and I felt Mill Town's pulse, its loss, ready to roll on
35mm film, a memory caught forever, directed by the kid who'd first
seen it through his dad's borrowed 8mm lens, now callin' the shots to
make it this Hollywood hit sing.

I stood by the dolly, headset on, clipboard tucked under my arm, the Mitchell 35mm glidin' smooth on rubber treads along chrome rails laid from the feed store to Chandler's Hardware.

"Ready on the set. Action!" I called, my voice cuttin' through the crew's rustle, and the dolly crawled slow, the camera's lens whisperin' across forgotten glass, its motor a soft purr.

Shop windows reflected sunlight like tired eyes, their panes smudged and cracked, holdin' shadows of Mill Town's past. We rolled by Elma's old bookstore with the lone handprint on the front window catchin the light, the lens peerin' inside, shelves sagged under a layer of dust, thick as snowfall, coverin' long-lost poems, the air inside smellin' of mold and forgotten ink. Faint footprints could be seen in the dusty floor, like a phantom customer looking for his lost book.

The camera pushed on, past Gable's Mercantile, where boxes lay strewn like the place was evacuated, not closed, twine tangled, receipts yellowed, rusted tins half-tumbled off a wire rack, their labels peeled like old skin. The lens lingered on the general store's heart: a lone baseball glove on the floor, its leather cracked, fingers curled inward like it was waitin' for one last catch, the faint whiff of oil and hide driftin' through a broken pane. I leaned in, my breath catchin', seein' Matt's grin as he tossed me the ball, our creek games, in that glove's quiet ache, the shot holdin' lingerin', illustratin' Mill Town's loss in a single frame.

We rolled past Chandler's Hardware, dad's old shop, part of its shattered front pane now boarded up, weathering quietly away. I motioned to the second unit, my hand quick, voice low through the headset: "Swing the boom mic wide, catch the rattle of loose nails, the wind through that glass." The Nagra recorder hummed, its tape spinnin' to grab the sound, a faint clink of metal, a whistle through jagged edges, raw as the town's wounds. Between takes, I stepped inside, the air cool and stale, carryin' the scent of sawdust and rust. Counters stood bare, pegboards empty, the front door frame still splintered from a

335

break-in, its wood jagged like a scar. I pointed to the old register, its keys stuck, dust thick. "Keep the frame tight on the register," I said, my voice low, steady. "Let it feel like what got left behind still matters." The crew nodded, adjustin' the Arriflex lights to cast a soft glow, the Mitchell's lens zoomin' to hold the register's weight, Dad's hands, mom's pride, a town's heartbeat.

I murmured into the headset, my voice low, "Pan up slow, tighten on the silhouette where that picture hung behind the register." The faded outline, a ghost of a frame long gone, spoke of a store that once pulsed with pride, cherished for decades, now left to dust and silence. Showin' that the owner of this store lost more than just a living, but a dream they were once proud of, a way of life.

"And...cut...You got it just right!" I whispered through the headset.

"Do you want to take another run, just in case?" Grant asked?

I looked at the empty street with the sunlight climbing higher. "Nope, we either got it, or we didn't. We ain't done quite yet." I solemnly replied.

Grant shrugged his shoulders, "yes sir!"

I smiled. "Lets set the next shot!"

The final shot was set, the dolly at the street's end, Main Street breathin' heavy in the late morning sun, a hush fallin' as the crew stilled.

I walked over to Ryan standin' by the camera, "You're doing great, now I want ya to roll up slow on that sign danglin' above the sidewalk until you see that flag in the background just so. Then, zoom in tight on the sign, focused on the sign, then we're going to just let it simmer for just a few seconds."

The operator smiled and nodded.

"Ready on the set!...Action!"

The sun was rising high, it was framed just so, the camera tiltin' up slow, the Mitchell's gears hummin' soft. Above Chandler's faded doorframe hung the old wooden sign, "Chandler's Hardware", clingin' by one rusted screw, its paint chipped, letters barely legible. It swung gently in the breeze, creakin' soft like a porch rocker with no one sittin' in it, the sound caught clean by the Nagra, a lonesome note in the street's silence. I didn't say cut for a long time, my eyes fixed on the sign nearly hypnotized, watchin' it sway, that sign, just hangin' on. The air held a faint tang of river mud from the Blackwater nearby, mixin' with the dust of Main Street, and I stood there, headset quiet, lettin' the shot breathe, knowin' this was the town's soul, caught on 35mm, a ghost walkin' memory's shoes, ready to remind the world what we've all lost.

"Cut!" I clapped my hands, "Great job everyone, lets get ready for this afternoon's shoot."

The sun was fallin' fast, its amber glow slantin' through bare oaks, castin' long shadows across the park just off Main Street, where the crew hustled to catch the magic hour. The air held a crisp bite, smellin' of dry leaves and river mud, the Blackwater's faint gurgle echoin' nearby. Lighting grips scrambled, adjustin' Arriflex lamps to bounce the sun's gold, their cables snakin' through the grass, while Ryan steadied the Mitchell 35mm on a tripod. I stood by framin' the shot, headset loose, clipboard in hand, my sneakers scuffin' the dirt as I watched the light hit the rusty swingset, its chains orange with corrosion, one swing movin' gentle in the breeze like a phantom was swayin' slow.

"Tight on the swing," I called, my voice steady, pointin' to the empty seat, "Ready on the set! Action!" its creak a soft ghost note caught by the Nagra recorder's mic.

Ryan pulled in close, the lens whisperin' as it framed the swing's lonely dance, Main Street's faded storefronts, cracked windows, peeled paint, blurrin' soft in the background, worn canvases of the town's

337

defunct gallery. Then he pulled out slow, the camera tiltin' up, capturin' the sun settin' just above the church steeple, its broken stained-glass window flashin' red and blue, reflectin' the light just right, like a fractured prayer flashin' in the lens. The glow painted the park, the swings, the street in gold, a fleeting requiem for the town's lost days, and I held my breath.

"Cut! That's a wrap for today!" I yelled as the light faded to a deep pink, the sun slippin' below the horizon, the park now a silhouette. The crew exhaled, clappin' each other on the back, their laughter breakin' the hush, grips high-fivin', Ryan wipin' the lens, the sound guy rewindin' the Nagra's tape with a hiss. Some stayed behind, breakin' down gear, the clank of tripods and rustle of cables mixin' with the evenin' chill, while I tucked my clipboard under my arm, Grant held a Coke into the air from across the set a quiet reassurance. The shot was in the can.

I met Grant at Benny's, its neon sign buzzin' faint, the smell of fry grease and coffee spillin' out as I pushed through the door. The waitress smiled at me, her eyes crinklin' like she'd known me forever. "Bobby Chandler, back to make us famous?" she teased, settin' down menus, her apron stained with years of service. I grinned, slidin' into a booth by the window, the vinyl creakin' under me, Grant slid in across from me, his notebook already open. A few minutes later, two plates of fried catfish, crispy and golden, sat between us, sweet tea sweatin' in tall glasses, the clink of ice a soft rhythm as the diner's jukebox hummed a low country tune.

Grant flipped a page, his pencil scribbles listin' schedules and names, his shaggy hair fallin' over eyes bright with purpose. "Tomorrow we start interviews," he said, tappin' the notebook, his voice steady but charged. "Real stories, Bobby. Real voices, folks like Mrs. Clara, your dad, maybe Lila if she's up for it. We get their perspective, it'll bring this home. We can use the voiceovers and images, just like you did."

338

I smiled, "well look at you Grant, I dare say I'm starting to rub off on you."

Grant smiled and gave a quick laugh "Well, I guess there's worse things, right?"

I nodded slow, the catfish's tang lingerin' on my tongue, the diner's warm light reflectin' in the window, the world beyond was dark with an occasional car passing by. "We'll do it right," I said, my voice low, firm, the resolve risin' like the river's mist.

Grant's grin flashed, his notebook closin' with a snap, "Then we agree."

I knew tomorrow's voices, the town's truth, my truth, may be tough for some to hear. It may be tough for me to hear, but we were gonna roll on film, one story, one shot at a time.

Chapter 42 - First Interviews
(November 1972)

The church basement smelled of old hymnals and lemon polish, its concrete floor cool under my boots as the crew hustled to transform it into an interview set. The air buzzed with the low hum of a generator truck parked outside, feedin' power to our gear through thick cables snakin' down the stairs. Two grips hung soft backdrops, gray muslin sheets pinned to wooden frames, to soften the cinderblock walls, while gaffers set up Arriflex lights, their beams diffused through silk scrims to cast a warm, even glow, no harsh shadows to spook the stories we'd hear. Ryan, our camera operator, mounted the Mitchell 35mm on a tripod, its lens glintin' under the lights, while the sound guy rigged a Sennheiser shotgun mic on a boom, testin' it with a soft tap, the Nagra recorder's reels spinnin' smooth, ready to catch every word. The setup was tight, intimate, like sittin' on Mom's porch, waitin' for truth to unfold.

I walked the set, clipboard in hand, headset looped around my neck, my flannel shirt clingin' to my back in the basement's stuffy heat.

"Shift that backdrop left a hair, and can we please turn the heat down?" I called to a grip, checkin' the frame through a grease-pencil-marked viewfinder, makin' sure the muslin didn't crease on camera.

I nudged the Mitchell's tripod, anglin' it to catch the interviewee's face dead-on, the 50mm lens set to f/2.8 for a shallow depth, lettin' their eyes tell the story.

"Light's too hot on the right," I said, pointin' to an Arriflex, and a gaffer spun a barn door, softenin' the beam.

This part felt different, closer to home, closer to truth, not just filmin' Main Street's decay but hearin' the town's thoughts from their own perspective. My chest tightened, thinkin' of what these interviews'd carry.

Grant leaned against a folding table, his shaggy hair tucked under a cap, watchin' me pace, his notepad scribbled with names, townsfolk ready to talk. He caught my eye, his grin steady, like he knew the nerves churnin' in me. "Whenever you're ready, Bobby," he said, his voice low, givin' a nod that felt like a hand on my shoulder. I exhaled, settin' my clipboard down, the basement's hush mixin' with the Nagra's faint hiss, the lights' soft buzz.

"Alright," I said, slippin' on my headset, my voice firm, though my hands shook a bit. "Let's roll tape. First up, Mrs. Clara. Frame her tight, Ryan, and keep that mic close, she's got stories that'll break your heart."

The crew snapped to, Ryan adjustin' the Mitchell's focus, the sound guy swingin' the boom, the grips steppin' back to the shadows. I stood by the monitor, the black-and-white image flickerin' with the empty chair waitin' for Mrs. Clara, her tales, her memories of the town's better days. This was it. I nodded back to Grant, feelin' the church basement's glow, knowin' these interviews'd make *or break the film.*

The Mitchell 35mm sat steady on its tripod, its lens glintin' under diffused Arriflex lights, their beams softened by silk scrims to wrap the interviewee in a gentle glow. A Sennheiser shotgun mic hovered on a boom, wired to a Nagra IV recorder, its reels spinnin' silent, ready to catch every tremble in a voice. Mrs. Eleanor Hartley, eighty-three, sat in a padded chair beneath a soft key light, her white hair pinned neat, her floral dress crisp but her hands fidgetin' in her lap, nervous under the crew's quiet bustle.

I crouched beside her, my headset off, my voice low and warm, like I was sittin' on her porch. "Mrs. Hartley, you're gonna do fine," I said, smilin' to ease her. "Remember that Fourth of July when your granddaughter, Annie, was seven? Set up that lemonade stand on the riverwalk, sellin' so much she ran outta sugar and tried usin' salt instead?"

Her eyes crinkled, a laugh breakin' through, soft and bright. "Oh, Bobby, that girl had folks puckered up worse'n a green persimmon!" she said, her shoulders easin'.

I nodded, pointin' to the camera. "Just talk like you're tellin' me that story. Start whenever you're ready."

"Roll it…" I said in a hushed tone.

She took a breath, her gaze driftin' past the lens, like she was seein' Mill Town through a window to 1905, her voice thin but clear, the Nagra capturin' its cadence, each word a thread of a world long gone. "Back in the early days, Main Street was alive," she said, her words paintin' a place I'd only heard in granddad's stories, but now bloomin' vivid from her childhood eyes. "I was just a girl, born in '89, runnin' barefoot down them dirt roads before they paved 'em. Main Street was a bustle, five-and-dimes with candy jars gleamin' like jewels, the A&P's coffee grinder churnin' out that rich, roasted smell, barber shops hummin' with clippers, and the Roxy Theater, oh, the Saturday matinees! Kids like me spillin' popcorn in the dark, laughin' at Charlie Chaplin's waddle, the organ playin' loud. Didn't lock our doors back then. Didn't need to, folks were family, whether kin or not."

The Mitchell rolled, Ryan adjustin' the focus slow, zoomin' tight on her hands, aged, tremblin', veins like rivers under thin skin, as she leaned forward, her eyes sparklin' with her best memories. "My favorite times? Summer picnics by the Blackwater River, the whole town there, spreadin' quilts under the trees, eatin' mama's fried chicken and fresh watermelon, the juice drippin' down my chin. Daddy won the watermelon spittin contest that year. We'd swim till dusk, the water cool, dragonflies skippin' over it, and my daddy'd play his fiddle, the notes dancin' with the fireflies. Life was hard, but we all felt warm and safe, every face a friend."

Her voice softened, her fingers twistin' the handkerchief, the camera catchin' its frayed edge as her worst memories crept in, darkenin' her eyes. "It wasn't all sweet. The flood of '07, I was eighteen, and the Blackwater rose angry, swallowin' half the town. Lost my best friend, Clara May, to the current, she was only sixteen, she was tryin to save her dog when her dress caught in the roots of a cypress. I can still see her face, scared' before the water took her. And the mill fire in '12, the smoke chokin' the sky, my uncle burned bad, never worked again. Folks rallied, rebuilt, but you felt the hurt linger, like a bruise under the town's skin. Still, we held on. We believed in each other. We all helped each other, that's how we made it."

She paused, the Nagra tapin' the faint crack in her breath, her hands still as she spoke of later years, the mill whistles blowin' at dawn, sharp and proud, callin' folks to work. Her voice trembled, the weight of change settin' in, but her memories, picnics and floods, fiddles and fires, caught vivid on 35mm, a girl's joy and pain now a woman's truth, holdin' the town's past alive.

"My husband, George, worked the same shift his daddy did, haulin' timber, comin' home with sawdust in his hair," she said, her fingers twistin' a handkerchief, the camera catchin' the cloth's frayed edge. "This town raised us, Bobby. And we tried to raise it back, church suppers, quiltin' bees, kids playin' free till dusk." Her voice dipped, heavy now, the basement's hush holdin' her words.

I then asked "what changes have you seen, between now and then?"

"Then the winds changed. The mayor sold the community piece by piece, land to outsiders, jobs to machines. I don't hardly recognize the place anymore." Her eyes glistened, the key light catchin' a tear, and the Nagra taped the faint crack in her voice, raw as Main Street's cracked windows.

Eleanor's eyes, bright with memories of 1905, dimmed, her brow creasin' as she leaned forward, the key light catchin' the lines etched deep in her face, like riverbeds worn by time. "The town's pulse... it's fadin', Bobby," she said, her voice low, crackin' soft, the Nagra tapin' the tremble. "Used to be, folks knew each other's names, their stories. We'd stop on Main Street, talk 'bout crops, kids, the weather, laughin' easy. Now? That's all gone, like a fire gone cold." Her lips pressed tight, a flicker of pain crossin' her face, her fingers clutchin' the handkerchief, its edges frayed, the camera zoomin' slow to catch the shake in her hands.

She shook her head, her gaze droppin' to her lap, then liftin' to meet the lens, her eyes wet but fierce. "The family stores, they're all closed up," she said, her voice risin' slightly, sharp with loss. "Gable's Mercantile, Elma's bookstore, your daddy's hardware, gone, boarded up, their windows dark. Them new stores, the chain ones poppin' up by the interstate? They're cold, Bobby. No soul, just bright lights and folks rushin' through, not even lookin' at each other. Everyone's in such a hurry now, heads down, movin' fast. Nobody talks to their neighbors no more, not like we did, sharin' coffee or a porch swing." Her jaw tightened, a flash of anger in her eyes, the Mitchell capturin' the way her shoulders slumped, like she was carryin' the town's weight.

Her voice slowed, softer now, heavy with sorrow, her face softenin' into a sad smile, the light catchin' a tear glistenin' on her cheek. "It's worse'n that, though," she said, her words slow, deliberate. "People see each other as competition now, not kin. Who's got the better car, the bigger house, the job that pays more. Ain't no 'we' anymore, just 'me.' The town's growin', sure, but from the outside in, newcomers buildin' on the edges, sprawlin' out, not joinin' us here in the heart." She paused, her breath shaky, the Nagra recordin' the faint rustle of her dress as she shifted, her eyes searchin' the air, like she could still see the town's old days.

Eleanor's brow furrowed deeper, her voice takin' on a note of regret, her hands stillin' in her lap, the handkerchief crumpled. "It ain't all the newcomers' fault, mind you," she said, her tone softer, almost pleadin'. "Lots of folks here don't talk to 'em, they treat 'em like invaders, like they don't belong. So the newcomers, they withdraw, keep to

344

themselves, build their own walls. And that's how the community's dyin', Bobby, nobody's reachin' out, nobody's holdin' on." Her eyes met the lens, steady now, a tear fallin' slow, the camera holdin' her gaze, her face a portrait of grief for a town she didn't recognize. "We used to lean on each other," she whispered, her voice barely audible, the Nagra catchin' the crack, "but now we're just... lettin' go."

I stood frozen by the monitor, my headset quiet, my throat tight, feelin', her heart breakin' through her story. "Keep rollin'," I murmured to Ryan through the headset, my voice thick, "let her sit in it." The Mitchell held her face, the Nagra her sigh, a raw lament for the town's fadin' pulse, caught on 35mm and tape.

The church basement was still, the air heavy with Eleanor's words, the soft hum of the Arriflex lights and the Nagra's reels fadin' into a sacred hush. Eleanor sat in the padded chair, her floral dress lit soft by the key light, her hands clutchin' the crumpled handkerchief, a tear still glistenin' on her cheek, her eyes distant, like she was still walkin' the streets of lost days. I stood by the monitor, my headset tight, my flannel shirt damp with sweat, my heart poundin' from her story. My breath caught, knowin' this was the soul of *what I was tryin to capture*, and I leaned into the headset, my voice low, steady but thick with emotion. "Cut," I said, the word soft, almost reluctant, like endin' a prayer. The Mitchell's motor slowed, its hum dyin', and Ryan eased back from the camera, his hand pausin' on the lens, while the sound guy lowered the Sennheiser boom, the Nagra's reels clickin' to a stop.

I slipped off my headset, lettin' it hang 'round my neck, and stepped toward Eleanor, my shoes quiet on the concrete floor, the basement's scent of hymnals and polish groundin' me. Her eyes lifted, meetin' mine, and I crouched beside her chair, my hand restin' light on the armrest, my face level with hers. "Mrs. Hartley," I said, my voice low, reverent, like I was speakin' to Mom or the river itself, "that was... powerful. You gave us your heart, the good and the gone. I can't thank you enough for sharin' all that." My eyes held hers, seein' the girl who'd ran through the reeds down by the river with her Sunday dress

345

on and still mourning for her loss, now an elder carryin' the town's truth. "Your words, they're gonna make folks feel this place, what it was, what we're losin'. You did somethin' real special today."

Eleanor's lips curved into a faint smile, her trembling hands easin', the handkerchief still in her grip. "Oh, Bobby," she said, her voice soft, weary but warm, "I just told it like I saw it. This town's been my life, and if my stories help your film, well, that's enough for me." Her eyes crinkled, a spark of her old fire returnin', and she patted my hand, her touch light but firm, like a grandmother's blessing. "You keep filmin', ya hear? Don't let it be forgotten." I nodded, my throat tight, swallowin' hard. "Yes, ma'am," I said, my voice barely above a whisper, "I promise, we'll do it right."

I stood, helpin' her ease outta the chair, her arm leanin' on mine as we walked toward the stairs, the crew movin' quiet, givin' her space, their usual chatter hushed outta respect. Grant leaned against the cinderblock wall, his shaggy hair fallin' over eyes wide with awe, his notepad clutched tight, unopened, like he didn't need to write to remember this. As Eleanor passed, he caught my eye, his grin gone, replaced by a slow nod, his jaw set, his gaze flickerin' with somethin' deep, pride, maybe, or the weight of her words hittin' him like they'd hit me. He stepped forward, his voice low, almost a whisper, as he reached me. "Bobby, that... that was heavy," he said, his hand grippin' my shoulder, firm, his eyes glintin' with the same fire I felt.

The church basement was a warm hum of activity, the soft buzz of Arriflex lights, diffused through silk scrims, castin' a gentle glow across the set. I paced the concrete floor, my shoes scuffin' soft, my headset looped 'round my neck, clipboard in hand, nerves buzzin' after Mrs. Hartley's heart-wrenchin' interview. Her words still echoed, and now I was settin' up for Mr. George Leonard, a man who'd lived here all his sixty-eight years, fought in WWII, and watched the town's changes over the years. I adjusted the muslin backdrop, smoothin' a crease, and called to Ryan, our camera operator, "Frame it tight on his face, 50mm, f/2.8, let his eyes carry it." He nodded, tweakin' the

Mitchell's focus, while the sound guy tested the Nagra, its tape hissin' soft.

Grant leaned against a cinderblock wall, his notepad open, scribblin' last-minute notes on Leonard's bio, born in Mill Town, enlisted after Pearl Harbor, worked at his war buddy's furniture store till it shuttered.

"He's a talker, Grant," I said lookin at Grant, his shaggy hair fallin' over a quick grin, "but he's got the town's bones in him. Let him roll."

Grant nodded, settin' his clipboard down. I slipped' on my headset, my flannel shirt clingin' to my back in the basement's heat.

"Alright," I said through the headset, my voice steady, "bring him in. Let's make it feel like home, and can we turn that heat off? Maybe open a window a bit?"

A grip ushered Mr. Leonard down the stairs, a wiry man with a limp, his gray hair combed neat, his flannel shirt pressed, his eyes sharp but heavy, like he'd seen too much but still stood tall.

I greeted him, shakin' his calloused hand, my voice warm, reverent, like talkin' to Dad. "Mr. Leonard, thanks for doin' this," I said, guidin' him to the padded chair under the key light. "Just talk like you're sittin' at the diner, tellin' me 'bout the town, the war, whatever comes. Good or bad." He nodded, settlin' in, his hands restin' on his knees, a faint smile creasin' his face.

"You're Thomas Chandler's boy, ain't ya?" he said, his voice gravelly but kind. "Your daddy'd be proud, filmin' this town's story."

I swallowed and smiled back. "I sure hope so, sir. Whenever you're ready." I stepped back to the monitor, givin' Ryan a nod, the Mitchell hummin' to life, the Nagra's reels spinnin' as Leonard began.

His eyes drifted, like he was being transported back in time, his voice steady but thick with memory, the Nagra catchin' every cadence. "I was seventeen when Pearl Harbor got hit," he said, his brow furrowin', a flicker of shock still in his gaze, the camera holdin' his face tight. "Heard it on the radio, December 7, me and my best friend Jimmy at the diner, eatin' fries. The news cut through like a knife, ships burnin', boys dead. I felt sick, angry, like I had to do somethin'. Next mornin', me and Jimmy drove to the recruitment office in Pensacola, lyin' 'bout our age. The line stretched two blocks, kids from all over, proud, all scared but actin' tough. We signed up, me and Jimmy. Jimmy wanted to join the Army, but I wanted to fight the Japs, so I convinced him to join the Marines. We shipped out by spring. We was just kids, not really knowin what we were doin'" His lips pressed tight, a shadow crossin' his face, the light catchin' the creases 'round his eyes, deep as riverbeds. "We were both sent to the pacific," his eyes turned black, "it was some tough work we did. Lost some good friends along the way."

He leaned back, his hands clenchin' slight, his voice softenin', the Mitchell zoomin' slow to his fingers, scarred from war and work. "Comin' home after the war in '45, steppin' off that train at the Mill Town depot… Lord, Bobby, I can't describe it," he said, his eyes glistenin', a smile breakin' through, faint but real. "I can remember it like it was yesterday. I can still smell the honeysuckle, the platform packed with folks wavin' flags, cryin', huggin'. I was twenty-one, skinny as a rail, my uniform hangin' loose, but I felt whole, alive. Jimmy was with me, both of us laughin', promisin' we'd stick together. This town felt like a promise kept, like it'd always be there waitin for us. Knowin' that got us through some really tough days." His smile faded, his gaze droppin', the camera catchin' the shift, the Nagra tapin' a soft sigh.

He straightened, his voice gainin' strength, his eyes meetin' the lens, steady now. "The '50s, them were our glory days," he said, a spark returnin'. "Main Street buzzed, five-and-dimes, the A&P, my buddy Jimmy's furniture store where I worked, managin' sales. Folks'd come in, not just to buy, but to talk, laugh, plan their lives, we were just happy to be alive. Like everyday was a gift. People'd buy oak tables for new homes, rockers for new babies. We built dreams right there,

Bobby, me and Jimmy, sawdust in our hair, coffee in our hands. We'd get most of the hardware from your granddaddy's store, and truck the mahogany in from Pensacola." His hands opened, like he was holdin' those days, the camera lingerin' on their tremble, the light soft on his knuckles.

Then his face darkened again, his brow creasin' deep, a tear wellin' as he spoke of the fall, his voice crackin', the Nagra catchin' the raw edge. "After Jimmy passed in 65, it was hard to keep things goin' but we promised each other in Guadalcanal, if one of us didn't make it, the other'd run the store until we couldn't no more. When the bank took the store a year ago, it was like losin' him all over again," he said, wipin' a tear with a shaky hand, the camera followin' the motion, unflinchin'. "They called it economics, big stores moved in, then interstates took the rest of the business to Pensacola, things just changed. There just ain't no jobs anymore or money circulating, families left, stores shuttered one by one. Gable's, Elma's, your daddy's hardware, all gone, like the town was bleedin' out." His jaw tightened, his eyes wet but fierce, the light catchin' the tear's fall. "Folks just stopped talkin', started fightin' over scraps. Community fractured, Bobby. Ain't just the stores we lost, it's us."

There was a long pause, I could tell he was spent. I stood by the monitor, my headset silent as I let the moment breathe. "Cut," I said softly, my voice thick, the Mitchell slowin', the Nagra stoppin'. I stepped to Leonard, standin' beside him, my hand on his shoulder, reverent, like touchin' history. I looked him in his eye, "Thank you for your service Mr. Leonard, that was... it's the town's truth, right there," I said, my eyes meetin' his, my voice low, warm.

Grant, by the wall, stood frozen, his notepad limp in his hand, his eyes wide, glintin' with unshed tears, his usual grin gone. He caught my gaze, he gestured that he wanted to talk, waving me over.

"Excuse me Mr. Leonard." I walked over to Grant, his hand rubbin' his jaw like he was holdin' back the weight of Leonard's words.

349

"Damn, Bobby," he whispered as I approached, his voice barely audible, His grip on my shoulder was tight, "This is great, but we're going to have to lighten things up a bit to keep people from jumpin' off the balcony at the premier."

I could tell he was tryin to suck his tears back in, I smiled back because I was doin' the same. I nodded, and walked back to my chair.

"I apologize Mr Leonard." I leaned forward, my voice soft through the headset, keepin' the moment intimate. "Mr. Leonard," I said, smilin' to ease him, "before we wrap, you got any funny stories you'd like to share? Somethin' to make us laugh, maybe from you and Jimmy?" The camera kept rollin', the Nagra tapin' the pause, Leonard's eyes flickerin' with a spark, his brow liftin' as a memory took hold. He paused for a moment, his lips twitchin' into a grin, his hands unclenchin', one finger tappin' his knee like he was rewound to his youth. The key light caught the crinkle 'round his eyes, a glint of mischief replacin' the grief, the Mitchell holdin' the shift in his face.

"Well, Bobby," he said, his voice gravelly but warm, a chuckle rumblin' up, the Nagra capturin' its low roll, "there was this one time, me and Jimmy, we was 'bout sixteen, summer of '40, before the war. Thought it'd be a hoot to mess with Sheriff Johnson, big ol' fella, always braggin' 'bout his shiny new patrol car." His grin widened, his shoulders easin', the camera zoomin' slow to catch the spark in his eyes, the way his hands gestured, lively now. "One night, we snuck out, moon high, air smellin' of fresh cut hay, and crept to the sheriff's house, where his car was parked out front. We had this crazy idea to let all the air outta his tires, every last one, just to see him huff and puff come mornin'."

He laughed outright, a short, barkin' sound, his hand slappin' his knee, the Nagra tapin' the joy, the Mitchell holdin' his face as it lit up, lines softenin'. "We was gigglin' like fools, me with a wrench, Jimmy holdin' the valve caps, crouchin' by them tires, lettin' the air hiss out, tryin' not to wake half the street. Took us near twenty minutes, sweatin', shushin' each other, 'cause Jimmy kept droppin' the caps in the dirt, mutterin' curses he learned from his pa. We thought we was slick as snakes, till we heard a screen door creak, Sheriff Johnson himself, standin' on his porch in his long johns, yellin', 'Who's out there messin' with my car?'" Leonard's eyes twinkled, his laugh deepenin', the camera catchin' a flush in his cheeks, the light glintin' off his glasses.

"We tore outta there, Bobby, runnin' like the devil was chasin' us, through the alley by Gable's, laughin' so hard we could barely breathe," he said, his voice lively, his hands wavin' like he was back in that moonlight. "Next day, Sheriff Johnson was red as a beet, pumpin' up them tires, cussin' to high heaven, and me and Jimmy just grinned at each other across the diner, knowin' we'd pulled it off. Never got caught, neither, though I reckon he knew it was us." His grin softened, his eyes distant, a touch of sadness creepin' in for Jimmy, gone now, but the story held its joy, the Nagra tapin' his final chuckle, the Mitchell keepin' his smile.

I stood by the monitor, my heart lighter, my headset quiet as I let the moment land. "That's perfect, Mr. Leonard." My solemn smile turned wider, "cause we just so happen to be interviewin' Sherrif Johnson next" The camera caught Mr. Leonards' expression change to that of a fifteen year old that had just been called to the prinicpal's office. I said smilin', my voice warm, a grin breakin' through. The crew snickered off camera, the basement's glow soft, caught on 35mm and tape, ready to make the town's heart sing, one laugh, one truth at a time.

I was settin' up for Sheriff Roy Johnson, seventy-two, a legend who'd patrolled this town's streets for thirty years. Grant, looked at me, "Heard he was the youngest sheriff elected in Florida back then. I can only imagine the stories he must have." I nodded, slippin' on my headset, my flannel shirt stickin' to my back in the basement's heat.

"Please bring him in, when he's ready," I said through the headset, my voice steady. A grip ushered Sheriff Johnson down the stairs, a tall man, stooped now, with a shock of white hair and a weathered face, his eyes twinklin' under bushy brows, his old sheriff's badge pinned to his jacket like a medal. I shook his hand, his grip firm, and smiled, I smiled back, "Sheriff Johnson, thanks for doin' this," I said, guidin' him to the padded chair under the key light. "Just tell it like you're at Sunday brunch, havin a coffee with me." He chuckled, settlin' in, his hands restin' easy on his knees. "Bobby Chandler, makin' movies now, huh? Your granddaddy would be proud," he said, his voice deep, rough with years. I grinned, noddin'. "Tryin', sir. Start when you're ready."

The Mitchell hummed to life, Ryan framin' his face, the Nagra spinnin' as Johnson began, his eyes sparklin' with pride, his voice steady, the camera catchin' the crinkle 'round his eyes. "I was elected sheriff in '36, just twenty-four years old," he said, leanin' forward, a grin tuggin' his lips. "Youngest in Florida at the time, maybe the whole South. Folks thought I was crazy, takin' on Santa Rosa County, but the town trusted me, and I swore I'd keep it safe." His hands gestured, broad and sure, the light glintin' off his badge. "Back then, Mill Town was small, maybe five hundred souls, tops. Main Street was the place to be, and the diner, all packed on Saturdays. Crime? Hardly any. A stolen pie from a windowsill, kids tippin' a cow now and then. We didn't need no big jail, folks sorted things out with a handshake or a switch, dependin' on the trouble."

His grin widened, his eyes twinklin' as he leaned back, the camera zoomin' slow to catch the mischief in his face, the Nagra tapin' a soft chuckle. "Lemme tell ya a funny one, Bobby, bout how we handled trouble back then," he said, his voice light, like he was back in the '50s. "Fall of '52, I was escorting the team back after the big football game with Pensacola, when I see two heads stick out the bus window, two high school seniors, star linemen, big as barns, hangin halfway out the window they shot two big ole windows out of Mr. Abernathy's feed store with a slingshot. They must have forgotten I was right behind them cause they got caught red-handed breakin' them windows. Now they was celebratin' a win, it seems them slingshots weren't the only

352

thing they snuck on that bus, we found a few mason jars of peach moonshine, but them boys were liquored up, slingin' rocks and laughin'… till I turned my siren on my patrol car, lights flashin'. Now, there was nowhere to run on a schoolbus, slingshot still in hand and moonshine spilt all over the back of the bus, faces redder'n a beet." He laughed, a deep, rollin' sound, his hand slappin' his knee, the camera holdin' his joy, the light catchin' a flush in his cheeks. "Now, Abernathy wanted 'em locked up for a night, but I knew their folks, good people. So I talked to Coach Daniels instead. Coach, he didn't mess around, he was madder than a hound dog at a cat parade, made the whole team, not just them two, plow Abernathy's field by hand that week, sunup to sundown, no tractors, no mules. Them boys was sweatin', cursin', but they fixed every window, and Abernathy got a free plowin', and they won state that year. That's how we handled crime back then, honest work, not jail, and a lesson that stuck."

"Oh, and on that note, I heard George's story earlier on bout flattnin' my tires" he smiled, "George Leonard and Jimmy thought they'd pull a fast one on me. I'd just got my new patrol car, a Ford V8, shiny as a new dime, parked out front my house. Them boys, 'bout sixteen, figured it'd be hilarious to let the air outta my tires, all four, mind you." His grin widened, his voice rich with amusement, the camera zoomin' slow to catch the crinkle 'round his eyes, a flush in his cheeks. He shook his head, laughin' soft, his hand wavin' like he was shoo-in' away the memory, the Nagra capturin' the warmth in his tone. "Now, George might tell it different, say they was slick, never got caught," he said, his eyes twinklin', a knowin' look crossin' his face, the camera holdin' his gaze. "But here's how it went, far as I recall. I was up late, cause it was so hot, there was a full moon lightin up the room like daytime, I had the window open readin in the moonlight, when I heard 'em out front, gigglin' like damn fools, the hiss of air comin' from my tires. I peeked through the curtain, saw George with a wrench, Jimmy droppin' valve caps in the dirt, both tryin' to keep quiet but failin' miserable. That full moon lit 'em up clear as day, and I coulda stormed out, hauled 'em to the station right then." His laugh deepened, a rollin'

353

sound, the light catchin' a gleam in his glasses, the Mitchell keepin' his joy.

"But I didn't," he said, his voice softenin', his grin fadin' to a thoughtful smile, his hands stillin', the camera lingerin' on their weathered knuckles. "See, Bobby, I was a kid once too, not long before them and I knew them boys, George and Jimmy, good kids, just full of vinegar, not mean. Their folks was hard-workin'. I'd seen both them boys helpin' at Gable's, carryin' sacks for old ladies, never causin' real trouble. I figured they was just blowin' off steam, testin' their mettle before the world got heavy, war was comin', we all felt it. So I let 'em think they got away clean, stood on my porch in my long johns, yellin' into the dark, 'Who's out there, even when I knew good n well who was out there, just to give 'em a scare." He chuckled, his eyes distant, the Nagra tapin' a faint sigh, the camera catchin' a flicker of sadness for those simpler days, "I think I made the right decision."

His laugh faded, his brow creasin', his eyes droppin' to his hands, the camera followin' the shift, the Nagra catchin' a heavy sigh. "Things ain't like that now," he said, his voice low, tinged with sorrow, his face tightenin', the light castin' shadows in his wrinkles. "The town's bigger, but it's colder. New folks movin' in, chain stores replacin' family shops, there's no community no more. Gable's, Elma's, all gone. Crime's up, break-ins, theft, kids on dope, not just slingshots, moonshine and flattenin' tires anymore. People don't know their neighbors no more, don't trust 'em, don't care bout em. Back then, we solved things together. Now? It's every man for himself, courts and lawyers, no community left to lean on." His jaw clenched, his eyes glistenin', the camera holdin' his gaze, steady but pained. "This town's losin' its heart, Bobby, and I don't know if we'll ever get it back, it's sad to watch it happen. I couldn't run no more, just seein what it's come to."

I stood by the monitor, "Cut…"

"Sheriff, that was incredible, thank you." I stood shakin his hand.

He nodded, his smile faint, pattin' my arm. "I always liked your daddy. Just keep filmin' son." he said, his voice rough but warm.

Lila's interview was next, and it felt personal, she'd been there with me, splashin' in Coldwater Creek, racin' bikes, her note still in my bag, her art helped guide this film. "Frame her soft," I murmured to Ryan, "50mm, f/2.8, let her eyes tell it." Ryan nodded, tweakin' the Mitchell, while the sound guy tested the Nagra, its tape hissin' soft.

Grant was still leaning against the cinderblock wall, his notepad scribbled with Lila's bio, twenty, artist, lifelong resident. "She's one of your friends, right?" he asked sarcastically, his shaggy hair fallin' over a quiet grin.

I nodded, slippin' on my headset, my flannel shirt clingin' in the basement's heat. "Bring her on in," I said through the headset, my voice steady but tight with nerves. A grip ushered Lila down the stairs, her dark hair loose, her denim jacket worn, her eyes bright but guarded, carryin' the same fire I'd known since we were kids. I met her with a smile, keepin' it warm, like old times. "Lila, you're gonna do great," I said, guidin' her to the padded chair under the key light. "Just talk like we're by the creek, sharin' stories."

She smirked, settlin' in, her hands foldin' in her lap. "You're all fancy now, Bobby, with your big camera," she teased, her voice light but shaky.

I chuckled, noddin', "Still just me. Start when you're ready."

The Mitchell hummed to life, Ryan framin' her face, the Nagra spinnin' as Lila began, her eyes soft, her voice clear, the camera catchin' the way her lips curved, nostalgic but tinged with loss. "I remember life as a kid here was difficult, but not in a bad way," she said, her gaze driftin', like she was seein' the '60s again, the Nagra tapin' her cadence. "Summers were magic, me, you, Eric, Matt, splashin' in Coldwater Creek, the water cool, minnows ticklin' our feet. We'd ride our bikes miles to the upper Blackwater River, pedals pumpin', laughin' till our sides hurt, racin' to the bend where the cypress hung low. We'd stay till dark, Bobby, not a worry, just the sky turnin' purple and Mom yellin' for me to get home." Her smile widened, her eyes sparklin', the camera zoomin' slow to catch the warmth in her face, the light glintin' off her hair.

She leaned forward, her hands unclenchin', her voice steady, the Mitchell holdin' her energy. "When I was twelve, I'd work at Mom's little store on route 90, stockin' shelves, sweepin' the floor, sneakin' a peppermint stick when she wasn't lookin'," she said, a laugh bubblin' up, the Nagra capturin' its lilt. "Folks'd come in, not just to buy, but to talk, gossip 'bout the harvest, plans for the church picnic. It felt like family, y'know? Like it wasn't really work, it was a social event where we traded things to help get us all through." Her smile faded, her brow creasin', the camera catchin' the shift, her eyes droppin' to her hands. "Then AG moved in, 'round '63. Town was split, Bobby. Some were excited, talkin' 'bout jobs, cheaper goods. Others, like Mom, were worried, knowin' their stores couldn't compete. It was like a storm brewin', and we were the only ones screamin' how bad it'd get."

Her voice softened, her fingers twistin' a loose thread on her jacket, the camera lingerin' on their nervous dance, the light castin' shadows on her knuckles. "Stores started closin' down, one store at a time," she said, her tone heavy, the Nagra tapin' a faint crack in her voice. "Mom's place went first, then Gable's, Elma's, your dad's hardware. It wasn't just shops, Bobby, it was us. The sense of community just... left, like a fog, slippin' away slow, and nobody noticed till it was gone." Her eyes lifted, meetin' the lens, wet but fierce, the camera holdin' her gaze, the light catchin' a glint of tears. "Folks don't gather no more, don't talk over coffee or help a neighbor fix a fence. I can remember mom given Jason's mama groceries for two months on just a handshake when his daddy hurt himself. They never could pay it back, but they sure put a new roof on the store as trade. Try that with AG?!" There was a fire in her eyes now. "New stores, new people, they're here, but it ain't the same. It's like we're all strangers now, livin' where

356

our home used to be. Now there's no work unless it's at one of those places. Mom's gotta work two shifts at AG to bring the same amount home, comes home empty every morning. Sleeps for a few hours, then does it all over again. She used to wake up early every morning with a smile, in a hurry to get to work cause she wanted to. Now, she's hollow, like this town has become. We got two choices, we can stay here, getting by, hopin' a miracle happens, or we can leave. I wanted to go to Auburn for art, but with the way things are here with Mom, I stayed to help, and now I'm just watchin things spiral down. Now I'm just wondering how far down the hole goes."

I muttered "Cut." but Grant gave Ryan the signal to keep rollin. I felt a sharp pang of guilt, and I had no idea things were that bad for Lila, and I felt awful for the fact that *I had no idea*. I hadn't taken the time to consider how deep the hurt ran for her, how Allied General's shadow had hollowed her mom, her dreams, her home. "Lila," I started, voice rough, lowerin' my headset, its weight pullin' at my arms, "why didn't you tell me it was this bad?"

She looked away, her braid swingin', fingers still tuggin' that thread, unravelin' her jacket's cuff like the town itself. "Didn't wanna burden you, Bobby," she said, soft, her eyes on the creek, its ripples catchin' the last of the sun. "You're out here filmin', tryin' to save us all with *Echoes*. Your mom is sick, the family store gone, I figured... my stuff could wait." Her voice cracked, and she swiped a tear, quick, like she hoped I wouldn't see. "But it's hard, watchin' mom come home, her hands raw, smellin' like chemicals, no light in her no more. I stayed for her, but sometimes I wonder if I'm just drownin' with this town."

"You ain't drownin'," I said, firm, meeting her gaze, her eyes wet but sharp, like Mom's when she'd talk about fightin' on. "You're Lila, toughest damn artist I know. Auburn's still there, waitin' for you." She laughed, short, bitter, shaking her head, "Easy to say, Bobby, but money's tight, and Mom needs me. I can't just leave her to AG's grind." I thought of Mom's quilt, her fierce "Small don't mean weak," and leaned closer, the fire's embers from our earlier game glowing faint, their smoky tang lingering.

"Then we fight for her, like we're fightin' for the town," I said, voice low, urgent. "*Echoes* ain't just my story, it's yours, your mom's, Eric's, Gable's. We make people face what's happenin, how it's killin' who we are, and maybe… maybe we wake folks up."

Lila's lips curved, a small smile breaking, her hand brushing mine, warm, steady. "You really think a movie can do that, Bobby?" she asked, voice soft but hopeful, the creek's flow a quiet promise. I nodded, "I know it can, 'cause it's got you in it."

She laughed, real this time, the sound bright, like the bells in *Echoes*. For a moment, I saw the same strength in her, I had seen echoin' in everyone else we talked to. Like the fire was still there, it just needed to be stoked a lil'.

The camera's whirr had become just noise in the background, but it's quick absence told me that it was still rollin when I was talkin' to Lila. I looked at Grant, he just smiled back. "I'm gonna have to put you down as co-director" I said smiling while shaking my head slowly.

"Don't know if this is an interview or a therapy session, but all's I can say, it's 100% real." Lila smiled, an I swear I heard a little laugh come out as she stood up.

The church basement was empty now, the crew packin' up, the last Arriflex light unplugged, its cables coiled like snakes in a crate, the room finally cool. The Mitchell 35mm and Nagra IV were cased, their hums silenced. I slipped off my headset, my flannel shirt damp from the basement's heat, and walked up the stairs, pushin' through the church doors into the twilight and the welcomed cool night air. The sky was a deep indigo, streaked with pink, the air cool and sharp with the smell of pine and river mud, the Blackwater's murmur a soft pulse in the distance. I leaned against a porch post, my shoes scuffin' the worn steps, my clipboard dropped to the ground with a thud.

Grant stepped out of the church doors, his shaggy hair catchin' the last light, his notepad stuffed in his jacket, a tired grin on his face. I turned, my voice low, a knot of worry in my chest.

"Grant, you think this town'll be transformed back ten years in just two days for shootin'?" I asked, picturin' everythin' shinnin' like it used to, Gable's open, the diner buzzin', a 1960s Mill Town reborn. "It's gotta feel alive, like Lila's stories, like Sheriff Johnson's days."

Grant clapped my shoulder, his grip firm, his eyes steady. "Bobby, Jesus has the crew workin' round the clock, signs repainted, windows cleaned, old cars lined up. The town's pitched in, too, Mrs. Clara's loanin' diner props, Abernathy's got his old ford for the street scene. It'll be perfect, man, trust me." His confidence eased me, and I managed a half-smile, noddin' back.

We walked through the quiet parking lot when Grant broke the silence, "we're starting to hear the same things over and over again with these interviews though. I'm a little concerned it will feel a bit repetitive."

"I was thinkin' the same thing" as he headed to his car, leavin' me to the night.

The world went quiet, just crickets chirpin' in the grass, frogs croakin' by the river, and the soft murmur of a town tryin' to sleep, its houses dark but for a few lit windows downtown, like eyes half-open. I sank onto the church steps, my hands clasped, still thinkin about the interview. Footsteps crunched behind me, and I turned to see Lila, her denim jacket loose, her dark hair catchin' the moonlight, her eyes searchin' mine. "You okay?" she asked, her voice soft, sittin' beside me, her shoulder brushin' mine, familiar like we used to do all the time.

"I should be askin you the same thing, but yeah," I said, my voice low, rough, starin' at the ground, the crickets fillin' the pause. "Just... hearin' it all out loud. Kinda makes it real again. I mean, that's why I'm here, but you're never really prepared. The town's mostly gone, and I'm tryin' to catch what's left." She nodded, her gaze on the stars, her voice quiet but sure. We sat there, just enjoying the silence, each lost in our own thoughts.

She nudged me, a small smile breakin' through. "Wanna grab dinner? Mrs. Clara's got catfish fryin', I think most of the crew is goin'." I shook my head, "Naw, I gotta go see an old friend tonight," I said, my voice firm, the need to face him stronger than hunger. "Been too long, and I owe him that." She nodded, no questions, just understandin', and stood, squeezin' my shoulder. "Good, go then. I'll see ya tomorrow." She walked off, her steps fadin', leavin' me with the crickets, the frogs, the town's whisper. I was actually nervous, can you imagine that? Nervous to go see your best friend, and I didn't even wreck his bike this time.

Chapter 43 - Visiting an Old Friend
(November 1972)

As I drove to Eric's house, the full moon shining above I smiled, remembering the thousands of times I had walked this road kicking cans or pulling rubber snakes across the road. I pulled into his drive, the bushes had grown, but otherwise looked the same. The lights were still on. I stood on the porch, the wood creakin' under me, my breath shallow, the cap tight on my head. I hadn't seen Eric since just before his deployment, back at the party on the creek after graduation. I could still see his grin wide, his voice loud with plans. Now, I didn't know what I'd find. Lila's words 'bout his silence, his pain, loomed large. I knocked, the sound sharp in the quiet, my heart racin' as the door creaked open.

Eric's dad, Mr. Tom, stood there, his face linin' with a tired but genuine smile, his eyes lightin' up. "Bobby Chandler, as I live and breathe!" he said, his voice warm, pullin' me into a quick, firm handshake that turned into a pat on the back. "Boy, it's good to see you, filmin' your big movie and all!" I took the hat off as I stepped in.

I managed a smile, my voice low. "Good to see you too, sir. Been too long."

Mrs. Fulton, Eric's mom, appeared behind him, her apron dusted with flour, her eyes soft but shadowed as she stepped forward and wrapped me in a hug, her arms tight, like she was holdin' onto a piece of the past. "Bobby," she said, pullin' back, her hands on my shoulders, her voice gentle but heavy, "you're a sight for sore eyes." She paused given me a big hug, then her smile fadin', her eyes searchin' mine. "Eric... he ain't been the same since he came back, honey. Some days are better'n others, but the war's still in him. Sometimes he screams in the night, nightmares so bad they wake the house. Just… be patient with him, alright?" Her voice cracked, her hands squeezin' my shoulders, and I nodded, my throat tight, the cap heavier in my hand. "Yes, ma'am," I said, my voice barely above a whisper, "I'll try."

Mr. Tom led me inside, the house smellin' of cornbread and woodsmoke, his bedroom dim, lit by a single lamp. Eric sat in a chair by the window, his silhouette sharp against the dusk, a blanket draped over his lap, hidin' the stump where his leg used to be. His hair was longer, his face thinner, his eyes fixed on the dark beyond the glass, distant, like he was somewhere else. Then his gaze shifted, lockin' onto the camo cap in my hand, his cap, the one he'd tossed me before shippin' out, sayin', "Keep it safe, Bobby, till I'm back." His eyes widened, a flicker of somethin', recognition, pain, maybe hope, crossin' his face, the first sign he saw me, really saw me. I froze, my heart in my throat, maybe this old cap was a bridge between where he is and where he was.

Eric's gaze flicked up to my face, a smirk tuggin' at his lips, faint but sharp, his voice rough, edged with somethin' bitter. "Look at you… big-time director now, huh?" he said, leanin' back in his chair, his eyes narrowin', the lamp's light catchin' the hard lines of his face, like he was testin' me, darin' me to flinch. I chuckled, tryin' to keep it light, my voice low, steady, hopin' to bridge the gap. "Naw, Eric, just tryin' to tell our story, y'know? Mill Town, like we always talked 'bout." I took a step closer, the cap tight in my hand, ready to say more, 'bout the film, 'bout missin' him, 'bout Mom, but he cut me off, his voice cold, sharp as a blade. "You can go now, Bobby."

The words hit like a punch, his eyes hard, turnin' back to the window, shuttin' me out, the blanket shiftin' slightly, revealin' the edge of his stump, a raw reminder of what he'd lost. I didn't move, my chest tight, my feet planted. I swallowed, my voice softer but firm, holdin' his cap like a lifeline. "Someone once told me, don't forget about the small-timers," I said, echoin' his old words, back when we'd fish the creek, dreamin' big laughin' larger, his grin wide under this very cap. "That was you, Eric. I ain't forgettin'. Not you, not this town, not us."

His smirk faltered, his eyes flickerin' back to mine, a glint of somethin', pain, maybe memory, breakin' through the wall he'd built. The room held its breath, the lamp's glow soft on his face, the cap a silent promise between us. I stood still, my heart racin', knowin' I couldn't push too hard, not yet, but refusin' to walk away. I knew he was hurtin, and I would gladly take whatever he was dishin out if it meant there was a chance I could get him out of whatever hell he was stuck in.

I moved slow, deliberate, not wantin' to spook him, like those bass we used to stalk as kids. I set his cap gentle on the arm of his chair, my feet quiet on the floorboards. I pulled a stool from the corner and sat beside him, close but not crowdin'. My hands clasped, my flannel shirt still damp from the day's interviews all still churnin' in me, mixin' with this moment with Eric. The room was quiet, save for the hum of a the TV in the livingroom. Outside, crickets chirped, frogs croaked, but here, it was just us, the silence heavy with what we hadn't said, what we might yet.

I looked at him, his face half-lit, his eyes still on the cap, his fingers twitchin' like he might reach for it but didn't. My heart pounded, but I kept my voice low, steady, like we were back at Coldwater Creek, skippin' rocks. "Been carryin' that cap everywhere, Eric," I said, noddin' to it, my words careful, hopin' to draw him out. "Kept it safe, like you asked. Figured it'd bring you back to me, one way or another." His lip twitched again, not quite a smile but close, his gaze flickin' to mine, holdin' a mix of pain and somethin' warmer, maybe memory, maybe the friend he'd been. "Remember where this hole came from?" I said, smiling pointing at the little hole in the side of his hat.

"Yeah, I remember that damn hole…you scared away the biggest bass I had ever seen when you hooked my hat." He said half smiling.

The door had cracked open…our voices soft, like whispers over Coldwater Creek, shared memories pullin' us back to the before times, before war, before loss. "Remember skippin' school to fish?" I said, a grin tuggin' my lips, leanin' closer. "That spring, what, '65? We snuck to the Blackwater, rods in hand, thinkin' we'd catch a bass big as a hog."

Eric's lip curled, a real smile breakin' through, his eyes sparklin' for the first time, the lamp's light catchin' a glint in 'em. "Yeah," he said, his voice rough but warm, "and we caught nothin' but mud and a lecture from your mom when we dragged in, smellin' like river slime."

We laughed, a low, shared chuckle, the sound fillin' the room, pullin' us back to bein' two kids, carefree, the world small and full of wonder.

"Or that time we outran the game warden," Eric said, his voice gainin' strength, his hand gesturin' slow, like he was back in the woods. "Summer of '66, sneakin' through the pines, tryin' to poach catfish from that restricted pond."

I nodded, "That's where the biggest catfish were." laughin' louder, the memory sharp. "Man, we heard his truck comin', and you grabbed my arm, yellin', 'Run, Bobby, he's got a shotgun!' We tore through them brambles, thorns rippin' our shirts, divin' into a ditch till he passed."

Eric's laugh was deeper now, a bark that shook his shoulders, his face lit up, the blanket slippin' slightly, unnoticed. "Thought we was outlaws, Bonnie and Clyde," he said, his eyes meetin' mine, bright with the thrill of it.

"And blowin' up cans of beans in the campfire!" I added, my voice risin', leanin' in. "Remember the stump thumpers we made? We'd swipe Dad's gunpowder, pack them cans, light a fuse, and boom, stump thumper', us hollerin' like we'd won the war."

Eric grinned, his hand slappin' his knee, the sound sharp in the quiet room. "Dad was madder'n a wet hen when he found out, grounded me

364

for a month," he said, his voice warm, the lamp's glow soft on his cheeks.

For a while, we were just two kids again, the years and wounds fallin' away, the livin' room a time machine, Mill Town's creeks and woods alive in our words, laughter returnin' like a long-lost friend.

But the quiet spaces crept back, the laughter fadin', leavin' gaps where the present crept in. Eric's smile dimmed, his eyes droppin' to the cap, his fingers brushin' its edge. I stayed put, my heart heavy but hopeful.

"We had some times, didn't we?" I said, my voice soft, tryin' to hold the light. Eric nodded, his voice barely a whisper.

"Yeah, Bobby. We did." The room held us, the noise of the TV and the crickets, and I knew these memories, this crack in Eric's shell, were a start.

I sat on a stool beside him, the quiet spaces had grown, heavy with what we hadn't touched: the war, his loss, the nightmares his mom had whispered about. Outside, crickets chirped, but here, the silence was loud, pressin' against us waitin' in the dark.

The room went quiet, both of us starin' out the window, the indigo sky studded with stars, the night's faint murmur a distant echo. Eric's face, half-lit by the lamp, was still, his earlier smile gone, his eyes fixed on somethin' beyond the glass, maybe the past, maybe nothin' at all. My heart pounded, with the need to know, to really know, the friend I'd missed. I swallowed, my voice low, careful, like steppin' onto thin ice. "Eric," I said, leanin' forward, my hands tight, "how are you *really* handlin' bein' back?" The question hung, raw and bare, the lamp's light catchin' the tense line of his jaw.

Eric's eyes lost their light, like a shutter closin', his gaze droppin' to the blanket, his fingers twitchin' toward the cap but stoppin' short. He exhaled, a sharp, shaky breath, a strand of his shaggy hair. "I'm not," he said, his voice flat, hollow, without expression, like he had just disconnected because it was too painful to bear. His face tightened, a flicker of anger, maybe shame, crossin' it, the lamp's glow castin' shadows in the hollows of his cheeks. "Ain't no handlin' it, Bobby. War took my leg, my sleep, my… me. Nightmares don't stop, and this town, it ain't the same, but neither am I." His words cut, sharp and final, his eyes meetin' mine, raw, unguarded, a wound laid bare, the blanket slippin' slightly, revealin' the stump's edge, a silent scream of what he'd lost.

I sat frozen, my throat tight, his answer heavier than I'd braced for. I wanted to reach out, to say somethin', but the weight of his truth pinned me, the cricket's song fillin' the gap. My hands unclenched, restin' on my knees, my voice gone for now, but my presence a promise to stay, to listen, to carry his. Eric turned back to the window, his face a mask again, but that crack, his stark "I'm not", was a door left ajar, a piece of his truth I'd hold, ready to build on.

The silence stretched, the cricket song outside the only sounds, until Eric's voice, low and strained, broke through, his eyes fixed on the floor, like he was seein' another place. "It was an ambush, Bobby," he said, his words slow, deliberate. "Some godforsaken jungle near Laos, rain pourin', mud suckin' at our boots. My squad was movin' through, quiet, rifles up, lookin' for VC. Then it hit, gunfire, tracer rounds flyin inches from my head, screams, the world explodin' all around me." His voice cracked, his hands clenchin' the blanket, the lamp's light catchin' the tremble in his fingers, his face tightenin', a sheen of sweat on his brow. "A mortar landed. The explosion… it tore through us. My leg was gone, just gone, blood everywhere, but I saw him, Sergeant Miller, just a few feet away, his eyes wide tryin' to get behind the log I was layin behind, then nothin', explosion and shrapnel took him, ripped him apart. At that exact time, the only difference tween him an me was three feet. I'm here, he ain't."

His voice broke, a sob chokin' out, his eyes glassy, starin' past me, the camera in my mind framin' the horror in his face, the lamp's glow castin' shadows in his hollow cheeks. "He was a good man, Bobby. A

366

good man. He would talk about his family all the time." He said, his words a whisper, heavy with grief, his hands shakin' as he gripped the blanket tighter. "Always checkin' on us, sharin' his smokes, tellin' awful funny stories 'bout his daughters back home. And just like that... gone. Pieces of him everywhere. Even on me." His voice faltered, a tear fallin', the light catchin' its path down his cheek, his body leanin' forward, head droppin' into his hands, fingers diggin' into his hair. "Why do people do that to each other?" he asked, his voice raw, muffled, a plea more than a question, the room holdin' his pain like a blanket.

I sat frozen, my throat tight, his words and pain slicin' through me. Eric straightened, his eyes meetin' mine, red but fierce, his voice steadier now, carryin' a hollow clarity. "I didn't even hate em, Bobby," he said, his hands unclenchin', fallin' limp. "The Vietcong, I mean. I was there because they told me to, but then when I got there, I was there to protect my friends, my squad. That's all. Keep 'em alive, get 'em home to see their families." He paused, his gaze driftin' to the window, the stars beyond. "But my friends said the same thing...we were all just fightin' to protect each other. And the other guys we were fightin'? I bet they were too, protectin' their own so they could get home. All of us, just... protectin', and losin' everythin' for it." His words hung, a bitter echo of his earlier philosophy, the weight of war's futility crushin', his face a map of loss, the blanket slippin' slightly, revealin' the stump's edge, a silent scar.

I didn't speak, couldn't, my chest achin' with his pain, the senseless cycle. I felt ashamed to not have acknowledged until now. My hands rested heavy on my knees, my breath shallow, knowin' this truth, belonged to him, to us, and I stayed, silent, my presence, a promise to carry his scars as if they were my own.

Eric's eyes fixed on the cap, his fingers still, the lamp's light catchin' the faint sheen of tears dried on his cheeks. I took a breath, leanin' forward, my voice low, warm, like we were kids plannin' a prank. "Eric," I said, pickin' up the camo cap, its fabric worn soft, holdin' it out to him, "you could use some luck back. This thing works pretty good." I smiled, hopin' to spark the old Eric, the one who'd tossed me the cap before shippin' out, grinnin' wide.

His eyes flicked to the cap, then to me, a smirk tuggin' at his lips, a glint of mischief breakin' through the pain. "Yeah, you son of a bitch," he said, his voice rough but light, takin' the cap, turnin' it in his hands, "had I been wearin' it, I might not be so lopsided now." His smirk grew into a laugh, a low, barkin' sound, and I joined him, our laughter fillin' the room, a burst of the before times, the lamp's glow warm on our faces, the blanket slippin' slightly, unnoticed.

The laughter faded, leavin' a comfortable quiet, Eric's fingers tracin' the cap's stitches, his smile lingerin', softer now. I stood, knowin' it was time to go, my heart lighter but still heavy with his pain.

As I slung my jacket over my shoulder, I turned, my voice gentle, a grin tuggin' my lips. "Eric, I'm doin' these interviews for the film, tellin' the town's story," I said, meetin' his eyes. "Will you do one? Tell your story? I'll make you a star, man." I winked, keepin' it light, not pushin' too hard.

He looked at me, his smirk fadin' to a thoughtful nod, his eyes searchin' mine, the cap still in his hands. "I'll think about it, Bobby," he said, his voice quiet but not closed off, a door left ajar, the lamp's light catchin' a flicker of possibility in his gaze.

I nodded, my grin holdin'. "Fair enough," I said, headin' for the door, my feet soft on the floorboards, the night's cool air waitin' outside. The crickets sang, the town slept, and I left with Eric's laughter, his cap returned to its rightful owner.

Chapter 44 - Second Day of Interviews (November 1972)

The church basement hummed with purpose by 9 AM, its concrete walls once again a makeshift studio for *Mill Town Echoes*, the air sharp with the scent of coffee and wax polish. Lights flared, Arriflex beams softened through silk scrims, castin' a warm glow over the muslin backdrop, its gray folds pinned tight to hide the cinderblocks. The Mitchell 35mm sat steady on its tripod, lens gleamin', while the Sennheiser shotgun mic, wired to a Nagra IV, hovered on a boom, reels spinnin' silent in test runs, the sound guy givin' a thumbs-up. Cables snaked across the floor, tethered to the generator's low rumble outside, and the crew moved sharp, testin' every bulb, every hum, ready for another heavy day of interviews.

I stood behind the Mitchell, my hands steady on the viewfinder, more confident, more focused than the interviews before, but bracin' myself for the weight of today's roster. Yesterday's interviews, Eleanor's tears, Leonard's war, Johnson's pranks, Lila's creek days, had carved deep, and today's list, scribbled on my clipboard, promised more: Mrs. Clara from the restaurant, Mr. Tatum with his cane, young Jenny who'd lost her dad to the mill's closure then the heavy hitters, Uncle Don, Mr Radcliffe, and Dad. Their stories would be Mill Town's heart, and I felt the weight, my pulse quickenin' as I adjusted the lens, settin' f/2.8 for intimacy.

"Lights good?" I called, my voice firm, echoin' off the walls. A gaffer nodded, tweakin' a barn door to soften a beam, the glow hittin' the empty chair where Mrs. Clara would sit first, her tales ready to spill. Ryan, at the camera, checked the Mitchell's focus, his fingers deft.

Grant leaned against a crate, notepad open, his shaggy hair fallin' over eyes bright with anticipation. "Clara's got stories 'bout feedin' half the town during the '50s floods," he said, grinnin'. "She's gonna steal the show."

I nodded, my lips tight, knowin' her warmth. I stepped back, headset loose 'round my neck, wipin' sweat from my brow, the basement alive with the crew's quiet chatter, the Nagra's faint hiss, the lights' soft buzz.

Mrs. Clara steps in, her presence filling the space like sunlight breaking through pines, her floral dress, pink roses on navy, hem brushing her knees, swaying as she moves, her apron traded for a pearl brooch pinned at her collar, glinting under the bulbs. Her hair, graying but curled tight from Saturday's salon, frames a face lined with years of laughter and loss, her eyes sharp, brown as the Blackwater River, twinkling with stories. She settles into the interview chair, its wood creaking, her hands folding in her lap, callused from years at the diner. I adjust the Mitchell, the lens framing her, the Nagra humming, ready to catch her voice, her truth.

"Alright, Mrs. Clara," I say, voice steady, leaning forward, the headset's foam warm against my ear, "let's start with when you were young, what was it like back then?"

She laughs, a rich, rolling sound, like gravel stirred by the creek, her hands unclenching, gesturing wide, the brooch catching light. "Oh, Bobby, when I was a girl, 'round the '40s, this town was alive, honey! Main Street bustled, folks in their Sunday hats, kids racin' bikes, bells jinglin'. My mama started the restaurant just after I was born. When I was old enough to stand, mama had me sweepin' the floor. I'd sneak a peppermint stick when she wasn't lookin', but I think she knew." Her eyes dance, the Nagra taping the lilt, Grant scribbling, grinning. "Wasn't just a restaurant, people lingered long after they were done eatin', talkin' crops, church suppers, who kissed who at the fair. Felt like kin, every one of 'em." Her smile softens, wistful, the basement's chill brushing her arms, goosebumps rising under her dress's cotton. "We were small, but tight, like a quilt stitched tight, y'know?"

I nod, the camera rolling. "What changes have you seen since, Mrs. Clara?" I ask, voice low, the lights' buzz steady, the crew quiet, Jesus adjusting a boom mic, his scarf dangling.

Her brow creases, fingers twisting a ring, gold worn thin, her voice dropping, heavy as the river's silt. "Biggest change came with Allied General, '63, '64," she says, eyes darkening, the Nagra catching a crack in her tone. "Town split like a log. Some saw jobs, cheap goods, progress. Others, like me, knew better, stores couldn't fight their prices. Most of downtown closed up in '65, then Gable's, Elma's, your daddy's hardware, one by one, like candles snuffed out. When AG moved in, our downtown died: folks quit comin', no customers, no sales; no sales, no stores; no stores, no restaurants, and before long the streets lay empty, our community was dryin up. Wasn't a matter of if, just when." She shakes her head, the brooch trembling, the air thick with her grief. "Ain't just the stores, Bobby, it's us. The stores just brought us together. Folks don't gather no more, don't swap stories over tea or help a neighbor like before. I work days at the Benny's just cause I miss it so much, but I gotta work nights at AG too, to pay the bills, scrubbin' vats, comin' home smellin' like bleach, bones achin'. Still love the diner shifts, servin' pie, chattin'. AG, it's just work, no time for anythin' else there. It's cold. Town's still here, but it's not, like it's forgettin' who we were."

"One more, Mrs. Clara," I say, forcing a smile, the Mitchell steady, "can you tell us a funny story, somethin' to make us laugh." Her face lights up, a spark flaring, her laugh bubbling again, rich, warm, the basement's damp fading under it. "Oh, honey, let's talk 'bout the hurricane flood, '54!" she says, hands waving, the Nagra taping her glee. "Now this town's seen plenty of floods, but the flood of 54' I'll never forget. Water came roarin' down the Blackwater, turned Main Street to a river, folks' homes swamped, furniture floatin' like boats. I was at the restaurant workin when I saw the water comin in under the

371

door the day after the storm. Luckily, that's as far as it came, but other's weren't so lucky. We turned the restaurant into a soup kitchen, me and the girls from church cookin' round the clock, pork and beans, cornbread, collards, pots big as washtubs, the air thick with bacon grease and steam. Fed near the whole town, Bobby, hundreds, crammed in, soppin' wet, eatin' on the counter, the floor, even the jukebox!" She grins, eyes glinting, the brooch flashing. "Funny part? Old Man Carter, stingiest cuss in town, tried sneakin' three plates, hid 'em under his coat like I wouldn't see! I hollered, 'Carter, you better pass them beans or I'll paddle you!' He turned redder'n a beet, dropped a dollar, and ran. Whole diner roared, even the preacher!" The crew laughs, Jesus muffling a chuckle, Grant's pen flying, the basement alive, her story a burst of light.

I leaned back, the headset slipping, her flood tale vivid, pulling me back too, I could still see its checkered floor slick and hear the jukebox still playin, plates clattering, Mill Town's heart beating through her hands, her pots, her love.

"Mrs. Clara, how'd you keep feedin' 'em all?" I ask, voice soft, the camera lingering on her hands, their calluses catching light.

She straightens, proud, her dress's roses vivid, her voice firm, "We didn't think how we could do it. I suspect if we did, we never would'a started. Bobby, we just did it. Mama'd bake fifty loaves a day, I'd stir beans 'til my arms burned, neighbors brought what they could, canned peaches, ham hocks, even a sack of rice from Miss Elma. Church ladies hauled water, kept the coffee hot, the air bitter with grounds. We set up tables in the street when the diner overflowed, folks eatin' under tarps, rain still drippin'. Fed 'em for weeks, 'til the water receded, no one went hungry, not one soul." Her eyes shined, wet, the Nagra taping a tremor, the basement's chill no match for her warmth. "That's what we were, Bobby, family, not just neighbors. I guess only time can take that away…but not if we hold on. We gotta teach the next generation, or they'll lose that somethin'. Somethin' they won't even know they've lost. They'll feel that hole inside, they just won't know what to fill it with, ya know?"

I nod, throat tight, the Mitchell rolling, her story woven permanently into *Echoes*, "Cut…Thank you so much Mrs. Clara, you really know how to tell it."

Grant closes his notepad, eyes soft, whispering, "She's gold, Bobby. Next up is Miss Baxter. I don't know if anyone can top that though."

Jesus adjusts a light, his scarf brushing a crate. The church basement glowed soft, the Arriflex lights' warm beams diffused through silk scrims, bathin' Miss Lorraine Baxter in a gentle light as she sat in the padded chair, her sharp eyes twinklin' under a neat bun of silver hair. At seventy-eight, she was spry, her floral dress crisp, her hands folded in her lap, fingers still nimble from years of needlework. The Mitchell 35mm hummed on its tripod, Ryan framin' her face tight, the Sennheiser mic hoverin' close, Nagra reels spinnin' to catch her voice, clear and lively despite her age. I stood by the monitor, headset loose, my flannel damp, heart steady but braced for her stories, knowin' they'd weave another thread into *Echoes'* tapestry.

Miss Lorraine leaned forward, her smile sly, the lamp's glow catchin' the crinkle 'round her eyes. "I owned the store on the corner by the bank, just off Main Street, across from the square," she said, her voice rich, like she was invitin' me into her shop. "Baxter's Boutique, we called it, though it was just a little place, racks of dresses I sewed myself, bolts of fabric stacked high, smellin' of starch and cotton. Women'd pass by, see my dresses in the window, chiffon for pageants, taffeta for church choirs, and they'd come on in, bells jinglin' on the door. I'd fit 'em for homecomin', weddings, Easter services, pinnin' hems while they chattered 'bout their lives."

Her hands gestured, mimickin' a needle's dance, the camera catchin' their grace, the Nagra tapin' her soft chuckle. "Folks didn't just come to buy, Bobby," she said, her eyes sparklin'. "They'd stop by to gossip, and gossip they did, oh, my! Who was courtin' who, whose crop failed, whose kid got caught sneakin' whiskey. My shop was like Mrs. Clara's restaurant, but with pins and thread. You'd be amazed what you learn 'bout people when you measure their inseams, secrets spill faster'n a ripped seam." She laughed, a bright, tinklin' sound, the camera zoomin' slow to hold her joy, the light glintin' off her glasses.

Her grin widened, her voice droppin' conspiratorial, the Mitchell keepin' her mischief. "Lemme tell you 'bout the time I saved the Mayor's hide," she said, leanin' in. "It was the summer of '55, big Fourth of July parade, first one since the flood, downtown was still a mess in spots, and he splits his pants right before the march, big ol' rip, right down the seat, from climbin' onto the float too fast. Comes runnin' to my shop, red as a tomato, parade startin' in ten minutes. I had him stand on a stool, bitin' my lip to keep from laughin', stitchin' that tear so fast my needle was a blur. Got him back out there, wavin' like nothin' happened, though he walked mighty careful rest of the day." She cackled, slappin' her knee, the camera catchin' the shake of her shoulders, the Nagra holdin' her delight.

Her laughter faded, her eyes softenin', droppin' to her hands, the camera lingerin' on their stillness, the light castin' shadows on her knuckles. "There were lots of good days, and some not so good. I was engaged once," she said, her voice quieter, a tremor in it, the Nagra catchin' the shift. "My Juel, one of three brothers, sweetest man I ever knew. He went off to college, '42, promisin' to marry me after he was through." She held up a solitary silver band still on her finger. But a bus accident, just beyond the city limits, took him on his way back for Christmas. Skidded off the road and went in the creek, they said, he saved two kids pinned up front." Her fingers twisted a ringless hand, her eyes distant, wet. "Never looked at another man. Nobody could hold a candle to my Juel." She paused, a tear glintin', the camera holdin' her grief, soft and raw, a seamstress's life stitched with love and loss.

I leaned forward, headset loose, the Mitchell still rollin', Miss Lorraine's story of Juel lingerin' heavy in the basement's glow. "Miss

Lorraine," I said, my voice soft, careful, "how'd things change for you, for the shop? Why'd you end up closin' Baxter's Boutique?"

Her sharp eyes clouded, her hands stillin' in her lap, the lamp's light catchin' a tightenin' in her jaw. "Oh, Bobby," she said, her voice low, tinged with regret, "the '60s brought new winds, chain stores, big lots out by the interstate, sellin' dresses cheaper'n I could sew. Folks stopped comin' to gossip, too busy, too rushed. My shop got quiet, just me and the thread, till '69, when I couldn't pay the rent no more. It wasn't just money, it was the town changin', like we just fell out of fashion."

"Thank you, Miss Baxter for tellin' your story." I said solemnly as I walked her out.

The church basement pulsed with quiet energy, the Arriflex lights' soft glow bathing Pastor Rayshawn Williams as he sat in the padded chair, his dark suit crisp, his eyes steady with a warmth that held the weight of decades. At sixty-two, his voice carried the cadence of Sunday sermons, rich and resonant, the mic catchin' every note, Nagra reels spinnin' smooth. The Mitchell 35mm hummed, Ryan framin' his face, the muslin backdrop a gentle gray behind him. I stood by the monitor, headset loose, my flannel damp already from the heat, heart braced for his stories, knowin' they'd carve deep into *Echoes'* soul after Miss Lorraine's tales of seams and loss.

"Pastor, can you please tell us about yourself, and your church, the roles you played in the community and the changes you've seen over the past twenty years."

Pastor Williams leaned forward, hands clasped, the lamp's light glintin' off his glasses. "The church was the town's anchor durin' desegregation," he said, his voice firm, grounded. "Back in the '50s and '60s, when the schools integrated, this place, First Baptist, was a refuge. Black folks, white folks, we didn't all agree, but we prayed together, argued together, tried to find a way. I was young, helpin' my daddy, the old pastor, hold meetin's here, where folks could speak

375

plain, anger, fear, hope. We'd sit in these pews, upstairs, singin' hymns to steady our nerves, knowin' change was comin', like it or not."

His eyes softened, a smile tuggin' his lips, the camera catchin' the shift, the Nagra tapin' his low chuckle. "There was resistance, sure, shouts at town halls, some white families pullin' kids outta school, some Black families scared to send theirs. But there was bravery, too, quiet kinds. Like Miss Etta, a Black seamstress, walkin' her daughter to the white school in '61, head high, ignorin' the jeers. Or Mr. Gable, white as flour, openin' his store to Black customers when others wouldn't, takin' heat for it too. And reconciliation, slow, messy. I saw enemies share coffee here after months of glares, not friends, but tryin'. The church held space for that, for hearts to bend."

His smile faded, his brow creasin', the camera lingerin' on his hands, strong but worn, the light castin' shadows on his knuckles. "It ain't all progress, though," he said, his voice heavier. "My family's BBQ joint, Shawn's, second generation, best ribs in the County, closed last year, '71. Couldn't compete with them fast-food chains, all grease and cheap prices, poppin' up by the interstate and in town. We'd been feedin' folks since Daddy opened it in '38, Black and white, laughin' over plates, sauce on their chins. Losin' it felt like losin' a piece of the town's soul, like when Main Street's shops started shutterin'. It's not just money, it was the heart of this community, what binds us, slippin' away."

He straightened, his eyes meetin' the lens, clear and fierce, the camera holdin' his gaze, the Nagra catchin' the resolve in his voice. "Forgiveness doesn't mean forgettin'," he said, his words deliberate, a sermon in miniature. "It means fightin' to remember better, to hold the pain, the bravery, the love, and build from it. The community's hurtin', but this church, these stories, they're still here, remindin' us who we can be." His voice settled, a quiet fire, the lamp's glow soft on his face, his truth a beacon for *Echoes*, ready to fight.

The church basement was windin' down, the air heavy with the day's stories, the scent of coffee and wax polish fadin' as the crew packed up. I stretched, my flannel shirt damp, bones achin' from hours of listenin' to people's testimonies, Miss Lorraine's dresses, Pastor Williams' reconciliation, my clipboard heavy with notes. I was about to call it a wrap, my voice half-formed, when the door creaked open, slow and deliberate.

Eric walked in, his limp markin' his step, wearin' his old Army uniform, the fabric worn but proud, his camo cap clutched in one hand, eyes alert, scannin' the room. "Ready to make me a star?"

I laugh, "Long as you don't outshine Mom," and point him to the chair, its wood creaking under his frame, the basement a cocoon for his truth.

I grinned, new energy surgin', my fatigue gone like a snapped film reel. "You betcha!" I said, clappin' my hands, the sound echoin' off the cinderblocks. The crew scrambled, movin' fast, gaffers flicked the lights back on, beams flarin' through silk scrims, castin' a warm glow; Ryan repositioned the Mitchell, lens snappin' into place; the sound guy swung the boom mic, Nagra hummin' alive. Within minutes, cameras were rollin' again, the basement alive, the muslin backdrop smooth behind the chair. Eric took a seat, his uniform creasin', his cap restin' on his knee, fingers tracin' its stitches.

"Don't really know what to say to a camera," he started, slow, his voice low, but it gained strength with each memory, the lamp's light catchin' the resolve in his eyes.

I leaned forward, grippin' the monitor's edge, my voice takin' on a playful radio announcer's boom, hopin' to ease him in. "Eric, I know we've known each other since before we can remember, but can you tell us a little 'bout the old days in Mill Town as you recall 'em?"

377

He smirked, a lopsided grin breakin' through, his shoulders easin' as he shifted in the chair, the lamp's light catchin' the crinkle 'round his eyes, a hint of the kid who'd raced me to the creek. "I think I can do that," he said, his voice rough but warm, a chuckle rumblin' low, the Nagra tapin' its grit.

His eyes flicked to me, then past the lens, like he was seein' the town's dusty foot paths again, his fingers tappin' the cap, the camera holdin' his nostalgia. "Remember that time we snuck onto the water tower, me, you, Lila and Matt?" he said, his grin widenin', voice alive with mischief. "Summer of '66, Fourth of July parade, Main Street packed, flags wavin', the high school band blarin' off-key. We were what, fifteen? Haulin' a sack of water balloons up that rickety ladder, slingshots stuffed in our jeans, sweatin' buckets in the heat. Planned to rain hell on them floats, thought we'd be legends. We were laughin' like fools, balancin' up there, till I slipped, one foot danglin', heart in my throat. Caught the rail just in time, you grabbin' my shirt, yellin', 'Don't die, doofuss!'" He laughed, a sharp, free bark, the Mitchell catchin' the shake of his shoulders, the Nagra holdin' the joy, the light glintin' off a bead of sweat on his brow.

He leaned back, his smile lingerin', hands grippin' the cap tighter, the camera zoomin' slow to their scarred knuckles, the blanket slippin' slightly over his stump, unnoticed. "Or that day we 'borrowed' watermelons from Mr. Collier's field," he said, his voice droppin' to a conspiratorial drawl. "Late July, '64, so hot the air shimmered, us out seinin' a catfish hole in the swamp that was dryin up, nets too heavy to pull from all the fish. We saw Collier's melons, fat and green, sittin' pretty across the fence, and Matt says, 'They're sweet as sin.' Nobody wanted to go, so I hopped that fence, thinkin' I was slick, Then Mr. Collier comes barrelin' outta nowhere, shotgun raised, hollerin' 'bout thieves. I ran fast as I could, with melons in that sack beatin me in the back as I did. Probably would have gotten away if I hadn't mooned him. He got the last laugh though, rock salt right in the butt, stung like a hornet's nest!" His laugh was louder now, head thrown back, the camera catchin' the flush in his cheeks, the Nagra tapin' the raw delight, the basement's hush amplifyin' his voice. Sure was good rippin' 'those watermelons open with our pocketknives down by the creek though, juice drippin' down our chins, laughin' till we nearly choked."

His laughter faded, his eyes growin' distant, the camera holdin' steady, the Nagra catchin' a quieter, heavier tone as he shifted to deeper ground. "We didn't have much growin' up," he said, his voice low, seein' our past in the air, his jaw tightenin', fingers still on the cap. "Hand-me-down clothes, one bike between us, meals stretchin' thin some weeks. But whatever we had in the community, we shared, no question. Food, tools, time, if your neighbor's roof leaked, you climbed up with a hammer. If their kid was sick, they brought soup. Mrs. Clara'd slip extra cornbread to families short on cash, no fuss. It was hard, sometimes, scrapin' by, but we did it together, leaned on each other, didn't ask for outside help, didn't want it. We knew then, that we were all only one mistake, one dry season, one tragedy away from bein' in the same situation, needin' help from them. Now, things are different. Everyone's in an invisible race, racin the clock, racin their neighbor, racin themselves. Everyone's out for themselves and whatever they can git…thinkin 'bout nobody but themselves. If someone needs help, well, they best look elsewhere." His voice grew firm, a soldier's resolve, the lamp's glow soft on his face, castin' shadows in the lines carved by war.

I frame him in the Mitchell, the lens catching the glint of his dog tags, the Nagra humming, ready for his voice, and lean forward, headset tight, "Eric, tell me 'bout protectin' each other, how you learned to fight for the ones you love, the lengths we go to."

His grin fades, his eyes dropping to his hands, callused fingers clenching, the bulb's light catching a scar on his knuckle, his breath slow, like he's pulling the words from a deep well. "Bobby, protectin' ain't just a choice—it's a fire in your gut, burns you up 'til you act," he says, voice low, rough, the Nagra taping its gravel. "We were in a God

379

forsaken jungle outside of Laos on a routine patrol, rain hammerin',
mud so thick it stole your boots. My squad, Miller, Jones, Tommy from
Ohio, we weren't just soldiers, we were brothers, sharin' smokes,
letters from home, laughin' 'bout dumb stuff like who'd eat the worst
C-rations. One night on patrol, VC hit us, gunfire rippin' through the
dark, screams, morters poppin' like firecrackers. Jones got pinned
behind a tree, bullets chewin' the dirt 'round him, cryin' for his mama,
his leg shot through. I didn't think, just ran, bullets be damned, dragged
him to cover, my heart poundin', blood soakin' my hands, his blood,
mine, didn't matter. Took a graze to my arm, didn't feel it 'til later. Got
him to the medic." His eyes lift, wet but fierce, meeting the lens, the
light catching a tear's glint, his voice steadying, "That's love, Bobby—
throwin' yourself in the fire for your people, knowin' you might not
come out, but doin' it anyway, 'cause they're yours. Learned it there,
learned it here, too—Mill Town's the same, fightin' for each other. I
saw the best and worst of human nature…on both sides. I saw what
we're capable of, capable of great evil, and great love, all on the count
of protectin' our own. Like nature was tryin' it's best to balance a scale.
You grow up in a place like this, you learn to fight for your neighbors,"
he said, his voice steady, burnin'. "Not out of duty, out of love. That's
the difference people don't understand. Duty's a contract, ends when
the job's done. Love? Love, for each other don't quit. It's why we
helped Miss Etta rebuild after the flood, why Gable kept his tabs open
so long, for folks who couldn't pay till harvest. It's why we stuck
together, no matter how tough it got. After those big stores moved in, it
got colder. Things got cheaper, and sure we each had a bike after, but
I'd trade every bit of those things for another chance to go back to how
we all were." His words landed heavy, echoin' the light catchin' a glint
in his eyes.

He paused, his eyes liftin' to mine, clear and fierce, the camera framin'
his gaze. "This film… this thing you're makin'," he said, his voice low,
raw, "it's the first real thing I've seen since I got back. The first thing
I've seen, that's worth fightin' for, and I'm damn proud to be part of it.
I realized, the only difference this time, is the enemy we're fightin' is

livin' inside each one of us. The good is fightin to get out, to do what's right, not what's easy or convenient."

The basement went still, the crew silent, my throat so tight I couldn't speak. I nodded, holdin' back emotions that were bubblin' up. "Cut..." The red recordin' light blinked, steady, then faded to black.

I shook my head, "You sure you didn't become a preacher while you were over there?"

"Bobby, you just keep doin' what your doin', I meant what I said, I'm damn proud." as he stuck his hand out to shake.

I gave him the biggest hug I had in me "It's great to have ya back."

I walked out with Eric talkin' bout meeting at home later, maybe bring Lila over too. As he drove away, I smiled, just happy to have my best friend back again. I knew he may not be completely out of the jungle yet, but I'd always be there fightin' to pull him outta it if he needed.

It was getting late and the night air was getting a chill when I saw Uncle Don talkin with the Reverand and Grant.

"Hey Uncle Don!" I said louder than I should have. His face lit up "Well look at you!" He said giving me a hug.

"Looks like one more, huh?" Grant said as he smiled at the crew. The crew stopped rolling up the wires and started unwindin' them again.

"It's late, y'all go home, I think we can handle it." as I looked at Grant with a grin.

Uncle Don had already started talkin about the ole' days like the memories had been crammed in a balloon that was about to burst, "Save it for the camera," I said with a smile, clappin his shoulder.

Uncle Don sat in the padded chair, a quiet, stern man in his early seventies, his flannel shirt buttoned high, arms crossed tight over his chest, gray hair cropped short, eyes sharp under bushy brows. The lamp's light caught the deep lines in his face, like a map of harvests and hard winters. "Didn't think you'd want an old mule like me on camera," he grumbled, his voice gravelly, a mix of reluctance and pride, his gaze flickin' to the lens, then to me, testin' my resolve. I chuckled, leanin' forward, my hands restin' on the Mitchell, keepin' it light but meanin' every word.

"You're a livin' archive, Uncle Don," I said, smilin'. "Ain't nobody knows this town's bones like you." His lips twitched, not quite a smile, but his arms loosened, the camera ready to catch his truth.

"and Action..." as I pressed record on the camera. "Tell us what was your memories of how town used to be."

He uncrossed his arms, leanin' forward, the lamp's light catchin' the lines in his face, his voice steady, like readin' an old ledger. "Mill Town in the '30s and '40s was different," he said, eyes driftin' past the lens, seein' fields and storefronts. "I was twelve, sweepin' the floor at daddy's hardware store, your daddy's store, well...old store. Where was I? Ah yes, I earned a nickel a day, pushin' a broom 'round, smellin' sawdust and oil, learnin' work's weight."

"Daddy showed me how to fix things, so that's what I did. I opened Dons-Fix-It. His hands moved, mimickin' a screwdriver's twist, calluses catchin' the light, the Mitchell holdin' their strength. "People took pride in fixin' things back then," he said, a smile tuggin' his lips. "Repairmen, carpenters, seamstresses, skills passed down like heirlooms. I'd watch Daddy show me how to rewire a lamp, solder a vacuum tube, his hands patient, steady. Folks brought in their old fans, fridges, phonographs, wantin' 'em to last, and we'd make 'em hum again. We'd always have neighbors droppin' by, laughin' over stories how their dog pulled the cord outta the radio runnin to catch a rabbit it saw outside eatin' the Mrs garden. Kids learnin' to tinker from their pa like my boy. Doin an honest day's work meant somethin', Bobby, meant family. God don't like it when people are just sittin' round." His voice warmed, the camera zoomin' slow to his eyes, bright with memory, the Nagra capturin' a town that mended its own.

"Before the mills, it was farmin', cotton, corn, folks scrapin' by on sweat and seasons. After the mills, the franchised superstores came in, big and cold, bleedin' Main Street dry." His brow creased, the camera catchin' a flash of disdain, the Nagra tapin' a faint grit in his tone. His smile dropped, his tone turnin' dark, the camera steady, the Nagra catchin' a heavier rhythm as he hit the breakin' point. "Then the closings came," he said, jaw tight, eyes fallin' to his hands. "Mid '60s, shops shuttin' one by one, Gable's, Elma's, then ours. Bank called in '70, threatenin' foreclosure. I had to close Don's Fix-It, after thirty-two years. Felt like losin' part of myself, Bobby, like I wasn't me no more. The only thing worse than the day after I closed the store wakin' up with nothin' to do, was havin' to tell my employees they wouldn't have nothin' to do either." His voice cracked, the light castin' shadows in his face's deep grooves. "It was worse for my workers, folks who'd been there decades, family. Old Hank, rewirin' motors since I was a boy, or Carl who could fix anythin', or Ellen who kept the books, she had her baby right there in the shop, gave birth to her lil boy right there in the office. Too late to take her to the hospital. Called the doc, and he delivered that baby right there. Four years later we was teachin' her son to strip wires, second generation up an comin'. Losin' the shop broke all their hearts, left 'em lost, took part of their identity too."

He leaned back, hands clenchin', the camera framin' his slump, the Nagra tapin' a bitter sigh. "They were more'n workers, they were family," he said, voice raw. "If somethin' big happened to one of us, a weddin', a sick kid, a new grandbaby, we all felt it, good or bad, we all shared it." He broke eye contact with the camera, began looking at the floor like he was ashamed of somethin'. "But folks stopped bringin' things to fix. Why mend a toaster when Allied General sold a new one for pennies? Everythin's disposable now, appliances, dreams, people. Toss 'em, get another one, a shinnier one for half off." His eyes hit the lens for a long pause, his eyes turnin red, like he had run out of words, or the will.

The red light blinked off and the screen faded to black…

Chapter 45 - Bringing it to Life
(November 1972)

The next day the air was crisp, the sun just peaking above the roofline of the old hardware store. The Mitchell's hum steadied, capturing the kids' laughter as they dodged around the soda shop's striped awning, their shadows dancin' on the cracked sidewalk. I crouched beside Ryan, squintin' through the viewfinder, the lens holdin' the elderly couple's slow shuffle, her scarf a soft blur of color. "Pan right," I whispered, my breath foggin' in the mornin' chill, "catch Abernathy's brushwork." Ryan tilted the camera smooth, the frame shiftin' to the hardware sign, wet paint glintin' under the rising sun, each stroke a quiet hymn to Dad's old days. The stray dog yawned again, stretchin' lazy on the bench, its fur catchin' flecks of dawn, and I grinned.

"Cut."

Grant jogged over, his steps kickin' up dust, his voice low but eager. "Bobby, we got more people coming, look."

He pointed down Main Street, where a woman in a housedress pushed a stroller, a toddler wavin' a pinwheel, its colors spinnin' wild. Behind her, old Mr. Tatum, cane tappin', tipped his hat to a passin' truck, its horn blarin' short and sharp. "Keep 'em in," I said, standin', my headset slippin' to my neck, "let 'em cross the frame natural." Grant nodded, wavin' to the woman, who smiled, steerin' the stroller slow, the pinwheel's whir a faint hum against the street's buzz. The mailman paused, stuffin' a mailbox, his cap tilted as he glanced at the camera, a half-smirk sayin' he knew he was part of somethin' now.

I stepped back, hands on hips, the air sharp with paint and coffee, feelin' the town's pulse in every motion, the kids' shouts, the couple's clasp, the dog's tail-thump. "Tighten up, Ryan," I called, "get the stroller and Tatum in one shot." The Mitchell whirred, the lens zoomin' slow, framin' the toddler's giggle, the pinwheel's blur, Tatum's cane scrapin' rhythm like a metronome. My chest tightened, this scene a livin' echo of their stories. Grant leaned close, his voice a whisper, "This is it, man, the town's singin'." I nodded, my throat tight, the camera rollin', the town wearin' its Sunday best, ready to burn bright on film, one frame, one life at a time.

The next day, it was Sunday morning and I was supposed to meet with Grant. The sun slanted through Benny's Diner, paintin' the Formica counter gold, dust motes dancin' in the light like fireflies caught indoors. The air smelled of fried okra and strong coffee, the jukebox hummin' a soft Merle Haggard tune, its notes curlin' around the clink of cups and Mrs. Clara's laugh from the kitchen. I sat in a corner booth, my notes scattered on the table, the window was reflectin' the neon glow of the "Open" sign. My notebook lay open, pages smudged with sketches of Main Street, barbershops buzzin', the square alive with Saturday night dances, each line drawn from the interviews we'd just wrapped. Miss Lorraine's lost love, Pastor Williams' fight for unity, Eric's war scars, Uncle Don's shop closin', their stories sat heavy in my chest, like river mud smoothed by time but too big to carry alone.

I traced a doodle of Gable's Mercantile, my pencil pausin' as a spark flickered. What if we didn't just *tell* these stories? What if we *showed* 'em, brought Mill Town's past back to life? The thought tightened my throat, Mr. Radcliffe's words echoin', "Remember who you are", and Eric's plea to fight for love, not duty. I was still turnin' it over when the diner door swung open, the bell jinglin' sharp.

Grant barreled in, his Converse scuffin' the linoleum, notepad pokin' outta his pocket, his shaggy hair bouncin' under a cap. "Yo, Bobby, you look like you're planning a funeral, man!" he said, his LA drawl quick and bright, cuttin' through the diner's calm. "We just shot *gold*, Lorraine's story, Eric's laugh. We're cooking!" He slid into the booth, wavin' to Mrs. Clara. "Coke please, ma'am!" His freckles caught the light, and he flipped open his notepad, rattlin' off edits: "Miss Baxter needs a soft fade, like a memory. Eric's war stuff? Hard cut, let it sting."

I nodded, half-listenin', my mind on the past, the diner's warmth a faint echo of Uncle Don's shop, where neighbors swapped stories over fixed radios. "Grant," I said, settin' my pencil down, my voice low, drawl thick with resolve, "what if we don't just talk 'bout the old days? What if we *show* 'em? Recreate 'em." I leaned forward, hands gesturin' like I was framin' a shot. "The '55 Fourth of July parade, Lorraine stitchin' the mayor's pants. Pastor Williams' church meetin's in '61, folks prayin' through desegregation. Me and Eric stealin', uh, 'borrowin', watermelons in '64. We dress up the storefronts, get folks to play their younger selves, shoot it like it's 1960. Make it *alive* again."

Grant's eyes widened, his Coke forgotten, his voice racin'. "Dude, that's *genius*! We're not just making a doc, we're building a time machine! Picture it: Main Street lit up, extras in poodle skirts, a brass band blaring, it's *American Graffiti* meets *The Last Picture Show*!" He scribbled frantic, ideas spillin' like creek water: "Vintage cars, period costumes, a tracking shot of kids in Gable's alley. We use locals, Mr. Abernathy, that skateboard kid, for real faces, real heart." His grin was infectious, his Hollywood savvy mixin' with a fire I hadn't seen before. "You're the director, Bobby, not just a kid with a camera. This is your *Citizen Kane*!"

Grant spotted Ryan at the counter, nursin' a coffee, his camera bag slung over a chair. "Ryan, c'mere for a sec!" Grant called, his voice eager. He ambled over, his calm eyes sharp, a cinematographer's mind already turnin'. Grant recapped the idea, he added: "We're going to stage scenes from the interviews, parades, church meetings, melon heists. Bring Main Street back to 1960."

I jumped in, hands mimickin' a dolly shot: "Dawn light, locals as extras, we'll make it pop!" Ryan sipped his coffee, brow furrowed, then spoke, his voice measured. "Ambitious, Bobby. Period details, costumes, cars, ain't cheap. The Mitchell's heavy, needs steady light. Parades want cranes, and we're tight on budget. But locals sell it. We shoot guerrilla-style, use dawn's natural light, save Arriflex for night. Watermelon heist's easy, kids, a field, handheld. Church scene's tougher, needs a crowd, may need the town's help."

Grant slapped the table. "Now you're talking, man! Mrs. Clara'll rally some extras, Lila's mom for costumes. I know a guy for cheap film stock!"

Ryan nodded, sketchin' a shot list on Grant's notepad, "We'll ask if we can get some of the people in church clothes, use Tatum's Ford for the parade. I think we can do it if we can get the town to help, and I don't even think we'll need to extend the budget." I felt a surge, my hands steady, the diner's warmth like the community we were fightin' for.

Lila passed, her braid swingin'. "Y'all plannin' to raise the dead?" she teased, her drawl playful. I grinned. "Somethin' like that, Lila. Wanna help?" She nodded, eyes sparklin', already in. The jukebox shifted to Johnny Cash, the diner alive with our plans.

Jesus walked in an noticed the commotion. "What's going on fellas?"

Grant told him all about the plan. The gears were already churnin' in Jesus's head. "Stay right here." Jesus said with a smile as he bolted out of the diner.

"Guess he has another miracle up his sleeve?" I said reflecting the rest of our looks, as we all continued to brainstorm ideas writing down set lists and scenes.

What seemed like only minutes had gone by, Jesus comes bargin' back in the door of the diner, "Good, you're still hereI"

I looked at Grant shruggin' my shoulders.

Jesus plopped down what must have been fifty professional lookin flyers on the table "I had stopped by the print store down the road the other day and made a few friends." I smiled.

Grant chimed in, "Tomorrow we'll go out to Mr. Radcliffe's place. He wanted to do his interview at home. Today we ralley the troops!"

We tore through town like kids on a mission, staplin' flyers to every lamppost and oak, their boots kickin' up gravel, flannels damp with sweat. The flyers, printed in color, hollered, "BRING MILL TOWN BACK! Volunteers, old cars, costumes for '55 Fourth of July parade reenactment!"

At Sunday service, after church let loose, I stood in the church pews, my voice echoin' off stained glass, "Folks, we're bringin' back the '55 parade for *Echoes*, we need your cars, your mom's old dresses, your spirit!" Grant, shaggy hair tucked under a cap, chimed in, "And if you got a trumpet, bring it!" The congregation chuckled, heads noddin', hands already riflin' through mental attics for mothballed treasures.

Next mornin', I rode with Grant and some of the crew out to Mr. Radcliffe's place, a small clapboard house off a gravel road, pines whisperin' secrets on either side. I could see Mr. Radcliffe clear as day, standin' tall at that town hall meetin' back in '65, when Allied General first slithered into our talks. His voice had been steady, cuttin' through the nervous chatter like a blade. "Once you let one in," he'd said, eyes sharp behind his glasses, "the rest'll follow like ants to sugar." Folks had nodded, but nobody listened. Not really. I was lookin' forward to talkin' to em.

The porch creaked under my feet, boards worn smooth by years of steps. Mr. Radcliffe opened the screen door, his handshake firm, his smile weathered like old leather. "I see you've upgraded your camera there Bobby," he said, his voice low but smilin', carryin' the weight of a man who'd seen too many seasons change.

We set up in his livin' room, Grant adjustin' soft lights till they glowed gentle on Mr. Radcliffe's plaid shirt and suspenders. He sat in a high-backed chair, hands folded, his face lined like a map of Mill Town itself. I nodded, and the camera hummed to life.

"Tell me 'bout the old days," I said, leanin' forward, my heart racin' like it always did when the truth was close.

Mr. Radcliffe sat under the Arriflex lights' warm glow, his plaid shirt tucked neat, suspenders taut, hands folded like he was holdin' onto the past. The room was quiet, the air thick with coffee and honeysuckle, the Nagra reels spinnin' to catch his every word, Ryan framin' his weathered face, sharp eyes glintin' with memory. I met his gaze, voice steady but reverent. "Mr. Radcliffe, you've lived in Mill Town all your life, tell us about how things were growin' up here."

He took a deep breath, his chest risin' slow, and his eyes drifted somewhere far off, to a time long gone. Mr. Radcliffe's eyes softened, a boyish glint breakin' through the weathered lines of his face, the Arriflex lights castin' a gentle glow as he leaned forward, hands loose on his suspenders, the Mitchell hummin' soft. "As a kid in Mill Town, 'round the early '30s, I was a scrawny little cuss, runnin' wild with my brothers, barefoot half the summer," he said, his voice warm, a chuckle rumblin' low, the Nagra catchin' its lilt. "We'd race down Main Street, dodgin' wagons, stealin' peaches from Carter's crates when he wasn't lookin', juice dribblin' down our chins. After chores, haulin' water or feedin' chickens, we'd sneak to the Blackwater, fishin' with bent pins and string, laughin' till the sun sank, our moms hollerin' us home for supper, cornbread and beans waitin'. Town was small, everybody's porch an open door, and I thought that's how the whole world worked, neighbors sharin' everything, trouble and all."

"World War II hit Mill Town like a storm in '41, boys leavin' for the fight, families rationin' sugar, prayin' over telegrams, but it knit us tighter, sharin' what little we had, plantin' victory gardens side by side," he said, the Nagra tapin' the faint tremor in his tone. "I was

390

sixteen when it ended, too young to enlist, but old enough to know I wanted more'n farmin' or mill work. Got a scholarship to Harvard, '47, economics, big shot dreams, I thought. Felt like I was betrayin' my family, leavin' Mom's biscuits for Boston's cold halls, but I went, heart racin', scared stiff. Comin' home in '51, degree in hand, I wasn't the same. Harvard taught me numbers, sure, but more'n that, it showed me what the pursuit of money can do to your soul, suits in boardrooms, wieldin' money like a blade, carvin' up towns like ours for profit. I'd had offers, investment banks, firms, fat paychecks, but I'd learned everything I needed, and I knew what mattered: people, honesty, the kind of work that builds a place, not the kind that tears it down for a buck. So I turned 'em down, came back to Mill Town, took a teacher's job at the high school, measly pay but real work, teachin' kids to think, to hold fast to what's true, 'cause that's the only way to really keep a person's soul alive."

"Back in the fifties, sixties, this town was alive, Bobby," he said, his voice rich, weathered, like oak polished by years, the Nagra tapin' its warmth. "When I got back, Main Street was a heartbeat, family stores on every corner, barbers snippin' away, razors flashin' under them red-and-white poles; tailors like Miss Lorraine, her needle dancin' through silk for pageant dresses; old man Carter's grocery, apples stacked high, red and glossy like jewels, smellin' so sweet you'd sneak a bite if he wasn't lookin'." His lips curved, a faint smile crackin' his stern face, the camera catchin' the crinkle 'round his eyes, the light glintin' off his silver stubble.

He leaned back, hands unfoldin', gesturin' slow, like he was paintin' the town for us, the Mitchell holdin' his every move. "Saturday nights, the square'd be bustlin', a regular hoedown," he said, his voice liftin', alive with the memory. "Folks spillin' outta their houses, cleaned up after a week's work, men in pressed shirts, women in skirts swirlin' like flowers, kids dartin' through the crowd, chasin' fireflies. The café'd fling its doors wide, music pourin' out, fiddles wailin', guitars strummin', maybe a banjo pluckin' fast, makin' your feet itch to dance.

391

Couples'd sway under the string lights, laughin', while old folks sat on benches, swappin' stories, passin' a jug of sweet tea. You could smell the fryin' catfish from Mrs. Clara's, hear the clink of glasses, the roar of a joke landin' just right." His chuckle was low, warm, the camera zoomin' slow to his hands, scarred from years of labor, now restin' easy, the Nagra capturin' the joy in his voice.

His smile softened, eyes still far away, the light castin' shadows in the deep lines of his face. "We didn't have much, Bobby, no fancy cars, no big bank accounts," he said, his voice quieter, earnest. "Most folks scraped by, farmin' or workin' the mills, hands callused, backs bent. But we had each other, and that was the real wealth. Neighbors weren't just names, you knew their kids, their troubles, their dreams. If a barn burned, the whole town showed up with hammers and lumber. If a family went hungry, Mrs. Clara slip 'em a pie, no questions. Just bout' every dollar we spent stayed right here, in Carter's, Gable's, Don's shop, your daddys, that money was circulatin' like blood, keepin' us strong." He tapped a finger on his knee, the camera catchin' the rhythm, the Nagra holdin' the resolve in his tone. "Made us tough as hickory, resilient, 'cause we leaned on our own, built our own, loved our own. That's what this town was, poor in pocket, rich in soul."

His voice darkened, like a storm rollin' in, eyes narrowin' under the Arriflex glow. "Then them franchise leeches showed up. One day, some slick-talkin' suit's out there, glad-handin' folks, grinnin' like a fox in a henhouse. Next thing, the pecan grove's bulldozed flat, Allied General's big box risin' up. Jobs, they promised, hah! What they delivered was a gut-punch. Sure, prices fell, but wages tanked worse. Shops, Gable's, Elma's, Don's, your daddy's, dropped like flies, dominoes in a row. You could damn near hear the cash drainin' outta Mill Town, near only a trickle comin' back, if that. It's simple arithmetic: take more'n you give, and the well runs dry eventually. Now, they'll pack up soon, leave us with what? Empty shells and broken spirits?" His hands clenched, knuckles white, the Mitchell catchin' the fire in his scowl. "Ain't just our money they stole, it's our soul. All so some Atlanta fat cats can buy another Cadillac. Progress? They can shove it. Back then, one store closed, ten others held strong, givin' us a buffer, a spread of roots when the storm comes callin. Now? We're hangin' on two big stores 'stead of thirty small ones. We're naked out here, Bobby, and we invited the wolves in with a parade, thinkin' they'd save us. Now folks got no choice but to prop 'em up, prayin' they don't leave."

Grant shifted behind me, scribblin' in his notebook, his pen loud in the quiet. "Heavy stuff, man," he whispered, his LA drawl sharp against the room's stillness. "This is gonna hit hard."

Mr. Radcliffe leaned forward, his eyes sharp despite the years. "Then that interstate came, just far enough to keep folks speedin' by. Truck traffic quit comin'. Tourists vanished. Main Street dried up like a creek in August. It wasn't just one big thing that killed us, Bobby. It was a few of 'em, each a little cut. And everybody outside of Mill Town kept callin' it progress."

I swallowed, my throat tight. "What do you hope folks take from this film, Mr. Radcliffe?"

He thought for a long moment, his gaze steady, like he was lookin' through me to the town we'd lost. "Remember who you are," he said, each word deliberate. "Don't sell your soul for convenience." He paused. "'cause once the lights go out on Main Street, it's damn hard to get 'em back on."

The room went still, the camera's hum the only sound. "Cut.."

Grant let out a low whistle, mutterin', "That's a wrap, man. Pure gold." But I just sat there, Mr. Radcliffe's words settlin' into me like stones in a riverbed. I saw Main Street in my mind, its laughter, its lights, its slow fade, and knew I'd carry this moment forever, long after the screen faded to black.

Chapter 46 – Dad's Interview
(November 1972)

The sun dipped low, paintin' the sky over the town a fiery orange as the crew hustled in the church basement, settin' up for the day's final interview, the air thick with the scent of wax polish and cooling coffee. Arriflex lights hummed, their beams soft through silk scrims, while Ryan tweaked the Mitchell 35mm on its tripod, lens gleamin', and the sound guy tested the Sennheiser mic, Nagra reels spinnin' quiet. I stepped outside, heart poundin', and took a long walk around the block, boots crunchin' on gravel, the Blackwater River's murmur mixin' with crickets, Mom's fight and Dad's quiet strength pullin' me back to face this one, personal, raw, necessary.

I returned to the basement, the glow welcomin' but heavy, Grant leanin' against a crate, his shaggy hair fallin' over worried eyes. "Want me to direct, Bobby?" he asked, voice low, sensin' the weight. I shook my head, my throat tight, hands flexin'. "This one's mine," I said, voice firm, slippin' behind the monitor, my flannel damp, ready to frame Dad's truth for *Echoes*. Dad eased into the padded chair, slow, deliberate, still in his work clothes, faded jeans huggin' his lean frame, boots scuffed from years at the hardware store, a button-down shirt with "Tom" stitched in red over the chest, sleeves rolled to his elbows, hands restin' heavy on his knees.

He glanced at the camera, its red light blinkin', then at me, his eyes, blue like mine, but weathered, searchin', a half-smile tuggin' his lips, creasin' the lines of a face that'd seen droughts and floods. "You sure about this, son?" he asked, voice low, gravelly, a mix of doubt and trust, the lamp's light catchin' the gray in his hair.

I nodded, grippin' the monitor, my heart racin'. "Yeah, Dad," I said, voice soft but sure, the Mitchell ready, Nagra hummin'. "I think I need it."

The basement stilled, the crew silent, the moment hangin' like dusk, Dad's story waitin' to unfold, ready to carve deep into *Echoes*, one word, one look at a time.

Dad leaned back, a faint smile creasin' his weathered face, the lamp's light glintin' off his grayin' hair. "Workin' in the hardware store with my daddy, your granddad, Bobby, was where I grew up," he said, voice warm, like he was walkin' those aisles again. "Back in the '30s, I was just a kid, luggin' sacks of nails, sweepin' sawdust, smellin' linseed oil and metal. He taught me the trade, how to cut a key, mend a shovel, size a bolt right. But more'n that, he drilled in honesty, the kind that don't bend. Business was handshakes then, Bobby, no contracts, just your word. You looked a man in the eye, and that was your bond." His hands gestured, slow and sure, the camera catchin' their callused strength, the Nagra tapin' his pride.

His eyes twinkled, meetin' mine past the lens, the Mitchell holdin' his warmth. "You knew every customer by name, son. Sometimes you knew what they needed 'fore they did, old man Tatum wantin' nails for his porch, Miss Etta needin' paint for her shed. Wasn't just sellin'; it was carin', knowin' their lives, their homes." His smile widened, voice droppin' to a chuckle, the light catchin' a spark in his gaze. "Take the summer of '60, hotter'n a skillet, air so thick you could chew it. We were puttin' up a new fence 'round the house, me, your granddad, your uncle Don. Neighbors showed up, hammers swingin', Gable, Carter, even Mrs. Clara with lemonade. We'd been restin' on an old bathtub under the big oak for days, usin' it as a bench. After lunch, your brother Matt, 'bout ten and full of vinegar, flips it over, bold as brass. Underneath's the biggest damn water moccasin I ever saw, coiled tight, hissin' like Satan himself, not thirty seconds after we'd been sittin' there! We scattered, hollerin', laughin' once the snake slithered off, neighbors clappin' Matt like he'd won a prize."

Dad's chuckle deepened, his hands slappin' his knee, the camera zoomin' slow to his grin, the Nagra capturin' the rumble of his laugh. "Or that time we went by Abernathy's lookin' for a new horse trailer, 'round '62," he said, eyes glintin' with mischief. "You and Matt, always chasin' trouble. Matt, maybe twelve, spots a buggy at the lot, jumps in like he's drivin' a chariot, not knowin' a hornets' nest the size of a melon's hangin' right by his head. He scrambles out, untouched, laughin' his fool head off. But you, Bobby, you couldn't let him have the glory, could you? You hopped in right after, all of eight, swingin' your arms like a king. Them hornets weren't keen on another rider, they lit into you, stings all over your arms and neck. You ran screamin', flailin' like a windmill, and I had to douse you with mud to calm the welts. Bet you still feel that one, don't ya?" He winked, the camera catchin' the crinkle 'round his eyes, the light warm on his face.

Dad's laughter faded, "We had lots of good times, but there were tough times too. The tornado that came through back in 58 took a lot of people's lives with it. We all thought it was just another summer squall, but we were wrong. That twister ripped through town like a buzzsaw. Lots of people lost their homes and everythin' they had, some their lives. The community was in shock, it was the Reverand that brought us all back together. His church was in the middle of that tornados path and it was completely untouched. Folks that lost everythin were welcomed in. We all brought food and clothin'. Government wouldn't do nothin for them since no government buildings were damaged. Folks back then didn't carry insurance. We all pitched in and rebuilt all those homes ourselves. One couple was even sleepin in the jail cause there was no more room at the church. We took them in for about six months, remember, Jamal and his family? I'll never forget their face when we pulled back into their driveway when their home was finished."

Dad's expression turned hollow, his hands stillin' on his knees, the Arriflex lights' soft glow castin' shadows across his weathered face, the Mitchell 35mm hummin' quiet, Ryan holdin' the frame on his eyes, now distant, heavy with memory. The church basement was silent, the Sennheiser mic catchin' the shift in his breath, Nagra reels spinnin' to tape the weight of his words. I stood behind the monitor, headset off.

He leaned forward, elbows on his thighs, voice low, like he was confessin' to the lens. "Times marched on and downtown started fadin' slow, sneaky, like a leak you don't notice till the floor's rotted," he said, eyes flickin' to the floor, the lamp's light glintin' off his gray hair. "The year that superstore, Allied General, rolled in, '63, it changed everythin'. Didn't matter if you weren't sellin' the same stuff; foot traffic dried up. Folks used to stroll Main Street, poppin' into shops, chattin', spendin' a dollar here, a dollar there. AG's out by the highway sucked 'em away, like a magnet pullin' iron filings. First, the bookstore went dark, Miss Ellie's place, where kids read comics in the back. Then the feed store, old man Carter's, shelves empty. By '70, even the barber shop, with its candy-stripe pole, closed up, chairs gatherin' dust." His jaw tightened, the camera catchin' the clench, the Nagra tapin' a bitter edge.

His hands rubbed together, calluses scrapin', the Mitchell framin' their slow dance, the light castin' shadows on his knuckles. "Used to be, a man could raise a family here, Bobby," he said, voice rough, eyes liftin' to meet mine past the lens. "Work hard, pay his way, put food on the table, maybe save for a new fence or a kid's schoolin'. Now? He's lucky if he can keep the lights on without takin a loan, prayin' the bank don't call him on it." He paused, eyes focusin' somewhere far away, past the basement's walls, maybe seein' Main Street's old bustle, the Nagra holdin' the silence, heavy as a held breath.

Dad's shoulders slumped, his voice softer, raw, the camera zoomin' slow to his face, etched with years of fight. "I kept the store's doors open long after it made sense," he said, a faint tremor in his tone. "Lost money hand over fist, but I wasn't ready to let go, not of what your granddad built, what we all built, me, you, Matt, Don. It was more'n a shop; it was us, our name, our home." His eyes glistened, the light catchin' a wet glint, his hands clenchin' tight. "When your granddad passed, '65, I promised him I'd keep the lights on, keep his store alive. I think he's lookin' down from heaven, sad to see it gone, but proud we fought, proud we held on till the end." His voice broke, the camera holdin' his gaze, steady and true, the Nagra capturin' his grief, his pride, a father's vow woven into *Echoes*, ready to burn for Mill Town, one promise, one light at a time.

I leaned forward, voice low, careful, knowin' this question would cut deep. "Dad, tell me 'bout the hard years, when things got tough at home," I said, mom's fight loomin' between us.

Dad shifted in the chair, his faded jeans creakin', boots scrapin' the concrete, his face tightenin', uncomfortable, like I'd asked him to open a locked door. He exhaled, slow, his eyes droppin' to his hands, then liftin' to meet mine past the lens, the lamp's light catchin' the gray in his hair. "I didn't know how to fix it, Bobby," he said, voice rough, crackin' like dry wood. "Not the store, bleedin' money as Allied General took our customers. Not your mom gettin' sick, her cancer eatin' at her, at us, while I worked late, tryin' to keep the lights on. Not you and Matt growin' up, pullin' away, Matt to college, you chasin' dreams in LA. I was losin' everythin', and all I knew was I couldn't use a hammer and nails to hold it together this time." His hands clenched, knuckles pale, the camera catchin' their tremor, the Nagra tapin' the ache in his words.

He leaned back, eyes glazin', starin' past the basement's walls, voice softer, almost a whisper. "How can you stop time? Progress?" he said, the words hangin' heavy, like dust in the air. "You just enjoy what you got when you got it, I guess, your mom's laugh, you boys wrestlin' in the yard, the store's bell jinglin' welcoming neighbors in and sayin' goodbye when they leave. But when it's slippin', it's like holdin' water in your hands, gone 'fore you know it." The camera held his face, etched with loss, the light castin' shadows in the lines carved by years, his truth raw, a father's quiet grief.

A long silence stretched, the basement still, the Nagra's faint hum the only sound, Dad's eyes lost somewhere in the past, maybe Mom's smile, maybe Matt's laugh, maybe the store's last day. I didn't interrupt, my throat too tight, hands grippin' the monitor, feelin' his pain. The silence held us, a shared ache, his words a wound that'd shaped us weather we liked it or not.

Dad cleared his throat, a rough, deliberate sound, his hands unclenchin', restin' loose on his knees, the lamp's light catchin' the gray in his hair. "But I watched you, Bobby," he said, voice low, warm, like a fire kindlin'. "Always watchin', always filmin', even as a kid, that little 8mm camera glued to your hand, catchin' everythin', Matt's grin as he figured out one of his physics problems, or Mom's smile as she plucked tomatoes from the garden, Main Street's bustle. I didn't understand it then, didn't get why you'd rather point a camera than swing a hammer. I used to get so frustrated, but I understand now." His eyes lifted, lockin' onto mine past the lens, blue and steady, the camera framin' their depth, the Nagra tapin' the quiet strength in his tone.

His gaze unbreakin', "You saw the town clearer than any of us did," he said, voice firm, proud. "You knew we were disappearin' before we did, somethin' in you told you to grab onto it while you could, shops closin', folks driftin' 'fore we could admit it to ourselves. You saw the heart of this community, what we were losin', and you held it in your films, every frame a fight to keep us alive. We made it through fires and floods with hammers and nails, but all the hammers and nails in the world ain't gonna put us back together this time." His lips curved, a small, rare smile, the light catchin' a glint in his eyes. "I'm proud of you, son. Not for leavin' to chase your dreams, not even for comin' back to make this. I'm proud 'cause you never stopped seein', never stopped carin'." His words hit like a wave, the camera catchin' the tremble in his jaw, and off-camera, a sniffle slipped from me, my eyes burnin'.

The camera kept rollin', the red light steady, even as I lowered my head, overcome, hands grippin' the monitor, tears stingin', Mom's fight, Eric's scars, Dad's love crashin' through me, all fightin to keep what they had. Dad leaned forward, his hand reachin' out, restin' firm on my knee, calluses rough through my jeans, groundin' me, the Mitchell capturin' the quiet strength in his touch. "You don't have to carry it all, Bobby," he said, voice soft, sure, like a promise. "Just carry what matters, the love." I nodded, throat too tight for more than a whisper, "I will," my voice barely audible, the Nagra tapin' its tremble, the basement still.

Grant motioned to Ryan to stop the recording…

Chapter 47 - Crazy Horse Saloon
(November 1972)

It was a cool November evenin' in '72, the kind where the air carries a bite but the stars burn bright enough to make you forget the chill. The Crazy Horse Saloon glowed like a lantern on Main Street, its neon sign flickerin' like it was decidin' whether to give up or keep fightin'. Inside, the jukebox hummed a low Hank Williams tune, and the smell of fried onions and spilled beer clung to the wood walls. We'd just wrapped a long day of interviews, Miss Eleanor's tremblin' hands, Mr. Leonard's tears, Lila's voice crackin' as she talked about the creek, and my head was spinnin' with stories, each one a weight I wasn't sure I could carry.

I was slouched in a corner booth, my notebook on the table like an old dog too tired to move. Lila sat across from me, her auburn braid frayed from a day of haulin' light stands, her hazel eyes dancin' with that mix of tired and stubborn that only she could pull off. Eric was next to her, his cap tipped back, nursin' a beer and starin' at the dartboard like it owed him money. Grant was sprawled beside me, his Converse tappin' the floor, a notebook scribbled with shot lists pokin' out of his backpack.

"Man, Bobby, you gotta chill," Grant said, his voice quick and sharp, like he was pitchin' a script on Sunset Strip. "You're, like, carryin' this whole town in your head, dude. I dig the passion, but you're gonna burn out before we cut the trailer."

I squinted at him, wipin' a smudge off my camera lens with my sleeve. "Ain't about burnin' out, Grant. These folks' stories, they're heavy."

Lila leaned forward, restin' her chin on her hand, a half-smile tuggin' at her lips. "Bobby's right, city boy. You can't just film this place and walk away. It sticks to you, like red clay after a rain. You'll see."

Grant grinned, unfazed, his freckles catchin' the bar light. "I'm not walkin' away, alright? I'm in, Lila. This is more real than any soundstage I've ever seen. But, you gotta pace it, you know? We got gold on that tape already. It's gonna hit like a Scorsese flick, but only if Bobby doesn't keel over first."

Eric snorted, settin' his beer down with a thud. "Scorsese, huh? You talk fancy for a fella who don't know a cottonmouth from a garden snake. Bobby's filmin' *us*, not some Hollywood picture. This ain't about hittin' big. It's about not lettin' this town and every other small town get sold out and thrown away."

"Fair, fair," Grant said, raisin' his hands like he was surrenderin'. "But dig this, man, Bobby's got a vision, right? That camera's his sword, and we're, like, the knights or whatever. We're fightin' for it, but we gotta make it *pop* for the world to care. That's my job, makin' sure the suits in LA don't bury this in some vault."

Lila laughed, a bright, sharp sound that cut through the saloon's hum. "Knights? M'Lord, Grant, you been readin' too many comic books. But you ain't wrong. Bobby's fightin' for somethin'. Always has." She nudged my foot under the table, her eyes soft but darin' me to argue. "Ain't that right, Bobby Chandler?"

I felt my cheeks heat up, the weight of their eyes on me. "Ain't tryin' to save nothin'," I mumbled, fiddlin' with the binding on the notebook. "Just... tryin' to show what's true. What we're losin' and why, then let folks make up their own mind, but I gotta make em feel it. If I can get that on film, maybe folks'll see it ain't just here. It's everywhere."

Eric leaned back, his grin slow and easy, like a cat stretchin' in the sun. "That's my boy. Always thinkin' deep. Like when we stole them

402

watermelons? Like we was Bonnie and Clyde. Even then, you was tellin' stories."

"Borrowed, not stole," Lila corrected, flickin' a peanut shell at him. "And I'm sure ya got caught 'cause you couldn't stop laughin'"

Grant's eyes lit up, leanin' forward like a kid hearin' a ghost story. "No way, man! You got that on tape? That's, like, pure b-roll gold! We could cut it in, show the town when it was alive, you know?"

I chuckled, shakin' my head. "Maybe. But that if I do it's buried in my room, under a pile of old reels and Matt's huntin' magazines. Ain't sure it's worth diggin' up."

"Worth it," Grant shot back, tappin' his notebook. "Every frame's a piece of this place, Bobby. You're buildin' a time machine, man. That's what this film is."

Lila reached across the table, her fingers brushin' mine, light as a breeze. "He's right, you know. You're keepin' us alive, I mean figuratively, Bobby. Not just the sad stuff, the good, too. Like them watermelons. Like today, sittin' here, laughin'." Her voice was soft, but it hit like a stone dropped in still water, ripplin' through.

Eric raised his beer, the glass catchin' the neon glow. "To Mill Town," he said, his voice low but steady. "To the Knights of Crazy Horse, we ain't done fightin'."

We clinked glasses, beer, sweet tea, and Grant's soda fizzin' like a sparkler. The jukebox switched to Johnny Cash, and for a moment, the saloon felt like the heart of somethin' still beatin'. I looked at my friends, Lila's quiet fire, Eric's stubborn grin, Grant's restless energy, and knew I'd film this, too, if I could. Not with the camera, but with my heart, where the light don't ever go out.

Chapter 48 – Mayor's Interview
(November 1972)

Dust motes danced in the slantin' light filterin' through cracked blinds in the mayor's old office, a forgotten corner of Mill Town's town hall, papers yellowed and curlin' on shelves, chairs draped in dusty cloths like ghosts of meetin's past. A faded town seal hung behind the desk, its eagle's wings chipped but proud, the only sign this room once held power. Ryan adjusted the Mitchell 35mm on its tripod, he was tweakin' the focus, while Grant rigged the Sennheiser mic, Nagra reels hummin' soft, the Arriflex lights castin' a warm glow over the clutter.

Mayor Heartwell, late seventies, still plump, shuffled in, his crisp white shirt tucked neat, a bolo tie gleamin' silver, his eyes tired, carryin' decades of fights won and lost. "Haven't sat behind this desk in a long time," he muttered, easin' into the creakin' chair, voice low, rough, as I framed him tight, my flannel damp, heart steady, ready to catch his story for *Echoes*.

Heartwell folded his hands, the lamp's light catchin' the creases in his knuckles, his gaze driftin' to the seal, a spark of pride flarin' in his eyes. "Mill Town's better days, Bobby, they were somethin'," he said, voice warm, thick with memory, the Nagra tapin' its cadence. "Fifties, early sixties, Main Street glowed, festivals every spring, floats decked in crepe paper, kids racin' with ribbons, the square packed with folks grillin' ribs, laughin'. School competitions, spellin' bees, science fairs, parents cheerin' like it was the World Series. Community events knit us tight: barn dances, church picnics, Fourth of July fireworks sparkin' over the Blackwater. We weren't perfect, son, had our squabbles, our divides, but we were united, one heartbeat, every soul pitchin' in, believin' in this place." His smile was soft, the camera catchin' the crinkle 'round his eyes, the light glintin' off his tie.

His hands shifted, fingers tappin' the desk, voice takin' a harder edge, the Mitchell holdin' his shift, the Nagra capturin' a wry chuckle. "Bein' mayor? Half facilitator, half firefighter, Bobby," he said, leanin' forward, eyes sharp despite his years. "You're runnin' meetings, cuttin' ribbons, but mostly you're fixin' messes, leaky pipes, feudin' neighbors, budgets that don't add up. Half the time, you're wrestlin' problems broke ten years 'fore you took the chair, left by some fool who kicked the can down the road. You do your damnedest, but it's like patchin' a boat with holes older'n you are." His lips pursed, the camera zoomin' slow to his face, etched with the grind of leadership, his truth a cornerstone for *Echoes*, Mill Town's glory and grit alive in his words.

"Mayor Heartwell, what happened when Allied General came to town?" I asked, voice low, careful, the basement's hush amplifyin' the moment.

Heartwell paused, his hands freezin' on the desk, eyes droppin' to a faded ink blotter, the lamp's light catchin' a tremor in his jowls. "I remember the first proposal, Bobby," he said, voice slow, bitter, like chewin' gravel. "I remember it well, Spring of '61, they sent their angel in to do the devils work, all flashy numbers and big, friendly smiles, promisin' the moon on a platter, jobs, growth, tax revenue to fix our potholes and schools. They had charts, glossy binders, handshakes that felt like traps." He shook his head, the camera catchin' the sag in his shoulders, the Nagra tapin' a heavy sigh. "Town was hurtin' and seemed like it was fallin' behind all the other towns round us, folks leavin' for work elsewhere. Me and the council, we were desperate, seein' families pack up, our tax base shrinkin'. We took the deal, Bobby. Didn't ask enough questions, didn't push back on their fine print. Thought we were savin' Mill Town, but we opened the gate to a wolf."

Heartwell's hands trembled on the desk, his voice low, almost a whisper, the lamp's light casting shadows in his wrinkles. "We thought we were savin' the town, Bobby," he said, eyes dropping to his clasped

405

fingers, the Nagra taping the crack in his tone. "Me, the council, we shook hands with Allied General, believin' their shiny promises, jobs, revenue, a future. Might just as well've signed Mill Town's death warrant instead." He swallowed, jaw tight, the camera catching the quiver in his lip. "I see it every day now, empty storefronts, boards where windows used to shine, young folks leavin' for cities, resentment simmerin' in the ones who stay. People want someone to blame, and sometimes, I think they're right to blame me." His voice broke, eyes glistening, the light glinting off a tear he didn't wipe, his guilt laid bare.

His fingers tapped the desk, restless, the Mitchell holdin' their rhythm, his voice growin' sharper, edged with regret. "Then the interstate reroute hit, '69, like a kick when we were down," he said, eyes narrowin', glintin' fierce in the light. "That interstate didn't just take traffic, it took hope, made us invisible overnight. Used to be, trucks and tourists rolled through Main Street, stoppin' at Clara's diner, Gable's store. They'd walk the riverwalk and picnic in the park. The new route swung wide, leavin' us a ghost town off the map. I fought it, Bobby, wrote letters to the state, held forums, begged for a damn exit ramp. Packed the hall with folks, all shoutin' we'd be erased. But no one listened to a town our size, not when big cities called the shots." His hands clenched, knuckles pale, the camera zoomin' slow to his face, etched with frustration, the Nagra capturin' a crack in his voice.

I leaned forward, throat tight, and asked softly, "What do you think of this documentary, Mayor?"

Heartwell's gaze lifted, a faint smile tugging his lips, weary but warm, the camera holding his fragile hope, the Nagra capturing his shift. "It's the first time we're facin' the truth out loud," he said, voice steadying. "Not hidin' behind excuses or old pride, just sayin' it, how we lost, how we hurt. Maybe that's how healin' starts, Bobby, not with fixin' what's broke, but with seein' it clear, understandin' it." His words landed like a quiet vow.

I called "cut," my voice thick, but Heartwell stayed seated, a beat longer, the camera still rolling, its red light steady.

He looked at me, eyes piercing, voice firm yet soft, the Mitchell catching his final charge. "Tell the story straight, son. Guess history will decide who's the hero and who's the villain, we were just doin what we thought was best for everyone." The room stilled, the Nagra taping the hush, his words a mandate, heavy with trust.

Chapter 49 - Evelyn's Interview
(November 1972)

The diner's chrome stools glinted under fluorescent lights, the air thick with grease and coffee as I slid into a booth, my notebook open. Grant plopped down across from me, his shaggy hair half-hidden under a cap, his eyes uneasy but sharp. "We got another interview this afternoon, Bobby," he said, voice low, almost a warning. "Mrs. Evelyn Carr." My pen froze. "Evelyn?", the woman tied to Allied General's chokehold on Mill Town, a name whispered like a curse at town halls. I met his gaze, heart racin'. "She's willin' to talk?" Grant nodded, lips tight. "Yeah. It isn't every day the devil asks to come to dinner." His words hung, heavy, as we headed back to the church basement.

The basement buzzed, Arriflex lights castin' a soft glow, the Mitchell 35mm hummin' on its tripod, Ryan tweakin' the focus, the Sennheiser mic rigged, Nagra reels ready. Grant stood off to the side at his usual spot at the wall, arms crossed, his face a mix of dread and pride, knowin' Evelyn was steppin' into a spotlight that'd burn. Evelyn entered, calm as a still pond, her gray blazer sharp but modest, skirt simple, her dark hair pulled back, no flash, no pretense, a woman who didn't need to prove herself. She paused by the chair, eyes flickin' to the camera, then to me, a wry smile tuggin' her lips.

"You sure you want me in this, Bobby?" she said, voice smooth, self-aware. "I was the villain in this story."

I nodded, throat tight, settlin' behind the monitor, my flannel damp. "Truth needs all sides, Evelyn," I said, voice steady. She sat, the lamp's light catchin' her clear, guarded eyes, ready to unravel her part in AG's shadow.

"I appreciate the opportunity to share my side then." She said smiling, but for some reason, I believed her.

Evelyn folded her hands, the camera framin' her poised frame, the Nagra catchin' the quiet power in her voice as she dove in with raw candor. "I joined Allied General in '55, straight outta college, all fire and ambition," she said, eyes steady, a faint pride edgin' her tone. "Rose fast, zoning, permits, site acquisition. I was good, Bobby, damn good. Could sweet-talk a council, slice through red tape, lock down a plot before anyone blinked. I made things move, kept AG's gears turnin' smooth." Her lips twitched, a shadow of regret creepin' in, the Mitchell holdin' her subtle shift, the Nagra tapin' her measured cadence.

She leaned forward, voice crisp, the camera zoomin' slow to her eyes, burnin' with memory. "AG's world was a race, fast, brutal, all metrics, no mercy," she said, an edge cuttin' through. "Meetings were a blur of quotas, spreadsheets, expansion maps. They called it revitalization, sold it as progress, modernizing, thought I was helpin' towns like Mill Town evolve, draggin' 'em into a shiny new era with jobs and big stores." Her hands tightened, the light castin' shadows on her jaw.

Evelyn paused, her hands clenching briefly, voice tightening, the lamp's light catching a flicker of shame in her eyes. "What AG never told folks," she said, words sharp, deliberate, "was the bonuses we got for every green light, zoning approvals pushed through, permits expedited, even community resistance squashed flat." The camera held her tense jaw, the Nagra taping the edge in her tone. "I once got a five-figure payout, Bobby, just for closin' a deal under budget, Mill Town's deal, I got twelve thousand, which was big money then. Every boarded-up mom-and-pop shop, every shuttered diner, meant we hit our efficiency targets, another notch on our belts, another check in our pockets." Her voice wavered, the Mitchell zooming slow to her hands, fingers twisting, the light casting shadows on her knuckles, her admission a gut-punch to Mill Town's story.

She exhaled, eyes dropping, then lifting to meet the lens, voice softer, raw, the camera framing her regret. "Years after, I went back to my hometown, a little place like Mill Town, thinkin' I'd quit the rat race and go back home," she said, the Nagra catching a tremor. "The fashion district, where I'd tried on prom dresses, was gone, empty stores, broken glass. The hardware store, where Dad bought nails? A pawn shop now, neon buzzin' over cracked pavement. I saw the same scars, hollowed cores, young folks leavin', childhood places erased, like my old soda fountain, just a memory." Her lips pressed tight, the light glinting off a tear she blinked away, the Mitchell holding her grief, raw and unshielded.

Evelyn leaned forward, voice breaking, the camera zooming to her eyes, burning with realization. "It hit me, Bobby, This was me, I'd helped do this," she said, words heavy, cutting. "Not to strangers, but to people like my neighbors, my family's friends, my own community. I'd pushed deals that turned towns into shells, thinkin' it was progress, cashin' bonuses while Main Streets died." Her hands unclenched, trembling, the light casting stark shadows on her face, her confession a mirror to Radcliffe's warnings.

Evelyn's hands tightened in her lap, her voice low, strained, the lamp's light casting shadows on her clenched jaw. "When I got back, I brought it up at a board meetin', '69," she said, eyes flicking to the floor, then hardening as they met the lens, the Nagra taping the steel in her tone. "I'd seen too many towns like Mill Town, like my own, gutted, left hollow. So I asked, point-blank, 'Are we trackin' the long-term health of these communities? We're bleeding them dry, shouldn't we stop or fund rejuvenation projects?'" Her words cut sharp, the camera holding her fierce gaze, the light glinting off her silver earrings, a spark of defiance in the quiet basement.

She paused, a bitter smile twisting her lips, the Mitchell zooming slow to her face, etched with betrayal. "Silence hit that room like a frost," she said, voice dropping, icy. "Then came the polite smiles, the kind that don't reach the eyes, heads nodding like I'd said something quaint.

Next day, I was out, replaced, my office cleared before lunch." Her hands unclenched, fingers trembling, the camera catching their shake, the Nagra taping a faint crack in her composure. "Officially, they called it 'strategy misalignment,' some corporate nonsense to save face. Off the record? I had grown a conscience and was a liability because I wasn't loyal enough, wasn't willing to keep my mouth shut and cash the checks while towns died." Her voice broke, eyes glistening, the light casting a stark glow on her cheekbones, her truth a wound laid bare.

Evelyn leaned back, exhaling, her posture softening, the camera framing her slump, the Nagra capturing the weight of her sigh. "That was my breaking point, Bobby," she said, voice quieter, raw. "I'd been part of their machine, pushing deals that shuttered shops, erased histories, all for a bonus. But questioning their game? That was my end at AG." Her eyes met mine past the lens, steady but haunted, echoing Dad's grief, Radcliffe's warnings, Mill Town's loss. Grant shifted, his face unreadable, but I felt the sting of her regret.

The lamp's light glinting off her silver earrings. "After AG cut me loose, I didn't crawl away," she said, eyes fierce, the Nagra taping the steel in her tone. "Now I campaign against corporate zoning corruption, advising local councils coast to coast, helping towns stand up to the likes of AG. I've spoken at more town halls this past year than I ever did pushing their deals, small rooms, angry folks, just like Mill Town's old meetings, but now I'm on their side, arming them with tools to fight." She paused, a faint smile breaking through, the camera catching the spark in her eyes. "Transparency's key, open records, public meetings, independent audits to catch the slick promises. But most of all, it's storytelling. Facts don't move people, Bobby. Stories? They stick, they rally, they save." Her words rang, echoing Dad's pride, Heartwell's truth, the Mitchell holding her conviction, a blueprint for resistance.

I swallowed, throat tight, and asked, "Evelyn, why'd you agree to this interview?" She looked straight into the lens, unflinching, her face raw, the camera framing her clarity, the Nagra catching the weight of her voice. "Redemption," she said, simple, heavy, eyes glistening but steady. "I owe it, to Mill Town, to every town I helped destroy with AG's deals, every shop I watched board up, every family I saw drift away. Redemption, Bobby, for the part I played. I could try to convince myself if it wasn't me it would have been somebody else, and that's probably right, but that's not justification, because it was me." She paused, her smile softening, voice dropping to a near-whisper. "And 'cause this time, someone's finally pointing the camera in the right direction, telling the story straight, showing what we lost and why."

The light on the camera turned dark.

I met Evelyn's gaze, her eyes still raw from her confession, the church basement's soft glow lingerin' on her face as the Mitchell's red light blinked off. "Thank you for doin' this, Mrs. Carr," I said, voice steady but thick. "We can thank Grant over there for gettin' you here, but now that you're here, after hearin' what I did, your part in AG, your fight now, I feel like I need to tell ya, I forgive you." Her lips trembled slightly, a nod her only reply, her hand grippin' mine, firm but brief, before she turned, blazer sharp against the dim hall. As she walked to her car, I caught the glint of tears on her cheeks through the window, her shoulders shakin' as she drove off.

Chapter 50 - Thanksgiving
(November 1972)

The Chandler house buzzed with purpose, the air crisp with November chill and the promise of a shared tradition that hadn't dissolved yet. This town's heart was beating strong after weeks of filming *Echoes*. Mom and Dad, were moved by the LA crew's kindness, Ryan' steady hands, and Grant's quiet loyalty. They knew they were all far from home away from their families for the sake of ours, so they decided to host a Thanksgiving dinner despite the lack of means or health. It was their way to thank em, and to weave them into the town's family. Mom stood in the kitchen, apron tied, her eyes warm as she chopped onions, saying simply, "No one should spend Thanksgiving without family." Dad nodded, his callused hands prepping a turkey with quiet focus, sage and butter scenting the air. Mom enlisted me and Lila, handing me a broom and Lila a stack of plates, her voice firm but fond, "Let's make sure our guests feel welcomed." I swept the porch, Lila arrangin' mismatched chairs, my flannel loose, Eric's cap and her note in my pocket, heart full of Mom's fight, Dad's pride.

The guest list grew fast, crew members, neighbors, old friends like Jason and Miss Lorraine, until mom, surveyin' the crowded dining room, laughed, "We might need a second table." Jesus, wiping his brow after hauling a cooler, grinned wide, his voice bright, "I don't think we're going to fit thirty people in here, Mrs. Chandler. I'll take care of it" he said with a wink. He took charge, organizin' a setup under the ancient oak in the yard, its gnarled branches spread like open arms. He strung twinkle lights through the leaves, their glow dancin' as dusk crept in, bringin' in folding chairs from the church, and borrowed long tables from the school cafeteria, their surfaces scuffed but sturdy. Lila and I helped drape them with checkered cloths, the yard transformin' into a communal hall, the crickets and frogs would provide the soft backdrop, *Echoes'* spirit alive in every knot tied, every chair placed.

Word spread through Mill Town like wildfire, pullin' folks to the Chandler yard with gifts and goodwill. Miss Elma arrived, her arms full of pecan and pumpkin pies, steam risin' from golden crusts, a stack of worn hymnals tucked under one elbow for a sing-along, her smile bright as she said, "Can't have Thanksivin' without a song." Uncle Don rolled up, pushin' a cart of hot apple cider, the sweet-tart scent waftin' from his back burner, his gruff voice mutterin', "Kept it warm for y'all." The local pastor, Pastor Williams, hauled in more folding chairs, a portable speaker hummin' soft gospel tunes, his nod quiet but warm. Gable shuffled in last, clutchin' jars of pickled okra, their green spears glintin' in the light, and a dusty record player, its needle ready for scratchy Hank Williams tracks. The oak's glow grew, tables laden, chairs filled, the town gatherin', crew, neighbors, friends, each contribution another frame immortalized in *Echoes'*, ready to feast, sing, and remember, one pie, one song at a time.

The yard pulsed with warmth under the ancient oak tree's gnarled branches aglow with lanterns and red ribbons, their soft light flickering like a memory of the communities brighter days. Neighbors poured in, their boots crunching on gravel and crisp leaves, hands clutching casseroles, creamy green bean, candied yam, cornbread dressing, steam curling into the chilly air. Kids in bundled coats chased each other, giggling, sprawling across patchwork quilts spread on the grass, while adults swapped tales of old harvests and lost summers, the air rich with sage, brown sugar, and woodsmoke from a crackling firepit. I stood near a checkered table, flannel loose, heart swelling as I watched Mom, move through the crowd, her face pale from cancer's grip but lit with joy, her apron dusted with flour, savoring this gathering, a sign not all was lost. Matt, home from college, lugged a cooler, his grin wide, was teasing Lila about her cornbread's crust.

The LA crew, usually sharp-edged, softened under the oak's spell. Ava, owner of Sun Studios, Grant's mom, and the film's sponsor, flew in to check on things and to join in the feast. She stood poised, her tailored coat open, bob loose, her sharp eyes softening as she watched mom weave through guests, a quiet awe in her whisper to Grant, "This is what home is, isn't it?" Grant, his shaggy hair free, nodded, chatting with Uncle Don about antique wrenches, his laugh easy, the weight of finishing the film lifted for a moment. Some of the crew members asked me if it was alright if they caught some of the festivities. I looked at them, they looked like boys askin' if they could go swimmin' in the creek on a hot day, "If you want to, but enjoy everyone's company too." I replied.

Ryan rigged a small setup on the porch, lens wide to capture the scene, tables heaped with food, quilts alive with kids, lanterns swaying, while the sound tech roamed, not because he had to, but because they wanted to. Donny, with headphone on, snaring Miss Elma's cackle, Pastor Williams' chuckle, clinking glasses, and cicadas' hum through the Sennheiser mic, the Nagra taping the night's pulse.

As the crowd settled, my dad, stood at the head table, his scuffed boots planted firm, wearin' his button down shirt, his weathered hands raised for silence, the lanterns' glow catching the gray in his hair. Mom sat to his right, her smile frail but radiant, Matt and I flanking her, our eyes on Dad. "Let's give thanks," he said, voice deep, steady, the Nagra catchin' its warmth, the Mitchell rolling quietly from the porch. "Lord, we're grateful for this life, this community, neighbors who share pies and stories, who hold each other up when the world tries to break us down. For every laugh, every tear, every moment we got together under this oak, we're truly thankful, 'cause each one's a gift, a spark of what this community is, what it'll always be." His voice cracked, eyes glistening, meeting mom's, then mine and Matt's, the crowd hushed, heads bowed, mom's hand squeezing mine, her joy a defiance of illness, proof hope endured. The "Amen" rose soft, the night was alive.

The ancient oak tree's lanterns casting soft gold across checkered tables laden with casseroles, pies, and cider, quilts blanketing the grass where kids tumbled in the warm glow, their laughter mixing with woodsmoke, sage, and pecan pie sweetness. Neighbors and the LA crew mingled, plates balanced on knees. Despite mom's cancer, her frail smile radiant as she hosted, proof hope hadn't faded. I moved through the crowd, flannel loose, Matt joking nearby, the oak's shade a bridge between the locals and the outsiders filming *Echoes*.

Mom, her apron still dusted with flour, leaned toward a young LA grip, her voice warm, teasing, "That oak's been shadin' dinners longer than you've been alive, hon." The grip grinned, fork mid-bite, as mom patted his arm, her eyes bright with memory. A young assistant, her notepad forgotten, sat on a quilt, watching families share stories, and murmured to Grant, "This ain't just dinner, it's rekindlin' a fire." Grant nodded, his shaggy hair catching lantern light, while Lila, sketching the table from a distance, pencil dancing, told him softly, "People think places die in silence, but they live on in a song." Donny walked quietly as he could, the Nagra catching nearby laughter. Mom, spotting Mike, the boom operator savoring her pie as he smiled. She raised her voice, "first time I made that pie was the day Thomas asked me to marry him. Glad to know it still works," her chuckle light, love enduring despite illness.

I grabbed my old 8mm handheld camera from my room, its weight familiar, and wove through the crowd, filming kids chasin' each other under the oak, their coats flapping, faces lit with joy, the lens catching their blur against lantern glow. I turned to Ava, sitting by the firepit, her tailored coat open, listening rapt as mom spun tales of Mill Town's old dances, the flames dancing in her eyes, the Nagra taping their soft exchange.

Steve, the second unit director, camera rolling, sat with Uncle Don and Aunt Debbie on a quilt, asking, "What's Thanksgiving mean here?"

Don's gruff reply, "Bein' thankful for what ya got."

Aunt Debbie looked at Steve, then directly at the camera "It's a tradition, not an obligation, it's about sharin' what ya got with those that may not."

As night deepened, hymns from Elma's hymnals faded to quiet conversation, a breeze carrying fallen leaves across the tables, rustling quilts. I stood, glass raised, voice thick, "To memories, echoes of the moments we can keep." Mom, beside dad, her hand in his, replied, voice soft but fierce, "And to the ones we never want to forget." Glasses clinked, the lanterns' glow warm, the crowd, locals, crew, Matt, Eric, Lila, united, the community's soul rekindled, bridging old and new, giving Ava and the crew a taste of what it's like to belong. The moment, unscripted, was *Echoes'* core, not just recording the decline, but recordin' what's worth preservin', captured in laughter, stories, and mom's enduring light, ready to shine, one toast, one song at a time.

Chapter 52 - Taking Mill Town Back
(December 1972)

It was cold, but Main Street glowed like a 1950s Christmas card plucked from a forgotten attic. Grant was right, Jesus was a miracle worker. This was the grandest shoot yet for Echoes, every inch of Mill Town reborn under the brittle December chill of 1972, the air biting with the crisp scent of pine needles, peppermint sticks, and the acrid tang of fresh paint slathered on old facades. The film crew had worked miracles, turnin' back time: classic cars, Chevy Bel Airs with tailfins sharp as knives, old F-100s, their chrome bumpers sparkling like polished silver, lined the curbs, their curves catchin' the golden halos of streetlamps strung with tinsel and frosted bulbs. Storefronts dazzled, alive with nostalgia: the soda shop's plate-glass window gleamed, reflectin' a chrome-plated fountain where glass Coca-Cola bottles stood in neat rows beside red-and-white candy canes and a pyramid of wax paper cups, the counter inside adorned with a garland of plastic holly. Gable's Mercantile shone next door, its mannequins draped in rich velvet dresses, emerald and ruby red, paired with wool coats and fur muffs, wide-brimmed hats pinned with silk poinsettias, evokin' Sunday-best winters long gone. The barbershop's red-white pole spun slow, hypnotic, its window etched with a frosted snowflake pattern, a tiny Christmas tree blinkin' with colored lights in the corner, invitin' passersby to a shave and a story. The hardware store, Dad's old pride, stood as the street's heart, radiatin' warmth through its hand-painted glass sign, Chandler's Hardware in bold, black letters, lit by buzzin' incandescent bulbs that cast a honeyed glow on the sidewalk, silver tinsel framin' the door, a wreath of pinecones and red ribbon hangin' proud, as if the store hadn't shuttered a decade ago. The crew hustled in the cold, their breaths puffin' white: Arriflex lights perched high on scaffolds, castin' a soft, cinematic sheen; the Mitchell 35mm sat steady on a dolly, its lens a hungry eye, Ryan kneelin' to check its focus, his scarf tucked tight against the wind; cables snaked across frost-kissed asphalt, taped down to keep the shot clean. I stood at the edge, flannel loose but not warm enough, my hands shovin' deep in my pockets. My heart was racin' like a kid on Christmas mornin', this shot more than a scene, a love letter to Mill Town's winter past, a plea to hold its soul in 35mm, every detail, every bulb, every wreath, a stitch in Echoes' tapestry, ready to burn bright, one frame, one frozen breath at a time.

I stood behind the A-camera, headset snug, breath fogging in my flannel, voice steady as I called, "Quiet on set! Ready positions!" Dozens of townspeople in vintage attire stood ready, kids clutching tin bells, sneakers swapped for polished boots; young men in wool service uniforms laughing coming out of the soda shop, caps crisp and new lookin', women in fur-trimmed coats, holding candles. Miss Lorraine tied a girl's scarf, Mr. Radcliffe adjusted his scarf, and Eric, in a borrowed Navy coat, stood tall despite his limp, camo cap tucked away, eyes alight with purpose. The street glowed, a ghost of 1950s cheer, every face a piece of *Echoes'* heart, ready to shine for the lens.

"Roll cameras!" I shouted, the Mitchell whirring, its lens drinking in the scene, the Nagra taping the jingle of bells. The recreated Christmas festival came alive, candles flickering in a soft breeze, their flames dancing against the night. A makeshift choir, locals with hymnals, sang "Silent Night" and "Jingle Bells," voices raw but heartfelt, kids ringing bells, giggling as they skipped. Women held candles high, men tipped caps, and classic cars crept forward, drivers in vests tossing candy from windows, a memory on loop. I moved with the dolly, calling, "Stay tight, Ryan, follow the kids!" my pulse pounding, seeing Dad's store glow, the town reborn.

The Mitchell 35mm swept wide, its lens drinking in Main Street's reborn magic, capturing the barbershop's red-white pole spinning lazily, its window aglow with a tiny Christmas tree's blinking multicolored lights and frosted snowflake decals; the soda shop's tinsel garlands glittering silver and gold, draped over a chrome fountain where candy canes stood like sentinels beside frosty glass bottles; the hardware store's festive warmth, its hand-painted *Chandler's Hardware* sign radiant under buzzing bulbs, one of mom's pinecone wreaths with red velvet ribbon swaying gently, every detail a vibrant detail of Mainstreet's history. "Keep the song, choir!" I called, voice cracking with awe, my headset tight, flannel damp under the December chill, the scene flawless, a moment stolen from 1950. The town's heart pulsing in every flicker. But then, a shift, like a candle snuffed by a sudden gust. Mrs. Ellie, her emerald velvet coat brushing the asphalt, stopped dead, her candle's flame trembling in its glass holder, wax dripping as her gloved hand covered her mouth, tears spilling down her cheeks, smudging the rose-petal rouge she'd painstakingly applied. Her sob, sharp and raw, pierced the choir's soft "Silent Night," the camera catching her shoulders heaving, the Nagra taping her choked gasp. Mr. Jennings in his wool uniform, his Navy cap tilted proud, froze mid-step, his hand half-raised in a salute, eyes glistening like frost, whispering, "Feels like yesterday, comin' home for Christmas." The Mitchell held his anguished pause, the crowd's rhythm fracturing, emotion rippling like a stone in a still pond, faces turning, eyes locking, memories of lost winters flooding back.

I saw the pain bloom, a wound torn open, and lowered my headset, its cord dangling, voice soft but firm, "Cut. Everybody take a break…" The dolly ground to a halt, Ryan easing off the lens, his scarf loose, but the tears kept flowing, unchecked. Mrs. Ellie in her velvet coat sank to the curb, her candle clattering to the ground, wax pooling, as Mr. Abernathy in his quilted jacket knelt, wrapping her in a tight embrace, their faces buried in shared grief. Mr. Jennings, in his uniform, leaned against a '57 Chevy's gleaming fender next to them, his medals glinting faintly, wiping his eyes with a worn sleeve, his breath fogging in the cold. Angie, in her red plaid skirt, her candle forgotten, its flame snuffed out, joined in, "I remember goin' carolin', real carols, door to door, by the town tree all lit up." Her voice trembled, the camera still rolling, catching her wistful stare into the dark. Another voice, low and rough, came from Mr. Danniels, wearin' suspenders perched on the soda shop's icy steps, his scarf loose, muttering, "Those were the days... folks together, singin' people would offer us hot cocoa and some would even join us." The Nagra taped their aching words, the Mitchell framing the crowd's quiet sorrow, kids pausing, tin bells silent in their mittened hands, the choir's song dissolving into the night. I stood frozen, hands gripping the camera rig, this unscripted truth rawer, truer than any planned shot.

I sat on the curb by Mrs. Ellie, her hand shaking as she gripped mine, muttering about Christmas Eves with her sister, gone now, the camera catching her knuckles, my nod. I gave her a soft hug, her coat crumpling, sobbing for her daughter, lost years ago, her tears soaking my flannel, the Mitchell framing us. I sat in the street with extras, Miss Lorraine, Mr. Mitchel, Mrs. Gables boy still playin' with a bell, but listening to tales of lost shops, old carols, the town they loved, the camera lingering on our circle, asphalt cold beneath us. Grant, arms crossed, watched me heal, not direct. Grant took over, whispering to the crew, "Don't stop recording. This is the real movie." The cameras rolled, capturing sobs, hugs, a veteran's tears, a woman clutching her candle, whispering of trees past, the light soft, stars bright above, no lines, just a community remembering, pain and unity woven tight tryin' to fill a hole.

As night deepened, the street hushed, cars still, bells quiet, then it happened, a whispered tale, a laugh. We watched as the joy rippled through the crowd now smiling and laughing with each other, no one leaving. I didn't know the cameras had kept rolling, didn't see Grant's signal, didn't realize this raw footage, Mill Town's heart laid bare, would be *Echoes'* truest pulse, outshining every planned shot, ready to burn bright.

The shop windows were still glowing, adorned with hand-cut paper stars, snowflakes and comets, pasted by Miss Lorraine's sewing circle, their edges curling against the glass. The soda shop's tinsel sparkled, the barbershop's pole spun lazily, and the hardware store's wreath gleamed, *Chandler's Hardware* sign buzzing bright, a heartbeat of

1950's Mill Town reborn. I stood behind the Mitchell 35mm, headset loose, flannel damp, calling "Cut!" as the kids stepped back, their mittens dusted with glitter. The crew cheered quietly, a soft whoop from Ryan, while locals clapped, scarves swaying, the smell of hot cider wafting from Mrs. Clara's diner, its neon sign flickering. I stood up, emotionally spent, chest tight with pride, having captured a town tryin' to remember its soul, every frame a prayer for *Echoes*.

As the crew packed gear, Arriflex lights unrigged, cables coiled, Grant leaned against a lamppost, his shaggy hair tucked under a knit cap, sipping coffee from a chipped diner mug, eyes thoughtful, distant. "You know what'd hit hard right now?" he said, voice low, steam curling from his cup. "Let's go shoot Allied General. Same day, same town. Total contrast." I was still a little raw. I hesitated, my bones heavy, drained from the emotions weight, Dad's store, but saw the value, the truth in it. "Yeah," I said, nodding slow, rubbing my jaw. "Show the cost of progress. Let it speak for itself." Grant grinned, tossing his coffee dregs, and we rallied the crew, piling into vans, the Mitchell and Nagra loaded, ready to face AG's shadow for *Echoes*.

The crew pulled into Allied General's massive parking lot, a gray sea of asphalt coverin' what used to be the orchard with our tree swing right about where we parked. Allied General was a stark contrast to Main Street's warmth, the wind howlin' off the concrete like a mournful ghost. Garish red and green banners snapped above metal shopping cart corrals, their plastic edges frayed, screamin' *Holiday Savings!* in block letters, the store's neon logo loomin' over a squat, beige building, its windows plastered with sale signs, *50% Off! Buy Now!* Rows of cars came and went as if in a silent parade, while shoppers pushed carts like race walkers, faces blank, scarves flappin', clutchin' bags of cheap tinsel and boxed toys. The camera rig felt heavy in my hands, the Nagra tapin' the wind's wail, Ryan framin' the stark sprawl, my heart sinkin' at the contrast, Main Street's hand-cut snow flakes versus AG's soulless glare, Mill Town's past against its present wound, Echoes ready to show the cost.

422

Grant, his shaggy hair tucked under a cap, scouted the first tracking shot, his eyes sharp, murmuring, "Carts moving like ants, synchronized chaos, not a damn smile in sight."

I nodded, heart heavy, Eric's cap and Lila's note in my bag, the crew's breath fogging as we prepped to capture Allied General's truth for *Echoes*, a raw contrast to the town square's hand-cut stars and carols.

I walked the shot, the dolly gliding smooth, the Mitchell tracing rows of carts rattling over cracks, shoppers' faces blank, eyes fixed forward, scarves flapping like surrender flags, no warmth, no pause. I grabbed the handheld Arriflex for B-roll, weaving through the crowd, lens catching fast hands snatching boxed electronics arguing over sale items, carts stacked with blenders, radios, flickering TVs, piled high in carts that bumped and jostled, wheels squeaking. Families moved in silence, isolated, parents gripping lists, kids trailing, no chatter, no joy, the Nagra taping the rustle of paper bags.

We overheard one couple talking, "What do you think Jake'll like?" "I dunno, maybe this radio, it's on sale."

My shoes scuffed the asphalt, the cold seeping through, as I muttered to myself, narrating for *Echoes*, "Downtown had lights, music, neighbors laughin' under the glow of the Christmas Tree in the square, sharin' cider... This feels like a timed drill, get in, get out as fast as you can, don't dawdle." The words stung, the lens framing the cost of progress, Mill Town's soul swapped for cheap efficiency.

A child in a reindeer hoodie wailed, tears streaking his face as his mother, head down, scrolled through a fistful of coupons, her lips tight, oblivious to his cries, the camera catching the disconnect, the Nagra taping his sobs against the wind. Nearby, two women reached for the last discounted coffeemaker on a display, their hands brushing, no words exchanged, just tight, forced smiles and averted eyes, a silent tug-of-war ending with one cart rolling away empty. A man in a bulky coat rushed past, his shoulder clipping another shopper's, no "excuse me," just a grunt, his gaze fixed on the store's neon glare, the Mitchell holding the fleeting collision, the crowd's rhythm unbroken, mechanical. I steadied the Arriflex, the town's warmth left behind on Main Street, this lot a graveyard of connection.

The sequence unfolded, cinematic and bleak, the dolly tracking the carts' relentless march, the handheld weaving through the chaos, capturing the isolation, hands grabbing, carts colliding, faces closed. The gray sky loomed, the concrete gleamed, the banners' red and green mocked the season, *Echoes* building its case, the town's heart, traded for this.

The wind stung my face as we wrapped, the lot's neon glare castin' long shadows. Ryan, scarf loose, turned to me, the Mitchell still rolling, his eyes bright despite the cold. "We got it, Bobby," he said, voice low, sure, patting the camera. "You can feel it in the footage, the emptiness, the temperature dropped twenty degrees." Grant, leaning on a cart corral, his shaggy hair dusted with frost, added quietly, "We didn't have to say a thing. They'll see it." No narration needed, the images would scream the trade-off, the life bled out for convenience.

We packed the gear, the crew piling into vans, the lot's wind howling as we pulled away.

I drove, glancing over my shoulder at the glowing Allied General sign in the rearview mirror, its red neon clawing the dark, a beacon of everything Mill Town had lost. "You can stack all the deals you want," I muttered, voice rough, my hands tight on the wheel, "but you can't buy back what's already been given away."

The words hung in the van's quiet, Grant nodding in the passenger seat, Ryan checking the Mitchell in the back, the road to Main Street stretching ahead, its faint glow calling us home. We arrived back on Main Street, where a crowd had started to gather, the town's folk were still sitting on benches drinking hot cocoa bathed in the overhead string lights.

Jesus looked at me "let's leave the lights on tonight."

424

Chapter 53 - Miss Baxter's Story
(December 1972)

Main Street in a golden haze, the air thick with dust, and the faint tang of Benny's diner fry grease waftin' down the block. Mrs. Clara, her apron dusted with flour, donated a stack of red-and-white checkered tablecloths from the diner, "Perfect for float skirts, boys, don't you dare stain 'em!" she teased, wavin' a spatula.

Gable, his suspenders snappin', rolled out his old mercantile cart, its wheels creakin' but sturdy, refurbished by the high school shop class into a "mayoral float" with fresh paint and a wobbly podium. Teenagers from the drama club, eyes bright with dreams of Hollywood, signed up as baton twirlers and scout troops, practicin' spins in the school lot, their sneakers squeakin'. Grant tracked down several vintage beauties: a cherry-red Plymouth Fury, its fins gleamin' like a shark's; a dusty Ford Falcon, waxed to a shine; and a turquoise Chevy Bel Air, its chrome winkin'. The owners, Mr. Tatum, Old Man Jenkins, and Miss Eula's nephew, grinned wide, insistin', "We drive 'em, Grant, or no deal!" their hands polishin' hoods like they were pettin' prized horses. Ryan had scouted lightin', squintin' at the sun's arc, while Lila, sketchpad in hand, had sorted the costumes, a borrowed mayor's sash of faded gold, oversized suit pants with a shiny seat, and a comically large tin "town key" for flair. "This key's bigger'n my head," she laughed, danglin' it, her braid swingin' as she pinned a hem.

Across Main Street, Lila, Miss Lorraine, and the set dressers worked magic, turnin' a boarded-up storefront into 1955's Baxter's Boutique, its window now gleamin' with bolts of calico and gingham, a working Singer sewing machine hummin' inside, its black enamel glintin' under a bare bulb, spools of thread in cherry red and sky blue stacked like candy. Miss Lorraine stood outside with her hands on her hips, her floral dress swishin', leanin' over to adjust a hem on the actress playin' her younger self, a spunky drama club girl named Jenny. "Not bad for a girl who didn't know a hem from a hash brown back then," Lorraine teased, her wink sharp, her needle flashin' as she tucked a stitch, the crew chucklin'. Jenny grinned, mock-curtsyin', "Learned from the best, Miss Lorraine!"

The shoot day dawned, Main Street alive with bunting, red, white, and blue streamers flappin' like a patriot's heartbeat. The real Mayor Heartwell, retired now, rounder and grayer, stood among the extras, arms folded, a knowin' smirk crinklin' his face, his plaid shirt stretched tight. Watchin' the chaos, kids droppin' batons, the Plymouth's engine sputterin', he leaned to Grant, mutterin', "That's exactly how it went in '55, 'cept I was even more red-faced, sweatin' like a hog." His chuckle rumbled, eyes glintin' with memory, the Mitchell 35mm hummin' nearby, catchin' the crowd's buzz, the Nagra tapin' the clatter of carts and kids' shouts.

The young actor playin' 1955 Mayor Heartwell, stuffed into comically tight pinstripe pants, climbed atop the mayoral float, wavin' to an imaginary crowd, his sash slippin', the tin key danglin' like a cartoon prop. He stepped too high onto the plywood platform, and, *RRRIIIPPP!*, a loud, unmistakable tear split the air, the seam of his pants givin' way with a cartoonish pop. The set exploded in laughter, batons clatterin' to the ground, Ryan near droppin' his lens, the drama club kids howlin'. "Oh, Lord, he's airin' out City Hall!" Grant hooted, slappin' his knee, while I tried my best not to laugh, grinned, callin', "Keep rollin'!" The real Heartwell doubled over, wipin' tears, his voice boomin', "I swear, it sounded just like that in '55, thought I'd die right there!" Jenny, as young Lorraine, rushed from the boutique, needle in hand, her gingham apron flappin', playin' up the rescue with a strut, hollerin', "Mayor, hold still 'fore you scandalize the scouts!"

Inside Baxter's Boutique, cameras rolled, the Singer's needle whirrin' like a tiny engine, Jenny's fingers flyin', thread snappin' taut as she stitched the mayor's pants, the young actor balancin' on a wobbly stool,

426

clutchin' his jacket 'round his waist, his face beet-red. "You got five minutes, Mayor, or you're marchin' moon-first!" Jenny sassed, her voice sharp, tossin' her braid, the crew stiflin' giggles. Bobby directed, leanin' in, "Close-up on the needle, Ryan, get her hands movin' fast!" The Mitchell zoomed, catchin' the glint of steel, the blur of fingers, the mayor's nervous grin, the shop's calico bolts glowin' warm, the Nagra tapin' the machine's hum and Jenny's mock-scoldin', "Next time, wear suspenders, ya big oaf!"

The float rolled again, pants patched, the mayor back atop, wavin' proud, the tin key gleamin' in the sun. The crowd, locals, drama kids, old-timers, cheered wild, patriotic brass blarin' from a borrowed record player, red-white-and-blue bunting flutterin' like a flag in a breeze. Ryan manned a crane shot, the camera soarin' over Main Street, catchin' the Plymouth's red gleam, the Ford's dust trail, the Chevy's turquoise shine, batons twirlin', scouts marchin', the float creakin' along, bunting snappin' all the while tryin not to capture all the dead grass and leafless trees. Miss Lorraine stood by her boutique, her floral dress bright, wavin' beside the real Heartwell, their hands high, their smiles twin beams of pride, the Nagra tapin' the crowd's whoops, the Mitchell holdin' the parade's heart, Mill Town alive in '55's echo.

I yelled, "That's a wrap!" my voice hoarse, the town eruptin' in claps, hats flyin', kids spinnin' batons for fun. Miss Lorraine dabbed her eyes with a hankie, laughin' soft, her voice warm, "Didn't think I'd see that day again." I walked over, boots scuffin', and hugged her gentle, her perfume like lilacs, my voice low, "You held the seams together, Miss Lorraine. Still do." She patted my cheek, eyes misty, "And you stitched us a picture, boy. Ain't that somethin'." The sun dipped, paintin' the street gold, the parade's echo lingerin', *Echoes* capturin' Mill Town's soul, ready to shine one stitch at a time.

Chapter 54 - Sherriff Johnson's Story
(December 1972)

Me and Grant were deep in prep for *Echoes'* next reenactment: Sheriff Johnson's legendary tale of the 1957 football team's mischief. Castin' was a town affair, high school football players, all lanky limbs and cocky grins, volunteered to play their '57 counterparts, their cleats scuffin' the lot behind the diner.

Even Coach Daniels' grandson, Tommy, a wiry kid with his granddad's squint, signed on to play young Coach, slingin' a whistle 'round his neck, hollerin', "I'll make Paw proud, Bobby, just don't make me run laps!"

Alumni, now paunchy but proud, joined in, their letterman jackets dug from attic trunks, faded red and gold, duct tape patchin' cracked helmets to match the era's grit. For the culprits, the boys who'd shot out Mr. Abernathy's feed store windows with a slingshot, Bobby cast Jason as Abernathy and the Miller twins, freckled terrors with gap-toothed smirks, already notorious for stealin' apples from Gable's. "We're naturals, Mr. Chandler!" they crowed, brandishin' a homemade slingshot, its rubber band twangin'.

We had to do this one on a budget, since we didn't account for it when we started, so we're gonna have to get it like we did Miss Baxter's story. All in one sequence. We thought it would be easier for the locals to follow as well.

The town lent a rattly old school bus, its green paint chipped, seats smellin' of stale gum and teenage sweat, parked by the set, a rejuvinated Abernathy's store, its windows rigged with sugar glass for shatterin'.

"Places everyone!" I belted from just out of frame lookin' over Ryan's shoulder in the bus. "Action!"

The filmin' had kicked off inside the bus, the air thick with the reek of moonshine sloshin' in Mason jars as the players passed 'mongst the rowdy players in the back of the bus, their hollers bouncin' off the metal walls. The Nagra pickin' up every hoot and helmets clankin' as they shoved and laughed. The Miller twins, eyes glintin' like raccoons, crouched by a window, slingshot taut, actin' like they were firin' rocks at the storefront as the bus rumbled past, the sugar glass explodin' in a glittery spray, their giggles wild, high-pitched. "Bullseye, Jimmy!" one whooped, high fivin' his brother, the Mitchell 35mm catchin' their glee, the Nagra tapin' the glass's tinkle and the team's cheers.

"Cut, let's get your response when you know you're caught. Go whenever you're ready. Roll it!"

The Nagra on the bus caught "Aw hell," Jimmy Miller muttered, as the camera got him slinkin' low, his brother's face pale, "We're dead meat." The bus lurched to a stop, the camera catchin the water spillin, supposed to be what was left of the moonshine all over the seat and floor.

"Cut! Nice job guys." I said clappin Ryan on the back. "Lets set up for the next scene!"

I whispered in the headset, "Jason, roll in quick, remember you're mad. Ryan pan to Jason as quick and as steady as you can. Jason, you ready?"

"Ready as I'll ever be. I've always been on the other end of this story." Jason replies with a nervous grin.

"Not this time." Jason turns the police lights and siren on.

I whispered in the headset, "Jason, roll in quick, remember you're mad. Ryan pan to Jason as quick and as steady as you can. Ready on the set! And...Action."

Ryan quickly pans to Mr. Abernathy through the bus windows as he drives up screechin' to a stop by the front of the bus.

"Cut, great job guys. Lets get ready for the next sequence."

The bus pulled over just inside the old tree lot downtown where Jesus had the second scene set up and ready to go. Ryan and I jumped off the bus and strode over to the camera already set up. Grant pointed over to Tommy who was standing in front of the school bus. Tommy gave a nod. Grant then pointed to the Sherrif sitting behind the wheel of the 1955 squad car. The Sherrif gave a nod indicating he was ready.

"Everyone ready?" as I put on the headset. Ryan nodded. "Action!"

The camera cut sharp to Sheriff Johnson's patrol car, a borrowed '55 Ford with a bubble light, screechin' 'round the back of the bus, red glow strobin' the set, its siren wailin' like a banshee.

"Get a closeup of his feet as he gets out of the squadcar, follow his feet all the way to the bus." I whispered to Ryan through the headset. "As he approaches the bus, pan up as he knocks on the bus door getting just his back." Mike held the boom microphone just behind the Sheriffs feet capturing the crunch of the gravel as he walked.

"Cut! That was just right. Everyone get ready for the next shot inside the bus."

Jesus backed a truck up to the back of the bus with the camera already set up. They opened the back door so the camera can poke through capturing the Sheriff walking down the aisle. Ryan and I climb on the back of the pickup. Grant is perched on a step ladder lookin in through an open back window.

The Miller twins are caryin' on in the back of the bus pretendin' like they had drunk all the moonshine. "Alright boys, y'all ready?"

"Ready on the set! Ryan, make sure you start with a wide shot then zoom in on the Sheriff's face. Action!"

The Mitchell starts whirring, the Sheriff boards the bus as the camera stretches out the Nagal catching the footsteps as the the Sheriff walks the aisle slowly.

Sherriff Johnson, with a jaw like granite, boarded, his boots thuddin', badge flashin', smellin the shine, his face went stone-cold. Johnson loomed over the twins, voice low, cuttin' through the silence, camera cuttin' from his face to the Miller twins, "Nice arm, boys. I saw ya hit both of them."

I whisper into the headset, "Now Sheriff, imagine you see Mr. Abernathy pullin' up fast stopping at the front of the bus."

Ryan pans to the Sheriff's face catchin' him lookin' out the window at an imaginary Mr. Abernathy, just as the Sheriff says "Y'all stay right there."

"Cut. Ok, everyone stay where you are, we have one more scene to shoot. Ok Sheriff, you just talked to Abernathy and you're tellin' em' to meet you in the morning to go plow the field." I said as the Sheriff nodded.

"Ready?" as I looked around and everyone shook their head.

"And…Action!" as the Mitchell began humming.

The Sheriff with a stern face looked at the twins, "See me tomorrow mornin', y'all, bright n early at Abernathy's field, let's see if ya can handle a plow half as good as ya can a slingshot."

The camera pans the players as their faces froze, the camera zoomin' on their wide eyes, the Nagra catchin' a nervous gulp, the set electric with the sheriff's calm menace.

"Cut. Did you get it Ryan?" I said lookin at Ryan.

"Of course I got it." Ryan said with a smile.

"That's what I like to hear, lets set up for the next shot." I said with a smile as I climbed out of the truck bed, with Ryan already breakin down the camera'.

"OK, lets get set up for the confrontation scene." I walked to the front of the bus where Jesus was already brining the camera from out of the truck mounting it to the tripod. "Remember, Jason, you're mad, some kids just shot out your windows. You're dead set to see them pay. Sheriff, this is your story, I don't need to tell you." I said with a smile. I looked to Ryan, already at the camera. He gave me a quick nod sayin' he was ready.

"Positions everyone. Quiet on the set! And…Action!"

I could hear the Mitchell hum. Ryan followin' the Sheriff as he stepped off the bus to quiet Abernathy who was screamin' bout his store windows.

"Now zoom in close capturin' both the Sheriff and Abernathy in one frame." I said whisperin' to Ryan.

"Now Mr. Abernathy, I know your upset, but kids are kids. They're good kids, just havin' a lil too much fun after the big game. These boys don't need nothin' on their record, that kind of thing will follow them round the rest of their life. If I remember right, you weren't always an angel in High School neither." Johnson said.

"Well, suppose you're right, well, even when I was in High School if I got caught, I had to make it right," said Abernathy.

"I know them and their folks, good people, but they ain't got much money." Johnson rubs his chin, " You still need your field done?"

"Now zoom in on Abernathy's face." I whispered to Ryan.

The camera cuts to Abernathy's face, where there's a hint of a smile, "uh, yeah, I do."

432

"Now pan back out to capture em both." I whispered to Ryan again.

"Meet us there tomorrow, let'm work it off," Johnson said with a questionin' look like he was hopin Abernathy said yes.

The camera follows Abernathy as he gives a nod, and walks back to his car.

The camera cuts back to Johnson, smiling, then it fades as the camera follows him walking back on the bus.

"Cut! Are you sure y'all aint professionals?" I said with a huge smile.

Grant looked around with a big smile, "Great job today everyone! That's a wrap for the day. We'll shoot again tomorrow at noon at Mr. Abernathy's field. Please get there at eleven."

Everyone started clapping, and high fiving.

Mike looked at his brother, "we're gonna be Hollywood stars!"

His brother looked back "I'm gonna have every girl in town callin' on me!" as Mike hit him in the shoulder.

The next morning the scene shifted to Mr. Abernathy's field, where Jesus had already set up a camera for a wide shot of the pasture as the sun came up. By eleven when everyone else got there under a merciless noon sun, the earth dry as bone, cracked like an old man's knuckles, dust risin' in clouds.

"Now, today is a little different, you're actually gonna plow part of this field while we get different angles. Now you don't mind the cameras, just focus on plowin' the field. The less real it looks, the longer ya gotta plow." All the players looked at me like I was playing a joke.

Tommy looked at the players, "No pain no gain!" which was greeted by several mumbles from the team.

Everyone ready?" I yelled out to everyone in the field looking around, everyone giving a nod. "And…Action!"

I heard the Mitchell begin to hum. The whole football team, Tommy as Coach blowin his whistle at some players that may have actually been throwin' up, the players, the twins, stood in a ragged line, grippin' the reins of Mr. Abernathy's old plow, rakes, and shovels, their letterman jackets tossed aside, T-shirts soaked, faces red as beets. We filmed it like a war montage, the Mitchell in slow motion, capturin' sweat beadin' on brows, dirt smearin' cheeks, players trippin' over gnarled roots, cursin' low, "Damn clods harder'n concrete!" One kid swung a hoe, missed, and sprawled face-first, his buddy cacklin', "Nice tackle, slick!" Mr. Abernathy, played by Jason, stood at the field's edge, arms crossed, his grin wide as a barn door, crow's feet crinklin'. "Best this field's been turned since '45, boys!" he called, spittin' tobacco, the camera catchin' his nod, the Nagra his low chuckle, the team groanin' but diggin' on.

The camera pans over to the real townsfolk gathered to watch, sprawled in lawn chairs under a sycamore, passin' jugs of sweet tea, ice clinkin', their laughter rollin' like thunder. Close-ups of Mrs. Clara, her apron swapped for a sunhat, hauled a tray of lemonade, her voice boomin', "Don't quit now, boys! Crime don't plow itself!" The crowd hooted and laughed, kids runnin' 'round, stealin' sips, old-timers like Miss Eula fannin' themselves, mutterin', "Serves 'em right, slingin' rocks like hooligans." The Miller twins, dirt-caked, glared at her, but their smirks betrayed 'em, shovels scrapin' slow. The community's joy, their teasin', wove into *Echoes'* heart, the Mitchell framins their faces, the Nagra tapin' their chatter, Mill Town alive in the spectacle.

The final shot came at sunset, the sky blazin' pink and gold, the field's furrows neat, the team spent. Ryan zoomed close on the Miller twins, their faces smudged with dirt, sweat streakin' through freckles, shovels leanin' on bony shoulders, their grins tired but proud. "Worth it," Jimmy muttered, collapsin' into the soil, his brother noddin', sprawl beside him, both laughin' soft, the camera catchin' their spark, the Nagra their wheezin' breaths. Ryan pulled back for a long shot, the team trudgin' off the field, tools slung over shoulders like farmhands from a lost era, silhouettes against the fiery sky, the Plymouth's chrome glintin' in the distance.

I leaned to Grant, voice low, reverent, "That's what justice used to look like, man, sweat, dirt, and a lesson you don't forget."

Grant nodded, scribblin' about music choices in his notepad.

"Cut! That's a wrap, great job everyone!" The crowd clapped, the player's just grumbled.

Chapter 51 - Mom's Interview
(December 1972)

The film was nearly complete, reels of Mill Town's soul, Main Street's twinkling Christmas lights, Allied General's barren lot, raw tears under the oak, stacked in dented metal cans, labeled in my scrawl, ready for *Echoes'* final edit. But that mornin', I stood alone outside the farmhouse, the air sharp with frost, my breath puffin' white as I stared at the porch swing, its rusted chains creakin' in a faint breeze, paint flakin' where Mom's hand used to rest, I could hear her voice hummin' "Amazing Grace" while she taught me to plant what I intended to reap. The swing swayed, empty, and a hole gnawed at the film's heart, somethin' vital missin'. Grant ambled up, his shaggy hair pokin' from a wool cap, leanin' against the crew's beat-up van, a chipped diner mug of coffee steamin' in his hand, his eyes squintin' against the low sun. "You okay, Bobby?" he asked, voice rough from a late night cuttin' footage.

I rubbed my neck, "I can't leave without her, Grant," I said, voice low, crackin' like dry wood. "Mom, she's the reason I ever picked up a camera, the reason I'm chasin' this. Her stories, her fire, that's what *Echoes* is built on. I owe her this, 'fore…" I trailed off, unspoken.

Grant's jaw tightened, his nod slow, knowin' mom's fight was the spark that lit this film, that landed him his first producer role, her voice needed to be the last piece to make it whole. "Then let's do it," he said, settin' his mug on the van's hood, his breath foggin'. "Soft, simple, just her. We'll make it right."

Inside, we turned the livin' room into an intimate set, keepin' it gentle, no Hollywood glare. No Arriflex lights on clankin' stands, just soft winter light pourin' through lace curtains, their edges yellowed, castin' dappled patterns across the worn floral sofa, its cushions saggin' from years of family gatherin's. Dust motes floated lazy in the pale beams, the air smellin' of Mom's lavender soap, a faint whiff of dad's reheated weak mornin' coffee lingerin' from the kitchen. I set the Mitchell on a low tripod, its black body hummin' soft, lens polished to catch every line in her face, my flannel loose, hands shakin' as I tweaked the focus, heart poundin' like a drum. "Keep it tight, Bobby," I muttered to myself, checkin' the frame, Mom's favorite armchair centered, a crocheted blanket draped over its back, her Bible on the side table, open to Psalms.

Grant worked audio from the hallway, his boots silent on the scuffed hardwood, riggin' the Sennheiser mic to a stand, its tip angled just so, Nagra reels spinnin' with a faint whir, givin' me and Mom space. He put the headset on, "Sound's clean," he whispered, his eyes soft, steppin' back to lean against the doorframe, his notepad tucked away, sensin' the weight of this moment.

Dad, moved quiet, deliberate, his work shirt tucked neat, his callused hands fluffin' the sofa's pillows, their faded roses bloom' under his touch. He steadied the mic stand, fingers brushin' the metal, then adjusted a framed photo on the mantel, me and Matt as kids, grinnin' with fishing poles by the Blackwater. "This good, son?" he asked, voice low, gruff, his blue eyes meetin' mine, holdin' a steady strength, no need for more words. I nodded, throat tight, "Yes sir, perfect."

The room settled, the tick of the mantel clock loud.

"She ready?" Grant asked, his voice barely a breath, checkin' the Nagra.

"Soon," I said, wipin' my palms on my jeans, heart racin' like I was sixteen again, showin' her my report card. This interview, her voice, was *Echoes'* final truth, the promise I'd made her when she first got sick, to tell Mill Town's story, her story, now ready to unfold.

The living room was a sanctuary of memory, steeped in the quiet glow of the soft winter light streaming through yellowed lace curtains, casting intricate shadows across the scuffed hardwood floor, the air thick with the comforting scent of Mom's lavender soap, a faint undercurrent of Dad's coffee from the kitchen, and the musty warmth of old books stacked on a side table. I sat across from mom like I had done millions of times before, on the sagging floral sofa, its faded roses barely holding their pattern, her frail body nestled into a nest of cushions, a crocheted afghan from Grandma, a quilted square from a church bazaar, and a lopsided heart-embroidered pillow Matt stitched in fifth grade, his clumsy stitches still somehow intact. Her illness was stark, her cheeks hollowed by cancer's toll, a knitted shawl of soft blue draped loosely over her thin shoulders, her graying hair tucked behind ears, but her spirit blazed, her blue eyes sharp and luminous, flickering with a defiant light no sickness could snuff, like those Christmas lanterns she'd place under the oak. The camera rested on a low tripod, its lens polished to a gleam, humming faintly, no clapboard, no countdown, just the gentle whir of the Nagra in the hallway where Grant stood. I leaned forward, flannel loose, heart hammering, throat so tight I could barely swallow. "Hey, Mom," I said, voice soft, cracking like thin ice, the camera rolling to capture her for *Echoes*, this final interview.

Mom's lips curved, a trembling smile, tears glinting in the corners of her eyes but her pride burning brighter, her hands smoothing the shawl, fingers bony yet graceful, nails still painted a faint pink from Lila's visit. "Oh, Bobby," she said, voice warm, a little hoarse, like a hymn sung through years of love, the Nagra taping its tender cadence. "I remember like yesterday, you were always seein' the world like a story, even before you could tie your shoes, narratin' every little thing like you were born to be behind a camera." Her eyes crinkled, a soft laugh bubbling up, the camera catching the glow in her face, the way her cheeks lifted despite the weight of illness. "You'd haul that camera your daddy won at the church raffle everywhere, pointin' it at everythin'. The dog chasin' his tail in the yard, Matt pilin' up mud pies

438

by the shed, even your bowl of cornflakes at breakfast, goin' on about how the milk swirled 'like a river in a picture show.' 'Look, Mom, it's an adventure!' you'd holler, draggin' that camera 'cross the grass, leavin' a trail in the dew." Her voice rose, bright with memory, the Mitchell framing her hands, gesturing lively, painting the past, the light dusting her hair with a silver halo, her shawl slipping slightly as she leaned forward.

She paused, her gaze drifting to the window, frost etching delicate patterns on the panes, her eyes being transported somewhere in the past. "I remember how this town was, back in the late '40s, '50s after the war, it was alive, Bobby, burstin' with life," she said, her tone rich, like she was unwrapping a gift. "Christmas pageants at the church, kids in tattered angel wings, trippin' over bedsheets, their halos crooked, the choir beltin' 'O Holy Night' till the rafters shook, folks packed in pews, passin' peppermint sticks, their wrappers crinklin'. Summers, we'd sit on the courthouse steps, eatin' sundaes from Clara's diner, vanilla ice cream meltin' down our wrists, laughin' as fireflies blinked in the dusk, the air sweet with honeysuckle. The town felt big when you were little, like it held the whole world in its arms, neighbors wavin' us in from porches for a chat that probably wouldn't end before the sun set. Shops hummin' with chatter, every corner a story waitin' for your lens." Her smile softened, tears spilling slow, tracing lines down her cheeks, the camera holding her gaze, steady and fierce, the Nagra catching a faint catch in her breath, a pause heavy with love.

I sat still, hands clenched in my lap, knuckles white, barely breathin', her spark ignitin' me, Dad's strength in the room's quiet. "You remember that first film you showed me?" she asked, eyes lockin' on mine, a tear fallin' but her smile wide. "You were eight, filmed your friend Lila walkin down Mainstreet laughin' and smiling at just bein', she didn't need a reason, then the splice you made to fade to that Blackwater, just bein' at sunset, all shaky, but you narrated it like a poet, 'The river's dancing too.' I knew then, you'd tell stories bigger'n us." Her voice trembled, proud, the Mitchell zoomin' slow to her face,

439

the light catchin' the fire in her eyes, this moment the soul of *Echoes*, her love, her fight, ready to shine, ready to live.

I leaned forward, a smile tugging my lips, voice soft, "Mom, any funny stories from growin' up in Mill Town you wanna share? Somethin' to make us laugh?"

Her eyes crinkled, a laugh bubbling up, her hands smoothing the shawl, fingers thin but lively. "Oh, Bobby," she said, voice warm, a touch hoarse, the Nagra catching its playful lilt, "Mill Town's seen its share, floods swamped Main Street knee-deep, hurricanes rattlin' shutters like they'd fly off. But those fade next to the good stuff." She paused, her smile widening, gaze drifting like she was seein' a different shore. "I was sixteen, out on Pensacola Beach, lovin' the Gulf, always did, the way the waves crash, salt stickin' to your skin. I'd just come outta the water, drippin' wet, hair a mess, sand clingin' to my legs, when this fella, your daddy, fresh back from the war, all tanned and cocky in his Navy whites, strolls up, hands in his pockets, and says, 'How's the water, miss?'" She mimicked his deep drawl, chuckling, the camera catching the mischief in her eyes. "I shot back, 'Wet, of course.' We talked for hours, Bobby, laughin' till my cheeks cramped, sittin' on the sand, him tellin' tales of ships, me sasssin' him about his sunburn. I knew right then he was trouble, and that trouble would be mine."

Her laugh softened, the Mitchell framing her hands, gesturing vivid, light dusting her hair silver. "Then there was Matt, '51, bringin' him home from the hospital," she said, voice tender, eyes glinting. "Lord, we were clueless, me and your dad, twenty-two, starin' at this tiny squallin' thing, no idea how to change a diaper. I'd rock him, singin' hymns off-key, while your dad fumbled with diaper pins, mutterin', 'This ain't no fence, Ruth!' We laughed through the panic, figurin' it out." She leaned forward, voice dropping, a grin breaking free. "And you, Bobby, '53, when I was pregnant, big as a house, I'd make your daddy drive us to Pensacola Beach every weekend. I loved layin' in the sun, but my belly wouldn't let me, hurt too much. So I'd boss him, 'Thomas, dig me a hole!' He'd grumble, 'Woman, I ain't a dog,' but he'd grab a shovel, dig a pit in the sand so I could lay on my stomach, feel the waves' hum. I'd lie there, you kickin' inside me, him sittin' beside, tossin' shells, both of us laughin' till we couldn't breathe."

I grinned, picturin' it, her joy infectious, the camera holding her glow, the Nagra taping her soft chuckle. "You never told me that one, Mom," I said, voice thick, leaning closer. "Dad diggin' holes like a kid?" She nodded, tears glinting but her smile fierce, hand reaching for mine. "Oh, he did, Bobby, 'cause he knew I'd fight for my beach. That's how it was, love and laughs, even when life's heavy." Her voice was a melody.

I swallowed hard, voice low, "Mom, what do you want people to remember about Mill Town?"

She grew quiet, her gaze drifting to the frost-etched window, then back to me, her eyes steady, voice soft but firm, like a hymn's final note. "That it was full of people who loved hard and worked harder," she said, the Nagra catching the weight of her words, the camera framing her hands, folded over the shawl. "Folks who'd share their last loaf, who'd hammer nails till dark to patch a roof before a storm rolled in, who'd hold each other up when the world got heavy." She paused, lips pursing, eyes glinting with memory. "That even when things broke, shops, dreams, hearts, we tried to fix 'em best we could. We patched, we mended, we stayed." Her hand reached for mine, frail but warm, squeezing with a strength that belied her illness. "Small don't always mean weak or ignorant, Bobby. It means close, close enough to know your neighbor's laugh, their hurt, their story." The Mitchell held her fierce gaze, light dustin' her gray hair silver, her wisdom forever etched in *Echoes*.

My throat tightened, tears burning, wanting to say so much, the camera was rollin', but knowin I may never get another chance and I broke a little, voice cracking, "You always believed in me, even when I didn't, when I ran to LA, when I doubted this film." Her smile bloomed, tender, tears spilling, her hand still in mine. "That's what moms do, baby," she said, voice a whisper, warm as a hearth. "We see what's there 'fore it blooms, your heart, your lens, your fight to save what really matters. I saw it when you filmed that river at eight, narratin' like a poet." The camera caught the love in her eyes, the Nagra her soft laugh. I gripped her hand, chest heaving, her faith the spark that carried me, Dad's steady nod behind her echoing her words, even if they didn't come from his lips.

Her voice grew softer, tired, her breath slower, eyes heavy. "You're tellin' the story right, Bobby," she murmured, a faint smile lingering. "You're showin' people what really matters, our town, our love, our try." She closed her eyes, not asleep, just resting, her face peaceful, the room still, the mantel clock ticking. I leaned forward, tears falling, and turned off the camera slow, the Mitchell's hum fading, her words the soul echoin' in me, ready to shine, one truth, one quiet breath at a time.

The Mitchell 35mm sat silent on its tripod, lens dark, the Nagra's reels still in the hallway, their hum gone, the room heavy with the weight of Mom's words, her stories of Main Street's pageants, sundaes on courthouse steps, a town that loved hard, now sealed in *Echoes'* final reel. Grant motioned to me, then slipped out, his boots whispering on the hardwood, pausing at the doorframe, his shaggy hair catching the last light, eyes soft with reverence for the moment.

"I'll check the gear," he murmured, voice low, giving me and my family this sacred space, the door clicking softly behind him.

Dad, eased onto the sofa beside Mom, his callused hand settling over hers, fingers lacing with a tenderness that spoke of decades, his thumb brushing her knuckles, a silent vow as steady as that great oak outside in the front yard. I stayed in my chair, flannel loose, hands clasped tight, knuckles white, heart swollen with her voice, every frame of her pride, her wisdom, etched deep, a film playin' in my chest, *Echoes* now complete but its pulse still racing, urging more.

Mom's crocheted blanket draped over her armchair, its colors soft, worn. I rose, knees creaking, and started packing the interview gear, my hands moving slow, deliberate, winding the rubber audio cables, their cool coils slipping through my fingers, stacking the Nagra's metal case, its edges scuffed from weeks of interviews, Each piece felt heavy, alive with the voices it held. Outside, the air was hushed, like it was settlin' down to hear what words were spokin', the distant hum of crickets beginin' to rise through the cracked window, joined by the faint bark of a neighbor's dog and the rustle of bare branches in a frosty breeze, the air sharp with pine and the promise of snow. "We're ready to wrap it up, but I just don't feel like we got everythin' yet. We got their stories," I said, voice rough, barely above a whisper, leaning against the sofa, the room dim, Dad's hand still over Mom's, her breathing slow, a faint smile lingering. "But now what, Dad?"

He looked up, his blue eyes steady, creased with years, reading the restlessness in me. "You tell me, son," he said, voice low, gruff, but warm, like a fire kindled slow. "If I know you, you got our souls in that film. What's it sayin' to you?" I rubbed my jaw, the stubble scratchin', my mind churnin', an internal monologue takin' hold. The stories, Miss Lorraine's cackle, Mr. Radcliffe's grit, Mom's love, weren't just preserved in those reels, locked away for some dusty archive. They were alive, breathin', clawin' at me to do more than show 'em on a screen. They were a call, a spark to bring a community back from the brink, not just in memory but in fightin' for what places could still be, shops open, neighbors laughin', kids chasin' fireflies. *Echoes* wasn't an epitaph; it was a seed, waitin' to grow, to rally, to build. "It's not enough to just try to save 'em," I said, half to Dad, half to myself, gripping the camera bag, its canvas rough under my palm. "I know lookin' back is a fools game, but I want these stories to live on, to show folks what we're losin', but at the same time showin em it ain't gone yet."

Dad nodded, slow, his hand tightening on Mom's, his eyes never leavin' mine. "Then do it, Bobby," he said, voice firm, a charge. "You always saw what mattered. Don't stop now." The crickets' hum grew louder, twilight deepenin' to a soft purple, the room's warmth holdin' us, Mom's breath a quiet rhythm. I slung the bag over my shoulder, restless, alive, knowin' the stories were just the start, *Echoes* a fire to kindle, one truth, one restless step at a time.

Chapter 55 - Last Night in Mill Town
(December 1972)

The holidays were upon us. There was just one week left in the year, and the church basement was a hollow shell under the dim flicker of a single bulb, the air thick with the musty scent of old hymnals, linoleum wax, and the stale ghost of coffee left too long in the pot, as the *Echoes* crew packed up the last of their gear in the fading December twilight of 1972. Metal equipment cases clanged shut, their latches snapping like tiny gunshots, while boots scuffed across the floor, kicking up dust that danced in slanted light.

Ryan, his red scarf half-untied, sweat beading on his brow despite the chill, wrestled a camera arm into its foam-lined case, its steel joints squealing as he muttered, "C'mon, you stubborn bastard, fold already!"

Lila watched humming a low blues tune, her braids swaying. Cables lay coiled in neat loops, their ends tagged with curling labels, *Mitchell 35mm*, *Arriflex Lights*, *Nagra Reels*, scrawled in Grant's messy Sharpie hand. I wandered the empty space one last time, flannel loose, my callused fingertips brushing the cinderblock wall, still tacky with tape residue from silver light reflectors we'd hung, their absence a quiet ache, like a stage after the curtain falls. The basement's silence pressed in, broken only by the creak of a forgotten folding chair and the faint hum of a distant heater.

Grant, his shaggy hair a wild halo, heaved a duffel over his shoulder, his voice gravelly but warm, "We got it all, Bobby, every tear, every damn carol, locked tight in them cans. Time to haul this treasure home, huh?" His tired grin flashed fierce, eyes glinting with the pride.

That evening, as the sky over the Blackwater River bled purple and gold, Lila stormed into the crew's makeshift HQ at Benny's diner, the bell jangling wild above the door, her denim jacket slung over one shoulder, dark hair spilling loose, eyes blazing like a lit fuse. "Alright, listen up, y'all!" she bellowed, her drawl thick as sorghum, boots stomping the checkered floor, cutting through the jukebox's mournful Johnny Cash croon, "One last round at the Crazy Horse tonight, no speeches, no weepy goodbyes, just family, and that's every single one of you, from townies to you fancy LA types!" Her laugh cracked like a whip, bright and bold, heads turning, forks pausing mid-bite.

Ryan, sittin' at the counter, whooped, "Heck yeah, Lila, I'm there, better have some Bacardi to warm my bones!" Ryan, cradling a chipped mug of diner coffee, smirked, his voice dry, "Long as it ain't that watered-down cider swill, I'm game."

The crew chuckled, exhaustion lifting, while Grant, rummaging through his duffle bag, yanked out two dented metal film cans, their scratched labels reading *Echoes Rough Cut: B Roll*, clips of Main Street's candlelit carols, Dad's Thanksgiving prayer, Evelyn's raw redemption. "We're bringin' the gold, Bobby," he said, winking, voice low like a conspirator, "Let's show 'em what we caught, make 'em cry into their whiskey."

I grabbed the second can, this one had some of my ole' 8mm clips, its cold weight grounding me, the Nagra's whispers of Mill Town's laughter, sobs, and songs locked inside, a treasure heavier than gold.

We spilled out of the diner, the crew's chatter a lively buzz, boots crunching gravel under a frost-bit sky, the Crazy Horse Saloon's neon sign pulsing ahead, red, blue, a defiant heartbeat in the dark. The air stung with winter's edge, carrying the diner's greasy warmth, the river's muddy tang, and a faint whiff of pine from wreaths still hung on lampposts.

Lila led the charge, hollering, "C'mon, slowpokes, drinks ain't gonna pour themselves!" as Ryan slung an arm around her, laughing, "You buyin', troublemaker?"

The night crackled with promise, one last chance to gather, to toast Mill Town's heart before *Echoes* carried its story west, ready to burn bright, one clink of glass, one shared memory at a time.

The Crazy Horse Saloon thrummed with life, its warped wooden walls vibratin'under the roar of laughter and clinkin' glasses, the air thick with the tang of spilled whiskey, smoke, and the faint sweetness of Mrs. Clara's cider still clingin' to coats. It was louder, brighter than I'd ever seen, every booth and barstool claimed, locals in scuffed shoes and faded flannels rubbin' shoulders with folks in Sunday-best dresses, their pearls glintin' under neon.

Old man Gable, his suspenders taut, leaned on the bar, hollering, "Another round, Sal, and make it quick 'fore I start singin'!"

While Miss Lorraine, her floral scarf loose, cackled, "Lord, Gable, your voice'd clear this place faster'n a fire!"

Ryan clapped my shoulder, grinning, "Man, you owe me a beer in LA for all them late nights!" while Ava smirked, "Make it two, hotshot."

The jukebox, usually blarin' Johnny Cash, sat unplugged, its lights dark, replaced by a clunky projector perched on a crate, its beam slicin' through the haze to splash flickerin' light on the wall above the dartboard, scarred from years of bad throws. I stood by the bar, flannel loose, Eric's cap and Lila's note heavy in my pocket, heart poundin' as the crew and town melded, *Echoes'* final night alive in the saloon's glow.

I stepped to the projector, the crowd's din softening, eyes turning, glasses pausin' mid-sip. "Alright, y'all," I said, voice rough but warm, a nervous smile tuggin' my lips, "we ain't done editin' *Echoes*, not by a long shot. But... we wanted you to see what you made, what this town poured into every frame."

My hand hovered over the play button, catchin' Lila's nod from a booth, her sketchpad tucked away,

Grant's grin flashin' beside her, Ryan raisin' a beer, shouting, "Hit it, Bobby, let's see the magic!"

I pressed play, the projector whirring, its bulb hummin' as the wall lit up, the saloon fallin' near-silent, save for the creak of barstools and a soft gasp from Miss Elma.

Clips rolled, raw and vivid: Eleanor's tremblin' hands, gnarled as oak roots, foldin' a quilt she'd sewn in '55, her fingers brushin' the stitches like a prayer, the Nagra's tape catchin' her shaky hum of an old hymn. Eric's voice, rough with pride, filled the room, recountin' the watermelon heist of '64, his teenage self sneakin' into Mr. Collier's field, laughin' as they hauled a prize melon, only to trip and smash it, the crowd chuckling, Eric himself in the back hollerin', "Still tasted sweet, damn it!"

Then, a rabbit, small and gray, frozen in a dusty road at dusk, its ears twitchin', caught by the Mitchell's lens durin' a quiet B-roll, a fleetin' symbol of the town's fragile life, drawin' a soft "aww" from Ava sittin at the table. Finally, a wide shot of Main Street, reborn as 1960, *Chandler's Hardware* glowing, soda shop tinsel sparkling, barbershop pole spinning, classic cars gleaming, every storefront a perfect echo of a lost era, the saloon eruptin' in cheers, glasses raised, Miss Lorraine yelling, "That's our town, y'all!" The clips flickered, hearts opened, *Echoes* weavin' our soul, ready to shine on the silver screen.

Locals packed the room, Gable in his saggin' suspenders, Miss Lorraine's floral scarf slipping, young Tommy Carter in scuffed boots, laughin' 'til their sides ached at stories they'd spun for decades, like the time Don's mule broke free at the fair, their guffaws drownin' the creak of barstools. Tears fell too, quiet and heavy, for memories long buried, old dances, lost shops, faces and friends gone too soon. Old man Tatum, his knuckles gnarled as oak, jabbed a finger at the screen, hollering, "Hot damn, that's my '59 Ford truck, right there by the soda shop!" his gravelly voice crackin' with pride, the crowd whooping. A woman in a faded shawl, Miss Etta, gasped soft, her hand clutchin' her chest, whispering, "Swear I saw my Henry smilin' in that crowd shot, right by Gable's… Lord, he's been gone ten years." Her eyes glistened, the saloon hushin' for a beat, the Nagra's ghost tapin' her awe.

I stepped back from the crowd, my flannel loose, lettin' them feel it, the joy, the pain, the ache, and the pride. The community's soul flickerin' on the wall. Grant sidled up, his shaggy hair wild under the neon's glow, clappin' a hand on my shoulder, his grip firm, voice low, "We did good, man. This, this is why we make movies, to tell stories, to make it live again, to make people feel something." His eyes shone, reflectin' the projector's flicker, and I nodded. Lila joined us, balancin' three whiskeys, her denim jacket scuffed, her grin fierce as she handed us glasses, the amber liquid catchin' the light. "Bobby, you didn't just film a town," she said, her drawl soft but sure, "you helped us remember it, every laugh, every scar, like we're still whole." Her words landed deep, the crowd's cheers swellin' as a clip of Main Street's 1960 glow faded, *Echoes* provin' there was still a spark there.

Eric, his limp forgotten, clambered onto a barstool, wobblin' but defiant, his jacket open, raisin' a glass high, whiskey sloshing. "To Mill Town!" he bellowed, voice rough, proud, "The one place that never needed a spotlight to shine, damn it!" The crowd roared, echoing, "To Mill Town!" glasses thrust skyward, laughter ringin' like a gospel choir, Miss Lorraine's hoot piercin' the din, "Hell yeah, Eric, preach!" Glasses clinked, rum burned throats, the saloon a livin' heartbeat, *Echoes'* spirit ablaze.

Chapter 56 - From Story to Screen
(January 1973)

The soft January sunrise of 1973 crept over Mill Town, paintin' the fields in hues of peach and gold, a delicate mist hangin' low, veilin' the earth like a bride's gossamer shawl, the air sharp with the scent of damp grass and distant woodsmoke. Inside our house, the floorboards creaked under my boots as I paused in the doorway of Mom's room, my flannel loose, heart tight with the weight of leaving. Mom was awake, propped against a mound of pillows, a faded quilt, patchwork of blues and yellows, stitched by her own hands, draped around her frail shoulders, her face pale from cancer's relentless march but her eyes bright, burnin' with a quiet fire. The room smelled of lavender from her bedside sachet and the faint medicinal tang of bandage adhesive and sterilization creme. I knelt by her bed, the mattress saggin' under my weight, and took her hand, her skin cool, delicate as onion paper, veins tracin' maps of a life hard-fought.

I leaned in, kissin' her forehead, her hair thin but soft, and whispered, "You taught me to see, to see what is right in front of us."

Her lips curved, a weak smile, and she whispered back, voice a raspy thread, "Just promise me you'll finish it, Bobby, make it sing."

I nodded, throat burning, and vowed, "You'll see it first, I swear," her hand squeezin' mine, a flicker of her old strength sealin' our pact.

At the small regional airport, a strip of cracked tarmac fringed by pines, a small crowd gathered under a sky bruised with dawn's last purples, their breath foggin' in the January chill, Lila in her scuffed denim jacket, Eric leanin' on his cane, Mayor Heartwell's bolo tie glinting, even locals like Miss Elma and Gable who'd hauled props or shared stories for *Echoes*, many of the crew members like Ryan, Jesus, and

Ava had already left to go home for the holidays. The air buzzed with murmured farewells, the scent of coffee from thermoses minglin' with the jet fuel's sharp bite.

Hugs were traded, fierce and lingering, Lila's arms tight around me, her hair smellin' of pine and diner grease, muttering, "Don't you dare forget to put us in the credits, Bobby Chandler!"

I laughed, squeezin' back, "Not a chance, troublemaker."

Lila pressed a folded note into my hand, again, her eyes soft but fierce, "Read this on the plane, alright? No peekin' till you're up there."

I tucked it in my pocket, nodding. Eric clasped my hand, his grip firm despite his limp, his voice low, steady, "We'll see ya soon, Hollywood."

I met his eyes, nodding. Thomas said little, his jaw tight, but he hefted my duffel, its canvas worn, and carried it to the gate, just like he had the first day I left for LA years ago, his silence louder than words, his eyes said all I needed to hear.

I boarded the plane, its metal skin cold under my hand, and settled side by side, the seats narrow, upholstery smellin' of old leather and faint cigarette smoke. I clutched my bag with my old 8mm film cans. More of *Echoes'* rough cuts, Mill Town's soul in silver halide, my knuckles white. The engines roared, a guttural hum vibratin' my bones, and the plane taxied down the runway, the tarmac blurrin' past. I pressed my face to the window, the glass cool against my cheek, watchin' Mill Town shrink below, the hardware store's faded sign, Main Street's deserted stretch, the Blackwater River's silver curve glintin' through pines. The crowd waved, specks now, Lila's jacket a blue smudge, Eric's cane a thin line, Dad standin' tall, hand raised. The town grew smaller, swallowed by the clouds and the haze of memory, my chest achin' with Mom's whisper, Dad's silence, Eric's charge, Lila's note burnin' in my pocket.

The plane climbed, clouds partin' like torn cotton, and I leaned back, the rumble of the engines steadyin' my pulse. I nodded, fingers tracin' the film cans, seein' the soda shop's tinsel, Eleanor's tremblin' hands, Eric's watermelon tale, the rabbit on the road, *Echoes'* heart, alive, ready to sing. Lila's note waited, unopened, a promise for the flight, but I knew what it said anyway.

I leaned back, the window's glass cool against my temple, nodding slow, my mind still tethered to Mom's room, her lavender sachet, her whisper, *finish it, Bobby.*

My gaze drifted to the clouds, thick as cotton, my heart stuck on the Blackwater River's shimmer, the church basement's dust, Eleanor's trembling hands folding her quilt. I saw Mom's eyes, fierce despite her pain, Dad carrying my bag to the gate, Eric's "soldier" ringing in my ears.

Hours later, the plane dipped through a layer of orange smog, LA's sprawl unfolding below, endless grids of concrete, neon signs blinking, cars crawling like ants, a world apart from Mill Town's pines and quiet. The landing gear groaned, the tarmac rushing up, and we touched down, the jolt shaking my bones, the film cans safe in my grip. At the gate, I was greeted with LA's brisk objectivity, porters hauling crates, clipboard-wielding assistants barking orders, no warmth, no hugs like the airport crowd back home. The contrast stung: Mill Town's laughter, Lila's fierce embrace, Eric's handshake, Dad's silent strength, all replaced by the city's cold efficiency, the air thick with exhaust and jet fuel, not cider or woodsmoke.

Ryan, his scarf still knotted, nudged me, muttering, "Feels like we left the real world behind, huh?" I nodded, clutching the cans, my eyes scanning the crates, *Mitchell 35mm*, *Nagra Reels*, ensuring every piece of *Echoes* made it safe to Sun Studios. We checked each label, counted every box, the crew's chatter clipped, tired.

Ava, her parka swapped back for a tailored coat, gave the all-clear, "We're good, boys. Let's call it." Her voice was sharp but warm, a flicker of Mill Town's glow in her eyes.

At the pool house Grant nudged me, his voice low, "You know, I've been on loads of location shoots, but never have I experienced anything like that." Grant, restless as a kid on Christmas, flipped pages, his pencil scratching furiously, sketching ideas, his voice cutting through the engine's hum. "Bobby, hear me out, what if we open with that rabbit, sittin' still in the road, all twitchy, eyes glintin' in the dusk? Boom, cut straight to Eric's slingshot story, him laughin' 'bout that watermelon heist, juice drippin' down his chin. Sets the tone, small town, big heart, right off the bat!" His eyes sparked, hands waving, the notebook nearly sliding to the floor.

"Yeah," I said, voice low, "that could hit hard."

Grant didn't pause, his pencil darting again, pages crinkling. "Then we go to the 60's Christmas re-creation, that Main Street shot with the hardware store glowin', tinsel shinin', cars rollin' slow. Crosscut it, his words over the barbershop pole spinnin', the soda shop's fountain fizzin', like the past is talkin' back to him. And then your dad's interview, man, his voice, all gravel and grief, talkin' 'bout losin' the store, your mom's sickness?" He grinned, tapping the page, his enthusiasm a live wire.

"Yeah... I like that," I said, a faint smile tugging my lips, Grant's ideas weaving into *Echoes*' pulse, but my soul still half in Mill Town, hearing their voices, Lila's laugh, Miss Elma's hymns, the saloon's roar.

Grant sensed it, his pencil pausing, his eyes narrowing as he leaned closer, voice softer. "You okay, man?"

I shrugged, glancing out the window, the sky an endless gray, my reflection faint, haunted. "Just... still hearin' their voices, you know?

Mom's whisper, Dad's quiet, Eric's stories, all of 'em." My fingers brushed the film cans, their edges cold.

Grant leaned back, his seat creaking, a knowing nod in his eyes. "Good," he said, voice low, firm. "Means you got it right, Bobby. You caught their soul, not just their faces." His words sunk in like a warm hand on my shoulder, easing the ache.

I nodded, "suppose you're right," the hum of the plane wrapping us, the cans under my seat a promise to Mom, to Mill Town, to finish what we'd started.

Grant snapped his notebook shut, a grin breaking wide, his energy snapping back like a rubber band. "My mom's gonna love this, you know," he said, chuckling, his voice bright. "Ava's tough, but she's a sap for stories like this, Evelyn's redemption, the oak tree dinner, all that heart. She'll probably cry and deny it."

I smiled faintly, picturing mom, her quilt around her shoulders her eyes shining. "So will mine," I said, voice steady.

 "And that means we got it right." Grant laughed, grabbing two soda cans from his bag, their aluminum glinting under the cabin's dim lights.

"To Echoes, then," he said, raising his can, the fizz hissing as he popped the tab. I clinked mine against his, the sound sharp, like champagne flutes in a smoky bar, and we drank, the sweet burn of cola remindin' me that sometimes good things sting a little.

That night, we gathered around the Klein family's dining table, a polished oak slab in their sprawling LA home. Grant smiled and said, "this is the first time we'd all sat together like this.", Grant, Ava, me, Ryan, Jesus, even a few crew hands. The table groaned with takeout, greasy pizza boxes, cartons of lo mein, soda cans scattered like confetti.

Grant looked up, "nothing like that Thanksgiving spread."

But the warmth felt close, the room alive with laughter, the clink of forks, the faint hum of a radio playing low jazz. Candlelight flickered, casting shadows on the walls, the air smelling of soy sauce, melted cheese, and Ava's rosewater perfume.

Grant leaned back, a slice of pepperoni pizza in hand, his voice thoughtful, "You know, we've never had dinner like this, all of us, just sitting, talking. Maybe Mill Town's rubbing off on us, huh?" He grinned, his shaggy hair catching the light.

Ava chuckled, her fork pausing, "Don't get soft on me, kid, but yeah, that oak tree vibe's got some pull."

Ryan raised a soda, smirking, "Yeah, teaching us city folks how to slow down!"

The table laughed, one of the crew chimed in, "Hell, I'm just here for the pizza, but, I know what you mean. That town did somethin' man."

We all caught his newly acquired southern accent, but nobody said anything.

"It ain't just me," I said, voice low, "it's all of 'em, Eric, Lila, Miss Elma, even your mom, Ava, spillin' her truth. They're the story." Ava's eyes softened, a rare crack in her steel, and she nodded, "I think you boys have a bright future, but we'll see how long it takes to shine."

The conversation flowed, stories spilling, Grant retelling Eric's watermelon heist, Ryan mimicking Gable's truck yell at the saloon, I was tellin' stories about sneaking into the Crazy Horse in High School. The candles burned low, wax pooling, the radio's jazz fading to static, but we lingered, plates empty, hearts full. I felt like we were closer somehow.

I stepped into the Sun Studios edit bay, the air thick with the metallic tang of overheated consoles, stale coffee, and the chemical whiff of fresh film reels, the hum of monitors vibrating in my bones. It's January 1973, and LA's smog feels a world away from home's misty fields, but my heart's still there. The bay buzzes, fluorescent lights buzzing overhead, casting a sterile glow on scuffed linoleum, their edges curling where boots have scraped for years. I see the timeline sprawled across the editing software, a quilt of *Echoes'* soul, interviews, B-roll, vintage re-creations flickering on screens. Clips flash: Eleanor's gnarled hands folding her quilt, Eric's grin as he spins his watermelon heist tale, Main Street's tinsel-lit Christmas glow, each frame raw, human, breathing like Mill Town's muddy river.

Grant, his shaggy hair wild, leans over a console, coffee mug steaming, and hollers, "Bobby, check this, your dad's interview cuts like a blade already!" His eyes are shadowed, tired, but his voice crackles with fire.

I nod, my throat tight, and mutter, "Damn, man, it's startin' to live, ain't it?" The monitors' hum wraps me, *Echoes* taking shape, its pulse my town's own.

I lead the way to the screening room, a dim cave of plush seats and soundproof walls, the air cool, heavy with the scent of worn leather and popcorn grease from late-night sessions. Ava, Sun Studios' iron queen and our sponsor, settles into the center seat, her blazer sharp as a blade, bob pulled up tight, her face a locked vault. I stand by the projector, Grant at my side, my fingers trembling as I hit play, the whir filling the silence, my chest tight with Mom's whisper, *make it sing*. The screen flares, and Mill Town breathes: the Christmas festival, kids hanging glitter-dusted ornaments on the square's spruce, as one fights with their gloves sticky with sap, candlelight dancing in their eyes as carols rise, the Nagra catching their giggles like bells. The Fourth of July parade rolls next, flags fluttering, classic cars gleaming, the barbershop pole spinning, Main Street a 1950s dream reborn, the crowd's hum a heartbeat. Mayor Heartwell's bolo tie glints as he spills his regret, voice gravelly, shoulders sagging, the Mitchell framing his pain. Then the slow fade to present day. The AG parkin' lot at Christmas where two cars are fightin' over a parkin spot. Mainstreet's broken windows. Evelyn's redemption cuts deep, her voice cracking over AG's bonuses, tears glinting as she drives off, dust trailing, the saloon's neon fading in her wake. The Crazy Horse roars, locals cheering their own stories, glasses clinking, laughter sharp as shattered glass. Dad's testimony lands like a stone, his work shirt patched, eyes wet as he talks of Mom's fight, the store's loss, Mill Town's soul, his words a quiet storm, the room still but for Ava's steady breath.

Silent shots of Main Street at dusk steal my air, storefronts dark, tinsel gone, a lone streetlamp flickering, the Blackwater River's murmur faint, the Nagra taping the wind's moan. Mom's final words close it, her voice a fragile thread from her quilt-draped bed, "Finish it, Bobby, make it sing," her eyes fierce despite cancer's grip, the screen holding her gaze like a vow. I glance at Ava, her eyes welling, a tear tracing her cheek, catching the projector's glow, her hands clasped, knuckles pale. The screen fades to black, the room silent but for the projector's dying hum.

Ava claps once, sharp, then again, slow, each clap a gavel. She turns, voice thick, "Bobby, it's powerful, honest as hell. I love it, every frame rips you open, shows what's lost, what's left."

She wipes her cheek, smiling rare, warm, "Add music, strings, maybe a lonesome guitar for them dusk shots. Layer voice-overs, let Eric's laugh, your dad's grit, Lila's fire carry it. And Bobby, use that old 8mm you shot, kids under the oak, your mom smilin' by the firepit, splice it in, make it home."

I nod, chest burning, Grant grinning, "Told ya, Ava's a sap for this!"

Ava swats him, laughing, "Keep talkin', kid, you're walkin' home!"

The edit bay turns into a war zone, monitors glowing into the night, the air heavy with pizza grease, smoke, and spilled cola's sticky bite. I hunch over a console, eyes stinging, splicing clips, the timeline a mosaic, Eric's slingshot tale fading into kids skipping, bells jingling; Eleanor's quilt folding into dusk, the river glinting; Dad's voice over the 1960s re-creation, the hardware store buzzing, tinsel sparkling.

Grant paces, scribbling, barking, "Slow that crosscut with your dad, Bobby, let his words sink, then hit 'em with the barbershop pole spinnin', like time's answerin'!"

I grin, fingers flying, muttering, "Got it, you pushy little goat, gimme that guitar track, let's make it bleed."

Even Ryan, sprawled with a beer, chimes in, "That rabbit shot's gotta open, quiet, then bam, Eric's laugh, like the town's alive!"

The room crackles, ideas sparking, the scent of film stock and sweat thick, *Echoes'* soul growing, raw, human, fierce.

Ava's words drive us, music, voice-overs, 8mm. I dig through crates, pulling my old handheld spools, their grainy warmth a hug compared to the Mitchell's polish. I thread a reel, the projector clattering, and there's Mill Town: kids chasing under the oak, coats flapping, laughter bright as lanterns; Mom by the firepit, her smile soft, eyes alive despite her illness, telling Ava stories, flames dancing in her gaze.

"This is it," I say, voice low, Grant nodding, "Splice that after the Christmas scene, let it carry the heart."

We layer a mournful guitar over Main Street's dusk, strings weeping, Eric's voice-over chuckling about the watermelon heist, Lila's drawl reading her note, *Keep us alive, Bobby, in every frame*, its words finally opened, a fire in my gut. The 8mm weaves in, kids' laughter fading into Dad's testimony, Mom's smile bridging the saloon's cheers, the film breathing like the Blackwater, its pulse unbroken. I play reel after reel of my old 8mm films, each one a piece of my memory faded, but not forgotten. I was looking for that one shot I took of us playin' in that old pecan tree with the tire swing and I found at least ten other's that we'll use.

Nights blur, the bay a cocoon of light and sound, pizza boxes teetering, ashtrays brimming, our voices hoarse but alive.

"Push that fade, Bobby!" Grant snaps, jabbing a monitor, "Let Evelyn's tears linger, then hit the Crazy Horse roar, make 'em feel it!"

I laugh, "Chill, man, gimme that track, let's make it ache."

Ryan, flipping a script, cackles, "This'll break hearts, my mom's gonna sob for weeks!"

Ava drops in, her presence a storm, watching a cut, her nod sharp, "Keep that 8mm raw, Bobby, let it be your eyes, like we're there." Her voice is steel, but her eyes soften, Mill Town's pull alive even in LA's haze.

The final cut looms, every clip a piece of home, Main Street's glow, the saloon's laughter, Mom's whisper, Eric's truth. I lean back, eyes red, the monitor's glow carving my face, the scent of film and coffee grounding me.

"We're close," I say, voice rough, "Mom's gonna see this, and it'll sing, like she said."

Grant claps my shoulder, grinning, "Damn right, she'll be proud, so's Ava. This is as real as it gets."

I sat in the Sun Studios screening room, the air heavy with the scent of worn leather seats and the faint tang of popcorn grease, my heart still racing from the rough cut of *Echoes* that just flickered across the screen.

Ava shifts, her posture stiffening, hands folding like a judge about to pass sentence. She leans forward, her gaze locking on me and Grant, serious, her voice low, cutting through the room's hush. "I love it."

Grant gives me a high five, "We can have it complete in a few weeks then!"

"There's one part I can't approve, not for public release," she says, each word deliberate, her eyes steady, unyielding. I freeze, my breath catching, the air suddenly sharp with the chemical whiff of film reels stacked nearby. "Eric's interview," she names it, and my gut twists, picturing Eric's weathered face, his limp, his voice cracking as he spoke of war's scars. "The war's too fresh, too divisive. People'll seize on it, twist it, and miss the rest of *Echoes*, the town, the heart, your mom's fight, Bobby." She pauses, her knuckles paling, her voice softening but firm, "I ain't worried about reviews. I'm worried about the company, about you two, about me. We can't risk it gettin' buried in politics." Her words land like a stone, the room silent but for the faint buzz of fluorescents overhead, the scent of coffee gone cold stinging my nose.

I'm stunned, my mouth dry, unable to speak, Eric's "worth fightin' for…" echoing in my head, his handshake at the airport, his truth a part of what makes the film real, an unpolished truth. Grant stands, his chair creaking, his lanky frame taut, voice calm but hard as iron.

He looked at me, "Mom, Eric gave us somethin' no one else could, not just pain, perspective." He steps closer, his boots scuffing the linoleum, his eyes burning, not defiant but fierce with conviction. "He talked about the cost of war, on soldiers, on families, on both damn sides, Vietnamese and us. Said maybe we wouldn't need to protect anyone if we all stopped hurtin' each other, if we listened. And what you're sayin is we bury it, so nobody has the chance to listen!" His voice cracks, raw, and I see Eric's cane, his grin, his story of dodging bullets and finding mercy in a stranger's eyes. "If we cut that, we cut the soul, the truth, and then I don't know what we're even doing here." Grant says, leaning toward Ava, his hands open, pleading, "We promised that town one thing, we'd tell it all, no sugar, no lies. You taught me that too, Mom, truth over safety." The room holds its breath, the projector's bulb ticking as it cools, the air thick with the weight of his words.

Ava studies her son, her eyes narrowing, then softening, a long beat stretching, the silence heavy with the faint hum of LA traffic outside. She exhales, slow, her shoulders easing, and nods, her voice quiet, warm, "I raised you to think like a strategist, Grant, all angles, know the risks. But damn, I'm glad you learned to feel like a storyteller, to

460

fight for what's real." She turns to me, her gaze steady, a faint smile breaking through, "Keep it, Bobby. Eric's story stays. If there's heat, I'll take it, me and Sun Studios, we've weathered worse." She leans back, her smile sharpening, a glint in her eye, "Maybe it's time people got uncomfortable, felt the sting of what's true."

I let out a breath I didn't know I was holding, my chest loosening, Mom's vow, Eric's courage, Lila's fire safe in *Echoes*. Grant grins, wide, boyish, and mutters,

"Hell yeah, Mom, that's the spirit!" Ava swats his arm, chuckling, "Don't push it, kid, or you're scrubbin' the edit bay floor."

With Ava's blessing, Grant and I head back to the edit bay, the air alive with the electric buzz of monitors, the scent of pizza grease and cigarette smoke curling through the room, the linoleum sticky under my boots. The timeline glows on the screens, a mosaic of Mill Town, Main Street's tinsel, the saloon's laughter, Evelyn's tears, and we dive in, locking Eric's segment into the final cut, his voice a cornerstone, unyielding. I lean over the console, eyes burning, splicing his interview between the Christmas festival and Dad's testimony, his words, "War don't pick winners, just survivors", fading into kids' bells, their joy a counterpoint to his pain. Grant paces, coffee mug in hand, his voice sharp, "Right there, Bobby, let Eric's line about mercy hit, then cut to the rabbit in the road, quiet, like the world's holdin' its breath."

I nod, fingers flying, muttering, "Yeah, man, let's make it ache, make it true." Ryan, sprawled in a chair, beer sweating, pipes up, "Y'all, that's gonna gut folks, my cousin'll bawl, and he's tough as nails!"

The room crackles, our laughter mixing with the click-clack of keyboards, the scent of film stock sharp in my nose, *Echoes*' soul growing fiercer, truer.

I add a voice-over, my own voice, rough, steady, to bridge Eric's words to *Echoes*' heart: "Sometimes the truth don't belong to the loudest voice. It belongs to the one who lived it." I record it, the mic close, my breath catching the Nagra's tape, the words a vow to Eric, to Mom, to Mill Town.

Grant listens, nodding, his voice low, "That's it, Bobby, that's the spine of the damn thing."

I splice it in, Eric's interview flowing into the 8mm of us kids under the pecan tree playin on the swing, the cut to the AG parkin' lot where the tree used to be, but can still be placed, with our laughter bright but fadin', Mom's smile by the firepit fading in, her eyes alive despite cancer's grip. The timeline locks, the cut tight, every frame a piece of home. I lean back, eyes red, the monitor's glow etching my face, the bay's hum wrapping me, the scent of coffee and film grounding me.

The night stretches, pizza boxes piling, our voices hoarse but alive. Grant jabs a monitor, grinning, "Push that fade after Eric's bit, let it linger, then hit the saloon's cheer, make 'em feel the hope!" I laugh, "You got it, pushy, gimme that guitar track, let's make it weep."

Ava pops in, her presence a quiet storm, watching the new cut, her nod sharp, "That interview of your mom, it's gold, like we're sittin' with her." Her eyes soften, the town's pull alive even in LA's haze. I smile, my chest tight, picturing Mom watching this, her quilt around her, her smile fierce, proud. *Echoes* ain't just film, it's raw, honest, human.

Chapter 57 - The Unwanted Call
(April 1973)

I'm hunched over a console in the Sun Studios edit bay, the air thick with the acrid bite of overheated circuits, stale pizza crusts, and the faint chemical whiff of film stock, my eyes burning from the monitor's glow. *Echoes* is so close I can taste it, but it's not done, not yet. The room hums, a chaotic symphony of post-production, timelines scrolling, voices overlapping, the clatter of typewriters like gunfire. I'm reviewing color grading notes, tweaking the dusk shots of Main Street to deepen the sky's bruised purple, while the sound designer, Ellie, adjusts the audio mix, Eric's voice-over, "Sometimes the truth belongs to the one who lived it", weaving into the mournful guitar strings.

Grant, his shaggy hair a mess, argues with a colorist, his voice sharp, "No, man, the soda shop's tinsel needs more sparkle, like it's 1960, not some dull '70s ad!"

Jesus, sprawled in a chair, chimes in, "Yeah, and pump up them kids' bells in the Christmas scene, make it jingle like my tía's tamale party!"

I laugh, scribbling a note, my flannel loose' The film's raw, human, almost there, but the final interview placements, Evelyn's redemption, Dad's testimony, still need cuts to breathe. The studio phone shrills, slicing through the din, and Sarah, our assistant, snatches it, her braid swinging. Her voice is clipped, "Sun Studios, yeah?" then softens, her eyes widening. She bolts from her desk, sneakers squeaking on linoleum, and bursts into the edit bay, her hand grabbing my shoulder, firm, urgent. "Bobby, your dad just called," she says, breathless, her words a punch. "He said you need to come home. Now." My throat tightens, a vise clamping my chest, Mom's pale face flashing, her eyes fierce despite cancer's grip, her whisper, *Finish it, Bobby*. I don't ask why. I know. Her time's slipping, fast, and every second in this bay is a second I'm not with her. I stand, my chair scraping, voice low, "I'll be there." The room quiets, Grant's argument pausing, Ellie's hands freezing on the console, the monitors' hum deafening in the silence, the scent of coffee gone cold stinging my nose.

I swallow, my heart pounding, and look up, meeting the team's eyes, Grant's furrowed brow, Jesus's wide stare, Ellie's parted lips.

"How long 'til the final cut?" I ask, my voice rough, barely mine.

Ellie glances at the timeline, her glasses slipping, and says, "At least another week, Bobby. Maybe more. We're close, sound's tight, color's almost locked, but it isn't quite finished yet." Her voice is soft, apologetic, the weight of it sinking me. A week. Too long. I shake my head, pacing, my boots heavy on the floor, the bay's fluorescent buzz drilling into my skull. Mom's waiting, her quilt fraying, her breath shallow, and I promised her she'd see *Echoes* first, and promised it'd sing.

"I understand, but I can't wait that long," I say, my voice cracking, hands clenched. "I need somethin' now, somethin' I can take with me, for her." My eyes burn, not from the screens but from the ache of her fading, the hardware store's glow, Main Street's dusk, all I've poured into this film for her, for all of us.

Grant steps closer, his lanky frame tense, his eyes searching mine, and I see he gets it, my promise, the ticking clock. "Bobby, we got you," he says, voice low, steady, his hand on my arm grounding me like Dad's quiet strength.

Ava strides in, her blazer sharp, braids tight, drawn by the commotion, her presence a storm breaking the bay's haze. She takes one look at me, my clenched jaw, my shaking hands, and her face softens, her voice firm but warm, "Give him a clean draft, whatever's ready. Now." She meets my eyes, her gaze steady, like she's carrying the weight with me,

"Go, Bobby. Be with her. We'll finish it here, polish every frame 'til it shines. I'll call you a ride to the airport."

I nod, my throat too tight to speak, gratitude flooding me, her words a lifeline, the scent of her rosewater perfume cutting through the bay's grease and smoke.

Jesus is already on the phone with the airline, "Bobby, your plane leaves in one hour!" he yells from across the hall.

The team scrambles, Ellie cans a rough cut to a reel, the timeline flashing, Christmas carols, Eric's war truth, Evelyn's tears, Dad's voice, Mom's final words.

Grant grabs a film can, muttering, "This one's for your mom, Bobby, gonna make her proud." Grant hovers, his voice soft, "We kept Eric's part, like you wanted, and your 8mm of them kids under the oak, you guys on the swing, it's all there, raw, real."

I clutch the can, its metal cold, heavy with Mill Town's soul, my promise to Mom locked inside. I think of her room, the lavender sachet, her frail smile, the way she held my hand, her voice a thread, *Make it sing*. I see Dad at the airport, carrying my bag, his silence louder than words, Lila's note, *Keep us alive*, burning in my pocket, Eric's "soldier" pushing me forward. The bay's chaos fades, the team's voices, Grant's fire, Ellie's focus, Ryan' heart, a chorus carrying me home.

I'm halfway out the door, the can under my arm, when Grant calls, "Bobby, wait!" He jogs over, his boots scuffing, and hands me a tape, "Audio mix, rough but good, your mom's voice, clear as a bell. Show her she's the heart of this." His grin is tired but fierce, and I nod, my voice a whisper, "Thanks, man. For all of it."

Ava's on the phone, barking, "Yeah, I need a car to LAX, stat, if they can't get one here in ten minutes, get the studio chopper, don't keep my boy waitin'!" Her smile flashes, rare, warm, and I feel a lil bit of Mill

Town in her, in all of them, the oak tree's glow, the saloon's roar. The bay's hum lingers as I step into the hall, the air cooler, the scent of LA's smog creeping in, but my mind's on Mom's bed, her quilt, her eyes waiting for *Echoes*. I'm going home, to hold her hand, to let her see what she gave me, a story, a town, a truth that sings, raw and human, like she always knew it would.

The ride to LAX is a blur, the city's neon smearing past, the driver's radio crackling low jazz, my fingers tracing the film can's edges, its weight anchoring me. I think of the rough cut, kids' bells, Main Street's dusk, Eric's war scars, Evelyn's drive away, Dad's patched shirt, Mom's fierce gaze. I see the church basement, the Crazy Horse's neon, Lila's sketchpad, Eric's cane, the river's shimmer. My throat burns, I just want to be home, to keep my promise. I promised her she'd see it first, and now, with the reel in my hands, I'm racing time to keep that vow. The airport looms ahead. The car slows. I step out, the jet fuel's bite sharp in my nose. My shoes heavy but sure. I'm carrying *Echoes*, carrying home, carrying Mom's story.

I clutch the film can tight as the plane lurches into the sky, its engines roaring, the vibration rattling my bones. The cabin smells of old leather and jet fuel, the air sharp, my flannel loose but not warm enough against the chill seeping through the window. The can's metal is cold, fragile as glass in my hands, but it's more than a reel, it's *Echoes*, Mill Town's soul, everything we tried to hold onto, now rushing home before it's too late. I press my forehead to the glass, the clouds below a torn quilt, my throat tight with Mom's whisper, *Finish it, Bobby, make it sing*. Her pale face, her fierce eyes, her quilt-draped shoulders haunt me, her time slipping like sand, and this rough cut, raw and human, is my promise to her, to let her see it first. The plane hums, my heart pounding. I'm racing time, carrying *Echoes* back where it's from, back home.

Mid-flight, back in LA, Grant slips into a quiet hallway at Sun Studios, the edit bay's buzz fading behind him, the air cooler, smelling of linoleum wax and distant smog. His shaggy hair falls loose, his boots scuffing as he dials a number on the rotary phone, its ring sharp in the silence. "Mr. Tolley? Remember me, It's Grant Klein, from *Sun Studios*" he says, voice low, urgent, his breath catching. "I need a favor, somethin' important, and fast."

Grant exhales, a faint grin breaking, "Thank you, Mr. Tolley. You're savin' us." He hangs up, the hallway's quiet wrapping him, his heart heavy with my pain, Mill Town's pull stronger than LA's neon.

In Mill Town, Mr. Tolley springs to action, he calls in a favor from the High School theater department, "You remember when I looked the other way when I caught you with Miss Lewis? Well, now I need ya to do me a favor too, but it's not for me."

He understands, and moves fast, dusting off their reel-to-digital hybrid, a beast of a machine used for special screenings, its casing scratched but reliable, glinting on a cart ready for him to pickup. "This'll do her proud," he mutters, wiping it with a rag, his voice soft, thinking of Ruth's smile, her pies at church suppers, the town's heart she carried. He packs extra cables, their rubber coils heavy, and a portable screen, its frame folding with a satisfying click, all stuffed into his beat-up pickup, its bed rattling with tools. The sky's bruising purple as he drives, the Blackwater River glinting, the scent of pine and frost sharp through his open window, his mission clear, Ruth will see *Echoes*, no matter what.

As the sun rises, painting Mill Town's fields in gold, Mr. Tolley pulls up to the farmhouse, the porch creaking under his boots, the air crisp with dew and the faint lavender from Mom's garden. He knocks softly, the door's wood worn, and Dad answers, bleary-eyed, his work shirt unbuttoned, his face etched with sleepless worry. "Mr. Tolley," he says, voice rough, grateful, stepping aside. Tolley nods, his cap tipped, and says gently, "Bobby's bringin' the movie, Thomas. We're gonna make sure Ruth sees it, you hear?" Dad's eyes glisten, his jaw tight, and he nods, "Thank you, Walt. Means the world." They share a look, two men carrying Mill Town's weight, the scent of coffee brewing inside

467

mixing with the morning's chill, their hands shaking as they grip each other's shoulders, a silent vow to hold Ruth close.

Inside, they move to Mom's room, the air warm, heavy with lavender and the medicinal tang of her pills, her quilt, blues and yellows, stitched with love, draped over her frail frame. Mr. Tolley and Dad rearrange the furniture, their boots soft on the hardwood, the dresser's edge catching a cable as they slide it aside. They set up the portable screen at the foot of her bed, its white surface taut, cables snaking neatly behind, taped down to keep the floor clear. The projector hums as Tolley tests it, its bulb casting a soft glow, the reel slot waiting for *Echoes*. Mom stirs, her eyes fluttering open, a faint smile breaking as she sees Tolley, his cap in hand, his grin wide.

"Mr. Tolley," she whispers, voice a fragile thread, "is the marquee still broken down at the theater?" Her tease is weak but sharp, her spirit unbowed, as she leaned forward to gently put her hand on his arm.

Tolley chuckles, his voice warm, "For you, Ruth, I'd climb up and light it myself, every damn bulb."

She laughs, soft, her hand reaching for Dad's, the room suddenly warm again.

I'm still hours away, gripping the film can of *Echoes* on a plane, racing time to keep my promise to Mom, but Matt is closer, his beat-up Ford Falcon rattling down the road from Tallahassee, the engine's growl a steady pulse after a sleepless drive.

He got the call from Dad last night, dad's voice low, cracked, over a crackling dorm phone: "Matt, it's your mom. She ain't doin' well. Come home, son."

Matt didn't ask questions, just threw a duffel in the backseat, his textbooks forgotten, the weight of Mom's cancer a stone in his chest. The drive's a blur, headlights cutting through fog, the radio's static humming low, the smell of stale coffee and leather seats grounding him. His hair's longer now, curling past his ears, his denim jacket frayed, but his eyes, like mine, carry Mom's fire, Dad's grit, and he's drivin as fast as he can to make it to her side, to see her smile before it's too late.

Matt pulls into the gravel drive, the tires crunching, the house looming quiet, its porch sagging under years of rain and love. The sky's bruising pink, the Creek glinting beyond the fields, its muddy tang mixing with the lavender from Mom's garden. He kills the engine, grabs his duffel, and steps out, his boots heavy, the cold biting his knuckles as he slings the bag over his shoulder. There's an unfamiliar truck in the drive. The front door creaks open before he knocks, Dad's there, bleary-eyed, his work shirt unbuttoned, his face carved with worry but softening at Matt's lanky frame. "You made it," Dad says, voice rough, pulling him into a hug, their arms tight, the scent of Dad's aftershave, Old Spice, sharp and familiar, mixing with the house's warm coffee haze. "She's holdin' on, Mr. Tolley is in there with her settin' up a projector" Dad adds, stepping back, his hand lingering on Matt's shoulder, "Bobby's comin' too, with the movie." Matt nods, throat tight, picturing Mom's quilt, her frail smile.

They step inside, the hardwood creaking, the air thick with lavender and the medicinal tang of antiseptic, her room a glow of sunrise spilling through lace curtains. Mr. Tolley's there, wiry and focused, his overalls dusted with sawdust, setting up the projector at the foot of Mom's bed, its hum a soft hymn. The portable screen stands taut, cables snaking behind the dresser, taped down neat, the room a sanctuary for Mom's wish, to see *Echoes*. The projector is set up, scratched but trusty, glints under a lamp, its bulb casting a warm glow, ready for the reel I'm bringing. Matt pauses in the doorway, his duffel slipping to the floor, heart lurching at Mom, propped on pillows, her quilt, blues and yellows, her stitches, draped over her, her face pale but her eyes sparking as she sees him.

"Matt, my college boy," she whispers, voice a fragile thread, a smile breaking, "you drove all night, didn't you?"

He crosses the room, kneeling by her bed, taking her hand, cool and delicate, and grins, voice thick, "Of course, Mom, couldn't let you have all the fun without me." She laughs, soft, her grip tightening, the room alive with her love.

Tolley looks up, his cap in hand, his grin wide as he adjusts a cable, the projector's click steady. "Matt, good timin'," he says, voice gravelly, warm, we're settin' up the big show right here."

Matt nods, his eyes flicking to the screen, picturing *Echoes*, imagining what I've put together. "You're a lifesaver, Mr. Tolley," he says, voice low, "she's gotta see this."

Tolley chuckles, wiping his hands on a rag, "For Ruth, I'd drag the whole damn theater over."

"That marquee's still busted, but this'll light up." Mom teases, her voice faint but sharp, "You better fix that marquee, Walt, or I'll haunt you."

They laugh, the sound bright, cutting the room's weight, Dad's eyes glistening as he leans against the dresser, watching his family hold tight.

Matt stands, his denim jacket creaking, and helps Tolley with the final setup, moving a chair to clear the projector's path, the wood scraping soft. "This thing ready for Bobby's reel?" he asks, tapping the projector, its metal cool under his fingers.

Tolley nods, "She's got lots of life left in her, she's solid, son. Ruth'll get her show, clear as day."

Matt glances at Mom, her smile unwavering, and feels the ache of her fading. He thinks of Tallahassee, late-night study sessions, but here, now, it's Mom's laugh, Dad's quiet strength, the town's heart in *Echoes*.

"Bobby's gonna make it, right?" he asks Dad, voice low, his hands shoving into his pockets, the denim rough.

Dad nods, his jaw tight, "He's on a plane, Matt. He'll be here." He looks at his watch, "speakin' of which, I better get to the airport to pick him up, can you stay with your mom?"

"My pleasure. Leave it to Bobby to steal the show," Matt says with a smile. Mom laughs.

I'm still airborne, the plane's rumble steady, the film can clutched like a lifeline, my mind flashing to Mom's room, her quilt, her fierce eyes. I don't know Matt's there yet, kneeling by her, or that Tolley's setting up, but I feel them, their love pulling me home. The clouds outside are endless, the cabin's leather scent grounding me, my heart pounding. Matt, in Mom's room, feels it too, his chest tight as he watches Tolley test the projector, a test reel flickering, shadows dancing on the screen.

"Looks good, Walt," he says, voice steady, but his eyes are on Mom, her hand in Dad's, her smile a beacon. He thinks of our childhood, running through fields, Mom's pies, Dad's stories, and now *Echoes*, our town's soul, her legacy, ready to shine.

The room settles, the sunrise gilding the quilt, the projector's hum a quiet pulse, the screen waiting for me, for *Echoes*. Matt sits by Mom, his hand on hers, Dad nearby, Tolley stepping back, his cap clutched, muttering, "This is for you, Ruth, all of it."

Mom's eyes gleam, her voice soft, "My boys, my town... it's gonna be beautiful, ain't it?"

Matt grins, teasing, "Just like ole time's, Mom, Bobby's bringin' the fireworks, just you wait."

She laughs, the sound a spark, the room a cocoon of love, hope, Mill Town's heart. They wait, the projector ready, my reel a gift, a vow, a song for Mom, for us, one moment, one tear at a time.

I'm still in the air watchin' the sun rise above the horizon, the plane's rumble steady, my fingers tracing the film can's edges, the clouds outside endless, my mind flashing to the edit bay, Grant's grin, Ava's nod, Ryan' "This one's for your mom." The whole crew pulled together to make this possible. I looked out the window, and could see the Gulf. Then I felt it, the plane dips, the seatbelt sign dinging, and I grip the can tighter, my heart racing, the scent of leather and fuel grounding me, Mom's smile waiting, *Echoes* ready to shine, one frame, one heartbeat at a time. I just hope I'm not too late.

Chapter 58 - Together Again
(April 1973)

The plane touches down in Pensacola under a heavy gray sky, the clouds low and bruised, pressing against the earth like a shroud. It's February 1973, and the air carries the damp chill of rain not yet fallen, the scent of jet fuel sharp in my nose as I step into the terminal, clutching the film can of *Echoes*, its metal cold, a fragile lifeline. The terminal's nearly empty, fluorescent lights buzzing faintly, casting stark shadows on scuffed linoleum, the only sound a distant janitor's mop sloshing in a bucket. No fanfare, no greetings, just the hollow squeak of my sneakers as I walk, my flannel loose. I spot Dad near the stairs, standing alone, hands shoved deep in his pockets, his face unreadable, carved like weathered oak. I wonder if I'm too late and the look on his face doesn't give me the confirmation I was lookin' for. I approach, my throat tight, and he nods, a silent acknowledgment, then pulls me into a hug, his arms strong but trembling, the scent of Old Spice that always takes me back to when I was a kid. He reaches for my bag with the film in it.

His voice is low, barely a murmur, as we head to the truck, "She's not doin' well, son. Just… don't be shocked." The words land like stones, the air between us heavy, the gray sky pressing harder.

We drive in silence, the old Ford's tires humming on wet pavement, no radio, no words, just the rhythmic thump of wipers clearing mist, the cab smelling of worn leather and Dad's coffee thermos, its metallic tang lingering. My mind churns, worry echoing, Mom's frail smile, her quilt, the reel I'm carrying for her. I stare out the window, the pines blurring, their needles glistening with damp, Mill Town drawing closer, its river's muddy scent faint in memory. We pass by Mainstreet, still painted and shined from the production. I gave half a smile when I saw there were a few people walkin' holdin hands. Dad's hands grip the wheel, knuckles pale, his silence louder than any speech, and I feel it too, the weight of what's coming, the fear of seeing her, the hope *Echoes* might light her eyes one last time.

Dad quietly said, "Mr. Tolley came over early this mornin' and set up the projector for ya."

I nodded and smiled, "Grant" I thought to myself.

The truck rumbles into the drive, gravel crunching. I see a familiar car in the drive, Matt's falcon, and I'm out before dad stops, my boots hitting the ground, the film can under my arm, the porch creaking as I push through the door, the house's warmth wrapping me, heavy with coffee and lavender, but undercut by the medicinal tang of Mom's illness.

I step into her room, my breath catching, the air thick with the soft scent of her lavender sachet and the sterile bite of anticeptic on her bedside table. She's in her bed by the window, sunken, pale, frail, her skin almost translucent with a greenish tint, veins tracing fragile paths under her cheeks, her once-fierce eyes half-closed, shadowed. The quilt, blues and yellows, her stitches, drapes her like a fading banner, its edges frayed, and I feel a gut punch of grief, her body failing her, betraying the fire I know still burns inside. I mask it, swallowing the ache, forcing my face steady, and kneel by her bed, my voice gentle, "Hey, Mom." I force a smile, my lips trembling.

She reaches for my hand, her fingers cool, delicate as moth wings, her grip weak but sure. "Bobby," she whispers, voice a fragile thread, her smile faint but real, "you brought it, didn't you?"

I look at her, "Brought what?"

Mom gave a half smile, "Of course I brought it, a promise is a promise."

She tries to laugh, but only half comes out.

I nod, my throat burning, the film can beside me, *Echoes*' weight her gift, her story.

The room's darkened, curtains drawn, the only light a warm glow from Mr. Tolley's makeshift screen at the bed's foot, its surface taut, catching the soft whir of the projector, a reel to reel sitting like a quiet prayer. The setup's beautiful.

I start winding the film, "Are you ready for this? Now, it ain't finished yet, but it's close enough."

I hope I'm doing this right. I click the play button, the leader starts feedin', clean picture, steady sound, a sacred hush settling over the space, the cables taped neatly behind the dresser, their rubber scent faint. Tolley's work is flawless, the screen ready to hold *Echoes*, to make Mom's wish sing, the projector's bulb casting a golden halo, its hum blending with the creak of floorboards under Dad's boots. Dad and Matt sit nearby in wooden chairs, their faces etched, Dad's jaw tight, his eyes glistening, the scent of his aftershave sharp. Matt's gaze fixed on Mom, worry carving his young face. I kneel beside her, holding her hand, my calluses rough against her skin.

My chest aches, not just for her fading, but for what she gave me, a town, a story, a fire to tell it true. I glance at Dad, his hands clasped, his silence a prayer, and Matt, his eyes wet, his breath shallow, both holding her as I do, our family a circle, unbroken despite the shadow. The projector's whir is steady, the screen waiting, the air thick with lavender, coffee, the faint rustle of Mom's quilt as she shifts, her eyes on me, trusting, fierce. "Well, show me, Bobby, can't wait forever." she smiles and whispers, and I nod, my voice gone, my hand squeezing hers, the reel a gift, a light, a song for her, for us, one frame, one tear at a time.

I kneel beside Mom, her hand cool and fragile in mine. Dad sits in a wooden chair, his eyes fixed on Mom. My throat burns, *Echoes* a vow I'm keeping for her, one frame, one heartbeat at a time.

The opening image piercing the dark, a rabbit, small and gray, nibbling grass sprouting through cracked asphalt, its ears twitching, caught in the dawn's amber glow, the soft rustle of wind as the camera zooms out showin' Mainstreet abandoned. The room stills, the air thick, Mom's eyes widening, her breath catching as the scene shifts to river mist curling over the Blackwater, its muddy scent alive in memory, swirling around pines. Faces fade in, Eleanor's gnarled hands folding her quilt, the scene fades to Christmas on Mainstreet in 1950, fading to the interviews, and voice overs, some over my old 8mm film, Eric's grin as he spins his watermelon heist tale, Miss Lorraine's scarf slipping as she laughs in the Crazy Horse, neighbors, their voices raw, filling the room like a choir. The stories unfold: Main Street's tinsel-lit Christmas, kids' bells jingling, the Fourth of July parade's flags fluttering, the hardware store's sign buzzing, a 1960s dream reborn. Mom's transported, her eyes bright despite her frailty, tears welling, catching the screen's glow.

She laughed watchin Sherriff Johnson makin' the boys plow Abernathy's field, "I remember that, it was hotter than the dickens that day."

Her voice a whisper, "That's Eleanor… and George. I can hear George again, his laugh," even though it was George's son in the film. Her words tremble, the scent of her quilt's cotton mingling with the room's warmth, Dad's hand clenching, Matt's eyes glistening, the film weaving Mill Town's soul, her soul, back to life.

The screen shifts to a dusk shot, Main Street's storefronts dark, a lone streetlamp flickering, and my voice narrates, rough, steady, "Sometimes the truth belongs to the ones who lived it, and hope belongs to those who refuse to forget it." Mom's hand tightens, reaching for me, her fingers trembling, and she whispers, "That's you, baby. You did it." Her voice cracks, tears spilling, soft sobs shaking her frail frame, overwhelmed, her town, her people, her heart. "It's beautiful, Bobby," she says, her words thick, "you made somethin' real…you showed us what you see, you made us feel what you feel." Her tears trace her cheeks, glinting like dew, her hand squeezing mine, a pulse of her old strength, the projector's hum steady, the screen's light bathing her, Dad, Matt, me, in a sacred glow.

The projector's glow bathes Mom's room, the screen flickering with Dad's interview, his work shirt patched, eyes heavy as he speaks of losing the hardware store, Mom's illness, Mill Town's heart. His voice, gravelly and raw, fills the air, thick with lavender and the faint tang of pills. Mom's hand trembles in mine, her quilt slipping, tears tracing her translucent cheeks. "That's my Tom," she whispers, a faint smile breaking, voice fragile but proud, "always carryin' us." I squeeze her hand, my throat tight, Dad's truth in Echoes echoing her love, the room hushed, sacred.

Her interview comes, her face onscreen, quilt-draped, her voice a thread but fierce, "Finish it, Bobby, make it sing," her eyes burning with love, with fight, preserved forever. She closes her eyes, tears slipping free, and laughs, soft, through the ache, "I still talk too much, don't I?" Her chuckle is fragile, a spark.

I lean close, my whisper fierce, "Every word counts, Mom. Every one." My voice breaks, my hand holding hers, the quilt's texture rough under my fingers, Dad's chair creaking as he shifts, Matt's breath hitching, the room a cocoon of her light, her legacy.

The projector whirs, the screen showing Eric's war truth. Evelyn's tears, the saloon's roar, but Mom's words linger, her laugh, her tears, *Echoes* a lasting gift. A mirror to her soul, shining for her, for us.

The final scene of Echoes fades in on the screen in Mom's darkened room. It's Thanksgiving under the old oak tree in our front yard, its gnarled branches sprawling wide, leaves a fiery mix of amber and crimson illuminated by hangin' lights, rustling in a crisp breeze that carries the smoky warmth of a firepit and the rich aroma of Mom's cornbread dressing, still steaming on the table. The camera pans across the scene, capturing Mill Town's heart through the community, kids chasing each other through the grass, their wool coats flapping, laughter bright as the tin bells they jingle, little Sarah tripping over a root and giggling as Eric, limping but grinning, scoops her up. Neighbors crowd around plank tables draped in checkered cloths, their plates piled with turkey, gravy pooling, green beans flecked with bacon, and pecan pie slices glistening with syrup. Lila, her denim jacket loose, sketches the scene on a napkin, the camera zooms in over her shoulder. It's a drawing of all of us at the table laughing in incredible detail. The camera zooms out and up, her dark hair catching the sunlight, while Miss Lorraine, her floral scarf slipping, passes a pitcher of sweet tea, its ice clinking. Dad stands at the table's head, his button down shirt, his voice steady as he offers a prayer, "...every laugh, every tear, every moment we got together under this oak, we're truly thankful, 'cause each one's a gift." His words, raw and reverent, hush the crowd, the Nagra taping the wind's soft moan, the fire's crackle, Mom's frail hand squeezing mine onscreen, her quilt-draped shoulders proud despite her illness. The camera lingers, the oak's shadow stretching long, then the screen fades to black, a quiet exhale, the projector's glow dimming. The final credit rolls, white text stark on black: This film is dedicated to Matt, Ruth and Thomas Chandler, my biggest fans. I kneel by Mom's bed, her hand cool in mine, tears tracing her translucent cheeks, Dad's eyes glistening, Matt's breath hitching, the room a sanctuary, Echoes' truth an eternal gift, one frame, one love at a time.

Mom exhales deeply, a sound like wind through pines, her eyes bright despite the pain, turning to me, their fire unbroken. "You told our story, Bobby," she whispers, voice a fragile thread, "you told it with love." Her frail hand brushes a tear from my cheek, her skin cool, trembling, her smile radiant, piercing my grief.

The room shifts, heavy, sacred, the projector's bulb dimming, the screen dark. Matt moves from the chair to the couch's edge, his boots scuffing the hardwood, his eyes wet, exhaustion etched deep. I stand, and we hug, no words, just the tight grip of brothers, his jacket's denim rough, his breath hitching, the scent of coffee and road dust clinging to him. We hold on, Mom's smile, Dad's silence binding us, the air warm, thick with her love, the faint creak of the house settling around us. Mom stirs, trying to sit up, her quilt slipping, but her face twists, and she vomits, sudden, uncontrollable, the acrid tang sharp, staining the quilt. I lunge for a basin, Matt grabbing a cloth, Dad's chair scraping as he stands, his voice low, urgent, "Ruth, hold on, darlin'." He grabs the phone, dialing, his knuckles pale, "It's Thomas Chandler, she's bad, real bad." The hospital's voice crackles, calm, "Bring her in, Mr. Chandler, now." Dad nods, his jaw tight, hanging up, the room spinning, the lavender fading under the sickness's bite, our family teetering on the edge.

We move fast, Dad lifting Mom, her frame light as a child, her quilt draped over her, Matt grabbing her pills. I held the door, feelin' helpless, like that was all I could do, hold a door. The truck's cab is cold, leather seats cracking, the engine's rumble loud as we drive, no words, just the hum of tires on asphalt, the faint scent of pine through the window, Mill Town's fields blurring past, the river's muddy tang a ghost in my nose. We arrive at the hospital, the ER's fluorescent glare stings, the air sharp with antiseptic and bleach, the linoleum slick under my boots. We're led to a room, Mom in a bed, IV lines snaking, her face pale, eyes half-closed, the quilt replaced by a thin hospital sheet, its starch stiff. We gather, Dad by her side, his hand on hers, Matt leaning against the wall, his jacket off, me standing close, my hands empty but heavy. The room's quiet, machines beeping soft echoing off the bare walls, the air cold, clinical, stripping away the lavender, the warmth of home.

Her oncology doctor enters, his white coat crisp, eyes heavy with years of delivering truths no one wants. "We'll do our best to make her comfortable," he says, voice low, steady, his clipboard clutched like a shield. "She's strong, but…" He trails off, the unspoken hanging, and we nod, slow, no one saying what we know, her time's near, cancer's grip too tight. Dad's shoulders slump, his Old Spice faint, his voice a whisper, "Thank you, Doc." Matt's eyes glisten, his jaw clenched, and I feel it too, the weight of her fading. The room holds us, the beeps a slow rhythm, the sheet's rustle as Mom breathes, her hand in Dad's, our family a circle, silent, loving, breaking, one breath, one tear at a time.

I sit by Mom's bed, her hand frail in mine, her face pale, almost translucent, but her eyes still flickering with the fire that shaped *Echoes*. Outside, Lila, her denim jacket frayed, moves through Mill Town's quiet streets, the scent of pine and river mud heavy in the dawn's mist. She spreads the news soft, voice low, to neighbors, shopkeepers, church folk, Ruth's fading, time's short. By morning, the hospital room transforms, flooded with flowers: vibrant roses from Miss Lorraine, daisies from the church choir, wildflowers from Eric, carnations from Gable's Mercantile, their petals crowding the walls, the windowsill, the foot of Mom's bed, their sweet, earthy perfume battling the antiseptic's bite. Bouquets spill over, a riot of color, reds, yellows, whites, vases and mason jars teetering, a testament to Mom's reach, her love woven into Mill Town's heart. Mom chuckles, weak, her voice raspy, "Good thing I ain't allergic to pollen." Her smile, faint but sharp, pierces the room's weight.

The flowers' glow holds us, but Mom's breath grows shallower, her eyes dimming, and she calls us close, Dad, Matt, me, to her bedside, the sheet rustling. She takes Dad's hand first, his calluses rough, pulling him into a soft hug, her arms trembling, "Thomas, my rock," she whispers, voice a fragile thread, her cheek against his, his aftershave sharp. She reaches for Matt, his eyes wet, and hugs him, "My dreamer, keep chasin'." Then me, her fingers cool, squeezing, her hug a fleeting warmth, "Bobby, my storyteller, you made it sing." Her voice breaks, tears tracing her cheeks, "You all made me proud. The loves of my life. Y'all watch out for each other." We nod, throats tight, Dad's jaw clenched, Matt's breath hitching, my chest caving, her words a vow, the room a sanctuary, the flowers' scent wrapping us, her love eternal.

Mom closes her eyes, wincing, pain twisting her face, and I lean close, holding her hand, its delicate weight grounding me, the sheet's starch faint under my fingers. "It's okay, Mom," I whisper, my voice cracking, "you've fought so hard. You don't have to fight anymore."

My tears fall, hot, and I add, soft, "We'll see you again soon. You can rest now." Her lips curve, a faint smile, her breath easing, the pain softening, *Echoes'* dedication, *to Ruth and Thomas Chandler*, alive in her, in us. The room quiets, just the monitor's slow beep and the distant hum of hallway life, nurses' shoes squeaking, a cart's wheels rolling, mixing with the flowers' perfume, the air heavy, sacred. Dad stands by her, his hand in hers, Matt wipes tears, his sleeve rough, and I hold on.

Mom lets out a final breath, slow, soft, almost a sigh, like wind through the oak tree's leaves, and the monitor flattens, its beep a piercing line, cutting the hush. No one moves. The flowers' colors blur, their sweetness choking, the antiseptic sharp again. Dad lowers his head, his shoulders shaking, Old Spice fading under grief's weight. Matt wipes his face, tears streaking, his breath ragged, his eyes on Mom, her peace a fragile gift. I hold her hand a moment longer, its coolness sinking in, my chest hollow, *Echoes'* final frame, Main Street's sunset, her story, playing in my mind, her smile, her love, her song preserved, living on in us. The room holds us, the monitor silent, the hallway's hum distant, Mill Town's heart in every bloom, every tear, one breath, one goodbye at a time.

Chapter 59 - A Town in Mourning
(April 1973)

The morning air hangs still and gray over Mill Town, heavy with the scent of damp earth and budding dogwoods, as church bells toll softly, their mournful notes drifting through the pines. I wake early in my childhood bedroom unchanged, the wallpaper's faded stripes a ghost of Mom's touch, the air carrying a faint trace of her lavender sachet, now mingling with the must of grief. I button a crisp white shirt, one mom ironed for my high school graduation, its collar stiff, the fabric cool against my skin, each button a quiet ritual, my fingers trembling. Downstairs, Dad stands at the kitchen counter, his flannel shirt swapped for a black suit his tea-like coffee untouched, steam curling in the dim light, the bitter aroma sharp against the silence. His face is carved, unreadable, his hands gripping the counter, knuckles pale, the creak of the floor under his boots the only sound. Matt, still home from Tallahassee, moves outside with the pastor, his denim jacket traded for a dark blazer, his hair tamed, eyes shadowed as he organizes seating under the oak tree, its branches bare, whispering in the breeze. "Didn't expect this many," he mutters, voice low, the pastor nodding, "Ruth touched more lives than we knew." The air feels fragile, the bells' echo a heartbeat, Mom's absence a wound in every silent breath.

By 10 a.m., we hadn't even gotten to the church yet and the cars lined the old country road, their tires crunching gravel, stretching past the river's bend, rusted pickups from Mill Town, sleek sedans with out-of-state plates, dusty vans from neighboring counties, their chrome glinting dully under the overcast sky. The crowd gathers, a solemn tide. The film crew from LA was there, Grant in a borrowed suit, Ryan with his scarf traded for a tie, Ava's blazer sharp, mixing with local business owners like Gable in a worn jacket, childhood friends like Tommy

Carter, his boots polished, my aunt Debbie and distant cousins from Mobile, their faces familiar but aged. They arrive dressed in black and Sunday clothes, dresses rustling, shoes scuffing, the air thick with the scent of starched cotton and faint perfume, voices hushed, hands clasping. Lila stands at the entrance, wiping tears, her denim swapped for a simple black dress, a clipboard in one hand, a crumpled tissue in the other, her dark hair loose, eyes red but steady. "Y'all find a seat, plenty of room," she says, voice gentle, grounded, her drawl a balm as she greets each guest, hugging Miss Lorraine, nodding to Eric, her grief a quiet fire, the tissue damp, the clipboard trembling, Mill Town's heart in her care.

Inside the chapel, the pews brim, worn oak creaking under the weight of mourners, the air warm with body heat and the sweet, heavy perfume of flower arrangements spilling over every ledge and windowsill, roses, lilies, wildflowers, their petals vibrant against the gray light filtering through stained glass. The scent of wax from flickering candles mingles with polished wood and old hymnals, the pages' musty tang a reminder of Mom's choir days. I sit in the front pew, clutching the folded program in my coat pocket, its paper soft, Mom's name in simple print, her story now eternal. My throat burns, the program's edge biting my palm, Dad's beside me, his suit stiff, Matt on my other side, his blazer tight, our shoulders touching, a silent anchor. The pastor steps to the pulpit, his robes rustling, his face lined with shared loss, and opens Mom's worn Bible, its pages marked by her hand. "From Proverbs 31," he says, voice steady, solemn, "'She opens her mouth with wisdom, and the teaching of kindness is on her tongue.'" The words, ones Mom underlined, fill the chapel, her voice echoing in them, her lessons, love, fight, truth, woven into every mourner, every bloom, every tear.

I think of *Echoes*, its final frame, Thanksgiving under the oak, Mom's smile, Dad's prayer, the town's laughter, now a light she saw, a song she heard. My chest aches, the chapel's hush wrapping me, the candlelight flickering, the flowers' sweetness choking. Dad's hand rests on his knee, trembling, Matt's breath hitches, Lila's clipboard lies forgotten outside, and I feel Mom's fire, her quilt's stitches, her whisper, *Make it sing*. The service begins, but she's here, in the bells' toll, the community's love.

The pastor opens the floor for remembrance, and the mood shifts, the solemn weight lifting like mist burning off the Blackwater River. Laughter ripples, soft at first, then bold, as Lila steps forward, her black dress swaying, a tissue crumpled in her hand, her drawl bright despite red-rimmed eyes. "Y'all remember Ruth's biscuits?" she says, grinning, "Burned a whole pan black as coal, swore it was the oven's fault, said it was 'bein' Democrat' and votin' against her!" The chapel erupts, chuckles bouncing off the rafters, Dad's lips twitching, Matt snorting beside me, Mom's mischief alive in the room, the air lighter, her love sparking joy.

Aunt Debbie, her floral shawl slipping, stands next, her voice warm, teasing, "When Ruth was a girl, we sat front row in church, like always, listenin' to Father John's sermon. Middle of the quiet part, Ruth, barely ten, jumps up, swings her rosary like a lasso, yellin', 'Hold on, Jesus, you're goin' for a ride!'" The crowd roars, Miss Lorraine's hoot piercing, even Grant from LA wiping a tear, laughing, the memory painting Mom young, fearless, the chapel's oak beams echoing her spirit. A local farmer, his overalls swapped for a stiff suit, rises, voice gruff, "Ruth sewed up my hen's wing with dental floss once, just to stop the kids from cryin'. Kept that bird alive 'til spring." Nods ripple, smiles spreading, the air sweet with flowers and memory. Tommy Carter, my old friend, stands, his tie crooked, "Ruth taught me to change a tire when I was sixteen, then sent me home with two jars of peach preserves and a lecture, 'Call your mom, Tommy, or I'll tan you myself!'" Laughter swells again, the pews creaking, Mom's kindness a thread weaving us, her lessons in every tale, the candlelight dancing, her fire undimmed.

An older woman in the back, her hat trembling, stands, voice quivering, "Seems like the only time we all get together these days is for funerals." The chapel falls silent, heads bow, the truth stinging, the flowers' sweetness choking, the air heavy again, my throat tight, Dad's hand clenching, Matt's breath still. Then Miss Elma, her scarf knotted tight, adds gently, "But Ruth would've found a way to make even this feel like a potluck, with her cornbread and a song." Soft chuckles break the hush, nods spreading, the air easing, Mom's oak tree Thanksgivings alive in our minds, her love pulling us close, even now.

The pastor signals, and the projector whirs, its bulb flaring, casting Ruth's segment from *Echoes* onto a screen above the pulpit, the chapel's hush sacred, the air warm with body heat and grief. Her face fills the frame, quilt-draped, eyes fierce despite cancer's grip, her voice a steady thread, "Small don't mean weak. It means close." The words land, raw, true, echoing her fight, her town, her heart, the Nagra's tape catching her breath's cadence, the river's murmur in her tone. Tears roll freely, Dad's shoulders shaking, Matt wiping his face, Lila clutching her tissue, even the LA crew, Grant, Ryan, Jesus, Ava, weeping quietly, strangers once, now bound to our town, *Echoes*' truth their own. My chest aches, the program in my pocket crumpled.

The service ends, and the police block intersections for nearly two miles, a solemn procession, cars with headlights on crawling through Mill Town, their tires humming on asphalt, the air thick with exhaust and the faint scent of rain. I ride with Dad and Matt, the truck's cab quiet, leather seats cracking, the coffee thermos's tang sharp. At an intersection, I glance right, spotting a motorist, his face twisted, honking, impatient, and I shake my head, his hurry, a stranger to Mom's world, her potlucks, her love. At the cemetery, under an oak older than the town, its roots sprawling, leaves rustling, Mom's laid to rest beside her parents, the earth soft, the air heavy with clay and grass. I kneel, my shoes sinking, and place a single strip of film reel in her casket, its silver glinting, Mom forever part of *Echoes*' frame and now Echoes will forever be part of her, her story, our story, preserved. The pastor offers a final prayer, his voice low, "May she rest in Your peace," but the wind carries the last line, a soft gust through the oak, almost as if Mom whispered it herself, her laugh, her fire, free. Dad's

485

hand grips my shoulder, Matt's arm brushes mine, the crowd silent, the oak's shadow long.

At home, the house hums with the weight of the loss, the air thick with the scent of casseroles, green bean, tuna noodle, their creamy warmth mingling with the sweet tang of pecan pies and fresh coffee brewing in Mom's old percolator. After her funeral, the living room's packed, porch, and even the front yard, neighbors and kin spilling across the sagging couch, folding chairs, even the staircase, their voices a low murmur, plates clinking, the hardwood creaking under polished shoes and Sunday dresses. Daisies and roses crowd every surface, their perfume heavy, battling the faint lavender ghost of Mom's sachet, her absence a shadow in every corner. I lean against the kitchen counter, Matt nearby, his hair curling wild, eyes shadowed, both of us hollowed by grief, dodging hugs and "She's in a better place" from well-meaning relatives. The front door swings open, and Eric limps in, his cane tapping, his dad's rusted Ford idling outside, Lila beside him, her denim jacket frayed over her black dress, a fierce glint in her eyes. "Y'all need air," Eric says, voice low, "Creek's callin'." Lila nods, "Come on, Bobby, Matt, let's get outta this zoo." We don't argue, craving escape, the house's warmth suffocating, her memories just too raw.

We pile into the truck, the cab smelling of old leather and motor oil, the engine's rumble a rough comfort as Eric drives, Lila cranking the window, letting the cool dusk air rush in, sharp with pine and mud. The road to the creek an adventure itself. It had been a long time since we memorized each of it's hazards. Time had marched on, the first big mud hole had been 'improved'.

"Damn, what's the fun in this?" Eric exclaimed finding that somebody had 'fixed' the mud hole.

The next hole came into view, and it did not disappoint. Eric hit the gas, the truck lurched forward as we were pressed back in the seat. The water and mud came in a wave so large it threatened to engulf the entire truck.

"Woohooo!" Eric screemed as the wave of mud and water came crashing back down onto the truck. Eric gassed it as a rooster tail of mud and water spewed from the tires. The truck inched forward as the engine raced, the anticipation crept in.

"We made it!" Lila screamed.

"Of course we did!" Eric yelled back.

"Good to see your confidence is still there." I said with a smile. I looked over and every face in the truck was lit up with a smile.

The road was overgrown with yaupons and wild blueberry bushes scraping and slapping the side of the truck. One more bend through the swamp and we would be back at our sanctuary. Then there it was, like a heavenly time capsule. The junipers and cypress branches drooping, framing the white sand of the sandbar. The water's glassy surface, the scent of swamp mud, earth and moss sharp as Eric cut the engine. We trek to our old spot, the ground soft, littered with driftwood, the creek's murmur a steady hymn.

"Like the old days," Matt says, voice thick, kicking a stick, and I nod, picturing us as kids, fearless, Mom's laughter trailing us.

Eric, grinning, starts a fire, gathering dry sticks, their snap loud as he strikes a match, the flames crackling, casting flickering shadows, the smoky warmth cutting the chill. Lila tosses in a log, sparks flying, "Still got it, soldier," she teases Eric, who salutes, "Damn right, ma'am."

Eric digs behind a stump, his cane propped, unearthing a rusty can of beans, our childhood stash. Matt laughs not believing it's still there.

"Last one," Eric says, eyes glinting.

"Wonder if it's still good?" Matt says looking at the rust around the lid.

A smile crosses Eric's face lookin' at the fire, "Well I know one thing it's good for."

We all move in closer surrounding the fire and smile.

Eric tossed it unopened into the fire's heart.

"Who's runnin' first?" he challenges, voice rough.

Matt laughs, sudden, bright, "Not me, old man, you'll limp away cryin'."

I grin, "Bet it blows before Eric can get out of the way," the fire poppin', the can makes a "Clink" sound.

Our laughter sharp, we sit, the flames' heat on our faces. Another "Clink" from the can. The laughter stops, we all look at each other. Then another "Clink."

"The hell with this!" Lila turns and begins runnin'.

We all turn just in time. "BOOM!" The sandbar is briefly illuminated with a spray of glowin' embers and beans as the can explodes.

A few second pass. I look up, I'm face down in the sand. "Everyone ok?"

Laughter is the only response I hear in return, it's the kind of laughter that doesn't need explainin' or a reason. It was just for us.

The laughter fades into silence.

The creek's ripples catching moonlight, and Lila points to a cypress tree, its bark carved with our initials, B, M, L, E, etched a decade ago, still sharp. "Look, Matt," she says, voice soft, tracing the letters, "we're still here."

Matt leans closer, his breath catching, "Damn, thought the tree'd outgrow us."

Eric chuckles, "Takes more'n time to erase us, kid."

The fire settles, embers glowing, beans are sizzling in the fire, and we fall quiet, the creek's murmur filling the silence, its water swirling, carrying silt and secrets.

I stare at the flames, seeing Mom's smile, "She'd love this," I say, voice low, "us here, laughin', not cryin'."

Lila nods, her hair loose, "She told me once after she started getting' bad when you guys were gone, 'Keep 'em together, Lila, no matter what.'"

Matt's voice cracks, "Miss her biscuits... and her yellin' when I got caught sneekin' out."

Eric, poking the fire, adds, "Remember, she's the one that patched my butt up after that watermelon heist, cussed me out, then fed me pie, cause she knew dad'd lay into me again."

We laughed, soft, the memories warm, like the fire, the can of beans still hissing. The cool air, the river's scent grounding, and I thought of her funeral, the chapel's flowers, Dad's bowed head, her legacy in every frame of *Echoes*.

I broke the silence, "I remembered years ago I had wished I could be like the creek, movin' forward, no matter what. Now I realize, the creek ain't steady. It swirls, it turns, and it always carries where it's been with it."

"Too deep for me, Hollywood." Eric says throwin a stick at me, which I dodged.

Eric stands, cane firm, dusting his jeans, "Time to head home, y'all. Your dad is gonna start thinkin' we got stuck again"

"Still might be true, we ain't made it home yet," I say pokin' at him.

Dad was sittin' on the front porch with his coffee cup in hand, waitin' on us to pull up. "I thought I was gonna have to come pull y'all out again."

Eric elbowed me in the ribs, "Told ya" he whispered.

Dad looked at Eric smilin', "I'll help you hose off your dad's truck before he tans your hide."

The dawns light creeps through the kitchen window of the house, soft and gray, the air heavy with the scent of damp grass and the faint tang of river mud from washin' off Eric's truck last night. Dad wakes early, his boots creaking on the hardwood, and moves to the counter, his hands steady as he pulls out the old waffle iron, its cord frayed, the metal warm from years of breakfasts. The kitchen smells of coffee brewing, bitter and sharp, and the sweet promise of batter as he mixes flour, eggs, and milk, the whisk's scrape a quiet rhythm of routine in the stillness. He sets the table like he's done a thousand times, blue ceramic plates, mismatched forks, a jar of Mom's peach preserves, its label faded, muscle memory guiding him, the clink of dishes soft, deliberate. He pauses, staring at the table, his breath catching as he realizes he's set one plate too many, the extra one glaring, empty, Mom's absence a fresh wound, but he can't bring himself to take it. The waffle iron hisses, steam curling, the air warm, but the house feels hollow, the echo of yesterday's funeral, her laughter, her voice *Echoes*, lingering like a ghost.

Matt's the first down, his footsteps heavy, his denim jacket slung over a chair, hair still curling past his ears, eyes shadowed from a sleepless night. He slides into a seat, the chair creaking, and grabs a waffle, its golden crust crisp, syrup pooling. "Smells like home," he says, voice low, a faint smile breaking, though his gaze flicks to the extra plate, untouched.

Dad nods, pouring coffee, the pot's gurgle filling the quiet, and says, "Figured we needed somethin' familiar."

They talk, halting, about Matt's drive back to Tallahassee, the words careful, skirting Mom's loss.

490

"Road's clear, should make it by noon," Matt says, forking a bite, the syrup's sweetness faint on his breath.

Dad leans against the counter, "Good. School's waitin'. You don't need to stay, son, I know ya got finals comin soon."

He understands, his eyes tracing Matt's tense jaw, the way grief clings, too many memories in these walls, the body's instinct to flee pain, to make it go away. The coffee's steam curls, the waffle iron clicks off, the air thick with what's unsaid, Mom's lavender sachet a ghost in the hall.

I finish packing then come down next, the stairs creaking under my feet, the kitchen's warmth wrapping me, the scent of waffles and coffee a fleeting comfort. I see Matt and Dad, their heads close, talking quietly about car maintenance, oil changes, tire pressure, their voices low, a lifeline to normalcy.

"Check the belts, too," Dad says, his hands gesturing, calluses catching the light, "squeakin' means trouble."

Matt nods, "Got it, Dad, I'll stop for supplies."

I slide into a chair, the extra plate a stab, Mom's absence louder than the clink of my fork. Dad looks at me, his eyes heavy, knowing I need to get back to California, to finish the movie.

"You got a flight, Bobby?" he asks, voice soft, the coffee pot trembling in his grip.

I nod, swallowing, "Nine o'clock, Dad. Gotta lock the final cut, add the music, like she wanted. Grant and Ava should be coming to pick me up soon."

He nods, understanding. Waffle's sweetness bitter on my tongue. We eat, the silence settling, broken only by the scrape of forks, the faint hum of a distant tractor outside, the air warm but thin, Mom's laughter just another echo. We say our goodbyes, standing in the kitchen, the table cluttered with plates, the extra one untouched.

Matt hugs me, his jacket rough, his grip tight, "Don't be a stranger, Bobby," he says, voice thick, his breath warm.

I nod, "You either, college boy."

Dad pulls us both in, his arms strong, Old Spice sharp, "Watch out for each other." His voice cracks, eyes wet, and we nod, throats tight, the house's warmth fading as Matt grabs his duffel, heading to his car.

As Matt is pulling out, I see a black car with Grant and Ava in it coming down the road. The tires crunchin' on the gravel as they park. Grant and Ava get out, heads held slightly low in respect. They all shake hands with dad, and express condolences again, but it's time to go. I throw my bag in the trunk, take one last look around, giving a half smile, I slide into the back seat and close the door.

I glance through the back window as Ava steers the car away from the old farm house, Grant in the front, the gravel crunchin' under the tires, the Oak Tree standin' resolute in the mornin' sun. Dad is still standin' on the porch, his hands shoved deep in his pockets, his face etched, unreadable, but his eyes, steady, heavy with grief and pride, following me, unwaverin'. His grayin' hair catches the light, his shoulders slumped, the scent of Old Spice lingerin' in my memory, the coffee thermos he held this mornin' now a ghost in his grip. As we turn onto the road, he lifts a hand, a slow wave, and I wave back, my throat tight, Echoes' film can beside me, my vow to make it sing pullin' me back to California.

Dad turns, his boots creaking on the porch, and steps inside, the door shuttin' soft, the house cloakin' him in an eerie silence, the air still, heavy with the absence of Mom's laughter, her lavender sachet's sweetness faded, replaced by the stale tang of untouched waffles, cold coffee and memories. Ruth's everywhere, her quilt's blue stitches on the couch, her handwritin' on a recipe card by the stove, the creak of her favorite chair. Mom's absence a shadow in every corner, her love, her story, lingerin', one forgotten plate, one goodbye at a time.

He pauses, his breath shallow, seein' her in the lamplight's glow, her fierce eyes, her smile, their late-night talks floodin' back, sittin' at this table, her hand in his, he remembers her voice firm, "Thomas, don't you dare be sad when I'm gone. Think of me and smile, love. I'll always be with you, in every sunrise, every story." Her words, a promise, an echo in the quiet, as he touches the recipe card, his fingers trembling, a faint smile breaking, her love echoing in the silence.

Chapter 60 - The Premier
(July 1973)

The edit bay at Sun Studios in Los Angeles hums with the electric buzz of monitors, the air thick with the metallic tang of incandescent lights, stale coffee, and the faint chemical whiff of film stock, the linoleum sticky under my feet. I pour every ounce of emotion into *Echoes'* final edit. My day and night blur, the bay a cocoon of light and sound, color grading Main Street's dusk to deepen its bruised purple, layering mournful guitar cues over the rabbit's twitchy ears, sharpening transitions from Eric's war truth to Mom's quilt-draped voice, "Small don't mean weak." Her words, raw and fierce, become the film's beat, pulsing through every frame, the Nagra's tape catching her breath's cadence, her fire. Grant checks in daily, his shaggy hair wild, lugging takeout, greasy burgers, lo mein, the soy sauce scent cutting the bay's haze.

"You're gonna win an award, Bobby," he says, grinning, tossing me a fry, "I told you, I'm just here for the snacks, man. I hear the snacks at the Chinese Theater are the best" I laugh again, my voice rough, his jokes a lifeline.

I'm still laughin, "What do you mean the Chinese Theater?"

Grant looks at me, "you mean she didn't tell you? The execs want her to book the Chinese Theater. We made it to the big leagues, Bobby!"

Across the lot, Ava's office crackles with plans, her desk buried under press releases, her bob tight, her voice sharp as she plans for the premiere, the air smelling of her rosewater perfume and fresh ink. She's mid-meeting, gesturing at a seating chart, when I barge in, my shoes scuffing, heart pounding. "Ava, wait," I say, voice low but firm, "can we have the premiere in Mill Town?" The room stills, her team glancing up, the hum of a ceiling fan loud in the silent pause. Ava leans back, her eyes narrowing, they all look to her, then a slow smile breaks, warm, knowing, like Mom's when I'd nail a story. I could see the wheels churnin' in her head, "You know, I think that's exactly where it should be," she says, her voice soft, the team nodding, the air shifting, Mill Town's pull stronger than LA's neon. *Echoes'* heart was calling us home.

Ava wastes no time, dialing Jesus, her voice crackling through the receiver, "You up for one last miracle, miracle man?" Jesus, his t-shirt stained with coffee, laughs, "For you? Always, boss." He flies to Mill Town the next day, clipboard in hand, eyes scanning rooftops and parking lots, the air thick with river mud and blooming dogwoods, the faint buzz of cicadas rising. He organizes a mix of local contractors and crew flown in from LA and transforms downtown, a maestro of revival, every awning freshly painted, their canvas taut, every lightbulb replaced, their glow banishing the dusk, Main Street reborn like *Echoes'* 1960s frames. The old Mill Town theater, once forgotten, its marquee broken, now gleams, its facade scrubbed, new bulbs twinkling, the scent of fresh paint sharp, the lobby's carpet vacuumed, popcorn machines humming, their buttery warmth a promise. Jesus, standing in the middle of Mainstreet, clipboard tucked underarm, grins, whispering to himself, "For you, we shine," the theater's neon buzzing, Mill Town ready to *Echo*.

The plane lands in Pensacola under a golden sky, the air hot and thick with the humid tang of gulf salt and blooming magnolias, the runway shimmering. Ava looks out the window at the mass of people crowding the terminal.

She looks at me, "You better go first."

As I step off, Grant and Ava behind me. My flannel's loose, but I'm already regretting not packing more t-shirts. The terminal buzzes, no longer quiet but alive, packed shoulder-to-shoulder with the town's heart, Lila in a bright skirt, her sketchpad tucked away, and there was

Eric leaning on his cane smilin', Miss Lorraine's floral scarf fluttering, Gable was wearin' his best jacket, kids waving handmade signs, "Welcome Home, Crew!" The air hums with voices, laughter, the scent of fresh coffee from thermoses and sugary donuts from the bakery, their glaze sticking to fingers.

Dad's at the front, his work shirt swapped for a clean button-up, his half-smile wide, eyes glistening as he pulls me into a hug, his Old Spice sharp, grounding. "Whole town's here, son," he says, voice thick, stepping back.

Lila barrels in, hugging me fierce, "You brought us back, Bobby!"

Eric salutes, "Now this is worth fightin' for," and the crowd cheers, hands clapping, kids giggling, the terminal's linoleum vibrating, a homecoming wrapped in love.

Reporters from across the country swarm the edges, mics thrusting, cameras flashing, NBC, CBS, a sharp-eyed woman from The New York Times, her notepad ready, all drawn to *Echoes*' story, a dying town revived by a boy with a camera.

"Ava, an interview for Channel 5?" one calls, voice eager, while another, from Atlanta, shouts, "How'd you capture Mill Town's soul?"

The New York reporter, her accent crisp, edges closer, "Mr. Chandler, what's *Echoes* mean to you?"

I nod, throat tight, waving them off gently, "Later, y'all, let me hug my people first."

Grant grins, his shaggy hair wild, nudging Ava, her blazer sharp, rosewater perfume cutting the jet fuel's bite, "Told ya, boss, this town's a circus!"

Ava laughs, rare and warm, hugging Miss Lorraine, who says, "You're one of us now, city girl."

Outside, a limo waits, Ava's doing, Ava slides in.

Grant looks at dad and looks back at Ava, "Let's take a real ride."

Ava, initially looks confused, then sees what Grant is lookin' at. Dad's truck idles nearby, tailgate down, and Grant calls, "Room for two more, Mr. Chandler?"

Dad chuckles, "Always, son,"

Ava smiles and exit's the limo with a smile. They all pile in, the cab warm with coffee's tang, the crowd waving, signs bobbing, reporters trailing, their pens scribbling. My heart is still pounding, our legacy ready to shine. Ava is gigglin' like a school girl on the first day of summer vacation.

Ava looks at Thomas, "How is Mrs Elma doing?"

Dad looks shocked she remembered her, "She's doing well, she's been reading for kids at the library every Tuesday and Thursday."

Ava looked at dad "Your son's film is the talk of Hollywood, Everyone is intrigued by something so genuine. Your son has a bright future ahead of him, and I'm not just saying that because you're his dad. You should have seen your son when he barged into our board meeting, insisting we have the Premier here."

Dad's smile of pride changed as he looked at me like I knew better manners than to barge in on a meeting.

Ava, an expert in reading peoples faces quickly retorted, "No it was great, not only does he have an eye for the artistic reality, but he has the gumption to speak up for it when other's may not. That's even more rare."

Dads expression eased back into a proud smile.

Ava continued, "Our son's have put together one hell of a film, it's gonna break peoples hearts then make them laugh about it, but they're going to walk away with a something."

Dad quietly replied, "It sure did for me."

Ava quickly remembering that I brought the draft film home for mom to see, "They have made a few tweaks since then, you're going to be impressed."

Grant was grinning, sitting beside me in the back just enjoying the ride.

"Sure you don't want to stay at our place, we have lots of room for you." Dad said as we pulled into their hotel.

"Thank you so much, you have done more than enough already. I have to talk with some of the crew and organize a few things, my job never seems to be done." She said with a smile. Dad gets out of the truck and we take their bags into the hotel lobby.

"See you later tonight!" Grant yells.

We get back into the truck and drive back home. Before we get into the driveway I can see Eric, Matt, and Lila standing on the porch. Eric and Matt run to the get an old red tarp from the side of the porch then hold the corners of it while Lila rolls it out on the steps like a redneck red carpet laughin'.

Dad smiles, "Sure is nice to have some laughter around here again."

As the sun set, Mainstreet came to life, the humid sweetness of blooming honeysuckle and the buttery warmth of popcorn drifting from sidewalk stands, their metal bins clattering as vendors scoop golden kernels. Main Street gleams, reborn as a 1960s dream, Jesus' miracle work painting every detail, red-and-white awnings taut, bunting swaying from lampposts, stars-and-stripes flags fluttering, the hardware store's hand painted sign lovingly brought back to it's former glory, the lights casting long shadows on the cobblestones. The old theater stands proud, its marquee blazing *Echoes Premiere*, bulbs twinkling like stars, the facade scrubbed clean, fresh paint sharp in the nose, the lobby's chandeliers sparkling, their light dancing on velvet ropes. But Jesus, our logistics wizard, knew the theater's oak pews couldn't hold the swelling crowd, so he'd conjured a giant outdoor screen across the lawn, its white expanse towering, tethered by ropes, glowing under strings of Edison bulbs strung between oaks, their amber hum a soft hymn. Folding chairs dot the green, creaking under families' weight, picnic blankets spread wide, patched and colorful, kids sprawling with lemonade-sticky hands. Lawn speakers, wired by Jesus' deft hands, crackle faintly with soft violin music, ready to carry *Echoes'* sound, the grass beneath them damp, smelling of earth and clover, the river's muddy tang faint in the breeze.

"Come on Bobby, we're gonna be late" Dad shouts from downstairs.

"I'm coming!" I get halfway down the stairs when I remember something. I turn around and run back up, I grab my old 8mm off my dresser. I burst out the front door screen door slapping back. Dad just shakes his head.

I climb in to dad's truck, the cab warm with coffee's bitter tang, the leather seats cracking, he leaned over, looking at my camera, "Got everything?"

"I think so," I reply smiling.

Dad's wearing a clean button-up stiff on his frame. I smile as the gravel crunches under the tires. The glow of Mainstreet can be seen for miles with searchlights flashing the sky. The closer we got, the more cars and trucks we saw parked on the side of the road. People walkin' with lawn chairs and coolers, all marchin' downtown.

Dad's face grimaces, "we're never gonna find a place to park. Look, they're even parked on the bridge. I've never seen so many people, not even at the Fourth of July."

I'm still watching the spectacle of people gatherin' out the window, "let's just drive to the hotel to meet Grant and Ava."

We arrive at the hotel, the parking lot is full there as well, the license plates were from all over the country. I even saw one from Alaska.

"There they are!" as I point to the entrance.

Ava is beautifully dressed in a silver sequined gown with black trim and the tallest heels I have ever seen. Grant is wearing a black tuxedo with patent black shoes.

"Guess I should have worn my jacket," Dad muttered.

"Yeah, me too," feeling completely underdressed, lookin' down at my tennis shoes.

Grant sees us and runs up to the window, "You guys want to ride with us in the limo?"

I look at dad, I can see him looking around the parking lot. "Nah, we'll just follow you."

Grant smiles, "Thought so."

As we were pulling up to the front of the theater, the red carpet was rolled out, dad asked, voice low, "Do we just leave the truck or should I park it first, Bobby?" innocent as a schoolboy on his first day, the theater looming ahead.

I smiled, "I think they'll park it for us, Dad."

He nodded, Old Spice sharp, the engine's rumble steady, The reporters flashbulbs twinkled like fireworks when we got out of the truck. I turned to see the crowd that spilled across the lawn, a sea of faces, The entire town's here, and more, families from neighboring counties, their pickups parked crooked, soldiers in crisp uniforms, students with notebooks, tourists snapping photos, their flashbulbs popping. I even saw Evelyn, standing quietly with her family as she raises her hand waving solemnly, her tailored coat swapped for a simple sundress, her kids tugging her hands, her face soft, *Echoes'* redemption, now hers too. The town, once fading, its storefronts shuttered, is now bathed in light.

Miss Lorraine's floral scarf slipping as she hugs a neighbor, Eric limping, cane tapping, grinning at kids chasing fireflies, their giggles bright as the bells in *Echoes*. They make their way towards us on the red carpet.

Lila weaves through, her bright skirt swaying, no clipboard now, just a fierce smile, stopping by a blanket to say, "Y'all brought the good quilt, huh, Miss Elma?"

Elma laughs, "Had to, Lila, Ruth'd want us comfy!"

Grant, his shaggy hair tamed, nudges Ava as they get out of the limo, her sequined gown catching every light in the marquee and then some, rosewater perfume cuttin' the popcorn's richness.

Grant mutters, "This sure beats Hollywood, huh boss."

Ava nods, her smile warm looking at the crowd and the downtown makeover results, "Damn right, kid. Now this is real. Your grandfather would be so proud. Now, I could live without the humidity though," she says smiling looking at Grant.

Reporters from NBC, CBS, even The New York Times, their lenses glinting, weave through, mics poised, scribbling, "A town reborn by a boy's camera," their chatter buzzing, the air electric, the lawn alive, every breath a celebration.

Inside the theater, the lobby's packed, the scent of polished wood and buttery popcorn thick, chandeliers casting prisms on the crowd, locals in Sunday best, cast and crew in borrowed suits, Aunt Debbie and cousins from Mobile, their voices a low hum. We all file down the red carpet, the seats creaking, flower arrangements spilling over ledges, daisies and roses sweet against the musty tang of buttered popcorn. Grant, Ava, Dad, Matt, Lila, Eric, and I take our seats in a reserved row up front, the oak seats smooth under my hands, my shirt getting hot, the program's paper soft in my pocket, *Echoes*' weight is now a vow kept.

I look to Grant, "we did it Mr. Producer."

"Yes we did, Mr. Director," as he smiled from ear to ear.

One seat next to dad remains empty, adorned with a small bouquet of wildflowers, daisies, her favorite, tied with a blue ribbon. Sitting right next to that bouquet was a small old bell with a note attached. Dad recognized it right away. Mom's seat, her presence palpable, I could almost smell the lavender and hear her laugh. With dad's hand on my shoulder, Matt's breath steady beside me, the theater became a sanctuary.

The lights dim, the crowd's boisterous laughter now a murmur fading, a hush falling like dusk over the river, the projector's hum rising, a solemn pulse blending with the faint creak of pews, the lawn's speakers crackling alive outside. The screen flares, inside and out as a violin plays softly, a rabbit hops into frame, small and gray, nibbling grass sprouting through the cracked asphalt on Main Street, its ears twitching in the dawn's amber glow, the Nagra's tape catching the wind's soft moan. The theater stills, the lawn outside quiets, blankets shifting, chairs creaking, the air thick with anticipation, the popcorn's warmth fading, the river's scent a ghost. I think of Mom, her frail hand, her final smile, *Echoes'* dedication, *"to Matt, Ruth and Thomas Chandler my biggest fans."* shows white on a black background.

Outside, the lawn breathes with the crowd, soldiers standing resolute, kids catching fireflies. The screen's glow bathes them, the speakers carrying Eric's watermelon tale, laughter rippling, then Mom's voice echoing, "Small don't always mean weak, it means close."

The End